Whispers in the Night

Adventures in the Enchanted Museum

Susie Bennett

BookPublishing.com

CONTENTS

INTRODUCTION

As the clock strikes midnight, the hallowed halls of the ancient museum awaken with a life of their own, their secrets previously concealed now yearning to be unveiled. Dust mites dance in the moonlight filtering through arched windows, illuminating forgotten relics and whispering tales of bygone eras. At the heart of this nocturnal exploration are Ellie Thompson, a sharp-witted historian driven by insatiable curiosity, and Professor Finch, a seasoned expert in the arcane arts of enchanted artefacts Professor Finch, a seasoned expert in the arcane arts of enchanted artefacts. Together, they embark on a perilous journey to unlock the past, piecing together fragments of forgotten narratives like a shattered mosaic.

Their quest echoes the daring exploits of Lady Arabella, a renowned explorer who disappeared centuries ago, and Finn, a cunning rogue whose legendary exploits are whispered in hushed tones. Like their predecessors, Ellie and Professor Finch must navigate treacherous shadows, decipher cryptic riddles etched into ancient stones, and figure out what's woven into the very fabric of the museum.

As the night deepens, trust becomes a fragile commodity. Alliances are forged and broken under the watchful gaze of forgotten gods, and the air crackles with the palpable tension of uncertainty. The possibility of awakening ancient curses, slumbering for millennia, hangs heavy in the air, threatening to consume them all.

The stakes are impossibly high. If they do not solve the museum's enigmatic puzzles before the first rays of dawn pierce the darkness, they risk becoming nothing more than footnotes in the annals of history, forever lost to the sands of time.

Step into a world where every artefact carries a story waiting to be revealed, where every shadow reveals a hidden truth, and where every moment brims with significance. Embark on an adventure that will ignite your imagination, challenge your perceptions, and leave you breathless, yearning for more of the secrets that lie hidden within the ancient museum's walls. Heed the call of the past, for its mysteries are waiting to be unearthed.

THE ENIGMA OF THE ENCHANTED MUSEUM

The night air was cool, a welcome balm against the lingering heat of the day, carrying the subtle, earthy scent of damp stone and the faintest whisper of petrichor. Ellie stood before the imposing façade of the city's ancient museum, a shiver of anticipation coursing through her. Tonight was the grand reopening, a moment she and many others had been eagerly awaiting. After years of neglect and hushed rumours of disrepair, the museum had finally opened its doors to the public once more, highlighting its towering, fluted columns that displayed signs of age, such as intricate cracks spiderwebbing across the marble and a soft green blanket of moss clinging to its northern side.

A historian by trade and a puzzle enthusiast at heart, Ellie felt a particular pull towards this place. It wasn't just the history it housed before its closure. Untold stories, etched into the relics within, awaited her decipherment. The thought of being among the first to explore the newly curated exhibits, to meet the unknown artefacts and unlock their secrets, sent a thrill of excitement through her. Ellie felt that tonight held the promise of something truly extraordinary. The anticipation was palpable, a buzzing energy that crackled in the cool night air, causing her pulse to quicken as she awaited the entry signal.

Renowned for its extensive collection of artefacts from ancient civilisations, the museum offered profound insights to those who were curious and eagerly expecting potential discoveries. Upon entering, Ellie detected the distinct aroma of polished wood and aged parchment. The grand foyer displayed a variety of items, including Roman statues and Egyptian artefacts. One exhibit in particular—a large lion statue named Azrael—captivated her with its intricate artisanry.

"Ah, there you are!" greeted Professor Finch, Ellie's mentor and an archaeologist. He appeared from behind a statue and commented on the value of learning from historical objects.

Ellie acknowledged the professor's statement, noting that every artefact has its own story. As they talked, a carved wooden fox named Finn seemed to draw their attention to another part of the hall where a strange glow was visible. Before further investigation, the lights flickered, creating a sense of unease. A low hum resonated through the building, followed by indistinct whispers suggesting a connection to the past. An authoritative voice then addressed them, saying,

"Welcome, esteemed visitors! You have awakened us!"

Ellie was nervous but curious about the situation; she sensed that the artefacts might be more than just objects. Oliver, the museum's guard, asked if the material was part of the exhibit, and Professor Finch commented on the rumoured enchantments. Just then, the clock tower outside chimed midnight, its deep tones echoing through the cavernous halls of the museum, momentarily silencing the hushed whispers and shuffling footsteps of the remaining security guards. Instinctively, Ellie turned back towards the lion statue, her heart pounding a frantic rhythm against her ribs.

To her astonishment, Azrael's stone form shifted and trembled, dust swirling as the granite groaned. With a loud crack, he sprang to life, landing softly on his paws. His golden hair, once the previously dull colours, now flowed vibrantly, contrasting with the museum's muted hues. A low growl rumbled, releasing power, and Ellie knew the night was about to become unpredictable.

"Fear not! For I am Azrael, guardian of these halls!" he declared, his voice deep and regal. "Tonight, we embark on an adventure steeped in time and mystery. You—the chosen few—are to explore the enigma that is this enchanted museum."

The entangled threads of fate intertwined tightly around the diverse group of companions. Ellie felt a thrilling surge of energy. "What is it we must do?" she asked, a fire igniting within her.

Azrael padded closer, eyes bright with wisdom. "Many paths lie ahead. To uncover the secrets embedded in these walls, you must solve the riddles of the past. However, be aware that others are also awake tonight."

In the shadows of the dimly lit chamber, a soft hiss appeared—a whisper that pricked the air with anticipation. All heads turned as one, drawn by the sound to a beautifully crafted bronze serpent. It was coiled gracefully near the base of an ancient Greek vase, its scales gleaming faintly in the ambient light. The vase itself, adorned with faded scenes of myth and legend, seemed to pulse with a hidden energy, mirroring the creature at its base.

Then, the serpent spoke. "I am Luci," she announced, her voice smooth and melodic, resonating with an ancient power that sent a shiver down their spines. Her words were hypnotic, both alluring and unsettling. "And I shall teach you the tales woven into the relics— tales that are not mere stories but keys to unlocking the past. The stories will lead you through the maze of time, shedding light on your future journey and unveiling secrets that have been long forgotten." Her golden eyes, glinting with an unnerving intelligence, seemed to pierce through them, seeing beyond the surface to the very core of their being. The air crackled with unspoken promise and a hint of danger as Luci, the bronze serpent, prepared to unveil the mysteries held within the heart of antiquity.

With a bond forming between them, Ellie felt invincible, a surge of confidence fuelled by the camaraderie of her unlikely companions. Together with the insightful Professor Finch, the ever-practical Oliver, the enigmatic Azrael, and the mischievous Luci, they were destined to traverse the museum's vast history, a labyrinth of artefacts and echoes of the past. Each of them, with their unique skills and perspectives, was a vital piece of the puzzle. They moved forward, not just as a group but as a team, ready to confront the challenges ahead and unravel the enigma within the museum's walls – a mystery that seemed to pulse with secrets, waiting to be unearthed. The weight of history, once daunting, now felt like a shared burden, a collective responsibility that bound them together in this extraordinary quest.

A sudden flapping interrupted their camaraderie, and from the rafters, Huckleberry swooped down, landing gracefully on a nearby pedestal. "Beware the labyrinth," he croaked, his dark eyes glinting like onyx. "Valen, the Timekeeper watches, and those who seek answers must prove their worth." He fluffed his feathers, bemused by the rapt attention of the group. "I have messages from the ages, lost fragments that offer wisdom if you dare decode them."

"What is the labyrinth you speak of?" Ellie asked, eagerness edged with trepidation. The mysteries and possibilities spiralled around her, electrifying her senses.

Azrael responded, his voice a low rumble in the echoing stillness of the Egyptian exhibit. Dust motes danced in the ethereal glow emanating from a sarcophagus, proof enough of the unnatural energy at play. "The museum is alive, a swirling vortex of temporal anomalies given breath by something... or someone.

But its life is fleeting, burning brightly only until dawn. If we are to restore balance and prevent the chaos that threatens to consume not just this place but the world beyond its walls, we must find Valen, the rogue sorcerer who dared to manipulate the threads of time itself. We must understand the importance of each artefact; each stolen relic pulsates with Valen's twisted magic. Only then will we solve the enigma of this enchanted museum and contain the storm before it breaks."

In that moment, Ellie felt the weight of their quest settle upon her shoulders, a tangible burden that threatened to bow her beneath its immense pressure. The fate of something or someone rested on their success and the realisation of her life, drawn to their allure like a moth to a flame, finding whispers of truths in dusty tomes and forgotten archives. However, she had never imagined that she would uncover them in such a remarkable way.

This was no ordinary investigation; it was a journey into the heart of legend, a dance with the impossible, and she, despite the daunting challenge, was ready to lead. The fantastical nature of it all, and the sheer improbability of their undertaking ignited a fire within her—a thrilling mix of fear and excitement that fuelled her determination.

"Let's not waste time," Oliver piped up, staring at the expanding shadows behind the exhibit walls. "What's the first riddle, or what do we do now?"

Dr. Mariana Bell, a figure usually more comfortable with the rustle of ancient texts than the clamour ana Bell, a figure usually more comfortable with the rustle of ancient texts than the clamour of academic debates, had been quietly watching from a nearby alcove. Her brow was furrowed in concentration, and her glasses, always on the verge of slipping from their position, slid further down her nose. Finally, she straightened, a spark of revelation flickering in her eyes.

"Just moments ago," she began, her voice a little unsteady, cutting through the ongoing discussion. "I realised that my conservation efforts may have awakened something incredible here." The words lingered in the air, heavy with unspoken implications.

Her voice trembled, a subtle vibration that betrayed the storm raging within her—a potent cocktail of anxiety and exhilaration. "I didn't intend for this to happen, of course," she continued, her gaze darting around the room, as if seeking reassurance or perhaps forgiveness. "But... perhaps I've sparked something wonderful." The 'perhaps' was a deliberate hedge, a shield against the immense responsibility that now threatened to engulf her, yet the underlying hope, the inherent optimism that had fuelled her life's work, shone through, illuminating the profound significance of her discovery.

"Your enthusiasm has contributed to this miraculous night," Professor Finch assured her with a gentle smile. "Whatever we meet, together we will traverse history's labyrinth. Let's go ahead!" As they began to move deeper into the museum's labyrinthine corridors, a disquieting chill settled around them like a shroud. They stumbled across what appeared to be the first of many exits. It wasn't a conventional doorway, however, but a hall lined with portrait-sized mirrors, each framed in ornate, tarnished silver.

The mirrors didn't simply reflect their images; they seemed to capture something more, a shimmering residue of the night itself, amplifying the surrounding darkness and lending it an almost palpable weight. Each reflection flickered with an unsettling animation, whispering half-formed memories that resonated deep within their subconscious. Faces both familiar and alien swarmed within the glass, beckoning them closer with promises of untold stories and long-forgotten secrets, their eyes gleaming with an unnerving, captivating allure. The air crackled with an unseen energy, a potent mix of curiosity and dread that urged them forward, deeper into the mirrored abyss.

"Each step we take unveils a fragment of history," Luci said, her eyes shimmering in the dim light. "We must heed the whispers."

Finn darted ahead, a playful blur of wood and spirit, leading the way. The atmosphere crackled with energy as Ellie recalled her studies: every artefact had a purpose, a reason for being in that place at that moment. This museum was a living entity, and it wished to be understood.

Suddenly, Oliver halted, his hand shooting out to stop Ellie in her tracks. He pointed a trembling finger at a small pedestal just beyond the distorted reflections of the hall of mirrors. Upon it rested a weathered book, its leather cover cracked and worn with age. The cover was embossed with a series of symbols, intricate and unfamiliar, yet they resonated deep within him, stirring a sense of déjà vu, an echo of something forgotten.

"It looks like something we must examine," Ellie suggested, her voice a hushed whisper that barely broke the eerie silence of the room. She stepped closer, her heart racing against her ribs, a drumbeat of anticipation and apprehension. "Perhaps it will help us understand the enchantment of this museum. These symbols...they might hold the key to breaking whatever spell has been cast here." She reached out, hesitant, drawn to the book like a moth to a flame, both intrigued and wary of the secrets it held within its aged pages.

With a gentle nudge from Finn, a subtle encouragement that settled the last of her apprehension, she opened the ancient book. The pages practically vibrated with unseen energy. The intricate illustrations seemed to shift and breathe; accompanied by texts in a language she barely recognised, they resonated deep within her, enchanting her mind with a dizzying array of possibilities, each more fantastic than the last.

"This could lead us to Valen!" she exclaimed, her voice barely a whisper, filled with both awe and a surge of determination. She flipped through the fragile, parchment-thin pages, a flurry of movement as she absorbed the cryptic content. Whispers of forgotten knowledge cascaded around them, a tangible presence that hummed with secrets untold, promising answers and hinting at perilous challenges to come. The air crackled with anticipation, the book a key unlocking a door to a reality beyond their wildest imaginings.

But before they could delve deeper, a shadow flickered behind them, a cloaked figure watching silently—Valen.

Ellie realised, lingering just a breath away, waiting for their first move.

With the thrill of adventure compounding with every heartbeat, Ellie and her companions prepared to navigate the secrets held within the Enchanted Museum. Dust mites danced in the ethereal glow of ancient artefacts, hinting at forgotten stories waiting to be unearthed.

Every step creaked with the weight of centuries, a constant reminder of the task before them. Whispers of long-dead curators and restless spirits seemed to swirl through the halls, urging them forward. They clutched their maps and tools, a motley collection of knowledge and their ingenuity lay in the understanding that every decision they made tonight would echo through history, altering the very fabric of time and transforming their destinies forever.

The air crackled with anticipation, a potent cocktail of fear and exhilaration that tasted sharp on the tongue. Every nerve ending sang with a heightened awareness, a primal instinct screaming both warning and invitation. Before them loomed a gilded doorway, shimmering with an almost unbearable light, a portal to unknown wonders and perilous challenges. Beyond its threshold, reality itself seemed to warp and twist, promising a spectacle that defied human comprehension and dangers that could shatter them irrevocably.

Their journey had only just begun; a fragile spark ignited in the vast darkness of the unknown. Each step forward was a gamble; some dice rolls against impossible odds. The weight of their mission, the sheer gravity of their task, pressed down on them, heavy and suffocating. For the stakes were impossibly high, far beyond personal glory or individual survival. The fate of the timeline itself, a delicate tapestry threatened by unravelling threads, inextricably intertwined their lives. The timeline itself is a delicate tapestry threatened by unravelling threads. threatened by unravelling threads. One wrong move, one miscalculated decision, could send ripples cascading through history, erasing everything they held dear, condemning countless generations to a future they could scarcely imagine, let alone control. Hope and fear battled within them, forging a steely resolve as they steeled themselves to face whatever lay beyond the shimmering gate.

THE MYSTERIOUS
INVITATION

Ellie stood frozen in the dim, filtered light of the museum, her heart a frantic drum against her ribs. Excitement, a giddy, swirling sensation, battled with a prickling apprehension that raised goosebumps on her arms. The air, heavy with the scent of aged paper, dust, and something indefinably ancient, thrummed with anticipation. She replayed the day's events in her mind, each moment a step closer to this very point. The grand reopening of the Blackwood Museum had drawn a curious crowd, a mix of local history buffs and wide-eyed tourists. But it wasn't the polite murmurs and champagne toasts that captivated Ellie.

The museum loom hung heavily in the air. It was the allure of the unknown that had drawn her here, a siren song sung by locked doors and hushed speculation. The whispered rumours surrounding the museum's long closure—tales of eccentric benefactors, forgotten expeditions, and the discovery of relics beyond comprehension—had fuelled her anticipation for weeks. Tonight, the curtain would rise. Tonight marked the unveiling of the mysterious artefacts, shrouded in secrecy for decades.

A shiver, not entirely from the autumn chill, ran down her spine as she stepped inside. The air was thick with anticipation, a tangible buzz that vibrated through the assembled crowd. Her fingers, trembling slightly, grazed the cool, smooth surface of a glass case, an unconscious act of grounding, of connecting with the reality of the moment.

Behind them, a collection of ancient artefacts lay bathed in a soft, ethereal glow cast by expertly placed spotlights. The light seemed to breathe life into the objects, illuminating their intricate details and hinting at the stories they held. Each piece was meticulously displayed, a testament to the curators' dedication, and clearly marked with labels detailing their provenance, their journey through time, and across continents. These small, informative plaques were gateways to other worlds, whispering tales of eras long since passed: dynasties risen and fallen in magnificent glory and cultures flourishing in the relentless march of time.

A chipped clay tablet hinted at the complex legal system of a lost Mesopotamian kingdom. A tarnished silver amulet whispered of forgotten gods and the rituals performed in their honour. A delicate porcelain doll, its painted face cracked with age, spoke of a child's laughter silenced by the passage of centuries. With each artefact, a fragment of history flickered into existence, a fleeting glimpse into the lives of those who had come before.

She felt a strange connection to these objects, a pull that resonated deep within her soul. It was more than just intellectual curiosity; it was a visceral understanding, a feeling that these objects were not merely museum pieces but conduits to the past. An invisible thread seemed to connect her to the artisans who had crafted them, the people who had used them, and the civilisations them, and to the civilisations that had revered them. An inexplicable urgency pulsed within her, urging her forward into the unknown depths of the museum, deeper into the heart of its secrets. The exhibit was more than just a viewing; it was an invitation, a call to adventure.

"Thank you, Dr Bell, for your dedication," Professor Finch's voice piped up as he pushed his glasses up his nose, peering closer at an ornate Egyptian vase. "But have we considered the consequences of awakening these relics? The historical significance can be profound, yet... dangerous."

Dr Bell bounded past them with a purposeful energy, her passion for conservation clear in every stride. She was a flurry of tweed and enthusiasm, her sensible walking shoes barely making a sound on the polished floor. "These artefacts deserve life, Harold! They've waited far too long to tell their stories. Just imagine!" She gestured animatedly towards a covered crate with her ever-present notepad, a small, leather-bound volume overflowing with sketches and notes. There was a spark of excitement in her eyes, a fervent glint that spoke of long hours spent poring over faded maps and crumbling documents. It wasn't just a job to her; it was a mission. She glanced at Ellie, whose own eyes were wide with a mixture of awe and understanding.

Moments later, the clattering of heels echoed in the corridor, sharp and insistent against the hushed silence of the museum. The museum guard ambled in, his shoulders slumped with the weariness of routine, appearing somewhat disgruntled. His uniform, usually crisp, now seemed rumpled, mirroring his lack of enthusiasm. "If I have to check the Hall of Ancient Warriors one more time..." he grumbled under his breath, the words laced with a familiar boredom. He adjusted his glasses, peering into the dimly lit hall, completely oblivious to the subtle hum that had begun to vibrate through the very floor beneath his feet. He was utterly unaware that he had unwittingly entered an exhilarating tipping point and space, a moment where the veil between realities thinned, and the past was about to bleed into the present in a way he could never have imagined. His mundane existence was on the precipice of shattering, and he was about to become an unwilling participant in a drama that transcended his understanding of history itself.

Ellie's nerves sparked as she glanced at Oliver. His presence was a surprise, a steadfast anchor that subtly shifted the vibe of their gathering from casual to something... more.

She hadn't expected him to join, and the warmth of his smile both comforted and unsettled her. "Oliver!" she exclaimed, perhaps a little too brightly, hoping to cover her surprise. "Did you get a chance to see the Egyptian lion in the main gallery? It's breathtaking! The detail is incredible, especially considering its age." She asked, her voice laced with genuine enthusiasm, hoping to draw him into their shared excitement and, perhaps, understand why he'd decided to come. His presence added a new layer to the day, and she was eager, yet apprehensive, to explore it.

"A lion statue that doesn't move? What can be seen?" He replied, folding his arms and leaning against the wall.

Before Ellie could answer, a sudden draught, icy and unexpected, swept through the corridor. It wasn't a gentle breeze; it was a gust, a purposeful push of air that whipped the heavy, velvet curtains lining the passage into a frenzy. The fabrics billow and snap like angry sails, their rich colours to the disturbance.

They flickered erratically, dipping in and out of brightness, casting long, dancing shadows against the aged, wallpapered walls. The shadows stretched and contorted familiar shapes into grotesque parodies, blurring the lines between what was real and what was merely imagined. A chill permeated the air, clinging to the exposed skin and raising goosebumps, adding an unsettling element to the already tense silence that seemed to last forever before the interruption.

"Did you feel that?" Ellie asked, her heart racing as she exchanged glances with the professor.

"Perhaps it's a sign!" Professor Finch exclaimed, the brilliance in his eye igniting a flicker of hope within Ellie. "Or simply a draft, wouldn't you say, Oliver?"

Snorting derisively, Oliver straightened to his full height, though his brow remained furrowed in deep suspicion. "I don't buy it for a second. The museum shows fundamental flaws, with telltale of dust mites dancing in the dim light and the faint, musty odour of old wood creeping into every corner! It reeks of neglect, not of hidden wonders. And what kind of invitation requires a sudden, suspiciously convenient breeze to deliver it? It resembles a simple magician's trick, an attempt to draw us into... what exactly? a trick, a sincere attempt to engage us in... what exactly?" He gestured dismissively, his eyes darting around the seemingly empty hall, searching for the hidden mechanics of the supposed invitation. "Someone's trying to pull a fast one, and I intend to find out who and why."

Ellie's curiosity deepened, a seed planted by rumour and watered by conjecture, now threatening to blossom into something all-consuming. She had spent endless nights hunched over dusty tomes and flickering screens, researching the museum's lore of whispers and wonders—the hushed tales of objects that moved on their own, the faint scent of forgotten perfumes that lingered in specific galleries, and the unsettling feeling of being watched by unseen eyes. But all her research, all the academic posturing, had been theoretical, a safe distance from the unsettling truth.

Now, they found themselves ensconced within its expansive walls, encircled by artefacts steeped in history and mystery, a palpable, pulsating life tugging at the boundaries of their comprehension. surrounded by artefacts steeped in history and mystery, with a palpable, pulsating life nudging at the edge of their understanding. The atmosphere was dense, imbued with an inexplicable energy. The museum was no mere collection of relics; this was something... more. And Ellie was determined to unravel its secrets, no matter the cost.

Before she could ponder further the implications of the strange symbols etched into the ancient stone or the heavy weight of the prophecy they were meant to fulfil, a shimmering light unfurled from the edges of a golden envelope resting atop a nearby pedestal, drawing the group's attention away from their thoughts and towards the ethereal display. The envelope glimmered with an otherworldly radiance, the gold catching the ambient light and refracting it into a dazzling spectacle of swirling colour, as if guided by an unseen energy, an intelligence beyond their comprehension. Everyone froze; each member of the party was caught in the mesmerising display, their breaths held captive in their chests, uncertain of what this magnificent and unnerving display might portend. They anxiously awaited the next development, suspended in a moment of anticipatory dread and cautious wonder.

"Look!" Dr Bell gasped, her excitement growing as she stepped closer to the pedestal.

With tentative steps, Ellie approached the envelope. It sat on the antique table like a captured star, the iridescent light reflecting shades of blues and greens, swirling and shimmering as if breathing, almost whispering secrets of its own. She lifted it cautiously, fingers trembling slightly, sensing that the message would be no ordinary invitation. The paper felt strangely smooth, almost alive beneath her touch, hinting at a world beyond the mundane. A faint, unfamiliar scent—a blend of ancient woods and blooming jasmine—emanated from within, further fuelling her anticipation and creating a prickle of undeniable unease. The fragrance wasn't merely an invitation; it felt like a summons.

"Have you ever seen anything like it?" she asked, her voice barely above a whisper.

Valen

"Well, it's beautiful, certainly," Professor Finch commented, peering over her shoulder. "But beauty often conceals mystery. Let us see what it holds."

Ellie carefully opened the font, its aged wood creaking softly in protest, and revealed a parchment scroll tied with a faded crimson ribbon. The paper felt delicate under her fingertips, as if it were poised to crumble into dust at the slightest touch. As she unrolled it, the ink, a shimmering, almost ethereal gold, seemed to writhe before her eyes. The letters danced as if alive, forming words that shifted and rearranged themselves with each glance, a mesmerising optical illusion. The message, penned in an elegant, yet unsettlingly fluid script, read: "To those who look for it, the adventure will beckon. Meet at the heart of the museum when the clock strikes midnight. Heed the whispers; they shall guide you." A chill snaked down Ellie's spine. The words were more than just an invitation; they were a promise, a dare, imbued with a strange, almost palpable energy. She wondered who "those who seek" were, what adventures awaited them at the museum, and what whispers she needed to heed. Could you please clarify what these whispers are that she should pay attention to? A knot of apprehension tightened in her stomach, but beneath the fear, a thrill of anticipation sparked. The present was no ordinary quest; this was something extraordinary.

"What does it mean?" Oliver asked, scratching his head. "Meet at the heart? Sounds like something out of a fairytale."

"If the clock strikes midnight..." Dr Bell began, her enthusiasm resuming with a fizzling excitement, "It suggests something is activated at that hour. Perhaps the artefacts?"

Ellie felt a rush of adrenaline surging through her veins. Valen, she thought. "Whatever it is, we can't pass up the opportunity to investigate."

"I'll stand watch," Oliver waved, a reluctant hint of responsibility appearing in his voice.

"Ah, but you must come with us!" Ellie insisted, determination creeping into her voice. "You'll never know what might unfold in this enchanted place. And we might need your strength."

"Strength?" Oliver chuckled. "I've got more than strength. I have–"

"A pinching suspicion that you're stalling," Finn interjected, appearing from behind a shadowy exhibit with his cheeky grin. "Come on, Oliver, fancy a bit of enchantment?"

Oliver scowled but engaged with a half-hearted smile, "Fine! Fine! However, if I find myself conversing with a lion statue, I will hold everyone accountable.

Azrael the Lion, an imposing, ancient statue carved out of stone, stood as a silent guardian just inside the grand entrance hall. Time had weathered his features, softening the sharp edges of his once fearsome mane and etching lines of untold stories onto his noble face. He exuded an aura of quiet power, his regal presence overshadowing the light-hearted banter and nervous chatter of those who passed beneath his stern gaze. Oliver, fidgeting slightly under the lion's stone scrutiny, met the knowing eyes of the elder who spoke. "There are far stranger things within these walls, Oliver," he said, his voice a low rumble that seemed to resonate with the very stones of the building. "There are things that defy logic and challenge your preconceived notions. If you are brave enough to look, you might even discover a new perspective and a glimpse beyond the ordinary.

Ellie clapped her hands together, the sound sharp and decisive in the hushed room. Excitement bubbled within her like a shaken soda, threatening to spill over into a giddy laugh as she surveyed the team. Faces, illuminated by the soft glow of the nearby lamp, mirrored her anticipation, a blend of thrill and nervous energy. "Then we have reached a resolution. " We explore at midnight!" she declared, her voice ringing with a confident enthusiasm meant to solidify their commitment. She turned back to the golden envelope, her fingers tracing the intricate embossed designs. A genuine, heartwarming excitement shone in her eyes, reflecting the promise held within. "This is our invitation," she murmured, almost reverently, "our invitation to uncover the mysteries that have been hidden away for so long— To peel back the layers of the unknown and finally understand what lies beneath."

As night's cloak wrapped around the museum, shrouding its grand halls in a hushed darkness, the atmosphere transformed. The echoing footsteps of daytime visitors faded, replaced by a palpable sense of anticipation. With their collective enthusiasm ignited by the day's discoveries and a shared purpose now binding them together, they spent their remaining time at the museum meticulously piecing together the history of its artefacts. Each worn inscription, each faded photograph, and each chipped ceramic shard became vital clues in their quest. Their minds buzzing with possibilities. Impatiently awaiting the appointed hour, a clock tower could be heard in the distance, marking the time as the moonlight crept through the stained-glass windows, painting the exhibits in an ethereal glow.

In the vast, echoing exhibition hall, the hushed reverence of the space seemed to coalesce around Ellie and the imposing statue before her. She stood transfixed, drawn in by an unseen force. Azrael, the mighty guardian, loomed, carved from dark, almost obsidian stone, its features both stern and strangely benevolent. The details, worn smooth by time and countless admiring hands, hinted at untold ages of watchful vigil. Ellie reached out, her fingers tracing the contours of a powerful shoulder and the curve of a sculpted wing. The chill of the stone seeped into her skin, a primal connection to the earth and the mysteries it held. "What stories do you hold, mighty guardian?" she whispered, her voice barely heard above the ambient hum of the hall. Her breath caught in her throat as a palpable shift occurred – the air thickened, the light softened, and a wave of potent enchantment washed over them, wrapping them in an inviting, almost suffocating embrace. The world around her seemed to fade, replaced by the promise of secrets revealed, of histories unearthed, and of a journey into the heart of Azrael's silent, stony soul.

In the dim light, where shadows danced like secrets, it felt as if Azrael could hear her words, not just with his ears, but with something deeper, more primal. His eyes flickered; a spark ignited in the darkness. It wasn't a simple glimmer of understanding; the power was an ancient magic, slumbering for centuries, now stirred awake by her voice, by the very air she breathed. The room seemed to pause, expecting his next move with this newly bought power.

"Look deeper," Luci's voice hissed from the shadows, her bronze form appearing from a disguise of light. "The night whispers secrets yet untold. Allow them to guide you."

As the excitement coursed through Ellie's veins like a potent elixir, a sense of camaraderie stirred among their eclectic assembly. They were a motley crew – a historian with a thirst for untold stories, a tech whiz whose gadgets hummed with latent possibilities, a seasoned adventurer with eyes that held maps of forgotten lands, and Ellie herself, drawn by a pull she couldn't quite explain. Time moves differently in this enchanted museum, its corridors echoing with secrets older than civilisations; its exhibits shift and breathe, with a life of their own. The excitement of the unknown beckoned stronger than any challenge ahead of them, a siren song promising both peril and unimaginable discoveries. As they ventured deeper into the museum, they entered a realm where the boundaries of reality became increasingly hazy, and their unwavering bond, forged in the face of the inexplicable, stayed the only constant.

"Let us embrace the magic of the night," Professor Finch said softly, his whimsical heart beating alongside the group's collective resolve. "Together, we shall not be mere spectators of history but participants in its wondrous dance."

As the clock struck twelve, the sound was slicing through the hushed museum halls; anticipation had settled in the air, thick and palpable like the scent of old paper and secrets. It was a tangible force, propelling them forward, pushing them past velvet ropes and darkened doorways towards the heart of the museum, the source of the legends they had come to explore. Their adventure had begun, a clandestine journey into the night where history came alive in the shadows. As each tick of the grandfather clock echoed like a heartbeat in the cavernous space, a steady drumbeat urging them onwards, they were ready to follow the whispers – the faint remnants of forgotten stories and unsolved mysteries – into the depths of the unknown, armed with nothing but their wits, their curiosity, and the faintest glimmer of moonlight filtering through the arched windows. The museum awaited, a labyrinth of secrets promising to test their courage and reveal its hidden truths.

A NIGHT LIKE NO OTHER

The museum loomed, a gothic silhouette against the inky canvas of the hangings, heavy in the air. It was the allure of the unknown that had drawn her here, a siren song sung by locked doors and hushed speculation. The whispered rumours surrounding the museum's long closure – tales of eccentric benefactors, forgotten expeditions, and the discovery of relics beyond comprehension – had fuelled her anticipation for weeks. Tonight, the curtain would rise. Tonight, the mysterious artefacts, shrouded in secrecy for decades, were to be unveiled.

A shiver, not entirely from the autumn chill, ran down her spine as she stepped inside. The air was thick with anticipation, a tangible buzz that vibrated through the assembled crowd. Her fingers, trembling slightly, grazed the cool, smooth surface of a glass case, an unconscious act of grounding, of connecting with the reality of the moment.

Behind them, a collection of ancient artefacts lay bathed in a soft, ethereal glow cast by expertly placed spotlights. The light seemed to breathe life into the objects, illuminating their intricate details and hinting at the stories they held. Each piece was meticulously displayed, a testament to the curators' dedication, and clearly marked with labels detailing their provenance, their journey through time and across continents. These small, informative plaques were gateways to other worlds, whispering tales of eras long since passed: dynasties risen and fallen in magnificent glory, cultures flourishing and dissolving like sandcastles in the tide, lives lived and lost to the relentless march of time.

A chipped clay tablet hinted at the complex legal system of a lost Mesopotamian kingdom. A tarnished silver amulet whispered of forgotten gods and the rituals performed in their honour. A delicate porcelain doll, its painted face cracked with age, spoke of a child's laughter silenced by the passage of centuries. With each artefact, a fragment of history flickered into existence, a fleeting glimpse into the lives of those who had come before.

She felt a strange connection to these objects, a pull that resonated deep within her soul. It was more than just intellectual curiosity; it was a visceral understanding, a feeling that these objects were not merely museum pieces of the museum, deeper into the heart of its secrets. The experience was more than just a viewing; it was an invitation, a call to adventure.

"Are you ready for this adventure, Ellie?" Professor Finch sat beside her, his spectacles glinting in the dim light. His excitement was palpable, and though he had a certain eccentric charm, there was something undeniably reassuring about his presence.

Ellie nodded, fighting off a wave of apprehension that threatened to swamp her. The air hung thick with anticipation, a palpable energy that prickled against her skin. It was one thing to be a historian, comfortably ensconced in dusty archives, meticulously piecing together fragments of the past from ancient texts and crumbling scrolls. It was quite another to be standing on the brink of something extraordinary, something that could rewrite history itself. A shiver traced its way down her spine, a mix of fear and exhilaration. She pictured the countless hours she and her team had poured into this project, the painstaking research, the late nights fuelled by lukewarm coffee and unwavering hope. Now, the decisive moment had arrived. "Let's see what mysteries await us," she replied, her voice surprisingly steady despite the whirlwind of thoughts spinning in her mind. She straightened her shoulders, pushing down the nagging doubts that whispered of unforeseen dangers and unimaginable consequences. This was it. It was time to face whatever secrets lie hidden in the depths.

As if in response to some unspoken plea, or perhaps the very presence of the adventurers themselves, Azrael, a grand statue carved from obsidian and gold, began to stir. He was a masterpiece of ancient Egyptian artistry, exuding an aura of timeless majesty, a silent sentinel guarding secrets for millennia. The air around him crackled with an unseen energy. Then, in a fiery spectacle that illuminated the darkened hall, the ancient Egyptian guardian came to life. Veins of molten gold pulsed beneath his obsidian skin, and his sculpted features glowed with a warm, ethereal light. His eyes, once lifeless gems, now burnt with ancient wisdom and a hint of warning. "Welcome to the night, brave adventurers," he rumbled, his voice a deep and resonant tremor that shook the very foundations of the museum. It was a voice like the grinding of pyramids and the whisper of desert winds. "The museum holds untold wonders, treasures beyond imagining, and knowledge lost to time. But tread carefully, for every shadow has a story etched in it and waits anxiously, yearning to unleash its secrets. Be warned, not all stories are meant to be heard, and not all secrets are meant to be unearthed."

Behind them, Oliver, the unsuspecting guard, rubbed his eyes, his lids heavy with the sleep he'd been fighting. "This is some sort of dream, right?" he murmured, his voice a low rumble, almost swallowed by the vastness of the hall. He squinted, trying to focus on the unfolding scene, the impossible dance of figures he swore to protect. "Statues don't come to life," he continued. He usually shows a stubborn nature, unwaveringly believing in the predictable order of things. He felt a strange pull, a magnetic force emanating from the animated sculptures, stealing the breath from his lungs and replacing it with a sense of wonder he hadn't experienced since childhood. He gripped his baton, a gesture more for reassurance than Defence serves as a tiny lighthouse against the encroaching tide of the unbelievable. Was he going mad? Or was something truly extraordinary happening before his very eyes?

"A dream? No!" Finn darted playfully around Oliver's feet, his wooden form infused with a mischievous spirit. "This is a night unlike any other! Time has turned, and your wildest fantasies may just come to life!"

Ellie chuckled at Finn's antics. "Let's focus on why we're here. Professor, what's first?"

Professor Finch pulled a small, worn notebook from the depths of his tweed jacket pocket. Its pages, thick with use, rustled as he flipped through them, revealing a chaotic mix of scribbled notes, faded ink sketches, and hastily drawn diagrams. His brow furrowed in concentration as he scanned the entries. "Right," he said, finally looking up, his eyes gleaming with a mixture of urgency and anticipation. "We need to find Luci. She, according to legend and these fragmented texts," he tapped the notebook, "holds the key to understanding the artefacts' past. Her knowledge is said to be unparalleled; she can guide us through their intricate tales and unravel them, weaving them. Everything hinges on it."

As they made their way deeper into the museum's labyrinthine halls, the air grew thick with the scent of aged paper and unseen wonders. The hushed reverence of the place pressed upon them, a palpable weight. Then, from a shadowed alcove, materialised Lady Arabella, a nobleperson made of marble, or so they had initially thought. An otherworldly shimmer surrounded her, a subtle distortion in the light that betrayed her true nature. "Young ones, heed my words," she intoned, her voice impossibly regal and yet calming, like a gentle breeze whispering through a grand cathedral. The sound resonated deep within their bones. "History and art intertwine like delicate threads, each carrying a tale and a secret awaiting discovery. Seek the wisdom that lies beyond mere sight. Do not simply see the surface; examine the hearts and minds of those who created these treasures and those whose lives they touched. For the true value of this place lies not in the artefacts themselves, but in the echoes of humanity, they hold within." Her eyes, usually unseeing orbs of stone, seemed to glow with ancient knowledge, beckoning them forward on a journey of understanding far deeper than they had expected.

Ellie turned her attention to Lady Arabella, feeling an almost magnetic pull towards the elegant figure. "Are you saying the artefacts have more to tell us?"

"Indeed," Lady Arabella replied, her eyes glimmering with depth. "Unlock their secrets, and you shall uncover the wonders hidden within this enchanted night."

Just then, a flurry of vibrant feathers—the colour of sunsets and storm clouds—fluttered past them, momentarily obscuring their vision. When the air cleared, they beheld Huckleberry , a magnificent creature of legend. He glided silently, his powerful wings barely stirring, before landing gracefully on a nearby pedestal, the ancient stone groaning softly under his weight. "I've been waiting for you all," he cawed, the sound surprisingly resonant and carrying a hint of impatience. His beady, intelligent eyes glinted with an inner light, assessing them with unsettling accuracy.

"You'll need my help to traverse the labyrinth of history."

He continued; his voice, a low trill, was interwoven with a melodic trill, like a predator purring. "This place", he hissed, the word hanging heavy in the air, "is a maze woven not of stone and earth but of shattered time itself, fractured memories echoing through eternity. And every turn, every forgotten corner, is guarded by perils so ancient, so deeply buried in the annals of reality, that they have been forgotten even by Death himself.

Follow my lead," he insisted, his eyes gleaming with an unnerving knowledge, "heed my warnings as if they were your very heartbeats. Trust that my instincts, honed by centuries of navigating these temporal currents, are your only compass. Then, and only then, will nothing – neither the ravages of time, which have crumbled empires to dust and turned gods to whispers, nor the guardians of the past, who hunger for new souls to drag back into their endless cycle – bar your path. But," he added, his voice dropping to a chilling whisper, "stray from my path, even for a moment, and the echoes of the past, the siren song of what was, will forever ensnare you, binding you to this broken reality, a prisoner of time for all eternity."

He paused, his gaze sweeping over them once more, challenging them to accept his guidance and the perilous journey that lay ahead.

agic lives not only in the artefacts and their inherent power but also in the bonds forged through adventure.

Ellie swallowed hard, exhilaration coursing through her as they followed Huckleberry deeper into the museum. The vast space transformed around them, each exhibit offering a glimpse into a different realm. They passed through a hall lined with ancient sculptures, their stony faces etched with the wisdom and weariness of forgotten ages; paintings that seemed to whisper the secrets of the past, the pigments subtly shifting as if the scenes depicted within them were still unfolding.

Displays laden with artefacts drawing the eye with their ethereal glow and promising untold power if only they dared to reach out. The air thrummed with palpable energy, a silent hum of magic that resonated within Ellie's very bones, urging her onwards energy, urging her onwards into the heart of the museum's hidden depths.

As they ventured into the Western wing, a chill permeated the air, heavier than the dust that coated the forgotten halls. The already dim light, struggling to penetrate the gloom, flickered erratically, casting dancing shadows that played tricks on their eyes. And then, they saw her. Coiled elegantly atop an ornate pedestal, like a living sculpture, was Luci. Her bronze scales, catching the light, shimmered like polished gold, each individual scale reflecting the surrounding darkness with an almost hypnotic gleam. Her head, held high with an air of ancient wisdom, regarded them with eyes that burnt with an inner fire. The silence deepened, broken only by the almost imperceptible hiss of her breath. Finally, her voice cut through the stillness, a low, resonant timbre that seemed to vibrate through the very stones of the room.

"Welcome, seekers of knowledge," she intoned, each word pregnant with meaning. "Time twists within these walls, a river flowing in circles. I am its keeper, the weaver of its threads, and I shall weave the tales you look for. But be warned," she added, her voice dropping to a conspiratorial whisper, "some stories are better left untold, and some knowledge comes at a price."

Intrigued, Ellie stepped forward, mesmerised by the snake's hypnotic gaze. "We need to learn about the Artefact of Echoes. Can you help us decipher its riddle?"

Luci nodded, her tongue flickering as if tasting the air. "To unlock the past, you must first understand the present. Tell me, what do you see?"

The group exchanged glances, the atmosphere thick with anticipation, a silent language passing between them that spoke of shared excitement and a touch of apprehension. Ellie considered the artefacts nearby, a curated collection of the ancient and the enigmatic, each more captivating than the last. Gilded statues gleamed softly in the low light, their eyes seeming to follow her; intricate carvings depicted long-forgotten rituals; and fragments of pottery hinted at lives lived centuries ago. "It's all interconnected, isn't it?" she asked, her voice barely a whisper, the pieces clicking together in her mind like tumblers in a lock. "The history of each object contributes to a larger narrative, weaving a tapestry of the past... a story that's been fragmented and scattered but is now, finally, beginning to coalesce." She gestured around the room, her eyes alight with understanding. "This isn't just a collection of relics; it's a puzzle, a testament to the enduring power of civilisation – a power we're only just beginning to grasp."

"Precisely," Luci replied, her voice flowing like silk. "Each artefact whispers a tale, but only those who listen can decipher the truth."

Magic lives not only in the artefacts and their inherent power but also in the bonds forged through adventure. Just then, an urgent flutter drew their attention.

Huckleberry, perched precariously on a crumbling ledge, flapped his impressive wings. The sound, a low, resonant thrum, pulled them closer, an undeniable signal in the oppressive silence of the ancient chamber. He landed gracefully on another pedestal, seemingly designated for objects of importance, and gestured with a hooked talon towards an intricate mask resting there.

"The Artefact of Echoes calls you," he encouraged, his voice a gravelly whisper that carried an unusual weight. He clearly believed in its power, or at least its significance. Prompted by his words, a mixture of awe and trepidation compelling them forward, they examined the mask. It was a masterpiece of artisanship, adorned with vivid colours that seemed to glow with an inner light even in dimness. Glistening stones, meticulously placed, caught and reflected the meagre light, creating a mesmerising dance of sparkle and shadow. They could almost feel the weight of history emanating from the object, a palpable hum that hinted at untold stories waiting to be heard.

Ellie reached out cautiously, her fingers brushing against the cool surface. "What can you tell us about this?"

"Ah, a mask of great power!" Luci hissed, her eyes narrowing with purpose. "To wear it is to hear the voices of those who once lived. However, keep in mind that time reflects and refracts, so one must exercise caution when posing questions. be careful what question one poses."

"What if we ask how to navigate what's ahead?" Oliver suggested, his eyes widening at the idea of conversing with the past.

"Caution, brave guard," Lady Arabella warned, stepping closer. "Echoes can be deceptive, leading one astray if not respected."

Ellie felt a powerful and irresistible tide of curiosity despite the cautionary words echoing in her mind like a persistent drumbeat. within Ellie, a powerful and irresistible tide. Instead of deterring them, the warnings made for excited rebelliousness. The risk, palpable in the air, wasn't a deterrent; it was exhilarating, a tingling anticipation that danced along her skin. The potential for discovery—

the tantalising possibility of unearthing something extraordinary—overshadowed her first hesitation, eclipsing the practical voice whispering about danger. She imagined forgotten secrets lying just beyond their grasp, waiting to be brought to light. Taking a deep breath, a determined glint sparking in her eyes, she spoke, her voice ringing with conviction. "Let's do it. We're not here to hesitate or let fear paralyse us; we're here to uncover! We are here to uncover the layers of mystery and uncover what lies beneath. We owe it to ourselves, and perhaps, to whoever came before us."

With a nod of approval from the professor, his eyes twinkling with a mixture of anticipation and thinly veiled concern, and a shrug from Oliver, who looked more amused than anything, Ellie held the ornate mask up to her face.

The moment it made contact, a rush of energy unlike anything she'd ever experienced enveloped her, a tangible force that felt both exhilarating and terrifying. She gasped, but the sound was lost in the swirling vortex of colours and sounds that erupted around her. The world as she knew it dissolved into a kaleidoscope of luminous greens, electric blues, and fiery oranges, all dancing and merging in a dizzying display. But the visuals were only the beginning. A cacophony of laughter, cries, and whispers, seemingly originating from both everywhere and nowhere at once, flooded her mind. Some were playful, some mournful, some laced with malice, and others spoke of long-forgotten histories. Secrets, spoken softly among the shadows, brushed against her consciousness, hints of truths she couldn't quite grasp, leaving her feeling overwhelmed and profoundly disoriented. The weight of the mask suddenly felt immense, as if it was not just an object but a conduit to a vast, unknowable realm.

"What question will you ask?" the whispers clamoured, vying for her attention.

"Guide us through the artefacts!" Ellie shouted, her heart pounding fiercely against her chest. "Help us discover their legends and the truth that binds them!"

There was a stillness, a pause laden with tension, before the voices answered. "Only with unity can the past be unlocked; only through balance can the story be told."

Abruptly, the world around her shattered like glass, accompanied by a cacophony of tinkling sounds and visual chaos, as the vibrant tapestry of the earlier reality fractured into countless shimmering fragments. These pieces, like miniature, self-contained universes, swirled around her—a disorienting ballet of impossible colours and shapes. Subsequently, they vanished into the realm of actuality, erasing all traces of their presence. Ellie gasped, her chest heaving, as she found herself abruptly back in the cool, sterile atmosphere of the museum, standing beside her friends.

The museum, with its hushed tones and static displays, felt jarringly normal after the extraordinary experience. She was breathless, not just from the physical sensation of displacement but from the sheer overwhelming intensity of what she had just seen, a secret world unveiled and then ripped away in an instant. The lingering echoes of the broken reality resonated within her, leaving her slightly dazed and desperate to understand what had just happened.

"What did you learn?" Professor Finch asked eagerly, his brow knitted with curiosity.

Ellie paused, her gaze sweeping over the assembled group, a mixture of scholars, adventurers, and mystics. She took a moment to collect her thoughts, piecing together the echoes of forgotten languages and fragmented visions that swirled within her. "I have something to say," she began, her voice resonating with newfound certainty.

To unlock their secrets and to understand the true purpose they serve, we must work together. Individual brilliance will only reveal fragments. It is through the combined knowledge and shared perspective of us all that we can truly decipher the patterns." She paused again, her expression hardening with a sombre understanding. "We carry the weight of their memories, the burden of the past. These artefacts are not mere relics; they are vessels holding the joys, sorrows, triumphs, and failures of those who came before them. We must respect them and be aware of their power, which can do great good or great harm. power they hold, for it is capable of both great good and devastating destruction."

"Together," Azrael affirmed, his voice a deep rumble. "That is the essence of this night. The museum reflects your unity—a bond that transcends time."

As if in agreement, the museum walls vibrated with a low, resonant hum that seemed to seep into Ellie's very bones, sending goosebumps prickling along her arms. The air thrummed with an unseen energy, a palpable confirmation of something significant. Finn, usually content to see from the sidelines, danced gleefully, a blur of orange fur weaving through their legs in excited, unpredictable patterns. He nipped playfully at Ellie's shoelaces as if sharing in a secret triumph. "Does that mean we nailed it?" Ellie breathed, her voice a mixture of hopeful anticipation and stunned disbelief. Her eyes, wide and shining, darted between the vibrating walls and Finn's ecstatic dance. "Are we the chosen ones?" The question hung in the air, heavy with implication, the possibility both exhilarating and terrifying. Had they stumbled upon something truly extraordinary, some forgotten power hidden within the museum's ancient heart?

A soft chuckle, laced with an undercurrent of something ancient and unknowable, broke through the tense air as Luci unfurled herself, her movements languid and hypnotic. Her eyes, like chips of obsidian, fixed on the chosen one. "You are chosen, indeed," she purred, the word hanging heavy with unspoken implications. "But responsibility – a burden you cannot yet comprehend – lies ahead. Seek the guidance of Valen to prevent the unravelling of fate. He holds the key to your journey, a key that could either save you... or damn you."

With renewed determination burning in her eyes, Ellie glanced at her companions. Liam, ever the eager historian, practically vibrated with anticipation, his fingers itching to uncover long-lost secrets. Across from him, Maya, their pragmatist and puzzle-solver, chewed nervously on her lip, a telltale sign of her excitement tempered by the unknown challenges ahead. Each face radiated a complex mixture of exhilaration and trepidation, a reflection of the daunting task they were about to undertake. Ellie straightened her shoulders, a surge of leadership coursing through her. "Then let's find Valen," she declared, her voice ringing with newfound conviction. "We have puzzles to solve, histories to unveil, and a timeline that depends on us. Let's not keep fate waiting."

Together, with each heartbeat resonating like a drum, they left the Egyptian wing behind, a primal rhythm against the unnatural stillness; they left the Egyptian wing behind, a sense of unease clinging to them like the desert dust. While traversing the vast expanse of the museum, shadows danced in their peripheral vision, deceiving their eyes. They were ready, or so they told themselves, to uncover its hidden labyrinth of history. But what if the legacies that whispered fervently through the night were not just stories but something far more...alive? What secrets slumbered within these walls, and what price would they pay to awaken them?

Together, with each heartbeat resonating like a drum, they left the Egyptian wing behind, a primal rhythm against the unnatural stillness. they left the Egyptian wing behind, a sense of unease clinging to them. While traversing the vast expanse of the museum, shadows danced in their peripheral vision, deceiving their eyes. They were ready, or so they told themselves, to uncover its hidden labyrinth of history. But what if the legacies that whispered fervently through the night were not just stories but something far more...alive? What secrets slumbered within these walls, and what price would they pay to awaken them?

SHADOWS AND SECRETS

The ancient halls of the Enchanted Museum were cloaked in an ethereal darkness, illuminated only by the faint shimmer reflecting off the polished marble floors. Dust motes, disturbed by unseen currents, danced in the silver light, lending the scene a surreal quality. As midnight approached, the air was thick with anticipation, a palpable hum that vibrated against the skin. Ellie felt her heart race with both exhilaration and trepidation; a thrilling cocktail of emotions Magic exists not only in the artefacts and their inherent power but also in the bonds forged through adventure. she couldn't quite tame.

They had already met the magnificent Azrael, a colossal marble statue that had come to life with an unexpected energy. Its gaze, once cold and lifeless, now held a spark of ancient wisdom, and a low rumble emanated from its chest, a sound that pulsed through the room and resonated deep within Ellie's bones. The encounter had left her breathless and questioning everything she thought she knew about the museum, about history, about reality itself. Now, with each ticking second, she wondered what wonders, or horrors, awaited them in the darkened depths of this magical place. What other artefacts were stirring, awakened by the same mysterious force that had animated Azrael? And what was their purpose in this nightly resurrection?

"Remember, everyone," Azrael's deep voice rumbled, "the museum holds many secrets, but each shadow also conceals a truth waiting to be uncovered." His golden eyes glinted mischievously as he beckoned Ellie, Professor Finch, and Oliver closer.

"Thank you for the helpful disclaimer, wise Azrael," Oliver said, brushing a hand through his tousled hair, trying to mask his unease with a smirk. "Is there a manual for dealing with enchanted artefacts? I don't have the necessary training for such situations.

"That's the beauty of adventure, dear guard!" Professor Finch chimed, adjusting his spectacles as he scanned their surroundings. "We learn by doing, and tonight? Well, tonight is full of delightful discoveries." He tapped his fingers against a dusty tablet nearby, drawing curious looks from the others.

"Speaking of delightful, let's not linger here too long," Ellie interjected. "Dr

From across the vast gallery, a hushed silence reigned, amplifying every minute sound. It was then that an inexplicably soft rustling, like the whisper of velvet curtains in a forgotten theatre, caught their attention. Eyes strained, they followed the subtle noise to its source: Finn. The creature wasn't just any fox, mind you. Finn was a scruffy, almost carelessly carved wooden figure, yet he owned an unnatural vitality, animated by an unseen spirit that hummed with untold stories. He darted out from behind a colossal statue of a pharaoh, its stoic face a stark contrast to the fox's playful demeanour. His painted eyes, usually dull and lifeless, twinkled with mischief, reflecting the flickering torchlight like captured stars. He tilted his head, a small, knowing grin spreading across his wooden snout. "If it's secrets you seek," he squeaked, his voice surprisingly high-pitched and clear, defying his rough construction, "follow me!" With a flourish, he pranced toward a dark corridor that seemed to breathe shadows. An oppressive chill emanated from its depths, hinting at mysteries that lay hidden within, waiting to be unearthed. The air was oppressive, thick with the scent of dust and forgotten ages, drawing them ineluctably toward the unknown. Was the situation a genuine invitation or a cleverly laid trap? They had no way of knowing, but the allure of the secrets Finn promised was too strong to resist.

"Lead the way, little guide!" said Azrael with enthusiasm, and the group followed Finn down the hallowed passage, where golden hieroglyphs whispered ancient tales through the cracks in the wall.

As the travellers moved deeper into the shadowed path, a subtle shift in the air heralded a change. From her perch coiled amongst the gnarled roots of an ancient, whispering tree, Luci uncoiled. The movement was liquid and mesmerising, a dance of scales and muscle as she slithered gracefully to join their company. Her bronze scales, usually a warm, earthy tone, glowed eerily under the filtered, dim light that pierced the dense canopy above, casting an unnatural sheen that seemed to emanate from within. She approached them slowly, a living statue of sinuous beauty and inherent danger.

When she was close enough that they could feel the faint, dry rustle of her scales against the earth, she spoke. "Beware what lies ahead," she hissed softly, the sound like wind whispering through dry leaves, yet carrying an undercurrent of profound warning. Her eyes, ancient and knowing, narrowed mysteriously, the pupils dilating to drink in every detail of their faces. "The secrets of the past", your intent, those whose hearts are free of malice and greed shall triumph. For all others, destruction awaits."

"What do you mean?" Ellie asked, her curiosity increasing. "What kind of secrets?"

"Shadows cast by regret, whispers of betrayal," Luci replied, flicking her tail. "Each artefact in this museum embodies a history—none are stagnant; they pulse with energy, shaped by those who have touched them." she paused, her serpentine form swaying gently. "Including you."

The group halted, boots scuffing softly on the marble floor, the silence amplifying the hum of anticipation that had been building with each passing exhibit. They exchanged glances, each face reflecting a complex mix of excitement at the threshold of discovery and a prickling foreboding, a sense that they were treading on hallowed, perhaps even dangerous, ground. Ellie's heart pounded against her ribs, a frantic drumbeat against the hushed reverence of the hall. She reached out, her fingertips hovering inches from a chipped clay tablet, and a shiver ran down her spine. Each artefact indeed felt alive, vibrating with a subtle energy, its surface a palimpsest of history. Its essence was undeniably intertwined with the potent emotions of countless souls throughout time – the joy of creation, the agony of loss, the burning ambition, the quiet despair. The museum was not merely a place of display, a sterile collection of relics encased in glass; it was a living testament to stories waiting to be told, a silent symphony of whispers yearning to be heard. It was a portal, perhaps, to something much more than just the past.

"Let's keep moving," Professor Finch urged, a hint of anxious recognition lingering in his voice. As they ventured deeper, the shadows thickened, and the whispers grew louder—a symphony of voices reminiscing about forgotten dreams and lingering fears.

Finn stopped suddenly, sniffing the air. "Hush!" he said, his ears perked. "I hear something!"

The echo of a solitary heartbeat rang in Ellie's ears as they moved closer to a nearby alcove. "What is it, Finn?" she whispered.

"There!" he exclaimed, darting toward an ornate wooden door, intricately carved with more hieroglyphics. "I can feel it. This door... it holds something important."

Determined, Ellie approached the door, tracing her fingers over the intricate carvings. The wood was ancient, darkened by time and weather, yet beneath its aged surface, she felt a strange warmth. It wasn't just heat; it was a subtle, pulsing energy, thrumming under her touch as though the carvings were alive, breathing with a hidden power. A shiver traced its way down her spine. Hesitation tugged at her, but the curiosity – the need to know – was stronger. "We need to see what's inside," she said, glancing back at the others. Her voice was steadier than she felt, a fragile shield against the unknown that loomed behind the silent wood.

"A puzzle perhaps?" said Professor Finch, his interest piqued. The anticipation in the air electrified their spirits.

"Or a trap," Oliver warned, his brow furrowing. "Let's be cautious."

"Caution is wise, but not as exhilarating!" Finn chirped, enticing them to explore further.

The air thickened, prickling against their skin, as if sensing their arrival. As if responding to their presence, the aged wooden door, its panels carved with forgotten symbols, creaked open with a groan that echoed the weight of centuries. The sound sliced through the silence. revealing a dark room shimmering with golden artefacts. Treasures piled haphazardly filled the space, reflecting the dim light in a chaotic yet breathtaking display of wealth. In the heart of this hoard, a statue of a regal 18th-century woman loomed at the centre, its marble form radiating an almost palpable aura. The artisanry was exquisite, capturing every delicate curve and subtle detail of her likeness. She was adorned with gems – rubies, emeralds, and diamonds – that sparkled like stars against the encroaching darkness, each facet catching the light and scattering it in a dazzling display. It was Lady Arabella, immortalised in stone, her expression strikingly serene despite the chaotic swirl of energies around her. A faint smile played on her lips, hinting at a secret knowledge, a power that seemed to emanate from the very core of the statue, drawing their gaze and holding them captive within the room's oppressive stillness. The air hummed with an unseen force, a tangible magic that both beckoned and warned.

"Welcome, travellers," Lady Arabella spoke in a melodic tone, her voice embodying centuries of wisdom. "You seek the shadows and the secrets they guard."

"What must we do to uncover them?" Ellie enquired, stepping cautiously into the chamber.

"First, reveal your intentions. Shadow and light must coexist; truth lies within balance," Lady Arabella replied, gesturing towards the artefacts surrounding her. "You have come to learn,

Finn bounded up to the statue. "Can you help us, Lady Arabella? We need to navigate the secrets of the night!"

With a subtle nod, almost imperceptible, Arabella turned her gaze to a shimmer in the corner of the room. It was a velvet curtain, the colour of midnight and dust, hung with deliberate carelessness yet radiating an aura of importance. It seemed utterly out of place amidst the modern, minimalist decor, a relic stumbled upon from another age. "Behind that curtain", she said, her voice dropping to a hushed whisper that amplified the air of mystery, "the enigma awaits. An ancient being, long forgotten even by the annals of history—Valen—holds the keys to your quest. He is resistant to influence and dislikes disruptions. Approach him with respect and be prepared to answer questions that explore the very fabric of your being. He communicates in cryptic ways and could discern lies. Your success, and perhaps your life, hinges on your ability to decipher his wisdom."

Azrael stepped forward, muscles taut with anticipation. "Then we must not waste time!"

Together, they moved towards the curtain, the anticipation hanging thick in the air like a tangible thing. Ellie's heart quickened, a frantic drumbeat against her ribs, as she reached for the heavy fabric. A nervous tremor ran through her hand, a testament to the unknown that awaited. This reveal could change everything. Ready or not, she was about to unveil whatever lay behind, and with each step closer, the gravity of the moment intensified. As they pulled the curtain aside, a tempest of vibrant light erupted, swirling around them in a dizzying kaleidoscope of colour. The unexpected brilliance washed over them, momentarily blinding and disorienting them. Intricate shadows danced to the rhythm of their racing hearts, thrown across the walls in a captivating display of light and dark. The air crackled with an unseen energy, a palpable sense of wonder and mystery that left them breathless and suspended in time, unsure of what awaited them beyond the blinding light.

"Cristal!" A wooden chest materialised before them, intricately carved with symbols that radiated history.

"Let's see what's inside!" Oliver exclaimed, but as he reached out to lift the lid, the shadows became restless, slithering along the walls like smoke, creeping closer.

"No!" Luci hissed, her posture rigid. "Do not disturb what sleeps! The shadows guard a truth not yet meant to be revealed."

The others stood frozen, each a statue carved from anxiety and disbelief. The air itself seemed to thicken, heavy with the weight of ancient secrets finally unearthed. Dust motes danced in the shafts of light piercing the gloom, illuminating faces etched with a mixture of fear and awe. They had stumbled upon something far grander, far more dangerous, than they could have ever imagined. Ellie, however, felt the urgency in the air like physical pressure. Time felt thin and weak; you've been silent since we opened the chamber. You knew what was down here, didn't you? Do you have anything to share? Anything that can help us understand what we've unleashed, or... how to hold it?"

The griffin cawed, the sound echoing through the ancient, crumbling ruins like a distant memory, a phantom chime from a forgotten age. Its piercing cry hung in the air, carrying a weight of untold stories and long-lost knowledge. "To understand the present", it rasped, its voice weathered and ancient, "one must acknowledge the past. To ignore the echoes of what came before is to walk blindly into a future forged in ignorance." Its golden eyes, like molten coins, narrowed slightly.

"Secrets entwined with the shadows hold profound wisdom and truths. It was buried deep beneath the surface, waiting to be unearthed. The griffin shifted its massive wings, a whisper of wind rustling through its sun-gilded feathers. " Heathens leading only to madness."

"Can we solve the riddle? Can we confront these shadows?" whispered Ellie, determination shimmering in her eyes. "If we work together, we can endure whatever lies ahead."

With a collective breath, the group prepared to face the unknown. A mix of anticipation and dread hung in the air, thick enough to taste. Oliver, despite his clear bravery in the lead, took a subtle step back, his eyes darting nervously around the dark entrance. He needed verification of his courage, a verbal boost to quell the bubbling anxieties swirling within him. He cleared his throat, forcing a light-hearted tone. "Okay, I'm in, but I'll need some reassurance that I won't turn into a toad or something..." The joke faltered in the tense atmosphere as he trailed off. He glanced at the others, hoping for a laugh, a playful shove, or anything to break the spell of unease. He added quickly, "Seriously though, is there any chance of... unexpected transformations? I just want to know what I'm getting into here.

Could you provide a quick rundown of the potential downsides? His bravado was cracking, revealing the genuine fear beneath.

"I've heard worse," Azrael teased. "If all else fails, I'll keep you company in your toad form!"

They laughed, a cascade of relieved and slightly hysterical sounds that echoed through the chamber. Just moments before, the tension that had been as tight as a bowstring started to release, dissipating like morning mist under a rising sun. Camaraderie, a feeling forged in shared hardship and mutual respect, wrapped around them like a warm blanket, a comforting weight against the chill of the unknown they had faced.

Together, their hands trembling slightly with anticipation, they lifted the heavy chest lid in unison. The ancient wood groaned in protest, and then, revealed in the dim light, a shimmering amulet rested upon a bed of plush, crimson velvet. The velvet, aged and worn, hinted at the long history of the object it cradled. The amulet, crafted from what appeared to be polished moonstone and intricately etched with symbols that seemed to shift and dance in their peripheral vision, pulsed with a soft, inner light. The moment it was fully unveiled, a palpable pulse of energy surged through the room, a vibrant, tingling force that pricked their skin and made the hairs on their arms stand on end.

The shadows, previously deep and brooding, writhed and twisted in what felt like joyful abandon, illuminated by the amulet's sudden radiance. The light danced across the stone walls, transforming familiar patterns into fleeting, ephemeral shapes, suggesting a hidden reality just beyond their grasp. The air crackled with untold possibilities, leaving them breathless and filled with a mix of awe and apprehension.

"Welcome back, Timekeeper," the shadows whispered.

"What is this?" Professor Finch marvelled while peering at the amulet. "Could this be the key to our journey?"

"Indeed," crooned the amulet, the voices of the past resonating through its core. "But only those willing to face their shadows shall unlock the truths within."

With newfound resolve, Ellie turned to her companions. "This is just the beginning. We solve these puzzles together."

"I don't know what lies ahead, but I trust in us," Oliver admitted, the fear in his voice tempered by a spark of bravery.

As they clasped hands, a jolt of energy, subtle yet undeniable, passed between them. It was as if their joined palms formed a conduit, a key unlocking the oppressive silence. The shadows that had clung to the ornate walls and shrouded the echoing halls began to recede, pulled back like a tide revealing a hidden shore. A path, previously obscured by darkness and the weight of unseen history, materialised before them. The path beckoned them forward into the heart of the museum's enigma. Dust mites danced in newly visible beams of moonlight, filtering through arched windows, illuminating forgotten artefacts and hinting at long-buried secrets. There was no doubt that the night had not yet end. The museum, far from being a silent tomb of relics, thrummed with an unseen energy. The whispers, barely heard before, now resonated with a newfound clarity, promising voices of the past still awaiting their adventure, eager to share their stories with those brave enough to listen. Their journey had only just begun, and the museum, a labyrinth of forgotten narratives, was ready to reveal its secrets.

They entered a labyrinth of intrigue and discovery, with a clear mission but a mysterious path to its completion. Ready to immerse themselves in the shadows and secrets that lingered like unanswered questions, they adjusted their cloaks, their hands instinctively reaching for the hilts of their swords – or the tools of their trade. Eager to unveil the wonders of the enchanted night that lay before them, not just for the sake of knowledge but for the sake of those who depended on them, they pressed forward with a determined resolve.

THE
WHISPERING PORTRAITS

The air in the Enchanted Museum was thick with anticipation, a palpable energy that settled on the skin like a fine mist. As the clock struck midnight, its chimes resonating deep within the building's ancient bones, a hush fell, broken only by the sounds of whispering. The whispers seemed to emanate from the very artefacts, drawing Ellie and her companions deeper into the museum's heart. Their guide, Azrael, a magnificent creature of myth and magic, visibly pulsed with excitement. He flicked his tail with a rhythmic thud against the polished marble floor, the golden fur rippling and gleaming under the dim, strategically placed light of the ornate chandeliers. Each flick seemed to urge them onwards, promising adventure and revealing mysteries that lay hidden within the museum's enchanted depths. A sense of both wonder and trepidation hung in the air, a promise that this night would be unlike any other.

"Stay close," he instructed, leading them towards a corridor lined with magnificent portraits. Each painting seemed to shimmer, as if the figures captured within were aware of the living world around them.

"Are you certain they talk?" Oliver, the museum guard, asked with a hint of scepticism. His grip on the flashlight tightened, illuminating the ornate frames that encased the portraits.

"They don't just talk, dear Oliver," Professor Finch chimed in, his eyes glowing with curiosity. "They whisper tales of history that could unlock the deepest mysteries of this place."

Ellie's heart raced with intrigue, a frantic drum against her ribs that echoed the silence of the ancient hall. She felt drawn, almost compelled, towards the portrait of a regal knight. His armour gleamed even in the dim light, and his face, stern and noble, was framed by thick, painted hair. But it was his eyes that held her captive. Deep and knowing, they seemed to possess a life of their own, following her every move with unsettling precision. A shiver traced its way down her spine. "What do you whisper?" she murmured, her voice barely heard above the imagined echoes of history. The words were more a plea than a question, born from a sudden and inexplicable yearning. She felt foolish, half expecting an answer – a rustle of canvas, a disembodied voice, a tale spun from the very fabric of the painting. But the silence persisted, thick and heavy, only amplifying the mystery that emanated from the knight in the portrait.

Suddenly, the knight's mouth twitched, a subtle spasm that belied the rigid stillness he'd kept for what felt like an eternity. Ellie, who had been cautiously studying the silent, armoured figure, staggered back in surprise. The twitch was followed by movement, a slow, deliberate tilting of the head, and then a voice, deep and resonant, boomed forth, shattering the silence of the ancient hall. "Seek the truths buried in shadows," he spoke, each word a carefully crafted stone in a building of mystery, his voice a deep rumble that resonated across the hall, vibrating in the very floorboards beneath Ellie's feet. "Only then shall you grasp the weight of time." The words hung in the air, heavy with untold meaning, leaving Ellie more confused and intrigued than before. The knight fell silent again, returning to his unmoving state, but the echo of his pronouncements lingered, bouncing off the high vaulted ceilings and swirling around Ellie like a tangible fog. She felt a frisson of fear but also a powerful pull, a magnetic draw compelling her to decipher the enigma he had just presented.

"Did you hear that?" Ellie exclaimed, her voice barely above a whisper, glancing at her friends. The others nodded, spellbound.

"Shadows? Luci, encircling the exhibit's pedestal, whispered in a deep voice. " This sounds like another riddle. The portraits appear to have a connection to our quest.

"Each one must hold a clue," Azrael suggested, his eyes sparkling with mischief. "Why not ask them directly?"

Ellie took a deep breath; the musty air of the museum was heavy in her lungs, and she stepped towards a nearby portrait. The lady depicted within was resplendent in opulent clothing—velvet the colour of midnight, adorned with shimmering pearls and intricate lace. Her painted gaze, though centuries old, seemed serene and knowing, holding secrets whispered from a bygone era. Ellie's heart pounded a nervous rhythm against her ribs. This was it. She had to try. Gathering her courage, she straightened her shoulders and addressed the painted figure. "Mlady," Ellie called, her voice steady despite the tremor in her hands. "We are...lost, in a manner of speaking. This museum holds its secrets close, shrouded in history and shadowed by forgotten tales. Can you help us unveil the truths hidden within these walls? Can you guide us, even if only with a whisper of insight, to remove the enigmas that bind us here?"

The lady's painted lips curved into a gentle smile, and a soft, melodic whisper filled the air. "Dearest child of time, the key lies within the heart that seeks."

"What does that even mean?" Oliver muttered, clearly more frustrated than intrigued. Ellie shot him a look of encouragement.

"Maybe", Professor Finch said, his brows furrowed in concentration, "the heart she speaks of is tied to the emotions and intentions behind our enquiries."

The portrait shimmered again, the canvas seeming to ripple like water disturbed by a gentle breeze. Faint, swirling colours danced around the edges, drawing the eye and blurring the lines between painted illusion and tangible reality. Then, with a final, almost imperceptible pulse of light, the figure depicted within stepped out of the frame. She wasn't a mere imitation of life but a breathing, radiant being. Her ethereal presence filled the room, casting a warm, comforting light that seemed to chase away the shadows and soothe the soul. Her features, delicate and timeless, held a deep well of wisdom and understanding.

"To understand the artefacts of the past," she continued, her voice a melodic chime that resonated with ancient power, "you must connect with them, not merely study them. You must feel their history, their purpose. Each was crafted with intention, imbued with the spirit of its maker, and shaped by the events it saw. Each has a soul yearning to share its story, waiting for a hand to touch it, a mind to perceive its essence, and a heart to understand its silent language. Approach them not as objects, but as echoes of lives lived, whispers of forgotten ages, and you will unlock secrets beyond your wildest imaginings."

With a flourish of her hand, a graceful, almost theatrical gesture that seemed to command the very air, the lady gestured to the adjoining portraits. They weren't mere paintings hanging on the wall; they were portals, conduits to another time. As her fingers danced in the air, an almost imperceptible hum resonated through the room, and the faces within the frames began to shift and morph. The colours intensified, the details sharpened, and the static images dissolved into something far more vibrant and alive. Arriving from their gilded prisons, figures materialise, stepping out of their painted worlds and into the present.

They were all historical beings come to life, their eyes gleaming with forgotten stories, their lips parted as if about to speak. Each one, a king in his crown, a queen in her jewels, and a scholar in his robes, was poised to share a fragment of their past, a secret whispered across centuries, and a truth waiting to be unearthed. The air crackled with anticipation, the weight of history palpable in the room, as the silent gallery was about to burst into a symphony of voices long silenced.

"Blimey!" Oliver gasped, taking an involuntary step back. "This is getting a bit too surreal for my taste."

Finn darted between the legs of the otherworldly figures, his excitement palpable. "Come, Oliver! When has a museum ever offered such a lively experience? Embrace it!"

One by one, the portraits unveiled themselves, their dust-laden canvases shedding years of secrets. Initially, a wise philosopher, his eyes glistening with timeless wisdom, uttered riddles and parables, implying the priceless lessons of the past and the cyclical nature of history. Then, a brave explorer, sun-weathered and scarred, appeared from his painted frame, regaling them with thrilling tales of perilous adventures across uncharted lands filled with strange creatures and forgotten civilisations.

A regal queen, a cunning inventor, and a stoic warrior followed, each embodiment stepping forward to share their wisdom, their follies, and their unique perspectives. Each held a fragment of truth, a piece of the intricate puzzle that Ellie and her carefully chosen team desperately needed to solve if they hoped to succeed in their quest. The air crackled with anticipation as Ellie meticulously documented every word and every gesture, knowing that a single missed detail could doom them all.

"All the while," remarked Lady Arabella, whose presence was now more majestic than ever, "we are drawn together by a common thread, our lives woven into a grand tapestry." She glided forward, merging with the whispers around them.

"Let us share what we know," encouraged Professor Finch.

Ellie found herself captivated by a portrait of a young artist. "What did you create to inspire?" she asked.

"Art bears witness to the spirit of the times," the artist replied with a paintbrush in hand. "Seek out the colours and stories they hold; their hues speak of joy, sorrow, and wonder."

"Perhaps each colour signifies a moment in history," Ellie thought aloud, recalling her studies. Each figure offered insights that hinted at their backgrounds, yet none fully illuminated the path they needed to follow.

"Time flows in the cycles of shadows and light," the knight said again, his voice resonating deeply. "Only by piecing together the echoes of our tales can you bridge the divide between past and present."

Oliver scratched his head. "Isn't time a bit more linear than that? I mean, centuries pass without much interaction."

Azrael chimed in, "True. However, the wisdom comes from these tales can alter your feeling of time itself. Let's not lose sight of our goal!"

The portraits, once vibrant depictions of stern lords and elegant ladies, began to fade, their colours bleeding into each other like watercolours left in the rain. As the details softened and blurred, the figures themselves seemed to recede into the canvas, leaving behind a soft, ethereal glow. This light, warm and inviting, emanated from what was suddenly revealed to be a narrow passageway hidden directly behind the portraits, a secret passage previously concealed by masterful illusion. "Follow the light, dear adventurers," echoed the disembodied voice of the lady from the largest portrait, her tone both encouraging and laced with a hint of playful mystery. "It will guide you, true. Hesitate not, for your path lies forward, waiting to be discovered," she urged, the resonance of her words pushing them gently to move ahead into the unknown.

"Keep your eyes peeled," Finn chirped playfully. "There might be more hints just waiting to be uncovered!"

As they turned toward the passage, the air grew heavy, a palpable shift in atmosphere that raised goosebumps on their skin. Shadows danced along the walls, elongated and distorted by the flickering torchlight, seemingly alive with an energy that both beckoned and warned. Each step echoed in the stillness, amplified by the tight confines and the thick silence that pressed in from all sides. Their hearts pounded with a mixture of excitement and apprehension, a primal rhythm echoing the anticipation that hummed in the very stones beneath their feet. What secrets lay hidden beyond the bend? What challenges awaited them in the darkness? The unknown stretched before them, a tempting and terrifying enigma.

"Remember, one mystery reveals another," Luci reminded them, her voice smooth. "As we delve deeper, the answers may lead us to the very heart of the Enchanted Museum."

They approached the illuminated hall, a beacon in the surrounding gloom. Ellie felt an ancient pull, a resonant hum that vibrated deep within her bones, as though the very walls were urging them onwards, compelling them to see what lay within.

As they stepped through an archway, a gallery appeared before them, stretching into the distance like a shimmering dream. It was lined with equally astonishing creations, each one a testament to forgotten artistry and unimaginable skill. Some glimmered and sparkled with an inner light, pulsing with vibrant energy that seemed to sing to the soul. Others were cloaked in darkness, shrouded in mystery, their secrets hinting at untold stories and forgotten tragedies. The air crackled with anticipation, a silent invitation to explore the wonders and unravel the enigmatic tales woven into the fabric of this extraordinary place.

"Every artefact has a story," Professor Finch whispered reverently. "We must listen closely."

But before they could step into the pristine, white-walled gallery, eager to immerse themselves in the art, an unexpected gust of wind, cold and strangely scented with dust and something akin to old parchment, flickered through the narrow passage. It whistled past their ears, momentarily disorienting them, and caused the flame of Oliver's flashlight to sputter violently, threatening to extinguish entirely.

The lights in the corridor, already dim and flickering from a faulty generator, dimmed even further, plunging the passage into near darkness. Eerie, distorted shadows, like grasping claws, crept across the worn stone floor, dancing in time with the swaying flashlight beam and transforming familiar shapes into menacing figures. A chill permeated the air, raising goosebumps on their arms and hinting at something unsettling lurking just beyond the reach of their vision.

"Stick together!" Azrael commanded, his voice steady, yet a tingle of worry threaded through it. As the darkness thickened, Ellie noticed whispers deepening, echoing through the air with urgency.

"There's... something here," she said, her voice barely heard amidst the rising anxiety. "Something that binds all these tales together—"

"Sheh!" Oliver interrupted, his face paling as he pointed to the far wall.

There, amidst the familiar collection of canvases and sketches, a new portrait had appeared. But this one was unique, unlike anything he'd seen before. It glimmered with an extraordinary, almost ethereal light, captivating and drawing the eye. Yet, despite the beauty and luminescence, the expression on its face was profoundly sorrowful, the lips curved downwards in a permanent, melancholic frown that hinted at a hidden story of pain and loss. The juxtaposition of light and sorrow was unsettling, a puzzle begging to be solved.

"What is it?" Ellie asked, stepping closer.

"It's mysterious," Finn chimed in, unusually serious. "There's something unsettling about it. It looks like it's hiding secrets."

Ellie studied the painting intently, sensing its connection to the others. "What are you trying to tell us?" she whispered, partly expectant and partly fearful.

To their astonishment, the figure spoke, its voice breaking through the silence like a chime. "Beware, for the truths you seek may reveal more than you wish to know."

"Do you know the whereabouts of Valen?" Professor Finch asked, emboldened by the ominous nature of the portrait.

"Knowledge of Valen comes at a price," the painted figure replied. "Only those with courage in their heart shall uncover it."

Ellie felt a shiver run down her spine. "What price must be paid?"

"The unearthing of a past long buried," the figure replied mysteriously. "And a heart transformed by the power of history."

Before they could enquire further, pressing for answers about its cryptic message or the figure it depicted, the vibrant colours of the portrait began to fade, draining away like water down a drain. The image, once so lifelike and compelling, reversed back towards its original inanimate state, with the brushstrokes becoming rougher and less defined. As the portrait retreated into its canvas form, losing its ephemeral glow, the surrounding shadows grew bolder, thickening and encroaching, as if eager to reclaim the space the portrait had briefly illuminated with its presence. A chill snaked through the room, a stark symptom of the encroaching darkness.

"What was that all about?" Oliver asked, bewildered. "This is beyond me!"

"Perhaps we must return to the figures we've met before," Ellie suggested, the adrenaline thrumming through her veins. "They may offer clearer guidance. It appears our answers lie within their whispers."

"Let's not waste a moment," Azrael urged. "If Valen is involved, we must hurry before night disperses into dawn."

The group retraced their steps through the seemingly endless corridor of whispering portraits, their gazes hardened, and their spines seized by renewed resolve. Each brushstroke seemed to follow them, the eyes of long-dead dignitaries and forgotten artists holding secrets just beyond reach. They were determined to gather more hints, to decipher the cryptic whispers and unlock the enigmatic clues scattered throughout the hall, before time, their relentless adversary, escaped them once again. The museum, a grand edifice of history and art, was undeniably alive with secrets, a breathing, pulsing entity teeming with forgotten truths.

Driven by a shared curiosity and a burning need to understand, they were determined to unveil each one, peeling back the layers of mystery like the delicate varnish on an ancient masterpiece. Along this perilous journey, they were forging bonds of trust and camaraderie, relying on each other's strengths and supporting each other's weaknesses. And as they plunged deeper into the labyrinthine depths of the museum, the tantalising possibility bloomed in their hearts: perhaps, just perhaps, they might reach the very heart of its enchantment, unravelling the core of the magic that held the museum, and themselves, captive.

Their journey had only just begun, a nascent adventure unfolding under the watchful gaze of a star dusted sky. The night, deep and velvety, held countless mysteries in its folds, secrets whispered in the wind and etched in the shadows. Ellie, her heart alight with a nascent optimism, could feel the warmth of hope glowing with each incremental discovery, each solved riddle, and each obstacle overcome. A sense of shared purpose bound them together, a silent vow etched in their eyes. Whatever awaited them next, be it peril or promise, they would confront it together, united in their quest. They were not alone; guided by the whispers that lingered in the ancient halls, echoes of forgotten ages and untold stories, the tales of the past were destined to intertwine with their own, weaving a tapestry of destiny that they were only now beginning to understand. The weight of history, the burden of prophecy, and the thrill of the unknown propelled them forward towards an uncertain future brimming with possibilities, both terrifying and exhilarating.

A GLIMPSE INTO THE PAST

The clock struck one, a deep, resonant boom that echoed through the dimly lit corridors of the enchanted museum. Each chime wasn't just a marker of time; it resonated with mystery, a palpable vibration that seemed to awaken the very artefacts around them. With each peal, a whisper of history, centuries dormant, begged to be uncovered, hinting at forgotten loves, epic battles, and the rise and fall of empires. Ellie, her heart racing with a cocktail of anticipation and trepidation, gripped her notepad a little tighter. The air crackled with an unseen energy, and she stared at her surroundings, her gaze sweeping across dusty display cases filled with enigmatic objects.

She felt like a detective on the verge of a breakthrough, hoping to glean the secrets that danced just beyond her reach— verge of a breakthrough, hoping to glean the secrets that danced just beyond her reach, secrets the museum had guarded for centuries. Standing beside her, Professor Finch, a man whose life was dedicated to the pursuit of the peculiar and the arcane, was the picture of unbridled joy. His eyes sparkled with an almost childlike excitement, reflecting the faint glow of the gas lamps, relishing every moment of this adventure, every potential discovery that lay ahead. He adjusted his spectacles, a mischievous grin playing on his lips, fully aware that tonight, the museum might just decide to reveal its most closely guarded truths.

"We're on the cusp of greatness, Ellie!" he exclaimed, brushing a hand through his tousled hair. "I can feel it – history is alive here, waiting for us to unlock its stories!"

As they stepped deeper into the museum, the breath of centuries old enveloped them, a palpable presence heavy with the echoes of lives lived and empires crumbled. The air hung thick, swirling with dust motes that glimmered like distant stars in the vast, unseen darkness. Each footfall resonated with an amplified silence, broken only by the faint creaks and groans of the ancient building itself. The walls, lined with tapestries and portraits, seemed to pulse with stories of the past, whispering secrets to those who dared to listen. Each artefact, meticulously preserved behind glass, was more than just an object; it was a key to a door long forgotten, a fragment of a narrative waiting to be pieced back together, promising glimpses into worlds that had vanished but whose influence lingered in the air. The weight of history settled upon their shoulders, a tangible burden and a tantalising invitation to explore the mysteries held within.

Azrael, majestic and formidable, stood at the heart of the museum, a silent sentinel of forgotten ages. But tonight, something was different.

The air crackled with an unseen energy, a subtle thrum that resonated deep within the ancient stone. "Listen closely, intrepid adventurers," he rumbled, his stone visage now animated with a warm, golden glow that pulsed like a beating heart. The light danced across his mane, transforming the hardened sculpture into something almost alive. "The past is a landscape of echoes, a tapestry woven with secrets just waiting to be unravelled. To navigate it, you must be willing to listen and look beyond the obvious. The surface whispers, but the depths roar. Seek the whispers, decipher the roars, and you shall unlock the knowledge you look for. But beware," he added, the golden glow flickering for a moment, "not all echoes are friendly. Some echoes jealously guard their secrets and will challenge your courage at every step.

Some guard their secrets jealously and will test your courage at every turn."

Ellie nodded, her historian's mind whirling. "What do you mean, Azrael?" she asked, eager for clarity amidst the enigmatic aura surrounding them.

"The answers lie within the shadows and lights of the artefacts," he replied, gesturing toward a pair of ornate Greek vases resting upon a pedestal. Their vibrant floral patterns seemed to dance under the flickering torchlight, each swirl telling a tale of ancient celebrations of gods and mortals intertwined.

Luci glided forward, her bronze scales catching the glimmer of the light, transforming her into a living sculpture of polished metal. Her eyes, twin chips of obsidian, held an ancient knowing that seemed to penetrate the deepest layers of the soul. "Each artefact has a spirit," she began, her forked tongue flicking almost imperceptibly, "stories woven into their very essence, like threads in a tapestry or rings in the oldest trees. Each one whispers of forgotten eras, of triumphs and tragedies, of love and loss." She paused and swept her gaze over the assembled seekers to gauge their interest and thirst for knowledge.

The seekers gauge their interest and their thirst for knowledge. "Would you like me to weave those tales for you?" The invitation hung in the air, heavy with the promise of revelations. Her voice was smooth, an enchanting melody that wrapped around the seekers like a soft shawl, a silken promise of secrets unveiled, and mysteries explored. It was a voice that could soothe the most savage beast or tempt the purest heart, a voice that spoke of centuries spent gathering lore and weaving narratives from the dust of time.

"Yes, please!" Ellie exclaimed, her interest growing as she crouched beside the vases. At this, Luci coiled around the pedestal, her form shimmering, and began to whisper secrets that only the night could reveal.

"Once, a great festival was held in honour of the goddess Athena," Luci breathed, her tone trailing like smoke. "In the flicker of torches and the laughter of guests, a secret love blossomed—a forbidden romance between a nobleperson and a servant girl". trailing like smoke "

"In the flicker of torches and the laughter of guests, a secret love blossomed—a forbidden romance between a nobleperson and a servant girl. Against the backdrop of the gods, their hearts defied time itself."

Luci glided forward, her bronze scales catching the glimmer of the light, transforming her into a living sculpture of polished metal. Her eyes, twin chips of obsidian, held an ancient knowing that seemed to penetrate the deepest layers of the soul. "Each artefact has a spirit," she began, her forked tongue flicking almost imperceptibly, "stories woven into their very essence, like threads in a tapestry or rings in the oldest trees. Each one whispers of forgotten eras, of triumphs and tragedies, of love and loss."

She paused and swept her gaze over the assembled seekers, assessing their interest and thirst for knowledge. "Would you like me to weave those tales for you?" The invitation hung in the air, heavy with the promise of revelations. Her voice was smooth, an enchanting melody that wrapped around the seekers like a soft shawl, a silken promise of secrets revealed, and mysteries explored. It was a voice that could soothe the most savage beast or tempt the purest heart, a voice that spoke of centuries spent gathering lore and weaving narratives from the dust of time.

Oliver, the unsuspecting museum guard, remained glued to the doorway, his boots practically fused to the ancient tiles. He peered into the vastness of the hall, its shadows stretching like grasping claws, uncertainty knotting his brow. The high, vaulted ceiling seemed to press down on him, amplifying the silence that thrummed in the air. Clutching his flashlight like a lifeline against the oppressive darkness, he tightened his grip on its cool metal casing. He called out, his voice echoing unnaturally in the cavernous space, "Are you lot sure this is a clever idea? I mean, it's just an old museum!"

He meant the words to sound confident; but his bravado faltered somewhat. A hint of doubt, cold and clammy, wormed its way into his words, betraying the unease that snaked through his gut. He desperately hoped someone would tell him they were joking, that they'd all just laugh and turn around, leaving this dusty, echoing mausoleum to its silent secrets.

Finn, who had been lurking nearby in the shadows of a towering display case, leapt forth with a cheeky grin that stretched from ear to ear. "Oh, Oliver, trust me!" he exclaimed, his voice a playful echo in the high- ceiled hall. "This old museum is anything but 'just' old! Every corner holds a new thrill, a whispered secret waiting to be uncovered! Join us, or you might miss the magic!" His eyes, bright and cunning like polished amber, twinkled with mischief and the promise of adventure.

Before Oliver could voice his hesitation, Finn tugged on his trousers with an insistent little pull, urging him to follow into the labyrinthine depths of the museum while a whirlwind of doubt and curiosity swirled within him. Finn tugged on his trousers with an insistent little tug, urging him to follow into the labyrinthine depths of the museum. The tug was light, but the weight of Finn's enthusiasm was undeniable, pulling Oliver towards the unknown wonders that supposedly lay within.

As they gathered around the vases, drawn in by their artistry and history, the cavernous museum seemed to flourish with life, no longer a static mausoleum of relics. Dust mites danced in the newly illuminated air, reflecting the soft glow cast by the display lights. The shadows extended from the pedestals and corners, becoming shimmering silhouettes that flitted through the air, mimicking the gestures of the living figures before them. It was as if the very memories of the ancient craftsmen – their hands shaping the clay, their meticulous brushstrokes painting each intricate detail, their hopes and dreams imbued within the form – were rejoicing in their resurrection, breathed back into existence by the attentive gaze of these modern admirers. The air crackled with an unseen energy, a tangible connection bridging millennia and uniting the creators with their audience, a silent symphony of artistry resonating within the silent halls.

"Look!" Ellie cried, her finger tracing a delicate pattern on the vase. "If we align the markings on the bottom with the constellations overhead..." Her voice trailed off into wild conjecture, but her companions leaned in, encouragement glistening in their eyes.

"Of course! The festival of Athena was celebrated under the stars!" Professor Finch added enthusiastically. "They believed the stars guided the actions of mortals. The stars could still be pointing us toward something significant!"

"Then let's match them," Ellie suggested, glancing up at the twisted beams of ancient wood that crisscrossed the ceiling.

The adventurers, their heads bent low in concentration, examined the intricate details of the vases, oblivious to the true power in the room. Lady Arabella, the majestic statue that loomed over them, was no mere decoration. She stood stoically nearby, her marble skin cool to the touch, her regal countenance emanating wisdom earned over centuries, perhaps millennia. "To see the past clearly, dear adventurers," she said, her voice seemingly coming from the very stone itself, "you must also understand the present and its shadows.

The past is not a static scene but a dynamic force that shapes everything around us. It is not just a tableau but rather a living, breathing entity that influences everything around us.

Let me unveil, there are more hidden narratives, secrets that the vases only hint at, and truths that are far more profound than you can imagine. profounder than you can imagine."

With a gentle nod from Azrael, a silent permission that seemed to settle the very dust motes dancing in the torchlight, Lady Arabella's voice enveloped the group. It was a voice rich and powerful, resonant with an age that seemed to breathe within the ancient stones of the hall.

"In this very hall," she began, her words hanging in the air like a palpable presence. "The plight of those who once walked these grounds dwells. This place weaves their joy, sorrow, hopes, and failures into its tapestry. Their failures are also woven into the tapestry of this place. She paused, her dark and knowing eyes sweeping over each of them in turn. "Remember, their footsteps echo through time, a constant reminder that the past is never truly gone."

Her words echoed ominously, not just in the cavernous hall but deep within Ellie's mind. They were a dark tide, pulling her back from the present and into the swirling currents of history. Before, the stories she'd unearthed felt like isolated fragments, shards of a broken mirror. But now, Arabella's words acted as a sort of spectral glue, drawing Ellie's attention back to the connections that fragmented hints in history created, which tied one story to another and created, which tied one story to another and that tied one story to another, one life to the next. The faces in the faded portraits on the walls seemed to shift and murmur, and Ellie could almost feel the weight of their unfulfilled dreams, their lingering regrets. The hall was no longer just a space but a living mausoleum, pulsing with the echoes of those who had come before.

Huckleberry, feathers ruffled by a non-existent wind, conveying an air both noble and subtly dishevelled, perched himself atop a nearby exhibit. Age and untold battles subtly marred his impressive form, which usually glowed with a symphony of gold and brown. It was subtly marred by age and untold battles. From his vantage point, his beady eyes, dark and sharp like polished pearls, glinted with an ancient wisdom and perhaps a touch of cynicism. A hush fell over the small crowd that had gathered as he spoke, his voice a dry, guttural rasp that resonated with the weight of ages. "Caw! Seek what was lost even in the echoes of triumph." he croaked. the sound echoing through the hall. "For every shade of light casts a shadow," he finished, his gaze sweeping over the onlookers, leaving a lingering disquiet in its wake. The words hung in the air, heavy with unspoken meaning, a cryptic warning delivered with the authority of a creature who had seen empires rise and fall and joys bloom and wither.

"Are you suggesting we find what remains—what belongs?" Ellie ventured, her excitement igniting anew, her fellow adventurers casting eager glances toward her.

"Precisely!" chimed Azrael, nodding vigorously. "The past is not merely a series of events, but a tapestry woven with choices. You'll need to unravel it carefully to navigate to the next chapter in our quest."

Finn, swishing his bushy tail, darted off across the hall, his energy infectious. "Let's solve the riddle first! What could our next step be?"

Ellie understood that every artefact they met was a part of a larger puzzle, a shard of a lost past aching to be reassembled. Each artefact they met stood for a piece of the larger puzzle, a fragment of a forgotten history that yearned for reassembling. The intricate carvings on the vases, the faded tapestries whispering of long-lost loves and tumultuous battles, and the lingering energy that clung to each object – they were all clues, breadcrumbs leading them towards a truth she could only glimpse at the edge of her mind.

Motivated by Finn's relentless enthusiasm, a bubbling energy that refused to be dampened by the dusty silence of the hall, and the comforting weight of Lady Arabella's wisdom, her guiding star in this labyrinth of the past, she took a deep breath and set her gaze around the hall. The scent of aged parchment and untold stories filled the air. "We have tales of magic from the vases, swirling with ancient power and unknown rituals, love and tumult intricately woven into the fabric of the tapestries, and now a powerful echo resonating from this latest find, a palpable sense of something significantly lost, but what stays? What crucial element are we missing for unlocking the full picture?

What is the single piece that will illuminate everything we've uncovered so far?" Although her voice was quiet, it conveyed a steely determination and a promise to discover what's hidden within these ancient walls. Although her voice was quiet, it still carried a steely determination and a promise to uncover the dark secrets that lay hidden within these ancient walls.

Whoosh! The air vibrated, and a sudden gust swept through the room, sending a pile of scrolls tumbling to the ground. Under the feather-like touch of the night's breath, one scroll unfurled to reveal intricate symbols.

"What's this?" Ellie stepped forward, squinting at the delicate detailing. "It's like a map of constellations, but with artefact imagery!" Slowly, it dawned on her that this artwork could reveal a location within the museum—one that might lead them to further enlightenment or new challenges.

Professor Finch crouched beside her, his tweed jacket rustling against the dusty artefacts. His eyes, magnified by thick spectacles, narrowed with a predatory intrigue, reflecting the flickering candlelight. "Ah! There it is! The inscription and the celestial alignment all seem to irrevocably point towards the East Wing of the museum!

Irrevocably point towards the East Wing of the museum!" He rose, a sudden burst of energy animating his usually stooped frame. "We must gather what we've learned—the sketches, the translated hieroglyphs, and the documented lunar cycles— and use them to unravel this!"

We are about to uncover the secrets hidden within those forgotten halls. The secrets that lie hidden within those forgotten halls are about to be revealed. He gestured urgently, his voice a hushed but excited whisper. "Come! Time is crucial. Let's see what mysteries await us in the East Wing!"

"Wait!" Oliver suggested, glancing nervously around, "Perhaps we should consider the matter more thoroughly?" We might become lost in the maze of history!

Ellie's eyes, usually soft and contemplative, hardened with a determined glint. She locked her gaze with theirs, a silent challenge in her expression. "Every step forward", she declared, her voice firm and resolute, "every painstaking piece of research, every connection we uncover, brings us closer to a comprehensive understanding." The museum, I believe, wishes to reveal its secrets to us. It's practically whispering to them, daring us to listen. Would you rather stay in the shadows, content with ignorance, when we have the potential for enlightenment?"

The idea of leaving their accumulated knowledge, shared dedication, and unique perspectives being left to wither and fade, unused and unappreciated, fuelled her resolve. It was a waste, a tragedy even, and the idea of letting it all go motivated her, driving her to push forward regardless of the risks. She wouldn't let fear dictate their path. She was determined to see the challenge through.

Azrael roared softly, "Fear not, brave hearts. It merely tests your resolve. The past is behind us, but the paths it creates lead us onwards."

With a newfound sense of purpose blazing within her, Ellie rallied her companions around her, her determination a tangible force field. Guided by Luci's quiet wisdom, a wellspring of ancient lore and sharp insights that cut through the noise; supported by Arabella's unwavering strength, a bulwark against despair and a champion of the vulnerable; and invigorated by the sparks of history that ignited with each hashed-out tale around the flickering campfire, they ventured beyond the realm of what lay immediately before them.

They were no longer simply reacting to the present but actively shaping a future informed by the past, a future rich with untold possibilities and fraught with unknown dangers—a future they were now irrevocably were now, irrevocably, prepared to face together. The weight of their quest settled upon them, heavy yet inspiring, as they stepped forward, bound by a shared destiny woven from courage, loyalty, and the echoing whispers of forgotten stories.

As they journeyed together towards the East Wing, the hushed atmosphere seemed to amplify, making Ellie feel the weight of time itself whispering through the air. It was palpable pressure, urging them onwards and fuelling a sense of urgency to seek out hidden knowledge and discover long-forgotten stories. The museum, which had initially seemed daunting with its labyrinthine corridors and towering halls, now transformed into a sanctuary of possibilities in her eyes. No longer a cold, indifferent institution, it beckoned her generation and her friends closer, promising enlightenment and adventure beyond the velvet ropes and behind the glass cases. The polished floors reflected not just the light fixtures but also the potential for connection to the past, inviting them to become active participants in a grand, unfolding narrative. The weight of expectation was now mingled with a burgeoning excitement, a belief that within those walls lay something profound waiting to be unearthed.

The heavy oak door groaned shut behind them, sealing them into a silence thick with anticipation. Each step echoed through the cavernous halls, not just with the sound of their footsteps but with the collective memories of explorers, scholars, dreamers, and all who sought knowledge within these hallowed walls. These echoes swirled around Ellie and her companions like a palpable presence, a symphony of hope, courage, and untold wonder. It whispered promises of discovery but also warned of the weight of the past. Just beyond the veil of the present lay a glimpse into the past that awaited them, a panorama of bygone eras, both daunting and splendid.

Ancient artefacts hummed with forgotten energies, portraits seemed to watch them with knowing eyes, and every exhibit held the potential to rewrite everything they thought they knew. This museum was more than just a repository of relics; it was a labyrinth of possibilities, holding the keys to a future yet unwritten, a future that hinged on understanding the echoes of yesterday.

Ellie and her companions paused in that enchanted museum, bathed in the ghostly glow of moonlight filtering through towering windows, as the hour slipped away like sand through their fingers and dawn inched ever closer. They took a collective breath, steeling themselves against the unknown. A sense of destiny settled upon them, a feeling that they were on the precipice of something monumental. They prepared for the revelations that would soon unfold—discoveries that promised to intertwine their fates with the unravelled that promised to intertwine their fates with the unravelled threads of history, binding them to the past in ways they could never have imagined. Would they be enlightened? Would they be burdened? Only time, and the ancient secrets held within these walls, would tell.

THE GUARDIAN OF TIME

The moon, a celestial coin of silver, hung high and bright, a solitary luminary within the star-strewn canvas of the night. Its light, a gentle, ethereal wash, cascaded down, casting silvery beams into the heart of the Enchanted Museum. Each beam, like a whispered secret, illuminated dusty artefacts and whispered promises of forgotten tales. Within these hallowed walls of history and magic, where time itself seemed to bend and play, Ellie felt a pulse, a subtle vibration resonating deep within her soul. It was a rhythm, a captivating beat that promised adventure and profound mystery, beckoning her forward into the unknown. The air was thick with anticipation, a palpable energy that crackled around them like static electricity. The group, a motley collection of curious souls, gathered in hushed excitement under the watchful gaze of the regal Azrael the Lion, a magnificent sculpture whose presence commanded respect.

His golden eyes, crafted centuries ago, glimmered with an ethereal glow, as if holding within them the secrets of a thousand ages, silently seeing, waiting to unfold his part in the unfolding drama. He was a silent guardian, a majestic sentinel, poised to witness and perhaps even guide the events that were about to happen.

Professor Finch's voice broke the night's stillness, his usually measured tone replaced by a vibrant urgency, filled with the eagerness of a child who had just discovered a treasure map. "Tonight, we'll visit the chambers that hold the essence of time itself!" His words hung in the air, the declaration amplified by the echoing silence of the hidden crypt. The seriousness of the mission ahead, which could either rewrite history or unravel it completely, bolstered the weight of his declaration. His eyes, usually hidden behind thick spectacles, gleamed with an almost manic energy in the flickering lamplight. He clutched a worn leather-bound journal, its pages filled with indecipherable symbols and faded diagrams, a testament to decades of obsessive research.

Oliver, still grappling with the bewildering notion of ancient artefacts coming to life and cryptic prophecies being fulfilled, stood slightly to the side, feeling like an unwilling participant in an extraordinary but bewildering dream. His sensible shoes and practical jacket felt woefully out of place in this subterranean labyrinth. He was a historian, not an adventurer, and the transition from dusty archives to perilous excavations was proving a difficult one. "All right", more importantly," he added, his voice laced with a touch of sarcasm, "is it going to involve any more sentient gargoyles?"

"Ah, my dear Oliver," interjected Lady Arabella, her marble visage softening in the moonlight. "In every object lies a tale waiting to unfold. All we need to do is listen closely."

With a flick of her wrist, Luci, a mechanical marvel of burnished bronze and emerald scales, uncoiled from the display case like a living thing. Her serpentine form shimmered under the luminous glow of the museum's energy crystals, reflecting the light in a mesmerising dance. "Ah, the Guardian of Time—a formidable entity we must look for. Legend says he alone knows the last riddle that will unlock the final passage through the labyrinth." Her voice, a synthesised whisper, echoed with ancient knowledge.

Ellie, her historian's brain already spinning with possibilities and historical precedents, thought aloud, her fingers instinctively reaching for the worn leather notebook she always carried. "A guardian... and riddles?" The very idea sent a thrill through her, a familiar mix of excitement and apprehension. She turned to Azrael, his features as sharp and enigmatic as the artefacts surrounding them, and noticed he appeared amused by her uncontained curiosity. "Do you think this guardian is someone— or something— we should be cautious about? Is it a creature? A construct? Or perhaps... a test, manifested by the labyrinth itself?" Her questions tumbled out in rapid succession, betraying her eagerness to uncover the truth. The potential dangers were secondary to the allure of the historical puzzle before them.

Azrael's deep voice resonated with a thunderous calm, each syllable carrying the weight of ages. The air around him seemed to vibrate with the low hum of ancient power. "Caution is indeed wise, young historian," he rumbled, his gaze piercing, yet not unkind.

"The threads of time are delicate, and to tug upon them haphazardly is to risk unravelling the very fabric of existence. But remember— the Guardian of Time watches over the past and the future alike; those pure of heart and with true intent may find an ally rather than an enemy. Fear not exploration but approach it with respect and a steady hand."

Just then, a whirlwind of movement and mirth disrupted the sombre, slow pokes. he chortled, his voice a playful melody. "Time bends with every tick of the clock! It's a river to be navigated, not a fortress to be stormed! Come on, let's dance through time! Let's chase the echoes of yesterday and whisper secrets to tomorrow!" He vanished as quickly as he appeared, a trail of shimmering leaves marking his ephemeral path.

"Finn!" chirped Huckleberry , fluttering onto a nearby statue. "Less merriment, more focus. We are nearing Valen's Chamber! The Guardian will only reveal himself to those who can interpret the vigils of time."

As they traversed the chilled marble halls, the cold seeping into their bones despite their thick cloaks, Ellie's heartbeat, the polished floor, the distant drip of water from unseen crevices, and the rustling of ancient tapestries – all coalesced into a symphony of the impossible. Every stride was like stepping into a realm where the laws of nature bent and fractured, where the impossible flourished like a strange, exotic bloom.

The coiling serpent, Luci, flickered at her command, her scales shimmering with an ethereal luminescence. She wove a pathway through the labyrinthine corridors, her serpentine body a living map as she directed them toward the chamber. "This way!" Luci hissed, her voice a low, sibilant whisper that carried on the still air, guiding them around the ornate fountains, their basins filled with stagnant, moss-covered water, and under the grand tapestries depicting scenes of forgotten battles and mythical creatures. The serpent illuminated the way with her folklore of the past, her explanations of the bizarre architecture and ominous symbols peppering the silence.

It was then that the shadows deepened, thickening and coalescing as if imbued with a life of their own. They whispered secrets in a language Ellie couldn't understand, secrets that seemed to mould the very air around them, solidifying into tangible shapes and textures, as if they were sealing a pact between the living and the long dead. They appeared from the constricted corridor and entered a vast room, a cavernous space that seemed to swallow sound and light. In the centre, dominating the entire chamber, stood a celestial clock tower of intricate designs. Its gears, crafted from shimmering gold and what looked like solidified starlight, spun with an almost frantic energy. Its hands, long and slender, moved against the passage of normal time, suggesting a manipulation of temporal forces that made Ellie's head swim. This room was not merely a place; it was a nexus.

"Every hour here holds a story," Professor Finch enlightened them. "The clock is the heart of the labyrinth, while within those walls lies the Guardian." He pointed to an archway draped in blue and gold. "Across the threshold of this magnificent clock lies the riddle."

The atmosphere thickened with anticipation, a palpable weight pressing down on them as they approached the entrance. The air, heavy with unspoken possibilities and the weight of the unknown, clung to their skin. As they stepped closer, a sudden, sharp chill swept through the chamber, a ghostly caress that raised goosebumps on their arms. Their breaths, normally invisible wisps, now lingered longer than expected, ghostly plumes hanging in the air, each exhaling a visual testament to the unsettling cold that had permeated the very heart of the space. The silence that followed was broken only by the soft rustle of their clothes and the frantic beat of their hearts; each sound amplified in the oppressive atmosphere.

"Who dares tread upon the path of time?" boomed a voice, reverberating from all sides. A figure cloaked in shadows appeared, its features obscured. Valen stood before them—a guardian of time, a sentinel of secrets.

Ellie swallowed hard, the confrontation sparking a web of courage within her. "We seek wisdom to restore balance to the museum's magic," she declared, her voice unwavering despite the tremor that went with her heart.

"Wisdom is often the result of trials," replied Valen, pointing a slender hand toward the clock. "If you wish to gain my trust, solve this riddle: I can be cracked, made, told, and played. What am I?"

The atmosphere thickened with anticipation, a palpable weight pressing down on the small band of adventurers. Each footfall echoed in the oppressive silence as they stepped closer to the entrance, a dark maw carved into the ancient stone. A sudden, inexplicable chill swept through the chamber, a biting cold that had nothing to do with the temperature. Their breaths, expelled as white plumes, lingered longer than expected, ghostly reminders of their mortality in this forgotten place.

A profound hush fell upon the group, even heavier than the silence that preceded it. They huddled together, their eyes darting from the ominous doorway to the cryptic riddle etched above it. The words, a twisting labyrinth of archaic language, seemed to taunt them. Pitfalls and confusion seemed to lurk not just in the inscription but in their thoughts. Doubts and anxieties, previously suppressed, now threatened to unravel their carefully constructed courage. Finn, ever vigilant, perked his ears up, straining to catch any subtle sound that might betray a hidden danger. Oliver, usually quick-witted, stood motionless, his brow furrowing deeper with each passing moment. The lines etched on his face reflected a fierce determination to solve the puzzle, warring with a growing sense of bewilderment. He chewed on his lip, lost in the complex structure that defined the riddle's meaning.

Ellie, the team's historian and linguist, stepped forward, her shoulders squared. The weight of the riddle, previously burdening her, seemed to lift as a spark ignited within her. Her historian's intuition, honed by years of deciphering forgotten languages and resolving ancient mysteries, was now ablaze. A sudden realisation

"A joke!" echoed Azrael, his voice booming like distant thunder.

Valen remained motionless, as if weighing her words against moments that had passed and yet to come.

"A joke it is," he finally intoned, a glimmer of approval shimmering in his eyes. The intricate clock resonated with a melodic chime, its hands spinning wildly before slowing to rest.

"This clock has been made anew," Valen intoned. "Your insight has revealed a wisdom that transcends time itself. Only by embracing joy can you navigate the paths ahead."

Luci, intertwining her bronze form, intertwined the importance of levity. "Good riddance to gravity! Let the joy of these riddles enlighten our path."

"Indeed," Valen confirmed, gesturing for them to approach the sides of the clock. "Now, you shall all bear witness. The Guardian entrusts you with the key to the future. You are guardians of the past, present, and future."

As the clock chimed thrice, a sound that echoed not just through the room but through the very fabric of time, the air shimmered like heat rising from sun-baked asphalt. This distortion wasn't just visual; it felt as if the fundamental rules of reality were momentarily suspended. Then, the shimmer solidified, coalescing into a breathtaking display. Pathways, inscribed in brilliant, almost painful light, materialised out of thin air, hovering before them like shimmering strands of fate. Each pathway, distinct in colour and intensity, pulsed with its own unique energy, beckoning and promising. Some glowed with a gentle, nostalgic warmth, hinting at idyllic pasts and lessons unlearned. Others blazed with an almost blinding intensity, radiating the potential for either glorious triumph or catastrophic failure in futures yet to come. The air crackled with the weight of infinite possibilities, the silent question hanging heavy: which path would they dare to tread?

"This is the Labyrinth of Echoes; each path leads to a moment, an experience," Valen explained. "Choose wisely, for time can only be rewritten in the name of unity and truth."

The team exchanged glances, the weight of choices ahead heavy in their chests. "What do we do?" Oliver finally broke the weighted silence.

"We choose a moment to uncover something that alters the course of the museum, perhaps something from its very foundation," Ellie replied, her voice steady now.

"Or perhaps we revisit the time before any of us found it," suggested Finn, a sparkle in his eyes.

As they contemplated the diverging paths that lay before them, each shimmering with the potential of untold stories, Valen, a figure both enigmatic and reassuring, subtly receded. He didn't simply walk away; instead, he seemed to distil himself into the very fabric of the museum. He melted into the shadows, the darkness embracing him until his form was completely encased, swallowed whole by obscurity. His essence seemed to merge with the museum's ancient stone walls, becoming part of its timeless structure. His essence seemed to merge with the museum's ancient stone walls, becoming part of its timeless structure. The air itself seemed to hum with a newfound energy, infused with the promise of wisdom gleaned from forgotten epochs and the thrilling allure of uncharted adventures.

With a collective breath, a shared understanding cementing their impromptu fellowship, they stepped forward. Their eyes were drawn to a path bathed in an ethereal, golden light. It beckoned them, a shimmering ribbon unfurling before them, leading to an artefact lost to the relentless currents of time. A lost treasure, a piece of history waiting to be rediscovered. Ellie's heart soared within her chest, a feeling of exhilaration mixed with a profound sense of purpose. They weren't just embarking on a quest for a forgotten relic; they were on a journey to uncover the secrets of the past, to breathe life back into history's silent narratives. And in doing so, they would create new memories, forging bonds stronger than time itself, sealing the unique and unexpected camaraderie they had found within the hallowed halls of the museum. Their adventure was more than a mission; it was the beginning of a legend.

"Together," Azrael declared, his strength encompassing the moment. "The Guardian of Time has seen our virtue. Let us explore the tapestry of our pasts and enlighten the future!"

Ellie and her resilient companions stepped into the unknown, embraced by the labyrinth's shifting time ways and surrounded by a swirling vortex of past, present, and future. The air crackled with anticipation, a symphony of the possible humming around them. They were armed with courage, driven by a shared purpose, and steeled by the trials they had already overcome. Each footstep echoed with the weight of history

The night deepened, ripening with whispers of adventures yet to come. The labyrinth held its breath, a silent observer to their unfolding saga. Around a crackling fire, fuelled by scavenged wood and shared stories, the bonds of friendship tightened. Laughter mingled with serious discussions of strategy, forming an unbreakable cord that illuminated the path ahead. They realised, perhaps with a touch of bittersweet understanding, that the greatest artefact of all was not some long-lost relic or a key to untold power hidden through the labyrinth's treacherous depths.

ECHOES IN THE HALLS

As the clock struck midnight, an eerie stillness enveloped the museum, absorbing sound and time alike, leaving a vacuum where only anticipation could thrive. Ellie stood at the threshold of the grand atrium, a cavernous space normally bustling with chatter and the shuffle of eager feet, now silent and watchful. Her heart raced, a frantic drumbeat against the unnatural quiet, as the echoes of the past whispered around her, not as a simple audio phenomenon but as tangible tendrils reaching from bygone eras, beckoning her deeper into the shadows of the enchanted museum. The air itself felt thick with history, heavy on her skin. The mosaics and murals that adorned the walls, usually static backdrops to the art on display, now glimmered with a life of their own.

Flickering candlelight, strategically placed for the late-night tour, danced across the tesserae and paint strokes, revealing glimpses of forgotten stories: heroic battles etched in stone, secret courtships painted in vibrant hues, and untold adventures waiting to be rediscovered in the museum's labyrinthine corridors. A shiver traced her spine, not entirely from fear, but from the intoxicating allure of the unknown, the promise of secrets unearthed, and mysteries solved within these hallowed halls. The weight of centuries pressed down on her, both a burden and a challenge. She took a breath, the scent of old paper and dust filling her lungs, and stepped forward, ready to embrace whatever the night held in store.

"Right then, team!" Azrael the Lion announced, his majestic form casting a powerful silhouette against the flickering light of the hanging chandeliers. "We must move swiftly and wisely. The echoes of the past guide us, but they can also mislead. Stay close!"

Ellie nodded, her historian's mind already beginning to unravel the ancient secrets held by the artefacts in the room. Images flashed through her head – faded weight of ages settled upon her shoulders, a thrilling burden she was eager to bear.

Beside her, Professor Finch adjusted his spectacles, a gleam of excitement glimmering in his eyes. The faint scent of aged parchment seemed to cling to him, a testament to the decades he'd dedicated to the pursuit of knowledge. "The acoustics in this hall are magnificent. They might just help us decipher the artefacts' tales," he said, a hint of a smile creeping onto his face. He tapped a slender finger against a nearby stone pillar, listening to the resonant hum that echoed through the chamber. "These stones... they remember. They vibrate with the stories of those who came before."

Oliver, the reluctant guard who found himself swept into this whirlwind of the extraordinary, scratched his head, bewildered by events unfolding before him. He'd expected a quiet night, maybe a stolen nap behind the Rosetta Stone replica. "Echoes and whispers? I thought I signed up for a night shift, not... whatever this is!" he muttered, glancing nervously at the glistening lion, its emerald eyes seeming to bore into him, and the imposing statues that loomed above him, their faces etched with serenity and secrets. A shiver ran down his spine. The task was not in the job description.

Finn darted between their feet, his wooden form animated by an unseen spirit. His paint was chipped with age, but his mischievous spirit shone through. "Stop worrying, Ollie!" he squeaked with mischievous delight, his tiny voice surprisingly loud in the echoing hall. "The night is just beginning! Besides, what's the worst that could happen? A little adventure never hurts anyone!" He winked, or at least, Ellie thought she saw him wink.

As if in reply, Luci slithered gracefully from behind a colossal, intricately carved column that reached towards the vaulted ceiling. Her bronze scales caught the light, shimmering like a thousand tiny stars, creating an illusion of movement and depth. Her voice, a low, melodic sibilance, resonated with an ancient wisdom. "Be wary, little fox. The past has a way of entwining the unwary in its coils. Centuries-old secrets often resist uncovering. Her forked tongue flicked out, tasting the air, a warning hanging heavy in the still air of the hall. The air itself seemed to thicken, charged with an almost palpable anticipation. The ancient hall's secrets stirred, ready to reveal themselves or perhaps to protect themselves.

"What do you mean?" Ellie asked, drawn to the serpent's wise but cryptic nature.

"The echoes you hear—" Luci began, her voice smooth as silk— "are fragments of stories long forgotten. Some will guide you, while others will entangle your minds in a web of confusion. Listen closely but tread lightly. Only those with purpose might discern the truth within."

At that moment, Lady Arabella stepped forward, her regal stature imposing yet comforting. Her silver hair, meticulously coiffed, framed a face etched with the wisdom of ages, and her deep-set eyes held a spark of profound understanding. "The key lies not just in listening but in understanding the history of the artefacts that surround us," she announced, her voice a low, resonant timbre that commanded attention. "Each has witnessed events that shaped destinies, empires risen and fallen, loves won and lost. They are not mere objects; they are echoes of the past, whispering secrets to those willing to hear."

Ezra, the once lifeless statue that depicted the grandeur of the 18th century – all powdered wig, ornate waistcoat, and knowing smirk – had come to life with a fervour that resonated through the air. He shifted on his marble plinth, the sound like grinding bones, and his previously vacant eyes now burnt with an almost manic energy. "Do they still teach about the Battle of Mortimer?" he demanded, his voice surprisingly robust for a figure presumed inanimate mere moments ago. "This very hall saw a clash between courage and treachery, a desperate gamble for survival against overwhelming odds. The walls themselves remember the blood that stained their stones!"

At the mention of the battle, the ambient sounds of the museum, previously a low hum of climate control and hushed whispers, shifted dramatically. Notes of distant trumpets, fractured and mournful, echoed from the high vaulted ceiling. The thunder of marching feet, a rhythmic cadence both powerful and terrifying, seemed to emanate from beneath the polished floorboards. The air grew thick with the phantom scent of gunpowder and damp earth, bringing an undeniable air of tension to the atmosphere. It was as if the museum itself was reliving the trauma of that long-ago battle, a silent testament to the echoes Lady Arabella spoke of. The very temperature seemed to drop, a chill that sank

"Listen!" Professor Finch exclaimed, his excitement mounting. "Those are the echoes. The echoes hold stories that yearn to reach their ears. are stories longing to be heard."

Ellie turned her focus inward, closing her eyes to home in on the reverberations. Within the layers of sound, she could almost visualise warriors and nobles parading through the museum—a lively procession weaving itself into existence. The tales were painted vividly in her mind's eye.

"Over here!" Azrael's call pierced through their concentration. They turned as he gestured towards a wide corridor that branched off from the atrium. Wisps of light drew them in like moths to a flickering flame.

"Just what kind of trouble lies ahead?" Oliver asked with a mix of trepidation and intrigue.

"The kind that leads to the reveal of Valen," Finn explained, wriggling at Oliver's side. "If we enter that corridor, we must be prepared to face the echoes of history. We could even see memories played out before our eyes!"

"Then there's no time to lose!" Ellie declared, determination fuelling her courage. "Let's uncover the mysteries that await."

As they ventured into the corridor, a palpable sense of history enveloped them. Ancient carvings, etched deep into the stone walls, adorned the passage, each telling a different story in a silent, visual language. Some depicted scenes of daily life, others of grand ceremonies and forgotten gods. A vibrant tapestry, remarkably preserved despite the passage of centuries, hung further down, its colours still rich and captivating. It depicted a swirling panorama of mythical creatures, their forms both terrifying and majestic, locked in legendary battles that seemed to spill off the fabric. Ellie, mesmerised, reached out, her fingers dancing over the textures. Each groove and contour, worn smooth by time and countless curious hands, ignited her imagination. She could almost hear the clang of steel, feel the heat of a dragon 's breath, and taste the dust of forgotten empires beneath her fingertips. The corridor wasn't just a passageway; it was a portal, pulling her into the heart of the past.

"Those who dare to dream", Luci whispered, "walk hand in hand with the past."

As they progressed deeper into the corridor, the air thickened with an otherworldly energy. The walls seemed to breathe, pulsating with the echoes of long-ago whispers.

Suddenly, a shadow flickered at the far end. En route to the depths of the museum, the group stumbled upon an ornate doorway that appeared to pulse with rhythm like a heartbeat.

"Here lies the Chamber of Echoes," Professor Finch murmured, awe-stricken. "Fabled to contain the voices of all who have passed through these halls."

"What are we waiting for?" Azrael bellowed. "Let us hear what stories lie there!"

Ellie stepped forward, her breath catching in her throat. The air in front of the ancient oak door crackled with unseen energy. Hesitantly, she placed her hand on the cold, smooth surface. As she did, a wave of warmth blossomed beneath her fingertips, spreading up her arm like liquid sunlight. The wood seemed to hum beneath her touch, vibrating with a low, resonant frequency that synchronised perfectly with her own pulse. The room beyond, previously a mystery, now seemed to thrum in resonance with her heartbeat, an irresistible siren song urging her inside, promising secrets and untold wonders.

With a gentle push, more of an instinctive reaction than a deliberate act, the heavy door swung silently inward, revealing an extravagant chamber bathed in an ethereal glow. It wasn't just a room; it was a treasury, a sanctuary, a portal to another time. Soft, diffused light emanated from unseen sources – enchanted orbs, she guessed, hanging suspended in the air like captured stars. The light danced across a breathtaking array of artefacts, each one whispering tales of forgotten civilisations and long-lost magic. Shelves, crafted from some wood as dark and smooth as polished obsidian, lined the walls, their surfaces overflowing with timeworn tomes bound in leather and clasped with silver. Dust motes, disturbed by the opening of the door, danced in the light, revealing objects that shimmered and sparked with history.

A vibrant feathered headdress from ancient Peru, its plumage an impossible array of colours, sat perched on a velvet cushion. Beside it rested a meticulously painted vase from the Ming Dynasty, its delicate porcelain depicting scenes of mythical creatures and serene landscapes. And then there was the hourglass, a slender, elegant masterpiece, filled not with sand but with glittering stardust. It seemed to defy gravity itself, the stardust swirling in a mesmerising dance as if held captive by some unseen force. Ellie felt a pull, a magnetic draw towards the room, a feeling that she had finally come home.

"Isn't it beautiful?" Ellie breathed, stepping into the chamber.

"Incredible!" Professor Finch echoed, his eyes gleaming with scholarly desire.

Suddenly, a rustling sound broke the silence. From the far side of the room appeared Huckleberry , his glossy plumage contrasting with the antiquity surrounding him. "Ah, the curious adventurers have found their way to the Chamber of Echoes," he croaked.

"What do you know about this place?" Ellie questioned, her heart racing at their new companion's arrival.

"Much and little. Huckleberry responded with a sly grin. even reveal the past to those who know how to listen,"

"Guide us, then," Oliver urged, stepping forward with newfound confidence. "We need to uncover the truth about Valen."

"A noble quest," Huckleberry nodded sagely. "But beware, for the echoes can be misleading. I shall guide you through, but you must listen not just with ears but with your hearts."

At that moment, a deep, resonating voice, imbued with the weight of ages, echoed through the ancient chamber. The very stones seemed to vibrate in response. From the deepest shadows, a figure coalesced, shimmering with an otherworldly light. It was Valen, The Timekeeper, his form partially obscured by swirling motes of ethereal energies that crackled with temporal power. He appeared slowly, deliberately, a sense of profound wisdom radiating from him like heat.

"You seek answers, seekers of truth," Valen intoned, his voice a low rumble that resonated not just in the ears, ding for a choice, a desire, or a regret. Understand these intentions, and you understand the forces that shaped what has been and those that continue to influence what will be. Only then can you truly grasp the nature of the echoes and find the answers you so desperately seek." The air crackled with anticipation as the Timekeeper paused, his gaze sweeping across the room, leaving each listener with the feeling of being individually assessed, their worthiness weighed in the balance.

Ellie stepped forward, emboldened by the challenge. "What must we do?"

"Each artefact within these walls contains a riddle," Valen explained, his hollow gaze settling upon them. "Decipher their tales, and you will unlock the pathways to both the past and your destinies."

With that, the chamber began to transform, as if awakened from a long slumber. Gears whirred deep within the walls, and the air crackled with an unseen energy. The bells of time, a series of resonant chimes almost too high-pitched for human ears, echoed around them, their melodies weaving a tapestry of past, present, and future possibility. Dust motes danced in newly unveiled beams of light, illuminating the silent sentinels – the artefacts.

These weren't mere relics; they responded to the activation, shimmering to life with inner luminescence. A sword pulsed with the heat of a forgotten forge, a scroll glowed with ancient prophecies, and a seemingly simple amulet radiated an aura of potent protection. The adventurers were enveloped in a kaleidoscope of stories, each artefact vying for attention, whispering tales of heroism, betrayal, and the relentless march of civilisations. The very air thrummed with the weight of history, threatening to overwhelm their senses and pull them into the echoes of ages long past. They were no longer simply standing in a room; they were standing at the nexus of time, poised on the precipice of untold adventures.

"Gather your wits!" Azrael proclaimed, his voice unfaltering. "It's time to unveil the guardians of history."

With that, the chamber began to transform. The air crackled with untold energy as the bells of time echoed around them, each chime resonating with the turning of epochs. The dormant artefacts, once silent witnesses, shimmered to life. Golden light pulsed from ancient goblets, tapestries woven with forgotten constellations glowed with celestial fire, and statues of long-dead heroes seemed to subtly shift and breathe. The adventurers were enveloped in a kaleidoscope of stories, each artefact vying for their attention, whispering promises of knowledge and power.

The shimmering chamber encapsulated them in its magic, a swirling vortex of chronal energy that pressed against their skin like a physical force. The echoes of ages past intertwined with their fates, binding them to the very fabric of the museum. It was more than just a room; it was a living, breathing entity, beckoning them to unlock the secrets that existed within its very walls. This was the heart of the Enchanted Museum, and it pulsed with a power that both thrilled and intimidated.

As the echoes reverberated, reaching into the deepest recesses of their minds, Ellie felt her connection to the artefacts deepen. A strange hum resonating from the objects resonated within her being, as if she was becoming part of the museum itself. Here, in the heart of history, they were destined to unearth the mysteries hidden within time's embrace. The challenge was clear: navigate the labyrinth, decipher the clues, and survive the unveiling of truths best left undisturbed. In the whispers of the night, the adventure had only just begun, a perilous journey into the past where the price of failure was not just defeat but erasure.

THE LANTERN'S GLOW

The clock struck midnight, its reverberations echoing through the hallowed halls of the museum like a solemn decree, a sound ripe with expectation and the promise of secrets unveiled. Shadows, elongated and distorted by the dim emergency lighting, danced along the polished marble floors, transforming familiar patterns into fleeting phantoms, as artefacts no longer frozen in time began their nightly transformations. Statues seemed to subtly shift, tapestries rippled imperceptibly, and the glint in the eyes of ancient portraits deepened. As the last resonant bell chimed, its dying note fading into the oppressive silence.

Ellie, hidden behind a towering suit of samurai armour, felt a tingling sensation ripple through her fingertips, spreading outwards to encompass her entire being. Anticipation, sharp and electric, flooded her veins, chasing away the creeping cold of the long night. The air was thick with the scent of ancient oils, papyrus and forgotten resins, mingled with the faint whispers of long-dead voices – voices that seemed to call to her from across the centuries. It was a palpable shift, a tangible change in the atmosphere. Something extraordinary was alive tonight within those walls, something beyond the realm of the mundane, and Ellie, the museum's junior research assistant, was about to see it, or perhaps become a part of it.

"Ellie!" called Professor Finch, his eccentric spectacles glimmering in the lantern light, "We must move quickly. Azrael mentioned a hidden chamber—one that reveals secrets forgotten with time!"

Beside them, a golden lion statue, once cold and still, sprang to life with a metallic groan. Its burnished fur shimmered in the flickering torchlight, and its eyes, previously unseeing gems, now burnt with a radiant, fierce intelligence. "Follow me!" commanded Azrael, his voice a low rumble that resonated with ancient power and undeniable authority. The sound seemed to vibrate in their chests, urging them forward. With a sweep of his stately mane, the golden hairs glinting like captured sunlight, he beckoned the group onwards into the gloom, his posture suggesting not just guidance but a regal expectation of obedience. Hope flickered in their hearts, tempered by the awe and trepidation that came with being led by a creature of legend.

"Wait!" interrupted Oliver, the stout guard, his uncertainty palpable as he adjusted the collar of his uniform. "Perhaps we should assess the situation instead of rushing headfirst into adventure!" Finn zipped past, darting between their legs, his carved wooden frame glowing softly in the dim light. His mischievous growl broke Oliver's resolve, drawing a reluctant smile from the guard. "Where's your sense of exploration, Jenkins?" Finn teased.

As they ventured deeper into the museum, the familiar order of exhibits dissolved into something altogether more mysterious. The air grew heavy with the scent of dust and forgotten incense, and the temperature dropped, raising goosebumps on their arms. The surroundings transformed from a curated collection to a living, breathing labyrinth. The flickering glow of lanterns, seemingly powered by some unknown energy, draped shadowy silhouettes across the walls, revealing ancient hieroglyphs and intricate carvings of long-forgotten tales. These weren't just static displays; the carvings seemed to writhe and shift in their peripheral vision, telling stories too complex to grasp in a single glance.

And then they saw her. Luci, a stunning bronze statue normally nestled in her display case, no longer stood immobile. She slithered forth, her bronze scales gleaming like a thousand polished coins catching the lantern light. Each scale seemed to move independently, reflecting the light in dizzying patterns. Her eyes, usually dull metal, now pulsed with an eerie, emerald light. "To the right, brave adventurers," she hissed, her voice a dry rustle that echoed unnervingly in the vast space. Her mouth curled into a knowing grin, revealing sharp, metallic teeth. "But beware, for time bends in this realm. What you see is not always what it was or will be. Tread carefully, lest you become lost in the currents of the past or swallowed by the shadows of the future." The grin widened, hinting at secrets and dangers beyond their imagining.

"What do you mean?" Ellie asked, feeling both thrilled and apprehensive.

"The past whispers secrets," Luci replied, her voice smooth like silk. "Unfortunately, it also guards its puzzles jealously. Each step could lead you closer to the truth—or further into the labyrinth."

"Let's not get lost," Oliver muttered, his instincts as a guard now in overdrive. "One wrong turn can lead to trouble."

"Trust me", Azrael said confidently, "Those who follow their hearts find their way."

As they turned the corner, the narrow passage opened slightly, revealing a stark contrast to the oppressive darkness they'd been navigating. A solitary lantern hung precariously from a rusted hook, its flame dancing with a peculiar, almost hypnotic rhythm. The light, weak as it was, painted the damp stone walls in shifting shades of amber and shadow, finally settling upon an ornate inscription carved into the wall directly behind the lantern. The script, unfamiliar and vaguely unsettling, hinted at a history long forgotten. Ellie, intrigued and perhaps a little reckless, felt a pull towards the inscription. She hesitated, her hand hovering, compelled to decipher the strange symbols.

Should she risk exposing the lies they held? Or should she heed the hushed warnings of her companions, urging her to go ahead with caution and leave the cryptic message undisturbed? The air hung heavy with anticipation, the flickering lantern The flame mirrored the internal battle that was raging within her. Each heartbeat seemed to echo the question: knowledge or safety?

"Listen," Professor Finch whispered, his scholarly voice quaking with reverence. "This could be a key to the entire night's mystery."

The soft glow flickered brighter, a mesmerising dance of light, as Ellie traced her fingers along the cool, moss-slicked stone. An ancient chill radiated from the surface, raising goosebumps on her arms despite the humid air. The inscription, etched generations ago by unknown hands, shimmered before her eyes, the letters catching the light and somehow seeming to breathe. She leaned closer, her breath catching in her throat as she finally deciphered the archaic script: 'Only those with true intent shall witness the glow that leads through shadows to the heart of the labyrinth.'

The words hung in the air, heavy with unspoken promise and veiled threat. Ellie considered them carefully, turning them over in her mind like a precious, fragile jewel. True intent. What constituted true intent? Was it simply a burning desire, or did it require something more – a pure heart, a sacrifice made, a destiny fulfilled? The weight of the inscription settled upon her, a tangible pressure in the cavernous space. The labyrinth, she knew, was more than just a physical construct of twisting passages and dead ends.

It was a trial, a test of character, a gauntlet thrown down by whatever power existed within. And the glow... The glow was the key, the guide, the whispering promise of what lay beyond, if only she was worthy. She took a deep breath, meeting the challenge in the glimmering stone, determined to prove that her intentions, whatever they were, were indeed true.

"True intent?" Ellie pondered aloud. "What does that even mean?"

"Perhaps it means your motives," Luci chimed in, weaving through the group. "Are you here for adventure, for knowledge, or something deeper?"

Oliver frowned. "What other reason would there be? This whole situation is perilous enough."

But Azrael defended Ellie, "She's a historian. Her heart beats for the tales of yore, for the essence of what has been lost."

"Exactly," Ellie affirmed, her excitement blossoming into determination. "If we want to unlock the next part of our journey, we have to be honest with ourselves."

Finn, in his playful manner, flicked his tail, "Then let us illuminate our intentions—who wants to go first?"

"I suppose I can start," Oliver said hesitantly, "I wanted to prove that I'm not just a guard but someone who can rise to challenges."

"Good!" Azrael exclaimed, "You need courage."

With a deep breath, Ellie stepped forward, the dust motes dancing in the faint light illuminating her determined face. "I look to uncover the truths hidden here—not just for myself, a personal quest to understand my own past, but to ensure their stories are remembered, honoured, and learnt from. History is a tapestry, rich and complex, and each thread, no matter how small or seemingly insignificant, has its place and contributes to the overall picture. To ignore even one thread is to weaken the whole." Her voice echoed slightly in the silent space, a promise and a challenge to the secrets held within its walls.

"Voila!" Finn exclaimed, "Next!"

"I... I look to preserve this museum's wonders," Dr. Mariana Bell spoke next, a sudden fire igniting in her expression. "I want the world to cherish these artefacts, to understand their value in today's context."

"Oh, lovely!" Finn danced around her, "Respect for history—a noble cause!"

"And I wish to share the wisdom of the past," Lady Arabella's voice floated gracefully, echoing from within her statue form. "The tales engraved in time are ripe with lessons for all."

The lantern flickered once more, casting dancing shadows that seemed to mimic the unspoken questions hanging in the air, as if even the inanimate object was leaning into their intentions, urging a confession. "What about you, Professor?" Ellie asked, her voice laced with genuine curiosity. The firelight painted her face with an innocent earnestness, a stark contrast to the complicated history she knew he carried. "What drives your scholarly heart? Is it the pursuit of pure knowledge, the thrill of uncovering forgotten truths, or something... more personal? I've seen the passion in your eyes when you speak of these old texts, Professor, a fire that hints at something deeper than just academic interest. Help me understand. What's the real reason you dedicate your life to this seemingly endless pursuit?"

"I look for, above all, adventure! The thrill of discovery is intoxicating," Professor Finch exclaimed, his eyes twinkling like constellations in the night sky. "But there's also an underlying wish—to share the wonders of history with the world, to inspire future generations."

"Wait!" yelled Oliver, interrupting the flow. "If we're sharing, I also want to be famous for protecting these treasures!"

As they exchanged their intentions, their voices hushed yet firm with conviction, the lantern blazed brighter, as though responding to the sincerity of their words.

The light, no longer a mere illumination, pulsed with a warm, inviting quality, painting the chamber in soft, golden hues and highlighting the earnestness etched on their faces. Then, in unison, a tangible shift enveloped them. The air, once still and heavy, now crackled with a subtle energy.

They felt a resonance, a deep and undeniable recognition of their shared purpose, vibrating through the very air between them, solidifying their bond and imbuing them with a sense of profound connection and anticipation for what was to come. It was as if the universe itself was acknowledging their agreement, lending its weight to their unified goal.

"I think we've unlocked something," Ellie declared, her heart racing. "This challenge is more than just about solving riddles."

Luci, her serpentine form gracefully coiling around the antique lantern, added her own piece of the puzzle, her voice a soft whisper in the echoing hall. "It's also about understanding each other, knowing our hearts. True connection unlocks more than dusty secrets; it unlocks us." She paused, her reptilian eyes shimmering in the dim light, conveying a deeper meaning that hung unspoken in the air.

Suddenly, as if responding to Luci's profound statement, the ancient inscriptions etched into the lantern's surface began to glow with an ethereal, inner light. The lantern trembled, humming with a latent power that had been slumbering for centuries. Before their eyes, it subtly, yet undeniably, transformed. Its intricate details sharpened, and a soft, warm light emanated from within, coalescing into a focused beam.

The beam struck the opposite wall, not just illuminating it but projecting an elaborate and intricate map of the museum's hidden chambers. The map revealed previously unknown secret passages, forgotten rooms, and subterranean tunnels in stunning detail. The map pulsed with a life of its own, highlighting potential pathways and suggesting the routes yet to be explored. The glow acted like a beacon, beckoning them forward, an outstretched hand welcoming them into the depths of history, promising adventure and untold stories waiting to be unearthed. It was an invitation they couldn't refuse, a silent promise of discoveries that would change them forever.

"Look there!" Azrael pointed with his paw, "That passage leads to the chamber of shadows—the next puzzle awaits us!"

Without hesitation, the group moved towards the passage, their footsteps echoing with a shared sense of purpose. The flickering light of their camaraderie, ignited by the shared illumination of their intentions and strengthened bonds of friendship, painted dancing shadows on the rough-hewn walls. Each step forward was fuelled by a silent understanding and fuelled by a silent understanding, a collective desire to unravel the mysteries that lay hidden within the passage's depths.

A sudden gust of wind, seemingly born from the depths of the earth, swept through with ferocious speed as they approached the entrance, mere feet from the promise of the unknown. It was a malevolent breath that extinguished the lantern in an instant, plunging them into an oppressive darkness. An eerie silence, thick and suffocating, enveloped them, amplified by the sudden absence of light. The darkness pressed in like an unwanted shroud, trying to smother their courage and replace it with creeping doubt.

The air itself seemed to vibrate with an unseen presence, and the only sound was the frantic beat of their hearts, each thud a loud reminder of their vulnerability in the face of the unknown. The passage, once a beacon of adventure, now loomed before them, a gaping maw of shadow and uncertainty.

"Flames have flickered and died," murmured Huckleberry, who had suddenly appeared, his voice low and melodic. "In the shadows, we hide. Hope may lie elsewhere—each must find their light."

"Each must find their light?" Fiona repeated, glancing at her companions. She sensed that inherent challenges lay ahead.

In that moment, they bravely entered the unexplored passageway, poised on the precipice of the unknown and guided solely by their unwavering resolve and the invaluable companionship of fellow adventurers. The cool, damp air at once enveloped them, and the pervasive shadows seemed to reach out like grasping fingers. Yet, within each heart, a steadfast determination fiercely burnt, though small, it would valiantly try to illuminate the winding path.

But they knew, deep down, that occasionally, it is not the physical light that truly guides us but the unwavering strength and support found within the hearts of those who walk together, forging a beacon that shines brighter than any artificial flame.

As Ellie stepped further into the inky depths, an exhilarating thrill coursed through her veins, a potent cocktail of anticipation and trepidation. It wasn't merely the allure of unearthing hidden historical secrets that drew her; it was the profound discovery of genuine camaraderie, forged in the face of ancient mysteries and shared dangers. More than just a team, they were bound together, not just by the formidable challenges they faced or the tantalising artefacts that whispered tales of forgotten ages, but by the subtle, almost imperceptible whispers of their own spirits, awakening within the enchanted embrace of the night. Each shared glance, each murmured word of encouragement, solidified the bond.

With a renewed sense of purpose and hearts ignited by their shared intentions, they resolutely forged ahead into the labyrinth of shadows, their footsteps echoing in the unnerving silence. They were ready to unravel the next layer of mystery that the enchanted museum held captive, to decipher the secrets hidden within its ancient walls, all before the inevitable dawn cast its revealing light upon them, potentially washing away the magic of the night and dispersing the secrets they looked for. They faced a pressing deadline, with the fate of their quest and possibly more at stake.

THE SPINNING CAROUSEL

The dim light of the Enchanted Museum flickered inconsistently, as if powered by the very magic it housed. Each hour, the deep, melodic chimes of the grandfather clock in the central rotunda echoed through its vast halls, their mournful sound a constant reminder of the relentless passage of time within these timeless walls. Ellie stood transfixed before the ornate carousel, a miniature kingdom frozen in a perpetual dance. Its woodwork was intricately carved, a dizzying array of flowers, mythical creatures, and swirling patterns that seemed to shift and breathe in the periphery. Dozens of animals, a vibrant menagerie of lions, tigers, griffins, and stags, were poised in mid-gallop, each a testament to the master craftsman who had painstakingly brought them to life. They glimmered faintly under the moonlight spilling through a nearby arched window, dust motes dancing in the pale beams like tiny sprites. The vivid hues of the carousel, once undoubtedly dazzling, were now dulled by time and a century's worth of dust, yet they still pulsed with a residual vibrant energy in the shadows. These faded colours seemed to whisper secrets of countless stories told through the years – tales of laughter, love, loss, and childhood dreams spun from the magic of the ride and the imaginations of generations past. Ellie could almost hear the faint strains of calliope music, a ghostly echo of the carousel's former glory, beckoning her to climb aboard and join the endless, silent journey.

"Can you believe this?" she murmured to Professor Finch, who was adjusting his glasses as he saw the delicate artisanry. "It feels as though each creature is waiting for its turn to spin and come to life."

"Ah, Ellie," Professor Finch replied, his eyes sparkling with enthusiasm, "the carousel has a rich history of its own. People once believed that the carousel held magic, spinning for children at festivals until time passed and they forgot about it. However, the enchantment it housed may awaken at midnight."

As if on cue, the clock struck midnight, a deep, resonant tone that wasn't merely heard but felt, a tangible vibration shaking the very air around them. The sound, aged and powerful, clawed its way through the silence of the abandoned amusement park. The last echo lingered, a phantom hum against the backdrop of the rustling wind, and with it, the carousel began to shudder. The once vibrant paint, now chipped and faded, seemed to peel inwards. Dust, disturbed from its decades-long slumber, danced in the air like the remnants of a long-forgotten spell, swirling and shimmering in the moonlight that streamed through the broken windows.

A whoosh of energy surged through the room, a sudden and palpable shift in the atmosphere. The air crackled with an unseen force. Ellie, the determined urban explorer, instinctively stepped back, her heart racing a frantic rhythm against her ribs. The intensity was far beyond anything she had predicted. Oliver, the unsuspecting security guard who had been dozing in his booth minutes earlier, rubbed his eyes in disbelief, his face a mask of bewildered confusion. "You're not seeing this, right? This can't be real... I must be dreaming," he stammered, his voice barely a whisper as he desperately looked to Ellie for reassurance, for any sign that his sanity hadn't completely deserted him. The absurdity of the situation battled with the genuine fear etched on his face. He tugged at the collar of his uniform, suddenly feeling stifled, trapped in a nightmare he couldn't wake from.

"Trust me, you're very much awake," Azrael the Lion boomed, his magnificent bronze form coming to life on a nearby pedestal. He leapt down gracefully, his powerful body radiating warmth. "The time has come for you to understand the significance of this carousel."

With a commanding gesture, a sweep of his hand that seemed to gather the very air itself, Azrael beckoned the group forward towards the spinning structure. It was a carousel, but unlike any they had seen before. The painted horses, usually frozen in mid-gallop, now seemed to breathe. As they approached, the wooden animals began to ride, lurching and dipping with unexpected life. Their painted eyes, once dull and lifeless, sparked with newfound energy, tiny pinpricks of light that danced with a strange sentience. Finn, a scruffy plush toy normally relegated to a dusty corner, watched the spectacle unfold. He straightened, his worn velvet fur seeming to smooth itself out. A mischievous glint, almost too bright to be real, ignited in his button eyes. He pranced closer, his stitched nose twitching with curiosity and perhaps a touch of something more...something akin to anticipation. He seemed drawn to the spectacle, as though compelled by an invisible force, ready to join the whirling, revitalised creatures of the carousel.

"Hey, don't you think we ought to give it a spin? What better way to travel through time!" Finn suggested bouncing on his paws, his enthusiasm infectious.

"Travel through time?" Oliver gulped, his fight-or-flight response flaring. "I'm just a guard! What's a carousel got to do with that?"

Luci, her scales shimmering like polished bronze in the dim light, coiled sinuously beside Finn. Her eyes, twin chips of obsidian, held a knowing glint as she addressed him. "Ah, young guard, this isn't merely a gaudy carousel for children's amusement. This is no ordinary ride. It has a power, a key, to unlock the echoes of the past. Each intricately carved animal is a different era, a distinct fragment of history frozen in time. When it spins, when the music swells and the world blurs, we may find ourselves drawn into those very moments, reliving them, seeing them firsthand. The question is, Finn, are you prepared to ride? Are you prepared to face the spectres of what was and what could have been?"

Lady Arabella, who had appeared lost in a waking dream only moments before, now sat bolt upright, her regal posture as sharp and defined as a queen's. The light of understanding flickered in her ancient eyes, lending her words the weight of centuries. "Every adventure, every journey into the unknown, has its inherent risks, Finn. Dangers lurk in the shadows, and the past is rarely as romantic as the stories portray. You can truly face the future with clarity and purpose only by understanding the victories and the mistakes, the triumphs and the tragedies, that have shaped the tapestry of existence. You must weigh the potential consequences against the potential rewards. You must decide, young guard, if you have the courage, the wisdom, and the sheer will to accept this perilous challenge and explore the swirling currents of time itself."

Ellie exchanged nervous glances with the others, the low light of the museum reflecting in her wide, apprehensive eyes. Her historian's instincts, usually a wellspring of measured analysis and academic caution, were now locked in a fierce battle against the growing curiosity that bubbled within her chest. The strange occurrences of the past few nights – flickering lights, echoing whispers, and the distinct feeling of being watched – were undeniably linked to the newly bought artefacts from the Valen excavation. "It could be the opportunity we need," she said, her voice surprisingly steady despite the tremor in her hands, "the chance to learn more about the artefacts themselves

The guard, a burly man named Oliver more accustomed to patrolling the perimeter than confronting the paranormal, scratched the back of his head. The fluorescent lights that usually illuminated the gallery were dimmed, casting long, dancing shadows that seemed to writhe with a life of their own. He weighed the risks – getting his trousers scared off by a ghost and a stern talking-to from his supervisor – against the thrilling, albeit terrifying, promise of a possible adventure. "Well," he drawled, a nervous chuckle escaping his lips, "I never thought I'd be chasing spirits in a museum, but what's the worst that could happen? Besides, if there are ghosts, they're probably bored stiff of looking at old pottery." He grinned, a hint of bravado masking his unease. "Let's do it."

The animals on the carousel began to lift their heads, their painted eyes seeming to gleam with newfound awareness, as if responding to Oliver's brave declaration. The wooden steeds pawed the air, the lions roared silently with bared, gilded teeth, and the swans arched their necks in elegant anticipation. The intricate mechanisms, long dormant, churned to life with a joyful groan and a whir of gears, sending a cascade of colourful lights dancing across the faces of the adventurers. The painted panels blurred into streaks of emerald, ruby, and sapphire, creating a dazzling spectacle. With each revolution, the magical aura enveloping them grew stronger, tinged with the scent of sawdust and dreams, pulling them deeper into the adventure that awaited beyond the whirling platform. They felt a strange pull, a dizzying sensation of being transported, as if the carousel wasn't just spinning.

"Hold on tight, everyone!" Azrael instructed as the carousel spun faster, its wooden beasts coming alive, whisking the group away into a whirlwind of history.

As the world blurred around them, a dizzying kaleidoscope of lights and sounds swirling into an indistinguishable mass, Ellie felt an electrifying sensation racing through her veins. It was more than just adrenaline; it was a tingling, almost painful, burst of energy that seemed to rewrite her very being. The whispers of the past, faint and fragmented at first, swelled into a chorus in her ears, snippets of forgotten melodies, echoing laughter, and hushed secrets carried on the wind. Before she could even grasp the changing reality, before her mind could process the impossible, the carousel, spinning with an almost frantic energy, had propelled them through a shimmering veil, a curtain of iridescent light that rippled and dissolved as they passed. One moment they were amidst the swirling madness of the ordinary, and the next, they found themselves standing in a sun-drenched field, the warmth soaking into their skin. The air hummed with life: the vibrant colours of a lively fair bursting forth in a riot of reds, yellows, and blues.

Tents stretched into the distance, adorned with fluttering banners, and the air was thick with the enticing aroma of popcorn, cotton candy, and something uniquely, tantalisingly unfamiliar. The clamorous cacophony of games, music, and excited chatter formed a symphony of pure, unadulterated joy, a stark contrast to the unsettling whispers that still clung to Ellie's memory. Where had they landed, and what secrets did this vibrant, otherworldly fair hold?

"Look!" Finn exclaimed, pointing to several children riding a smaller version of the carousel nearby, laughter mingling with the sweet sound of music. "The 18th century " This must be the festival Lady Arabella spoke of!"

"Everything seems lovely," Oliver remarked, still trying to adjust to the recent turn of events. "But are we stuck here?"

Huckleberry , a magnificent creature with eyes like molten gold, pools of liquid fire that seemed to see straight into the soul, and feathers shimmering with every colour imaginable – emerald green melting into sapphire blue, ruby red fading into amethyst purple, and streaks of sunshine yellow highlighting the ebony black of its primary flight feathers – flew down from an unseen perch high above, a citadel perhaps, carved into the face of a sheer, windswept mountain. Its powerful wings, each spanning the length of a small cart, beat the air with a soft, almost melodic rhythm, a gentle pulse that belied the immense strength contained within.

Dust mites danced in the shafts of light that pierced the courtyard as Huckleberry descended a living kaleidoscope against the aged stone. It landed with a graceful thud, unusual for such a powerful being, its talons, sharp as obsidian daggers, gripping the ancient stones of the courtyard with a gentle precision, as if aware of their delicate age. The passage of countless years had worn the stones smooth, etched with glyphs hinting at a forgotten history. Then, it spoke with a charismatic caw that echoed through the space, not a harsh screech, but a resonant baritone that rippled outwards, filled with both unquestionable authorities, honed over centuries of wisdom and experience, and an underlying warmth, a hint of benevolence that softened its otherwise imposing presence. The very air seemed to still as Huckleberry spoke, waiting to hear the pronouncements of this ancient guardian.

"Do not fear, brave adventurers!" Huckleberry declared, its voice resonating This world, woven with threads of forgotten magic and untold stories, is yours to see. This world, woven with threads of forgotten magic and untold stories, is yours to see. But your time here is fleeting, like a dream fading at dawn. You must uncover the secrets that lie hidden within these ancient walls, solve the riddles whispered on the wind, and understand the truths that echo in the very stones before the final chime calls you back to your reality." The griffin paused, its gaze sweeping over the assembled adventurers, a hint of urgency in its brilliant eyes. "Do not waste this precious opportunity. Seek knowledge, for knowledge is the key to unlocking the mysteries that bind this realm."

"What does that mean?" Ellie asked, feeling a knot of worry forming in her stomach.

Huckleberry tilted his head, his obsidian eyes glinting mysteriously in the fading light of the ancient forest. A subtle smile played on his lips, a smile that promised both knowledge and peril. "Only by tracing the origins of this carousel can you truly grasp its power, a power that both creates and destroys, heals and corrupts. It is not a simple toy but a key. Seek the tales told long ago, whispers on the wind, etched in the bones of the earth, for they hold the answers you need. Listen to the legends of the artisans who crafted it, the sorcerers who enchanted it, and the empires that rose and fell under its influence. The carousel is more than just wood and paint; it's a living tapestry woven with history, soaked in magic, and stained with blood. Be warned," he added, his voice dropping to a low rumble, "the threads of its past are tangled, and some are best left undisturbed."

With a newfound determination hardening her gaze, Ellie led the group deeper into the vibrant chaos of the fairgrounds, where the infectious clang of laughter echoed around them like wind chimes. They navigated a maze of stalls bursting with life and colour, from pyramids of freshly cut flowers radiating intoxicating perfumes to tables overflowing with sugary sweets, their iridescent wrappers glinting in the afternoon sun. Snippets of conversations, like whispers carried on the breeze, brushed past them: tales of miraculous wins at the ring toss, hushed accounts of its wonders beyond imagination.

"Maybe the juggler knows something," suggested Oliver, nudging Ellie in excitement. "They're the ones captivating the audience, after all!"

They approached the tent, its vibrant, striped fabric billowing rhythmically in the gentle breeze, a welcoming beacon against the dusty landscape. Hesitantly at first, then with growing anticipation, they pushed aside the heavy canvas flap and stepped inside. The interior was a scene alive with festivity and wonder, a kaleidoscope of sights and sounds that at once enveloped them. Banners strung with glittering sequins crisscrossed the space, casting dancing patterns of light. Laughter echoed off the tent's high roof, mingling with the lively music of a nearby oud. At the centre of it all, a juggler, his movements fluid and mesmerising, spun not only colourful props – gleaming clubs, shimmering scarves, and bouncing balls – but also captivating tales of faraway lands and daring adventures, his voice rising and falling with each toss and catch, holding the audience spellbound.

"Welcome, seekers of the past!" the juggler exclaimed, his voice echoing as he tossed a set of neon balls into the air with deft precision. "What brings you to our realm of magic?"

"We seek knowledge about the enchanted carousel," Ellie responded, steeling herself. "It was once a beloved part of this fair, wasn't it?"

"Ah, yes. The carousel holds memories of love and loss," he replied, his hands. Many celebrations were held until darkness fell upon them, curses hidden in joy. Its magic can only be summoned by those who uncover the truth of its past."

"What darkness?" Finn piped up, his playful nature now tinged with a hint of concern.

"If you listen closely to the whispers of the wind, you will discern the stories waiting to be unveiled," the juggler advised cryptically, his hands continuing their ballet of colour. "In every spin, there's a tale lurking, waiting for those eager enough to unravel it."

Suddenly, Azrael stepped forward, his regal presence demanding attention. The air crackled with anticipation as the celestial being, wings shimmering subtly in the firelight, addressed the assembled crowd. His voice, a low and resonant baritone, cut through the murmur. "We wish to learn of this darkness that has festered and begun to spread its tendrils. To understand its nature is to understand how to return it to the light. How do we unearth these tales? What keys unlock the secrets buried within this cursed carnival?"

The juggler, mid-cascade with flaming torches, paused, the weight of the room shifting from playful amusement to sombre intensity and unwavering on Azrael. "But be warned," he added, a flicker of apprehension crossing his face, "the past is a hungry beast, and it may not want to let you go."

With their task clear, the adventurers, spurred by the urgency in the juggler's voice, sprinted out of the tent. The flap slammed shut behind them, plunging them back into the chaotic, yet strangely subdued, atmosphere of the night fair. The air floated. In the dim light, cast by flickering gas lamps and the macabre glow of the funhouse, they could see the carousel in the distance, a beacon of garish light against the receding darkness. It glimmered tauntingly against the backdrop of the pastel sky, its painted horses frozen in eternal gallop, promising both joy and untold sorrow. The faint strains of its calliope music drifted on the wind, a siren song drawing them closer to the heart of the mystery and perhaps to their doom.

"Let's ride it again!" Oliver exclaimed, newfound confidence roiling within him. The group hurried towards the carousel, hearts racing with the anticipation of untold stories waiting to unfold.

As they reached the grand spinning structure, the air around them crackled with anticipation. Ellie, her eyes wide with a mixture of awe and excitement, noticed an ornate disc embedded in the centre of the carousel, where whimsical horses should have lived. Swirling designs and symbols, ancient and enigmatic, were etched into the surface, giving it an almost living quality. "This must be the wheel of fate!" she said, pointing eagerly, her voice barely a whisper above the gentle hum emanating from the machine. "We need to spin it and see what story it tells. What mysteries it will unravel for us."

The carousel's lights flickered again, momentarily plunging them into near darkness before surging back to life, bathing the scene in an otherworldly glow. Azrael, ever the observant protector, nudged Ellie gently with his side. "You must lead the spin," he rumbled, his voice a low, comforting vibration. "It is your historian's heart, your deep connection to the past, that can sense the pulse of its magic. You are the key to understanding what lies ahead."

Feeling the weight of her friends' eyes upon her, Ellie stepped forward, her earlier excitement tempered with a sudden dose of responsibility. A slight tremble ran through her hands as she approached the disc, her breath catching in her chest. This wasn't just a game; she could feel the power radiating from the ancient artefact. She placed her hand against the cool, smooth surface of the wheel and closed her eyes, drawing strength from the moment, from her friends, and from the very air around her. Visualising the stories she'd dedicated her life to preserving, she channelled her knowledge and her hope into a single, focused intention. With a determined push, she spun the disc, setting it into motion with a low, resonant hum that seemed to echo through the very foundations of the abandoned amusement park.

In an instant, the world around them warped, the cotton candy scent of the fair replaced by the metallic tang of ozone, the cheerful music dissolving into a dissonant symphony of chimes and whispers. The vibrant fair, a kaleidoscope of colours and bustling crowds just moments ago, dissolved into a shimmering haze, like a painting left out in the rain. Images flickered past Ellie's eyes with dizzying speed: childhood birthday parties, sun-drenched picnics, tearful goodbyes. Memories tangled in time, blurring the line between reality and illusion, tales of joy and sorrow intertwining before her in a chaotic ballet of emotion. She felt herself swept up in a whirlwind of sensations – the giddy laughter of children, the sharp sting of heartbreak, the hushed weight of untold secrets whispered in the wind. The ground vibrated beneath her feet, a low hum resonating deep within her bones.

As the spinning slowed, the chaotic visual storm began to coalesce, the swirling colours resolving into sharper forms. Ellie opened her eyes cautiously, her head still swimming, to see a new vision before her. Standing beside the now-still carousel was a noble couple, dressed in elegant attire that hinted at a bygone era. Their faces were lit with a love and joy so profound it seemed to radiate outwards, illuminating the air around them. Ellie knew these were the carousel's creators, the architects of this magical place. However, the idyllic scene was marred by an unsettling element. Shadows, thick and oily, lurked behind them, clinging to the edges of their smiles and obscuring the edges of their fine clothing. Dark tendrils, like creeping vines born of malice, seeped from the carousel's ornate base, twisting and writhing like living things, a silent testament to a darkness that threatened to consume the light. The joyous scene felt fragile, as if a single breath could shatter the illusion and unleash the darkness fully.

"The curse!" she gasped, turning to the others. "They were consuming the happiness of others for their own! If we don't break this cycle, it will repeat itself indefinitely!"

Oliver's eyes widened, "What do we do?"

"We must confront the darkness," Ellie declared. "We'll find a way to turn their sorrow into joy; we must make their hearts sing once again!"

With fierce determination, the group returned to the spinning carousel, the haunting melody now almost a taunt. They knew this was their focal point, the nexus of the strange energy that had gripped the abandoned fair. They combined their strengths, a united front against the unknown: Ellie's encyclopaedic knowledge of local folklore and arcane symbols, Professor Finch's historical insight into the fair's origins and the rumours surrounding it, Azrael's unwavering bravery, honed by years of facing down dangers both seen and unseen, Luci's quiet wisdom, capable of cutting through deception and revealing the truth, and Finn's surprisingly potent playful spirit, a beacon of hope and lightness that kept despair at bay.

As they danced around the carousel, not in joyful abandon but with deliberate intention, each step resonated with the magic of their newfound friendship. Ellie chanted a forgotten rhyme, Professor Finch directed their movements with the authority of one who understood the history they were rewriting, Azrael stood guard, his gaze sharp and alert, Luci offered silent guidance, her hand gently correcting their course, and Finn danced with a mischievous grin, channelling the forgotten joy of the fair itself. Their combined energy, a swirling vortex of knowledge, courage, wisdom, and laughter, created an unbreakable bond that lit the once-dark corners of the fair. The oppressive atmosphere seemed to thin, the weight on their shoulders lightening with each completed circuit.

The shadows began to recede like frightened creatures, driven back by the growing light. The air, thick with dread just moments before, now filled with the tentative sound of laughter, first hesitant whispers, then building to a chorus that echoed through the deserted grounds. Joy, long absent from this place, flooded the scene, expanding and enveloping the couple in warmth – a radiant shield against the lingering darkness. At that very moment, the carousel glowed brilliantly, the painted horses shimmering with an ethereal light, the music swelling to a crescendo as the platform spiralled even faster, blurring the figures upon it into streaks of vibrant colour. They were on the verge of something momentous, on the cusp of either triumph or utter failure, and the air crackled with anticipation. The fate of the fair, and perhaps more, hung in the balance.

They had broken the cycle, the endless loop of sorrow and despair that had plagued the enchanted fair. As the final echoes of the spell dissipated, like whispers fading on the wind, the fair began to transform. The melancholy hues that had cloaked everything softened, replaced by vibrant colours that pulsed with newfound life. The couple, once trapped in an eternal reenactment of heartbreak, stood together, their faces radiant, the weight of the curse lifted from their shoulders. Their eyes shone with a genuine joy that hadn't existed moments before. Ellie felt a thrum of triumph course through her, a wave of satisfaction washing over her as she realised the impact of their actions.

As she stepped back, seeing the revitalised scene, she saw the juggler reappear, no longer a shadowy figure burdened by sorrow. The light of joy radiated from him, an almost palpable aura of happiness that filled the air. He beamed at them, his voice ringing with gratitude. "You have done well, brave adventurers. Your courage and compassion have saved us all. This carousel once again spins tales of love and laughter instead of despair, weaving dreams of happiness instead of nightmares of regret. You have restored balance in time, mended a tear in the very fabric of reality."

With a victorious smile, Ellie and her friends exchanged glances, a silent understanding passing between them. They had succeeded. As if summoned by their shared feeling of accomplishment, the carousel began to spin faster, its horses glowing with an ethereal light. A swirling vortex of colours enveloped them, and they felt the carousel swallow them whole, spirited them back to the museum. The familiar scent of aged wood and dust filled their nostrils, but the echoes of their adventure still hummed within the walls, a silent testament to the magic they had unleashed and the balance they had restored.

The carousel's world may be unchanged, but they were forever altered by the adventure and the knowledge that they could make a difference.

They appeared in the familiar yet mystical halls, the night's magic lingering like a soft embrace.

"Well, I suppose we might have a few more stories to uncover," Oliver muttered, his previously guarded spirit now infused with a sense of wonder.

"Indeed", Professor Finch said with a beaming smile, "who knew an old carousel could weave such rich tales? Onwards to the next mystery!"

As they ventured further into the museum, driven by curiosity and camaraderie, Ellie knew with certainty that together, they could conquer whatever challenge lay ahead. The carousel had not only shown them history, but also sealed their bond, launching them into adventure with the night still echoing around them.

THE MAP OF
FORGOTTEN REALMS

As the clock struck one, the museum transformed. No longer a repository of silent history, it became a cacophony of echoes and whispers, the building itself seemingly breathing secrets into the still night. Ellie, drawn in by the hushed energy, found herself almost alone in the vast hall, surrounded by artefacts bathed in an ethereal, moonlit glow filtering through the high, arched windows. She moved with a quiet reverence, her footsteps barely disturbing the dust motes dancing in the beams of light. Drawn as if by an invisible thread, she brushed her fingertips against the cool glass enclosure of a particularly captivating display.

Inside, nestled upon a velvet cushion, lay an ancient map that had ensnared her curiosity from the moment she'd seen it. Aged and delicate, the parchment was brittle with time, its surface a tapestry of cracks and faded ink. Yet, despite its fragility, it pulsed with an undeniable power. The map displayed intricate drawings that twisted and wove through a landscape of forgotten realms, a cartographer's fever dream of mythical beasts, impossible mountains, and rivers that bled into the sea. Strange symbols, unlike any she had ever seen, adorned the borders, hinting at a language lost to the ages.

A tingle danced down her spine, a sensation both exhilarating and unnerving. It wasn't just the allure of the unknown; it was something more profound, something almost tangible. She could almost hear the map calling out to her, whispering promises of adventure and peril, beckoning her to find out what's hidden within its ancient folds. The air around her seemed to crackle with anticipation, the silence amplifying the unspoken invitation. She felt an irresistible urge to reach out, to touch the parchment, to somehow connect with the hand that had drawn it centuries ago, and in that moment, Ellie knew her comfortable life was about to take an unexpected and potentially dangerous turn.

"Ellie!" Professor Finch called out, adjusting his spectacles and peering over her shoulder. "I do believe that's the legendary Map of Forgotten Realms. It's said to reveal routes to lost cities and hidden treasures throughout history. But be warned—it is notoriously fickle and shrouded in enigmas."

"Fickle how?" Ellie asked, her interest piqued.

"The map alters depending on the beholder's intent," he explained, pacing excitedly. "Only those with a pure heart and a noble mission can decode its secrets."

Just as Ellie, her eyes wide with burgeoning curiosity, was about to venture deeper into the labyrinthine halls of the old museum, the overhead lights sputtered and flickered erratically, casting long, dancing shadows that writhed across the dusty exhibits. A low hum, almost imperceptible at first, vibrated through the very floorboards beneath her feet. The walls themselves seemed to breathe, expanding and contracting in a subtle, unsettling rhythm that made her skin crawl. And then, he was there. Finn, a meticulously crafted wooden sculpture she'd admired earlier, darted into view from behind a towering display case. His once-static form was now animated by a mischievous energy, his painted eyes gleaming with an unnatural light. His sly grin, previously a charming detail, now seemed almost predatory, hinting at secrets and untold stories about to unfold.

"Ready to play a game, Ellie?" he teased, eyes sparkling. "The map wants to share its secrets, but it's up to us to coax them out. Shall we?"

"Of course!" Ellie responded with enthusiasm. She turned back to the map, noticing that the ink shimmered slightly as if alive.

Azrael the Lion, a legend whispered in the rustling leaves, stood before them. He was a titan of muscle and fur, his ancient glory palpable in the very air. Moonlight painted his golden mane in shimmering hues, making him appear almost ethereal. He had a regal bearing that commanded attention and respect, a king surveying his domain. His voice, when he spoke, resonated with the weight of centuries, a low rumble that seemed to vibrate in their bones. "Let us unite our powers," he declared, his amber eyes gleaming with purpose.

"Each of us has a gift to share, a unique strength that can illuminate the path ahead. With the unparalleled expertise of Professor Finch, whose knowledge spans forgotten languages and arcane sciences; the sharp insight from Lady Arabella, whose intuitive mind unravels the most intricate webs of deceit; and the profound wisdom of Luci, whose spirit connects us to the ancient rhythms of the earth, we can unveil what lies beneath the surface and confront the mysteries that shroud our world."

"First", murmured Luci, sliding from her pedestal, her bronze body glimmering. "We must understand the languages of the past. The map speaks in riddles, embellishing forgotten tongues."

"Then we'll need Huckleberry ," Ellie thought aloud, a sense of determination igniting within her. "His knowledge of history will guide us through the riddle's shadows."

Just moments later, a shadow detached itself from the dusty shadows clinging to the topmost shelf. Huckleberry, the raven familiar, descended in a graceful flutter of black feathers. Light caught on them, making them gleam with an almost oily, unnatural sheen. "Did someone mention riddles?" he cawed, his voice a peculiar blend of melodious tones and piercing sharpness, like wind chimes made of polished obsidian. "I have whispers that brush against the truth, echoes of solutions carried on forgotten winds."

The group, huddled around the ancient, parchment map spread across the worn wooden table, instinctively drew closer. Ellie took a deep breath, pushing aside the lingering anxiety that coiled in her stomach. Reaching for a semblance of calm, she focused her mind, willing herself to be receptive. "Alright, Huckleberry, what do we need to do? Where do we begin?"

As if in answer, an inscription began to coalesce along the faded edge of the map, the ancient script shimmering into existence. It writhed and pulsed with a barely perceptible energy, as if the words themselves held a secret. Luci's eyes, usually warm and inviting, glinted with a sudden, almost predatory intensity. "These writings need deciphering, but they're not in plain sight," she murmured, her fingers tracing the barely visible symbols. "They remain obscured, concealed beneath layers of illusion or possibly misdirection." The answer isn't just in understanding the words but in finding where they truly lie."

"Leave it to me!" Finn piped up cheerfully, his small stature teleporting him to various points on the map, playing with features hidden from view. He pressed his wooden paw against a river that flowed across the parchment.

The map responded instantly, a living thing beneath Finn's fingers. It shifted and undulated, swirling topographical lines morphing and reforming as if it had some innate, magnetic intelligence. Mountains crumbled and reformed, forests thickened and thinned with a silent rustle of ink. "A little dab here, and voila!"

Finn exclaimed, his eyes gleaming with mischievous delight as he touched a specific point on the aged parchment with a charcoal stylus. The river beneath his touch started whispering secrets of its own, its course deepening and branching out, revealing hidden tributaries and forgotten canals. These waterways, now vivid and clear, led to sprawling cities, their forms architecturally alien, where marble towers kissed the clouds, reflecting a light that seemed to originate from within.

Professor Finch leaned closer, his breath catching in his throat. "This map appears to have been drawn in an era long lost, a time when geography and myth intertwined." He traced a trembling finger along the now-illuminated course of the Orinoco River. "Look at that—a remarkably correct sign of the Orinoco River, far more advanced than any cartography of its time! And following its course...it leads to the legendary City of Gold, El Dorado itself!" His voice reverberated with excitement, a low, rumbling tremor that shook the dust motes dancing in the shaft of sunlight illuminating the map. He gripped the edge of the table, his knuckles white, his gaze fixed on the swirling network of rivers and cities, the promise of great wealth and forgotten knowledge flickering like a beacon in his eyes. The air in the room crackled with a palpable energy, a sense of impending adventure and the unravelling of a centuries-old mystery.

"They say the city is a mirage!" Oliver chimed in from the corner, his bravado cutting through the warmth of camaraderie. "It's all myths, isn't it?"

Ellie's eyes sparkled with wonder as she spun towards him. "Not anymore! The map is revealing it to us right now! It's offering us a glimpse of what was and what might still be."

Sweet sounds of collaboration drifted through their discussions, fiery enough to ignite old ambitions. They had been brought together by fate, and their disparate paths intertwined in this enchanted night.

"What's our next step?" Lady Arabella asked, her voice smooth like silk. "We need to focus. There's more hidden in these folds than anyone dares imagine."

The map glimmered once, wrapping tendrils around their collective hopes, as it began to pulse.

"Let it guide us by the sincerity of our dreams," Azrael urged. "Whisper your wishes to it!"

Ellie closed her eyes, a nervous flutter in her chest mirroring the anticipation that danced beneath her skin. Inspiration wrestled with her apprehension, a thrilling tug-of-war between the allure of the unknown and the fear of failure. Taking a deep breath, she articulated her desires, her voice a little shaky but firm with conviction, "I wish to explore lost wonders—to uncover the truths of time and bring history back to life." The ancient map, fragile and parchment-thin under her fingers, seemed to hum in response. As she spoke, it absorbed her words like a thirsty sponge, the ink shimmering for a moment before a stunning transformation began.

Vibrant colours surged through its surface, flowing like molten lava deciding its course, revealing contours of forgotten lands and hinting at paths leading to mysteries untold. The air crackled with energy, the scent of aged paper mingling with the metallic tang of adventure. A new era was dawning, not only on the map but in Ellie's very soul.

"History is a tale waiting to be told anew," Luci added.

"Adventure awaits," Azrael encouraged.

As their heartfelt wishes cupped the map, a series of cryptic symbols materialised at the corners, each illuminating their surroundings.

"Can you decipher that, Huckleberry?" asked Professor Finch, eyes now sparkling with intrigue.

"Of course," said Huckleberry, tilting his head. "Let me commune with the whispers of time."

He spread his wings, the sound like rustling parchment in a forgotten library, and the air thickened with the essence of antiquity. It wasn't merely a scent; it was a feeling, a palpable weight of ages past settling upon the room. In a harmonious rhythm, almost a heartbeat echoing through time, he began to chant in an archaic tongue, a language lost to all but the most ancient of beings. The words, guttural and melodic, resonated with a power that defied definition. The room fell silent, the very air holding its breath, the dust motes suspended in the fading light seeming to pause mid-flight as if listening intently. The raven's call, a low, sonorous croak, danced amid the intimate atmosphere, adding a layer of mystique to the unfolding ritual.

Just then, the map, spread out on the worn wooden table, transformed dramatically. What were once simple lines and faded ink now had a life of their own. The markings wriggled, swirling into a fantastical tableau, like stars re-arranging themselves in the night sky. Pictures, previously unnoticed, morphed into vibrant scenes of lost tribes performing forgotten rites, mythical creatures stalking through primeval forests, and sprawling landscapes that defied the laws of geography and time. Finn, perched on the edge of the table, his button eyes wide, perked his ears, his attention rapt, completely consumed by the spectacle. Each flutter of his wooden tail, usually a subtle tick, became a rhythmic dance of uncontainable excitement, a silent applause for the magic unfolding before him. The air crackled with unseen energy, and Finn knew, with a certainty that resonated deep within his clockwork heart, that something extraordinary was about to happen.

"Look!" he exclaimed, pointing with a paw as the images crystallised into a more defined map. "There! The Valley of Shadows! And beyond it, the Ruins of Eldora!"

Ellie's heart raced. It had been a mere legend whispered among scholars. "Ruins of Eldora? That's where the ancients believed the spirit of lost wisdom rests!"

"Bingo!" Finn chimed. "And you need only to decipher the riddle that has kept it hidden for centuries."

"What riddle?" Oliver questioned, somewhat sceptical yet intrigued.

A new engraving appeared on the map, a riddle woven into the terrain, encompassing their very surroundings.

"To find the path to the Ruins of Eldora, seek the light that mends the shadows, where whispers chase the falling leaves, and time holds still. Only then will the way be revealed."

"Whispers and shadows?" Ellie pondered aloud, piecing the riddle together. "It's a poetic paradox. But what does it mean?"

"Perhaps the answer lies within the museum itself," Professor Finch suggested, his keen intellect firing. "We should explore further, seeking components of the riddle. The artefacts may hold the key!"

Emboldened by his leadership, a confidence that seemed to ripple through the very air, Ellie rallied the group, her voice a beacon in the echoing halls. "Let's explore every section of this museum," she urged, her mind racing with possibilities, conjuring up images of hidden compartments, overlooked clues, and subtle symbols, "Maybe there's something, some artefact, some forgotten detail that resonates with the riddle, some piece that will unlock the next step."

As they ventured deeper into the museum, a labyrinth of history frozen in time, the artefacts seemed to watch them with expectant gazes. Each display case held a rusting remnant of stories untold, whispers of lives lived, battles fought, and secrets buried. They visited the priory dedicated to ancient warriors; its stone walls were lined with weathered statues. The figures, etched with the enduring marks of time, echoed the valour of men long left, their silent strength a tangible presence. As they stood before them, bathed in the dim light filtering through the arched windows, they spoke silent promises of bravery, a vow to face the challenges ahead with the same unwavering spirit that had defined these legendary figures.

"Be mindful," Luci whispered as they passed an ornate case displaying delicate porcelain leaves fluttering as if alive. "The past is fraught with shadows, and they can swallow the unwary whole."

Returning to their quest, they gathered in the gallery of echoes. The faint hum reverberated as voices swept around them, warm as a summer breeze.

"Perhaps it is in this very chamber that we'll find the light," Azrael proposed. "Where the whispers dwell—an artifice of sound."

Ellie felt compelled to listen closer, a subtle shiver dancing across her skin. The air, thick with the weight of history and untold stories, seemed to hum around her. Her heart synchronised not just to a general rhythm but to a specific cadence, a time-worn beat echoing from the very artefacts that surrounded her. As the museum, usually bustling with curious chatter and the shuffle of feet, fell into an almost unnerving silence, a single, perfect leaf from the exquisite porcelain tree, perched precariously on a high branch, dislodged itself and drifted silently to the polished, wooden floor. The delicate thud of its landing resonated in the stillness, amplifying its significance.

Where shadows had reigned, the fallen leaf seemed to draw in the faint, ethereal moonlight streaming through the high, arching windows, creating a focal point – a solitary path illuminated by the soft, otherworldly glow. It was as if the leaf had chosen her, marking a specific direction, beckoning her deeper into the museum's secrets.

"Follow that light!" whispered Oliver, stepping with conviction toward the radiant leaf that glimmered with an enchanting gold hue.

When they reached the centre, the room transformed in an instant—the walls shimmered with celestial designs, the air thick with a new energy. The group exchanged glances of wonderment—the shadows around them seemed to whisper secrets rooted deep in history.

"Now, Ellie, what do you see?" Lady Arabella asked, her voice imbued with a wise reverie.

"I think... I think the light is mending the shadows!" Ellie exclaimed, stretching out her hand toward the golden leaf that danced back and forth as if beckoning.

Building moments upon her voice and presence, the shadows began to recede. The figure of Valen manifested briefly, cloaked in ethereal robes, illuminating the path forward.

"You have come far, brave souls," Valen the Timekeeper's echoing voice beckoned through the chamber. "But only those who can read the heart of time will find the Ruins of Eldora. The path lies within your earnest quest—unveil the truth, and the shadows shall yield."

Ellie nodded, a fire igniting in her eyes, radiating determination that matched the flickering candlelight. "Together, we can do it! Let's carry the lessons of tonight, the trust we've forged, and the burning curiosity that drives us. Let's unveil the riches that bind our pasts, the stories whispered on the wind, etched in the stone, and hidden within the layers of time. The map, this ancient tapestry, holds the knowledge, and now, finally, we have it too!" Her voice resonated with newfound conviction, electrifying the air around them.

With hearts united and minds attuned to the riddles of time, a shared purpose thrumming in their veins, they took their first tentative steps along the illuminated path.

The Map of Forgotten Realms shimmered mischievously in their grasp, its age-old ink gleaming as if relishing the prospect of release. The Map whispered tales of yearning, long-lost civilisations, daring adventures, and the profound promise of history, ready for unveiling, testing, and perhaps rewriting. Each ripple in the parchment seemed to urge them forward, promising answers to questions they hadn't even dared to vocalise just hours before.

As they continued their journey, deeper into the labyrinthine museum, a palpable excitement grew with each passing moment. They uncovered long-buried secrets hidden behind dusty artefacts, deciphered cryptic symbols etched into forgotten corners, and pieced together fragments of a narrative that had been fragmented for centuries. The night was filled with promise, each discovery a spark igniting their passion. The museum, no longer a silent tomb of relics, felt like a living, breathing entity, guiding them further into the complexities of time, destiny, and the interwoven threads of their lives with the past they were resurrecting. The weight of history settled upon them, a responsibility and a privilege they embraced with unwavering resolve. Every shadow seemed to hold a secret, every echo a clue, and their adventure had only just begun.

A DANCE WITH
THE FAIRIES

The moon hung high in the sky, a perfect silver coin tossed into the inky velvet above, casting a shimmering, ethereal glow throughout the Enchanted Museum. The ancient stone walls seemed to absorb and reflect the moonlight in equal measure, painting the corridors with dancing shadows that whispered secrets only they knew. Dust motes, disturbed by unseen currents, swirled like tiny galaxies in the luminous beams. As the clock struck midnight, its resonant chimes echoing through the silent halls, Ellie felt a shiver of anticipation course through her. It wasn't a chill of fear but a thrilling awareness, a tingling sense of possibility that prickled her skin. The adventures they had embarked upon so far – the stolen artefact from ancient Egypt, the escape from the animated Roman statues, and the riddle solved within the Van Gogh painting – had been remarkable, testing their courage and wits. But something about this moment, the stillness, the moonlight, and the palpable weight of history thick in the air, felt distinctly magical. Beside her, Professor Finch adjusted his spectacles, the faint click of metal against metal the only sound besides their breathing. His normally pale face was flushed with exhilaration, and his eyes, magnified by the thick lenses, were sparkling with excitement, betraying the carefully cultivated image of a reserved academic.

He looked less like a scholar and more like a child on Christmas morning, utterly captivated by the unfolding mystery. He clutched a worn leather-bound journal in his hand, its pages filled with cryptic symbols and handwritten notes, a key, perhaps, to unlocking whatever wonders awaited them in the heart of the museum.

"Tonight, my dear Ellie, we shall traverse realms beyond our wildest imaginings," he said, almost to himself, as Azrael the Lion prowled ahead, his golden fur glistening in the moonlight. The statue of Azrael had become a steadfast guide, embodying both courage and ancient wisdom. The team hadn't yet fully grasped the wonders yet to unfold.

"Where to next, Azrael?" Oliver, the unsuspecting museum guard, asked, his posture a mix of eagerness and trepidation.

"Follow the sound of the music," Azrael replied, his voice deep and resonant, "for the fairies beckon us with their dance, and only through their enchantment can we unlock the next piece of our journey."

As they moved deeper into the museum, the hushed reverence of the crowd faded, replaced by the soft notes of a delicate melody that drifted through the air like a gentle breeze. It wasn't a defined tune, more a series of harmonious whispers, a symphony of subtle chords that seemed to resonate with the very walls of the ancient building. The music wrapped around them like a fine silk thread, clinging to their skin and drawing them further into its ethereal embrace.

Ellie closed her eyes for a moment, a faint smile playing on her lips. She let the music wash over her, feeling its gentle currents pull her away from the mundane. It spoke of freedom, of untamed landscapes and boundless horizons, a stark contrast to the enclosed space of the museum. It sang of joy, not the boisterous kind, but a quiet, contented happiness that bloomed from deep within. And most profoundly, it hinted at a world where dreams danced on the tip of reality, where the impossible seemed not only plausible but inevitable, a world where the boundaries between what was and what could be blurred into a breathtaking, iridescent haze. The weight of the everyday lifted from her shoulders, replaced by a lightness, an anticipation for the wonders that awaited them further inside. The music was a siren's call, beckoning them onwards into the heart of the museum's secrets.

"Can you hear it?" Finn chirped as he darted ahead, his wooden frame glowing faintly. "It's the Fairies of the Forgotten Gallery! They strike a dance at midnight but rarely offer their secrets to the uninvited."

"What's the Forgotten Gallery?" Oliver asked, glancing at the eclectic group. He had always considered himself a man of logic, yet now his heart raced with an exhilarating mixture of disbelief and wonder.

"It's said to be a realm where forgotten stories linger, a space blessed by the fairies who have safeguarded the tales of lost moments,"

Luci slithered closer, her bronze scales shimmering in the dim light, "but only those pure of heart and curious of soul can glimpse their dance."

"Then we must be worthy," Ellie declared, her voice rich with determination. She felt an unspoken bond with her newfound companions, a connection fortified by their shared desire to unveil the museum's mysteries.

"Very well! Onwards," Azrael commanded, leading them towards an intricately decorated wooden door. Deep carvings of fantastical creatures adorned its surface, swirling vines and floral motifs that seemed to shimmer under the moonlight.

As Ollie pushed the heavy oak door open, a cascade of colourful light spilt out, enveloping them in a gentle luminescence that felt like a warm embrace. Hues of emerald, sapphire, and ruby danced across their skin, promising wonders beyond. The sight that met them was utterly otherworldly: the Forgotten Gallery was a vast, ethereal ballroom, stretching further than seemed possible. Dozens of ornate, glistening chandeliers, each a masterpiece of forgotten artistry, hung from the high, vaulted ceiling, casting shimmering patterns on the polished floor. The walls were draped with enormous tapestries, their threads woven with gold and silver, depicting scenes of bygone eras, of legendary heroes and mythical beasts, of pure, unadulterated magic. The very air shimmered and vibrated, thick with an enchantment that tickled the senses and made the hairs on their arms stand on end. It felt ancient and alive, a silent hymn to the power of imagination.

At the centre of the hall, a myriad of tiny figures flitted about, their gossamer wings catching the light like dewdrops under a rising sun. These were fairies, each one a miniature beacon of light, swirling and darting with playful energy. They spun and danced in intricate patterns, their movements precise and graceful, illuminating the room with their luminescent presence. Some chased each other through the air, leaving trails of sparkling dust, while others perched delicately on the chandeliers, their laughter a faint, melodic chime that echoed through the silent hall. It was a scene of breathtaking beauty, a vibrant testament to the enduring power of magic in this forgotten place. Ollie couldn't help but gasp, completely mesmerised by the spectacle unfolding before them.

"Prepare yourselves for a dance unlike any other!" Azrael called, his eyes gleaming with mischief.

Dr Bell, her heart a hummingbird trapped in her chest, step A mixture of anxiety and exhilaration furrowed her brow. Anxiety and exhilaration furrowed her brow. Her efforts, spanning years of research and whispered theories dismissed by her colleagues, had finally awoken these magical beings. A shiver, not entirely unpleasant, danced down her spine. "I read about this!" she said, her voice barely a whisper carried on the twilight air. "The ancient texts spoke of the Fae, of beings bound to this land. They possess ancient knowledge, lost to the passage of time, yet we must approach them with grace and respect for their ancient ways."

With a subtle gesture from Azrael, his face unreadable in the fading light, the group lined up, a motley collection of adventurers, academics, and the perpetually enthusiastic Finn. They resembled nothing so much as a ragtag dance troupe about to face their toughest critics. Finn, ever the mischievous spirit, couldn't hold his enthusiasm. His tail twitched with barely suppressed energy. "Let's show them our best moves!" he declared, a wide grin splitting his vulpine face. His words, however, were laced with a genuine desire to connect, to bridge the gap between their world and this magical realm.

Ellie, usually so stoic, couldn't help but giggle at Finn's antics. The absurdity of the situation – dancing for fairies in the hopes of unlocking ancient secrets – was almost too much to bear. A gentle breeze stirred the leaves of the ancient trees surrounding them, carrying the scent of wildflowers and damp earth. As the fairies continued their intricate dance, weaving patterns of light and shadow in the air, the melody pulsing through the very ground beneath their feet

As Ellie joined the dance, the pulsating energy of the makeshift ballroom enveloped her. She felt as though she were not merely taking part; she became one with the rhythm of the fairy lights, their gentle glow mirroring the spark igniting within her. Spinning and twirling, she let the music, a vibrant melody woven from forgotten instruments and rustling leaves, guides her movements. Her heart was alight with possibility, a kaleidoscope of dreams swirling in her chest with each graceful leap. She was a dancer unbound, a spirit freed by the magic of the night.

Professor Finch, initially reluctant, his posture stiff and disapproving, soon found himself swept up in the intoxicating current. He mirrored Ellie's movements, at first awkwardly, then with growing confidence. With each step, he seemed to shed a layer of his usual stoicism, his face softening, his eyes widening with a childlike wonder he hadn't felt in decades. The transformation was enchanting; the rigid professor was dissolving, replaced by a man rediscovering joy in the simplest of pleasures.

Oliver, still uncertain, remained at the edge of the impromptu dance floor, his gaze fixed on the wondrous scene unfolding before him. He watched Ellie's fluid movements and the Professor's surprising transformation, a mixture of longing and trepidation swirling within him. "I've never danced in my life!" he confessed, his voice a nervous tremor, half-laughing to mask the underlying fear. He felt the pull of the music, the allure of the liberating dance, but the ingrained patterns of self-doubt held him captive, tethered to the sidelines of the magical night. Would he find the courage to break free and join them?

"Just follow the beat!" Finn encouraged, bounding back to his side with playful enthusiasm. "Feel the magic."

To his surprise, the fairies, until now flitting around the edges of the festivities, suddenly abandoned their playful chase of butterflies and turned their collective attention to Oliver. A thousand points of light coalesced and focused on him, sparking around him in a merry whirl of iridescent wings and glittering dust. He felt a warmth spread through him, not just from their luminous presence but from a deep, underlying current of joy that resonated from their tiny forms. Sensing the quiet strength, the unwavering loyalty, and the unexpected wellspring of joy and passion hidden within the seemingly stoic guard's heart, they beckoned him to join in the dance. It wasn't a command but an invitation, a silent promise of belonging and release from the rigid confines of his duty. Oliver, usually so disciplined and reserved, felt a pull, a magnetic force drawing him towards the swirling lights and the promise of something magical.

"Alright, let's see what this little ball is all about!" he declared, his burgeoning spirit flooding through him.

As he moved in time with the fairies, feeling the rhythm of their ancient dance resonate deep within his soul, Ellie felt her heart swell with pride for her friends. He watched them, illuminated by the ethereal glow of the fairy ring, and saw not just individual beings. it ignited a sense of belonging amid the enchantment. He had never felt closer to them, never more connected to the magic that thrummed through the forest.

But suddenly, the enchanting melody shifted. The lively, intricate tune that had fuelled their movements and sparked joy within their hearts faltered. The fairies' joyous laughter, which had echoed through the glade like tinkling bells, faded into a soft, almost mournful hum. The vibrant light that danced around them, painting the leaves and faces with otherworldly colours, began to dim, its brilliance slowly ebbing away. With a sudden jolt of fear that ran cold through his veins, Ellie realised they were losing the magic, that the very source of their power was fading. "What's happening?" he exclaimed, his voice tinged with panic, the question echoing in the sudden, unsettling quiet that had descended upon the fairy ring. He looked around wildly, searching for an explanation in the faces of his friends and the swirling darkness that was beginning to encroach upon them.

"Perhaps they need a reason to share their secrets," Lady Arabella's stately voice echoed from a nearby sculpture, her features imbued with wisdom.

"Something itches in my memory," Professor Finch pondered. "The dance requires more than mere participation; perhaps they seek a story of our own, a moment of authenticity from each of us."

The group paused, exchanging glances of understanding. They had all travelled unique paths, filled with trials and discoveries that had led them here.

"I remember the first time I unearthed a forgotten history," Ellie began, her voice steady. "It was awakening a piece of myself that had been lost in time. It was a thrilling adventure, uncovering the past intricately woven with my present."

As Ellie shared her heartfelt story, the fairies danced closer, drawn to the essence of her words. Each reflection offered warmth in the cool air, urging the others to share their tales.

"I, too, had a moment of discovery," Professor Finch added, his face lighting up with nostalgia. "The day I first touched the tablets of an ancient cave—time froze as I connected with the ancients' wisdom. It is that feeling of connection that leads to true discovery."

Oliver, now at the heart of the unfolding magic, took a tentative step forward, the wonder of the evening etched on his face. "And me?" he began, his voice barely a whisper at first, then gaining strength as he found his words. "I always thought guarding was about standing still, a silent, unwavering presence. But tonight, I've learnt that duty can be an adventure, a vibrant tapestry woven with unexpected moments and shared experiences. The joy of sharing these moments, this enchanted night, with my friends – I've never felt so alive, so connected to something bigger than myself. It's like the world has opened up, revealing secrets whispered on the wind."

As he spoke, a soft, ethereal light began to emanate from him, a visible manifestation of the newfound energy coursing through his veins. It enveloped him in a luminous aura, a gentle, pulsating glow that reflected the joy radiating from within and brought visible delight to the fairy folk gathered around. The light seemed to respond to his words, intensifying as he acknowledged the magic he'd found within the seemingly mundane duty he'd always performed.

The air around them thrummed with untold stories. Luci, a whirlwind of shimmering wings and sparkling dust, wove through the air, her animated tales of ancient battles and forgotten heroes imparting enchanted threads of history to the growing tapestry of the night. With each loop and pirouette, she spun narratives of bravery and sacrifice, weaving them into the very fabric of the evening. And then Lady Arabella, her voice a melodic echo in the stillness, spoke of love that bloomed in the face of adversity, of the sharp sting of loss, and above all, of the enduring beauty of courage – a courage that resided not just in grand gestures but in the quiet steadfastness of everyday acts, like guarding a gate with an open heart and an awakened spirit. The magic of the night intensified, binding them all together in a shared moment of wonder and understanding.

Through their collective stories, the Forgotten Gallery began to glimmer anew, its long-dormant spirit stirring with vibrant energy. The dust motes danced in the air, suddenly illuminated with a thousand hues, reflecting off the polished surfaces of forgotten relics and transforming tarnished frames into shimmering gold. The colours shifted and swirled in a breathtaking display, a kaleidoscope of emerald greens, sapphire blues, and ruby reds painting the walls with ephemeral artistry. The fairies, emboldened by their shared narratives, flitted about like living constellations, beams of light cascading around them, a whirlwind of light and laughter echoing through the echoing halls. It was as if the museum itself breathed along with their tales, the stone and mortar responding to the rekindled magic, alive with the magic forged in friendship and unity. The very air crackled with possibility, the silence of centuries replaced by a symphony of whispers and giggles.

Just as the dance reached its peak, the music, a soaring melody woven from the rustling of silk wings and the chime of tiny bells, crescendo in a wave of harmonious power. And from the heart of the swirling light, a figure began to solidify, materialising from the very essence of the rediscovered magic. An ethereal fairy appeared—a figure dressed in shimmering silks that flowed and shifted like liquid moonlight. Her skin glowed with a gentle luminescence, radiating warmth and wisdom. This was no ordinary fairy; her presence commanded respect, her eyes held the secrets of ages, and a gentle smile hinted at the profound joy she felt at seeing the Gallery's rebirth. She was the embodiment of the forgotten stories, the guardian of the museum's soul, and her appearance marked a new chapter in its long and silent history.

"Brave explorers of the Enchanted Museum," she sang, her voice like a soft bell. "You have offered your stories, and in turn, the stories have brought light to our dance!"

She paused, her voice echoing slightly in the grand hall, and the music, which had been a constant, ethereal hum, faded ever so slightly, as if taking a breath. Then, it resumed, swelling back to life with a melody now laced with a deeper, more heartfelt emotion. The notes danced with an urgency, a sweet sorrow, and a promise of hope. "We shall share our knowledge," she continued, her eyes gleaming with an ancient light, "guiding you in your quest. Heed our words, for the tapestry of time is intricate and easily frayed.

Seek the paths that weave through time, for answers lie hidden in the dance of these tales. Understand the rhythm, and the truth will reveal itself."

With that pronouncement, the fairies, radiant in their iridescent gowns, drifted together, forming a circle bathed in soft, golden light. They extended their shimmering hands, inviting the adventurers to join them in a final, swirling dance. Hesitantly at first, then with growing enthusiasm, Ellie accepted, taking a fairy's hand. She twirled under the enchanted light, her laughter bubbling up like a spring, perfectly harmonising with the tinkling laughter of her friends. Each step was not just a movement but an affirmation, emboldening their bond, weaving them tighter into the fabric of this magical encounter.

With every graceful move and every perfectly synchronised spin, the museum shimmered with a newfound energy. The portraits on the walls seemed to see with knowing smiles; the ancient artefacts pulsed with a quiet hum. Their connection to the fairies, to the history held within these walls, strengthened with each passing moment as they embraced the magic that swirled around them, tangible and intoxicating. The fairies spun faster, their movements blurring into streaks of light, and soon, Ellie could barely distinguish between reality and enchantment. The line between the mundane and the marvellous dissolved, and a profound sense of joy bubbled within her, a feeling of belonging and purpose she had never felt before.

As the final notes of the melody echoed through the air, resonating, their eyes crinkling at the corners, their whispers exuded understanding and wisdom that spanned centuries. They had imparted not just information, but a key, a way of seeing, a deeper appreciation for the interconnectedness of all things. The adventure had only just begun.

"Thank you!" Ellie exclaimed, breathless, as she felt the presence of the fairies receding, leaving them enriched with purpose and knowledge.

With a wisp of shimmering, iridescent light, the ethereal fairy faded like a dream, her form dissolving into the very air around them. Though her physical presence was gone, her words, imbued with ancient wisdom and a touch of magic, remained resonant in their hearts, echoing the profound truths she had unveiled. Together, they stood in the fading, otherworldly glow of the Forgotten Gallery, the dust motes dancing in the last rays of light filtering through the crumbling architecture. Each of them was lost in their own thoughts, contemplating the profound experience they had shared – the secrets revealed, the bonds forged, and the path forward now illuminated by the fairy's ethereal grace. The weight of their shared journey pressed upon them, a mixture of awe, responsibility, and a quiet understanding that their lives would never be quite the same.

"We are part of a tapestry far greater than we realised," Azrael remarked, his voice a blend of pride and regard. "What lies ahead can be revealed, but unity remains our most potent gift."

As they made their way back through the museum's echoing halls, the weight of the night's magic settled around Ellie like a comforting cloak. A sense of excitement, vibrant and promising, bubbled within her, fuelled by the afterglow of their ethereal dance with the fairies. The fairies' ancient wisdom, imparted through laughter and shimmering movements, had planted a seed of confidence and anticipation. They had not only woven their own unique narratives into the rich tapestry of the enchanted night, becoming characters in a story far grander than themselves, but had also begun to embrace the limitless potential truly that stretched before them on their extraordinary journey. The museum, once a static repository of the past, now felt like a launchpad into the future.

And in that moment, under the low, hushed lighting, Ellie understood with a clarity that resonated deep within her soul: the greatest treasures weren't merely the meticulously preserved artefacts locked inside the museum's imposing walls, the ancient relics behind glass cases, or the historical documents bound in leather. No, the true riches lay in the intangible bonds forged, the friendships formed in the crucible of shared experience, and the stories shared under the watchful, silvery gaze of the moon. Each whispered secret, each shared laugh, and each moment of bravery had contributed to a treasure more valuable than anything crafted from gold or adorned with jewels. A whisper of destiny, subtle yet persistent, lingered in the air, a silent promise of wonders yet to come, guiding them toward their next magnificent adventure, beckoning them onwards into the unknown. The possibilities stretched before them, vast and glittering, like a star-strewn sky waiting to be explored.

THE CURSED ARTEFACT

As the clock struck midnight, an eerie stillness enveloped the Enchanted Museum. The ornate doors, usually bolted shut and silent, now creaked subtly, whispering secrets only the magical architecture could understand. The once-silent halls, now pulsing with magic, beckoned Ellie and her companions to explore more of their quest – a mission to retrieve the Sunstone, a relic of unimaginable power stolen by the malevolent sorcerer, Malkor. Shadows danced in the flickering light of the museum's grand chandelier, its crystal prisms reflecting the swirling, unseen energies that permeated the air. The air itself hummed with a palpable energy, tingling against their skin and raising goosebumps despite the unseasonably warm night. It was then that Azrael the Lion, his golden fur shimmering in the ghostly glow, rallied the group with a low, resonant growl. His eyes, usually warm and playful, burnt with a fierce determination as he surveyed Ellie, the brave but apprehensive historian; Ben, the ingenious inventor armed with a backpack full of enchanted gadgets; and Maya, the nimble rogue whose knowledge of ancient languages was proving invaluable.

"The magic is growing stronger," Azrael rumbled, his voice echoing slightly in the vast hall. "Malkor is aware of our presence. We must be swift and decisive if we are to succeed." He pointed with a massive paw towards a hidden passage, barely visible behind a tapestry depicting a forgotten pharaoh. "The Sunstone awaits us beyond. Prepare yourselves."

"Listen closely," Azrael's deep voice reverberated through the chamber, "tonight we must confront the Cursed Artefact, a relic soaked in the misfortunes of its past. It can unwittingly unleash chaos upon us if we are not careful."

Professor Finch, adjusting his spectacles, leaned forward, his eyes alight with intrigue. The dim, flickering candlelight cast dancing shadows across his wrinkled face, emphasising the earnestness in his expression. "The Cursed Artefact is said to have belonged to an ancient sorcerer, Zarthus the Unmaker. It was imbued with dark magic, a power that twisted the fates of those who had it, leading them down paths of madness and despair. Legends speak of whispers, haunting melodies that emanate from it, capable of driving men to the brink of sanity." He paused, letting the weight of his words sink in. "Some say it grants wishes, but at a terrible, unforeseen price."

Oliver, the reluctant guard of the museum, leaned against a towering display case filled with dusty pottery shards. He rolled his eyes, the gesture barely visible in the gloom. "Great, just what we need—more trouble. We've already had Mrs. Higgins report a talking gargoyle last week, and now this? How will we locate this artefact? The museum is like a maze designed by a caffeinated architect. Even trying to find the break room, let alone a cursed thing, leaves me lost. cursed... thing." He sighed, pulling his ill-fitting uniform jacket tighter around himself. The compensation he received was insufficient.

Luci, the mystical serpent, a creature of myth and legend, was reluctantly employed by the museum as a... well, no one was quite sure what she did, but she was undeniably useful, slithered forward. Her bronze scales gleamed under the candlelight, reflecting the eerie light like living jewels. Her forked tongue flicked in and out, tasting the air, a silent dance of sensory input. "Fear not, little Oliver. I have knowledge of the whispers that guide us, echoes of forgotten magic woven into the very stones of this place. Tonight, they are unusually clear, a chorus leading us to our destination. The artefact calls to me, a discordant note in the symphony of the ages. Follow me." With a flick of her powerful tail, she led them deeper into the museum's labyrinth, past towering sarcophagi and relics of forgotten civilisations, the shadows stretching and twisting around them like grasping claws. The air grew colder, and a faint, unsettling hum filled the silence, promising danger and untold secrets ahead.

As they entered the dimly lit Egyptian wing, the air grew thick with the scent of aged papyrus and dust, a fitting prelude to the mysteries held within. Finn, a whirlwind of auburn fur and boundless energy, darted playfully around their ankles, his bushy tails a blur against the ancient mosaics. "Come on! This way! The more we delay, the more restless the night becomes," he urged, his voice a high-pitched chirp that echoed strangely in the cavernous hall. A mischievous twinkle danced in his amber eyes, hinting at some knowledge beyond his seemingly youthful demeanour.

Suddenly, a palpable shift occurred in the atmosphere. The very walls seemed to breathe, exhaling secrets that had been trapped for millennia. Whispers, like the rustling of desert sands, filled the air, carrying fleeting tales of a long-lost artefact – a sorcerer's trinket, imbued with power and steeped in dark legend. Ellie, ever the historian, her mind a library of forgotten lore, stood rooted to the spot, her breath catching in her throat. Her heart raced as she listened, piecing together the fragmented echoes, fragments of a forgotten story. "The artefact was buried with the sorcerer, hidden away deep within his tomb to prevent its curse from awakening. But it seems something... some disturbance... has stirred it from its slumber," she murmured to herself, her brow furrowed in concentration. The implications were chilling. If the artefact was truly awakening, the consequences could be catastrophic.

Lady Arabella, a life-sized statue of a regal Egyptian queen, adorned with lapis lazuli and gold, stood upon a towering pedestal overlooking the hall. Her carved features, usually stoic and unyielding, softened as she offered a subtle, almost imperceptible, regal smile directed at Ellie. Her voice, surprisingly melodic and resonant, echoed through the hall, seemingly originating from the stone itself. "My dear Ellie, such artefacts are never far from their tale. To find it, we must understand the story that binds it. Each artefact in this museum holds a piece of history, a thread in the tapestry of time.

The Cursed Artefact will respond only to those who truly look to understand it, to those who are willing to delve into the depths of the past and uncover the truth behind its creation and its curse." Her words hung in the air, a haunting invitation to unravel a mystery that had slept for centuries, a mystery that now threatened to awaken and unleash its dark power upon the modern world.

With renewed determination burning in her eyes, Ellie turned to her companions, her voice ringing with newfound resolve. "Then we must piece together the legend, brick by brick, word by word, until we have a clear picture of what we face. We must find every clue we can, no matter how small or insignificant it may seem. Professor Finch," she continued, fixing her gaze on the elderly scholar, "do you have any texts or notes about its history? Anything that might shed light on the sorcerer's motives or the nature of his creation?"

Professor Finch nodded eagerly, his spectacles nearly slipping off his nose in his haste. "Indeed, my dear Ellie! I've dedicated years to studying such arcane matters. There is a tome, a rather ancient and significant one, nestled within the dusty shelves of the university library. It speaks of the sorcerer's tyrannical reign, detailing the rise and fall of his power, and, most importantly, it speaks of his cursed creation. But," he added, his brow furrowing with concern, "it lies hidden, shrouded in puzzles and riddles, deliberately protected by intricate magical wards. Accessing it won't be easy, I'm afraid."

"More puzzles!" Oliver groaned, though a hint of excitement crept into his voice. "Alright, lead the way, then! Let's hope it's not the end of us."

As they forged ahead, the tunnel opened into a wider chamber, revealing a large mural dominating one entire wall. It depicted the sorcerer, not as a man, but as a figure of terrifying power, his presence looming ominously over a solemn procession of villagers. Each villager was made with painstaking detail; their faces etched with a mixture of fear and resignation. The colours of the mural were vivid, almost unnaturally so, as if time had no effect on them; their brightness contrasting sharply with the deep, encroaching shadows that clung to the edges of the chamber and seeped into the corners of the artwork, hinting at a darkness underlying the scene and the sorcerer's reign. The vibrant hues seemed to vibrate against the cold stone, creating an unsettling dissonance that heightened the sense of dread that permeated the air.

"Look!" Ellie exclaimed, her eyes widening. "The artefact is positioned at the heart of the mural. It was meant to be a protector, yet it ended up becoming a curse."

"A classic tale turned dark," Luci saw, inching closer. "But perhaps the answer to breaking its curse lies not in fighting it but in understanding its origins."

With Azrael's encouragement, they began to decipher the symbols and clues etched within the mural. Huckleberry , perched nearby, cawed loudly, breaking their concentration. "Time is fleeting! The artefact lives in the Echo Chamber, guarded by riddles only the worthy may solve," he remarked cryptically before taking to the air.

"Echo Chamber? Oliver muttered, feigning enthusiasm, "Sounds riveting." With a shared glance of resolve, the team followed Huckleberry, who led them down a winding corridor lit by sporadic lanterns etched with ancient hieroglyphs.

After what felt like an eternity, they reached a heavy stone door inscribed with swirling patterns that seemed to pulse with life. "This must be it," Ellie breathed, touching the cool surface. Luci coiled around her arm, her eyes sparkling with anticipation.

"The entrance to the Echo Chamber will only open to those who can answer its riddles," Azrael warned, positioning himself as the temporary leader of the group.

Oliver shot him a sceptical glance. "Riddles? You're joking, right? I barely passed my maths!"

"Focus, Oliver! We're not here to throw jokes," Ellie said, her voice steady. "Together, we can do this."

As if summoned by a whisper of destiny, the Earth rumbled slightly beneath their feet, a subtle vibration that resonated with an unseen energy. The air shimmered, and the ancient stones of the doorway seemed to pulse with a faint, inner light. Then, from the threshold, a voice boomed, not from a throat, but from the very fabric of existence itself. It was a voice that spoke of ages past and futures yet to come. "To enter, answer me this: What is a facet of time that can be twisted but never broken?"

"The answer must be 'memory'," Professor Finch interjected confidently. "It is the essence of time, intertwining our pasts with the present."

The door rumbled again, and a profound silence followed. Moments later, it creaked open, revealing the heart of the museum— the Echo Chamber. As they stepped inside, the shadows danced wildly, and enigmatic whispers surrounded them.

"Welcome," the voice echoed around them. "What do you seek?"

Ellie, seizing the opportunity, stepped forward. "We seek the Cursed Artefact that binds the fates of its holders."

"Only a heart true in purpose may hold it without succumbing to its curse," the voice warned. "Are you prepared to face the darkness within?"

Without hesitating, Ellie replied, "We are united by purpose, willing to confront whatever darkness guards the artefact."

In perfect synchrony, the ancient glyphs etched into the walls of the chamber began to glow, reflecting off the polished surfaces of the scattered artefacts. Each object, from the tarnished silver chalice to the petrified wooden staff, pulsed with its own distinct energy, yet now these energies were harmonising, coalescing into a unified whole. A wave of golden light, both warm and strangely unsettling, washed over the chamber, pushing back the oppressive darkness that had clung to its corners for centuries. In the centre of the room, bathed in the radiant glow, lay the object of their perilous quest: the Cursed Artefact. It was a beautifully crafted amulet, its gold intricately woven around a central gemstone that pulsed with a dark, inner light, gleaming ominously and radiating an almost palpable aura of power.

But as they approached the shimmering amulet, drawn forward by an irresistible force, the shadows around them stirred. They twisted and writhed, coalescing from the very fabric of the darkness into a tangible form. A menacing figure appeared, tall and gaunt, wreathed in an aura of despair. Its face, barely discernible within the gloom, was contorted in a perpetual scowl, its eyes burning with ancient malice. "You dare seek the truth that lies hidden within this chamber?" the figure boomed, its voice echoing with the weight of ages. "You think yourselves worthy to wield the power of the Cursed Artefact? The curse is powerful, a force that has broken empires and shattered destinies! You will face trials that test your unity and resolve, trials that will push you to the very brink of sanity!"

Fear, cold and sharp, pricked at the edges of their courage, but the lure of the artefact, the promise of its power, held them fast. Finn, despite the gravity of the situation, couldn't resist a mischievous grin. He whirled around, his emerald eyes wide with a blend of playful audacity and genuine bravery. He brandished his trusty rapier, its polished steel catching the golden light. "Let's see what you've got, then, Shadow Man!" he quipped, his voice echoing with unexpected confidence. "Life's too short to back down from a little adventure, especially when there's potentially untold power at stake!" He winked, a flash of defiance in his eyes. "Besides", he added, under his breath, "I've always fancied myself a bit of a curse-breaker."

"Together!" Azrael roared, his voice booming. "We'll face this challenge as one."

As the spectral figure advanced, the team regrouped, each member resonating with their strengths. Ellie's intellect, Professor Finch's knowledge, Oliver's bravery, Luci's wisdom, and the mischief of Finn combined created an aura of courage.

The spectral entity shimmered, its form coalescing from the shadows, a cold light emanating from its depths. It paused, a moment stretched thin with anticipation. Its smile didn't reach its eyes; instead, it was a chilling, predatory curve that hinted at unimaginable power. "The first trial", it echoed, the voice resonating with an unearthly timbre that seemed to vibrate in Ellie's very bones, "shall be your greatest fear—what haunts your past? What festering secret keeps you shackled to the mortal realm?" The entity gestured with a skeletal hand, and the air around Ellie grew thick and heavy, laced with the scent of decay and forgotten memories.

Ellie stepped forward, the ancient stone floor cold beneath her worn boots. Her heart hammered against her ribs, a frantic drumbeat against the silence. But beneath the fear, a steely resolve had begun to form. "I've always feared", she admitted, her voice surprisingly steady despite the circumstances, "that my inadequacy—that I'm not clever enough, not strong enough, not enough—will prevent me from uncovering the truth. My inadequacies could lead to the loss of countless others. But tonight," she continued, her gaze meeting the entity's unblinking stare, "I stand resolved. Not simply for myself, to prove my worth, but for those whose stories have been swallowed by time. I refuse to allow their stories to fade into oblivion. A faint light began to emanate from Ellie, a spark of defiance against the encroaching darkness.

The figure recoiled slightly as Ellie spoke, feigning arrogance. "Is that all?" it taunted.

Professor Finch quickly followed, his voice resonating with purpose and a hint of desperate urgency. "Knowledge is my passion, the fuel that drives me, the compass that guides my hand. But I fear that even my accumulated wisdom, the years spent deciphering ancient texts and unravelling arcane mysteries, may not be enough to save those I care for from the encroaching darkness. Yet, despite this daunting uncertainty, I willingly accept the challenge. I will delve deeper, learn quicker, and fight harder than I ever have before, for their sake."

Slowly, the spectral figure's form began to fade, its ethereal grip on the chamber weakening, its power visibly diminishing under their combined resolve. Encouraged by this shift in momentum and empowered by Finch's declaration, Oliver, confident now, shouted, "And I fear losing those I have come to trust! I fear the emptiness they would leave behind! But tonight, I choose solidarity over solitude! I choose to stand with them, to fight with them, and to face whatever horrors lie ahead together!

We will not break; we will not yield; we will not let fear dictate our choices!"

"That's the spirit!" Finn chimed in, bounding beside Oliver. "Let's show this ghost what we're made of!"

With the battle drawing on, each clash of steel and surge of magic fuelling their resolve, a remarkable shift occurred. A collective strength pulled them together as the tide of the struggle and an unspoken agreement vibrated in the air. This shared purpose, this unified front against the encroaching evil, began to have a tangible effect: the oppressive darkness that had clung to the battlefield started to dissipate, retreating like a wounded beast. Breathless but resolute, faces streaked with grime and sweat, they turned their focus back to the Cursed Artefact, their shared victory offering a glimmer of hope.

The shimmering amulet, once a source of dread and corruption, now glowed brightly, its surface pulsing with a newfound energy. It seemed to respond to their unity and unwavering belief in the truth, as if woven with their declarations of allegiance and defiance. Hesitantly at first, then with growing confidence, they reached out together, hands meeting on the cool, smooth surface of the artefact. Their energies, no longer fragmented and scattered, began to entwine within it, a vibrant tapestry of light and power gathering around the amulet's heart. A feeling of immense potential, both terrifying and exhilarating, surged through them, promising a turning point in the fight against the curse.

Suddenly, a powerful surge of energy enveloped them all, a raw and untamed force that crackled in the air. The once imposing shadowy figure screamed as the artefact violently pulled it into its swirling vortex of light. "No! You cannot hold its power!" it shrieked, its voice a distorted echo of defiance, laced with terror. "It will consume you all!"

But the bonds forged that night—the shared sacrifice and unwavering trust that blossomed in the face of overwhelming darkness— proved stronger than the artefact's malevolent influence. A protective shield of camaraderie shimmered around them, deflecting the worst of the surge

THE QUEST BEGINS

The hall was steeped in shadows as the last rays of twilight slipped away, ushering in the enchanted evening that marked the grand reopening of the museum. Ellie stood at the centre of the Grand Atrium, her heart pulsating with anticipation. The air buzzed with whispers of stories waiting to be uncovered, tales preserved within the artefacts poised to go with their tales of history into the night.

"Are you ready for this?" Professor Finch, his tweed jacket slightly askew, adjusted his spectacles and beamed at her. The excitement in his voice was palpable, and Ellie couldn't help but smile back.

"Ready as I'll ever be," she replied. For Ellie, this was more than just an assignment; it was a dream come true. The museum held secrets that had long been buried in the annals of time, and tonight promised to unearth them.

However, as the final ceremonial speech ended, Dr. Mariana Bell, the passionate conservationist whose tireless work had single-handedly revitalised the museum, stepped forward. Her eyes, bright with pride and a fervent belief in the power of the past, scanned the assembled dignitaries and eager onlookers. "Let us preserve not just the artefacts, the tangible remnants of bygone eras, but also their stories," she exclaimed, her voice echoing with conviction. She was blissfully unaware that her words, an earnest plea for historical understanding, would soon awaken something far beyond her control, something slumbering deep within the museum's ancient heart.

A flicker of energy, subtle yet palpable, shimmered through the room as the grand clock tower outside began its measured descent toward midnight, the chimes promising a whimsical hour filled with celebration. Champagne flutes tinkled, laughter bubbled, and a general air of festivity permeated the hall. Yet, lurking among the jubilance was Oliver, the museum guard, a man of habit and unwavering routine. He continued to pace the perimeters with a furrowed brow, his hand instinctively resting on the walkie-talkie clipped to his belt. He was oblivious to the unfolding magic, more concerned with potential late-night rowdiness than spectral awakenings. He suspected tonight would be a long one.

As the clock struck twelve, midnight's resounding chime reverberating through the stone corridors, a sudden, almost suffocating hush enveloped the surroundings. The joyous cacophony abruptly ceased, replaced by an unnerving quiet that hung heavily in the air. Instantly, the stone lion statue — Azrael, as the museum's curators affectionately called him — situated majestically at the far end of the hall, rumbled to life. The very foundations of the building seemed to tremble as the ancient stone shifted. His golden fur, previously dull and lifeless, now twinkled in the dim light, vibrant and alive with an otherworldly luminescence. Gasps erupted, filling the space where silence had once dwelled, a chorus of astonished whispers and disbelieving murmurs rising to meet the newly awakened lion's gaze. The party was undeniably, irrevocably over.

"Fear not, brave souls!" roared Azrael with a voice like rolling thunder. "I am here to guide you on a quest through the realms of time! It has begun!"

Ellie's eyes widened in disbelief. She exchanged glances with Professor Finch, whose usual scholarly composure crumbled into childlike wonderment.

"Extraordinary! He murmured, adjusting his glasses yet again, "A living statue." "This can't possibly be real!"

"It is, Professor," Ellie said, her voice firm despite the whirlwind of thoughts racing through her mind. "And we need to follow him. This is precisely what we came for!"

"Always jumping into danger, aren't you?" Oliver grumbled, though a spark of curiosity flickered in his eyes.

Before they could argue further, Azrael, the ancient guardian of the crossroads, gestured with a slow, deliberate sweep of his paw, beckoning them closer to the heart of the moonlit grove. The air crackled with unspoken power, thick with the scent of damp earth and forgotten magic. "The night holds riddles and treasures, shimmering illusions and concrete realities, all intertwined," Azrael rumbled, his voice like the grinding of mountains. "But beware! For only those who understand the past, those who can decipher the echoes of yesterday woven into the tapestry of today, will prevail. Ignorance is a dangerous burden in these shadowed paths."

Suddenly, Luci, a mystical bronze creature, materialized from the deepest shadows. Her scales, shimmering with an otherworldly light, curved elegantly as she moved, weaving in and out of the floor like flowing water given form. Her presence felt both alluring and unsettling, a paradox of beauty and venom. "Allow me to lend a hand," she hissed softly, her eyes glinting with mischief and a knowing that stretched back through centuries. "Time is but a fabric of history's weave, a complex and often misleading pattern. Let's unravel it together! I can guide you through the threads, expose the hidden knots, and reveal the true design."

Finn, a miniature whirlwind of fur and energy, even smaller than a child's fist, darted between the group's feet, his tiny paws kicking up dust. He teased tugged at the edges of Ellie's skirt, his playful nature barely concealing a sharp intelligence. "Come on! There's no time to waste! The longer we linger, the harder the riddles become!" he urged, his voice laced with excitement and a hint of impatience. "The shadows are shifting; the paths are changing! We need to move, to explore, to *discover* before the night swallows its secrets whole!" His tail flicked back and forth, a tiny beacon urging them forward into the unknown.

"Stick with them, Oliver," Ellie said, her voice steady yet reassured. "This adventure could be our chance to preserve the stories the artefacts have to tell."

With a reluctant nod, Oliver joined their motley crew.

"Onward, brave adventurers!" Azrael exclaimed, his roar echoing through the hall as they moved into the depths of the museum. They navigated through the dimly lit corridors, the glimmering eyes of portraits watching their every move. Each step resonated with an ancient energy, drawing them further into the heart of the enchanted realm.

Suddenly, they entered a vast chamber filled with exhibits from eras gone by. The walls appeared to throb with energy. At its centre stood a great mural depicting the creation of the universe, ink flowing in brilliant strokes and light.

"It looks as if it comes alive," whispered Professor Finch, mesmerised. "Where shall we start?"

"Let us begin with the Riddle of the Sphinx," Azrael instructed solemnly, gesturing toward a large pedestal where a sandstone Sphinx statue seemed to blink in alignment with the flickering torches around them.

Ellie approached cautiously, the words "To enter the realm of night, answer me true, what walks on four legs in the morning, two at noon, and three in the evening?" echoing in her memory. "It's a classic!" she exclaimed.

"Humanity's riddle," Luci confirmed, her scales shimmering brightly as she hovered nearby.

"Good, good!" Oliver grumbled. "But what if we can't solve it?"

"Then we must think," urged Ellie, tapping her chin thoughtfully. "A creature that crawls as a baby, walks as an adult, and uses a cane as an elder."

"The answer is... man," Professor Finch affirmed. "It sits at the very core of our existence, a journey through life!"

With trembling anticipation, Ellie uttered the answer aloud. "Man!"

At once, the Sphinx's eyes glowed, not with the warmth of fire, but with a chilling, ethereal luminescence. The ancient stone seemed to absorb and amplify some unseen energy, casting the chamber in an otherworldly light that danced with hues of cyan and violet. A low rumble, like the groaning of the earth itself, echoed through the vast space, vibrating in the bones of anyone present. As the dust motes settled, a previously unseen passageway yawned open at the far end of the room, revealing a darkness that seemed to swallow the light itself.

"Excellent!" Azrael proclaimed, his voice booming as they prepared to venture deeper.

"Well done, but don't celebrate just yet," warned Huckleberry , flapping down from a rafter. His feathers were dulled with age but shimmered with a profound wisdom. "Many more riddles lie ahead, and not all are so straightforward."

Finn circled the group, his glee palpable. "Let's go! The night is young, and who knows what treasures lie ahead!"

As they stepped closer to the newly revealed passageway, Ellie felt a thrill dance along her spine, a shiver that was equal parts exhilaration and trepidation. It was exhilarating to stand on the precipice of the unknown, to be the first in what felt like centuries to gaze upon what lay hidden. But it was also terrifying. What dangers lurked in that inky blackness? What ancient guardians might still protect the secrets it concealed? The darkness itself seemed to beckon them, a silent invitation to a world beyond the familiar. It was an allure born of the unknown, the intoxicating promise of secrets and histories waiting to be unfurled, like a long-forgotten scroll being slowly unravelled. The air hung heavy with the scent of damp earth and something else, something indefinable and undeniably ancient. This wasn't just a passage; it was a gateway, and Ellie knew, with a certainty that resonated deep within her bones, that crossing its threshold would change them forever.

"Remember," Azrael reminded them, his gaze steady. "Stay close. The adventure is about to begin, but it can only be completed if we work together."

"What are we waiting for?" Oliver declared, finally shedding his guard demeanour as the awe of adventure embraced him fully.

With hearts pounding a frantic rhythm against their ribs and spirits ignited by the thrill of the unknown, the group strode purposefully into the depths of the museum. Each step echoed in the cavernous halls, amplifying the sense of adventure that coursed through their veins. The quest for undiscovered truths, for knowledge hidden beneath layers of history, illuminated the shadows surrounding them, painting the dusty corridors with an aura of anticipation.

Together, they ventured deeper into the unknown, leaving the familiar world behind with every footfall. They prepared themselves for the challenges that lay ahead - riddles etched in ancient languages, traps triggered by forgotten mechanisms, guardians protecting secrets that had slumbered for centuries. A sense of camaraderie, unexpected yet undeniably present, began to blossom among the peculiar group: Ellie, with her sharp wit and insatiable curiosity; Professor Finch, his mind a labyrinth of historical facts and forgotten lore; Oliver, whose uncanny ability to decipher codes seemed almost supernatural; Azrael, quiet and observant, possessing a knowledge of the museum's architecture that bordered on the uncanny; Luci, whose mischievous spirit and quick thinking often proved invaluable; Finn, a master of disguise and infiltration; and Huckleberry, the enigmatic raven, whose presence seemed to herald both auspicious and ominous tidings.

As echoes of nervous laughter and whispered theories danced off the aged walls, the mysteries of the museum beckoned. Each artefact, each painting, each relic held a piece of the puzzle, promising discovery that shimmered like distant stars in the vast night sky. They were united, bound not just by a shared quest, but by the deep-seated magic that seemed to permeate the very air within the hallowed halls. Each artefact whispered a silent call to adventure, urging them forward, tempting them with the promise of profound revelations. The air crackled with unseen energy, a palpable sense of history holding its breath, waiting to be awakened.

And so, fuelled by adrenaline and a shared thirst for knowledge, the quest began. An odyssey through time, a perilous journey filled with nail-biting excitement, unforeseen danger, and the tantalizing promise of extraordinary revelations. They were not just explorers; they were guardians, entrusted with unlocking secrets that could reshape their understanding of the past, and perhaps even the future. Their path was fraught with peril, but their resolve, strengthened by their burgeoning bond, burned brighter than any torch, illuminating the darkness that lay ahead.

THE RIDDLE OF
THE SPHINX

As the clock struck midnight, each chime echoing through the cavernous space, the air within the vast halls of the Enchanted Museum shimmered with an otherworldly energy, a palpable vibration that tickled the skin. Dust motes, usually invisible, danced in the moonlight streaming through the arched windows, swirling like miniature galaxies. Unbeknownst to the casual visitor, those who merely strolled through during daylight hours, ancient secrets lay dormant within every exhibit, slumbering giants ready to unfurl beneath the silver light of the moon. Tonight, the veil between worlds was thin, and the artefacts hummed with a power only accessible under these specific celestial conditions. Ellie felt her heart race with anticipation, a potent mix of excitement and trepidation, as she stood at the grand entrance of the Egyptian gallery. Hieroglyphs seemed to writhe on the walls, whispering forgotten prophecies. To her right stood Professor Finch, his spectacles perched precariously on his nose, his eyes gleaming with intellectual fervour. He clutched a weathered leather-bound book; its pages filled with arcane symbols and hand-drawn diagrams. To her left, ever vigilant and regal, was Azrael the Lion, a magnificent creature whose presence exuded both power and a sense of ancient guardianship, his golden eyes fixed on the gallery's depths, a silent promise of protection against the unknown. The air crackled with anticipation, a silent prelude to the mysteries they were about to uncover.

"Here we are," Azrael said, his voice a deep rumble, reverberating off the walls. "The Sphinx awaits. It holds the key to our next leg of the journey."

Ellie's mind buzzed with questions, a swarm of historical enquiries taking flight as she took a step closer. The massive stone figure of the Sphinx loomed over them, a colossal guardian appearing from the sandy landscape. Its carved features, sharp and enigmatic, were bathed in moonlight, the silvery glow emphasising the fine lines of its ancient face and casting deep shadows that danced in the sand around its base.

This interplay of light and shadow created a hauntingly majestic silhouette against the velvet sky, a timeless spectacle that both intimidated and intrigued. "How does it work?" she asked, her voice a hushed whisper lost in the vastness of the desert night, her historian's curiosity piqued. How did this colossal monument, a testament to human ingenuity and ancient beliefs, stand for millennia? What secrets lay hidden within its stone heart? How did it function as a symbolic and possibly literal guardian of this sacred place? The question hung in the air, pregnant with the weight of history and the promise of untold discoveries.

"The riddle of the Sphinx is as old as time itself," Professor Finch explained, adjusting his glasses with a twinkle in his eye. "It is said that only those who understand its secrets can pass unscathed."

Before they could ponder further, a low tremor vibrated through the sand beneath their feet. A subtle ripple, like heat rising from a forge, twisted and distorted the air around the Sphinx's ancient, weathered paws. The sand itself seemed to swirl in miniature vortexes. Then, with a silent grace that belied her size, Luci rose from the shadows. Bronze scales, polished by centuries of cool darkness, caught the fading light of the desert sun, glinting like a thousand scattered coins. Her eyes, twin embers of intelligent fire, fixed on the adventurers.

She moved with a liquid smoothness, coiling gracefully around the Sphinx's giant sandstone pedestal, as if claiming it as her throne. "Listen closely, brave adventurers," she whispered, her voice a sibilant murmur that seemed to resonate not just in their ears, but in their very bones. "The riddle is not merely a riddle; it embodies the essence of life. To discover the truth, you must speak the answer and mean it. Feel it in your heart; let it guide your tongue."

"What kind of riddle?" Oliver, the reluctant guard, interjected. His voice echoed against the stone walls, laced with apprehension.

"Time is fluid, always advancing. But the Sphinx revels in reflection. What walks on four legs in the morning, two legs at noon, and three legs in the evening?" Luci's eyes sparkled with mischief and wisdom, inviting them to think.

Ellie pondered the riddle for a moment. "It's a classic!" she exclaimed. "The answer is a human—crawling as a baby, walking on two legs as an adult, and using a cane in old age."

The Sphinx's lips, cracked and weathered like ancient papyrus, parted with a slow, rumbling chuckle that seemed to vibrate the very air. Dust motes danced in the shafts of sunlight that penetrated the gallery, illuminated by the echoing sound. "Well done, historian," it boomed, the voice resonating deep within the listener, a low thrum that settled in their bones. The words reverberated off the stone walls, creating an almost hypnotic effect. "But wisdom in the heart must reflect in the mind. Your knowledge is impressive, yes, but it is merely the surface. Answer again, this time, truly. Shed the learnt pronouncements and speak from the core of your being. Let your reply be more than just recitation; let it reflect your soul." The immense, unblinking gaze of the Sphinx intensified, holding the historian captive in its ageless scrutiny, patiently awaiting the answer that would unlock not only the secrets of the past but also the truth within.

Ellie frowned, a knot twisting in her stomach. The words hung in the air, heavy with implication. "Truly?" she murmured, her voice barely a whisper. She glanced at her companions, Azrael, his brow furrowed in concentration, and Professor Finch, whose spectacles seemed to magnify the worry lines etched around his eyes. "What does it mean... to answer truly?" The weight of the challenge, the labyrinthine complexities it hinted at, pressed down on her.

Finn, who had been quietly watching from a shadowed corner, his lithe form practically melting into the gloom, sprang forward with an unexpected burst of energy.

His eyes, usually guarded and sly, were bright with enthusiasm, almost manic. "It means you must understand the essence of the riddle," he declared, his fox ears perked up, twitching with excitement. He padded closer to Ellie, his gaze intense. "Try to see beyond the surface, Ellie. What if it's not just about the stages of life? What if it's about something more... something hidden within the words themselves?" He paused, a mischievous glint in his eye. "Think about the asker's intent. Think about *why* they would phrase it that way."

Professor Finch scratched his beard thoughtfully, the gesture a habitual punctuation mark to his deepest thoughts. "Perhaps we should consider what it means to be human—to embody our fears, challenges, and triumphs through time and experience. We've seen empires rise and fall, saw the creation of breathtaking art borne from desperate hardship, and felt the echoes of love and loss carved into ancient stones. What binds us to those who came before? What makes us uniquely *us*, yet inextricably linked to the tapestry of history?" He paused, his gaze distant as if contemplating the very essence of existence. "The answer, I suspect, lies not just in our achievements, but in how we navigate the complexities of being."

As Ellie stepped closer to the Sphinx, its weathered face a silent guardian of millennia, she took a deep breath, the dry desert air filling her lungs. She was no longer just a student on an assignment; she was a participant in a conversation that spanned centuries. The whispers of the museum, the low murmur of history, echoed in her mind, each artefact presenting a layer of understanding, each inscription a cryptic verse in a sprawling epic. "The riddle is not just a representation of life stages – the crawl, the walk, the cane – but an invitation to accept the inevitability of change," she said slowly, her voice barely a whisper against the immensity of the monument. "It's about embracing our journey and honouring our growth, understanding that each phase, each challenge, contributes to the person we become. It's about recognizing the beauty in the ephemeral, the strength in vulnerability, and the wisdom gleaned from weathering the storms of life. It's about understanding that humanity isn't a static state, but a perpetual evolution, a constant dance between who we were, who we are, and who we aspire to be."

The Sphinx's eyes, ancient and knowing, glimmered with a light that seemed to penetrate Ellie's very soul, an expression that hinted at both approval and lingering scrutiny. "Your answer bears truth, child of the past," the Sphinx rumbled, the voice echoing with the weight of millennia. "But still… it needs a close reflection. A single side polished until it shines with unparalleled brilliance. What, then, do you *truly* cherish most about the journey?"

Ellie's heartbeat quickened, a frantic drum against her ribs. The air around her seemed to thicken, charged with the Sphinx's expectant gaze. She realised the gravity of the question, the depth of understanding it demanded. This was not a simple test of knowledge but a probe into the very core of her being. Her mind raced, replaying scenes from the long and arduous quest. She thought of Liam, whose unwavering courage had pulled them through countless dangers; of Maya, whose sharp wit had unlocked ancient riddles and navigated treacherous political landscapes. She thought of the newly discovered constellations, the breathtaking sunsets over alien terrains, and the spine-tingling thrill of deciphering forgotten languages.

It was not just about the destination, she realised with sudden clarity, the ultimate prize at the end of their path. That was merely a point on a map. The true treasures lay scattered along the way, glittering fragments of experience that had slowly coalesced into something far more valuable. It was the unbreakable bonds formed in the face of adversity, the whispered confidences shared under starlit skies, and the inside jokes that had become their own unique language. It was the stories woven together, thread by thread, until they formed a vibrant tapestry, a testament to their shared struggles and triumphs. The journey, she understood now, was not about where they ended up but about who they had become along the way and the indelible marks they had left on each other's hearts.

"It's the connections we make, the people we meet, and the legacy we leave behind," she said, her voice steady. "Each part of our journey teaches us and shapes us. Time itself is a tapestry of experience, intertwined with love, loss, and everything in between."

The Sphinx, ancient and weathered by millennia of sun and sand, nodded with glacial slowness. The movement, barely perceptible, sent a tremor through the air, a subtle shift in the desert's equilibrium. Its monumental frame, a fusion of lion and human, seemed to subtly relax, the rigid lines of its carved features easing as Ellie spoke.

"Your words resonate with wisdom, Ellie," the Sphinx intoned, its voice a low, rumbling echo that seemed to emanate from the very earth beneath their feet. "In the midst of darkness, light stays. Find the centre, and you shall find the key." The words hung heavily in the still air, laden with layers of meaning Ellie struggled to grasp.

With a soft hiss, like escaping steam from a long-dormant furnace, the Sphinx moved. The colossal statue shifted, grinding against the ages-old stone beneath, revealing a glinting doorway behind its stone silhouette. It wasn't merely an opening, but a shimmering, iridescent portal, humming with a low, vibrant energy. The light within pulsed like a living thing, beckoning and warning in equal measure. It was a portal to the next chamber of discovery, a new and unknown trial lying in wait.

"Enter, if you dare," the Sphinx continued, its voice regaining its ancient, almost weary tone. "Remember this lesson, for not all riddles yield answers in haste. Some truths require patience, perseverance, and a willingness to face the shadows within yourself." The glint in its eyes, ancient and knowing, held a silent challenge. The path ahead was open, but the journey would be far from easy.

With a newfound confidence, Ellie turned to her fellow adventurers, her voice ringing with a resolve that only the past few perilous trials could forge. "Shall we?" she asked, her eyes gleaming with a mixture of anticipation and cautious optimism. The daunting threshold before them pulsed with an energy that both thrilled and warned.

Azrael nodded, the affirmative movement causing the long strands of his golden mane to sway, catching the ethereal moonlight streaming in from the entrance behind them. "Let's explore what lies beyond," he rumbled, his voice a low, comforting resonance that settled the nerves frayed by the journey so far. He carried himself with a quiet strength, a silent promise of unwavering support.

As they stepped through the threshold, leaving the familiar behind, the chamber sprang alive, bathing them in a kaleidoscope of colours and a symphony of unheard sounds. The air vibrated with an ancient energy. Ornate hieroglyphs, carved with meticulous detail into the walls, danced and shimmered, animated by unseen magic. Faces of gods and mythical beasts seemed to wink at them, their painted eyes following their every move. It was a room of wonders, utterly captivating and undeniably dangerous. The very stones seemed to pulse with the echoes of forgotten ages, encapsulating tales of pharaohs and their grand ambitions, the capricious whims of powerful gods, and the struggles of mortals caught in the crosscurrents of fate. Each glyph, each carving, each carefully placed artefact seemed to whisper its narrative into the air, creating a swirling vortex of history and legend that threatened to overwhelm the senses. They had entered a living museum, a repository of secrets waiting to be unlocked.

Finn, a blur of youthful energy, darted ahead, his nimble feet barely disturbing the dust motes dancing in the faint torchlight. His enthusiasm, fuelled by an innate, almost fox-like curiosity, beckoned him deeper into the forgotten tomb, eager to uncover the mysteries that lay hidden within. He moved with an instinctive grace, his senses alert to the nuances of the aged stone and the faint whispers carried on the stagnant air.

Oliver, in stark contrast, cautiously eyed the encroaching darkness, his hand instinctively resting on the hilt of his worn sword. Every shadow seemed to writhe with unseen menace, every creak and groan of the ancient structure amplified by his mounting unease. He was no stranger to peril, yet the oppressive atmosphere of the tomb pressed down on him, a palpable weight of forgotten ages. "We've come this far without any mishaps," he muttered, his voice barely above a whisper, trying to reassure himself despite the earlier trepidation that still clung to him like a shroud. Each step was measured, a deliberate act against the growing urge to turn back and flee.

Suddenly, a shadow fell over them, eclipsing the flickering torchlight. Above them, perched precariously on a crumbling display of ancient artefacts, landed Huckleberry. His powerful wings, feathered in hues of midnight and storm cloud, flapped once, sending a fresh wave of dust cascading down. He settled with surprising lightness, his keen, golden eyes fixed on the two adventurers. "Seek the pharaoh's crown," he croaked, his voice a melodic tone, strangely soothing yet laced with an underlying mystery that sent a shiver down Oliver's spine. "It is not just an artefact; it is a part of history, a piece needed to navigate your journey." The words hung in the air, a profound pronouncement that both intrigued and unsettled, leaving Finn bouncing on the balls of his feet with anticipation and Oliver staring up at the majestic creature with a mixture of awe and apprehension. The quest had become more than just a treasure hunt; it was now a path ordained by something ancient and powerful.

"Where do we find it?" Ellie asked, feeling excited by the prospect of further unravelling the museum's mysteries.

Huckleberry tilted his head, black eyes shining with an unnerving knowledge that seemed to penetrate their very souls. "It lies in the Pyramid of Souls," he rasped, his voice like the rustling of dry leaves. "But only those worthies may enter. The path is guarded not by stone or steel, but by choices. You must choose wisely what to leave behind – for the Pyramid consumes that which is considered unworthy." His gaze swept across the group, lingering on each of them in turn, a silent challenge hanging in the air.

The air thickened with anticipation, heavy with the weight of Huckleberry's words. A palpable tension crackled between the adventurers, a sense of foreboding settling deep in their chests. Luci hissed softly, drawing closer to Oliver. "The choice must come from within," she murmured, her voice barely heard. "What are you willing to sacrifice for the truth? The Pyramid demands not trinkets or treasures but something far more precious – a piece of yourself." Her emerald eyes searched theirs, reflecting the flickering torchlight and the dawning understanding of the trials ahead.

The adventurers shared hesitant glances, each grappling with the implications of Huckleberry's pronouncement and Luci's cryptic warning. Doubt clouded their faces, a stark contrast to the fierce loyalty that had driven them this far. Oliver scratched his chin, his brow furrowed in thought. "Knowing what the pharaoh represents – the embodiment of absolute authority and unwavering control – could this crown, recovered from his tomb, symbolise power at a cost? Perhaps it is the suppression of individuality, the crushing weight of responsibility, or the insatiable hunger for dominance. We can't simply abandon a physical object; it's more than that. It's the *meaning* behind it we would have to relinquish." He looked at his companions, seeking confirmation, "Are we willing to let go of our desires for power, ambition, and control to gain access to the truth we seek?"

"Perhaps it represents responsibility," Professor Finch suggested, his archaeologist's mind stirring. "To wear the crown means bearing its weight and suffering the consequences of leadership. What are each of us willing to embrace?"

Ellie felt the warmth of camaraderie around her. "I would cast aside the fear of failure. I want to embrace the truth of who I am and what I can become."

"For adventure", Azrael added, "I would leave the burden of the past behind. We cannot forge ahead if we cling to what once was."

Finn's tail gave a sharp, excited twitch, betraying his barely contained enthusiasm. An impish grin, wide and mischievous, spread across his face, crinkling the corners of his eyes. "Count me in, absolutely! Curiosity's sake alone is worth the risk! I'd gleefully trade my measly caution for a glimpse of uncharted horizons, a taste of the unknown. What's life without a little adventure, eh?"

Oliver paused, running a thoughtful hand along his chin. The silence hung in the air for a moment, thick with anticipation. Finally, he chimed in, his voice carrying a newfound conviction. "I'd readily sacrifice the predictable comfort of routine for a life overflowing with unexpected events. This night, this...feeling has awakened something within me. A yearning for more than the mundane, a hunger for the unpredictable splendour of the world beyond."

Nodding solemnly, Luci wrapped her tail around the two of them, a gesture of profound affection and unwavering support. Her eyes, ancient and knowing, held a deep well of wisdom. "Together, you shall find fulfilment. For the bond you share, forged in this moment of shared aspiration, overcomes all tribulations. Trust in each other, support each other, and remember why you embarked on this journey. Now, face the pyramid, that silent sentinel guarding secrets untold, and let truth, and truth alone, guide your steps there."

With spirits buoyed by a newfound unity, forged in shared trials and whispered hopes, they turned towards the ethereal glow emanating from the far end of the chamber. The luminous light, a beacon in the ancient space, pulsed with an almost palpable energy, drawing them forward. Their hearts were poised, not just for more mysteries to unravel, but for a deeper understanding of the forces at play. They ventured forth, with each step echoing in the hallowed silence, ready to decipher not only the intricate legacy of the crown, etched in forgotten languages and veiled symbolism, but also their own destinies. These destinies, they sensed, were inextricably entwined in the ever-expanding tapestry of history, a grand narrative woven with threads of power, sacrifice, and ultimately, connection.

The night awaited them; a canvas painted with shadows and secrets. It was a night filled with whispers of forgotten kings and queens and the echoing laughter of long-gone celebrations. They would soon discover that together, bound by their shared purpose and unwavering belief in each other, they could conquer even the mightiest of riddles, unravelling the most complex of enigmas. They were not just explorers; they were truth excavators, unearthing the profound connections that surrounded them, connections between the past and the present, between themselves and the ancient power that thrummed beneath their feet, and ultimately, between each other. Their journey was just beginning, and the answers, they knew, lay just beyond the ethereal glow, waiting to be discovered.

The adventure through the enchanted museum had transformed them, forging bonds stronger than any artefact within its walls. They had entered as separate individuals, each carrying their own unspoken hopes and fears, but appeared intertwined, their lives indelibly marked by the shared experience. The echoing halls, filled with whispers of forgotten kings and queens, had not merely presented tales of the past, but illuminated a timeless journey into the intertwined realms of love, friendship, and self-discovery.

Each exhibit, a window into another era, had also reflected onto them, revealing sides of their personalities they hadn't known existed. The riddles weren't just puzzles to be solved, but opportunities to peel back layers of their own identities, to confront anxieties and embrace vulnerabilities.

With every step deeper into the labyrinthine corridors, they ventured further into a world where the imagination thrived, where the very air hummed with possibility. They learnt the language of empathy, understanding each other's silent signals and unspoken needs.

The enchanted museum, it turned out, was merely a conduit, a catalyst for a more profound exploration: the depths of their souls. The magic wasn't confined to the ancient relics or fantastical creatures depicted in the artwork; it resonated within them, ignited by the shared pursuit of knowledge, the thrill of discovery, and the unwavering support they offered each other. The adventure had not only brought them closer; it had revealed the power of connection, the beauty of vulnerability, and the enduring magic that blossoms when hearts open to understanding, acceptance, and genuine affection.

THE LABYRINTH BENEATH

S ure, I can help refine the selected text. Here is a more concise and polished version:

The echoes of laughter and startled gasps, remnants of Azrael's dramatic awakening, faded into the cavernous silence of the Enchanted Museum's grand foyer. Dust motes danced in the moonlight filtering through the arched windows, illuminating the stunned faces of Ellie, Professor Finch, Oliver, and the magnificent, newly awakened Azrael the Lion. The clock, perched high above the entrance, ticked with deliberate slowness, its hands creeping inexorably towards midnight. The sound was amplified in the stillness, each tick a sombre drumbeat marking a threshold – a transition from the known to the unknown, from reality to the realm of magic and secrets long buried beneath layers of history. Ellie, ever eager, took a deep breath, the scent of old parchment and forgotten magic filling her lungs. Excitement, vibrant and untamed, bubbled within her. She could practically taste the adventure, feel it woven into the very fabric of the museum's ancient stones and whispered in the rustling tapestries. The experience was more than just a field trip; this was the beginning of something extraordinary. The weighty silence of the foyer hinted at untold stories waiting to be unearthed, and Ellie, with her insatiable curiosity, was ready to unearth them all.

"Azrael", she began, her voice steady but laced with anticipation. "Where do we start?"

Azrael, a being of such radiant presence he seemed to shimmer with golden light, stood before them. His form, impossibly tall and powerful, radiated an ancient authority. He paused, the silence broken only by the soft rasp of his clawed foot against the cold stone floor, a sound that echoed strangely in the vast hall. "The labyrinth lies beneath, veiled in mystery and shadows.

" His voice resonated with an otherworldly timbre, a sound that seemed to vibrate in Ellie's very bones. "Follow closely, for the path is treacherous, a twisting descent into the forgotten. But fear not, for I will lead you." The promise, even uttered with such imposing gravity, offered a sliver of comfort in the face of the unknown.

As they descended the spiralling staircase that wound relentlessly downwards beneath the hallowed halls of the museum, the atmosphere underwent a tangible shift. The air grew heavy, thick with the dust of ages and the weight of untold stories. The familiar hum of the city above faded into a muffled whisper, replaced by an unsettling silence that seemed to press in on them from all sides. Every damp, moss-covered stone seemed to whisper secrets of the past, every flickering shadow danced with phantoms of forgotten histories. Ellie could feel the weight of history pressing against her, a palpable force urging her onwards into the depths. A shiver traced its way down her spine, a mixture of trepidation and exhilaration. The labyrinth awaited, and she was about to enter its embrace.

"Fascinating," Professor Finch murmured, adjusting his spectacles as he took in the intricately carved walls that seemed to pulse with a life of their own. "This must be part of the museum's original design. It's designed to evoke wonder and stimulate the intellect. Each curve and turn conceals yet another layer of its purpose."

"Or its dangers," Oliver grumbled under his breath, trailing closely behind. His sturdy frame seemed incongruous within the maze of beauty and ancient fear.

As they ventured deeper into the labyrinth, the air grew noticeably cooler, clinging to their skin like a damp shroud. An insistent rustling, like whispering secrets, caught Ellie's attention. It seemed to emanate from the very walls themselves. Finn, his ever-playful demeanour undeterred by the oppressive atmosphere, darted ahead, a blur of russet fur weaving in and out of the lengthening shadows cast by unseen sources of light. "Over here!" he beckoned, his voice echoing faintly, a glint of mischief in his eye that belied the growing unease prickling at Ellie's senses.

Ellie exchanged hesitant glances with the others – Maya, the pragmatic healer, and Azrael, the stoic warrior – before rushing after Finn, her heart racing a frantic rhythm against her ribs. Each echoing footstep seemed to amplify the silence that pressed in around them.

The labyrinth was a maddening puzzle, its passageways twisting and turning with illogical geometry, corridors branching out like the tentacles of an ancient creature, a slumbering titan ready to ensnare them in its dusty, forgotten mysteries. The air floated with the scent of damp earth and something else, something indefinable and unsettling that spoke of ages long past.

"Keep your wits about you," Azrael warned, his voice, deep and resonant, echoing strangely through the cool stone corridors. His hand rested on the pommel of his sword, his eyes narrowed, scanning the intricate carvings that adorned the walls. "These walls remember. They have seen things, felt things... and they don't easily forget."

An inscription caught Ellie's eye in a dimly lit alcove, tucked away from the grand halls of the museum. Ellie's eye. It pulsed with a faint, ethereal shimmer, the source of its luminescence a mystery. The air around it felt cool, almost charged. "What does it say?" she asked, her voice hushed with a mixture of curiosity and apprehension, stepping closer to decipher the strange symbols etched into the ancient stone.

A voice, smooth as polished jade and laced with ancient wisdom, echoed through the chamber. "The Serpent will guide the minds, but only to those who seek." As the words faded, a figure uncoiled from a darkened nook – Luci, her scales gleaming like burnished bronze in the ambient light. She was magnificent, her serpentine form having an almost regal bearing. Her eyes, like chips of obsidian, regarded them with quiet knowing.

Professor Finch, a man whose brow was perpetually furrowed in thought, tilted his head, his gaze fixed on the inscription. "It seems we must think critically, not just observe. The inscription implies a condition, a prerequisite. But what, precisely, do we look for? The 'seeking' feels deliberate." He rubbed his chin, his fingers tracing the lines etched by years of academic pursuit.

"Knowledge!" Ellie exclaimed, her enthusiasm bubbling to the surface. "We're here to uncover the museum's treasures, to piece together its history, to understand the stories etched into its very stones. It's what we do! It's why we're here, braving dusty corridors and cryptic clues!" She gestured around the chamber, her excitement momentarily eclipsing the solemn atmosphere. "We seek the truth behind the artefacts, the secrets of the past!

"In a sense, we seek understanding." Lady Arabella's stately form materialised from a shadow, her voice rich and comforting. "These artefacts have stories of their own, tales interwoven with time itself."

"Great, but we also need to find a way through this labyrinth!" Oliver interjected, impatience edging his tone.

Finn, nimble as a squirrel, scampered up to one of the age-worn walls, his fingers dancing across the cool, rough stone. He leaned closer, his ear pressed against the surface. "There's something here, something hidden," he announced, his voice hushed with anticipation. "Listen closely, and you might hear the whispers."

The rest of the group, their curiosity aroused, homed in on the silence. The air hovered with expectation, stretching the moments between breaths. After a heartbeat that felt like an eternity, faint murmurs appeared from the stone, like the rustling of forgotten leaves. They were fragments of history, swirling around them like a spectral mist, hinting at secrets long buried. "These walls remember," the voices seemed to sigh, a chorus of echoes from the past. "The path is veiled, its entrance obscured. But the truth shall come to light if you are brave enough to seek it."

The whispers were more than just words; they were riddles, wrapped in layers of allegory and enigma. Azrael, his brow furrowed in concentration, moved closer to the wall, his massive shadow enveloping them, casting long, dancing silhouettes in the flickering torchlight. The air grew colder, imbued with a sense of profound mystery. "We must decipher what history offers," Azrael boomed, his voice resonating with authority. "Let us listen to Huckleberry; he once served as a messenger between realms, a confidante to kings and shadows alike—he knows the languages of the past, the secrets whispered in the dark." The mention of Huckleberry hung in the air, a promise of guidance and a chilling reminder of the potent magic that permeated their quest. The weight of their mission pressed down upon them, heavy and inescapable.

"Huckleberry!" Ellie called out, scanning the intricate designs of the walls. Suddenly, from the depths of the shadows, Huckleberry appeared with elegant grace, his obsidian feathers gleaming.

"It's wonderful to see you again!" he croaked, flapping his wings as he perched on a nearby ledge. "A riddle lies ahead, a test of your resolve. Solve it, and the passage will be yours."

"Go on then," Professor Finch encouraged, leaning closer. "What is the riddle?"

"Three I am, the past, present, and future entwined in a single thread. Please identify the moment that is frozen in time, Find the artefact that holds this mystery, then speak its name, and you shall find your way!" Huckleberry explained, a glint of excitement in his eye.

Ellie furrowed her brow in concentration. "The three... past, present, and future? It must refer to something significant, something that embodies those concepts."

"The Hourglass!" Azrael exclaimed suddenly, muscles rippling with urgency. "It represents the passage of time across the ages!"

"Indeed," Luci confirmed, her serpent's gaze piercing. "But which hourglass? This labyrinth is filled with myriad artefacts."

"Then we must look!" Ellie declared, her heart steering her forward. "Split up—look for anything that resembles or evokes the essence of time. Finn, stay close to me. Oliver, you stick with Professor Finch and Luci. Azrael can guide us."

As they each ventured into different passages, Ellie's mind raced, the silvery walls alive with history, whispering tales of forgotten empires and long-lost secrets. The chill air hummed with an energy that both thrilled and unsettled her. She recalled the glimmering display from earlier in the museum, a golden hourglass encased within a glass prism. It was it—the artefact that held memories of time cascading like grains of sand; not just a record of events, but a tangible representation of moments passing, lives lived, and futures yet to unfold. The image of the hourglass, its delicate frame radiating warmth against the cool glass, burnt in her memory, a beacon in the labyrinthine depths of the museum. What stories did it hold within its glistening grains? And, more importantly, what secrets would it reveal to her now?

"This way!" she yelled, rushing down the twisting corridor.

Finn bounded alongside, his clever eyes sparkling with determination.

Rounding yet another bend in the labyrinthine corridors, they erupted into a chamber that stole their breath away. Gone were the drab greys and browns of the tunnels; here, the air thrummed with rich colours, a vibrant symphony of forgotten hues. Every surface seemed to spin with treasures from eras long past: gleaming golden artefacts, intricate tapestries depicting scenes of mythic grandeur, and shelves overflowing with ancient tomes bound in leather and clasped with precious stones. In the very centre of the chamber stood a magnificent pedestal, carved from a single piece of obsidian and polished to a mirror sheen. Upon it rested the hourglass, the object of their perilous quest. Its sands weren't merely grains of silica; they shimmered and danced like captured starlight, swirling within the glass as if alive.

"There it is!" Ellie gasped, her voice a mixture of awe and anticipation. She moved forward almost unconsciously, her fingers brushing against the cool, smooth glass of the hourglass. A jolt of energy, subtle yet undeniable, ran up her arm. "But how do we activate it?"

Luci slithered closer, her scales catching the light and scattering rainbow patterns across the floor. Her voice was low and melodious, a hypnotic whisper that seemed to resonate deep within Ellie's bones. "We must speak its name, the essence that binds the threads of time, the key that unlocks its power. We must utter the 'Virtue of Continuity'." She enunciated the words with a reverence that suggested ancient knowledge and profound understanding.

Ellie's heart pounded against her ribs, a frantic drumbeat against the silence of the chamber. The fate of everything rested on this moment. She turned to Finn, her eyes searching his face for reassurance. "On the count of three, then," she said, her voice trembling slightly despite her best efforts. She took a deep breath, steadying herself. "One... two... three!"

"Virtue of Continuity!" they shouted in unison, their voices layered with courage and belief. An electric pulse rippled through the air, enveloping them in a cascade of luminous sparkles.

The hourglass hummed with a low, almost palpable energy, its glass frame vibrating against the ancient stone floor. Inside, the swirling sands, no longer behaving according to the laws of gravity, twisted and contorted into intricate shapes that mirrored the impossible. They danced, coalescing into fleeting visions, each a window into moments that had long since faded into legend. Great warriors clashed on sun-drenched battlefields, their bronze armour gleaming under a forgotten sky. Ancient discoveries unfolded before their eyes – the construction of magnificent pyramids, the unveiling of forgotten constellations. And within the swirling chaos, they could almost hear the faint echoes of lives lived long gone – laughter, sorrow, triumphs, and tragedies woven into the fabric of time itself.

"Profound!" exclaimed Professor Finch, his voice echoing through the cavernous chambers, a blend of awe and intellectual curiosity. Oliver, Lady Arabella, and the remaining members of their expedition hurried towards the group, drawn in by the spectacle of the magical display. The air thrummed with potent energy, thick with the weight of history.

"I can see the way!" yelled Oliver, his voice laced with a mixture of excitement and disbelief. The visions within the hourglass seemed to be responding to something – to him, perhaps? The sands, as if guided by an unseen hand, were now actively shaping their path.

The sands of time, shimmering with an ethereal light, coalesced and formed an illuminated trail, a pathway woven from the very essence of the past. It drifted through the labyrinthine corridors, beckoning them to follow, a luminescent thread leading them deeper into the heart of the ancient structure. "We can navigate the labyrinth!" Azrael crooned, his excitement infectious, his eyes gleaming with anticipation. "Let's hurry before the magic wanes! The hourglass won't hold this intensity forever. We need to seize this opportunity while we can!"

The group coalesced into a tight circle behind the shimmering, ethereal path, its edges crackling with untold energy. Their breaths came in ragged gasps, a mixture of fear and exhilaration clinging to the air. The hourglass, held aloft by Elara, pulsed with a soft, internal luminescence, its golden sand a constant, silent reminder of the precious time slipping away. It illuminated their faces, highlighting the determination etched onto Liam's brow, the nervous anticipation fluttering in Chloe's eyes, and the unwavering resolve in Elara's own gaze. They raced deeper into the labyrinthine museum, a chaotic maze of forgotten artefacts and swirling timelines. Ancient pottery whispered forgotten stories as they brushed past; shadows danced with the echoes of long-dead pharaohs. They rushed around corners, their footsteps echoing in the vast, silent halls, a counterpoint to the frantic beat of their hearts. Each successful navigation of the treacherous paths was met with a shared gasp of relief, a fleeting moment of rejoicing in the enchantment, the magic that clung to everything like glittering dust.

"Look!" Finn chirped, his voice a youthful burst of energy in the oppressive atmosphere. He pointed towards a doorway shimmering with an ethereal light, a beacon in the surrounding gloom. "It leads deeper into the museum's heart! The energy is... intense!" He swallowed nervously, his first enthusiasm tempered by a hint of trepidation.

"It feels like we are on the cusp of something extraordinary," Lady Arabella said, her regal presence unwavering even amidst the frenzy. Despite the chaotic rush and the undeniable danger, she kept a sense of composed authority, her voice calm and steady. Her eyes, however, betrayed a hint of wonder, a spark of the same excitement that coursed through the others. "A convergence of timelines. A nexus of possibilities. We must be cautious, but bold."

As they approached the glowing doorway, pulsating with an ethereal light that seemed to beckon them forward, Ellie could feel a powerful sense of unity enveloping them, a tangible bond forged in shared struggle and burgeoning triumph. The air thrummed with an energy that resonated deep within her bones. They were not merely solving riddles etched into ancient stone; they were weaving their own stories, their individual threads intertwining to craft a vibrant and resilient narrative that would echo through time, its resonance mirroring the enduring legacy of the artefacts surrounding them - relics of forgotten civilisations, testaments to the power of collaboration and courage. Each solved puzzle, each overcome obstacle, had strengthened their connection, moulding them into something more than just a team. They were becoming a legend in the making.

Across the expanse of the chamber, a cavernous space filled with the hushed whispers of ages past, came a familiar voice, deep and resonant, a comforting rumble that vibrated in the very foundations of the temple: the call of Valen. His words, imbued with ancient wisdom and a hint of veiled warning, resonated with an almost paternal authority. "Do you have the courage to face what lies ahead? The tests you have endured have proven yourselves worthy but keep your wits perpetually sharp and your hearts vigilant; shadows linger even in the brightest light, and the night, though seemingly waning, is still young and full of unseen dangers." The implication was clear: the true trial was yet to begin.

"Together, we can overcome anything!" Ellie declared, her voice ringing with newfound conviction, amplified by the echoing chamber. She felt the warmth of friendship and unshakeable resolve radiating from her companions, a tangible energy that fuelled her own determination. It was a feeling of interconnectedness, a shared purpose that transcended individual fears and anxieties. They were a force, a collective will be capable of confronting whatever darkness lay beyond the glowing doorway, bound together by an unbreakable promise to protect each other, and to face the unknown as one. This wasn't just a quest; it was a testament to the enduring power of human connection.

With newfound determination burning in their hearts, they stepped closer to the radiant doorway. It wasn't merely an exit, but a shimmering passage, a gateway that promised secrets

ALLIES OF THE NIGHT

The moon hung high, a celestial pearl suspended in the inky canvas of the night sky, casting shimmering beams of silver through the towering, arched windows of the Enchanted Museum. Each sliver of moonlight painted the polished floors with an ethereal glow, highlighting the intricate carvings and centuries-old dust motes dancing in the air. The air itself was thick with a palpable excitement, a vibrant energy that tingled on the skin and resonated with the promise of adventure. Tonight was different. Tonight, as the grand clock in the hall chimed its final, resonating dong, marking the witching hour of midnight, the magic began. Ellie , a bright-eyed and eager intern, her notebook clutched tightly in her hand; Professor Finch, the museum's eccentric curator, his spectacles perched precariously on his nose and a gleam of childlike wonder in his eyes; and Oliver, the sceptical security guard, his usual stoic expression replaced with a mixture of fear and fascination, stood in the great gallery. They were surrounded by the silent yet watchful artefacts – relics from forgotten civilisations, enchanted objects whispering untold stories, and portraits whose eyes seemed to follow their every move – all of which had come alive just moments ago, their dormant magic now surging through the hallowed halls. The museum, once a bastion of history, had transformed into a playground for the mystical.

"Where do we go from here?" Oliver asked, his voice a mix of awe and anxiety. The once-stalwart guard was now an unwilling participant in an unfolding tale far beyond his comprehension.

Before either Ellie, her heart pounding with a mixture of fear and exhilaration, or Professor Finch, his monocle gleaming with academic curiosity, could respond, a great roar echoed through the hall, shaking the very dust motes dancing in the air. It wasn't just any roar; it was the kind of sound that resonated deep within your bones, a primal call that spoke of power and ancient authority.

At the centre of the gallery, illuminated by the ethereal glow of the moon filtering through the arched windows, stood Azrael the Lion. He wasn't just any lion, either. He moved with the grace of a king, stretching majestically, rippling muscles flexing beneath his golden fur. On his broad chest, an ancient Egyptian insignia, a symbol of power and protection etched in polished lapis lazuli, gleamed in the moonlight, pulsing with a faint, inner light. With a shake of his shaggy mane, a cascade of gold that seemed to possess a life of its own, he turned towards the others, his eyes, like embers, fixing them with an intense, knowing gaze.

"Fear not, friends!" Azrael proclaimed, his voice deep and resonant, a rumbling baritone that filled the vast hall. The sound seemed to vibrate through the very stones of the gallery, silencing the last vestiges of their fear. "We are destined for a grand adventure," he continued, his voice softening slightly, taking on a tone of almost paternal reassurance. "Our first ally has come to guide us, a beacon in the encroaching darkness. But be mindful; the night is filled with both danger and wonder, shadows that whisper secrets and challenges that will test our very souls. We must be vigilant, brave, and above all, trust in the path that has been laid before us."

Ellie stepped forward, her heart racing with curiosity. The air crackled with unspoken tension, and a thrill, both exhilarating and slightly terrifying, shot through her veins. "Who else will join us?" she asked, her voice barely a whisper in the hushed stillness of the night. A lifetime of studying forgotten lore and arcane secrets wove a rich tapestry of history into her mind, making her eager to unravel this unfolding mystery and understand the forces at play and her own role within them. Each new revelation felt like a piece of a puzzle she was desperate to solve.

"Patience, young historian. The night reveals its allies slowly, like the dawn after a long, dark journey," Azrael intoned, his voice a low rumble that resonated deep within her chest. His stone eyes, normally as cold and unyielding as granite, now sparkled with ancient wisdom, a depth of understanding that spanned millennia. He seemed to be weighing her, assessing her worthiness for the task that lay ahead. Ellie held her breath, hoping she wouldn't disappoint.

As if summoned by a whisper of the night, a slithering form appeared from the shadows, fluid and mesmerising. It was Luci. Her bronze scales glinted brilliantly under the pale moonlight, catching the light like a thousand tiny mirrors. She unfurled herself, weaving through the air with serpentine grace, her movements both elegant and predatory. The air grew thick with an earthy scent, a primal aroma that spoke of power and untamed wildness. Ellie felt a shiver run down her spine, a mix of fear and fascination, about to begin.

"Ellie, Professor Finch, Oliver, it is time for you to embrace the treasures of the past," Luci hissed, her voice smooth yet commanding. "You will need each other and the allies who will soon reveal themselves."

"But how do we know whom to trust?" Oliver interjected, his brow furrowing with concern.

"Trust is forged in the fires of adversity," Luci replied, her amber eyes holding a flicker of mystery. "But I can assure you, not all who dwell in shadow wish to harm."

As her words hung in the air, still echoing slightly on his wooden face. Light glinted off the polished wood of his snout, highlighting the mischievous sparkle in his painted eyes. "Allies? Did someone say allies? Count me in!" he chirped, his voice surprisingly resonant for such a small, wooden figure. "A fox is always useful when the moon rises! We know the shadows, the secret paths... and where the best cheese snacks are hidden, of course."

Ellie chuckled, the unexpected appearance and enthusiastic welcome easing the knot of nervousness in her stomach. The lively creature darted around her feet, his small wooden paws clicking softly against the marble floor. "Finn, what adventures await us?" she asked, her voice now brimming with a mixture of excitement and anticipation.

Finn grinned wider, a dazzling, almost manic expression that displayed his spirit, bright and mischievous. "You won't believe what treasures lie hidden in the museum! Not just dusty old artefacts, mind you, but secrets whispered from the past, waiting to be rediscovered! And I've gathered clues from all corners, from the whispers in the sarcophagus chamber to the graffiti hidden behind the dinosaur exhibit, clues that will help us find our way." He pulled a tiny, rolled-up parchment from a hidden pocket in his miniature coat, wiggling it excitedly. "I even stole this from the Curator's desk! Don't tell him!"

Before they could go ahead any further, a sudden, powerful fluttering sound filled the space, drowning out the murmur of other patrons and the distant hum of the museum's ventilation system. Huckleberry , a majestic creature of bronze feathers and keen, golden eyes, swooped down from a high ledge near a replica of the Rosetta Stone, landing elegantly on Azrael's back, his talons barely making a sound. The air shimmered slightly around him, hinting at untold power. "A riddle awaits you, friends," he croaked, his voice a deep rumble that resonated through the hall, a knowing gleam flickering in his eye. "Only those who solve it, only those who can unravel the threads of time, shall earn the aid of Valen, your most valuable ally of all. But be warned, time is a fickle friend, and its secrets are not easily revealed." He paused dramatically, his gaze sweeping over Ellie and Finn. "Are you ready to play?"

"What's the riddle?" Ellie asked, eager to absorb any scrap of wisdom available.

Huckleberry puffed his chest. "Listen closely:
In the heart of the night, I hold the key,
A past unseen, yearning to be free.
With whispers of time, I weave a thread,
To the lands of lost treasures long thought dead."

"So, we must locate something at the heart of the museum related to time," Professor Finch mused, his mind already racing with possibilities.

"Precisely, Professor!" Finn chirped, twitching his bushy tail. "The heart of the museum could be the central chamber! Let's go!"

With renewed enthusiasm, the unlikely allies moved through the galleries, each step guided by the moon's silvery glow that filtered through the high, arched windows. They traversed rooms filled with ancient sculptures frozen in time, relics whispering tales of forgotten empires, and tapestries depicting scenes of glory and ruin. Finn, ever the jovial guide, led the way, displaying artefacts with playful banter and surprisingly insightful observations, transforming what could have been a sombre trek into an engaging adventure. He pointed out the mischievous glint in the eye of a Roman bust, guessed on the secret ingredients of a crumbling pharaoh's balm, and even debated the true purpose of a particularly bizarre-looking ritualistic object, always punctuating his explanations with a wink and a grin. The moonlit silence, punctuated by Finn's lively commentary and the soft echo of their footsteps, created an atmosphere of both mystery and camaraderie, forging a stronger bond between the unlikely companions with each passing artefact.

"Careful not to touch the porcelain dancer!" Finn warned, darting ahead. "She's known to give quite the fright if startled!"

"Right," Oliver said, trying to stay focused. As he dd so, he couldn't shake the feeling that they were being watched.

Upon reaching the entrance of a vast chamber draped in shadows and illuminated by a single beam of moonlight, Ellie paused. "What could be behind those doors?"

"Just beyond lies the Celestial Chamber," Azrael explained, his voice a low rumble. "It's a secret most do not know—within it are the stars of history. But be cautious, for the passage may hold unforeseen trials."

"What do you mean by 'trials'?" Oliver asked, crossing his arms defensively.

"Trials of history! A test of your wits and courage," Luci whispered, her voice full of intrigue. "Each artefact has a tale—a riddle must be solved."

The air crackled with anticipation, thick and palpable like an electrical storm about to break. Ellie took a deep breath, the cool air doing little to settle the frantic fluttering of her heart. Her historian instincts, honed through years of dusty libraries and forgotten texts, kicked in, pushing aside the creeping tendrils of fear. This was it. The culmination of years of research, dead ends, and whispered rumours.

"'Then let us enter," she announced, her voice resonating with a newfound steeliness, "and may our allies hold true. Each artefact may hold a key to our riddles, a fragment of the truth we look for." She gestured towards the imposing entrance, the words a rallying cry for her companions, a silent promise of shared success or shared failure.

A breathtaking spectacle greeted the group as they passed through the tall, arching doors, their shadows stretching long and distorted before them. A breathtaking spectacle greeted them. A breathtaking spectacle greeted them. Gone was the cold stone they expected. The great dome above mapped a panoramic display of glowing constellations, a celestial tapestry woven with shimmering light. Each star pulsed with a vibrant energy, reflected in the wide, awestruck eyes of the entering group.

Beneath the stars lay a circular platform, crafted from a material that seemed to absorb and refract the surrounding light. Encircling this platform, like silent guardians, were towering displays of artefacts, each meticulously presented. They were from different times, disparate cultures, and seemingly unrelated origins: a gleaming Roman gladius, a feathered Mayan headdress, an intricately carved Egyptian sarcophagus, and a strangely humming device crafted from polished obsidian. Each emanated a palpable aura of history, of stories waiting to be told.

"Just like the riddle!" Ellie exclaimed, her heart racing against her ribs like a trapped bird. The weight of responsibility, the sheer audacity of their quest, threatened to overwhelm her, but the sight before her reignited her passion, her unwavering belief. "We must unlock the secrets of these artefacts and decipher their hidden meanings to uncover the next path. The riddle spoke of a convergence, a point where past, present, and future intertwine. This... this must be it!"

Above them, the stars twinkled with a knowing glint, as if sharing an ancient secret, their light casting an ethereal glow upon the scene. Suddenly, the room shifted, a subtle but undeniable tremor that ran through the ground and up the walls, as if the very structure was alive, breathing, and reacting to their presence. The artefacts, silent until now, started to hum softly, a chorus of ancient voices rising in unison. Whispers filled the air, unintelligible yet profoundly evocative—a language of the past echoing through time, beckoning them closer to the heart of the mystery. The air thrummed with power, a palpable energy that promised both revelation and peril. The game was afoot.

"Welcome to the Celestial Chamber," a voice appeared, deep and melodic. Valen The Timekeeper stepped forward, cloaked in shadows. "You summon history's allies, yet those who arrive must prove themselves worthy of the knowledge that resides here."

"They test us," Professor Finch murmured with eagerness, nodding towards the display of artefacts. "Look! Each artefact seems to lead to a specific place in time."

Huckleberry, a creature of immense power and ancient lineage, spread his impressive wings, each feather tipped with iridescent moonlight. The leathery expanse moved with a soft, almost silent rustle, creating a fleeting eclipse as he fluttered to a nearby artefact. It was an astrolabe, crafted from polished obsidian and inlaid with veins of pure gold. The intricate device gleamed under the ethereal glow of the cavern, radiating an aura of forgotten knowledge. "We must decode its purpose," Huckleberry declared, his voice a resonant baritone that echoed through the chamber. "Only then will we access the wisdom necessary to navigate through this night. Our path lies hidden within its celestial mechanics."

Unwavering, Ellie stepped closer to the astrolabe, her eyes wide with a mixture of awe and determination. Spells of excitement twisted within her like the ancient scrolls she had studied for years, finally coming to life before her. "This astrolabe—it's a tool for determining latitude and time, isn't it?" she pondered aloud, her fingers itching to trace the delicate markings on its surface. "It measures the angles of celestial bodies. If we align it with the right constellation... we can unlock the map it holds. But which constellation? Should we align it with a specific time? it with?" She paused, her brow furrowed in concentration, the gears of her mind whirring as she tried to piece together the astrolabe's secrets and the cryptic clues that surrounded them. The fate of their quest, she knew, likely hinged on the accuracy of their interpretation.

"Wonderful!" Luci interrupted, slithering closer. "But be meticulous, for one wrong step could alter our fate forever."

Oliver's heart hammered against his ribs, a frantic drumbeat against the tense silence as they huddled in the museum's shadowy alcoves. Each whispered word of their strategy felt electric, charged with the thrill of the unknown. The event wasn't just another night; it was a convergence, a moment where the ordinary dissolved into the extraordinary. They, a band of unlikely heroes, heeded the night's silent, insistent call for unity – adventurers not by profession, but by circumstance, forging their destinies together. Their paths, once separate, are now intertwined, weaving a tapestry of history and heart within the museum's majestic, awe-inspiring spaces.

The astrolabe, a swirling vortex of brass and starlight, lay before them, its intricate carvings hinting at the secrets it held. Around it, Ellie, ever the pragmatist; Professor Finch, his eyes twinkling with intellectual fervour; Oliver, grappling with a mixture of fear and excitement; Luci, her quiet confidence a reassuring presence; and even the ever-playful Finn, momentarily subdued by the gravity of the situation, all took a deep, collective breath. They were ready, or at least pretending to be, for the revelations the museum, a silent sentinel of ages past, had in store. Time itself seemed to warp and bend around them, the echoes of forgotten eras resonating through the labyrinthine corridors, each turn a potential portal to another world. With mounting anticipation, they prepared to confront whatever magical trials, ancient guardians, or mind-bending puzzles lay ahead, defences raised against the unseen.

Together, bound not only by a shared goal but also by the intangible whispers of the night, they stood poised on the precipice of their adventure. This was not merely a quest; it was a story unfolding in real-time, a narrative written in moonlight and whispered secrets. This would be a night filled with heart-stopping moments, bursts of unexpected laughter, and the blossoming of an unexpected camaraderie – a bond forged in the crucible of shared experience. It was a night that promised to illuminate the uncertain path forward, guiding them not with blazing torches, but with the soft, steady glow of the constellations above, mirroring the intricate map of fates etched within each of their hearts.

"Onward!" Azrael boomed, and with that, the allies of the night set forth—each step leading them deeper into the heart of the enchanted museum, where every artefact held not just a riddle, but a fragment of their blossoming destiny.

THE MIDNIGHT MASQUERADE

The grand hall of the Enchanted Museum was a remarkable sight at midnight. Moonbeams fractured and kaleidoscopic from their journey through towering stained-glass windows depicting mythical beasts and long-forgotten heroes, spilled across the polished marble floor. They illuminated the dust motes that danced in the cool, still air, each speck shimmering like a tiny, suspended star. Statues of emperors and gods, silent sentinels of history, seemed to lean in and whisper secrets of the past, their carved lips barely moving in the dim light. Ancient artefacts, trapped within glass cases or perched on pedestals, added their voices to the chorus, their stories woven into the very fabric of the room. This created an ethereal atmosphere, thick with the weight of centuries and pulsing with a subtle, almost sentient life. Shadows stretched and writhed, playing tricks on the eyes, and the air itself seemed to hum with a low, resonant energy. At the centre of it all stood Ellie, her breath catching in her throat, her heart racing with a mixture of fear and exhilarating anticipation. The thrill of the unknown coursed through her veins as she turned to face her companions, a question and a challenge burning in her bright, inquisitive eyes. The adventure was about to truly begin.

"Are we really doing this?" she asked, her voice barely a whisper. The thought of the Midnight Masquerade sent a thrill of excitement through her.

"Of course, we are!" exclaimed Professor Finch, his eyes gleaming with fervour. "This is a once-in-a-lifetime opportunity to unearth the hidden narratives of these artefacts. Besides, when else will we have the time to enjoy such a mysterious event?"

Oliver, the bemused museum guard, stood rooted to the spot, his eyes wide with a mixture of fear and disbelief. Still reeling from the impossible sight of a lion statue brought to life, he stammered, "You...you mean to say that we're going to...attend a masquerade ball? Hosted by...enchanted statues?" He scratched his head vigorously, as if to dislodge the surreal scene from his mind. "I thought I was going crazy."

Azrael, now fully animated and radiating an almost palpable aura of majesty, let out a low, rumbling chuckle. He swept a paw, heavy with the weight of ages, toward the ornately carved archway that led to a second chamber. "Not just attend, my friends! We shall be the stars of the show! Imagine! Humans, attending the most exclusive event of the century! Follow me!" His voice, a rich baritone that resonated through the hall, held a playful note of anticipation.

As they ventured into the adjoining hall, a collective gasp escaped their lips. A breathtaking transformation had occurred. The previously bare, utilitarian walls now gleamed with opulent colours, rich jewel tones woven into intricate patterns. Swathes of shimmering silks, the colour of twilight and dawn, draped from the soaring ceilings, catching the light from the countless flickering candlelit chandeliers that now hung suspended in perfect symmetry. The air itself was alive with whispers, a symphony of hushed anticipation that tickled the skin and sent shivers down their spines. It was as if the very walls were eager to share their stories, eager to reveal the secrets they had guarded for centuries.

Stepping fully into the hall, Ellie's eyes widened in astonishment. Row upon row of tables stretched before them, each laden with an array of exquisitely crafted masks. Every single one was unique, a testament to the artistry of a bygone era, and steeped in its own history and legend. Some were feathered and jewelled, shimmering with an ethereal glow; others were carved from dark wood, their faces etched with expressions both whimsical and haunting. "This is astounding!" Ellie exclaimed, her fingers dancing across the delicate surface of a beaded mask, its intricate design depicting a constellation of stars. "What do these masks signify? Are they... important?" She looked at Azrael, her curiosity piqued, sensing that these were more than mere party favours. They were imbued with something...more.

"It's said that each mask carries the essence of its previous owner," Luci coiled at her feet, gliding gracefully into view. "They hold the memories of the past and wearing them might allow you to glimpse into their lives."

Ellie's pulse quickened as she pondered the implications. "What if we find a mask that connects us to an important moment in history? It could be a key to solving a puzzle!"

"Focus, Ellie!" Professor Finch urged, his hat almost slipping from his head as he turned eagerly toward the din. "We must not lose sight of our goal. We need to find Valen if we are to solve the riddles and restore the balance."

"To find him, we'll need the masks that align with our deepest curiosities," said Lady Arabella, her statue-like form exuding a regal grace. "Each of you must choose one that resonates with your story. That will guide us to Valen."

As Ellie scanned the vast selection of masks, a dizzying array of colours, textures, and shapes vying for her attention, her eyes finally landed on one that seemed to hum with a quiet energy. It was a celestial masterpiece, adorned with intricate patterns of stars and constellations painstakingly etched onto its surface. Each tiny point of light seemed to shimmer, depicting familiar constellations like Orion and the Big Dipper, alongside swirling nebulae painted in shades of deep blues and purples. It called to her, resonating with a deep-seated part of her soul and igniting her passion for history and exploration, a yearning to understand the stories hidden within the cosmos and the echoes of civilisations long past. Carefully, almost reverently, she slipped the mask onto her face. A strange and unfamiliar sensation washed over her – a surge of energy flowed through her, tingling at her fingertips and causing the constellations on the mask to seem to glow even brighter.

Around her, the others made their choices in a silent, almost ritualistic fashion. Professor Finch, ever the scholar, selected a mask etched with swirling ancient runes, their meanings lost to time but promising untold knowledge and forgotten magics. The runes pulsed with a faint, inner light, hinting at the potent power held within. Oliver, ever the stoic and dependable one, chose a simple yet striking design that resembled a knight's helm. Forged from what looked like blackened steel, it radiated a sense of strength and unwavering resolve, its austere lines a perfect reflection of his own character. Luci, drawn to intrigue and hidden knowledge, chose a serpent-patterned mask, its scales shimmering with an unnatural sheen. Emeralds, cool and calculating, glinted from the serpent's eyes, promising power and cunning. Azrael, a warrior at heart, picked one decorated with motifs that celebrated strength and bravery. Depictions of legendary heroes and mythical beasts adorned the mask, radiating an aura of invincibility and unwavering courage.

Finn, a whirlwind of restless energy, scurried around the group, bouncing from mask to mask, his bright eyes darting from one design to the next. He sniffed, pawed, and examined each one with meticulous curiosity, his tail twitching with anticipation. Finally, with a delighted yip, he donned a mischievous, painted fox mask. The mask, decorated with playful swirls and bright colours, perfectly captured his playful spirit and inherent trickster nature, promising adventures and unexpected turns. With their masks chosen, a palpable sense of excitement and anticipation filled the air, the room buzzing with unspoken questions and the promise of an unforgettable journey.

"Now, let the Midnight Masquerade begin!" Azrael announced, his voice booming with excitement.

As the midnight hour chimed, its resonant boom vibrating through the very foundation of the ancient hall, the space erupted in a flurry of colour and movement. Gone was the formal stillness, replaced by a vibrant, chaotic ballet of swirling silks and shimmering jewels. Figures appeared from the shadows, drawn forth as if by the chime itself, ethereal guests from various times and places. Some were grand, their costumes whispering of forgotten empires; others whimsical, adorned in garb that defied earthly logic. Each wore a mask, a meticulously crafted facade that adorned their own unique tales, hinting at secrets and long-lost identities hidden beneath. Gentle laughter, light as a feather, mingled with music that seemed to echo from every corner, not merely played, but emanating from the walls themselves. The melodies pulsed with life, weaving a tapestry of sound that enveloped Ellie and her friends in a marvellous celebration, a dreamlike spectacle that blurred the lines between reality and fantasy. The air crackled with magic, and the scent of exotic spices hung heavy, promising a night unlike any other.

"Look! Oliver exclaimed, pointing toward a group of Renaissance courtiers, their movements fluid and elegant as they danced. Ellie could hardly believe her eyes; they were not mere illusions but a tapestry woven from the threads of history coming alive.

"Dance with them, Ellie!" Professor Finch encouraged, pulling her into the throng. The music swirled around them, and Ellie began to lose herself in the rhythm. Each twirl sparked a new insight about the stories hidden within the museum walls. With every movement, she felt the trust of countless souls who had walked before her.

"Remember to seek!" Finn's playful voice chimed in, leaping beside her as he nimbly darted through the dancers. "This night is not merely for fun but for discovery!"

Determined to honour Finn's last words and continue their quest, Ellie felt a pull away from the swirling revelry of the dazzling dance floor. The music, the laughter, the glittering gowns – all faded into a background hum as she stealthily slipped away. She ventured toward an elaborately carved column that had snagged her attention from across the room. The artisanry was exquisite, the stone cool beneath her fingertips.

The engravings shimmered faintly under the soft light of the ballroom, catching and reflecting the ambient glow. Upon closer inspection, she noticed a connected series of symbols, each distinct and intricate. A jolt of recognition shot through her; they resembled different artefacts they had met in their travels, relics from fragmented moments in history brought together in this grand, almost impossible place.

Excitement bubbled within her, a renewed sense of purpose overriding the lingering sadness of Finn's sacrifice. "Professor Finch! Come here!" she called, her voice hushed but urgent. She beckoned him over to her discovery with a wave of her hand. "I think these might be clues, Professor! Clues to the riddle we need to solve to find Valen!"

Professor Finch, ever the dedicated scholar, hurried over, his face lighting up with scholarly curiosity. He examined the engravings closely, his brow furrowing with concentration as he traced the lines with a trembling finger. His spectacles perched precariously on his nose. "Indeed, Ellie," he murmured, his voice laced with awe. "These symbols represent items from different eras. That's a Babylonian astrolabe, and next to it, a feathered cloak from the Aztec Empire! Each is a piece of history, a resonant echo that connects to a specific moment. If we decipher their meanings and unravel the narrative woven into this stone, perhaps we can unlock the next step in our journey and finally find Valen." His eyes gleamed with a renewed hope, mirroring Ellie's own. The quest, despite its perils, continued.

As they shared their findings, a collection of ancient runes and cryptic symbols scattered across the worn stone table, Luci, the serpentine scholar, slithered forward, her scales shimmering with an inner excitement. "I can weave tales from these symbols, feel the echoes of forgotten eras resonating within them. I believe I can draw out the historical connections, mapping the complicated fabric of the past. But we must hurry," she cautioned, her voice a low, melodious hiss, "for the Midnight Masquerade is fleeting, and with it, our chance to learn the truth about this legend mystery."

Just then, a sharp, guttural caw ripped through the hushed atmosphere, shattering their intense focus. Huckleberry , a creature of legend and shadow, landed atop the crumbling column beside them. His dark feathers, the colour of midnight, glistened in the faint, ethereal light filtering through the ancient temple. "Seeking Valen, are we?" he croaked, his voice a rasping whisper that seemed to carry the weight of ages. His intelligent, piercing eyes, usually devoid of warmth, now sparkled with a mischievous glint. "I know where he lurks, the master of temporal currents and forgotten lore. But knowledge comes at a price. You must answer a riddle to find him; prove your worthiness to stand before the Timekeeper himself."

"What must we solve?" Ellie asked, her heart pounding with a mix of anticipation and trepidation. The prospect of meeting Valen was both terrifying and exhilarating. Excitement, that familiar, bubbling feeling, rose within her, pushing back against the fear. This was it, the decisive moment.

The raven extended his magnificent wings, the shadows of their span momentarily engulfing the group. He circled them once, a silent, predatory dance, before settling back on the column, his gaze unwavering. "Listen well," he commanded, his voice echoing through the ruins. 'In darkness I shine but vanish from sight, only to reappear in the warmth of daylight." What am I'"

Ellie furrowed her brow, her mind instantly racing. She closed her eyes, allowing the enigmatic words to float through her mind like wisps of smoke, searching for a form, a meaning, a connection.

The fate of their quest, and perhaps the fate of something far greater, hung in the balance, dependent on the answer to this ancient riddle. The pressure was immense, but the burning desire to uncover the truth fuelled her resolve.

"A star!" exclaimed Oliver suddenly.

"No, no," Professor Finch said, shaking his head. "Stars are visible at night, not hidden until the day. Think deeper, everyone."

"Hmmm ..." Luci pondered, her eyes gleaming with mischief. "What disappears in darkness yet is revealed in light " What, indeed?"

Ellie's eyes widened, pupils dilating as the realisation hit her with the force of a physical blow. "It's a shadow!" she exclaimed, her voice a breathless whisper. "Shadows can only exist when there's a light source!" The implication hung in the air, thick and pregnant with possibility. If she were to identify the light source, she might gain an understanding of... what?

Could she discern the essence of the deception?

Could she uncover the truth underlying Huckleberry's statements?

"Correct!" Huckleberry screeched, his voice echoing through the chamber. The sound was grating, like nails dragging across slate, yet a hint of delight, a sliver of genuine amusement, laced his tone. "Valen awaits you beyond the enchanted curtains where shadows whisper their secrets. But beware—time is not as linear as you think!" The words vibrated with an ominous weight, adding another layer of complexity to the already bewildering situation. Time, the very fabric of reality, was suspect.

Fingers trembling with a mixture of excitement and trepidation, Ellie gestured toward the flowing drapes that hung like curtains of twilight across an arched doorway. The fabric shimmered with an ethereal quality, the colours shifting and swirling like a captured nebula. She could almost hear whispers emanating from their depths, promises of knowledge and warnings of danger. Taking a steadying breath, she squared her shoulders, trying to ignore the frantic hammering of her heart. With a shared glance of determination, she and whoever went with her moved as one towards their new aim, curiosity burning in their hearts like a newly kindled flame. The unknown beckoned, and despite the inherent risk, they couldn't resist its pull.

What secrets lay hidden beyond the veil of shadows and whispered time?

There was only one way to discover the truth. As they stepped through the silken veil, a ripple of cool air brushed against their skin, and the very atmosphere seemed to thicken, becoming heavy with an unspoken history. The ornate gallery, just moments before filled with the murmur of tourists and the gleam of polished brass, vanished entirely. It felt timeless, as though they were no longer in the museum, bound by its earthly constraints and ticking clocks, but rather suspended in a moment that existed outside of time itself – a pocket of stillness where past, present, and future blurred into a hazy, indistinct canvas. The air hummed with a low, almost imperceptible vibration, a subtle symphony of epochs colliding.

There, in the dim, ethereal light that seemed to emanate from nowhere and everywhere at once, stood Valen—a cloaked figure, his garments the colour of twilight, perpetually shifting in patterns that hinted at swirling galaxies. His face was a canvas of shadows, obscuring his features and making it impossible to discern his age or intentions. An hourglass, crafted from obsidian and filled with sands that shimmered with an inner luminescence, hung suspended near his wrist. Its sands trickled gently in an eerie silence, each grain a whisper of moments slipping away, a tangible representation of the relentless march of time. The silence surrounding the hourglass was profound, swallowing any sound and amplifying the anticipation that thrummed in their veins.

"Welcome, seekers of time," he spoke, his voice resonating not just in their ears but within their very bones. It was a voice that echoed with the weight of ages, a voice that had seen the rise and fall of civilisations, the birth and death of stars. It had a timeless quality, devoid of inflection yet imbued with an undeniable power. "You have passed the first test, a mere threshold meant to deter the casual observer and proved your worth. But to discover the deeper truths about this museum, to utterly understand the mysteries woven into its very fabric, you must confront your shared pasts. Prepare yourselves, for the journey ahead will demand not only courage and intellect but a willingness to face the echoes of what once was."

"What do you mean?" Ellie asked, defending against the sudden intensity of the moment.

"This masquerade is not for distraction alone," he explained, his gaze piercing through the shadows. "It is a path to understanding. The masks you wear connect you to the tales that bind your spirits."

"Then how do we unravel the mysteries?" asked Azrael, his lion heart beating with determination.

"You must share your stories — the tales that shaped your journeys, the secrets that lurk beneath the surface. Only through these bonds can you unveil the heart of the museum," Valen the Timekeeper replied, gesturing toward a shimmering tapestry that hung nearby, its threads intertwining like lives interwoven through time.

As Ellie and her friends exchanged glances, a shared understanding bloomed in their eyes, a silent acknowledgement of the extraordinary circumstances that had drawn them together. Each one felt a rush of recognition wash over them, a comforting wave that dispelled the first unease and uncertainty. They were not alone in this adventure; they were united not just by proximity but by a common thread woven from their shared curiosity, their willingness to brave the unknown, and the inexplicable magnetism of the Midnight Masquerade. The whispers of the night, carrying secrets on the cool museum air, and the echoes of the past, resonating within the ancient artefacts, bound them together, transforming them from mere acquaintances into a clandestine fellowship.

Thus began their journey of revelations, a cascade of unearthed truths and long-forgotten narratives. Stories tumbled forth like raindrops in a storm, some gentle and poignant, others forceful and electrifying, each one enriching their understanding of who they were, the dormant potential that resided within them, and what they sought – not just within the walls of the museum, but within the depths of their own hearts. Each whispered confession, each shared theory, each collaborative decoding of cryptic clues, solidified their bond, creating a tapestry of shared experience that would forever connect them.

And though the Midnight Masquerade was but a fleeting moment, a single, shimmering night suspended in time, the connections they forged within its enchanting embrace would echo far beyond the museum's stately walls. The thrill of the chase, the camaraderie of the puzzle-solving, the shared vulnerability of revealing their deepest selves – all of it would leave an indelible mark. Their fates, once separate and distinct, were now inextricably entwined in a weave of adventure, a vibrant and complex pattern that promised challenges, triumphs, and a lifetime of shared memories, forever linking them to the magic they discovered under the veil of the midnight hour.

A SORCERER'S TALE

The echoes of earlier adventures lingered in the vaulted halls of the museum, their weight hanging in the air, thick with possibility and a faint scent of aged parchment and exotic spices. Each creak of the floorboards, each rustle of unseen fabric, seemed to murmur of daring escapades and narrow escapes. As the hands of the grandfather clock in the main gallery inexorably edged towards midnight, the flickering light of ornate sconces cast a warm golden glow over the artefacts. This light danced across polished surfaces and glinted in the depths of glass cases, making the treasures within appear almost alive, pulsing with untold stories waiting to be unearthed. Shadows stretched and contracted, playing tricks on the eye, transforming ancient statues into watchful guardians and dusty relics into instruments of untold power.

Ellie stood before a magnificent tapestry, its sheer size dominating the room. The threads, woven with dyes long lost to time, shimmered with an ethereal luminescence, catching the light and reflecting it in a spectrum of otherworldly colours.

The intricate images depicted scenes of forgotten kingdoms and breathtaking acts of sorcery: valiant knights battling mythical beasts, wise women communing with nature's spirits, and cities shimmering like mirages in the desert. It whispered to her in a language of colour and texture, a dialect of time encapsulated within its woven form, hinting at secrets buried deep within the fabric of history. She felt a strange pull towards it, an almost hypnotic allure that resonated within her very soul.

Beside her, Professor Finch adjusted his spectacles, the lenses magnifying his already keen eyes. He peered at the intricate details of the tapestry with the patience of a scholar enthralled by the mysteries of the past. His fingers, gnarled and stained with ink, traced the contours of the woven figures, as if trying to decipher their hidden meanings. He ran a hand through his thinning, silver hair, a familiar gesture when he was deep in thought. He muttered to himself, snippets of ancient languages and historical dates forming a low, almost unintelligible hum. The tapestry, he knew, held the key to something extraordinary, something that had eluded scholars for generations. Tonight, he felt closer than ever to unlocking its secrets.

"This tapestry represents a sorcerer's journey," he said, his voice a quiet reverence. "It is said the thread he used was infused with enchanted elements, capable of rendering his spells untouchable by time itself..

Suddenly, a soft rustle broke their focus, drawing their attention to Azrael, who had leapt down from his pedestal, shaking off the remnants of stone dust like a dog emerging from a swim. The colossal feline moved with surprising agility for a creature seemingly carved from granite. "Ellie, Professor, gather round," he said in his deep, rumbling voice, vibrant and alive. The sound vibrated through the hall, making the display cases hum faintly. "Tonight, the fabric of this museum harbours secrets of a sorcerer who once walked these very halls. His magic is intertwined with the artefacts around us, a dormant power waiting to be reawakened."

Ellie, wide-eyed with a mixture of awe and apprehension, shuffled closer to Professor Armitage, her hand instinctively reaching for his reassuringly familiar tweed sleeve. The Professor, usually a bastion of scholarly calm, adjusted his spectacles with a nervous gesture, his gaze darting around the shadowed corners of the grand hall.

"I believe I know whom you speak of," said Lady Arabella, her stately figure stepping forward with grace. The faint moonlight filtering through the high arched windows illuminated the intricate embroidery on her long velvet gown. "He was a formidable sorcerer, revered yet feared, for his power was both a blessing and a curse. Master Eldrin, they called him. Only those worthies could understand his art, and many have tried to seize it, driven by greed and a thirst for dominion. All have failed, meeting with... unfortunate ends." Lady Arabella paused, her expression turning melancholic, as if recalling long-forgotten tragedies. "His magic stays elusive, guarded by trials and riddles, woven into the very essence of this place. We must tread carefully, for Eldrin's legacy is not one to be trifled with."

Oliver remained sceptical, the flickering gaslight reflecting in his narrowed eyes. He shifted his weight, the polished floor echoing the movement in the otherwise hushed hall. "Essence? Are these tapestries reminiscent of enchanted nights? Sounds like a load of romantic claptrap to me. We've got rogue automatons, paintings that bleed, and a whole museum gone haywire. Seems a bit... esoteric to focus on a fairy tale right now." He gestured vaguely with his chin towards the chaotic scene beyond their small circle, where a robotic knight was currently engaged in a clumsy duel with a bewildered marble statue.

Finn, however, remained unfazed by Oliver's pragmatism. He twirled a tiny wooden staff, catching the light. "My dear Oliver, sometimes the most practical solutions lie within the seemingly impractical. Think of it as... reverse engineering. We dissect the narrative, find the core components of Alaric's magic, and then... poof! ...

We comprehend the interconnectedness of this entire mess. is connected." He winked, his painted eyes gleaming with mischief. "Besides, who doesn't love a delightful story? Even stubborn museum guards, I presume."

Ellie adjusted the strap of her bag, her expression thoughtful. "Finn's right, Oliver. We've tried brute force, we've tried logic, and we've gotten nowhere. There's clearly a magical influence at play here, something tying everything together. Alaric's story might be the thread we need to pull to unravel the entire knot." She glanced at the tapestry, a vast and intricate weaving that seemed to pulse with a faint inner light. "And it's not just a fairy tale, Oliver. It's history, magic, power... all woven into a narrative. We just need to learn how to read it."

As Luci, a creature of pure, fluid motion, coiled closer, her scales shimmering in the dim light, a palpable hush fell over the group. She raised her head, her forked tongue tasting the air. "I sense him," she hissed, her voice a low, mesmerising rumble. "Alaric... yes. He was a weaver of worlds, a shaper of destinies. But his name... it's more than just a name. It is a key. Alaric. He whispers from the tapestry if you know how to listen." She turned her obsidian eyes towards Ellie. "He awaits."

"Alaric..." murmured Professor Finch, his brow furrowing as he recalled tales of the sorcerer hidden in the pages of his texts. "Yes, he mastered the art of illusion, bending reality to his will. His power was so great that it is said he could navigate the very fabric of time."

"But Alaric was also a victim of his ambition," Lady Arabella continued, her voice a song saturated with wisdom. "In seeking eternal dominance, he lost sight of the importance of companionship and humility. His deepest fears eventually materialised into shadows that haunted his every step."

"Perhaps we could encounter these echoes as we navigate the labyrinth," Ellie suggested, her excitement palpable. "If Alaric left behind traces of his magic, we might unlock more than history—perhaps we can unlock the keys to our own fates."

Just then, Huckleberry, an imposing raven, landed with a soft thud on a nearby, weathered pedestal. His iridescent feathers, shimmering with deep blues, greens, and purples in the dim light, caught the eye like scattered jewels. He ruffled his impressive wings, each movement a subtle display of power and wisdom. "A wise thought, Ellie," his voice resonated, a low, gravelly croak that seemed to carry the weight of ages. "The shadows of Alaric's past can show us not only the path ahead but also reveal the trials that one must endure to emerge unscathed. To survive the future, we must study the past. they often hold the key to surviving what is yet to come."

"We'll need to tread lightly," Azrael cautioned, his voice a counterpoint to Huckleberry's, laced with a tangible sense of urgency. "If indeed Alaric's essence lingers within these ruins, we must be prepared for tests of our resolve. His spirit, broken and twisted by his experiences, may not welcome intruders. We must be wary of illusions, temptations, and trials designed to break us, just as they broke him." He paused, his gaze sweeping over his companions, making sure they heeded his words. "Our strength will be tested, both individually and as a group."

With the decision made and the weight of their undertaking settling upon them, the group stepped forward, a mixture of fascination and intrepidity etched on their faces. The air crackled with anticipation, the silence broken only by the rustling of unseen creatures and the distant howl of the wind. Determined to weave their adventure into the rich tapestry of the night, they ventured into the heart of the forgotten place, ready to face whatever secrets and dangers lay hidden within Alaric's haunted past.

As they approached the heart of the tapestry, colours began to morph, revealing the haunting visage of Alaric—the sorcerer drawn as if he were spellbound into the very fabric itself. His eyes glimmered with a light reminiscent of distant stars, while strange symbols ebbed and flowed in the background, dancing provocatively as if inviting them closer.

"With approaches carefully spun, you seek the lessons of the one who could manipulate time," Alaric's voice resonated softly, weaving through the air like a caress. "But be wary, for magic borne of hubris can distort the very essence of existence. What is your desire, brave seekers?"

Ellie stepped forward, emboldened by a mix of desperation and determination. The flickering torchlight danced across her face, highlighting the resolve in her eyes. "We seek knowledge, wisdom gleaned from the tapestry of your stories, ancient one, to navigate the mystical labyrinth of this night. Your past holds the answers to our lost journey. She paused, taking a deep breath, the air thick with the scent of old parchment and forgotten magic. "Specifically,", she continued, her voice gaining strength, "we want to learn the lessons of friendship and sacrifice that you, in your pride, failed to understand. We hope to succeed where you stumbled, to choose a different path, guided by the ghosts of your mistakes."

The tapestry rippled, mimicking the tremor that ran through Ellie and the subtle currents of the ancient room. mimicking the tremor that ran through Ellie.

Alaric regarded her with an intensity that made her heart quicken, his gaze piercing the carefully constructed walls she presented to the world. His eyes, the colour of a storm-tossed sea, seemed to see straight through her, acknowledging the vulnerability she fought so hard to conceal.

A slow smile, more knowing than welcoming, touched his lips. "Ah, so you do not come to conquer, as so many have before, driven by greed or ambition, but to understand," he said, the words laced with a hint of surprise, perhaps even a sliver of approval. "Very well. The first shadow, the prelude to the trials ahead, speaks of a choice—a conundrum you must embrace, a decision that will define the path you tread: to follow the threads of fear, allowing them to unravel you and bind you to the darkness, or to weave the fabric of courage, strengthening yourself with each brave act, each challenge overcome." The air crackled with unspoken warnings, emphasising the weight of the choice. He paused, letting the gravity of his words sink in, before adding in a soft, almost conspiratorial tone, "Choose wisely, Ellie, for the shadows are long and unforgiving."

"The first puzzle," Finn chimed, a twinkle of mischief in his wooden eyes. "What do you see when you look deeper into fear?"

"Perhaps", Ellie pondered, "we must confront our fears, not flee from them."

"You may be right," Professor Finch replied. "To learn from the past, we should not shy away from its darkest corners."

Alaric's visage flickered with approval. "Such insights will serve you well. Now, unravel the riddle of fear within these hallowed walls."

With that pronouncement, the tapestry shifted, its intricate patterns dissolving and reforming like a dream in flux. The meticulously woven scene of pastoral beauty was abruptly rent asunder, the threads splitting and fraying to reveal a darkened corridor that pulsed with an unsettling energy. This passage was shrouded in equal parts intrigue and dread, a tangible miasma that clung to the air and sent shivers down their spines. As if beckoning with a silent, irresistible call, the shadows coiled and writhed about them, their depths concealing unknown dangers and untold possibilities. Whispers, like the rustling of unseen leaves or the sighs of long-dead spirits, filled the space, promising secrets and sowing seeds of uncertainty, threatening to unravel the very fabric of their resolve. The very air hummed with a low, persistent thrum, a vibration that resonated deep within their bones, warning them of the path they were about to tread.

"Here lies your first trial," Azrael announced, his voice steady as they took their first hesitant steps into the dim corridor. "Embrace your fears, confront them head-on, and learn what Alaric failed to grasp."

The group advanced, hearts racing in unison, a frantic drumbeat against the encroaching silence. Initially shrouded in uncertainty, a mist of trepidation clinging to them like a damp shroud, they noticed the faint sound of anguished cries mixed with laughter echoing in the depths of the corridor. It wasn't just noise; it was a haunting symphony of rhetoric, a macabre opera played out in the shadows. The cries were sharp and piercing, laced with a desperate plea for release, while the laughter that entwined with them was hollow, mocking, and tinged with a manic energy that sent shivers down their spines. The sound reverberated off the cold, unforgiving walls, creating a disorienting echo that amplified the sense of unease. Each footstep forward was met with an increase in volume, a promise of confrontation with whatever madness lay ahead, and a stark realisation that their first uncertainty was rapidly solidifying into a chilling fear. The corridor seemed to breathe with the unsettling melody, drawing them deeper into its unsettling embrace, promising a revelation that they might not be ready to face.

"What is that sound?" Oliver whispered, instinctively stepping closer to the others.

"Fears brought to life," Luci elucidated. "They're manifestations of regret and forgotten enigmas—shadows that Alaric once let slip away. To unlock the door ahead, we must face these echoes together."

Ellie recalled the time when her passion for history had been challenged, when the opinions of doubters stung like bees in the back of her mind.

"I fear being unworthy, of never measuring up to the scholars I admire," she confessed, her voice trembling slightly.

"I share a similar trepidation," Professor Finch admitted, eyes shining with a flicker of vulnerability. "My biggest fear has always been being overshadowed in the pursuit of knowledge."

As Ellie and Professor Finch confided in each other, sharing the weight of their individual burdens, the oppressive shadows that had clung to them both began to recede. The internal murmurings of doubt, fear, and regret that had plagued their thoughts subsided like a distant tide, slowly ebbing away from the shore of their minds. In its place arose something profound and unexpected: a universal resonance of understanding, a shared experience that transcended their individual circumstances and connected them on a deeper, more fundamental level. It was a silent acknowledgement of shared humanity, a recognition of the inherent struggles and vulnerabilities that bound them together, offering solace and a newfound sense of hope.

"Together we are strong," Lady Arabella chimed, her voice regal and kind, encouraging further revelations. "What binds us as companions is greater than any individual fear we carry."

As each fear was voiced, hesitant at first and then with increasing conviction, the lingering shadows that clung to the edges of the corridor swirled and twisted, agitated by the light of their shared vulnerability. With each confession, the menacing shapes wavered, revealing their true forms – mere wisps of self-doubt, puffed up by isolation and uncertainty, that once had seemed so insurmountable. Finn, energized by the collective cleansing, cackled with delight. the sound echoing through the hallway as the darkness dissipated, not with a bang, but with a soft sigh of surrender, transforming into laughter and shared understanding. The weight lifted from their shoulders, replaced by a lightness they hadn't realised they were missing.

Suddenly, amidst the echoing laughter and the comfortable silence that followed, the corridor brightened, bathed in a soft, golden light that seemed to emanate from the very stones themselves. Suspended mid-air, bathed in this ethereal glow, was a glimmering key – an intricate piece of artisanry that pulsed with a gentle warmth. It was an ethereal prize, a tangible reward for their courage, a symbol of the obstacles they had overcome together. As Ellie, drawn by an irresistible force, reached out to claim it, her fingers brushed against the cool metal. At that moment, she felt a profound spark of connection with her companions, an invisible thread of unity, forged in the crucible of shared vulnerability, that twisted around them like the intricate threads of a tapestry, strengthening their bond and weaving them together into a single, resilient whole. She knew, with unwavering certainty, that whatever lay ahead, they would face it together.

"It appears we've solved the first riddle," Azrael noted with a proud smile. "But Alaric's tale is only beginning. We must keep our minds sharp, as the heart of the sorcerer's magic pumps through this museum."

With a nod of resolve, Ellie tucked the shimmering key securely in her pocket, the warmth of newfound bravery filling her spirit.

"What next?" Oliver asked, his earlier doubts beginning to fade.

Luci gestured meaningfully towards the withdrawing shadows, the first rays of dawn painting the cavern walls in streaks of grey. "With each step", she said, her voice hushed with reverence, "we'll need to attend to the sorcerer's lessons. The magic of the night will reveal itself only to those who seek understanding—not power. Alaric was a master of the subtle arts, a weaver of destinies, but he was ultimately undone by his ambition. Let us learn from his mistakes and listen to the whispers of the night."

As they appeared from the realm of shadows, stepping onto ground warmed by the burgeoning sunlight, Ellie felt a thrill coursing through her veins, mingling with the lingering chill of the dark places they had traversed. The tale of Alaric, the once-revered sorcerer, was no longer merely a story trapped in history books and dusty scrolls; it was alive, breathing with the same air they breathed, carrying the echoes of their adventures within its complex framework.

The air thrummed with anticipation, promising that further adventures lay ahead, adventures that would test their courage and push their limits. Treacheries, lurking in the shadows like ancient curses, were poised to ensnare them, forcing them to confront not only external threats but also the darkness within themselves. Yet, amidst the looming perils, the true power of companionship awaited them, a bond forged in shared danger and unwavering loyalty, the very anchor that would keep them grounded as they navigated the treacherous currents of time itself. They knew, with unwavering certainty, that their success, perhaps even their survival, depended on the strength of their unity and the unbreakable connection they shared.

THE BOOK OF SHADOWS

The museum, usually a mausoleum of quiet contemplation, hummed with a mystical energy tonight. Moonlight, fractured by the gothic windows, painted silver streaks across the polished marble floor, highlighting dust motes dancing in the air like captured spirits. Ellie, her eyes gleaming with intellectual fervour, circled the ornate pedestal. Professor Finch, his white beard a beacon in the dimness, adjusted his spectacles and leaned closer, his breath fogging the air around the ancient artefact. Oliver, a historian by trade but a sceptic by nature, fidgeted nervously beside him.

The object of their collective attention was the Book of Shadows, an ancient tome that lay ensconced in a pool of inky shadows. Its cover, crafted from what looked like petrified wood, was bound with tarnished silver clasps. The whispers they had followed, whispers swirling through academic circles and whispered in dusty libraries, suggested the book held secrets that transcended time itself. Secrets capable of shaping destinies or unravelling the very fabric of reality.

"Are we certain about this?" Oliver questioned, his voice a nervous tremor in the otherwise silent hall. He hadn't initially planned on being embroiled in a night filled with enchantments and puzzles, a world he'd only ever met in fictional narratives. Now, staring at the book's spine, etched with cryptic symbols that seemed to writhe in the low light, he felt a pang of trepidation that went beyond simple professional curiosity. The air itself felt thick, charged with an unseen power that made the hairs on the back of his neck stand on end. He swallowed hard, suddenly aware of the vast, silent museum looming around them, a labyrinth of forgotten stories and perhaps, tonight, of awakening magic.

"Absolutely," responded Harold, his eyes gleaming with excitement. "This is our chance to uncover the missing pieces of history! The artefacts have guided us here for a reason. The Book of Shadows could reveal the story behind each one of them."

"Just be cautious," Ellie added, adjusting her glasses as she stepped closer to the pedestal. "The last thing we need is to awaken something we can't control."

As the clock struck midnight, its chimes echoing through the silent halls of the museum, a shaft of pearlescent moonlight pierced through the tall, arched windows. The silvery beam landed directly upon the ancient tome resting on its velvet pedestal. Almost at once, its leather-bound cover, worn smooth with age and countless hands, began to tremble. Then, as if compelled by an invisible force, its pages flittered open, the delicate parchment rustling softly like whispers from a forgotten language. A silent, unseen breeze seemed to dance within the book, causing the illuminated text to shimmer and blur. With the pages unlocked, the room itself began to transform. A gentle, ethereal glow, born from the interaction of moonlight and ancient script, filled the space, casting long, dancing shadows on the walls and transforming the familiar museum artefacts into ghostly sentinels. The air crackled with an unseen energy, hinting at secrets untold and powers awakened.

"Azrael, is this normal?" Ellie asked, her heart racing with anticipation.

Out of the corner of her eye, she saw Azrael the Lion—his majestic form unmistakable—appearing from the shadows, his golden mane shimmering in the moonlight.

As the clock struck midnight, a shaft of pure, silver moonlight streamed through the tall, arched windows of the museum, cutting through the velvet darkness like a celestial blade. It fell directly upon the ancient tome resting on the pedestal, bathing it in an ethereal glow. Its leather-bound cover, etched with symbols that seemed to writhe in the shifting light, pulsed with a faint, inner energy. The pages, brittle with age and whispered secrets, flittered open as if stirred by an unseen breeze, revealing intricate illustrations and cryptic text that danced before the eye. The room, once silent and still, now buzzed with a palpable sense of anticipation.

"Normal? I believe the term here is 'extraordinary'!" Azrael replied, a hint of amusement lacing his deep voice. His imposing figure, cloaked in midnight blue, seemed to absorb the surrounding shadows. "The Book of Shadows is a portal, dear friends, to realms unseen, to realities beyond mortal comprehension. It is more than just ink and parchment; it's a key, a bridge, a gateway to the very heart of our quest. It will guide us through the labyrinth of challenges that lie ahead, illuminate the darkest corners of our path, if we dare to heed its call, if we are brave enough to face the truths it holds."

Huckleberry perched atop a nearby statue of a forgotten deity, flapped his immense, feathered wings, sending dust motes swirling in the moonlight. His golden eyes, sharp and ancient, scanned the group with a profound solemnity. A low, guttural caw echoed through the hall, laced with a warning ancient. "Beware, mortals, for knowledge comes at a price. Each secret revealed demands a sacrifice, and only the worthy, the pure of heart and strong of will, may seek its wisdom without being consumed by its power. The book judges, it tests, it breaks those who are not ready."

"The Book of Shadows is bound by ancient magic, woven from starlight and the essence of forgotten gods," Luci hissed, her voice a sibilant whisper that seemed to slither into the mind. Her bronze skin, shimmering with an almost hypnotic gleam, rippled as she slithered closer to the tome, her forked tongue tasting the magical energy in the air. "We must answer its riddles, decipher its veiled prophecies, to unveil the truth that lies hidden beneath the surface. Only then, when we have proven ourselves worthy, can we navigate the challenges that await us in the shadows. Only then will we understand the true nature of our enemy and find the key to his defeat."

Harold's enthusiasm was palpable as he leaned over the tome's pages, his breath catching in his throat with each new discovery. The ancient leather felt warm beneath his fingertips, and the aged parchment crackled softly as he turned each leaf, scanning the exquisite illustrations and intricate texts. He traced a finger along a depiction of a jewelled dagger, then another of a celestial map etched onto a silver plate. "Look!" he exclaimed, his voice barely above a whisper, as if afraid to disturb the silent stories held within the book. "Each illustration corresponds to an artefact in the museum, tied to a different story! It's a key, a guide to unlocking the secrets hidden within those objects!"

Finn, never one to be left out of the excitement, darted between their legs, his bushy tail twitching with anticipation. His amber eyes, wide with mischief and curiosity, gleamed in the dim light of the room. "Maybe I can find out if one of those stories involves a cunning fox!" he yipped, imagining himself as the hero of a long-forgotten legend.

Ignoring Finn's antics, Oliver, ever the pragmatist, pointed to a vivid illustration of a serpent, scales made in shimmering emerald ink, entwined around an ancient staff crafted from what looked like petrified wood. "What's this? Is that related to you, Luci?" he asked, his brow furrowed in thought. He remembered Luci's enigmatic nature, the hints she'd dropped about a past and a purpose beyond their understanding.

Luci nodded slowly, her usually playful eyes shimmering with a distant, weighty memory. The air around her seemed to subtly shift, and the flickering candlelight cast long, dancing shadows across her face. "Long ago," she began, her voice softer than usual, "I was the guardian of the staff that maintains the balance between realms. It's not merely a weapon or an artefact, but a conduit for the energies that hold the world together. When the time grows disordered, when the threads of fate begin to unravel, it is my duty to restore harmony." A hint of sadness tinged her words, as if the weight of that duty had been a burden for centuries.

Harold rubbed his chin thoughtfully, the stubble scraping against his fingers. "If we can find that staff, we may be able to influence the outcome of our adventure. It could be the key to... well, everything." He trailed off, gazing into the flickering firelight, his mind already picturing the ancient artefact and the power it might hold.

"Let's focus on the answers the book provides first," Ellie interjected, her voice sharp and practical against Harold's more fanciful musings. She flipped through the thicker pages; her brow furrowed in concentration until a particular section caught her eye. "Here! It speaks of a riddle—a way to unlock the knowledge we look for. It says understanding it will reveal the staff's true location."

"Gather 'round, everyone!" Azrael beckoned, his deep voice resonating in the small clearing. He extinguished a nearby torch, letting the remaining firelight cast long, dancing shadows. "Let us hear the riddle whispered from the pages of shadows. Prepare yourselves; these are not words to be taken lightly."

With a collective breath, the group huddled closer. Harold, Ellie, and even the usually stoic Azrael leaned in, their faces illuminated by the crackling flames. Ellie began to read, her tone hushed and reverent, the words unravelling in haunting, echoing tones, as if the book had a life of its own:

"In darkness I dwell, in secrets I wait,
To seek the light, you must tempt fate.
The knowledge I hold, a treasure unseen,
To unlock the past, keep your heart keen."

"Tempt fate, eh?" Oliver muttered, the scepticism still nagging him. "What does that mean?"

Ellie pondered, her brow furrowed in thought as she reread the cryptic inscription. "It doesn't mention a specific key, but rather a willingness to explore what we fear. Perhaps we need to confront our doubts, the insecurities that gnaw at the edges of our resolve." The weight of the unknown settled heavily in the ancient chamber, amplified by her words.

Finn, always the playful spirit, though often masking a deeper anxiety, leapt up onto the pedestal with an exaggerated flourish. "Time for some bravery then! Should we close our eyes and dive into the unknown, like jumping into a bottomless pit of... well, whatever scares us most?" He struck a heroic pose, but a flicker of unease betrayed his forced levity.

Azrael chuckled, his deep voice reverberating around them, a sound that seemed to both soothe and unsettle the very stones around them. "Bravery isn't closing your eyes and hoping for the best, but facing what lies ahead, even in darkness, with unobstructed vision and a steady hand. But it won't be easy; the trials that await will likely prey on our weaknesses, exploit our vulnerabilities. We need to work together, support each other, and expect the challenges."

"Agreed," Ellie said, her voice gaining strength. She took a deep breath, drawing courage from the determined faces of her companions. "Let's each focus on what we fear most and share it. Opening, exposing our vulnerabilities to each other, could unlock our way forward, forging a bond strong enough to overcome whatever awaits us." She looked from Finn to Azrael, a silent plea for their trust and honesty. The air crackled with anticipation, the unspoken fears hanging heavy between them, a tangible obstacle they needed to dismantle.

Harold nodded excitedly, "Excellent plan! What about you, Oliver? What do you fear?"

"I fear getting trapped in all this madness!" Oliver spat, his stubbornness still clinging. "What if we can't reverse whatever awaits us?"

"Fear can result in misunderstanding," Lady Arabella's shimmering voice cut into the conversation, echoing wisdom from centuries past. "Remember that while exploring the unknown may bring chaos, it also brings understanding."

"Insight from a statue!" Oliver exclaimed sceptically, though deep down he felt the weight of her wisdom. "What do you fear, then?"

"I fear that people will forget the stories these artefacts tell," Lady Arabella replied, her statue-like form regal yet vulnerable. "If we do not listen to their whispers, we lose our connection to the past. Each piece beholds a legacy we must honour."

"And what about you, Finn?" Ellie probed, wanting the dialogue to continue.

The lively fox, its russet fur practically glowing in the dappled sunlight filtering through the trees, paused mid-stride. Its lifelike eyes, a mesmerising shade of amber, sparkled with an almost mischievous glint. A playful twitch of its nose preceded its words, delivered in a voice surprisingly smooth and articulate. "I fear the dullness of the mundane! The predictable rhythm of sunrise and sunset, the unchanging paths... ugh! Adventure drives me, fuels this very fire within. But I admit," a slight tremor entered its voice, "sneaking through shadows at night, the rustle of unknown creatures in the undergrowth, it does make my heart race! A thrilling, delicious fear, perhaps, but fear nonetheless."

The fox's confession hung in the air, breaking the tension that had clung to the group like morning mist. One by one, they began to speak. The gruff bear, usually a bastion of stoic silence, admitted his fear of being alone, a vulnerability reflected in his lowered gaze. The nimble squirrel, always seemingly fearless as it leaped from branch to branch, confessed to a paralyzing fear of heights, a secret carefully guarded. The wise old owl, who dispensed wisdom with effortless grace, revealed her fear of losing her memory, of the knowledge she held fading into the twilight. Each confession was laced with vulnerability and raw honesty, stripped bare of pretence or bravado. In that shared space of fear, a newfound sense of unity blossomed, forging an unexpected bond between creatures who, until now, had only been acquaintances, bound together by circumstance rather than genuine connection. The rustling leaves seemed to whisper secrets of understanding, and the silent forest bore witness to a moment of profound intimacy forged in the crucible of shared vulnerability.

"Now, we conjure the courage to face this," Ellie concluded. Together, their voices rose as they spoke, "We will embrace the shadows!"

As they declared their resolve, their voices echoing with newfound determination, the Book of Shadows reacted in kind. Its ancient, brittle pages fluttered violently, as if an invisible hand were flipping through centuries of accumulated knowledge. Then, as abruptly as it began, the furious movement ceased, and the Book settled down, a warm, inviting glow emanating from its very core. This light wasn't merely illumination; it felt like a pulse of raw power, radiating outward to fill the room. The air itself thickened, becoming heavy with unseen energy, a tangible manifestation of the magic they were about to unleash. And as the energy intensified, the shadows in the corners of the room, usually static and benign, began to twist and dance with a life of their own. They writhed and coalesced, swirling into ghostly, ephemeral images – fleeting glimpses of forgotten battles, whispered secrets, and times long gone – offering a tantalising, and perhaps cautionary, preview of the forces they were now about to wield.

"Watch!" exclaimed Professor Finch, his eyes wide with astonishment. "The book is guiding us!"

Suddenly, the illustrations came to life, not gradually or subtly, but with a jarring, unexpected burst of energy, drawing them into a swirling vortex of light. It was a dizzying, disorienting sensation, a rush of colour and movement that stole their breath and blurred their vision. They were no longer in the museum's quiet chamber, a space of hushed tones and reverent whispers that now seemed a distant, faded memory; rather, they found themselves amidst a grand hall, a breathtaking and impossibly opulent space. Towering pillars, crafted from a material that shimmered like polished moonlight, lined the hall, reaching towards a vaulted ceiling lost in shadow. The pillars, draped in delicate, golden filigree, seemed to weave themselves into intricate and impossible patterns, adorned with cultured flowers unlike any they had ever seen. These flowers had impossible patterns and were adorned with cultured flowers unlike any they had ever seen, flowers that pulsed with an otherworldly glow, casting ethereal shadows that danced on the polished floor. The air hummed with a low, resonant energy, a tangible force that vibrated in their bones and hinted at the magic that permeated this extraordinary place.

"Where are we?" Oliver gasped, startled.

"This is the Keeper's domain," Azrael said solemnly. "We have ventured beyond ordinary realms; this place is held together by the wisdom of time and existence."

As they stepped forward, each movement a subtle dance of ambition, vying for focus amidst the breathtaking splendour of the gilded hall, their eyes were drawn to a disturbance in the periphery. A figure, impossibly still, stood silhouetted against a tapestry woven with scenes of forgotten epochs. Slowly, their attention coalesced, and they caught sight of an imposing figure shrouded in a cloak that seemed to merge seamlessly with the shadows clinging to the corners of the room. The very air around them seemed to hum with an unseen energy.

It was Valen the Timekeeper, is a legendary curator of destinies and a guardian of moments lost in the river of time. Their face, usually hidden, was partially illuminated by the soft glow emanating from the hall, revealing an enigmatic smile dancing on their lips—a smile that hinted at knowledge beyond comprehension and a power that could unravel the fabric of reality itself. The silence that followed was thick and heavy, punctuated only by the frantic beat of their hearts as they wondered what purpose lay behind this unexpected encounter.

"Welcome, brave souls," Valen's voice resonated through the grand hall like echoes in a canyon. "You have dared to tread where others falter."

"Guide us, please!" Ellie exclaimed, her voice unwavering despite their surroundings. "We seek knowledge about the artefacts we guard. We wish to learn their tales through the Book of Shadows!"

"Ah," Valen spoke with a knowing glint in their eye. "Every artefact has a piece of your hearts' desires, yet not every tale is one of comfort. Are you sure you wish to hear their secrets?"

The group exchanged glances, each pulse of courage surging through them like electricity. "We are ready!" they declared in unison.

"With courage as your key, the shadows will unveil what lies beneath."

Valen then gestured towards the Book of Shadows, a subtle movement that unleashed a cascade of light, sending shimmering ripples dancing across the room's surfaces. "Open it again, brave ones," he urged, his voice imbued with a power that resonated deep within them. "Let it show you the origins that bind each artefact to your quest, the threads of destiny woven through time that connect you all."

Ellie, the encouragement warming her resolve and strengthening the unseen bonds they shared, stepped forward once more. The weight of responsibility settled upon her shoulders, but fear was overshadowed by a profound sense of purpose. With a steady hand, she opened the Book of Shadows. It responded to her touch, the ancient pages turning with a life of their own, whispering secrets only she could now perceive.

Each mystical image materialised active journey of Luci, breathing life into forgotten histories of guardianship and even the unexplained fears that haunted Oliver, etched within the very fabric of his being—each story resonated with a chilling clarity. Each narrative, no matter how disparate on the surface, echoed their shared purpose, a purpose that spanned centuries and bound them together through the relentless currents of time. The Book revealed the intricate connections, the hidden lineage of their power, and the undeniable truth that their destinies were inextricably linked.

Ellie felt the connection deepening with each shared story, each carefully examined artefact. A sense of purpose, profound and undeniable, resonated within her. "We must embrace all parts of ourselves—the joys, the fears, the histories," she declared, her voice echoing slightly in the vast hall. "Each artefact tells a story not just of the past, of bygone eras and forgotten lives, but of who we are meant to become! They are echoes of potential; whispers of future selves forged in the crucible of experience."

With each revelation, with each whispered secret gleaned from the ancient objects, the shadows began to lift, swirling around them like a phosphorescent mist responding to the unveiling of truth. The darkness, once oppressive and daunting, now seemed almost... sentient, a living entity reacting to their journey. The more they learnt, the clearer their path became, as if the very artefacts were guiding their footsteps, illuminating the way forward with their hidden knowledge.

"So, this is it!" Finn exclaimed, his energy bubbling over, darting around in a playful circle. He ran his hand over a weathered tapestry, his eyes alight with understanding. "The shadows unite us through the narratives shared! We're not fighting the darkness; we're understanding it! We become stronger together, bound by the threads of history and empathy!"

Indeed, for in that sprawling hall, amidst the dust and the echoes of ages past, they realised that darkness held not just fear but the power of unity—the power of sharing history, acknowledging pain, and forging friendship in the face of the unknown. United through understanding, they became willing bearers of the artefacts' legacies, not just custodians of the past, story by story.

With each heartbeat, the anticipation thrummed a little louder, drawing them closer to the precipice of understanding. Ahead lay not just a world but a boundless expanse brimming with infinite possibilities, each one a glittering star in the vast cosmos of the unknown. Time, usually a relentless river, yielded to their purpose, bending gracefully as if charmed by their quest. Whispered tales, like fragments of a forgotten melody, illuminated their journey, patiently unravelling layers of forgotten history, revealing the intricate patterns of events long past. And the Book of Shadows, ancient and knowing, was ready to reveal even more, its pages shimmering with untold secrets waiting to be unlocked.

As they paused, poised to uncover their next step, a palpable sense of magic enveloped them, a comforting and empowering aura that settled like stardust on their shoulders. This magic wasn't just a spell or an enchantment; it was the invisible force forging unbreakable bonds between them, laying a solid foundation of trust and camaraderie that would carry them forth, together, throughout their adventurous quest. They knew, with a certainty that resonated deep within their souls, that they were stronger together than they could ever be apart.

For in the depths of the Enchanted Museum, a place where reality blurred with legend, they were not merely passive seekers of secrets. They were active participants, the very threads weaving the intricate and vibrant tapestry of a night destined to be rich with adventure, danger, and discovery. And as the shadows danced in the flickering candlelight, swirling around them like playful spirits, the Book of Shadows whispered promises, a soft murmur of hope for a destiny yet to be fully realised. It offered a tantalising glimpse of a fabled passage, a gateway to the wonders of mysteries still yet to be discovered, secrets that would perhaps reshape their understanding of everything they thought they knew.

ENCOUNTER AT
THE EXHIBIT

The air in the Enchanted Museum, a palpable blend of anticipation and a prickling unease. As Ellie and her companions cautiously ventured into the heart of the enormous hall, the scent of aged parchment, polished stone, and something indescribably magical permeated the air. It clung to the back of the throat, a lingering aftertaste reminiscent of a half-remembered dream. Flickering shadows danced against the marble walls, cast by ornate sconces that lined the corridor. These weren't mere light fixtures; they pulsed with an inner light, bathing the hall in an ethereal glow that both revealed and obscured. The museum had transformed, no longer a static repository but a realm of possibilities, an expansive tapestry of history woven together by the whispers of those who had walked before. Each footstep echoed, stirring dormant energies, awakening the spirits trapped within the artefacts.

At the towering entrance to the Ancient Civilisations Exhibit, Ellie paused, her heart pounding against her ribs. The archway was constructed from colossal blocks of granite, etched with hieroglyphs that seemed to writhe and shift beneath her gaze. "This is where we'll find the key," she declared, her mind racing to decipher the untold stories encoded within the artefacts. She felt a pull, a subtle magnetic force emanating from within, urging her forward. The air here was different – heavier, charged with the weight of forgotten rituals and long-dead kings.

Professor Finch, perched precariously, adjusted his glasses on his nose, peering intently at the large stone tablets adorning the walls. Intricate carvings depicting scenes of life, death, and the gods covered their surfaces. He traced a finger along the cool stone, muttering about forgotten languages and lost empires. "Indeed, Ellie. But we must tread carefully; each artefact holds a fragment of history laced with enchantment." His voice was a blend of caution and excitement, reflecting the thrill of uncovering forgotten lore. He knew the museum was more than just a collection of relics; it was a living, breathing entity, its magic potent but unpredictable, even dangerous in the wrong hands. He gripped his worn leather satchel tighter, a silent prayer on his lips for a safe and successful expedition into the heart of the past.

The air in the exhibit vibrated with anticipation, each member acutely aware of the weight of their mission. As if summoned by their hushed deliberations, Azrael the Lion stirred to life. Majestic and imposing, his massive frame cast long shadows in the dim light. He stepped forward, his paws silent on the ancient stone floor, his emerald eyes gleaming with an ageless wisdom that seemed to penetrate their very souls. "We must awaken the spirits of this exhibit," he intoned, his voice a resonant rumble echoing through the vast hall. Each word carried a solemnity that elevated their quest from a mere exploration into a sacred undertaking. "They will guide us to the secrets that lie within, secrets long dormant, waiting to be unveiled."

As the group prepared to move forward, heartened by Azrael's pronouncement, an unexpected sound echoed through the exhibit – a low, intriguing hiss, like wind whispering through dry leaves. From the shadows, Luci coiled herself around one of the ornate displays. Her bronze scales shimmered and rippled, reflecting the soft light with a hypnotic beauty. She raised her elegant head, her forked tongue flicking out, tasting the air, sampling the energies swirling around them. "Ah, young adventurers," she hissed, her voice a silken whisper that belied the sharpness of her words, "I sense your quest is searching for significance, a meaning woven into the fabric of this place. However, exercise caution, as not every enchanted entity can serve as your ally. The exhibit's very stones etch tales, cautioning against the perils of overconfidence and the hubris of the seeker of overconfidence, the hubris of the seeker."

Ellie, the de facto leader, straightened her shoulders, meeting Luci's gaze with unwavering resolve. "We understand," she said, her voice clear despite the underlying tension. "This is more than just a treasure hunt, a frivolous pursuit of trinkets. We are seeking knowledge and genuine understanding. She paused, adding with quiet sincerity, "We appreciate the warning. Caution will be our constant companion."

Before Luci could retort, a sudden rustling sliced through the hushed atmosphere of the ancient Egyptian exhibit. Oliver, the museum guard assigned to babysit the peculiar group, jumped visibly. He had been trailing them with a mixture of apprehension and reluctant fascination, his flashlight beam nervously dancing over the hieroglyphic-covered walls. "Could we please try to keep it down?" he whispered, his voice barely heard above the hum of the museum's ventilation system. He glanced around, his eyes wide and darting, as if expecting the ghosts of pharaohs to materialise from the shadows. "This all feels like a bad dream, and I'm really not sure I want to be in it. Yesterday, it was just touring groups and dusty artefacts. Now... presently, this."

"It's hardly a dream, Oliver," Finn chimed in, his voice a cheerful counterpoint to the guard's anxiety. The small, articulated wooden fox darted playfully between their legs, his polished joints clicking softly against the marble floor. A cheeky grin seemed permanently etched on his painted wooden face. "It's an adventure! A thrilling, one-of-a-kind adventure! And you've got to admit, where else can you chat with a majestic lion and a slithering serpent? It's not exactly your average Tuesday, is it?"

"A lion and a serpent? What nonsense!" Oliver retorted, though a reluctant smile tugged at the corners of his mouth. He folded his arms, trying, and failing, to look stern. The sight of the talking fox, the regal lion statue now animated, and the serpent carving that had inexplicably come to life was still playing havoc with his sense of reality. He couldn't help but feel a spark of the magic enveloping them all, a tiny ember of wonder flickering in the face of his ingrained scepticism. Perhaps this 'bad dream' wasn't so bad after all.

Professor Finch, completely oblivious to the museum guard's hesitant expression and the uncertainty flickering in his eyes, pointed enthusiastically at the artefacts filling the exhibit. His spectacles gleamed under the warm light, reflecting the excitement bubbling within him. "Look at this! Ancient scrolls! We might decipher languages long forgotten! Imagine the knowledge we could unlock!" He rushed over to the scrolls, his fingers trembling slightly as he adjusted his glasses and began examining them with feverish fervour, mumbling incantations of academic delight. He was a man consumed by the allure of history, lost in the whispers of the past.

Ellie and her companions, a diverse trio ranging from the studious to the pragmatic, followed at a more measured pace, their eyes wide with a mixture of curiosity and caution. But Finn, ever the impish spirit and the resident wildcard, darted ahead with a mischievous grin to investigate a nearby display of bejewelled daggers and ceremonial masks. "I'll see what treasures I can uncover; just follow the trail of mischief! If there are any riddles to solve or traps to trigger, you know I'll find them!" he exclaimed, his voice echoing slightly in the vast hall as he vanished around the corner, leaving a lingering sense of playful anticipation hanging in the air. He thrived on the unknown and the thrill of the unexpected, a stark contrast to the Professor's methodical approach.

As the group proceeded towards the exhibit, leaving the familiar hum of the city behind, the atmosphere underwent a subtle, almost imperceptible shift. The warm glow of the sconces, previously a comforting presence, seemed to brighten unnaturally, casting exaggerated shadows that danced across the walls. The light illuminated a vast mural stretching across an entire wall, depicting the rise and fall of countless civilisations in a swirling panorama of vibrant colours and intricate details. It felt as if the very walls were whispering secrets, unravelling their epic stories of triumph and tragedy, a silent symphony of history played out in stone and paint. The air grew thick with the weight of ages, pressing down on them with the untold tales of empires long gone. A sense of both wonder and unease settled upon them, a poignant reminder of the fleeting nature of existence.

Beneath the mural, a tapestry of faded glories and cryptic symbols, a massive stone pedestal awaited, cloaked in an ethereal mist that swirled and danced like restless spirits. The air thrummed with an almost palpable energy, a hum resonating deep within their bones. At its centre sat a delicate hourglass, defying the immensity of its surroundings. its crystalline structure, unlike any crystal Ellie had ever seen, sparkled with an inner fire, mimicking the constellations above them. It was as if stars had been plucked from the night sky and imprisoned in time within its fragile form.

"The Hourglass of Echoes," Ellie breathed, her voice barely a whisper lost in the vastness of the chamber. Astonishment painted her features, her eyes wide with awe and a touch of trepidation. "Legends say it reveals the past through whispers to those who dare to listen. That it can unlock forgotten memories and show the true faces of those long gone."

Azrael stepped closer, his imposing figure casting a long shadow that momentarily swallowed the hourglass in darkness. A rumbling growl, deep and guttural, vibrated through the stone beneath their feet. "We must commune with it," he said, his voice a low, commanding baritone. "It holds the lore of these artefacts, the secrets of their creation and purpose. And it might, just might, lead us to Valen. He is the key to stopping this madness and restoring order."

Ellie, the Professor, and Oliver stood shoulder to shoulder, forming a united front against the unknown as they cautiously approached the hourglass. Oliver cautiously approached the hourglass. The air grew colder, the mist thickening around their feet as they drew nearer. "We need to ask the right questions," Ellie said, her voice ringing with a newfound determination. The first awe had faded, replaced by a steely resolve. "Dr Bell's awakening was no mere coincidence – it was a tremor, a ripple in time caused by the artefacts. This hourglass is our key, our compass in this labyrinth of the past. We need to understand what happened to Dr Bell and, more importantly, how to prevent it from happening again." She reached out a tentative hand, hovering just above the shimmering surface, ready to examine the echoes of time.

At that moment, Lady Arabella's statue— having stood quietly in the corner of the hall for centuries, a marble sentinel of forgotten stories— shifted. A low, grinding sound echoed as the stone figure seemed to awaken, its eyes, previously dull and lifeless, now gleaming with an inner light. "In every artefact lies a truth," she spoke, her voice melodious yet commanding, resonating with the weight of ages. It was a voice that both soothed and challenged, a siren's call to the inquisitive mind.

"What do you mean?" Ellie asked, captivated by the depth of Lady Arabella's words. She felt a shiver run down her spine, a blend of fear and exhilaration. This was no ordinary history lesson; this was something profound, something magical. Her heart pounded in her chest, eager to find out what was missing.

"The past is not just a collection of dates and facts," she replied, the statue's gaze seeming to pierce through Ellie, seeing something deep within her soul. "It is entwined with emotion: joy, sorrow, love, and loss. Every artefact knows its bearer's story, the triumphs and tragedies woven into its very essence. To unlock its wisdom, you must connect to the heart of history, feel the pulse of the past, and understand the human spirit that breathed life into these objects. Only then will the truth reveal itself." A faint, sweet fragrance, like dried roses and ancient parchment, filled the air, further intensifying the surreal atmosphere. The statue remained still once more, but the echo of her words lingered, a tantalising invitation to further investigate the mysteries dormant within the ancient hall.

Ellie's brow furrowed in thought, a network of tiny wrinkles forming above her intense gaze. The ancient hourglass, with its rumoured secrets hidden within its swirling sands, weighed heavily on her mind. "We must open our hearts to the stories of these artefacts, not just see them as relics of a forgotten past," she declared, her voice hushed with reverence. "Perhaps then, and only then, the hourglass will share its secrets, revealing the truths it has guarded for centuries."

Huckleberry, the raven familiar who always accompanied Ellie on her historical escapades, shifted his weight on the hourglass's pedestal. He ruffled his obsidian feathers, the movement a subtle gesture of approval. "Approach it with respect, little historian," he croaked, his voice raspy with age and wisdom, each word echoing slightly in the cavernous exhibit hall. "Let the echoes guide your inquiry. The past speaks in whispers, if you only know how to listen."

A palpable tension filled the air as Ellie, Huckleberry, and the others surrounded the hourglass. The heavy, still atmosphere was shattered by a rush of wind, swirling within the sealed exhibit. A faint, ethereal mist lifted, dancing with the wind, coalescing into strange, shifting shapes. The shapes twisted, resolving themselves into fleeting images and whispers. The whispers, fragmented at first, began to form words, faint and fragile, lingering momentarily before dissolving back into the mist. The air crackled with unseen energy, the past reaching out to meet them.

"**What do you look for?**" the voices intertwined, questioning yet inviting.

Ellie exchanged glances with her group. "We seek knowledge of the past—answer our questions, guide us to Valen."

"**The hold of time is both a burden and a gift," **the whispers replied.** "To move forward, you must first confront the past. What truth do you wish to behold? **"

Professor Finch stepped forward, apprehension masking his excitement. His fingers, gnarled and stained with ink, twitched at his side. "The artefacts—their origins, their legacies. We wish to know their stories!" He addressed not just the hourglass but the Archives themselves, steeped in history and whispering secrets. He had dedicated his life to unravelling mysteries, and the energy emanating from the hourglass promised a tale unlike any other.

The hourglass shimmered brilliantly, an ethereal beacon, and the whispers intensified, wrapping around the group like an old tune, both comforting and unsettling. The air crackled. "In the shadows of the past, find the guardian; in the echoes of time, search for the thread. Only then may Valen reveal their tale." The words resonated with a power that bypassed intellect and struck at the soul. The pronouncement felt less like a riddle and more like a key.

Suddenly, the ground trembled beneath their feet, the subtle vibrations escalating into a low, resonant hum. The hourglass began to glow with an increasingly intense light, swirling with iridescent colours that defied earthly categorisation. It was as if a miniature galaxy had been captured within its glass confines. The whispers transformed into vibrant images – scenes materialising before them, projected upon the very air. Long-forgotten moments, frozen in time, unfolded before their astonished eyes: warriors in gleaming armour preparing for battle, artists lost in inspiration, families woven through the tapestry of history. The images flickered and shifted, promising a journey through time itself, guided by Valen and the secrets hidden within the guardian and the thread.

"We see!" Ellie gasped, mesmerised by the images. "Each artefact carries the essence of those who crafted it."

Oliver stared, slack-jawed, as a soldier raised his sword in triumph. "This is amazing! They're all living their stories..."

"Yes," Finn chimed in, returning from his mischievous escapades. "Stories sleeping, waiting for you to wake them!"

"**And here lies the guardian,**" the whispers said—stronger this time.

The chamber seemed to warp and bend as unseen energies gathered. A swirling vortex of dust motes and memories danced, coalescing into discernible shapes. Then, the magnificent guardian took form.

He was a towering being, cloaked in the absence of light. Shadow clung to him like a second skin, obscuring details yet accentuating raw power. His face was hidden, yet his gaze pierced through the obscurity, holding the weight of centuries.

His voice was a resonant hum, laced with the rustle of parchment and the distant tolling of bells. "I am the Guardian of Time. To learn from the past is to carry the light of knowledge into the future. Ignore the lessons from the past, and you will inevitably replicate their errors.

Ellie's heart raced. The sheer size of the being was overwhelming. Yet, she found her voice. "We wish to understand. We seek Valen."

The guardian nodded, a slow movement of considered wisdom. "Then embrace the echoes in your hearts. Allow yourselves to be swept away by the currents of what was and what might have been. Only in understanding the complex tapestry of moments past, in grasping the consequences of choices made and unmade, will the path before you lead your way to Valen Timekeeper." He paused, his gaze intensifying. "But be warned, children of the present. The past is a treacherous sea. Lose yourselves within its depths, and you may never find your way back."

As Ellie and her friends focused their energy, the hourglass began to spin with increasing ferocity. The fine grains of sand within became a blur, mirroring the dizzying sensation as they were drawn into a transfixing whirl of light and sound. All around them, history unfolded like a thrilling tapestry.

At that moment, a chill swept through the air, sharper than any winter wind. A palpable sense of gravity settled in the room as a new presence approached. Oliver turned instinctively, his eyes widening. At the edge of the scene stood a figure clad in robes of deep indigo and silver – Valen, the Timekeeper. His presence radiated an ancient power, a silent authority that commanded respect.

"I am here," he announced, his voice deep as the silence of time itself. "You have awakened the murmurs of history, disturbed the sleep of ages. Are you ready to embrace your destiny? To face the consequences of your actions?" His gaze swept over each of them, piercing any doubt.

Ellie felt a knot of clarity form in her chest, a sense of purpose solidifying. The swirling chaos seemed to still, allowing her to focus. New resolve pulsed within her. She nodded firmly. surrounded by her friends. The magic of the museum was irrevocably intertwining their fates. They stood firm, a united front, ready to confront whatever awaited them.

As the light intensified, bathing them in an ethereal glow, they took their first step. It was a deliberate stride towards unravelling history's secrets, understanding its burdens, and unveiling their true destinies. The journey had begun, and there was no turning back.

THE WEAVING OF FATES

The Hall of Intertwined Destinies held its breath, the myriad orbs pulsing with a softer, gentler light. Exhaustion, both physical and emotional, began to creep into the group. The sheer size of the place, the weight of history, and the dizzying visions of what could be had taken their toll.

"We need to focus," Ellie said, her voice firm, though laced with fatigue. "We can't just wander aimlessly through the timestream. We need a goal, a destination."

Professor Finch, ever the pragmatist, adjusted his in time where they are significant."

Lady Arabella, ever the observant and wise one, floated closer to the shimmering mirror, her regal aura radiating an ancient understanding. "Look," she said, her voice echoing with an otherworldly resonance. "The threads... they are beginning to converge. The tapestry is revealing a location."

Everyone turned their attention back to the mirror, where the swirling colours were now coalescing, forming a more distinct image. The chaos was subsiding, replaced by a clearer picture of a bustling city, a marketplace filled with vibrant colours and exotic smells. The architecture was unlike anything they had ever seen, a blend of ancient and futuristic styles. The air hummed with an energy that felt both familiar and alien.

"What is this place?" Mariana asked, her eyes wide with wonder.

"I believe", Azrael said, his voice low and resonant, "we are looking at Alexandria, Egypt. But not Alexandria as it exists in your present. This is Alexandria during the reign of Cleopatra, a time of immense learning, innovation, and political intrigue."

Oliver shifted nervously. "Egypt? Isn't that...dangerous? I mean, pyramids and sand and... mummies!"

Ellie ignored Oliver's apprehension, her mind already racing. "The serpent and the key... what significance could they have in Cleopatra's Alexandria?"

Huckleberry, ever the observant, interjected, understanding of magic. The serpent, a symbol of wisdom and power, could stand for her reign. The key... perhaps it unlocks a secret, a hidden knowledge that Cleopatra possessed."

"But what secret?" Mariana asked, "Could you explain what we should expect to find?"

"A new image rippled across the surface of the mirror, this time a close-up of the key from the tapestry. It was intricately designed, with hieroglyphs etched into its surface. One hieroglyph stood out: a symbol of a phoenix rising from the ashes.

"The Phoenix", Professor Finch breathed, his voice filled with awe. "The Phoenix symbolises rebirth and immortality." Could Cleopatra have been searching for the secret to eternal life?"

Azrael nodded gravely. "It is a possibility. Cleopatra was known to dabble in alchemy and other esoteric arts. The key could unlock a secret chamber, a hidden library, containing the secrets of the Phoenix.

Ellie felt a surge of excitement, tempered by a healthy dose of trepidation. "So, our destiny is to travel to Cleopatra's Alexandria, find the key, and uncover the secrets of the Phoenix. But what if it's a trap? What if Cleopatra herself is guarding this secret?"

Lady Arabella smiled enigmatically. "That, my dear Ellie, is for you to discover. The tapestry has revealed the path; it is up to you to walk it."

Finn darted to the front. "Let's go! Let's go! What are we waiting for? Adventure awaits!"

"Patience, Finn," Ellie said, "We need to be prepared. We don't know what we're walking into."

She looked around at her companions, their faces reflecting a mixture of excitement and apprehension. She knew that they were all in this together, bound by fate and a shared sense of purpose.

"Alright," she said, her voice resonating with newfound resolve. "Let's gather our strength, prepare our minds, and step into the heart of Cleopatra's Alexandria. The secrets of the Phoenix await us, and we will be ready to face whatever challenges lie ahead."

With a deep breath, Ellie stepped forward, her hand outstretched towards the shimmering mirror. The others followed suit, their hearts pounding with anticipation. As their fingers touched the cool surface of the glass, the world around them dissolved once again into a swirling vortex of colours and sensations.

They were on their way to Cleopatra's Alexandria, ready to find out the truth about the past and forge their destinies in the sands of time. The stakes were high, the dangers were real, but they were not afraid. They were the museum's guardians, protectors of history, and ready for whatever the tapestry had in store. were ready to face whatever the tapestry had in store for them.

The air crackled with anticipation as they embarked on their next chapter, a thrilling journey into the heart of ancient Egypt, where the secrets of the Phoenix awaited their discovery.

THE MOONLIT ESCAPE

The clock in the grand hall chimed midnight, its twelve melancholic bongs reverberating through the hallowed spaces of the Enchanted Museum. The sound bounced off centuries-old tapestries and polished marble floors, creating a ghostly echo that seemed to whisper forgotten secrets. Shadows, long and distorted, danced across the walls as the cold, ethereal moonlight streamed through the tall, arched windows, painting silver streaks on the dust motes swirling in the air. This filtered light illuminated the faces of three unlikely companions: Ellie , a bright-eyed history student with an insatiable curiosity; Professor Finch, a renowned but eccentric antiquarian, his tweed jacket perpetually rumpled and his spectacles perched precariously on his nose; and the reluctant guard, Oliver, a middle-aged man whose dreams of a quiet night shift were about to be thoroughly shattered. The air grew thick with anticipation, a palpable tension that hummed beneath the silence. Then, it happened. With a low growl that vibrated deep within the museum's foundations, Azrael the Lion, the museum's star attraction – a meticulously crafted automaton of solid gold – stirred. His golden eyes, previously lifeless and still, shimmered with a sudden, unnerving life. A low, mechanical whirring filled the air, gears grinding to life after decades of slumber. And with that single, breathtaking moment of animation, a new adventure, fraught with mystery and danger, unfolded before them, promising to unravel the very fabric of the Enchanted Museum.

"Quickly! We have but a fleeting hour before dawn," Azrael rumbled, his voice echoing like distant thunder. Ellie's heart raced at the prospect of the night's escapades, the sense of urgency intoxicating.

"I can't help but feel we're being watched," muttered Oliver, peering into the dark recesses of the museum. The once-quiet halls now felt alive with unseen presences.

"Perhaps it's the spirits of history, urging us on," Professor Finch chuckled, adjusting his spectacles. "Or maybe the enchantments of the museum itself." He stayed undeterred by the unease that clung to Oliver like a heavy cloak.

Just then, Luci, a creature of myth and legend, unfolded from her resting place atop a weathered stone pedestal. Her bronze scales, catching the faint light, glimmered under the moon's ethereal glow like a thousand polished coins. The air around her crackled with an unseen energy as she straightened, her serpentine grace a captivating paradox of power and fluidity. "Fear not, brave souls!" her voice resonated, a low, hypnotic hum that seemed to vibrate in their very bones. "The paths we traverse tonight will reveal secrets beyond your wildest dreams; truths etched in the fabric of time itself. But you must heed my guidance, for these secrets are guarded by trials and veiled in illusions." With a sinuous movement that defied gravity, she slithered gracefully through the air, her form almost disappearing into the swirling mist before reappearing, presenting a rolled scroll made of ancient parchment. The scroll etched a complex puzzle; the age-worn ink had faded and cracked, a testament to the centuries it had endured was etched a complex puzzle; the ink had faded and cracked with age, a testament to the centuries it had survived. Ellie, her eyes wide with a mixture of awe and trepidation, leaned forward. Her historian's mind, a labyrinth of dates, languages, and lost civilisations, raced to decipher the cryptic riddle. The thrill of the chase, the allure of the unknown, washed over her, momentarily eclipsing her fear. Squinting in the dim light, she read aloud, "'In the embrace of night, where shadows meet, find the heart of the lion beneath the unseen.' What could it mean?" She chewed on her lip; her brow furrowed in concentration. "A constellation? Could it possibly be a hidden chamber? Could it be a symbolic depiction? symbolic representation? The 'unseen' implies something hidden, something beyond plain sight... This job will be challenging." "Follow me!" Azrael beckoned, leading the way toward the museum's vast heart, where the colossal murals of past legends covered the walls. The trio hurried after him, Oliver stumbling slightly, hesitant about the path ahead.

As they moved deeper into the museum, a palpable sense of ancient magic thickened the air. Finn, no longer just a wooden carving brought to life but a creature imbued with boundless energy and mischievous spirit, darted past, a streak of polished wood and foxy enthusiasm. He was their guide, their beacon, leading them further into the labyrinthine museum, a maze of wonders both beautiful and unsettling. "Over here!" Finn chirped, his voice a high-pitched melody, almost gleefully. "The way forward is through the Gallery of Echoes. Shadows speak and secrets murmur in the Gallery of Echoes, where time itself seems to bend and whisper its forgotten stories. The Gallery of Echoes, where shadows speak and secrets murmur, appears to bend and whisper its forgotten stories. The group, a motley collection of brave souls and curious onlookers, followed Finn, their hearts pounding with a mixture of excitement and trepidation. They entered the Gallery of Echoes, and true to Finn's word, the air shimmered with unseen forces. A cacophony of whispers lingered, swirling around them like a restless wind. Tales from the past unfurled like a tapestry woven from countless voices, a symphony of forgotten moments and half-remembered desires.

Light played tricks on their eyes, creating phantoms and fleeting glimpses of figures long gone. At the far end of the gallery, Lady Arabella stood poised in her alcove, a statue of remarkable grace and power. Her regal features, usually stoic and impervious, were now illuminated by the flickering and dancing shadows, giving her an air of ethereal beauty and haunting sadness. The shadows seemed to cling to her, highlighting the fine lines etched around her eyes, hinting at the weight of centuries and secrets she had borne. A hush fell over. The group watched as Lady Arabella's gaze, sharp and knowing despite her stony form, settled on Ellie. "Child of Time", she addressed Ellie, her voice a low, resonant echo that seemed to vibrate from the very walls of the gallery. "The whispers are here – listen closely. Time", she addressed her, her voice a low, resonant echo that seemed to vibrate from the very walls of the gallery, "the whispers here – listen closely. The key lies within their grasp. They'll help you find the truth hidden in darkness, obscured by time and those who want to control it.

They urge you to find the truth hidden in darkness, obscured by time and the deceit of those who seek to control it. But be warned, child, for some secrets are best left undisturbed, and the path to truth is often paved with peril."

"What truth?" Ellie asked, captivated by the statue's composure.

"The truth binds the past to the present; it holds the key to your escape." Her voice flowed like a gentle stream, calming Ellie's racing thoughts. "But beware, for only the brave will tread into the depths of the unknown."

A sense of responsibility, heavy and profound, washed over Ellie, settling deep within her bones. She could feel the weight of history, not just the dusty tomes and forgotten kings, but a living, breathing entity beckoning her forward. The fate of something, maybe even everything, rested on her shoulders. "We must solve this riddle," she declared, her voice ringing with newfound conviction, "then move towards the heart of the lion." She glanced back at Azrael, whose gaze was unwavering, a silent promise of support etched on his face. His presence was a grounding force, a reminder that she wasn't alone in this daunting task. The whispers, a chorus of voices both ancient and ethereal, continued to swirl around them, urging them towards the next chamber. It was an exhibition of artefacts, each piece shimmering with an unearthly light that seemed to pulse with a life of its own. Intricate carvings adorned the walls, depicting scenes of long-forgotten battles and mythical creatures. And perched atop a display case, as if guarding its secrets, was Huckleberry. His ebony feathers caught the moonlight filtering through a high, arched window, giving him an almost spectral appearance. "Caw! The heart you seek lies beneath, but be cautious," he cawed, his voice a low, gravelly rumble that echoed through the chamber. "Time is not your ally," he added, his eyes sparkling with a strange mixture of mischief and ancient wisdom, hinting at a hidden danger. The presence of Valen, the one who had set this all in motion, loomed larger in Ellie's mind. She could almost feel his dark influence, a chilling presence that threatened to suffocate them. He was a formidable opponent, and she knew he wouldn't hesitate to use any means necessary to achieve his goals. If they were to overcome this obstacle, if they were to claim the heart of the lion and prevent Valen from unleashing its power, they needed to solve the enigma before the first rays of dawn shattered their enchanted night, revealing them, vulnerable, to the coming day. The stakes were higher than ever, and every second counted. "Underneath what?" Oliver asked, glancing nervously around the chamber, sensing the urgency pulsing through the air.

"Look here", Ellie pointed to a pedestal bearing the inscription carved in a forgotten tongue, "This symbol—it's the same as the one from earlier! The heart of the lion." She knelt, tracing the outline of the symbol with her finger.

"It's a mechanism, isn't it?" Professor Finch exclaimed, his eyes alight with intrigue. "A hidden passage—perhaps leading to the lion's core."

With steady hands that belied the frantic hammering of her heart, Ellie pressed at various points of the intricate symbol etched into the ancient floor. Each touch was deliberate; a memorised sequence gleaned from crumbling scrolls and whispered legends. Gears, long dormant, groaned and creaked in protest, their rusty voices echoing in the otherwise silent chamber. Dust motes danced in the air as a hidden trapdoor, seamlessly integrated into the stone, slowly revealed itself beneath their feet. A faint, ethereal glow radiated from within the newly opened passage, painting the faces of the assembled group in an otherworldly light. The air grew thick with anticipation, a palpable wave of excitement and trepidation washing over them as they stared into the unknown depths. This was it. This was the moment they had risked everything for.

"Prepare yourselves," Azrael growled, stepping closer, emanating warmth and protection. "We shall enter the lion's heart together."

They descended into the narrow stairs, each step echoing like thunder in their ears, amplified by the oppressive silence and the unknown that awaited them below. Dust motes danced in the light filtering from above, momentarily illuminating their anxious faces. The dim light of the moon barely reached this lower realm, a subterranean world where shadows clung to the walls like secrets. It illuminated strange, ancient carvings that vibrated with an almost palpable energy. These weren't mere decorations; they were stories etched in stone, tales of kingdoms and civilisations long gone whispered through time, their grandeur and follies frozen in silent testimony. The very stone seemed to hum with the weight of forgotten rituals and the ghosts of long-dead kings. As they reached the bottom, the cramped confines of the staircase gave way to an expansive chamber that unfurled before them like a forgotten dream. It was a space of immense proportions, glimmering with the remnants of lost treasures—shards of pottery, fragments of shimmering metal, and the ghostly outlines of what must have once been magnificent tapestries. This wasn't just a room; it was a cathedral of history, a testament to ages past. The air was thick with enchantment, heavy with the scent of damp earth and the lingering aroma of incense used centuries ago. It reverberated with the call of epochs long past, a symphony of whispers that stirred the imagination and hinted at the untold stories hidden within these ancient walls. A sense of awe and trepidation settled upon them, for they knew they were standing on hallowed ground, a place where time itself seemed to have taken a breath. "Can you feel it?" Ellie murmured, catching sight of ethereal threads weaving through the air, connecting the artefacts to each other. "This... this is where time converges."

Finn leapt onto a pedestal, his eyes sparkling with mischief. "Look! The heart of the lion!" he squeaked, pointing to a colossal statue of Azrael, his spirit captured in stone.

"But what does it mean? What are we supposed to do?" Oliver fretted, glancing around nervously, as shadowy figures began to swirl in the chamber.

"Focus on the riddle, Ellie!" Professor Finch encouraged. "What does it say about the heart?"

"In the embrace of night, where shadows convene..." Ellie repeated, her eyes scanning the room, "We need to perform an action! It must be a way to channel the energy!"

With newfound determination, she approached the statue, her fingers brushing against the lion's thick fur. It was like striking a tuning fork—a resonance filled the air. The echoes of time grew louder, the shadows coalescing.

"Everyone, join in!" she called, gesturing for the others to gather. "We must stand together, embodying the courage of the lion!"

In that moment, they formed a circle, each person stealing strength from one another. Azrael, Finn, and even Oliver lent their energies to Ellie, who centred herself amid the flow of time.

"Together, we are strong!" Ellie cried, summoning the spirit of unity. The museum surged with life, energised by their collective resolve.

Suddenly, the chamber brightened, illuminating the heart of the lion. A glowing orb pulsed in the lion's chest, radiating warmth and a calming presence that encompassed the entire room.

"Quickly! Speak the words!" shouted Professor Finch as the shadows closed in.

"May history remains alive!" they echoed as one, their voices intertwining.

With a blinding flash that seared afterimages onto Ellie's retinas, the orb pulsed with raw power, propelling the encroaching shadows back into the recesses from which they'd spawned. The very fabric of time seemed to unravel itself, the ages unfurling like an aged scroll revealing its secrets. Ellie felt the weight of epochs crash over her, an overwhelming sensory bombardment. She glimpsed the clash of ancient battles; the spectral legions locked in eternal combat. Visions of long-lost realms, shimmering with forgotten magic and whispered promises, danced before her eyes. And beneath it all, the faintest echoes, the sorrowful whispers of every soul who had ever walked, loved, and suffered within these walls brushed against her consciousness, leaving her breathless and disoriented. The chamber trembled, the stone floor vibrating beneath their feet. Reality itself seemed to buckle and sway, mirroring the temporal chaos unleashed by the orb. The air crackled with unstable energy, a tangible force that threatened to rip them apart. "Now! Move!" Azrael bellowed, his voice a gravelly shout cutting through the disorienting whirlwind. He gripped Ellie's arm, his eyes blazing with urgency, guiding them back toward the narrow passageway. The spatial relations of the chamber seemed to shift with each pulse of energy, making navigation a dizzying challenge. They scrambled up the treacherous, dust-choked stairs, each step a battle against the temporal currents. Oliver's face was scrunched in fierce concentration, his brow furrowed as he strained to keep pace with the thrumming beat of history pulsing violently through them. He seemed to be anchoring them, his will a fragile shield against the chaos. There was no time to waste. The shadows would regroup, the temporal distortions would intensify, and failure meant being lost forever in the labyrinthine echoes of the past. Just as they burst back into the expansive gallery, the delicate chime of dawn, amplified a thousandfold by the residual energy, echoed through the museum. It was a sound of hope, a promise of renewal, but also a warning. A final surge erupted from the lion statue, a blinding light emanating from its very heart. This wasn't the chaotic burst of the orb, but a focused, controlled release. The light cascaded through the museum like a wave of golden energy, washing over the artefacts, the walls, and finally, over them. Leaving behind... something different. The air crackled with anticipation; the game, it seemed, was far from over. "Quickly!" shouted Luci, as the light danced around them, illuminating the artefacts and breathing life back into them. "To the exit! Before we lose the magic!"

With Azrael leading the way and the rest united in purpose, they rushed through the corridors, shadows fading before them, the enchantment weaving around them like a gentle breeze.

Finally, bursting out the main doors, they found themselves bathed in the soft hues of dawn. The world was awakening, and the magic of the night gracefully retreated, concealing itself until the moon's next ascent.

"We did it!" Ellie exclaimed, breathless and exhilarated, her heart racing with the thrill of adventure.

"Indeed," Professor Finch replied, slightly out of breath but elated. "The whispers of the night have guided us true. We are bound by history and friendship."

"Now, let's not forget what we've learnt," Olive said, a newfound respect for the museum glowing in his eyes. "There's still so much more to uncover."

As they turned back towards the museum, the rising sun cast a golden glint off the polished stone of the entrance, each reflective surface hinting at the countless mysteries still nestled within its walls. The adventure they had just experienced, thrilling and perilous as it was, felt not like an ending, but a prologue. It was only the beginning, not just of their exploration through the labyrinthine corridors and forgotten chambers, but of the relationships forged in the crucible of shared danger and uncertainty. Together, they had braved the shadows that clung to the ancient artefacts, deciphered the cryptic riddle of the stone lion, and appeared not only victorious but deeply connected. A bond, stronger than any they had known before, had been forged; a silent pact of trust and camaraderie that surpassed the limitations of time itself. In the hollow silence of the dawning morning, a stillness broken only by the chirping of birds and the distant hum of the city, the very stones of the Enchanted Museum seemed to vibrate with a subtle magic. It whispered a silent, yet undeniable, promise for countless adventures to come - adventures that awaited them just beyond the threshold, beckoning them into a future shimmering with possibility and untold wonders. The museum held its breath, waiting for their return, a silent invitation to delve deeper into its captivating embrace.

SECRETS OF
THE COLLECTOR

The grand hall of the Enchanted Museum had transformed into a kaleidoscope of shadows and light, each flicker and whisper hinting at the secrets slumbering within its ancient walls. Moonlight, fractured by the stained-glass windows depicting forgotten lore, painted dancing patterns on the marble floor, illuminating dust motes swirling like tiny, restless spirits. Cobwebs, usually the mark of neglect, now shimmered with an ethereal glow, woven with threads of captured magic. As the clock in the tower struck the first hour of midnight, its chimes echoing with a hauntingly melodious resonance, a hush enveloped the artefacts. Silent suits of armour seemed to straighten their shoulders, forgotten portraits watched with newly animated eyes, and the very air crackled with untapped power, allowing Ellie and her companions to pause and absorb the mystical ambiance. A sense of anticipation, thick and palpable, hung in the air, promising both wonder and peril.

"Did you hear that?" Ellie whispered, her voice barely heard above the beating of her own heart, as she squinted at the darkened corners. The sounds of her friends around her – Oliver's nervous shuffle, Mariana's quiet murmurs of scientific curiosity – faded into the backdrop of hushed anticipation. A subtle scratching, like a quill writing on vellum, seemed to emanate from the Egyptian exhibit.

"What did you hear?" Oliver, the reluctant museum guard, asked, rubbing his eyes, his uniform rumpled and stained with what appeared to be ectoplasmic residue. He had barely managed to keep up with the whirlwind of magical events unfurling since Dr Bell's blunder – a carelessly recited incantation during an unauthorised investigation of a cursed amulet – had awakened the museum's enchanted inhabitants.

Now, gargoyles winked, tapestries whispered secrets, and paintings stepped out of their frames for midnight strolls. He just wanted to go home and forget he'd ever seen a sentient suit of armour.

"It sounded like... secrets," Ellie murmured, her historian's intuition prickling at the edges of her consciousness.

"Secrets indeed," came a silky voice. The figure of Lady Arabella shifted elegantly from her statue state. "There are tales woven into the fabric of each artefact, and tonight they beckon you closer."

Professor Finch stepped forward, his eccentricity shining like a beacon in the dimly lit chamber. His tweed jacket, patched at the elbows and adorned with a constellation of mismatched buttons, practically vibrated with nervous energy. "Ah, secrets! This is the essence of discovery! For every artefact holds a narrative, a reflection of the collector's intentions, a whisper of the past yearning to be heard. A tarnished coin might reveal a lost empire, and a chipped vase, a forgotten love story. But we must tread carefully, for not all secrets are benign. Some are guarded by shadows, by regrets, by the very fabric of time itself. Some are best left undisturbed, sleeping in their dusty tombs." He adjusted his spectacles, his gaze sweeping over the assembled group, a motley crew of historians, linguists, and adventurers.

Azrael, the ancient sphinx who served as their guide, gave a low growl, a sound that resonated deep within their chests, vibrating the very stones beneath their feet. His amber eyes, gleaming with an ancient wisdom that spanned millennia, focused on the array of objects before them. "The greatest treasure, my friends, lies not in the artefacts alone but in the stories that bind them. The Collector, who gathered these wonders, has his tale; one of ambition, of obsession, perhaps even of heartbreak. We must uncover his motivations and understand the threads that connect these disparate objects. For within his story lies the key to unlocking the true power, and the true danger, of this collection. He looked to understand the past, to control it perhaps. But did he succeed? And at what cost?" Azrael paused, his gaze growing distant, as if he could see echoes of the past swirling around them. "His legacy waits to be judged, and we, it seems, are the jury."

"Who is this Collector?" Finn enquired, his wooden form darting around the group, eyes bright with curiosity.

"An enigma wrapped in riddles," Luci slithered closer, her bronze scales shimmering under the faint light of the museum's flickering torches. "He traversed time, seeking relics from forgotten realms. Yet his secrets account for more than history; they speak of ambition and consequence."

"Then we must find this Collector's puzzle," Ellie said with determination, her voice steady. "If we unravel his story, we might piece together the mysteries of this night."

With a shared nod of determination, the adventurers set off, the weight of their quest settling firmly upon their shoulders. Leading the way, Huckleberry , a magnificent beast with feathers the colour of midnight, flapped his wings lazily. The air around him shimmered as a flickering wisp of light, born from his very essence, danced ahead, illuminating the path that snaked before them into the museum's depths. "Follow my lead, dear friends!" he called back, his voice a low rumble that resonated through the echoing halls. "The truth is never simple to grasp, especially when it's been veiled for so long. But the Collector's essence lingers deep within the Museum's heart, a residue we must find and understand if we are to unravel his mysteries."

They navigated through the museum's vast chambers, each a testament to the passage of time, filled to the brim with carefully curated artefacts from different eras. Egyptian relics, entombed for millennia, stood beside medieval relics, weapons gleaming with a long-lost sheen, and imposing statues adorned with jewels. These gems, emeralds, rubies, and sapphires, glimmered like stars in the velvet night, adding an ethereal quality to the already overwhelming collection. But as they journeyed deeper, pushing past the opulent display and into the museum's shadowed underbelly, they began to perceive the fine threads of connection binding the disparate items together. It was more than just a collection; it was a tapestry woven with history, a pulse of history vibrating with each step, growing stronger as they approached the Collector's core. They felt the weight of forgotten empires, the whispers of ancient secrets, and the echoes of countless lives lived and lost.

"Look!" Oliver exclaimed, his voice hushed with a mixture of awe and apprehension, stopping abruptly in front of an intricately designed cabinet. The wood was aged, darker than oak and polished to a mirror sheen by centuries of handling. Yet, it was meticulously carved, the artisanry breathtaking in its detail. The carvings weren't merely decorative; they displayed illustrations, not just of individual artefacts, but scenes depicting the very artefacts scattered throughout the museum, arranged in symbolic patterns and sequences. Some objects were highlighted; others were shrouded in shadow. It was as if the entire museum, its contents and its history were distilled into this single, unassuming piece of furniture. A shiver ran down Oliver's spine. The item was more than just a cabinet; it was a Rosetta Stone, a key to unlocking the Collector's secrets.

"That's not just any cabinet," Professor Finch explained, his eyes gleaming with excitement. "That was crafted by the Collector himself, a man of both skill and vision. The artwork on the cabinet is the very essence of what kept him motivated throughout his lifelong journey of collecting."

Finn leapt up, his eyes alight with sudden inspiration, and began circling the ornate cabinet. He examined the minute details etched into its surface – the subtle shifts in perspective, the recurring motifs, and the almost imperceptible changes in the expressions of the figures carved into the wood. "What if the illustrations tell a story? Could the illustrations depict a series of events or a progression of symbols that guide us towards comprehending his intentions?

Perhaps they depict pivotal moments in his life or key steps in his grand design. Each illustration could be a breadcrumb on a trail leading to the Collector's ultimate ambition."

Dr Bell, captivated by the history practically radiating from the ancient cabinet, leaned in closer, her brow furrowed in concentration. Her fingers, gloved to protect the delicate wood, brushed lightly against the carvings, tracing the lines of a particularly intricate scene. "This resonates with the items we've met so far! We have manipulated each item, not merely storing it away for posterity. They've been carefully curated, arranged with intention, almost like pieces in a complex puzzle. The Collector wasn't just gathering artefacts; he was orchestrating something."

"That is precisely the term," Lady Arabella added regally, her statue-like posture exuding an almost unnatural charisma. She saw the cabinet with a knowing gaze, as if she could already perceive the secrets it held. "The Collector looked not only to preserve history but also to harness the magic that infuses each artefact. He believed these objects held power, and he looked to unlock and wield that power. To reveal the Collector's story, to utterly understand his motives and his goals, we must first decipher this cabinet. It is the key, I believe, to unlocking the mysteries that surround us."

With an air of excitement, Ellie stepped closer, her eyes gleaming with a mixture of anticipation and intellectual curiosity. "Maybe each section is a different artefact or perhaps even a collection of artefacts from a specific civilisation. If we align them based on their origins – their geographical location, their cultural significance, and their estimated age – we might unveil a hidden message! A password, a location, a clue... something that will guide us."

The group gathered around the enigmatic display; their faces etched with concentration. Azrael, with his extensive historical knowledge, and Luci, with her sharp analytical mind, provided insights and contextual information, while Ellie, brimming with enthusiasm, pointed to various elements, her finger tracing the intricate designs. "Look here! The depictions shift subtly in design and tone as we move across the sections. This one clearly is Egypt; its golden hue isn't just decorative; it almost vibrates with the power of the sun god Ra. Then there's a Celtic pattern over here, steeped in mysticism and interwoven with ancient lore, hinting at something deeper, perhaps a connection to the otherworld." She paused, a thoughtful frown creasing her forehead. "And notice how the Mesopotamian section uses cuneiform, not just as decoration, but almost like it's trying to tell a story..."

As they meticulously examined the illustrations, comparing stylistic choices and searching for hidden patterns, a guttural caw echoed through the chamber. Huckleberry , perched atop a nearby pillar, fixed them with his piercing gaze. "Beware!" he rasped, his voice resonating with ancient wisdom. "The path ahead is fraught with enigmas, cloaked in shadows and obscured by layers of misdirection. But heed the wisdom of the collector. He valued cleverness more than anything else. He wouldn't make it simple. You must think like him, expect his traps, and unravel the threads of his design with both intellect and intuition."

With renewed determination, Ellie traced her fingers along the intricately engraved wood, feeling a tingle of source energy below her fingertips. "Let's focus on the first artefact—the Sphinx. We need to ask the right questions."

"A riddle, then!" Azrael proclaimed, his eyes gleaming like gemstones. "If the Collector was as intelligent as you say, he surely spun challenges woven into the essence of his creations."

"What was seen and unheard, shrouded in riddles, awakens the spirit of the Collector!" Luci's voice vibrated with anticipation. "Let us summon his essence."

At that moment, the cabinet, no longer a mere piece of furniture, emanated a soft, ethereal glow. It pulsed with a gentle, almost sentient energy, a subtle pull urging them closer, inviting them to whisper their queries into its ancient heart. Ellie stepped forward, her heart pounding a frantic rhythm of excitement and trepidation against her ribs. The air around the cabinet crackled with unspoken stories, promising answers to questions that had haunted her for weeks. "What drives a collector to gather? What insatiable desire fuels their obsession? And more importantly," she added, her voice barely above a whisper, "what must he hide? What secrets might be carefully preserved within these dusty acquisitions?

The wood responded, almost as if it had been waiting for the precise phrasing of their need. The grain seemed to writhe and breathe, and a series of shifting images materialised on its polished surface, morphing and blending like watercolours in a dream. At first, they were abstract shapes, hinting at the Collector's motivations. But then, each illustration became more intricate, painstakingly detailed, depicting the multi-faceted nature of his existence. They showed scenes of relentless searching, tireless bargaining, and the quiet, lonely satisfaction of discovery. But intertwined with these were visions of responsibility, of the burden of preserving history, of the constant fear of loss or damage. The cabinet painted a portrait not of a man had by greed but one burdened by the weight of the past, a solitary guardian entrusted with safeguarding fragments of a forgotten world. He wasn't simply collecting; he was preserving, protecting, and perhaps, hiding something far more profound than mere objects.

"Look!" Oliver cried, "The collector stands among his treasures! But these shadows? They seem like burdens..."

"Indeed," Professor Finch nodded sagely. "His ambitions may have led to unforeseen consequences. The shadows signify what he feared most—failure, loss, and regret. However, each shadow also serves as a reminder of his triumphs, as his thirst for knowledge and beauty drove him.

Ellie felt a pang in her heart, a sharp sting of empathy mixed with a dawning comprehension, upon realising the multifaceted nature of the Collector. He wasn't a simple greedy hoarder, as she had initially assumed. He was a paradox, a walking contradiction. "He was both a seeker and a prisoner in his pursuits," she mused, the weight of his obsession settling heavily on her own shoulders. The relentless drive to get, to discover, to have, had seemingly built gilded bars around him. "Maybe that's why he was so secretive, afraid that his ambitions would overshadow the very treasures he cherished." He likely saw the inherent irony: the more he amassed, the more enslaved he became to its preservation, its security, its very existence. The beauty he craved, the knowledge he looked for, had become chains, anchoring him to a life of solitude and paranoia, forever guarding his hoard from prying eyes and envious hands. His carefully constructed facade of aloofness and disdain was perhaps just a desperate shield, protecting a vulnerable core from the judgement that he, himself, feared he deserved. The treasures weren't just things to him; they were extensions of himself, pieces of his very soul, and exposing them meant exposing his own deep-seated vulnerabilities.

"Yes!" Lady Arabella responded emphatically. "Now we must uncover the implications of these revelations. For within the tales of a Collector lies the key to the artefacts themselves. Let's continue unravelling the cabinet!"

With every sentence uttered, a new image illuminated before them, each a fleeting glimpse into the Collector's eccentric life and vast holdings – a snow-capped mountain range, a bustling alien marketplace, a chamber filled with shimmering artefacts. Finn, captivated by the changing tableau, darted back to the ornate cabinet, his fingers tracing along its intricate carvings. He was particularly intrigued by a curious mechanism nestled within its design: a small, circular indentation with a button crafted from polished wood. A wave of curiosity, laced with a tremor of apprehension, washed over him. "What's this button for?" he asked, his voice hushed with a mixture of wonder and trepidation, as he pressed the polished wood carefully.

Suddenly, a low rumble echoed through the hall, vibrating through the floorboards and sending a shiver up Finn's spine. The previously static images on the wall shifted again, resolving into a single, awe-inspiring vista. The cabinet, with a groan of ancient hinges and hidden gears, swung silently inward, revealing a spiral staircase hidden behind it. Carved from what looked like obsidian, it spiralled downwards into the inky darkness, an endless descent that swallowed the light. The air around it hummed with a barely perceptible energy, suggesting a portal to the very heart of the Collector's world, a place where secrets slumbered and mysteries waited to be unearthed.

"Should we explore?" Oliver asked nervously, glancing towards the shadows.

"Yes!" Ellie declared. "If we 're to understand the Collector truly, we must delve deeper."

Azrael nodded, the movement rippling through his magnificent mane, causing its silver strands to shimmer like captured starlight in the museum's dim, filtered light. The air hung thick with anticipation, a tangible tension that pressed down on them all. "Fear be not your guide," he declared, his voice a low rumble that resonated with ancient power. "Let it be the curiosity forged by hope, the burning desire to understand that fuels our steps. Together, we shall uncover the truth of the Collector's secrets, no matter how deeply buried they may be."

Finn, ever the eager and fearless one, barely waited for Azrael to finish before racing ahead, his youthful energy a sharp contrast to the weighty atmosphere. He bounded down the darkened corridor, an explorer driven by pure, unadulterated excitement. Meanwhile, Luci, the serpentine guardian, slithered gracefully beside Ellie, her scales whispering against the ancient stone floor. The professor, usually so calm and collected, now walked with a hesitant uncertainty, relying on Luci's guidance through the oppressive darkness. "We are the echoes of history," Luci hissed, her voice a soft sibilance that seemed to emanate from the very walls. "We are alive within these walls, carrying on the breath of forgotten lives. What happened next, the choices made, and the deeds done will shape the stories yet unheard, the present that hangs in the balance."

With hearts steady yet wild, a mixture of trepidation and fierce determination coursing through their veins, the adventurers began their descent down the spiralling staircase. Each step was a conscious act, a testament to their united quest for knowledge and understanding. The worn stone beneath their feet spoke of countless journeys taken before, of secrets whispered and then lost. They were no longer merely a historian, a guard, and a professor; they were a band of seekers, bound by a shared purpose. They were determined to unveil the echoes of the past, to excavate the mysteries that clung to the museum like shadows, and to understand the enigmatic figure of the Collector. His secrets, they suspected, defined not just the fate of the museum but the journey of all that had come before them, the very fabric of their shared reality. The deeper they ventured, the more they felt the weight of history pressing down on them, a silent promise of revelations to come.

As they ventured deeper into the shadows, the air thickened with intensity, and they felt the enchantment wrapping around them like a tapestry.

"Remember," murmured Huckleberry, who had perched himself atop a carved dragon's head along the staircase. "Understanding the secrets of the Collector is but the first step. What he holds tonight plays a part in a greater cycle—a journey tethered to your own."

"We're ready," Ellie affirmed, clutching the knowledge they had gathered so far. The weight of history hung in the air, and together they would unravel the fables—their whispers harmonising with the very essence of the night.

In that moment, Ellie understood something profound: every artefact they met within these ancient ruins, every chipped pottery shard, every faded inscription, was more than just a relic of a forgotten past. They were reflections of their lives, mirroring the hopes, fears, and aspirations that drove them forward. Each object whispered of potential futures, a collection of dreams shaped by the choices they made and the stories they had yet to write upon the world. They were not simply archaeologists, digging up history; they were gazing into a mirror that reflected the very essence of their being. And as the oppressive darkness, thick and heavy as velvet, enveloped them, stealing the light and promising unknown challenges, each adventurer stood tall, resolved and prepared to embrace the shimmering, alluring mysteries that lay ahead, knowing that the answers they sought might hold the key not only to the past but to their own destinies as well.

THE PUZZLE OF THE PORCELAIN DANCE

As the clock struck midnight, its chimes echoing eerily through the cavernous halls, the dimly lit interior of the enchanted museum pulsed with life, an energy thrumming beneath the surface that was imperceptible to the casual observer. Ellie, her heart racing with a mixture of excitement and trepidation, stepped cautiously into the grand atrium. Dust motes danced in the slivers of moonlight that pierced through the high, arched windows, painting fleeting patterns on the marble floor. Her gaze, like iron filings drawn to a magnet, was drawn to the glimmering glass case in the centre.

Within its confines lay an exquisite porcelain figurine—a dancer caught mid-pirouette, her delicate form seemingly frozen in time. The porcelain, aged and yet impossibly pristine, glowed with an inner luminescence. Her painted eyes, a vibrant sapphire blue, seemed to follow Ellie's every move. The air shimmered around her, not just with dust, but with a palpable magic, whispering secrets of a forgotten ballet and a mystery waiting to be unveiled. The secrets hinted at a tragic love story, a hidden curse, and the dancer's eternal imprisonment within the fragile form. Ellie felt a pull, an irresistible urge to understand the story held within the figurine, unaware of the perilous journey that awaited her as she delved deeper into the museum's enchanted secrets.

"Look at her!" exclaimed Professor Finch, adjusting his round spectacles as he stepped closer, his voice tinged with awe. "The Porcelain Dancer... legend has it that she held the key to one of the museum's most complex puzzles."

Ellie approached, enchanted by the graceful curves and intricate details of the dancer. The smooth, almost luminescent porcelain captured the light, highlighting the delicate flow of her sculpted robes and the serene expression on her face. Ellie's fingers itched to touch the cold surface, to trace the lines of her raised arm as if frozen mid-waltz. "But what puzzle could she possibly hold? Can you decipher it, Professor?" she asked, her curiosity piqued. Her eyes searched Professor Finch's face, hoping to find a reflection of the dancer's enigma.

Before Professor Finch could respond, a faint rustling sound caught their attention. Finn appeared from the shadows, his playful eyes sparkling with mischief. His russet fur seemed to glow in the dim light filtering through the arched windows. "I overheard you, and I think I can help!" he chimed cheerfully, darting around the pedestal on which the dancer stood. He feigned a dramatic bow, his bushy tail sweeping the floor. "There's more to her than meets the eye! She's not just standing there; she's practically vibrating with secrets!"

As they gathered closer, Luci coiled gracefully around a nearby marble column, her scales catching the light like scattered jewels. Her forked tongue flicked out, tasting the air, as her gaze shifted to the porcelain figure. There was an ancient wisdom in her reptilian eyes. "She is much more than a mere artefact," Luci hissed softly, the sound barely heard above the quiet hum of the museum. "She holds the stories of those who have danced before her—stories interwoven with the fabric of this museum's history. Her form echoes with each pirouette, arabesque, and whispered laugh, waiting to awaken." " She paused, her gaze meeting Ellie's. "Listening carefully is key."

Oliver leaned against the cold stone wall, his arms crossed in a gesture that telegraphed his scepticism. A single, carefully groomed eyebrow arched high above his eye. "And how exactly do we unlock her secrets?" he drawled, the question laced with a mixture of doubt and reluctant curiosity. "Is there a riddle etched on her petticoat? Or perhaps some sort of arcane incantation I should know about, passed down through generations of enchanted artefact handlers?" He eyed the porcelain dancer, a masterpiece of artistry and latent magic, with a wary gaze. The flickering torchlight cast dancing shadows that seemed to animate her delicate features, making her appear both alluring and unnervingly lifelike.

At that moment, Huckleberry, a creature of both majestic power and unsettling familiarity, flitted down from his high perch amidst the rafters. His descent was surprisingly graceful for such a large creature, each powerful wingbeat creating a subtle gust of wind that rustled Oliver's dark hair. He landed delicately beside the porcelain dancer, his sharp talons barely disturbing the dust motes swirling in the air. "Riddles are indeed her language," he croaked, his voice a strange blend of gravel and melody, a sound that resonated deep within the chamber. A glint of mischief danced in his beady eyes, hinting at the complex games he often enjoyed playing. "But remember, fledgling adventurers," he continued, tilting his massive, feathered head, "not all puzzles are spoken aloud. Some are felt beneath your fingers, etched into the very essence of her form. The statue holds more than meets the eye, if you have the wit to perceive it."

Ellie, ever the pragmatist and detail- orientated member of their trio, had been quietly seeing the dancer since they entered the chamber. She examined the statue closely, her fingers, slender and surprisingly strong, brushing against the cold, smooth porcelain surface. She moved with a reverence that Oliver lacked, treating the statue less like an obstacle and more like a delicate work of art. Finally, she stopped, her brow furrowed in concentration. She noticed something unusual, something easily overlooked in the dim light of their torches: tiny, almost imperceptible symbols inscribed along the base of the statue. These markings were so fine, so intricately woven into the design, that they appeared to be nothing more than decorative flourishes. "Look here!" she exclaimed, her voice a soft but urgent whisper. She traced a delicate line with her fingertip, illuminating the subtle carving. "These markings... they aren't just decoration. They must be part of the puzzle! They're far too deliberate to be accidental." A spark of excitement lit her eyes, a hunter's gleam in the face of a promising clue. The dancer, once a silent enigma, had begun to whisper her secrets.

Professor Finch squinted, his brow furrowing with concentration as he moved closer to scrutinise the ornate designs etched into the ancient artefact. Dust motes danced in the beam of his flashlight, illuminating the intricate carvings. "They appear to be musical notes, potentially part of a score. Observe the positioning, the specific symbols... if I recall correctly, there's a melody associated with the dancers of this era! Perhaps it's a forgotten waltz, perhaps, or a lively jig. We may need to recreate the music, to faithfully interpret its rhythm, to unlock the next part of her mystery."

Finn bounced excitedly, his brown fur shimmering in the soft light filtering through the forgotten chamber. "Let's make some music! I know a few tunes! A sea shanty, a victory march, even that little ditty about the badger and the bell!" He puffed out his chest, eager to contribute.

Taking a moment, Ellie and Professor Finch exchanged an understanding glance. Finn's enthusiasm was endearing, but they both knew the task ahead needed more than just a catchy tune. The assignment was not just a riddle challenging their minds with logic puzzles; they were about to embark on a sensory journey.

VALEN THE
TIMEKEEPER'S WARNING

The museum, a mausoleum of forgotten empires and whispered secrets, echoed with a symphony of whispers. Footsteps faded into the plush carpets, rustling programmes fluttered in nervous hands, and the low murmur of hushed conversations created a constant hum – each sound a note of history resonating through the dimly lit halls. Dust motes, illuminated by strategically placed spotlights, danced in the still air, like miniature time travellers revisiting their past. The archaic structures loomed taller than they should, monuments to ambition and artistry, their weathered surfaces bearing the silent testimony of centuries. Shadows, elongated and distorted by the uneven light, danced like phantoms, swirling in the soft glow of Azrael the Lion's golden light, a watchful protector cast in bronze and bathed in carefully curated illumination.

Ellie, a wisp of a girl with eyes that devoured information like a starving artist, felt a shiver of anticipation crawl down her spine. It wasn't just the chill of the ancient stone seeping into her bones but the thrill of the unknown that hummed beneath her skin. She stood beside her companions in the Hall of Time, a vast rotunda dedicated to the relentless march of chronology. Around them, artefacts pulled from across the ages stood sentinel: a Roman sundial, a Victorian chronometer, and a gleaming, futuristic time-measuring device that pulsed with an eerie, internal light. Overhead, a monumental clock, its gears exposed and intricate, ticked away with a deliberate, almost sentient rhythm, as if aware of the impending prose of destiny about to be written in the very air around them. Each tick was a beat of the universe's heart, a countdown to something extraordinary.

"Isn't it extraordinary?" Ellie remarked, her eyes gleaming like the ancient artefacts surrounding them. "Each piece tells a story, but tonight, they have a voice."

Professor Finch adjusted his glasses, the last remnants of his scholarly composure slipping as excitement took hold. "Quite so, Ellie! Each artefact is a key, unlocking the mysteries of our past. But we must tread carefully; time is a delicate fabric, easily torn and irreparably damaged. Handle these with respect, with understanding. One wrong move could unravel the very threads of history!" He gestured wildly, almost knocking over a meticulously crafted vase.

Oliver stood bewildered, trying to wrap his head around the enchanting occurrences that had unfolded since Dr Bell's accidental awakening of the artefacts. Sarcophagi glowed with an inner light, hieroglyphs danced on the walls, and the air thrummed with an energy he couldn't understand. "Why do I feel like we're in way over our heads?" he muttered, glancing at the life-sized statues that seemed to breathe alongside him. Their eyes, carved from obsidian, followed his every move, sending shivers down his spine. This wasn't a museum anymore; it was a portal.

"It's all part of the adventure, isn't it?" Finn chimed in, darting mischievously between their feet. His fur shimmered with an unnatural sheen, and his bright eyes sparkled with ancient wisdom. "More than just the stories, it's about feeling the pulse of those who lived through these moments! Imagine walking in the sandals of a pharaoh or feeling the weight of a Roman legionary's armour! It's tangible history, right here, right now!" He nipped playfully at Oliver's shoelace, urging him to embrace the chaos.

A low growl reverberated from Azrael as he stepped forward, his marble whiskers capturing the flickering light cast by a nearby brazier. The lion, a magnificent creation from a bygone era, exuded an aura of power and ancient knowledge. "And moving forward in time may come at a cost," the lion warned, his voice a deep rumble that resonated through the chamber. "The past is not meant to be trifled with. You must prepare for Valen the Timekeeper's warning—it is near. Heed his words, for they hold the key to your survival and the preservation of the timelines." He paused, his gaze fixed on a far-off point, as if listening to a voice only he could hear. "Heed them well, for the sands of time are shifting, and danger is on the horizon."

Ellie raised her brow, suddenly aware of the shifting energy in the air. The playful banter that had filled the chamber moments ago seemed to dissipate, replaced by a tangible sense of anticipation and unease. "What do you mean? Who is Valen?" she pressed, her gaze sharp and unwavering. The name, though unfamiliar, resonated with a primal feeling of significance, like a forgotten echo in the depths of her being.

Before Azrael could respond, an ethereal wind rustled through the chamber, the once-still air now charged with an electric tension that prickled against their skin. Dust motes danced in the sudden gusts, swirling like miniature galaxies. Luci, usually languid and indifferent, coiled even tighter around a nearby pedestal, her bronze scales shimmering with an unusual brilliance, reflecting the collective uncertainty hanging heavy in the air. "Legend whispers of him, cloaked in shadows, guardian of temporal continuity," Luci hissed, her forked tongue tasting the changes in the atmosphere. "He harbours great power, the ability to unravel and reshape moments themselves, but his knowledge is not given freely. You must earn his favour and prove yourselves worthy of his attention." Her voice, low and sibilant, sent a shiver down Ellie's spine.

Oliver crossed his arms defensively, a flicker of apprehension crossing his usually confident features. "And how exactly do we do that? Survive the night? Stay out of trouble?" he asked, his tone laced with a healthy dose of sarcasm. He clearly wasn't convinced this 'Timekeeper' was going to be throwing a welcome party.

"Trouble is the essence of adventure," Professor Finch chimed in, his voice brimming with scholarly enthusiasm, momentarily eclipsing the underlying tension. His eyes, usually hidden behind thick spectacles, were wide and alight with a fervent light. "But heed the warning from the past, for in histories far older than ours, a price was always paid for meddling with time. The gods themselves were wary of its manipulation." He adjusted his spectacles, seemingly oblivious to the dread that had settled in the room. "Think of the paradoxes! The ripples! The potential for...unforeseen consequences!"

As if summoned by their discussion, a ripple of light warped against the far wall, twisting and bending the stone. The light coalesced, resolving into the unmistakable figure of Valen himself. Cloaked in a robe woven from the very essence of night, a garment that seemed to absorb all the light around it and shimmer with impossible constellations, the figure radiated an aura of immense power and ancient wisdom. His face was shadowed, but even in the dim light, Ellie could sense the weight of ages etched onto his features. He beckoned them closer with ageless fingers, a silent invitation that both intrigued and terrified. "Seek not just the answers you desire, but the questions that lead you, for true understanding lies not in destination but in the journey," Valen's voice echoed, a resonant baritone that seemed to vibrate within their very bones. "Your fates are intertwined, threads woven tight into the grand tapestry of existence, and tonight, the fabric of time hangs precariously. Choose wisely, for your choices will determine not only your destinies but the fate of timelines yet to come."

Ellie felt her heart quicken, words swirling in her mind like restless spirits. "What must we do?" she asked, stepping forward, her historian's instincts pushing her to understand.

"Time flows in currents, my dear historian," Valen intoned, his voice low and resonant. "To navigate its waters, you must solve the Riddle of Reflections. Each reflection shall show you the paths not taken and the choices you could have made. But beware—the shadows carry whispers of regret."

"Where do we find this riddle?" Azrael demanded, his lion form emanating strength and leadership, eyes burning with an intensity that matched the weight of their quest.

Valen, his face etched with the wisdom of ages, raised a hand adorned with rings that shimmered with trapped starlight. The gesture unleashed a cascade of spectral images, a whirlwind of swirling colours that resolved into fleeting scenes: children laughing, artists sculpting, lovers embracing. A palpable sense of shared history, of lives lived and lost within the museum's walls, flooded the room. "The riddle", Valen's voice resonated, deep and resonant, "lies within the Mirror of Moments. It is not merely a looking glass but a portal to the past, a repository of time itself." He paused, his gaze sweeping over the assembled group, a flicker of concern in his ancient eyes. "But the mirror will not yield its truth without first seeing the purity of your intentions. It sees beyond the surface, into the very core of your being."

Luci, ever the wise guide, her own aura radiating a gentle, calming light, stepped forward "Valen speaks truly," she affirmed, her voice like the chime of distant bells. "The Mirror of Moments is a powerful artefact. It reflects not just your physical form but also mirrors your heart's desires, your deepest aspirations… but also your fears and doubt, the shadows that cling to your soul. Be warned. Go forth, unravel your truths, and confront the vulnerabilities you hold within. Only then, perhaps, shall you find what you look for, and only then will the mirror reveal its secrets."

Oliver, the pragmatic one, the voice of reason amidst the fantastical, threw his hands up in exasperation. The disbelief was thick enough to cut with a knife. "Wonderful. So not only are we solving riddles concocted by a probably-slightly-mad Timekeeper, but we also must dive headfirst into our emotional baggage? Confront our deepest insecurities in front of a magical, judging mirror? Great," he repeated, the sarcasm practically dripping from his voice like condensation on a cold glass. He glanced nervously at the swirling mass of memories lingering in the air.

Ellie, the determined heart of the group, placed a reassuring hand on Oliver's arm. Her voice was firm, filled with a conviction that radiated outwards, pushing back against Oliver's cynicism. "Yes, Oliver," she encouraged, her focus unwavering. "And I know it's daunting. But it's about more than just ourselves, more than just a personal journey into our psyches. This expedition is about the museum, about preserving its magic, and about protecting the history it holds within these walls. We need to find a way back before dawn's light erases everything, before all the past is lost forever. Remember why we're here."

As they moved deeper into the labyrinthine corridors of the museum, the air growing colder, heavier with the weight of untold stories, Finn, a blur of russet fur and mischievous energy, darted ahead. His playful nature, usually a beacon of light-heartedness, seemed strained by the gravity of their mission, but he still managed a playful flick of his tail. "Follow my tail!" he yipped, his voice echoing slightly in the vast space. "The Mirror of Moments lives in the Chamber of Echoes! But be warned! The path there… well, let's just say it's not exactly a straight line!"

Navigating through twisting corridors, illuminated by the faint glow of magical artefacts and the dust motes dancing in the meagre light, they soon arrived at an imposing door. It was unlike any they had seen before, crafted from a dark, obsidian-like material and adorned with intricate carvings. These weren't static images; they seemed to shift and change as they regarded them, depicting scenes of battles, celebrations, and strange, otherworldly rituals. Ellie stepped forward, her historian's mind racing, a thrill of anticipation coursing through her veins. "This must be it! The Chamber of Echoes", she declared, her voice barely a whisper in the heavy silence of the corridor.

Inside, the room unfolded into a vast expanse of reflections. Mirrors of all shapes and sizes lined the walls, some towering giants, others tiny and ornate. Each surface flickered with glimpses of events long past – fleeting images of robed figures, echoing laughter, and the clash of steel. The air shimmered with history and nostalgia, heavy with the weight of untold stories. Each ripple in the reflective surfaces seemed a testament to time itself, a reminder of moments lost and forgotten. The very atmosphere hummed with a low, resonant energy, tickling the skin and raising goosebumps.

"Look," Finn piped up, his furry nose twitching as he pointed towards a grand mirror dominating the centre of the room. It was much larger than the others, its frame crafted from silver that seemed to absorb the light around it. "That one seems special! It's... brighter, somehow."

Approaching the mirror cautiously, Ellie felt an undeniable draw towards it, a resonance almost beckoning her existence closer. She had the impression that something in the mirror recognised her, or maybe something inside of her did. recognised her, or perhaps something within her recognised it. As they gathered around, their breath held in anticipation, words began to appear from the reflective surface. They weren't spoken aloud but formed as glowing script upon the silvered glass, ethereal and haunting, as if whispered from the depths of time itself. The words shimmered, resolving into a single, chilling phrase: "The Past is Never Truly Gone."

"Through the looking glass, your essence I shall show,
There are adventures past and futures yet to unfold.
Be true in heart, unveil your deepest quest,
Only then shall you see the time's true zest."

With a collective breath, a shared moment of profound understanding washed over them. The riddle, they realised, wasn't a dry exercise in historical trivia or a simple recitation of well-worn tales. It pierced deeper, demanding a level of vulnerability they hadn't expected. It was a call to exhume the secrets they had carefully buried in the shadowed corners of their hearts, secrets they had often refused to even acknowledge to themselves.

"What are we afraid of? What regrets haunt us in the quiet hours of the night?" Ellie posed, her voice steady, yet softened with an unexpected tenderness. The question hung in the air, a challenge and an invitation.

Professor Finch looked grave, his usually bright eyes clouded with a melancholic contemplation. His mind, a labyrinth of historical facts and theories, now swirled with more personal, more vulnerable dualities. "I've always feared that my discoveries... that all my years of toil and dedication... will only fade into the annals of forgotten lore, a footnote in some obscure text. It's the fear that I haven't, and perhaps will never, make an indelible mark on history, that my life's work will ultimately be inconsequential."

Oliver, always the observer, the quiet philosopher, started slowly, carefully choosing his words. "I fear", he confessed, his voice tinged with a familiar sadness, "that I'll never truly belong, that I'm destined to remain perpetually on the outside looking in. I fear that I have become a lonely observer, detached from the vibrant tapestry of life, while others actively weave themselves into its intricate patterns."

Luci curled protectively around them, her eyes reflecting an ancient and knowing wisdom, offering a gentle perspective. "The key to unlocking deeper connections lies not in grand pronouncements or shared victories but in the intimate sharing of these fears. In being vulnerable, in allowing yourselves to be seen, flaws and all, you strengthen your bonds, forging unbreakable links of empathy and understanding."

Ellie, inspired by the bravery of her companions, felt a surge of courage, a wave of resolve washing away her own lingering hesitations. "I've often feared that my all-consuming passion for history, the very thing that defines me, inadvertently isolates me from genuine human connection, from true friendships. I worry that I get so lost in the labyrinthine corridors of the past, endlessly chasing echoes and shadows, that I tragically neglect the beauty and immediacy of the present." She paused, taking another deep breath.

"That I become a ghost in my own life, haunted by stories instead of living one."

The reflections of their words danced within the glass, a swirling kaleidoscope of shared anxieties. The image wasn't static; it breathed, absorbed, and magnified their vulnerabilities and fears, a tangible manifestation of the weight they carried. Each whispered secret, each hesitant admission, seemed to ripple across the surface, distorting their faces into fleeting masks of anguish. At once, Azrael stepped forward, his imposing figure casting a shadow that momentarily stilled the turbulent reflections. His voice, a resonant growl that vibrated through the room, cut through the tension. "We all are intertwined, each reflection essential to the tapestry. Trust in each other and speak your truths. Only by acknowledging the darkness can we truly find the light."

The air thickened with purpose, charged with an almost palpable energy. The mirror, no longer just a passive observer, seemed to pulsate as if alive, its surface shimmering with an inner light that both beckoned and intimidated. It urged them to confront the shadows they harboured within their hearts, to drag their deepest insecurities into the open and expose them to the healing power of shared vulnerability. The silence that followed Azrael's words was thick with anticipation and trepidation.

Finn, usually the embodiment of levity, hopped on the edge of the mirror, his playful demeanour now shed like an unwanted skin. His eyes, usually sparkling with mischief, held a surprising depth of earnestness. "Let's face it together! Let's stop hiding and pretending. We stand as one, so let's share what makes us – us! We should share everything that makes us unique, including our strengths and weaknesses. Let's get it all out there." He offered a nervous grin, hoping to inject a sliver of his usual cheer into the heavy atmosphere.

With newfound resolve, fuelled by Azrael's stoicism and Finn's unexpected sincerity, each of them began to speak. Hesitant at first, then with growing confidence, they bared their truths, their stories weaving together like strands of a complex braid. The room seemed to absorb their confessions, the very walls resonating with the weight of shared experience. Their reflections, initially distorted and fearful, began to subtly transform, softening as each truth was spoken, each burden laid down. As Ellie spoke her final words, her voice trembling but firm, the mirror shimmered brightly, bathing the room in an ethereal glow. The reflections within shifted dramatically, the distorted images of fears and anxieties melting away to reveal visions of hope, resilience, and newfound camaraderie. The tapestry, once frayed and dark, was now interwoven with threads of light, a testament to the strength they had found in their shared vulnerability. The mirror, no longer a reflection of fear, now reflected their true selves: flawed, yes, but strong, united, and ready to face whatever lay ahead.

And then, Valen reappeared, his eyes twinkling with knowing, a subtle smile playing on his lips. "You have shown your hearts and unveiled your depths," he declared, his voice resonating with a gentle power. "The riddle, a mere catalyst, has brought forth the bond you share, a connection forged in shared experience and burgeoning trust. Now, dare to move forward, for the threads of time have revealed your path, albeit a path wreathed in uncertainty and brimming with potential."

The mirror, no longer a simple reflection, rippled with unseen energy. Light, an ethereal ballet of cerulean, crimson, and gold, swirled in vivid colours, painting the air with its luminescence before subsiding, releasing a soft, otherworldly glow. As the light faded, a doorway materialised, arching into a vast expanse of infinite time streams. Each stream shimmered and pulsed with its own unique energy, carrying echoes of the laughter, tears, triumphs, and tragedies of the past. The air hummed with the weight of history, a tangible reminder of the consequences of choices made and the power of actions taken.

"Now you must recite your bond aloud," Valen said, his gaze sweeping over each of them with an intensity that hinted at the seriousness of the task ahead. "The currents of time are turbulent and unpredictable. Only by speaking your shared commitment, by solidifying the foundations upon which your partnership is built, shall you navigate them safely. Your words will act as a compass and an anchor, guiding you through the temporal storms and preventing you from being swept away by the relentless tide of history."

Taking a deep breath and steeling themselves for the unknown, Ellie, Professor Finch, Oliver, and the enchanted artefacts – the ancient compass whispering secrets of forgotten voyages, the quill humming with the untold stories it longed to write, and the hourglass shimmering with the remnants of countless passing moments – pledged their commitment to each other. Their voices, though distinct, blended in a tapestry of sound, weaving together a symphony of loyalty, camaraderie, and shared purpose. Ellie's youthful optimism intertwined with Professor Finch's scholarly wisdom, Oliver's unwavering courage, and the artefacts' ancient knowledge, revealing a shared determination to protect time and unravel its mysteries, whatever the cost.

Valen, his face a roadmap of ages lived and lessons learnt, watched them with knowing eyes. A deep sigh, a sound akin to wind whispering through ancient ruins, escaped his lips, tinged with both relief and a touch of melancholy. Finally, he gave a slow, deliberate nod. Satisfaction, as palpable as the ticking of a grandfather clock, etched itself upon his weathered features. "Then voyage forth," he intoned, his voice resonating with the weight of centuries, "for your adventure has only begun. The tapestry of time awaits your touch, and its threads are yours to weave."

As they stepped through the luminous doorway, hand in hand, Ellie felt a rush of exhilaration pulse through her veins, chasing away the lingering anxieties of their past trials. The light was almost tangible, a shimmering curtain parting to reveal the unknown. They were united in spirit, their bond forged in the crucible of shared experiences, armed with understanding gleaned from victories and defeats. Ready to face whatever shadows lay ahead, they stood on the precipice of a new beginning, their hearts beating in unison.

From a point somewhere both within and beyond the doorway, Azrael's majestic voice boomed, resonating around them with the force of a celestial symphony. His words, pregnant with wisdom and authority, echoed through the very fabric of the space. "Time is a river, my friends," he declared, the sound a clarion call to action. "And together, we shall ensure that its history flows onwards, unhindered by the shadows of the past. Protect its currents, safeguard its tributaries, and fight to keep its waters pure."

With hope alight in their hearts, like twin embers glowing in the twilight, the adventurers crossed the threshold into the unknown. The air shimmered with possibility, a kaleidoscope of realities waiting to be explored. This world was a living tapestry, where memories, struggles, and friendships wove the very fabric of time itself. Each thread stood for a life lived, a choice made, a moment cherished. They were set to embark on yet another chapter of their enchanted journey, armed with the unwavering trust they had in each other and a fragile glimmer of hope – a small but potent light against the formidable shadows that awaited them, lurking at the edges of the River of Time. Only time, ironically, would tell if their light was strong enough to prevail.

A HEART DIVIDED

The moon hung high over the Enchanted Museum, a celestial pearl suspended in the inky velvet of the night sky. Its light, cool and ethereal, cast silvery beams through the intricate latticework of the glass ceiling, painting geometric patterns on the polished marble floor below. Inside, gathered from the far corners of the world and carved from a forgotten age, ancient artefacts stirred with an almost imperceptible life. Clay tablets whispered half-forgotten epics, jewelled daggers hummed with dormant power, and statues of long-dead gods seemed to shift in the periphery, surrounded by the hushed whispers of their individual histories – tales of triumph, betrayal, love, and loss, all etched into their silent surfaces.

Yet, as Ellie nervously glanced at the grandfather clock standing sentinel in the grand foyer, a palpable tension filled the air, thick and heavy as a shroud. The clock's pendulum swung with a hypnotic rhythm, each tick echoing the growing unease in her stomach. It was close to midnight, a time known for its secrets, a witching hour when the veil between worlds thinned and the ordinary became extraordinary. And tonight, the heart of the museum, usually a place of quiet contemplation and scholarly pursuit, felt irritable and restless, like a slumbering beast about to awaken. A low hum vibrated through the very foundations of the building, a discordant note that set Ellie's teeth on edge. Something was about to happen; she could feel it in the prickle of goosebumps rising on her arms, and she knew, with a certainty that chilled her to the bone, that she was about to see it firsthand.

"Where is everyone?" Ellie asked, pulling her cardigan around her shoulders as a draught flowed through the gallery. She hadn't seen Oliver for a while and was starting to get concerned.

"He should be here," replied Professor Finch, adjusting his glasses and flipping through an old tome that had been opened on a nearby display stand. "He was meant to help us solve the riddle of the Sphinx."

"Oliver isn't exactly the most reliable of guards," laughed Luci, her bronze scales shimmering in the moonlight. "But it appears even guardians need a little excitement in their lives!"

"I hope he's not getting into trouble," Ellie added, anxiousness gnawing at her. She didn't want the bond she'd forged with Oliver, through their shared adventures in this magical place, to be broken.

"Do not fret, dear Ellie," chimed Azrael the Lion, who saw the worry on her face. His golden eyes twinkled with wisdom. "Our adventures are intertwined; he would not stray too far from the ties that bind us as we venture this night."

Just as Azrael finished speaking, the clock struck midnight, each chime resonating with a deep, almost sentient quality, echoing through the vast, silent halls of the museum. The sound wasn't merely auditory; it seemed to vibrate within the very bones of the building, a tangible presence that settled over them all. A palpable energy, thick and tingling, swept over them, causing the artefacts on display – ancient pottery, gleaming jewels, and forgotten relics – to hum with vitality. A faint, ethereal glow emanated from some, casting flickering shadows that danced on the walls. Ellie's heart raced, a frantic drumbeat against her ribs, a mixture of breathless excitement at the prospect of discovery and chilling apprehension at the unknown dangers that might lie ahead. This split, this internal conflict, grounded her in the moment, anchoring her to the reality of the extraordinary events unfolding around them.

As the last stroke of the hour faded into the cavernous space, a sudden commotion erupted from the main entrance, shattering the expectant silence. In strode Oliver, his usually impeccable attire slightly rumpled, his expression a chaotic mixture of exhilaration and disarray. A fine sheen of sweat glistened on his forehead, and his eyes shone with an almost manic intensity. "I'm back! You wouldn't believe what I just met," he exclaimed, his voice raspy, hardly catching his breath after what was clearly a frantic run. He gestured wildly with his hands, his usual composure completely abandoned.

"And what, pray tell, was *that*?" Professor Finch enquired, raising a distinguished eyebrow, his attention drawn to the subject. He carefully closed the ancient, leather-bound tome he had been studying, marking his place with a delicate silver bookmark. His eyes, usually obscured by thick spectacles, now held a spark of anticipation.

"There's a riddle... lurking in the West Wing. I could *hear* it — like a voice calling me, beckoning me closer," Oliver recounted, his voice hushed with awe, wide-eyed and visibly shaken. "It's... intricate, complex. But I believe it could lead us to something significant, something that connects all these seemingly disparate artefacts we're trying to understand. Something... bigger."

Ellie felt her heart flutter, a nervous, hopeful bird taking flight. "We have to go there!" she declared, the words tumbling out almost involuntarily. A sense of unity ignited a shared purpose that momentarily eclipsed the anxieties that plagued her. She took a decisive step towards Oliver, an unspoken agreement passing between them. However, alongside that burgeoning hope sprouted a seed of uncertainty, a creeping tendril of doubt. What would happen if they followed this riddle, if they uncovered a truth so profound, so disruptive, that it shattered their fragile bond, leaving them irrevocably changed and forever divided by the secrets they unearthed? The prospect was both terrifying and irresistibly alluring.

"Follow me, then!" Oliver said, his enthusiasm infectious. They turned to Azrael, ready to follow his lead.

In winding through the darkened museum passages, Finn darted about playfully, his small paws padding softly on the marble floors. He wove between towering exhibits, a vibrant splash of orange against the sombre backdrop, guiding them with a flick of his bushy tail. "Hurry!" he chimed, his voice a cheerful melody in the echoing halls. "There's much to uncover and not a moment to lose!" He paused, looking back at Ellie and Oliver, a mischievous glint in his bright, amber eyes. "The artefacts within hold secrets whispered through centuries, but time, as always, is a slippery foe!"

As Finn led them deeper into the museum, the shadows danced around them, swirling like phantom figures in the periphery. The flickering ancient lanterns, hanging precariously from the high, arched ceilings, cast elongated, distorted shapes on the walls and illuminated their path with an eerie, mesmerising glow. The air grew heavier, thick with the scent of dust, aged parchment, and something indefinably ancient. They reached the West Wing, a section rumoured to house the museum's most enigmatic treasures, where the riddle awaited. They stood before an imposing bronze door, its surface polished with age, etched with intricate images of the Sphinx, its knowing gaze seeming to penetrate their souls.

"This is it," Ellie whispered. Her trembling fingers touched the cold, resonant metal door. As her palm pressed against it, warmth spread through her fingertips, igniting a sense of anticipation and trepidation. "Can we trust what lies beyond?" she asked uncertainly. "What if this riddle is more than just a game?"

Oliver, serious now, placed a hand on her shoulder. "We must be ready for both light and dark, Ellie," he said. "Darkness can lead to light. We'll face it together." He looked at Finn, who was focused on the bronze door. The air was thick with anticipation; their quest depended on what lay beyond.

"Goodness gracious," Professor Finch said, shaking his head as he adjusted his glasses. "It isn't just a riddle; it's a mind-bending gate that can change everything."

"The heart of the museum is divided—reveal the truth, and it will bring unity," Luci hissed, sensing the weight of the moment. "But in revealing it, one must confront their own shadows."

As Ellie took a step back, she felt an unfamiliar tug within her. It was as if the door beckoned her to act while warning her of the possible consequences. "What if unearthing these truths forces us to choose sides?" she pondered aloud, conflicting emotions flooding her mind.

"Whatever we find, we face it together," Oliver affirmed, stepping forward. There was a glint of determination in his eyes, yet beside it, she sensed vulnerability, a flicker of fear about the task ahead.

Azrael roared softly, a sound that seemed to vibrate through the very stone beneath their feet. In response, the ancient bronze door, etched with hieroglyphs that seemed to writhe in the flickering torchlight, creaked open with agonising slowness. The threshold revealed a dimly lit room, pulsating with an unseen energy that prickled the skin. Dust motes danced in the air, illuminated by an unknown source that cast long, distorted shadows across the chamber.

At the centre of the room, dwarfing everything else, stood a gigantic stone Sphinx. Its lion's body was weathered and worn, marked by the passage of untold centuries, yet its human head remained eerily serene. Its eyes, crafted from polished obsidian, seemed to bore into them, piercing not just their physical forms but extending to the deepest recesses of their souls, exposing their fears and desires.

Suddenly, the air crackled with an almost palpable power. The Sphinx stirred, and a voice resonated through the chamber, deep and hypnotic, a sound that bypassed the ears and settled directly into their bones. "Answer my riddle," it intoned, the words echoing with an unnatural clarity, "and you may gain passage to the artefacts' truth. Fail, and be forever lost within your shadows." The threat was still in the air, a chilling promise of a fate worse than death.

Ellie's heart raced, a frantic drum against her ribs. She found herself staring into the Sphinx's unyielding gaze, trying to decipher the secrets held within those ancient, unblinking eyes. A wave of anxiety washed over her. What if the riddles revealed were more than just intellectual challenges? What if they forced her to confront hidden truths about herself and those she held dear? Would the answers shatter her fragile ties with Oliver, the man she was beginning to fall for? Would they expose vulnerabilities within their group, dividing her friendship with the others and jeopardising their mission?

"What is the riddle?" Professor Finch pressed, his voice trembling with a mixture of trepidation and, unsettlingly, a palpable excitement that surpassed the gravity of the situation. He adjusted his spectacles, his eyes gleaming with an almost manic fervour.

The Sphinx leaned closer, its massive head moving with a ponderous grace that belied its stony composition. Its golden eyes, reflecting the strange light of the room, gleamed with an infuriating wisdom, a knowing that bordered on mockery. "I speak without a mouth and hear without ears. I have no body, but I come alive with the wind. What am I?"

The words, ancient and enigmatic, reverberated within Ellie's mind. They danced around her like restless spirits, teasing and taunting. Fragments of memories, half-formed ideas, and lingering suspicions swirled through her thoughts. The pressure mounted, the silence in the chamber becoming almost unbearable. Finally, something clicked into place, a sudden spark of recognition that ignited within her. "An echo!" she shouted, the word bursting from her lips with a force that surprised even herself. It wasn't a conscious decision, but a primal instinct, a desperate gamble thrown into the face of eternity.

"Correct," replied the Sphinx, though its voice held no warmth; it felt almost chilling. "But remember, echoing images in your life may not always align with your heart's desires. Choose wisely how you answer the next question."

"Next question?" Ellie echoed, panic bubbling beneath her composed exterior.

"Yes, for the heart of the museum lies divided, as is the heart of those who seek its truth," the Sphinx prompted.

"What do you mean?" Oliver stepped forward, frustration creeping into his voice, but the Sphinx merely stared in silence before continuing.

"There exists a choice: to cling to the past or forge a new path. What weighs more, the truth you uncover or the bond you share?"

Ellie blinked slowly, the Sphinx's words sinking deeper, an anchor dragging against the seabed of her resolve. "It's not just a choice of loyalty; it's about... us?" she echoed, the question hanging in the air, thick with unspoken anxieties. The implications resonated within her with an intensity she had never felt before, a chaotic storm of possibilities swirling around the comfortable, familiar harbour of her friendships. Was the artefact, the quest, about to expose something raw and dangerous she'd carefully kept buried?

Finn looked from Ellie to Oliver, sensing the subtle, almost imperceptible undercurrents of unspoken feelings guiding their minds; a silent dialogue conducted through glances and guarded expressions. He knew them both, perhaps better than they knew themselves. "The 'I' between you two is as powerful as the waves of history that surround us," he quipped lightly, trying to alleviate the tension, to inject a dose of his trademark humour into the increasingly fraught atmosphere. He hoped a light-hearted remark might break the spell before they all succumbed to the weight of the unknown.

"What if there's something that could tear us apart?" Oliver murmured, his voice barely escaping his lips, a fragile confession lost in the vastness of the chamber. He avoided Ellie's gaze, focusing instead on the intricate patterns carved into the temple floor. The vulnerability in his tone struck Ellie like a lightning bolt, igniting her uncertainty, turning her carefully constructed sense of security to ash. She had always seen Oliver as a constant, a reliable anchor in her life. Now, he was admitting to the potential for catastrophic change.

"The artefacts possess profound truths, but they could lay bare more than we wish to know," the Sphinx challenged, its voice a low, rumbling echo that seemed to vibrate through their very bones. Its eyes, ancient and knowing, locked onto each of them in turn, piercing through their facades. "Will you risk your friendship to unearth painful secrets? Will you prioritise the pursuit of knowledge over the fragile bond you share? The past rarely stays buried; be prepared for what it might reveal." The Sphinx's pronouncements hung heavy in the air, a stark warning that the path they were choosing was fraught with peril, not just from external forces, but from within themselves.

Ellie took a step back, the gritty sand crunching beneath her boots, her heart pounding a frantic rhythm against her ribs. The weight of the moment, the sheer impossibility of what they were facing, settled heavily on her shoulders, threatening to crush her. She felt dizzy and disoriented, as if the very ground beneath her was shifting. Turning to Oliver, her gaze frantically searched his face, desperate for a flicker of recognition, a glimmer of understanding. Could he understand the chaotic storm of thoughts raging within her? Would he share the same bone-chilling fears that were threatening to consume her? Or was she alone in this terrifying new reality?

Before them stood the Sphinx, an ancient sentinel guarding secrets untold, its enigmatic smile only deepening the mystery. Before her were her feelings, a tempest of confusion, anxiety, and a faint, flickering hope. Gathering all her courage, she planted her feet firmly on the earth, drawing strength from the palpable history emanating from the monumental statue. "We have to remain united," she replied, her voice trembling slightly, a fragile thread of defiance in the face of overwhelming uncertainty. "Whatever the truth, however bizarre or frightening, it's ours to face together. I won't let fear dictate my choices. I won't let it tear us apart."

From its perch high above them on the Sphinx's weathered head, Huckleberry, the ancient raven companion, cawed gently, its obsidian eyes gleaming with an unnerving intelligence. "They say a heart divided cannot stand. In unity, there is strength to overcome the shadows of doubt that whisper insidious lies in the darkness. The world, in its ignorance or malice, may look to divide you; do not succumb! Cling to each other, for in your bond lies your greatest weapon."

Ellie felt her resolve solidifying, hardening like steel in a forge. The raven's words resonated deep within her, striking a chord of truth and reminding her of the strength she found in their shared journey. Beside her, Oliver nodded slowly, his first shock giving way to a burgeoning determination. He was finding his footing again, pulling himself out of the dizzying whirlpool of revelation. Before them lay a world of uncharted mysteries, unexplored emotions, and the intriguing, yet daunting, promise of discovery. The road ahead was uncertain, fraught with peril, but they would face it together, united against the unknown.

"We will face whatever follows, as friends," Oliver said, a quiet strength returning to him.

The Sphinx remained still, a monument of enduring power, its lion body sculpted from the very earth, its human face an enigma etched in stone. It was impressive in its sheer size, dwarfing the figures who stood before it, and regal in its silent authority, a silent guardian of secrets untold. "Then embrace your hearts," its voice resonated, a low hum that seemed to vibrate through the very sand beneath their feet, "for they must endure the storms to unveil the treasures that lie ahead." The words hung in the desert air, heavy with meaning, a prophecy and a challenge woven into one.

With those final, enigmatic words, the Sphinx shifted. The shift was not a violent tremor but a subtle, almost imperceptible movement, akin to a waking giant stretching after centuries of slumber. Dust cascaded down its flanks as a section of the monolithic structure slid back, revealing a hidden passageway. It was a dark, gaping maw in the stone, obscured by layers of time and the relentless kiss of the desert wind. This passageway was more than just a path; it was an invitation, a dare, to continue their journey deeper into the unknown. But going with this invitation was a subtle, unspoken warning, a chilling realisation: companionship, the very bond that had brought them this far, could prove to be just as intricate a puzzle, just as perilous a challenge, as the ancient artefacts they looked for.

The treasures they sought were not only in gilded chambers but also in their delicate trust and understanding.

Feeling empowered by their shared resolve, despite the underlying tension, Ellie took a deep breath. The air was thick with the scent of dust, decay, and the promise of untold wonders. Her heart, still reeling from the recent revelations, steadied itself for the adventures yet to come. Yes, it was a heart divided, torn between the past and the present, loyalty and longing. But within that world of chaos, within the tangled web of emotions that threatened to ensnare her, lay the undeniable promise of building a connection that could transcend all boundaries.

Not only could this connection guide them through the perilous path ahead, but it could also illuminate both their journeys, unveiling truths about themselves and the hidden world. The journey was far from over; in fact, it felt like it had only just begun.

"Together?" she asked, extending her hand towards Oliver.

"Always," he replied, clasping it firmly as they stepped into the unknown, the tug-of-war between past and future curling into a bond filled with both hope and courage.

And so began the next chapter of their adventure—a quest to discover not only the secrets of the artefacts but the depth of their own hearts.

THE VORTEX OF DREAMS

The clock struck one, the sound echoing strangely in the vast hall, as Ellie stood in the heart of the Enchanted Museum. Once a repository of dusty relics, it had transformed into a wondrous, albeit perilous, realm since Dr Bell's mishap had awakened its artefacts. Now, long, dancing shadows stretched from the exhibits, and hushed whispers seemed to emanate from the very walls, murmuring secrets only the enchanted could understand. The weight of the night's adventures, a chaotic tapestry woven with close calls and baffling riddles, pressed upon her shoulders, a tangible burden that mirrored the uncertainty swirling in her gut.

"Where to now, Azrael?" she asked, her voice laced with determination, a shield against the creeping tendrils of fear. But beneath the resolve, a distinct uncertainty lingered, betraying the exhaustion that threatened to overwhelm her. The stone figure of Azrael the Lion, normally a stoic guardian, now radiated an almost palpable energy. Regal and fearsome even in his animated state, he had just revealed, with a rumble of ancient stone, the entrance to what he called the Vortex of Dreams. It was a swirling, iridescent portal shimmering with impossible colours, a gateway said to hold the secrets of time and possibility and the key, perhaps, to undoing the chaos.

Azrael lowered his massive head slightly, a gesture of both respect and reassurance, revealing a surprising warmth that belied his intimidating features, which seemed perpetually etched in a frown, a testament to ages of guarding.

"This path, little champion, leads to the heart of the sanctuary – an intersection of dreams and memories, a nexus point where timelines converge. In here, we may find what we need to confront Valen, the knowledge or the weapon necessary to restore balance to this place and to the world beyond." His voice resonated with a deep, earthy timbre that seemed to vibrate through the very foundations of the museum.

Professor Finch, forever the scholar even in the face of the utterly impossible, adjusted his spectacles, which tended to slip down his nose during moments of high excitement. His eyes danced with a manic gleam, reflecting the swirling vortex before them. "The Vortex is referenced in countless ancient scrolls and fragmented texts, often veiled in metaphor, of course. They say that it weaves realities together, presenting not only vivid and perhaps terrifying visions from the past, but also tantalising glimpses and agonizing choices concerning the future," he explained, his voice quivering with enthusiasm, barely having a tremor of fear. "Imagine, Ellie, the chance to see the consequences of our actions before we take them! But... the scrolls also warn that prolonged exposure can blur the lines between reality and illusion, leaving a traveller lost in the labyrinth of their own mind."

As they stepped into the vortex, the air crackled with an unseen energy, pressing against them like the weight of oceans. Flashes of vivid imagery, fragmented and fleeting, assaulted their senses: a Roman legion marching, a Viking longship cresting a wave, a futuristic city bathed in neon. Then, as abruptly as it began, the chaotic kaleidoscope coalesced. Ellie gasped, finding herself standing in a vibrant marketplace of ancient Egypt. The sun beat down with relentless intensity, baking the sand-coloured stalls that overflowed with wares. Exotically dyed cloths, shimmering blues, reds, and golds, hung from the stalls, fluttering as if a gentle breeze caressed them, a welcome respite from the oppressive heat. The scents of spices, sweet dates, and freshly baked bread mingled in the air, creating a rich and intoxicating aroma. The sounds of bartering, the bleating of goats, and the rhythmic chanting of merchants echoed in her ears, a cacophony of ancient life.

"Look!" cried Azrael, his eyes wide with wonder, nodding toward figures in the distance. A procession, adorned with elaborate headdresses and draped in flowing robes, wound its way toward the riverbank. "Isn't that a description in your book about the Festival of the Nile? I remember you mentioning the sacred barges."

Ellie squinted, shielding her eyes from the glare, her heart racing with a mixture of excitement and apprehension. "Yes! I've read about this – the celebrations of abundance and life, a tribute to the river that sustains them. The legend says the gods themselves bless the waters for fertility and prosperity." She paused, a tremor in her voice. "But how...? How is this real?"

Suddenly, Luci unfurled from her brass form, her scales shimmering with an ethereal light. Her voice, usually playful and teasing, was now smooth, yet laced with an uncharacteristic urgency. "We can't linger here, Ellie.

The vortex grants us glimpses, echoes of potent moments. This vision exists to guide us, to reveal a crucial piece of the puzzle we look for, but we must decipher the truth before it slips away before the vortex closes its door."

Sounding almost as though she had been holding her breath, a fear she hadn't realised she was harbouring now surfacing, Ellie turned away from the mesmerising spectacle of the ancient festival. The vibrant colours and enticing sounds seemed to fade slightly, replaced by the pressing weight of their mission. "Right, you're right. How do we go ahead? What are we looking for?" Her eyes darted around the marketplace, searching for a clue, a symbol, anything that might unlock the secrets held within this fleeting vision.

The serpent, scales shimmering with an ethereal light, coiled gracefully around Ellie's wrist, a living bracelet of wisdom and mystery. Its wise, ancient eyes, flecked with gold, gleamed in the dreamy ambience of the chamber, reflecting the swirling energies that danced within. "The Vortex", it rasped, its voice a low, melodic hum that seemed to vibrate through Ellie's very bones, "shows us paths—futures and pasts intertwined. From the echoes of those who walked before us, we must take the fragments that resonate with our purpose." The serpent's words hung in the air, heavy with meaning and hinting at the perilous journey ahead.

Before Ellie could fully grasp the serpent's cryptic pronouncements, a flash of russet fur and a burst of excited yips announced the arrival of Finn. He made his dexterous entrance, darting around Ellie's feet in playful circles, his tail a blur of orange. "A riddle awaits! This is truly a mind-bender!

I heard Huckleberry cawing around! Something about a gate and a key..." He chattered excitedly, his sharp nose twitching with anticipation, clearly relishing the challenge.

"Huckleberry!" Oliver, the normally stoic museum guard, exclaimed, his carefully composed facade cracking to reveal the anxiety churning within. He wrung his hands, his eyes wide with a mixture of apprehension and relief. "I'd almost forgotten about him. Of all the inhabitants of this place... Will he help us here? Or lead us further into danger?" His voice trembled slightly, betraying the weight of his responsibility for the group's well-being. The mention of Huckleberry seemed to stir a deep-seated fear, a reminder of the unpredictable nature of the dream world they had entered.

Oliver received the ancient stone before anyone else could. His eyes, sharp and black as obsidian, scanned the group with a piercing intelligence that made Ellie feel as though he could see straight through her. "The dreamscape is fickle," he boomed, his voice echoing through the chamber with an authority that demanded attention. "Listen carefully to the echoes of the past, for they hold the key. To pass through this realm, a riddle must be solved! Answer incorrectly, and you risk being lost forever between the threads of time itself." A single feather, dark as midnight, drifted from his wing, a silent promise of the trials to come. The group fell silent, as if the air had been sucked from the room.

Every eye was fixed on Huckleberry, their faces etched with a mixture of trepidation and hope. They were utterly reliant on his guidance, the fate of their quest, perhaps even the world, feeling heavy and precarious upon their shoulders. The raven, perched atop a weathered obelisk, preened thoughtfully, carefully fluffing his obsidian feathers. Then, with a deliberate tilt of his head and a sharp beckon of his beak, he directed their attention to the swirling, kaleidoscopic visions that churned around them. "In the fabric of oblivion woven tight," he croaked, his voice a low, resonant rumble, "what flies without wings but carries the night?"

Ellie's pulse quickened, a frantic drumbeat in her ears. "It's time," she thought fervently, her mind a whirlwind of half-remembered passages from ancient texts. She clawed at the recesses of her memory, searching for the key. The answer lay dormant, obscured by layers of anxiety and the sheer weight of the moment, but a faint light, a glimmer of recognition, beckoned her forward. "It's time! The answer is dreams!" she proclaimed triumphantly, the words bursting from her lips with a desperate urgency.

"Indeed!" Huckleberry cawed, a note of undeniable satisfaction dancing in his voice. He ruffled his feathers again, the gesture almost a congratulatory one. "Now tread lightly, for every answered riddle unlocks a new path, and with each path, new dangers and new choices await."

As if in direct confirmation of her successful deduction and Huckleberry's cryptic warning, the vortex of visions shimmered and shifted with renewed intensity. The chaotic swirl coalesced into a clearer image, resolving into another series of scenes. They depicted the glimmering Lumière, the

"Lady Arabella must have graced this hall," Professor Finch remarked, his voice awed.

"Shall we step into those dreams?" Azrael enquired, his golden eyes alight with curiosity.

"Indeed, we shall," Ellie replied, grinning at the prospect of stepping into history once more. With determination, they approached the swirling images, breaking through the barrier of illusion.

The air shimmered, a dizzying swirl of colours, and then, with disorienting abruptness, they were there. The sudden change transported them into the grand ballroom, echoes of laughter, like a thousand tiny bells, wrapping around them like firm, welcoming arms. They marvelled at the chandeliers, colossal structures of crystal and light, glimmering high above, casting a warm, honeyed glow on the polished floor. This world felt so close, so vividly real, yet impossibly distant—a place where dreams were stitched together in a tapestry of bygone elegance, a world preserved in amber, untouched by the relentless march of time.

Finn, ever the explorer, darted about, his fingers tracing the intricate designs of the gilded corners. He peered behind velvet curtains, his eyes bright with insatiable curiosity. Oliver, a figure of steadfastness, his posture radiating quiet strength, stood rooted near the entrance, surveying the scene with a keen, intelligent gaze. He took in the swirling dancers, the elegant gowns, and the hushed conversations, all with a sense of bewildered awe. "This is more enchanting than I imagined," he murmured, his voice barely a whisper, a glimmer of wonder replacing his earlier apprehension. The first fear in his eyes had been replaced by a light of tentative delight.

At that moment, Lady Arabella appeared from the shadow of a nearby statue, the cold marble of her form inexplicably softening into the warm flesh of life. Her features, impossibly serene, held a wisdom that seemed to span centuries. Wise eyes, the colour of aged brandy, glistened in the soft glow of the chandeliers, reflecting the ballroom's ethereal light. With a voice as smooth as velvet, she spoke, her gaze locking onto Ellie. "To enter the Vortex is to reflect upon choices long forgotten. Each step taken within these walls echoes with the weight of decisions past. You hold a purpose here, Ellie. A memory of deeper significance, a truth long buried, lies beneath the glamour of this dance." Her words hung in the air, a riddle wrapped in silk, promising both revelation and peril. The music swelled, a haunting melody that seemed to resonate deep within Ellie's soul, hinting at the secrets yet to be uncovered.

Ellie watched the elegant lady, captivated by her aura. "What do you mean, Lady Arabella?"

With a graceful motion, Arabella gestured around the ballroom, her hand a delicate conductor leading Ellie's gaze through the swirling scene. Crystal chandeliers cast a warm, inviting glow on the polished floor, reflecting the opulent decorations that adorned the walls. The music played, a lilting waltz that filled the air, but it grew softer, almost imperceptible, as if bowing its head in reverence, nodding to the unspoken truths woven into the tapestry of history. "Every choice made shapes the future, Ellie," Arabella said, her voice low and resonant. "Here, in this dream, you may see defined paths – bridges that were built with ambition and hope, and those that were washed away by the tides of time, swallowed by regret or swept aside by circumstance. Observe them closely, for they hold the echoes of what could be."

The weight of her words struck Ellie, a profound understanding blooming amidst the lingering confusion. The dazzling spectacle of the ballroom seemed to fade slightly, replaced by a sharper focus on the implications of Arabella's words. "I must choose wisely, then," Ellie replied, her voice tinged with a newfound seriousness. "The shadows of history guide us, whispering cautions and offering lessons, yet the yearning for discovery propels us forward, urging us to forge our path."

Just as she spoke, faint silhouettes began to drift through the ballroom, materialising from the edges of Ellie's vision. These were figures dressed in the elegant period attire of bygone eras, men in tailcoats and women in sweeping gowns, twirling in an intricate waltz, a silent, spectral dance. They moved with an ethereal grace, seemingly oblivious to the world outside the confines of their memories. Each dancer appeared as if caught in a frozen moment of time, a miniature tableau vivant, stories wrapped within their steps, secrets hinted at in their lingering glances. Ellie felt a pull, a powerful and almost irresistible desire to join them, to lose herself in the swirling dance of history, to understand the narratives etched into their movements. But she hesitated, a knot of apprehension tightening in her stomach. To join them meant to step into the past, to potentially alter the threads of time. Was she ready for the weight of such a decision? What consequence would her presence bring to the delicate balance of this historical dream?

"I cannot lose myself in this dream," she thought. "We have a mission."

"Focus!" Luci's voice broke through Ellie's thoughts, a sharp reminder of their quest. "What lurks behind this illusion could bind us forever. Seek the clues hidden among the dancers—the truth must become your anchor."

With newfound resolve hardening her gaze, Ellie turned to face her companions. The weight of their quest and the urgency of their situation pressed upon her, demanding action. "Gather around me, everyone!" Her voice, though soft, carried a thread of steel that cut through the ambient music. "We'll explore together. No one wanders off. Pay attention to whispers in the dance—to fleeting gestures, hushed words, and subtle shifts in energy. That is where our next riddle lies, hidden within the rhythm and flow."

Immediately, the group, a mix of anxious and determined faces, began to blend with the dancers. They moved cautiously at first, then with increasing confidence, letting the rhythm guide them. The spirits of the night, both ethereal and grounded, resonated within the enchanting atmosphere, a vibrant tapestry woven with music, movement, and unspoken stories. The pulsating heart of the night echoed through them, each step resonating with possibility, each breath a shared experience. The air itself thrummed with secrets waiting to be uncovered.

As they navigated through the moving sea of elegance, a kaleidoscope of swirling gowns and graceful movements, Ellie's keen eyes scanned the crowd. Amidst the swirling colours and shifting forms, she noticed a peculiar figure—a silhouette subtly different from the rest. It was the distinct shape of a raven, its head bobbing rhythmically, its movements somehow sharper, more deliberate than the others. Its presence felt like a dissonance in the otherwise harmonious dance. "There!" she whispered, pointing with a trembling hand barely visible through the crowd. "Huckleberry!"

A name that carried the weight of lore and whispered warnings, a name that promised answers and perilous challenges.

"Go on, follow your instincts!" cried Finn, his heart racing.

Rushing toward the hazy figure, they slipped through the other dancers until they reached Huckleberry. The raven fluttered his wings playfully, as if inviting them to partake in the dance of fate.

"Seek the mirror that reflects your truth, for therein lies the key to unravel the tapestry," he cawed, his tone playful yet urging.

Ellie brandished resolute determination. "A mirror! It must be an artefact hidden within this vision—a reflection of our choices."

Without a moment's hesitation, they began searching. The grand ballroom, usually a beacon of celebratory life, now felt like a labyrinth of echoing secrets. The room began to spin ever so gently, the music, a haunting waltz emanating from unseen speakers, swaying with an ethereal rhythm that tugged at their subconscious. Each glance turned into a deluge of reflective surfaces – polished chandeliers, ornate picture frames, and even the gleam on the marble floor – each shimmer inviting their gazes, distracting them with their alluring but ultimately empty promises.

At the centre of the ballroom, a grand mirror adorned with intricate engravings beckoned. It wasn't just a mirror; it felt like a portal, a gateway to something more. Its surface shimmered like stars in the night sky, adorned with swirling designs that seemed to shift and change with every breath. It hummed with a silent energy, pulling them closer.

"This is it!" Ellie exclaimed, her voice barely a whisper in the vast space, yet filled with a newfound determination. She couldn't explain how she knew, but the mirror felt like the key. "We have to confront our dreams!" she declared, leading the way forward, her steps echoing softly on the marble.

"We've come too far to falter now," Oliver affirmed, his usually jovial face now etched with a seriousness that mirrored Ellie's. He stepped up beside her, his hand instinctively reaching for hers, a silent gesture of support in the face of the unknown.

As they approached the mirror, it began to resonate, a low thrumming vibration that pulsed through the floor and into their bones. Before them, images of their past and potential futures cascaded and twisted in a vortex of shimmering light. Scenes flashed by – moments of joy, crushing failures, whispered promises, and unspoken fears – all intertwined in a chaotic dance.

"Step forward and face what you see," Azrael encouraged, his voice a calming balm amidst the swirling chaos. His presence was soothing, a grounding force as he stood tall beside them, his eyes filled with understanding and a quiet strength that reassured them they weren't alone.

With hearts pounding a frantic rhythm against their ribs, each member of the group took a place before the mirror. The surface rippled, responding to their presence, morphing and swirling like a living entity. It reflected their deepest dreams and aspirations, shimmering with the potential of what they could become, while simultaneously merging with the stark silhouettes of their past, the experiences that had shaped them into who they were.

Ellie saw visions of herself poring over ancient texts in dimly lit libraries, her heart steeped in scholarly pursuit, each word she read a step closer to unlocking forgotten knowledge. This image seamlessly blended into her future – working alongside her friends, solving ancient riddles, piecing together fragments of forgotten history, her passion ignited by discovery.

And then, from the depths of the mirror, shadows appeared – doubt, whispering insidious lies about her abilities; fear, paralysing her with the potential for failure; and the heavy weight of responsibility, threatening to crush her under the burden of expectation. These shadows, born from her insecurities and anxieties, latched onto her dreams, forming a formidable barrier, a dark cloud threatening to extinguish the brilliant light of her potential.

"Believe, Ellie!" Luci urged, coiling around her wrist for strength. "These shadows hold no power over your essence."

Ellie inhaled deeply, the air catching in her lungs like liquid courage. She focused, feeling the cool marble beneath her bare feet, grounding her whirling thoughts. The grand ballroom, once a scene of shimmering elegance, now felt heavy, haunted by the ghosts of futures feared and mistakes regretted. However, this was no longer the case. "I embrace my past", she declared, her voice resonating with newfound strength, "my allies, and the path ahead!" Each word was a hammer blow against the encroaching darkness, each syllable infused with the conviction of her spirit, dispelling the shadows that clung to the edges of the room.

One by one, her friends followed suit, their hesitations melting under the heat of Ellie's resolve. Oliver, his youthful face etched with the weight of responsibility, faced his burden of duty – the crown, the kingdom, and the lives entrusted to his care. Azrael, his eyes ancient and knowing, accepted his place as a guide, shedding the cloak of aloofness to embrace the role of protector. Each acceptance was a spark, igniting a flame of hope that merged with the burning determination in their hearts. As they spoke, the visions reflected in the ornate mirrors surrounding them grew brighter, clearer, untangling the threads of dreams from the tangled knots of doubt. The fractured images began to coalesce, revealing a mosaic of their intertwined fates, a complex picture of sacrifices and triumphs yet to come.

With each pulse of the unseen energy that thrummed through the ballroom, the vortex in the centre spun faster, weaving vibrant threads of light throughout the chamber. The air crackled with anticipation, elegantly summoning the truth that lay entwined within them, the secret bond that connected their destinies. It was a symphony of shared purpose, resonating with the echoes of battles fought side by side and the promises whispered in the darkest hours.

"Together, we forge our destiny!" they shouted in unison, their voices blending into a powerful chord that shattered the oppressive atmosphere. The mirror, no longer reflecting their individual fears, erupted with a kaleidoscope of colours – emerald, green, sapphire blue, ruby red, and shades beyond human comprehension. The light pulsed, pushing back the encroaching darkness, liberating them from the confines of past anxieties and the shackles of self-doubt.

Suddenly, the vortex widened, yawning open like a gateway to another realm. The swirling energies surged, drawing them back and away from the heavy opulence of the ballroom, pulling them into a bright, boundless expanse where time flowed freely. The room was no longer a gilded cage but a tapestry of dreams, memories, and choices, each thread shimmering with possibility and crackling with raw, untamed magic. They stood at the precipice of their destiny, ready to leap into the unknown, together.

In that moment, Ellie grasped the sheer energy of their unity, a palpable force that resonated within them all. It was more than just camaraderie; it was a deep-seated understanding; a woven connection forged in shared experiences and unwavering support. This understanding was a potent reminder that as they embraced their individual destinies, accepting the paths laid before them with courage and determination, they were never truly alone. They had each other, a constant anchor in the turbulent sea of life.

The vortex, a swirling tapestry of light and shadow, glimmered with renewed intensity. It offered intoxicating glimpses of possibilities yet to unfold, tantalising visions of futures shaped by their choices and actions. They felt the encroaching dawn, a subtle shift in the air that signalled the return of the mundane world. The world outside, with its familiar routines and everyday concerns, beckoned them home, pulling them back from the extraordinary. Yet, even as the sun threatened to break the spell, they stayed illuminated within the enchantment they had forged, bathed in the lingering magic of their shared adventure.

As reality seeped back in, like morning mist dissolving under the rising sun, Ellie felt the warmth of companionship wrap around her like a comforting blanket. It was a quiet reassurance, a silent promise of unwavering support as they prepared to face whatever challenges, whatever obstacles, lay ahead. Together, they were bound by adventure, their hearts intertwined through the vibrant threads of dreams woven in the swirling, mesmerising Vortex. The memories of their shared experiences solidified their bond, creating an unbreakable chain of loyalty and affection.

With a final, lingering glance, they acknowledged the mysterious energy still swirling within the vortex. The shadows twisted and danced within its depths, performing a silent ballet of untold stories and hidden potential. Then, slowly, gracefully, they subsided, leaving nothing but a soft, ethereal glow, a gentle whispering of promises of further adventures to come. These whispers were not just empty hopes but a confident expectation born from the certainty of their shared fate. The enchanted museum, with its endless corridors and echoing halls, eagerly awaited their next journey, their next foray into the unknown. The echoes of the night, the whispers of magic, lingered in the air as they traversed through the historical labyrinth, a place brimming with tales yet to tell, secrets waiting to be unearthed, and destinies longing to be fulfilled.

And in that profound moment of clarity, they knew, with an unwavering conviction, that they were more than mere spectators of time, passively seeing history unfold. They were its architects, its sculptors, actively shaping the narrative, writing the next chapter of their collective story with every step they took, every choice they made. They were the masters of their own destinies, bound together by fate, and ready to face whatever the future held, together.

THE RISE OF
THE SHADOWS

As the night deepened, shadows began to stretch and merge in the dimly lit halls of the museum, transforming familiar exhibits into grotesque parodies of themselves. The gentle echo of footsteps, usually swallowed by the daytime cacophony, now seemed to carry whispers of ancient secrets, rising from the cold stone floors into the vaulted ceilings, where they mingled with the dust mites dancing in the faint light. Ellie, her heart racing with a desperate urgency, quickly glanced at the sudden flickering of the lights overhead.

The erratic illumination cast long, dancing shadows that momentarily illuminated the path ahead, only to plunge it back into deeper obscurity seconds later. Doubt gnawed at her, whispering insidious questions about the sanity of their quest.

"We need to keep moving," she urged her companions, her voice, though strained, steadying the creeping unease that threatened to envelop them all. The oppressive atmosphere, thick with the scent of old parchment and something indefinably ancient, pressed down on her, making it difficult to breathe.

Azrael, no longer a mere statue but fully alive and seemingly brimming with the wisdom of centuries etched into his golden eyes, nodded in sombre agreement. His massive form seemed to radiate a faint, inner light. "The shadows are thickening, becoming more... sentient. It is a clear sign that the guardians are waking. We must find Valen before the darkness consumes us entirely and the balance is irrevocably shattered. Every moment we delay empowers them and weakens Valen's defences." He shifted his weight, a low growl rumbling in his chest, a sound that resonated with the primal power he now had. "The air itself tastes of forgotten magic and impending doom."

Oliver, still reeling from the night's impossible events, found himself in the echoing chamber's air. But Ellie's determined gaze, unwavering and bright with a strange mixture of fear and excitement, spurred him on, reminding him he wasn't alone in this escalating madness.

"No, Oliver," Professor Finch interjected, his voice laced with the academic authority that had always both comforted and intimidated Oliver. He adjusted his spectacles, the lenses magnifying his already intense gaze as he peered at the engraved mural on the wall, a complex tapestry of symbols and figures that seemed to writhe before his eyes. "The artefacts have awakened for a purpose, and whatever lies ahead, however perilous, could hold the key to restoring balance. This isn't some random occurrence, Oliver. This is destiny, unfolding before us."

Nearby, Luci, her voice a melodious whisper that seemed to slither through the air, twisted and turned on her bronze pedestal. Her scales shimmered in the torchlight, and her eyes glinted like polished emeralds, holding an ancient wisdom that both fascinated and terrified Oliver. "To face the shadows, we must understand their origin," she intoned, her forked tongue flicking out. "They are echoes of the past, born from the artefacts' long-forgotten tales, fragments of a narrative lost to time. Follow me, and together we shall unravel their secrets, piece by piece, until the whole picture emerges."

As the group, a motley crew bound together by the bizarre circumstances, reluctantly followed Luci, Finn darted around them, his playful antics momentarily alleviating the oppressive tension. He was a whirlwind of orange fur and boundless energy, a stark contrast to the sombre mood. "This way! This way!" he squeaked, his tail wagging furiously. "There's something shiny over here! And maybe some treats!" He scampered ahead, leading the way into a newly discovered chamber adorned with ancient relics – dusty scrolls, tarnished weapons, and strange, unidentifiable objects that hummed with a low, almost imperceptible energy. The air thickened with anticipation, the sense of purpose, and a growing feeling of dread. The secrets they looked for were close; Oliver could feel it, but he couldn't shake the feeling that some secrets were best left undisturbed.

Entering the chamber was like stepping into a dragon's hoard made of liquid gold. The air thrummed with a palpable energy, a low hum that resonated deep within their bones. Glimmering treasures piled high, not just gold and jewels, but artefacts of impossible beauty: shimmering orbs that seemed to contain miniature galaxies, intricately woven tapestries depicting forgotten battles, and weapons forged from metals unknown to modern science. The walls themselves pulsed with a deep amber light, emanating from veins of luminescent crystal embedded within the stone. This ethereal glow cast shifting silhouettes that danced across the surfaces, transforming familiar shapes into monstrous illusions that played tricks on the eye. At the far end of the room, dominating the space, a massive sarcophagus stood sentinel. Intricately carved from a single block of obsidian, it depicted scenes of a long-lost civilisation, their stories etched in painstaking detail. Its lid was slightly ajar, hinting at the secrets hidden within.

"Look!" Ellie exclaimed, her voice barely a whisper, yet echoing in the vast chamber. Her eyes, wide with wonder and a flicker of apprehension, were fixed on a section of the sarcophagus. "That inscription—it has been partially uncovered! Perhaps we can finally understand the purpose of this place!"

Approaching the sarcophagus with reverence, Professor Finch carefully brushed away centuries of accumulated dust. Beneath his touch, ancient hieroglyphs, crisp and sharp as the day they were carved, were revealed. He traced the symbols with his aged fingers, his brow furrowed in concentration, muttering to himself in a blend of ancient languages and scholarly speculation. "This... this refers to the Keeper of Secrets... the guardian of lost memories. A being charged with safeguarding something of immense importance... something that could rewrite history itself." He paused, his voice taking on a hushed tone. "The text speaks of a power that can unlock the past, but at a terrible price."

Oliver felt a chill creep up his spine, a sensation far colder than the damp air of the tomb. He glanced back at Azrael, their usually taciturn companion. In the amber light, Azrael's eyes gleamed with an unearthly light, a strange, almost predatory hunger that sent a shiver of unease through Oliver. They seemed to reflect the light of the crystals in a way that was... wrong.

"What do you think this phrase means?" he asked hesitantly, his voice catching in his throat.

He felt Azrael knew more than they were saying, that this was more than a historical find; it was something more important and possibly dangerous. He wondered if they had stumbled upon something they weren't meant to find.

"It means that if the shadows are rising, they are linked to someone who wishes to reclaim their forgotten stories," Azrael explained, a hint of urgency carving his voice deeper. "We must decipher the riddle inscribed on this sarcophagus before it's too late."

Luci runs her hand smoothly around the artefact, her form a mesmerising dance of light and shadow. The air crackled with anticipation, a subtle hum vibrating from the ancient object. "Let me assist," she purred, her voice resonating with an otherworldly cadence. "Tales and meanings are woven together, inextricably bound, and their very essence shall guide us. Recite the unspoken, give voice to the silent narratives etched upon this relic, and the path forward shall reveal itself, illuminated by the understanding you unlock."

The group, a huddle of adventurers drawn into this enigmatic quest, leaned closer. Each held their breath, captivated by Luci's presence and the potential answers held within the artefact. As Luci began to unravel the threads of mystery, her voice became like silk through the air, each syllable carefully chosen, each intonation imbued with power. The words seemed to dance around them, weaving a tapestry of arcane knowledge. As she spoke, the symbols etched into the artefact began to shimmer and shift, previously inert glyphs now pulsating with nascent energy, revealing hidden meanings like secrets whispered from the ages. "In the darkness, where shadows creep and nightmares hold dominion, the light of truth is yours to keep. But it is a fragile flame, easily extinguished. Speak the name of that which binds, the key to its construction and purpose, and open the door to the secrets you seek." She paused, her luminous eyes surveying their faces, a silent challenge hanging in the air.

"What could it be?" Ellie mused aloud, her fingers tapping a nervous rhythm against her chin as she concentrated, her brow furrowed in thought. "A name... a title? Could it be something more abstract? A concept deeply intertwined with the artefact's function?" She paced a short distance, her mind racing through possibilities, the weight of the task settling upon her shoulders. The answer, she knew, lay hidden within the riddle, a linguistic puzzle box waiting to be unlocked.

Finn, ever the lively spirit, perked up, his eyes gleaming with a sudden spark of inspiration. "What if it's not something we have to find but something already here? Could it be something that already exists here? Something intrinsic to this place, something that keeps all these stories alive, breathing and vibrant?" He gestured around the chaotic room, littered with ancient relics and forgotten wonders.

"Indeed," Lady Arabella chimed in from her pedestal nearby, her voice a melodic echo in the vast space. Her regal posture, a testament to generations of refined lineage, kept an air of dignity despite the surrounding chaos and the palpable tension. "Ask yourselves, who is the Keeper of Secrets? What unites all the artefacts beneath this roof, binding them together in this collection of whispered histories?" Her gaze swept across the assembled group, a silent challenge in her knowing eyes.

The air thrummed with energy, a tangible hum that resonated with the ancient power contained within the museum's walls. Ellie's mind raced through the possibilities, a whirlwind of theories and half-formed ideas colliding in her thoughts. "It has to be something fundamental," she said, her voice barely a whisper as she tried to grasp the overarching concept.

Then it hit her, the realisation dawning like a sunrise. "The Museum itself! It's not just a building; it's... it's the keeper of our history; it protects these stories, safeguards their essence, and allows them to be shared."

"Then let us speak its name," Azrael encouraged, his voice a low, resonant rumble that seemed to vibrate through the very floorboards. "In the heart of shadows, where secrets slumber and history whispers, speak it aloud. Acknowledge its power and let the magic respond."

Taking a deep breath, Ellie stepped forward, the weight of the moment settling on her shoulders. She felt the eyes of everyone in the room on her, expectant and hopeful. Her voice, though initially trembling, grew stronger with each syllable as she declared, "Museum of Enchantment, Keeper of Secrets!"

As the last syllable fell from her lips, a rush of wind, ancient and powerful, filled the chamber, swirling the dust of centuries into miniature tornadoes that danced across the stone floor. The hieroglyphs carved into the walls seemed to writhe in the sudden gust, their secrets stirred awake. With a deafening crack, the sarcophagus, once a silent container of death, erupted into a blinding light, bathing the chamber in an ethereal glow. From within this radiance, shadows, thick and tangible, began to coalesce, twisting and stretching until they formed distinct shapes. They solidified into spectres of ancient guardians, their faces frozen in expressions caught between the agony of despair and the fragile glimmer of hope, as if they had been waiting an eternity for this moment.

"Seekers of truth," the spectres intoned in unison, their voices a haunting harmony that resonated deep within Ellie's bones. The sound was not one voice multiplied but a single, unified entity speaking through many vessels. "You awaken us from our slumber, a slumber enforced by duty and fuelled by regret. What is it you want that breaches the sanctity of this tomb?"

Ellie felt a wave of apprehension wash over her, a chill that had nothing to do with the tomb's coldness. The weight of history and the power of the unknown pressed down on her. But beneath the fear, a core of determination blazed. "We seek to understand the shadows that plague our world," she declared, her voice ringing with a newfound strength that surprised even herself. "We seek to unravel their origins and put an end to their insidious rise before they consume all that we hold dear."

A whisper, like the rustling of papyrus scrolls in a forgotten library, danced in the air around them, rippling with the echo of forgotten promises and broken vows. The temperature in the chamber dropped noticeably. "Then you must face the guardian of shadows," the spectres warned, their figures flickering uncertainly, losing and regaining their form as if tethered to this reality by a fragile thread. "A trial awaits, one that tests not only your strength but also your courage, your wisdom, and the very purity of your intentions. Before dawn, Valen Timekeeper, the master of temporal currents and keeper of forbidden knowledge, will unveil the final challenge. Prepare yourselves. The fate of your world hangs in the balance."

Azrael's mane bristled with anticipation, the fine hairs standing on end as a low growl rumbled in his chest. "We are ready," he affirmed, his voice echoing slightly in the chamber, looking towards the doorway that led deeper into the labyrinth of aisles and treasures. His eyes, pools of molten gold, scanned over his companions, Oliver and Finn, a silent reassurance passing between

251

them. He could practically taste the magical energy emanating from the depths of the labyrinth, a siren's call to the adventurous, or perhaps, the foolish.

As they exited the chamber, the atmosphere underwent a dramatic shift. The warm, inviting light that had bathed the room receded, leaving them standing on the precipice of an encroaching darkness. It wasn't merely the absence of light; it was a palpable presence, a suffocating weight that settled upon their shoulders. Shadows, previously benign, began to whisper among themselves, their voices a low, sibilant chorus that slithered around them. They tightened around them like a shroud, a suffocating embrace that hinted at the dangers that lay ahead.

"Stay close," murmured Oliver, his voice low but firm, a thread of warning woven into its texture. He reached out, his hand brushing against Finn's shoulder. "I can feel it... something's watching." His eyes, narrowed and focused, darted from shadow to shadow, trying to discern the unseen observer. A primal instinct screamed at him to turn back, but the lure of the treasures, and perhaps a touch of reckless curiosity, kept him rooted to the spot.

Driven by a sudden, almost frantic instinct, Finn darted ahead, his footsteps echoing in the oppressive silence. He seemed compelled forward, pulled by an invisible tether. The flickering light from Oliver's lantern barely pierced the gloom, casting elongated, grotesque shadows that danced across the walls. Soon, they found themselves inside an expansive gallery, its dimensions vast and imposing. Lining the walls were monstrous statues, figures sculpted with a disturbing blend of artistry and malice. Each loomed with an animated expectancy, as if poised to come to life at any moment. The lights, previously a source of weak comfort, now flickered ominously, their erratic dance illuminating the sculptures in fleeting glimpses that shifted between grandeur and decay, beauty and horror. The overall effect was unnerving, a visual symphony of dread that resonated deep within their bones. The gallery felt less like a place of display and more like a waiting room...for something terrible.

A faint echo pierced the silence—the sound of rustling wings. Suddenly, Huckleberry appeared, his ebony feathers glinting in the low light. "Beware the shadows, adventurers! They are drawn to fear, relishing despair. We must stay united against them!"

Ellie steadied herself, heart pounding. "What do we do?"

"Follow the light!" Huckleberry cawed, flapping towards a luminescent orb hovering above one of the statues. It pulsed in rhythm, casting a glimmering pathway that fractured into two directions ahead.

"Two paths," Finn noted with keen interest, his tail twitching. "Which one do we take?"

"You must choose wisely," Lady Arabella advised, her voice echoing like a distant memory. "The left leads to knowledge, whilst the right harbours hidden dangers."

"Knowledge!" Ellie blurted, her instincts screaming for them to tread carefully. "We came to unravel the past, not confront danger."

But even as she spoke, a cold gust of wind swept through the gallery, sending a chill straight to her bones. Shadows spiralled around them, converging along the right path where laughter, tinged with malice, echoed distantly.

"Do we go towards the laughter or the knowledge?" Oliver questioned, uncertainty gnawing at him.

"The choice is yours alone," Huckleberry cautioned, his voice laced with gravity. "Choose wisely, for the shadows thrive on hesitation."

"Only time can tell which path holds the truth," Azrael pondered, pushing through the uncertainty surrounding them. "Ellie, the decision lies with you."

As the echoes of laughter, hollow and distorted, danced mockingly in the air, Ellie bit her lip, her thoughts tumbling like stones in a chaotic river. The laughter, a remnant of happier times, now felt like a taunt, a cruel reminder of what they were fighting to preserve. Her innate desire for knowledge, a lifelong thirst for understanding and truth, spoke loudly, a beacon in the swirling darkness. Yet, the shadowy allure of danger, the exciting whisper of shortcuts and forbidden power, tempted all too readily. The museum, steeped in history and secrets, offered both enlightenment and perilous paths. But the burden of leadership, a weight she hadn't asked for but now carried with unwavering resolve, called to her. The choice she made now, in this moment of terrifying uncertainty, would shape not only her fate but the fate of everyone who had placed their trust in her.

"Towards knowledge!" she declared, her voice ringing with a conviction that surprised even herself, cutting through the oppressive atmosphere of fear. She stepped forward, her chin lifted, a single point of defiance against the encroaching darkness. "We must remember that all shadows conceal a story. Every whispered secret, every forgotten truth, every artefact shrouded in mystery... it all holds knowledge. There lies our weapon against the darkness. Understanding is our armour, wisdom our shield."

With that affirmation, a surge of hope, fragile but undeniable, rippled through the group. They aligned themselves beside Ellie, a motley collection of scholars, adventurers, and guardians, each bound by a shared purpose and a fierce determination to protect the museum and its invaluable contents. Shoulders touching, they moved together, a united front, towards the path of light – a literal path illuminated by flickering lanterns and a metaphorical path guided by the promise of enlightenment.

Suddenly, as they took their first tentative steps upon that path, an uproar of shadows erupted, a cacophony of hisses and growls that sent a shiver down their spines. The darkness, previously lurking in the corners, now poured from the depths, a viscous, oily substance given terrifying life. It twisted and whirled, coalescing into grotesque forms – spectral figures with clawed hands and burning eyes, a malevolent manifestation of the museum's fears and regrets, the embodiment of all the pain and suffering that had been locked within its walls for centuries. The air crackled with unseen energy, and the scent of decay filled their nostrils.

"Stay together!" Azrael commanded, his voice like thunder, a booming roar that momentarily eclipsed the fear. He raised his own weapon – an antique staff topped with a shimmering crystal – brandishing it like a conductor leading an orchestra of defiance. "Embrace the knowledge; hold onto the light! Remember why we are here! Fear is their weapon, but knowledge is our power! Do not let them consume you!" His words served as a rallying cry, a reminder of their shared purpose and the power that lay within them. The battle had begun.

As they advanced, their resolve lit a spark, a defiant flicker against the oppressive darkness. The shadows writhed, like sentient tendrils, pushing against their every step, whispering insidious doubts and conjuring illusions meant to break their will. But unity among the adventurers, the unspoken pact forged in shared trials and mutual respect, fuelled their progress. It was a tangible force, a shield against the encroaching despair.

"We are bound by history!" Ellie shouted, her voice ringing out, a clear, unwavering beacon in the suffocating gloom. Determination lifted her voice, lending it a strength that defied the shadows' tries to smother them, to silence their hope. "Together, we are stronger! The past lives within us, a reservoir of courage and knowledge that this darkness cannot extinguish!"

Bit by bit, their shared courage, their unwavering belief in each other, carved openings in the thick darkness. These weren't just gaps; they were breaches, wounds inflicted on the oppressive entity that allowed glimmers of light, stolen from forgotten eras and preserved within their hearts, to pierce through. They pressed on, deeper and deeper into the heart of the gallery, a labyrinthine space filled with echoing silence and half-seen artefacts. They ventured into the unknown, where ancient echoes woven in time, the whispers of empires and the sighs of long-dead heroes awaited their arrival.

The rise of the shadows, once an overwhelming force that threatened to consume them entirely, was no longer an insurmountable obstacle. Instead, it became a canvas, a dark and foreboding background waiting to be painted with tales of courage, friendship, and discovery. Each step forward was a brushstroke, each shared glance a vibrant hue, transforming the oppressive gloom into a testament to their resilience.

As the light, painstakingly coaxed from the depths of their spirits, began to vanquish the darkness, the air thrummed with anticipation. Then, horns echoed within the hallowed museum halls, ancient and sonorous, heralding not the end of their journey but the beginning. Their current struggle was merely a prelude, setting the course for the true confrontation that awaited them with Valen, The Timekeeper, a being whose power warped reality and threatened to unravel the fabric of existence.

And as dawn approached, painting the sky with hues of hope and renewal that mirrored the burgeoning light within the museum, the building itself seemed to surge with untold potential. It pulsed with the promise of new stories yet to be told, of legends waiting to be written. The museum enfolded Ellie and her friends in an adventure unlike any other – one where the whispers of the night, the chilling pronouncements of despair, would transform into the whispers of destiny, guiding them towards their final confrontation and the fate of time itself.

BOUND BY
ENCHANTMENT

The air inside the Enchanted Museum crackled with an unfamiliar energy, thick and buzzing like a disturbed hive. Ellie stood in the centre of the grand hall, the ornate mosaic floor cold beneath her boots. Surrounding her were the artefacts – Egyptian sarcophagi gleaming with an eerie gold, suits of armour reflecting fractured moonlight, and glass cases filled with objects that hummed with restrained power. Each glimmered with secrets waiting to be unlocked, whispering promises of forgotten stories and perilous quests. The strokes of midnight had come and gone, their resonating chimes replaced by a growing cacophony.

Whatever enchantment Dr Bell had inadvertently unleashed, a mystical experiment gone awry, now thundered through the museum like an awakening storm, shaking the very foundations of the building. Shadows flickered against the walls, dancing in grotesque shapes as if mimicking the awakening of something ancient and malevolent. Creatures long dormant within their preserved states – taxidermied beasts, fossilised skeletons, and even the mannequins in historical attire – began to stir with unsettling life. And above it all, Ellie felt an undeniable pull, a magnetic force drawing her toward her next adventure, a thrilling and terrifying prospect all at once.

Professor Finch, his customary tweed jacket now ruffled and his hair askew, paced nervously beside a display case having a shimmering Aztec headdress. He distractedly adjusted his spectacles, pushing them up his nose with a trembling hand. "We must find Valen," he insisted, his voice a high-pitched tremor. "He holds the key to restoring order, the linchpin in Bell's temporal equations! Without him, we may find ourselves lost in a tangle of time, our very existence rewritten." He wrung his hands, a picture of scholarly distress.

"Easy for you to say, Finch. You've been dreaming of night adventures like this forever," Oliver remarked, scratching his head beneath his security guard cap, his youthful face creased with uncertainty. The museum guard hadn't signed up for this level of excitement, of cosmic disruption, when he'd stumbled upon his midnight routine. He'd envisioned quiet patrols, maybe a rogue teenager sneaking a peek at a dinosaur bone. "But we're up against enchanted artefacts, ancient mysteries, and potentially angry Egyptian gods. Not exactly in my job description, is it?" He nervously adjusted his holster, the weight of his flashlight feeling woefully inadequate against the power swirling around them.

Before Ellie could respond, a dramatic voice cut through the escalating tension. Azrael crashed into the conversation, an almost theatrical entrance. As the clock struck two, its chimes warped and distorted by the magical surge, his golden eyes began to glow with an incandescent light, illuminating the dim hall and casting long, dramatic shadows. He stood tall and imposing, a figure who barely had energy. "Fear not, brave souls!" his voice echoed like rolling thunder, resonating deep within their chests. "This night holds the answers you look for, and I, Azrael, shall guide you through the perilous passages of time. But beware, the road ahead is perilous, and your choices will determine the fate of this museum and maybe the world!"

He swept his arm dramatically, and a gust of wind seemed to answer, swirling dust motes into miniature vortexes around him. The adventure had truly begun.

Finn, a whirlwind of boundless energy, burst into the room, his every movement a testament to his tireless nature. He zipped and zagged, his inherent playful spirit at once lifting the atmosphere, infusing it with an almost childlike sense of wonder. "What's the master plan, then, you brilliant lot?" he chirped, his voice bubbling with excitement. "Are we going to crack this puzzle like walnuts under a sledgehammer, or are we diving headfirst into the lion's den, claws and all?" He punctuated his question by darting playfully between Ellie's and another's legs, a flash of bright clothes and boundless energy.

"Our immediate priority", Ellie announced, her voice firm with determination, "is to locate Luci. She holds the key to understanding this place." She paused, her eyes gleaming with purpose. "I intend to weave my knowledge of history, gleaned from countless hours of study, with the living artefacts that surround us. Luci has the unique ability to unravel the riddles barring our path. If we can solve them, if we can truly understand the threads that bind this place, perhaps we will draw closer to Valen."

As if summoned by the sheer force of Ellie's conviction, Luci appeared from the shadows, slithering gracefully into a pool of dappled light. Her bronze scales, catching the light, shimmered and rippled like ancient scrolls unfurling. The effect was mesmerising, lending her an aura of timeless wisdom. "You have made a wise and prudent choice, Ellie," she hissed, her voice smooth and flowing like silk draped over polished stone.

"Follow me, and I shall weave the tapestry of knowledge you require, binding together the threads of past and present."

With newfound resolve, the group fell into step behind Luci, following her into a narrow, winding corridor. The walls were lined with incredible paintings, but these were no static artworks. They shifted and breathed, reacting to the ambient light and the group's presence, becoming like living memories playing out before their very eyes. As they walked deeper, the shadows themselves seemed to dance, morphing into fleeting figures from the past, their silent forms whispering secrets of long-forgotten times.

A voice, rich and resonant, echoed through the corridor, seemingly emanating from everywhere and nowhere at once. "Remember, Ellie," the voice boomed, found instantly as belonging to Lady Arabella. Even from her stony pedestal, where she stood frozen in time as a regal statue, her presence commanded attention. "History is not a simple story; it is a complex tapestry, embroidered with tales of both triumph and unspeakable despair. Do not let its harsher threads frighten you, child. Learn from them."

The regal statue, seemingly oblivious to the passage of time, saw the shifting murals as they passed, her wisps of hair painstakingly painted in delicate marbled hues. It was then, in that moment, bathed in the ethereal glow of the corridor's living paintings, that Ellie utterly understood the purpose of their quest. It was not merely a thrilling adventure, a childish game of hide-and-seek. It was something far more profound: a communion with history itself, a chance to understand the echoes of the past and, perhaps, to shape the future.

"Do you feel it?" Ellie turned to her companions, her heart racing. "These artefacts—they're living, breathing stories. Each holds its magic. If we can connect with them, perhaps they will reveal the path we need to take!"

Her fervour—a contagious blend of desperation and hope—ignited a spark within Oliver. He straightened, his shoulders squaring. He'd been hesitant, unsure of their mission, but seeing Luci's passionate commitment erased his doubts. "Right! We've got to unlock these secrets before dawn. Every second counts. Let's not waste another moment on strategising; acting is paramount!" He clapped his hands together, a sound that echoed in the cavernous space.

They pressed onwards, Luci leading them with the confidence of one who knew the land intimately. She navigated through a labyrinth of corridors, her hand brushing against cold stone walls etched with forgotten languages. Finally, she stopped before an enigmatic door. It was made of an obsidian-like substance, and upon its surface pulsed ancient symbols, their meaning lost to time but radiating an undeniable power. With a deep breath, she touched a specific sequence, and the door groaned open, revealing the room beyond.

The room heaved with a thousand days of history, pressing down on them with the weight of ages past. A grand tapestry, vast and breathtaking, was draped across the high ceiling. It wasn't woven in typical fashion; rearrange at will, as if reflecting the ever-changing flow of time itself.

"Deciphering this tapestry lies at the heart of our adventure," Finn squeaked, his voice barely above a whisper, his eyes wide with a mixture of fear and unadulterated excitement. He pointed a trembling finger towards the centre of the tapestry. "Look at the centrepiece! Constellations surround it. surrounded by constellations. Perhaps it can guide us! Each star seems to align with a specific purpose or meaning.

Indeed, the constellations glimmered like stars under a night sky, each one pulsating with an inner light, as if it held recounted stories yearning to be told. The constellations were not static images; rather, they were living representations of celestial events, with each shimmer being a forgotten moment. They were not mere images but living representations of celestial events, with each shimmer symbolising a forgotten moment in time. They were living representations of celestial events, with each shimmer being a forgotten moment. But before they could explore their hidden meanings, a presence interrupted their concentration.

A shadow stirred in the far corner of the room. Huckleberry , perched for too long in still silence, unfolded his massive wings. The movement sent dust motes dancing in the air, and a low, guttural caw echoed through the chamber, commanding their attention. His eyes, ancient and knowing, seemed to penetrate their very souls.

"Answers lie in what you seek, woven into the fabric of legends past," he croaked, his voice a rasping echo of forgotten kings. "Two riddles shield Valen; only with their answers may the path unfold anew. Beware, for failure invites chaos and the unravelling of time itself."

Ellie stepped forward, her scholar's mind already racing, piecing together the fragmented pronouncements. Her fingers twitched, eager to transcribe and understand. "What are the riddles? We will solve them together, Huckleberry. Tell us what we must know."

Huckleberry spread his wings further, the shadows of the tapestry seeming to entwine and deepen around him, magnifying his imposing figure. A chilling wind swept through the room as he pronounced, his voice reverberating with ageless power, "First, we must honour the sun yet embrace the night." I give you this: What flies without wings? Valen is hanging in the balance.

"A shadow", Ellie replied instinctively.

At her words, the ancient tapestry, hanging heavy with age and untold stories, rippled as if disturbed by a sudden, unseen wind. Beams of ethereal light, like captive sunbeams long imprisoned within the woven threads, extricated themselves from the intricate designs. They converged upon a previously obscured section of the tapestry, illuminating it with an otherworldly glow. This new section revealed intricate inscriptions, alien in their script yet strangely familiar, pulsating with a vibrant golden hue that seemed to breathe with life.

"Excellent, my historian," Luci remarked slyly, a hint of amusement dancing in her crimson eyes. "Your knowledge serves us well. But solve the second riddle so we may turn the key and unlock what lies beyond."

"I'm ready," Ellie affirmed, her voice barely a whisper despite the adrenaline coursing through her veins. Her heart pounded with anticipation, a frantic drumbeat against the rising excitement and a prickle of apprehension. The weight of responsibility settled heavily upon her, knowing that their success – or failure – rested on her shoulders.

Huckleberry, the gargantuan raven with shimmering obsidian feathers, shifted his gaze, his intelligent eyes pinning Ellie to the spot. "Though it is light as a feather, the strongest man cannot hold it for long. What is it?" His voice resonated with the age of mountains and the secrets of forgotten empires, each syllable a challenge and a test.

Ellie closed her eyes for a moment, focusing her mind, recalling ancient texts and forgotten lore. The answer flickered at the edge of her consciousness, then blossomed into certainty. "The answer is... breath," she declared triumphantly, her voice ringing with newfound confidence.

With that final word, an eruption of golden light surged into the chamber, bathing everything in its radiant glow. They felt a rush of air, not a gentle breeze, but a powerful swirling vortex that tugged at their clothes and whispered unintelligible secrets in their ears. Suddenly, the very fabric of reality felt thinner, as if a veil had been lifted, revealing the raw, untamed power beneath. Time itself seemed to shift and pulsate, accelerating and slowing in erratic bursts, opening a shimmering, ethereal doorway – a gateway into another realm entirely.

"Into the sanctum of Valen," Azrael proclaimed in astonishment, his usual stoic demeanour momentarily shattered by the sheer spectacle. The glory of their triumph was clear in his stance, his shoulders squared, his chin lifted in anticipation. "But beware! The labyrinth of time holds traps and uncertainties beyond your wildest imaginings. Turn not against the heart, for it will lead to dire fates!" His warning hung heavy in the air, a sombre reminder of the dangers that lay ahead, even in the face of their hard-won victory. The golden doorway beckoned, promising untold power and unimaginable perils.

"Together, we can do this; we are bound by enchantment!" Ellie shouted, inspiring confidence in her friends. Their camaraderie shone like a beacon, pushing aside lingering doubts.

They entered the shimmering realm – the hall of Valen – a vast, breathtaking chamber that seemed to breathe with the passage of epochs. Intricate gears, some the size of carriages, others no larger than a watch's pinion, spun and meshed in a mesmerising dance of perpetual motion. Gleaming brass cogs ground against polished steel, their rhythmic ticking a symphony of precision, each beat a testament to the meticulous order that reigned within. Delicate pendulums swung in hypnotising arcs, their movements echoing the ebb and flow of history itself. Steam hissed softly from ornate pipes that snaked across the ceiling, adding a layer of mystique to the already surreal atmosphere.

At the very centre of this mechanical marvel, bathed in the ethereal glow emanating from the intricate machinery, stood a cloaked figure. Valen. Their face remained hidden in the deep shadows cast by the cowl, obscuring any trace of identity or emotion. An aura of immense power radiated from them, making the very air crackle with anticipation.

"You have found your way to the heart of the museum," Valen spoke, their voice resonating like a peal of thunder through the hall yet having an undercurrent of ancient wisdom. The sound seemed to vibrate within their bones, carrying the weight of countless ages. "But knowledge unchains only those who prove their unity. The past guards its secrets jealously. What binds you, brave adventurers? What is the common thread that has led you to this precipice of revelation?"

Ellie stepped forward, her gaze unwavering, her voice ringing with conviction. She drew upon the collective experiences of their arduous journey, the lessons etched into their hearts through trials and triumphs. "We are woven from stories of the past; each thread connected to the other. We share laughter that echoes through the ages, overcome fears that have haunted generations, and embark on adventures that write new chapters in the grand narrative. It is not just about individual accomplishments; it is our bond, our shared humanity, that brings us strength. History isn't just about objects and artefacts locked away in dusty rooms; it's about connection, empathy, and the understanding that we are all part of a larger story."

"Wisdom lies not in the solitude of one but the harmony of many," Valen mused, tilting their head slightly as if considering the implications of Ellie's words. A subtle shift occurred in the air, a softening of their rigid posture, a hint of approval perhaps. "Only thus will time reveal its secrets to those who seek it with open hearts and united spirits. Your understanding pleases me. But words are fleeting. Only action can truly prove your worth. Your final challenge awaits!"

Certainly! Here is a refined version of the selected text:

As the last word echoed through the chamber, the very fabric of reality seemed to warp and bend. The intricate machinery around them churned and whirred with increasing intensity. The hall itself began to morph, the walls dissolving and reforming, shifting like the sands of time in an hourglass. Before them, in the space that had been a meticulously ordered workshop, a labyrinth began to materialise.

It was no ordinary maze. This was a shimmering, ethereal construct, its walls composed of pure light and shadow. The corridors darted in and out of existence, solidifying and dissolving with a disorienting rhythm. The architecture seemed simple at first glance yet quickly proved to be perplexing and deceptive. Shadows flickered in every corner, playing tricks on the eye. Some paths glistened with an inviting, golden light, promising progress and enlightenment. Others, however, swallowed light whole, beckoning with a dark and ominous allure, hinting at dead ends and hidden perils. The air thrummed with an energy that both thrilled and terrified. Their ultimate test had begun.

Entranced, Finn exclaimed, "Look! Only one path glimmers invitingly, while others fade into darkness!" His voice echoed slightly in the cavernous space, carrying a note of both wonder and trepidation. He pointed towards the single corridor radiating a soft, ethereal light, a stark contrast to the oppressive blackness that consumed the rest of the labyrinth.

Ellie squinted, understanding something clearly at last was faint, almost pulsating at the edges of uncertainty. "Together, we must navigate this maze—not just as individuals, but as one!" Her words were firm, a beacon of resolve in the face of the unknown. She recognised the fragility of the light, how easily it could be extinguished. This wasn't a challenge to be faced alone; it demanded constructive collaboration and unwavering trust.

They held hands, forming a united front, and stepped into the labyrinth's embrace. The glow of the artefacts flickered around them, whispering encouragement. The touch was a silent promise, a conduit for shared strength. As they crossed the threshold, the enchanted artefacts lining the walls seemed to respond, their gentle luminescence intensifying, casting dancing shadows that seemed to murmur secrets of guidance and hope. The shadows seemed to retreat, pinned back by their determination and unity.

Together they manoeuvred through the maze's twists and turns, every corner challenging their resolve but never blurring the bond they forged. Under the eerie light of the enchanted artefacts, every laughter shared, every nagging fear vanquished, reinforced their collective strength. The labyrinthine corridors tested them with illusions and dead ends, whispered temptations and sudden drops in temperature. But with every puzzle solved and every obstacle overcome, their camaraderie deepened. A nervous joke from Finn, a reassuring hand squeeze from Ellie, and the Professor's calm directives—each small act wove a stronger tapestry of reliance.

As they reached the centre, an ethereal door appeared before them, shimmering with endless stories yet to be explored. With one final glance at each other, Ellie, Finn, and Professor Finch pushed open the door together. The door pulsed with raw energy, hinting at the countless possibilities and untold adventures that lay beyond. A wave of anticipation washed over them; the successful navigation of the maze had been merely the prologue. Sharing a brief, meaningful look—a silent acknowledgement of their shared journey and mutual readiness—they gripped the cool, smooth surface of the door and pushed it open, stepping into the next chapter of their extraordinary quest.

Uniting under the banner of friendship forged through adventure, they stepped beyond the threshold of Valen's domain, plunging headfirst into the beautiful chaos of unfolding destiny, forever bound by the enchantment of the night.

I hope this refinement captures the essence of your original text while enhancing its flow and clarity. Please let me know if there's anything else you'd like to adjust!

Trials of Courage

The quiet hum of the museum, usually a soothing drone for Ellie, was now a tense undercurrent, a subtle soundtrack to the gathering storm. The sound was disrupted as Ellie, Professor Finch – his brow furrowed in scholarly concern – Oliver, the museum guard, and their newfound companions huddled in the echoing semicircle of the Great Hall. Above them, suspended from the immense domed ceiling, the hourglass hanging in the museum's centre ticked ominously, each grain of sand a relentless countdown, signalling the rapidly dwindling hours of mystery left to unravel. The midnight sun, that bizarre anomaly that had bathed the city in ethereal light, had now abandoned the sky, plunging the museum into an unnerving darkness. A haunting stillness draped the exhibits, the silent statues and ancient artefacts seeming to hold their breath, covered in an unseen cloak of anticipation.

"Are we ready for what lies ahead?" Ellie's voice trembled slightly, betraying the fear she desperately tried to conceal. Her gaze flitted from one flickering candlelight to another, the dancing flames casting elongated, grotesque shadows that seemed to writhe with a life of their own. Each shadow seemed to whisper of hidden dangers and unknown consequences.

"Ready?" Oliver scoffed, his bravado bubbling to the surface like a shaken soda. He puffed out his chest, momentarily forgetting the strange occurrences that had led them here. "I was born ready. What could be more dangerous than working the night shift in a museum filled with dust and the occasional pigeon? Besides, I've got my trusty flashlight and my years of experience handling unruly school children on field trips!" He brandished his flashlight with a flourish, the beam cutting a weak swathe through the darkness.

Finn, the mischievous sprite they had recently met, ever playful and immune to the gravity of the situation, darted in and out of shadows, a phantom blur of motion. He seemed to delight in tackling Oliver's bravado head-on, nipping at the guard's shoelaces with mischief glinting in his beady eyes. He was a whirlwind of impish energy, a stark contrast to the growing tension in the room.

"Indeed, dear guard," chimed Azrael the Lion, his deep voice resonating across the hall, a rumble that seemed to vibrate the very foundations of the museum. His golden eyes, usually warm and benevolent, now held a glint of solemn understanding. "Courage is not born of reckless bravado, young one. It is measured by the heart's resolve when faced with trials. We must tread carefully; darkness often holds more than mere shadows. It holds secrets, and secrets, as we are about to discover, can be quite dangerous." He shifted his massive weight, his gaze sweeping over each of his companions, assessing their readiness.

Ellie nodded, feeling the weight of the lion's words as if they were a stone resting on her chest. The easy confidence she had tried to muster crumbled under the weight of Azrael's pronouncement. The journey ahead promised challenges that would test not only their courage but their very spirits.

She knew the night was far from over and that the museum held secrets darker and deeper than they could have imagined.

"Then it seems we have a trial of courage ahead," Professor Finch remarked, his voice a curious blend of apprehension and barely had glee. He adjusted his spectacles, which perpetually threatened to slide off his nose, as his eccentric excitement peaked. A faint flush rose on his cheeks, betraying the gravity of the situation warring with the thrill of academic discovery. Flipping open the ancient tome he had discovered earlier, its leather brittle with age and smelling faintly of dust and forgotten magic, he found an inscription detailing a series of trials intrinsically linked to the artefacts they had inadvertently awakened.

"Valen", he announced, his voice echoing slightly in the cavernous hall, "oversees this ancient test—a series of riddles and challenges designed to gauge not only our physical prowess but, more importantly, our resolve and wisdom. The inscription speaks of impossible choices, deceptive illusions, and tests of character that will push us to our very limits. To go ahead, to secure the power these artefacts hold, we must embrace these trials and confront our deepest fears." He looked around at the group, his bespectacled gaze hopeful, almost pleading.

Luci uncoiled herself elegantly from the top of a weathered pedestal. Her bronze scales, each the size of a florin, glinted like liquid gold in the soft, ethereal light filtering through the hidden chambers. She moved with a sinuous grace, a living embodiment of ancient wisdom. "Let me whisper the secrets of the past," she hissed, her voice a low, hypnotic rumble that seemed to vibrate within their very bones. "Courage, my dear companions, often lies not in brute force or reckless abandon, but within the stories we tell, the bonds we forge, and the truths we uncover about ourselves."

As her words wafted through the hall, carrying the weight of centuries, the statues surrounding them seemed to subtly lean in, their stony faces almost animated, as if eager to take part in the discourse. Legends whispered that these statues were not mere decoration but the petrified remains of past challengers, forever bound to see the trials. Lady Arabella, a woman of quiet strength and unwavering loyalty, stepped forward, her presence radiating a calm that belied the daunting task ahead. Her voice, smooth and melodic, carried a reassuring tone that helped to quell the growing sense of unease. "Long ago, I bore witness to those who sought strength and knowledge within these trials. Each proved their worth not through individual brilliance but through laughter shared in the face of adversity, the unwavering support of friendship, and the undeniable bravery needed to face their own inner demons. Together," she concluded, her gaze sweeping over each of their faces, "We will forge our path, not as individuals, but as a unified force, ready to face whatever Valen Timekeeper has in store for us."

The group exchanged knowing glances, a silent language passing between them. The weight of their shared purpose settled upon them, solidifying their resolve. No longer were they just individuals; they were a collective, bound by a mission.

A steely determination replaced any doubts that had persisted moments earlier. This was where they proved their mettle, drawing strength not just from within but from the unspoken support radiating from one another. They were connected: a chain of courage forged in the face of the unknown.

"Then let us begin," Ellie declared, her voice ringing with a newfound confidence. An inner fire ignited within her, fuelled by the shared resolve and the challenge that lay ahead. As she took a resolute step forward, the very air around them seemed to respond. Shadows writhed and danced, mimicking their anticipation, twisting into grotesque shapes that hinted at the dangers to come.

Before them, the air shimmered and shifted, bending the light into a kaleidoscope of swirling colours. Slowly, painstakingly, the distortion coalesced, revealing a colossal archway of ancient stone. Hieroglyphs and cryptic inscriptions covered its surface, a silent testament to a forgotten age. Finn, ever the impulsive adventurer, bounded through the archway with a playful yip, his tail wagging with deceptive nonchalance. "Come on, slowpokes!" his voice echoed from the other side, laced with a mock impatience. "Waiting will just make the trials even scarier!"

Ellie turned to Professor Finch, his face illuminated by the ethereal glow emanating from the archway. He stood transfixed, his fingers hovering inches from the ancient carvings, as if afraid to break the spell. "Professor?" she prompted, her voice laced with urgency. "What do they say?"

The professor shook his head, his eyes wide with a mixture of awe and apprehension. "It speaks of a creature feared and revered... a guardian of the future, bound to these trials since time immemorial." His finger, trembling slightly, traced the intricate carvings, deciphering the symbolic language. "To pass through, we must awaken its spirit. Only then shall we be deemed worthy to face the first trial."

Huckleberry cawed from a nearby statue, his voice a ghostly echo. "To summon the guardian, you must answer truthfully. Fear is but an illusion; it is in your hearts where clarity lies."

"Fear... illusion..." Ellie whispered, mindful of the depths of courage needed to move forward. "Perhaps our fears hold more power than we care to admit."

At that moment, the archway illuminated brilliantly, bathing the clearing in a light so intense it seemed to hum with power. The air thrummed with anticipation, a palpable energy that prickled their skin and quickened their pulses. The beckoning light drew them closer, an irresistible force promising challenge and reward. "Let us descend into the trial," Azrael announced, his voice resonating with the weight of the impending ordeal. With a deep breath, Ellie steeled her nerves, her heart pounding against her ribs. She stepped through the shimmering portal, feeling a pull of energy envelop her entirely, a disorienting swirl that tugged at her very being.

They landed with a soft thud in a vast chamber carved deep within the earth. A flat expanse of ancient stone stretched before them, its surface intricately carved with swirling patterns that seemed to shift and writhe in the dim light. Dust motes danced in the air, illuminated by an unseen source. In the centre of the chamber, an enormous stone statue towered, its scale dwarfing them into insignificance.

It was the embodiment of the guardian they had awoken, a sentinel forged from the very bedrock of the mountain. Its fierce visage, etched with lines of ancient wisdom and untold battles, glimmered with the essence of countless souls who had faced their fears across time. Each crack and crevice in its stony form seemed to tell a silent story of courage and despair.

"Your trial shall begin now," the statue boomed, its voice echoing through the chamber with the force of a thunderclap. The sound vibrated through their bones, a resonant pronouncement that left no room for doubt. "Face your innermost fears, and only then shall you prove your valour. Step forth, one by one, and confront the demons that lurk within." The statue's gaze, though unseeing, seemed to pierce directly into their souls, demanding a reckoning with the shadows they had long tried to ignore. The true test had begun.

"What does that even mean?" Oliver asked, his bravado faltering for the first time.

"It means", Professor Finch replied, "we will be subjected to flashes of our fears—visions of what haunts us most. Trust in one another; that will see us through."

"Trust is only the beginning," Luci added, her voice laced with an enchanting mystique. "Strength grows in unity. May the tides of courage engulf your hearts."

The stone guardian's gaze, ancient and unwavering, fixed on Ellie. Its eyes, seemingly carved from the very mountains themselves, held an unnerving intelligence. "Step forward, historian," the statue boomed, its voice a resonant rumble that vibrated through the ground and up Ellie's spine. "Show me your courage."

Her heart hammered against her ribs, a frantic drumbeat against the otherwise silent pronouncements of the stone sentinel. Swallowing hard, Ellie forced one foot in front of the other, each step a heroic effort as she drew closer to the guardian. She felt the weight of countless past souls, the hopes and fears of generations who had stood before this very test, pressing against her like a suffocating shroud. The air crackled with an unseen energy, and she could almost hear whispers carried on the wind – warnings, encouragements, and the chilling echoes of failure.

The moment she reached the guardian's base, the world dissolved. One moment she was standing in the sun-drenched clearing; the next, she was thrust into a swirling vortex of mist and shadow. Images, fragmented and terrifying, flashed before her eyes, a chaotic slideshow of darkness enveloping her mind. A deep, primal fear clawed at her, threatening to drag her under.

Then, just as suddenly, the chaos subsided. She found herself standing before a dilapidated, crumbling building. Its paint peeled, its windows were boarded up, and a heavy sense of desolation hung in the air. Despite the decay, the building was hauntingly familiar. It was... her childhood home. The recognition slammed into her with the force of a physical blow. And then she heard it.

"Ellie!" a small, plaintive voice cried out, laced with terror. She saw a younger version of herself, maybe eight years old, standing near a broken window, tears streaming down her cheeks. "Help me! I'm trapped!" The child's voice was a dagger twisting in Ellie's heart, a reminder of a vulnerability she had long tried to bury.

The scene morphed again, this time to a horrifying panorama bathed in the lurid glow of flames. Her childhood home was now an inferno, engulfed in a raging fire that devoured everything in its path. The air crackled with heat, and the smell of burning wood and acrid smoke filled her nostrils. From the heart of the blaze, voices rose, cold and accusatory. "You failed then, and you have failed now!" the voices of guilt taunted, their words echoing the deepest insecurities she harboured. The memory, raw and painful, overwhelmed her. Ellie stumbled back, breathless, the phantom heat scorching her skin.

Panic threatened to consume her. She wanted to run, to escape the suffocating weight of her past. But a flicker of defiance ignited within her. She couldn't let these spectres control her.

"NO!" she shouted into the void, the sound echoing with surprising force. She shook her head violently, trying to clear the lingering images, the insidious voices. She planted her feet firmly on the ground, anchoring herself in the present, in the woman she had become. "That's not who I am! That was then; this is now. I have learnt; I have grown! I have faced my demons and come out stronger. I will not let my past define me!" The words poured out of her, a declaration of independence, a defiant roar against the darkness that looked to claim her. The fire in her eyes mirrored the flames she had just seen, but this time, it was a fire of determination, of unwavering resolve.

In an instant, the oppressive mist receded like a drawn curtain, revealing the majestic chamber around her once more. Sunlight, previously obscured, streamed through unseen apertures, illuminating the swirling dust motes in the air. The guardian, a being of immense size and sculpted stone, roared in approval, its gruff voice, a sound like grinding mountains, echoing through the vast hall. "Well done, historian," it boomed, the sound vibrating in her very bones. "You have faced what you feared and emerged unbroken. Your spirit shines brighter than the sunstones that adorn this place."

As the suffocating tension lifted, a wave of relief washing over them, the others cautiously stepped forth, each bracing themselves for their own harrowing trials. Oliver, plagued by the insidious self-doubt that whispered he would never be enough, vanished into a swirling vortex of shadow. Professor Finch, a man whose life revolved around the validation of others, was next, swallowed by a mirage that flickered with the faces of his past malicious critics, their barbs sharper and crueller than he remembered. Even Finn, the ancient golem, usually stoic and unwavering, was pulled into the swirling mists, forced to confront the crushing loneliness of being a forgotten artefact, relegated to the shadows of history.

One by one, they appeared, reborn from the crucible of their personal nightmares. Oliver, no longer shrinking under the weight of expectation, stood taller, his eyes filled with a newfound self-assurance. Professor Finch, though still bearing the faint tremor of the experience, held his head high, his gaze clear and unburdened by the need for approval. Finn, shedding the veneer of stoicism, evinced a flicker of warmth in his ancient, gem-like eyes. Each victory, each shattered illusion, interwove their spirits further, strengthening the fragile threads of connection that bound them together. A web of trust and companionship, spun from shared vulnerability and hard-won courage, grew stronger with every challenge faced.

At last, only Azrael, the enigmatic leader, remained. He approached the colossal statue with a deep, steadying breath, the air around him crackling with barely had energy. "Guardian", he said, his voice resonating with an inner strength that belied the vulnerability in his words. "You know me. I embody courage, I wield power, and I have faced countless dangers. Yet, I often quake at the idea of not fulfilling my destiny, of failing to live up to the prophecy that hangs over my head like a sword." He paused, his gaze unwavering, fixed on the ancient eyes of the guardian. "My fear is not of death, Guardian, but of inadequacy. Show me what I must overcome."

The statue, carved from a stone that seemed to absorb the noticeable light of the chamber, regarded him solemnly. Its features, etched with ageless wisdom, held no judgement, only an unwavering focus. "What do you fear more than failure, noble lion?"

Azrael, a warrior known for his strength and unwavering resolve, stood before it, his usual composure momentarily fractured. He hesitated, the question striking a chord deep within his soul. He was used to facing external threats – beasts, armies, impossible odds. But his situation was different. This task was a challenge to his very being. "Being without purpose, losing those I cherish," he finally answered, his voice a low rumble that echoed in the vast chamber, his heart bared. "I fear being alone." He confessed the stark truth, the vulnerability raw and exposed. The words tasted like ash in his mouth.

A silence fell, heavy and profound, as the guardian's gaze seemed to soften, a flicker of understanding in its ancient, stone eyes. "Your fear is valid, Azrael," the statue finally resonated, its voice a deep, resonant hum that vibrated through the floor and up into his bones. "It is a fear shared by many who walk a path of valour. But recognise—those who are bound by love and respect, by shared trials and unwavering loyalty, will always walk beside you. Their presence is not defined by physical proximity but by the unbreakable threads that bind your souls."

A sudden rush of warmth filled the previously cold and austere room. It wasn't just physical warmth, but a feeling of profound comfort, a sense of belonging that resonated deep within Azrael. Drawing upon the guardian's words and fuelled by the memory of his companions, Azrael summoned the energy from within, channelling courage like never before. It pulsed through him, a radiant force pushing back the shadows of his fear. With a final roar that shook the very foundations of the chamber, he unleashed the power, a blinding surge of light and determination. The guardian vanished, its form dissolving into shimmering particles, leaving behind only an echo of laughter and light, a silent promise of guidance and strength.

As he rejoined Ellie and the others a few moments later, breathless yet triumphant, Ellie's heart swelled with gratitude for each of her companions. She saw the subtle shift in Azrael, the newfound lightness in his eyes.

The trials in this forsaken temple had not only tested their physical and mental strength but also reaffirmed their bond and loyalty.

It was a tapestry woven from threads of fear and courage, sacrifice and unwavering support, a testament to the power of their camaraderie.

Their next obstacle awaited, a looming archway leading into another unknown chamber. Time's infinite labyrinth promises to unveil another mystery. But now, fuelled by the trials they had conquered, inspired by the wisdom of the guardian, and strengthened by the unwavering belief in each other, they strode forward with sturdy spirits, ready for whatever lay ahead. The unknown no longer held the same terror, for they knew they would face it together, a united front against the darkness.

"Together, we can face anything," Ellie declared, her eyes sparkling with newfound determination.

And with those words, the echo of their courage lingered in the air, promising adventures beyond the enchanted museum walls.

THE KEEPER'S CHALLENGE

The grand hall of the Enchanted Museum was a tapestry of shadows and light, a silent testament to centuries of whispered secrets. The soft glow of ancient lanterns, suspended from the vaulted ceiling by chains thicker than a man's arm, cast an ethereal dance upon the stone walls. Each flicker teasingly revealed glimpses of forgotten languages – letters and runes wrought not just by the hands of artisans but by the patient work of time itself, etching stories into the very fabric of the building. Just moments prior, Ellie Thompson, a young archivist with a thirst for the unknown, had felt the spark of possibility ignite within her. The whispers and rumours that had drawn her to this place had proven true. The opportunity to unravel the Keeper's Challenge, a legendary trial said to guard the museum's most potent secrets, lay just beyond the golden archway, an invitation shimmering with untold potential.

"Are you ready?" Azrael the Lion's voice rumbled melodiously, a sound that echoed through the vast hall, pulling Ellie and her small group from their reverie. The majestic statue, more than just stone and metal, stood proud and sentient. The golden sheen of its coat, impeccably kept despite its age, glistened in the muted light, catching the warm hues and reflecting them back in a dazzling display. He radiated an aura of wisdom and anticipation, a guardian eager to fulfil his purpose.

"I've been waiting for decades for someone brave enough to face the Keeper's Challenge," he continued, his amber eyes, normally still, now alight with a palpable excitement. They burnt with an inner fire, hinting at the power living within the enchanted construct, and the sheer joy he derived from finally witnessing someone step forward to accept the challenge. He was a gatekeeper, and his gate was about to be opened.

"I'm ready," Ellie declared, determination imbued in her voice, a clear, steady sound that cut through the silence. It wasn't bravado, but a quiet confidence born from years of preparation and a deep, abiding love for the mysteries of the past. It was her intrinsic love for puzzles, the thrill of the chase, and a profound connection to history that had drawn her into this enchanted realm. And now, having crossed the threshold, she was prepared to dive deeper, to risk everything to uncover the secrets that the Enchanted Museum held within its heart. The weight of the challenge, and the potential reward, settled upon her shoulders, a burden she readily embraced.

Professor Finch adjusted his glasses, the anticipation practically crackling in the air around him. He tugged nervously at his tweed jacket, his eyes wide with a mixture of scholarly fervour and genuine apprehension. "The Keeper's Challenge is steeped in mystery, a trial shrouded in the mists of forgotten ages," he added, his voice trembling with a potent cocktail of excitement and fear. "The last historian who tried it...vanished.

Never returned, or so the legend goes, swallowed whole by the challenge itself, leaving behind only whispers and unanswered questions." He paused for dramatic effect, allowing the weight of his words to sink in.

"Perfect," quipped Oliver, the normally stoic and stubborn museum guard who had, to his terrible misfortune, unwittingly joined their otherworldly escapade. He shifted uncomfortably, adjusting the holster that normally held his taser but now felt strangely inadequate. His brow furrowed with a mixture of trepidation and a surprising sense of urgent determination. "I always wanted my name in the history books – but not like that. Preferably not etched on a tombstone as a cautionary tale." He cleared his throat, trying to inject a bit more bravado into his voice.

"Focus!" exclaimed Luci, her emerald scales shimmering as she effortlessly wove her way between the two men. Her forked tongue flicked out, tasting the lingering fear in the air. "The Keeper is neither cruel nor malevolent, but he demands respect, a profound understanding of the past, and a profound respect for its secrets. He tests not just knowledge but the very essence of your being. Solve his riddles, and the path forward shall be revealed, a key to unlocking the next stage of your journey. Fail, and you risk...far more than just getting lost."

The group, a motley crew united by circumstance and a shared, albeit reluctant, need to solve the Keeper's Challenge, gathered before an imposing door at the far end of the hall. The stone of the archway seemed to hum with an unseen power. Ornate carvings, depicting forgotten gods and long-dead heroes, spiralled around the door's edge, pulsing and flickering with the ethereal glow of ancient magic. Dust motes danced in the light, adding to the otherworldly atmosphere. Above the door, etched into the stone in a language that seemed both familiar and utterly alien, a faded inscription shone faintly: "In the realm of echoes, find your truth; each answer a key to unveil your youth." The challenge had begun.

Finn peered from the shadows, his wooden form momentarily illuminated by the shimmer of passing moonlight. His button eyes gleamed with excitement, his painted smile widening. "It's a riddle! We need to figure out what the Keeper is asking," he chirped playfully, his voice a light, bell-like tone that cut through the tense silence of the ancient chamber. He bounced on the balls of his tiny, carved feet, entirely unfazed by the ominous atmosphere surrounding them.

"Echoes and truth," mused Ellie, her brow furrowed in concentration. She paced back and forth, her flashlight beam dancing nervously across the damp stone walls, revealing grotesque carvings that seemed to leer at them from the darkness. "We're not just looking for words. We need to study our very own experiences." The air was laden with the weight of the Keeper's challenge, and she felt the pressure mounting. This challenge wasn't just about intellect; it was personal.

"Exactly!" Professor Finch exclaimed, adjusting his spectacles, which had slipped down his nose in his agitation. His tweed jacket was rumpled, and his usually neat hair was slightly dishevelled. "Echoes can also refer to stories from our past. Maybe we need to think about moments that shaped us, events that reverberate through our lives even now, influencing our decisions and perspectives." He tapped a finger against his temple, his gaze distant, lost in a web of memories.

"Hang on a moment... let's talk about echoes," Oliver said, his voice laced with scepticism. He crossed his arms, his muscular frame radiating a quiet strength that belied his youthful appearance. "If we think of ourselves, our pasts, maybe the Keeper wants us to share tales of courage. Moments where we faced fear or hardship and appeared stronger. Echoes of bravery, resonating through time." He looked at each of them in turn, his eyes challenging and encouraging.

"Courage..." Ellie repeated, her heart pounding with both anxiety and exhilaration. The prospect of sharing her own vulnerabilities filled her with dread, but the stakes were too high to hesitate. "What if we each share something about our past that shaped who we are? A moment of courage, a defining experience, a truth echoed from within. It could be our key. It must be." She stopped pacing and looked directly at her companions, a newfound resolve hardening her features. "Are we willing to open ourselves up like that? To trust each other with our vulnerabilities?"

"Very well, I shall go first," Azrael began, his voice resonating through the hall like the deep hum of ancient obelisks. Dust motes danced in the light as the power in his words stirred even the stone. "I was once a protector of the Temple of Amun, a bulwark against the encroaching darkness. For centuries, I stood sentinel, my gaze sweeping over hieroglyph-etched walls and through echoing chambers, a living embodiment of the pharaoh's will. Many looked to plunder the sacred relics, to steal the power held within the golden sarcophagi and the scrolls of forbidden knowledge. They came bearing promises of wealth, whispering temptations of earthly glory. It took immense courage to remain steadfast, to resist the allure of power and the siren call of greed. My loyalty to the gods, to the ancient ways, echoed through the ages, a testament carved into the very fabric of time. It is an honour I still hold, a burden and a sacred trust."

"A noble tale, Azrael," Luci said, her serpent body shimmering in the reflected light of a thousand unseen candles. Scales the colour of amethyst and jade rippled as she shifted, her gaze sharp and intelligent. "I, too, have my story, though perhaps less... monumental. Once, amidst a battlefield still smoking with the embers of war, I found myself coiling around a peace treaty, a simple scroll bearing the fragile hopes of a fractured world. Two warring factions, their hands-stained crimson with the blood of generations, stood poised to tear each other apart once more. It was courage – not mine alone, but that of the scribes and diplomats who dared to dream of peace – that compelled me to safeguard those precious words. To ensure history recorded not only the brutality of conflict, but also the hard-won victory of unity. The ink was barely dry, the parchment still warm, yet it held the power to rewrite the future. That moment, cradling the weight of hope amidst the ruins, taught me the invaluable, often overlooked, power of resolution. For it is easier to break than to build, easier to hate than to forgive, and easier to wage war than to forge peace."

"I... I can share something," Oliver began hesitantly, his voice softer than usual, almost a whisper in the echoing library. He shifted in his seat, the firelight glinting off the nervous flicker in his eyes. "It's not something I often talk about." He paused, gathering his thoughts. "I once stood up to a thief. It wasn't some grand, dramatic showdown like you read about. It was chaotic, messy... and terrifying. Someone was attempting to steal valuable artefacts from the city museum – ancient relics, priceless sculptures, things that belonged to everyone." He swallowed hard. "I put myself in harm's way to protect those treasures. I knew they were more than just objects; they were fragments of history, pieces of our shared identity. I managed to disrupt him, to slow him down... but I didn't succeed completely. He got away with one of the smaller items. It was a moment that changed me forever. That fear," he said, his voice gaining a little strength, "taught me that true bravery isn't the absence of fear, but the will to act despite it. Even knowing I could fail, even feeling my heart hammer against my ribs, I couldn't stand by and watch him loot our past."

Professor Finch nodded slowly, his brow furrowed in thought. He removed his spectacles, polished them absentmindedly with a corner of his tweed jacket, and replaced them, causing them to slide precariously further down his nose. "Those are profound stories of courage, both of you," he said, his voice a warm rumble. "My turn then," he said with a small smile. "I have spent my life in the pursuit of knowledge. As a historian, I once unearthed a lost scroll while working on an excavation site in Egypt. These scrolls detailed ancient rituals forbidding the misuse of powerful artefacts – rituals designed by a civilisation long since crumbled to dust. It was a risk digging deeper; the location was unstable, and I had the feeling that I was being watched, but I couldn't allow history to remain buried, even if it meant confronting uncomfortable truths. I knew that this document held the key to understanding a forgotten chapter of human history. This dedication to preserving knowledge, to unearthing and understanding the past, has shaped my career and, I believe, my very being."

Ellie felt a swell of pride in her companions. The flickering candlelight danced across their faces, highlighting the sincerity etched within them. They had each faced moments that tested their mettle, moments that revealed the true depths of their character. Their shared passion for history had brought them together, but these revelations were forging a more profound bond, something more akin to family. Inspired by their courage, she took a deep breath, the musty scent of old books filling her lungs. "I always wanted to be a historian because I believed there was truth in every artefact, every inscription, every faded photograph. Every time I unravelled a mystery—from painstakingly piecing together fragmented tapestries to deciphering ancient scripts carved into forgotten temples—I felt a deep connection to the past, a responsibility to give voice to those who could no longer speak for themselves. My courage", she said, her voice ringing with conviction, "lies in my unwavering desire to tell those stories, to ensure that the voices of the past are not silenced, that the lessons learnt, and the sacrifices made, are not forgotten. It is a quiet courage, perhaps, but it fuels everything I do."

As their shared stories filled the space, weaving a rich saga of laughter, sorrow, and triumph, the very air thrummed with palpable energy. The inscriptions on the ancient door, once static symbols of forgotten lore, pulsed with a vibrant, newfound life. The intricate carvings, depicting scenes of long-lost civilisations and mythical creatures, sang softly – a low, melodious hum that seemed to echo the profound sentiment of their interwoven truths. Their voices, resonating with honesty and vulnerability, intertwined into a magical tapestry, binding them together in ways they couldn't have imagined.

With a groan and a creak that echoed through the vast hall like the sigh of a slumbering giant, the door slowly began to open. Dust motes danced in the sliver of light that pierced the darkness beyond, revealing a darkened chamber steeped in an aura of mystery. The air hung thick with anticipation, heavy with the weight of untold secrets and the promise of untold wonders. A chill permeated the air, raising goosebumps on their skin, a testament to the potent magic that permeated every corner of the space.

"Keep moving," Azrael urged, his voice low and steady, a beacon of calm amidst the rising tension. Stepping forward, he projected a protective aura, a warm, shimmering shield that enveloped him and radiated outwards, offering reassurance to his companions. Behind him, ethereal streams of light, like captured stardust, began to coalesce, revealing a magnificent array of historical artefacts. Each object pulsed with its own unique energy, whispering silent stories of forgotten heroes, devastating wars, and groundbreaking discoveries – their histories begging to be unveiled, their secrets yearning to be heard.

As they stepped through the doorway, leaving behind the familiar solidity of the hall, the Keeper materialised. He was a looming, cloaked figure, draped in shadows that seemed to cling to him like loyal servants. His presence dominated the chamber, silencing the soft hum of the artefacts. But it was his eyes that deeply held their attention: two shining stars, burning with ancient wisdom and an otherworldly understanding, piercing the gloom and fixing them with an unwavering gaze. "You have shared your truths and demonstrated courage," the Keeper intoned, his voice a deep, resonant rumble that echoed in the chamber's high ceiling, vibrating through the very foundations of the place. "Further challenges await, and only through unity, through the unwavering strength of your bond, shall you overcome the trials ahead." He paused, the starlight in his eyes seeming to intensify. "The past is a mirror to the future. Heed its lessons or be doomed to repeat them."

Ellie's heart hammered against her ribs, a frantic drumbeat against the sudden, breathtaking vista. Just beyond the threshold of the chamber lay not empty space but a new realm entirely, woven from the threads of history and enigma. She could just make out the layout: a series of ten intricate puzzles, each a shimmering mirage of logic and lore, dispersed throughout the landscape. More intriguing still, each puzzle seemed to directly involve the very artefacts that encircled them, ancient relics humming with untold stories. They couldn't tackle this task alone. They had to work together, weaving their individual talents into a cohesive whole, using each of their unique strengths—Ellie's keen observation, Luci's raw power, and Finn's unwavering courage—to advance and to survive.

"Are you ready for the challenges that lie ahead?" the Keeper asked, his voice a deep, resonant rumble that echoed through the chamber. His eyes, ancient and knowing, shifted between the group, taking in their apprehension and their resolve.

"Ready as we'll ever be!" Ellie proclaimed, her voice ringing with newfound confidence. The presence of Luci, her bronze scales shimmering with an inner fire, and Finn, his youthful energy bubbling with restless anticipation, bolstered her, filling her with a strength she hadn't known she had. They were a team, bound by circumstance and a shared purpose.

"The myriad paths of history are rife with trials," the Keeper revealed, his words hanging in the air, heavy with meaning. "Only by recalling the past while embracing the future will you find your way through." His gaze swept across them, imparting a silent warning and a subtle encouragement.

With a low, grinding rumble, the chamber walls receded, expanding outwards to reveal ten distinct corridors, each leading into the unknown. Each passage was marked by lavish mosaics and vibrant depictions of historical events: eras of unparalleled bravery, triumphant moments of unity forged in the face of adversity, and sombre tales of strife and loss that tested the very limits of the human spirit. The air thrummed with the weight of these stories, a tangible presence that both inspired and intimidated.

"Which path do we take?" Luci asked, her bronze scales glinting intensely under the unseen light, reflecting her inner turmoil. The choice felt monumental, each corridor being a unique and potentially perilous journey.

Finn, never one to shy away from a challenge, darted forward, his gaze fixed on a particular mural. It depicted a grand battle, an epic clash of armies locked in a desperate struggle for survival. "Let's start there! What better way to test our bravery than with a fight? If we can conquer the challenges there, we can conquer anything!" His enthusiasm was infectious, but Ellie couldn't shake the feeling that their journey wouldn't be decided solely by brute force. Knowledge, strategy, and understanding would be just as crucial in unravelling the mysteries ahead. The real question was, could they learn to master all three before it was too late?

"No," Professor Finch interjected, shaking his head, his spectacles glinting in the dimly lit chamber. "Not every challenge is one of brute strength – heaving boulders, shattering obstacles. Wisdom and insight often lead to greater rewards, revealing secrets that mere muscle could never unearth. We must approach this Keeper's Challenge with our minds as our strongest weapons."

Ellie nodded, her brow furrowed in contemplation. "Professor Finch is right. We shouldn't rush headlong into danger. We should choose a path guided by the lessons of history – one that embodies courage, of course, but also understanding and unity. A path that honours those who came before us and the sacrifices they made."

"Agreed," Oliver said, swallowing hard, his Adam's apple bobbing nervously as he glanced at the various corridors branching out before them. They yawned into the darkness, each promising untold dangers and potential rewards. His earlier trepidation was slowly fading, replaced by a growing sense of purpose. His courage was rising with every moment, fuelled by their shared commitment and Professor Finch's unwavering faith. "Let's move towards the door adorned with the symbol of unity then – an emblem of those who fought side by side, regardless of their differences. It's a testament to the power of collaboration, a trait we'll undoubtedly need to succeed."

With a decisive motion, born not of recklessness but of considered choice, they ventured towards the corridor embellished with intricate carvings. Knights in shining armour stood shoulder to shoulder with wizened scholars holding quills and parchments and rugged warriors with scarred visages, all joining hands under the same banner – a tapestry of interconnectedness, a symbol of strength forged in alliance.

As they stepped further into the corridor, the walls seemed to breathe, vibrating with subtle energies, whispers of ancient tales unfolding around them. Each step resonated with their resolve, echoing through the stone passageway, pulsing with the essence of their individual stories, now interwoven into a single, unified narrative. The air grew thick with the weight of history, guiding them toward new realms of understanding and discovery, promising to unlock the secrets of the Keeper's Challenge.

And so, their odyssey continued, knitting the individual threads of courage, knowledge, and unity together into an unbreakable cord. They transformed from mere adventurers, driven by curiosity and the allure of the unknown, into allies on a quest not just for answers but for the enduring connection that history hoped to preserve in their hearts – a legacy of cooperation and mutual respect.

"Let the Keeper's Challenge truly begin," Ellie said, a smile illuminating her face, banishing the shadows of doubt and replacing them with the radiant glow of anticipation. As they embarked together into the unknown, hearts alight with the magic of possibility, they knew that their journey was more than just a test of skill; it was a testament to the enduring power of human connection.

THROUGH THE
GLASS DOOR

Certainly! Here is a refined version of the selected text:The hall of the Enchanted Museum sighed with an air thick with anticipation and adventure, the silence punctuated only by the distant tick-tock of grandfather clocks guarding forgotten artefacts. Dust motes danced in the shafts of moonlight filtering through the high, arched windows, illuminating the secrets held within these hallowed walls. Ellie stood before a magnificent glass door, intricately etched with swirling patterns and symbols that shimmered in the moonlight. The symbols pulsed with a faint, inner light, hinting at the powerful magic that lay beyond. The door glinted like a million stars had been trapped within its surface, a siren calls to the curious historian in her, promising untold knowledge and the thrill of discovery. She felt a pull towards it, a magnetic force drawing her ever closer to unravelling the mysteries it concealed.

"Isn't it beautiful?" Ellie murmured, her voice barely above a whisper, reverential in the face of such artistry and potential. She reached out a hand, hesitating just before her fingertips brushed against the cool, smooth surface of the glass.

Professor Finch adjusted his glasses, perched precariously on the bridge of his nose, and nodded appreciatively; his gaze fixed on the door as if it held the answers to every riddle ever posed in human history. The lines on his face, etched by years of scholarly pursuits, deepened as he studied the intricate carvings. "Indeed, Ellie. The artisanry is exquisite, a testament to an age long past. But what lies beyond it may be even more fascinating. Legends speak of... well, let's just say extraordinary things." He trailed off, a twinkle in his eye suggesting he held more than he was letting on.

"Shall we find out?" Ellie replied, her heart racing with the thrill of exploration. The promise of the unknown, the potential for groundbreaking discoveries, fuelled her excitement. She could almost taste the adventure, the weight of history resting on her shoulders.

Before the professor could respond, a low rumble echoed through the museum halls, vibrating through the very floor beneath their feet. It deepened, growing into a resonant growl that seemed to emanate from the door itself, causing the glass to tremble slightly. With a deliberate grace, like a slumbering giant awakening, the door swung open, groaning on ancient hinges. It revealed a corridor dimly lit by floating motes of light, like will-o'-the-wisps beckoning the adventurers forth. An alluring aroma, a blend of ancient parchment, exotic spices, and something indefinably magical, wafted from the corridor, tantalizing their senses and promising a journey into the heart of the Enchanted Museum's most guarded secrets. The air crackled with energy, a silent invitation to step into the unknown and face whatever wonders, or perils, lay in wait.

"Or perhaps it is a trap..." Professor Finch added, his voice a low murmur, his gaze sweeping across the shadowy corridor with a palpable mix of excitement and caution. He adjusted his spectacles, the lenses glinting in the dim light. He wasn't afraid, not exactly, but decades of exploring forgotten places had taught him that anticipation should always be tempered with prudence.

"Only one way to discover," Ellie said with a grin that was as infectious as it was daring. Without hesitation, she stepped into the passage, her hand instinctively reaching for the flashlight clipped to her belt. She trusted her instincts, and they were currently humming with a potent blend of curiosity and anticipation.

As they walked deeper into the corridor, the silence was broken by a rustling sound that seemed to dance along the edges of their hearing. Suddenly, Finn appeared, darting playfully among the elongated shadows cast by flickering sconces. His movements were fluid and unpredictable, a blur of russet fur against the dusty stone. With a mischievous glint in his wooden eyes that somehow seemed impossibly real, he bounded ahead, his articulated limbs clicking softly against the floor, urging them to follow.

"Come on, slowpokes! There's much more to see!" Finn chirped, his voice a surprisingly melodic blend of gears and recorded sounds, his playful spirit infectious. He was a marvel of clockwork engineering, a gift from a long-dead inventor, and always eager for adventure.

"Finn, wait!" Ellie called out, her voice carrying warmth and authority, a tone that suggested a long and affectionate acquaintance. She didn't want him to stumble into anything dangerous; his enthusiasm could sometimes outpace his caution.

Finn paused abruptly, his pose dramatic, looking back at them with an exaggerated pout that was clearly manufactured but undeniably charming. "What? Don't want to miss the adventure of a lifetime, do you?"

Ellie smiled back, her spirits buoyed by his irrepressible delight. He was a constant reminder to embrace the unexpected. The trio forged ahead, leaving the comparative safety of the earlier room behind. As they moved deeper into the museum's heart, the atmosphere shifted perceptibly. The air was no longer still and dry; it was thicker here, almost viscous, swirling with echoes of forgotten times and whispered secrets that tickled the back of their necks. The scent of dust and decay was overlaid with something else, something subtle and indefinable, a hint of something ancient and powerful that made the hairs on Professor Finch's arms stand on end. He reached for the worn leather-bound journal in his pocket, a familiar comfort in the face of the unknown.

This was more than just a museum exhibit; it was something... else. Just as they rounded a sharp corner, the labyrinthine tunnel giving way to a space unlike any they had met before, they stumbled upon a chamber bathed in a soft, ethereal glow. The source of the light remained hidden, yet it cast an otherworldly luminescence upon everything within. The walls were not stone or brick but lined with countless mirrors, each framed in intricately carved obsidian. These were no ordinary reflections; each mirror presented a slightly different image, a window into another time and place. Historical figures, frozen in mid-conversation, gestured emphatically. Epic battles unfolded in miniature, armies clashing under smoke-filled skies. Serene landscapes from another era stretched beyond the confines of the chamber, offering glimpses of civilisations both familiar and utterly alien.

"Striking, isn't it?" Professor Finch marvelled, his eyes wide with academic wonder. He stepped closer to one of the mirrors, his fingers hovering just inches from the cool, smooth surface. "These reflections are more than mere glass; they encapsulate moments suspended in time. Fragments of history, echoes of possibilities... an extraordinary feat of temporal magic!"

Just then, a deep, rumbling voice, seemingly emanating from the very walls themselves, echoed through the room. It resonated with an age-old authority, sending a shiver down Ellie's spine. "Only those who seek with pure hearts may pass, for the truth unveiled can be burdensome."

"Who's there?" Ellie demanded, her voice trembling slightly despite her best efforts. Her pulse quickened at the sudden, disembodied presence. She gripped the handle of her satchel, her eyes darting nervously around the chamber, trying to pinpoint the source of the voice.

From the deepest shadows, where the ethereal light struggled to penetrate, appeared a creature of legend. Huckleberry , a magnificent being with the body of a lion and the head and wings of an eagle, soared gracefully through the chamber's stillness. His feathers, a tapestry of midnight blue and shimmering silver, rippled in the unseen breeze. He circled once, his golden eyes, wise and ancient, sweeping over the group before landing softly on a nearby pedestal carved from a single block of jade. "I am Huckleberry," he announced, his voice now clearer and closer, "the keeper of whispers, and I guide those brave enough to venture through the glass doors." He swept a wing towards the mirrors, acknowledging their unique properties.

"Ooh, a riddle!" Finn exclaimed, bouncing with excitement. All traces of apprehension had vanished, replaced by an almost frantic enthusiasm. "Can we solve it? I love riddles!

Is the pure heart thing, like, we must be nice? Or does it mean, like, literally, no bad cholesterol?" He looked expectantly at Professor Finch, then back at Huckleberry, practically vibrating with the anticipation of the challenge.

"Indeed," Huckleberry replied, his coal-black feathers glistening in the ethereal light filtering through the chamber's high, unseen windows. The air hung heavy with anticipation, thick with the scent of ancient stone and forgotten magic. "But beware, for the reflections are not always what they seem. Mirrors, like memories, can be deceiving. To reveal the path forward, you must answer wisely, discerning the kernel of truth hidden within the shimmering facade."

Ellie exchanged knowing glances with Professor Finch. He adjusted his spectacles, his brow furrowed in thought, his worn leather satchel swinging gently against his tweed suit. Together, they had faced countless puzzles during their globe-trotting adventures: riddles carved into forgotten obelisks, cryptic maps etched on crumbling scrolls, and treacherous traps guarding long-lost treasures. And yet, the weight of this moment filled her with a sense of urgency that eclipsed all prior challenges. This experience felt different, more profound. The stakes, she suspected, were higher than ever before.

"What must we do?" Ellie asked, her voice echoing slightly in the cavernous space, stepping forward as courage—a familiar companion during their expeditions—mounted within her. She straightened her shoulders, pushing aside a nagging feeling of unease.

"Gaze into the mirrors," Huckleberry instructed, his voice a low rumble that seemed to vibrate through the very stone beneath their feet. He gestured with a clawed wing towards a series of ornate, silver-framed mirrors lining the far wall. "And speak the truth of what you see. Not what you wish to see, or what you fear to see, but the unvarnished truth. The answers will guide you; the reflections tell tales long forgotten, secrets buried deep within the heart of time. Only by acknowledging the past can you hope to shape the future."

Ellie drew a deep breath, the air cool and damp in her lungs, before cautiously stepping closer to the nearest mirror. The surface shimmered like the surface of water disturbed by a gentle breeze, and for a moment, she saw only her own reflection, slightly distorted and wavering. Then, as she focused, the image morphed, dissolving into a swirling vortex of colours before solidifying into a vision of her younger self. She was barely a teenager, perched on the floor of her grandmother's dusty attic, poring over ancient texts filled with arcane symbols and forgotten languages. Her brow was furrowed in concentration, her cheeks flushed with excitement, and her heart blazed with an insatiable curiosity, a burning desire to find out the truth about mysteries of the world.

"I see..." Ellie hesitated, her voice barely a whisper, caught between wonder and a sense of vulnerability. "Myself, searching for history; a reflection of my passion. A thirst for knowledge that has driven me my entire life."

As soon as the words escaped her lips, hanging in the air like visible sparks, the mirror glowed brighter, bathing the chamber in an ethereal, silver light. The air crackled with energy, and soft whispers, like the rustling of ancient pages, filled the air, recounting the tales of those who came before her: explorers and scholars, each driven by the same unwavering pursuit of knowledge, each facing their own trials and tribulations. Ellie felt a connection to them, a sense of belonging to a lineage of truth-seekers, a legacy that stretched back through the ages. The whispers faded, but the memory of them remained, a subtle shift in the atmosphere, a promise of revelations yet to come. The path, it seemed, was beginning to unfold.

"Good," Huckleberry hooted approvingly, the sound echoing through the cavernous chamber. "You are close. Now, share the truth of your companions! The mirrors reveal not just reflections but the very heart of each being. Speak what you see, and the path forward shall illuminate itself."

Ellie glanced at Professor Finch, who was already engrossed, almost hypnotised, by his own reflection. The ornate, silver-framed mirror revealed a younger version of himself, perhaps twenty years younger, his brow furrowed in concentration as he excitedly unearthed archaeological treasures in some forgotten corner of the world. His love for history was ablaze in his youthful eyes, his face filled with pure, unadulterated joy at the thrill of discovery. Dust and sweat clung to his brow, but his spirit shone brighter than any jewel.

"I see the professor not just as he is now, but as he was," Ellie said, her voice steady, resonating with the power of truth. "A youth driven by an insatiable thirst for discovery and the endless pursuit of knowledge. A man whose heart beats in time with the echoes of the past." The air around them shimmered, a visible manifestation of the magic at work, acknowledging her true insight. Threads of light danced around the professor 's reflection, weaving a tapestry of his youthful passion.

Finn hopped closer, his wooden form glowing with an increased intensity, a sign of his eagerness and anticipation. "My turn! I know what I see!" He approached a mirror depicting a young, energetic fox, its fur a vibrant red- nded, its tail held high, embodying pure, unbridled freedom and playful mischief. The reflection seemed to capture the essence of everything Finn aspired to be.

"I see myself!" Finn exclaimed, his voice brimming with excitement, a wide, carved grin stretching across his wooden face. "Always exploring and playing, never weighed down by worries, never held back by fear! Free to run, free to jump, free to be me!" The mirror sparked as his truth resonated with the image, solidifying the connection between the wooden puppet and the wild spirit he embodied. Tiny leaves and blades of grass seemed to spring up around the fox's paws in the reflection, a testament to Finn's vibrant energy.

"Very well," Huckleberry said, nodding with approval, a hint of amusement in his ancient, knowing eyes. The chamber vibrated with a low, resonant energy, and the mirrors flickered, their surfaces rippling like water disturbed by a pebble. The air grew thick with anticipation. "But now the final truth beckons – the culmination of your journey. A riddle must be answered, a secret unveiled. What binds these tales, yet stays unseen, heralding adventure both wild and keen?" Huckleberry's voice took on a dramatic, almost theatrical quality, the words echoing with the weight of centuries.

"The bonds of friendship!" Ellie shouted, the answer erupting from her as a wave of understanding washed over her. She felt a surge of connection to Finn and Professor Finch, a tangible feeling of warmth and shared purpose. "Our combined love for history, exploration, and above all, our affection for each other, is what brings us to life and emboldens our path! It's what makes us brave enough to face whatever challenges lie ahead!"

Huckleberry, the avian guardian, spread his immense wings, each feather catching the reflected light from the surrounding mirrors. Their glow intensified, bathing the chamber in an ethereal luminance. The air thrummed with magical energy as the colossal raven opened his beak, a deep, resonant caw echoing through the stone walls. "You have spoken truthfully!" he proclaimed, his voice imbued with ancient authority. "You may proceed."

The air itself crackled with unseen energies, the residue of Huckleberry's judgement. With a grinding rumble, a hidden door at the opposite end of the chamber slid silently open, revealing a staircase spiralling downward into the inky blackness below. A cool draught, carrying the scent of damp earth and forgotten things, wafted upwards.

"Shall we?" Ellie grinned, the successful completion of the riddle buoying her spirits. A triumphant spark danced in her eyes, eager to uncover the mysteries that lay ahead.

"After you," Professor Finch replied with a theatrical bow, his grin flashing beneath his neatly trimmed moustache. He gestured towards the staircase with a flourish, a hint of playful anticipation in his hazel eyes.

The trio descended the staircase, their footsteps echoing in the confined space. Each step resonated with an unspoken anticipation, a shared excitement at the prospect of discovering the secrets hidden below. As they reached the bottom, the air became noticeably cooler, the scent of ancient parchment growing stronger, almost overwhelming. The atmosphere was charged, crackling with a palpable sense of the profound history that surrounded them.

The staircase opened into a breathtaking chamber, a dazzling room filled with artefacts from various epochs, each glowing softly under the light of a thousand unseen stars. The source of the illumination stayed a mystery, adding to the otherworldly atmosphere. Statues of long-forgotten pharaohs stood tall and proud, their impassive faces etched with the wisdom of ages. Adorned with jewels that gleamed like captured starlight, they served as vivid reminders of their past glory and the civilisations they once ruled. Hieroglyphs, faded yet still discernible, covered the walls, hinting at untold stories and forgotten rituals.

"Welcome to the Hall of Whispers," a majestic voice announced. Azrael, a towering figure clad in shimmering robes, appeared grandly at the threshold, seemingly materialising from the shadows. His presence exuded regal assurance, his posture radiating power and authority. His eyes, deep pools of ancient wisdom, sparkled with an understanding that transcended time.

"What stories do they tell?" Ellie asked eagerly, her insatiable curiosity igniting once more. She took a tentative step forward, her fingers itching to touch the nearest artefact.

"Each artefact bears witness to the events that shaped history," Azrael replied, his voice resonating with gentle authority. "They whisper to those who listen, revealing insights and lessons from the past. But beware, for not all stories are mirrors; some may conceal more than they reveal, leading the unwary astray." He raised a cautionary finger. "Discernment is key in this hall. Trust not everything you hear."

Finn, the youngest of the group, scampered close to a magnificent golden sarcophagus, his eyes wide with wonder. The sarcophagus was intricately carved with scenes of gods and goddesses, their forms both familiar and alien. "Can we hear them? Can we listen to their tales?" he asked, his voice filled with innocent excitement. He reached out a hand, hesitating only for a moment before gently touching the cool, smooth surface of the gold.

Azrael nodded, his gaze unwavering, guiding them deeper into the echoing hall. The air grew thick with anticipation, the silence a deceiving veil over the burgeoning symphony of whispers.

As they passed by various artefacts – dusty tomes bound in dragonhide, gleaming swords inlaid with forgotten constellations, intricately carved idols of long-dead gods – the soft murmurs grew clearer. It was a cacophony of voices, a chorus of echoes, each seemingly emanating from the relics around them, vying for their attention.

Ellie, her curiosity piqued, paused before a beautifully crafted vase, its porcelain surface painted with scenes of a bustling, ancient city. A faint, almost imperceptible hum vibrated from it, a palpable energy that tickled her fingertips as she reached out. "What secrets do you hold?" she wondered aloud, her voice barely a whisper, focusing her attention on the vessel. The air around it seemed to shimmer, distorting the light.

To her astonishment, the vase shimmered more intensely, the colours on its surface swirling like trapped starlight. Then, an ethereal voice, ancient and resonant, resonated within the chamber, seeming to bypass her ears and speak directly to her mind. "I was once held by a great empress, whose story was woven with power and ambition. Her reach extended across continents; her name was whispered in awe and fear. Beware the lust for triumph, for it blinds the heart. She sacrificed everything – love, loyalty, even her own humanity – to claim the throne, only to find herself alone and consumed by the very hunger that drove her."

Ellie stepped back, entranced by the vase's recollections and the empress's tragic tale, as a chill traced its way down her spine. The Empress 's tragic tale painting vivid images in her mind, stepped back, a chill tracing its way down her spine. "Each artefact tells its truth, but we must listen carefully," she said, turning to her companions, her eyes wide with the realisation of the power they were surrounded by. "These aren't just relics; they're living memories."

"Indeed," Professor Finch mused, stroking his beard, his gaze sweeping over the vast collection. "Some tales linger long after their owners are gone, etched into the very fabric of these objects. And in these echoes lie vital lessons for us, warnings and wisdom gleaned from the past, if only we are astute enough to perceive them." He adjusted his spectacles, his eyes gleaming with intellectual excitement.

As they ventured deeper into the hall, further into the heart of this repository of history, she shouted a melodic, almost hypnotic summons that cut through the other whispers with ease, her regal presence commanding attention even in stone. She was a marble statue, life-sized and exquisitely detailed, depicting a nobleperson in elaborate finery.

"Ah, my dear adventurers! Come closer, for I have a tale to share," she beckoned, her marble-like eyes, impossibly, glimmering with an uncanny life, suggesting a sentience that defied logic. A faint smile played on her lips, hinting at secrets untold.

Ellie and the others, drawn by the allure of Lady Arabella's voice and the promise of more captivating histories, moved towards her, drawn almost unwillingly by her presence. "What wisdom do you possess, Lady Arabella?" she asked, eager to gain insights that may aid them in their quest, her voice filled with a mix of apprehension and fierce curiosity. The air around the statue crackled with a silent energy, waiting for the story to unfold.

"Beyond every object of beauty lies a history woven like a tapestry," Arabella began, her voice as smooth as silk, its tone resonating with the weight of untold stories. "Treasures are not merely trinkets of the past; they are fragments of time, solidified memories. They are portals to what was, offering glimpses into the lives, loves, and losses of those who came before, and they are also echoes of what may yet be, prophecies etched in metal and stone. Understanding them, deciphering their narratives, allows you to master the art of truth – to see beyond the superficial and grasp the profound currents that shape our world."

Ellie felt invigorated, a spark ignited in her soul by Arabella's words. She recognised that the journey ahead was far deeper than a mere exploration of artefacts and ancient relics. It was a quest for understanding, a bridge to the past meticulously constructed from curiosity and determination. This bridge wouldn't just lead them backward; it would illuminate their future, providing context and perspective that could guide their choices and define their destinies.

"Let us uncover these truths together," she encouraged her friends, her voice ringing with newfound resolve. The bonds of friendship felt stronger than ever, tempered by shared excitement and a burgeoning sense of purpose. Their individual strengths, she knew, would be amplified by their collective spirit.

"I'm all in!" Finn chimed, his spirit undaunted by the mysteries they would face. A mischievous glint sparkled in his eyes, betraying his excitement for the puzzles and challenges that lay ahead. He thrived on the unknown, and the prospect of unravelling history's enigmas fuelled his adventurous heart.

Pushing forward, the adventurers united under a common purpose, their footsteps echoing in the grand, silent hall. They stepped further into the depths of the Hall of Whispers, a chamber renowned for its secrets and shrouded in legend, ready to unlock the secrets hidden beyond the ornate glass door. Each breath they took was filled with anticipation; each glance exchanged a silent pact of unwavering support.

Little did they know, the true challenge awaited them just beyond the horizon of that enchanted chamber. It wasn't a monster to slay or a trap to disarm, but something far more complex and demanding— a test of unity, courage, and their shared passion for the stories that shaped their world.

The hall held not just secrets of the past but a mirror reflecting the very essence of their character, forcing them to confront their own beliefs and the strength of their commitment to each other and to the truth. The treasures they looked for were not gold or jewels, but the wisdom to navigate the trials that lay ahead.

A WHISPER OF BETRAYAL

The moon, a silver disc pregnant with secrets, hung low over the Enchanted Museum. Its ethereal glow spilt through the towering arched windows, painting elongated, dancing shadows across the pristine marble floor. Inside, the air hummed with a low, almost palpable energy. The echoes of distant footsteps, perhaps lingering memories or perhaps something more, reverberated through the grand hall, bouncing off the high, vaulted ceilings and the silent displays. Each corner held its breath, expecting the unfolding drama of the night, a drama woven from the threads of history, magic, and perhaps, danger.

The enchanting artefacts, each a relic whispering tales of forgotten empires and long-lost arts, seemed to pulse with an inner light, awaiting their moment to reveal their hidden truths.

Ellie, her brow furrowed in concentration, adjusted her spectacles, their lenses magnifying the intricate details of a shimmering obsidian amulet displayed before her. Her fingers instinctively traced the protective barrier. Deep in thought, she perused the cryptic inscriptions etched into its surface, her heart quickening with each newly deciphered symbol. "These symbols", she murmured, her voice barely heard above the museum's subtle hum, "they hint at something more profound than mere decoration. They speak of ancient guardians, a binding spell... I can feel it. A powerful force lies dormant, just waiting to be awakened."

Professor Finch, a whirlwind of tweed and nervous energy, paced nearby with a wild glint in his eye, his grey hair askew. He eagerly joined her; his excitement barely held. "Magnificent, Ellie, absolutely magnificent! Each of these artefacts holds a secret, a whisper from the past waiting for us to uncover it! A puzzle box, waiting for the key to be formed. But beware, my dear," he cautioned, his voice dropping to a conspiratorial whisper, "not every tale is woven with the threads of truth. Some are spun from illusion, from desire, and from the darkness that can lie dormant within even the brightest of legends."

As the clock struck midnight, its twelve chimes boomed through the silent halls and shattered the quiet anticipation, causing Azrael, the magnificent, life-sized bronze lion statue that guarded the entrance to the Egyptian exhibit, to spring to life.

Its metal jaws opened in a majestic roar that echoed through the museum, shaking the very foundations. The sound startled Oliver, the museum guard, a young man more accustomed to the quiet rustle of history books than the roar of mythical beasts.

He had been awkwardly trying to muster the courage to approach the esteemed academics, clutching his flashlight like a lifeline. "By the gods!" he exclaimed, his voice cracking with surprise and fear, fumbling with his flashlight, its beam dancing erratically across the walls. "What is happening?

The answer isn't in the training manual!"

"Fear not, brave guard!" Azrael proclaimed, his golden mane shimmering in the moonlight. "Tonight, we embark on an adventure through time and mystery!"

The first excitement of the museum's hidden chambers adventure began to wane, replaced by a creeping sense of foreboding. Whispers of unease began to drift among the group, like cobwebs clinging to their adventurous spirit. Luci, the serpentine oracle, sensed this growing tension. She glided forward, her bronze coils glistening under the eerie glow emanating from unseen sources, her movements sinuous and mesmerising... "Listen closely, my friends," she hissed, her voice a sibilant whisper that somehow carried through the cavernous space, the tone echoing both ancient wisdom and urgent caution. "The night holds more than mere riddles and arcane puzzles. We seek knowledge, yes, but some secrets are best left undisturbed. Some advise caution, urging us to tread lightly and respect the boundaries of what we find, while others, driven by ambition, seek self-serving destinies that could endanger us all."

As the adventurers gathered at the base of the staircase leading to the museum 's hidden chambers, Lady Arabella, the enigmatic historian, stepped forward. Her porcelain face, usually serene, was etched with concern. "Trust is as fragile as glass, dear companions, easily shattered by suspicion and deceit. To progress, to unlock the secrets that await, we must unite, sharing our strengths and protecting each other's weaknesses. Yet shadows of betrayal hover ever so closely, whispering promises of power and tempting us to stray from our collective purpose. Be vigilant and trust your instincts."

Ellie, the group's resourceful inventor, nodded, feeling a knot of trepidation tugging at her stomach. Lady Arabella's words resonated with her own doubts. Yet, through the layers of anxiety, it was curiosity, an insatiable thirst for discovery, that burnt bright within her. Oliver, the stoic protector of the group, adjusted his stance, his hand instinctively going to the hilt of the blade concealed beneath his tunic. His fingers grazed his belt, a silent promise to defend his comrades should the need arise, though he knew that some battles were fought not with steel, but with vigilance and discernment.

The team began to descend, each step echoing in the unsettling silence. Their guide was Finn, a whimsical clockwork automaton. He darted playfully down the stairs, his wooden form surprisingly agile and spirited, gears whirring softly with each energetic bound. "Follow me! Follow me! I've sniffed out the secrets that lie ahead! The air down here is thick with magic and mystery, and I can practically TASTE the adventure!" he yipped, boundless enthusiasm emanating from his every movement, a stark contrast to the growing apprehension among the other members.

The corridors twisted and turned, a labyrinthine descent into the museum's forgotten depths. The walls were adorned with ancient tapestries, their vibrant colours surprisingly well-preserved, depicting scenes of both joy and sorrow, triumphs and tragedies, hinting at the complex history of the museum and its enigmatic founder. Suddenly, Huckleberry, the wise and slightly cynical raven familiar, swooped down from his perch high above, his feathers shimmering in shades of onyx, catching the meagre light. "Beware, dear fellows! Beware the allure of the forbidden! A flicker of greed, a moment of weakness, can turn the most loyal heart into one filled with betrayal. Are all present for the right reasons? Or does ambition lurk beneath the surface, ready to consume even the closest of allies?" His beady eyes scrutinised the group, each member feeling the intense gaze, a silent challenge lingering in the air, forcing them to confront their own motivations and question the loyalty of those around them. The adventure had begun, but the true test, it seemed, was about to begin.

Oliver exchanged glances with Ellie, suspicion beginning to lace through their camaraderie. "Not everyone is trustworthy, are they?" he asked cautiously, voice barely above a whisper.

"Is it you who feels the need to guard secrets?" Huckleberry cut in, peering into Oliver's eyes as if searching for hidden truths.

"It's not me!" Oliver protested defensively. "I merely wish to protect what's right! We're all on the same side, aren't we?"

"Side?" the serpent interjected smoothly. "What do you know of sides? Each of us has a purpose this night; let it not be clouded by doubt."

As they ventured further, their path led them into a vast room illuminated by the soft glow of enchanted lanterns. Intricate carvings adorned the walls, intricacies intertwining history and myth. In the centre, a stone pedestal bore an ancient tome, its pages whispering to be opened.

"Something doesn't feel right," Ellie said, unease creeping into her voice. "What if this is a trap?"

"Or a test," Professor Finch mused, his brow furrowed in contemplation. "The secrets of the museum are layered; we must be vigilant."

As Ellie stepped closer to the tome, drawn by an irresistible pull, the faintest flicker of light caught her eye. The light did not originate from the ancient book itself but rather from a nearby statue. It was an inscription, barely visible in the dim light, that suddenly seemed to glow with an ethereal luminescence. The statue itself was a grotesque depiction of a traitor, eternally frozen in stone, his face contorted in a silent scream of betrayal. It felt as though the statue's hollow eyes bore witness to their every move, a silent sentinel warning her of impending trouble, a subtle hint of discord in their midst.

Azrael, sensing the palpable tension in the air, stepped forward, a strained, low growl emanating from deep within his throat. "We must remain a united front," he urged, his voice resonating with a forced calm. "We can't allow mistrust to seep into our hearts. That's what it, they, want. Focus, friends; we have a challenge to tackle, a task that requires unwavering faith in one another." He gestured towards the tome, trying to redirect their attention.

However, without warning, the enchanted lanterns that lined the chamber dimmed, casting long, dancing shadows that amplified the unease. A hushed silence fell over the group, swallowing the sounds of their breathing between one moment and the next.

In that disorienting moment, an unsettling vibration in the air, a palpable hum of unseen energy, thrummed through Ellie, compelling her to turn back. Her gaze landed on Finn, usually a beacon of playful energy, his demeanour wilting under the crushing weight of something unseen, something terrible. The ever-present twinkle in his eyes was gone, replaced by a flicker of fear. Suspicion, a lingering scent in their shared space, the very toxin she had spoken of only moments before, seemed to have found purchase.

Dr Bell, who had been meticulously guarding the entrance to the chamber, suddenly appeared, her face etched with lines of deep worry. Sweat beaded on her brow as she rushed towards them. "You must hold together!" she exclaimed, her voice laced with urgency. "The museum, this place...it's fragile. It's more than just stone and relics. It's woven with magic, powered by belief. And should these artefacts, these ancient energies, discover mistrust amongst you, their power could become chaotic! Unpredictable! We risk unleashing something we can't control!"

"What do you know, Mariana?" Ellie challenged. "You awakened them—was it intentional?"

The conservationist flinched, taken aback. "I acted with the best of intentions! But I didn't expect..."

"Didn't anticipate what?" Oliver interrupted impatiently. "What else may you be hiding?"

Silence, heavy and absolute, descended upon the chamber. It was a silence so profound it seemed to press in on them, stealing the air from their lungs. As one, they took two steps backward, instinctively creating distance, a physical manifestation of the growing chasm between them. Tension rippled through the group like a visible wave, each member radiating suspicion and unease. The earlier whispers, hushed and clandestine, now echoed aloud in their minds, each syllable a barbed wire of betrayal. Trust, once the bedrock of their alliance, began to fracture, hairline cracks spiderwebbing across its surface.

"Azrael", Luci interjected, her voice sharp and clear, cutting through the suffocating atmosphere. Her metal body, usually a testament to strength and resilience, shimmered under the flickering, spellbound light of the cavern, reflecting the uncertainty in their eyes. "We must not let ourselves be governed by mere shadows," she continued, her voice gaining strength. "Someone here might be acting contrary to our common goal! Allowing doubt to fester will only serve the true enemy."

Azrael, leader of their disparate band, lifted his head, his golden gaze sweeping across the tense faces before him. Resolve, hard and unyielding, began to fill his chest, pushing back the encroaching despair. "Enough!" he roared, his voice resonating with primal authority. "Whoever is causing this division shall be cast out—or worse—if we do not unite against the true threat that lurks in the darkness! We swore an oath, and we will see it through, together, or not at all!"

Each member of the party stood rigid, a wall of uncertainty growing impossibly thick around them, suffocating the camaraderie they once shared. Ellie's heart raced, a frantic drum against her ribs. She glanced at everyone – friends, confidantes, allies – now potential foes, their faces masks of apprehension and suspicion. What would happen to their quest and shared purpose if paranoia severed their bonds?   they could not keep unity. The weight of their mission, of the world's fate perhaps, pressed down on her with crushing force.

Before the mounting anxiety could suffocate the team entirely, Huckleberry cawed, a resonant, ancient sound that filled the void with unexpected clarity. The sound cut through the murmur of doubt, demanding attention. "Look beyond, dear allies!" he boomed, his voice echoing with the wisdom of ages. "History is rich with lessons! The darkness you feel will pass if you choose to seek the truth together. Doubt is a poison, but truth is the antidote. Seek it, and you will find strength."

As Ellic looked at the pages of the ancient tome, its worn leather and faded script whispering secrets of forgotten ages, a realisation began to dawn. The symbols blurred, then sharpened, revealing not just the prophecy they looked for but a more profound understanding of their purpose. "We're here to uncover mysteries," she murmured, her voice barely heard but resonating with newfound certainty, "not just of the artefacts, but perhaps of our own selves! Trust lies interwoven within choices made, within the willingness to face the darkness not just outside but within. We must be worthy of this quest, worthy of each other." The weight on her chest lessened, replaced by a fragile ember of hope. The path forward was unclear, fraught with danger, but perhaps, just perhaps, they could find their way back to each other.

Finn, his earlier despondency replaced by a spark of renewed determination, let the whispered hope resonate within him. A genuine smile spread across his face as he chimed in cheerily, "Let's get on with it, shall we? The night is still ours for the taking!" His voice, filled with optimism, acted as a beacon, drawing the others back from the precipice of despair.

Reinvigorated by Finn's infectious enthusiasm, the group, momentarily fractured by suspicion, instinctively gathered. They realigned, not just physically, but in purpose too. Each glanced at one another, a tentative smile breaking through the lingering tension, a fragile promise of forgiveness and renewed camaraderie. The air, thick with the residue of betrayal, began to thin, replaced by a burgeoning sense of unity.

Facing the ancient, glowing tome that held the key to their shared mystery, Ellie took a deep, steadying breath. Her eyes scanned each of their faces, looking for and finding a reflection of her own newfound resolve. "Together, then," she declared, her voice stronger now. "Let's reveal our truths as we delve deeper. What's done is done. Now, we face what's to come...together."

"Together!" they chimed in unison, the word a powerful affirmation, a symbolic cleansing. The oppressive weight of betrayal slowly lifted, like a suffocating blanket being pulled away, as they instinctively took their positions beside one another, forming a united front. The shadows of doubt still lingered, but they held them at bay, their collective strength a shield against the encroaching darkness.

With the first fragile, parchment-thin page of the tome turned, ancient script illuminated by the ethereal glow, secrets were ready to flow. They felt a profound strength building within them, a reservoir of resilience they hadn't realised they had. While shadows may whisper betrayal, trying to sow discord and seed doubt, they recognised the enduring bonds they had forged, the memories shared, and the battles fought side by side. These connections were safeguarded in their hearts, a testament to their loyalty, a fortress against any trial the night might throw their way.

As the whispers of betrayal faded, they were gradually replaced by a shared resolve. The first shock and hurt gave way to a quiet understanding, a deeper appreciation for the fragility of trust and the importance of forgiveness. The ocean of time loomed vast before them, its depths concealing mysteries both beautiful and terrifying. Yet, they ventured forth, brave and resolute, ready to uncover the secrets of the past. The resilient spirit of trust had slowly, painstakingly, become their greatest strength. They were not just a group of individuals; they were a team, bound by shared experience and a common goal.

The echoes of the night awaited exploration amidst the enchanted exhibits of the museum, where history whispered through dust-laden artefacts and forgotten lore clung to the very air. The echoes of the night awaited their exploration. The adventure was far from over; it was merely the beginning of something extraordinary, something that would test their limits, challenge their beliefs, and ultimately forge them into something stronger, more resilient, and infinitely more connected than they ever thought possible. The secrets of the past beckoned, and they were ready to answer.

UNLIKELY ALLIES

The museum was an imposing presence, a monolithic guardian looming over Ellie and her unlikely fellowship. Its weathered stones, each etched with the silent stories of ages past, seemed to hum with a palpable energy. They huddled near the grand atrium, its soaring arches disappearing into the inky blackness above. Midnight had struck, bathing the artefacts within in an ethereal, almost feverish glow. The air itself thrummed with the intoxicating promise of adventure, a relentless pulse that quickened their senses.

Azrael, resplendent in his ancient, golden armour, moved with a newfound fluidity, shaking off the metaphorical dust of centuries. He turned towards his companions, his eyes, like molten gold, reflecting the reflected gleam of the atrium. "Listen closely, my friends," he began, his voice resonant and commanding. "Our quest has only just begun, and at this juncture, our reliance on one another will be paramount. Time, that insidious thief, is our greatest adversary. And I sense, with a certainty that chills me to my very core, that a riddle lies ahead, a formidable challenge designed to test the strength, the very fabric, of our nascent partnership."

Ellie nodded, a surge of exhilaration battling with a knot of apprehension in her stomach. "Earlier, we witnessed how the whispers of the past spoke to us through those portraits. They led us here. I believe that together, we can unravel any enigma, no matter how complex or obscure." Her voice carried a conviction that belied her first trepidation.

As if summoned by her confident declaration, Luci, the Serpent, gracefully slithered forward. Her bronze scales, catching the oscillating light from the enchanted artefacts, shimmered like a living tapestry. "Do not forget", she hissed, her voice smooth as silk and laced with an ancient wisdom, "that the power of the artefacts amplifies exponentially when united. But what truly binds us is more than just our shared determination; it is the intricate tapestry of stories etched within each of us, the echoes of lives lived, and lessons learnt. For each riddle solved, a nine-hued thread, vibrant and strong, weaves itself tighter around the grand tapestry of fate, shaping not only our destinies but the destiny of all."

Oliver, ever the pragmatist, fought back a yawn that threatened to undermine his resolve. His unwavering loyalty had already been tested, pushed to its limits. Yet, something deep within him, an instinct he couldn't quite explain, urged him to stay the course, to see this effort through. He crossed his arms defensively, a gesture that betrayed both his scepticism and his preparedness. "Alright," he enquired, his tone laced with a mixture of resignation and curiosity. "Spare us the poetry for a moment. What exactly are we facing? What's this riddle all about?"

"An intricate puzzle," Professor Finch replied, excitement gleaming in his eyes. "This museum stands on secrets. Each artefact holds clues to its earlier owners and their destinies—knowledge that can sever time's hold on us if we untangle the strands."

"Untangling?" Finn could not have his amusement. He darted around the group playfully, his wooden form animated with spirit. "More like a game of cat and mouse! I've always been half of one, you see."

"Focus, Finn!" Ellie said, with a soft chuckle. "We must be serious. Valen awaits. But are we truly ready to face whatever lies ahead?"

Just then, a soft croak echoed through the hall, abruptly silencing the murmur of anticipation. Every head swivelled towards the source of the sound. Huckleberry , majestic and unsettling in equal measure, perched ominously atop a weathered stone pedestal. His feathers, the colour of midnight and storm clouds, ruffled slightly as he surveyed the assembled group. His beady eyes, like polished obsidian, gleamed with a palpable mischief, hinting at the trials to come. "Ready, you say?" he rasped, his voice a gravelly counterpoint to the hall's hushed atmosphere. "Valen has spoken of trials that may bind you further or strengthen your alliances. Seek the riddle hidden within the artefacts that guard the paths of the past. Only by deciphering these mysteries can you hope to navigate the shifting currents of time."

"Guardians, you say?" Lady Arabella's voice chimed in, smooth and authoritative, cutting through the air like the finest crystal. All eyes now turned to the ornate 18th-century statue that moved gracefully to the forefront. Her porcelain face, illuminated by the soft glow of the enchanted torches, exuded an elegance that captured Ellie's heart. Every detail, from the lace at her collar to the delicate curve of her hand, seemed imbued with centuries of wisdom. "Many versions of the past exist in shadows, fractured and fleeting. Each time shifts, each alliance forged, each choice made defines the trajectory of events. Choose wisely, for in every decision, destinies intertwine, linking us closer together or tearing us irrevocably apart. The past is not a fixed point, but a tapestry woven with endless possibilities, waiting to be unravelled."

With a surge of inspiration blooming in her chest, Ellie stepped forward, the thrill of the challenge invigorating her senses. "Let's travel to the grand hall," she proposed, her voice ringing with newfound confidence. "Last time we were there, we found portraits that showed varied elements of history – a combination of past visions revealing potential paths. Perhaps within their brushstrokes, their hidden details, and the stories they silently whisper, we'll find the clues we need to unlock the secrets of the Timekeeper's trials and choose the right path through the labyrinth of the past."

"Indeed! Professor Finch praised Ellie's brilliant idea. "The grand hall has always been the museum's beating heart, after all."

And so, the unusual band of allies set forth, thumbing the very fabric of destiny swirling around them like a vibrant, unpredictable tapestry. Each footstep echoed with the weight of untold futures, a symphony of potential victories and devastating failures. Wandering through the labyrinth of time and possibility, a journey far more literal than metaphorical, Azrael led the way confidently. His eyes, sharp and knowing, constantly scanned the shifting realities that bled through the cracks in their temporal pathway. Glancing back at his companions, a warrior's grim determination etched onto his features, he spoke with a quiet authority. "Stay attuned to one another. Feel the pulse of our shared purpose. It is together, bound by this improbable alliance, that we can weather the trials ahead, for the path ahead will test us beyond measure."

As they traversed the arches of history, each archway a portal to a different era shimmering with its own unique energy, Oliver fumbled nervously with his museum-issued flashlight. The beam, a meagre attempt to pierce the oppressive darkness, danced wildly across the walls, painting grotesque shadows that seemed to writhe with forgotten secrets. "This newfound teamwork is certainly not what I expected when I took on my guard duty tonight," he admitted, his voice barely a whisper above the hum of temporal energy. A mixture of discomfort and intrigue was clear in his voice. "One moment I'm making sure no one gets sticky fingers on the artefacts; the next I'm... well, I don't even know what I'm doing, to be honest. But it's certainly an upgrade to polishing display cases!"

Finn, the historian with a thirst for knowledge that bordered on obsession, stopped suddenly. His ears perked up like a curious fox, tuning into the whispers of the past that resonated deep within the very stones. "Just imagine the tales the statues must hold!" he exclaimed, his eyes gleaming with excitement as he gestured towards a towering figure frozen mid-stride. "They've witnessed empires rise and fall, love and war, the relentless march of time itself. And look at us! Each of us has vast treasures of history within our own experiences, our own memories.

We are each a soldier of legend, a humble museum guard, and a scholar engrossed in the lore. Indeed, we form an unlikely alliance! But perhaps," he added, a thoughtful frown creasing his brow, "that's precisely what makes us strong. Our differences are our greatest weapon."

"An incredible one," Luci added, her eyes sparkling in shared mirth. "But friends or allies, we shan't be dismissed. We are all now bound to this unfolding story."

Ellie hesitated for a moment, her gaze flickering between the Lion of Luxor, its granite mane somehow shimmering with temporal energy, and Seraphina, the serpent whose scales seemed to whisper forgotten tales. Their quirks were undeniable, almost laughable in their absurdity, yet here they were, her unlikely allies against forces she was only beginning to understand. Who would have thought a stoic lion statue could prove itself through time, leaving trails of sand and shimmering paradoxes in its wake? Or that a serpent, usually associated with cunning and deceit, could have such an intricate understanding of narrative and a genuine desire to aid them in story-weaving, crafting narratives that could either save or damn worlds?

And then there was Oliver, dear, perpetually bewildered Oliver, still grappling with the uncontainable chaos that had ripped him from his mundane life of fence-guarding and thrown him headfirst into a world far beyond mere guarding. The sheer scope of their adventures seemed to weigh him down, the weight of forgotten histories and potential futures pressing on his shoulders. He looked like a man trying to hold back a flood tide with a teaspoon, a testament to how far they had all come and how much further they still had to go.

"Perhaps the very fabric of our narrative is calling out for these unlikely alliances," Ellie mused, excitement bubbling within her as they neared the grand hall.

As they entered the hall, a hush fell over them, broken only by the soft padding of their footsteps on the ancient stone floor. Towering statues, silent sentinels of a bygone era, loomed above, their carved faces impassive yet somehow knowing. Each figure was a masterpiece of artistry, adorned with intricate carvings that seemed to writhe and shift in the dim light, telling stories of forgotten kings and mythical beasts. The hall was suffused in an ethereal glow, not from any mundane source, but from delicate fae lights strategically placed alongside each artefact. These diminutive, shimmering orbs lent the space a magical ambience, as if the very air thrummed with unseen energy. Whispered secrets, echoes of past events and forgotten rituals, collided within the air, like motes of dust dancing in a sunbeam. These subtle hints, teasing amidst the stillness, spoke of mysteries waiting to be unlocked.

"I sense we're on the brink of discovery," Professor Finch declared, his voice barely above a whisper, yet filled with an excitement that radiated off him like heat from a forge. His eyes gleamed with anticipation as he gestured forward. "Look here—"

His voice trailed off, lost in awe, as they stood before a grand mural that dominated the far wall. It depicted the history of the museum itself, chronicling its journey through time from its humble beginnings to its current grandeur. The mural was not merely a depiction but a living tapestry of history, its enigma-laden imagery coming alive with each step they took closer. Within the vivid strokes of the artist's hand lay definitions of artefacts long lost, their purpose obscured by the passage of centuries. The whispers of their use, their powers, and their fate were woven into the very fabric of the story.

"Look!" Azrael exclaimed, his voice ringing with a newfound understanding. His stellar energy, usually had, now pulsed outwards, illuminating the space like a beacon in the darkness. The soft, cool light bathed the mural, revealing details previously unseen. "Each artefact depicted in the mural is marked by shadows—a reflection of their past guardians! Look closely at the patterns; they shift and change, reflecting the personalities and powers of those who protected them. This mural itself offers the answer we look for, a key to unlocking the secrets held within these walls!"

Ellie traced her fingers along the cool, aged surface of the artefact, a low hum vibrating beneath her touch. She could feel the energy thrumming in response, a palpable pulse that resonated deep within her bones. "The guardians of the past hold the key to the next link in our path," she murmured, her voice barely heard above the ambient whisper of ancient magic. She stepped back, her gaze sweeping over the intricate carvings. "What would a gathering of partners uncover? What secrets are revealed when we bring together those connected to these powerful entities?"

Finn, ever the exuberant one, jumped into the air, displaying his joyful spirit. His eyes shone with excitement. "More than a riddle, Ellie! This is a chance to truly connect! Let's unleash puzzles of proportion, divided between vessels and carriers. Imagine the insights we could gain if we could understand the relationship between those who carried the power and those who channelled it!" He landed with a flourish, already picturing the complex challenges ahead.

Oliver, despite his earlier cynicism and scepticism towards anything remotely mystical, found himself inexplicably drawn into the spectacle. The palpable energy in the air was undeniable, and even he couldn't deny the pull of the ancient artefact. "Look closer," he urged, his usual dry tone tinged with genuine curiosity. "Who are these guardians, exactly? The mural suggests protectors, but what did they protect? Surely, they must hold wise counsel, if only we can decipher their language...or their purpose."

No sooner were the words uttered than the mural began to glow brighter, the painted colours intensifying until they seemed to burn with inner light. Translucent forms, ethereal and shimmering, began to appear where the painted shadows had lain dormant for centuries. Like phantoms of history, vestiges of various guardians drifted forth, their forms coalescing slowly, revealing fragments of armour, flowing robes, and faces etched with wisdom and sorrow. They were entrancing, captivating the allies assembled before them and silencing all doubts with the undeniable power of their presence. The air crackled with anticipation, the promise of answers hanging heavy in the suddenly charged atmosphere. The journey to uncover the next link had begun, and the guardians of the past were ready to guide them.

"Well, well, well," the first ghostly figure chirped with joviality. It was a young scholar adorned in antiquated attire, quill in hand. "You come seeking wisdom, don't you? But wisdom must be won! What is it you've learnt?"

"Time binds the past, future, and present," Ellie replied, her mind darting between possibilities. "We are all part of a greater narrative—united, we unravel truths."

The mural flickered, responding to her words. "Then an ally must offer the willow of wisdom. Give the answer to the riddle bound in arrows."

"Arrows?" Professor Finch repeated, processing swiftly. "Are we to draw from our alliances? The union of our histories must lend credibility to the strength of the present!"

With a sigh that carried the weight of generations, Lady Arabella stepped forward, her presence radiating a palpable sense of regal power. She seemed to gather the very air around her, pooling her energy into a concentrated force of will. "One must meditate on their role as a guide," she began, her voice resonating with an almost otherworldly timbre, "The noble must cradle the sharp edge of their destiny, understanding that true leadership lies not in wielding power but in bearing the burden of its consequences. We are not just rulers but shepherds, and the path ahead will be fraught with thorns."

The shadows in the chamber flickered again, deepening and swirling, as if responding to Lady Arabella's words. The air crackled with an aura of anticipation, a silent promise of revelation. "Speak this matter of importance, dear candidates," the shadows seemed to whisper, their voice a chorus of ages, "and let it resound among your kindred souls. For unity and understanding are the foundations of empires, and they will protect you from the coming darkness."

In that moment, a flicker of movement, almost imperceptible, caught Ellie's keen eye. Across the vast mural, which stretched across the entirety of the chamber wall, a series of glowing arrows began to appear. They appeared as if drawn by invisible hands, each one a precise, luminous pathway. The arrows pointed towards distinct sections of the intricate artwork, depicting scenes of ancient battles, forgotten rituals, and mythical creatures. They intertwined and wove, converging and diverging in a complex tapestry, until they formed a web of light that pulsed with an almost sentient energy. "Could these be the artefacts and their guardians?" she whispered, her voice barely heard, her breath catching in her throat with a mixture of excitement and trepidation. A wave of realisation washed over her, the potential of this discovery overwhelming her senses.

"Yes!" Azrael exclaimed, his voice ringing with fervent conviction. He stepped forward, his eyes shining with a newfound understanding. "The artefacts themselves might hold the knowledge we desperately look for! They are not mere objects but repositories of ancient wisdom, fragments of a forgotten age. When united, their power will resonate, guiding us through the chaos that awaits us. We must remember that relying on each other's strengths, acknowledging our weaknesses, and forging unbreakable bonds will be the key to overcoming Valen's challenge. He looks to unravel the fabric of time itself, and only by working together, imbued with the knowledge of these artefacts, can we hope to stand against him." The urgency in his voice was palpable, a clear indication of the perilous journey that lay ahead.

In that illuminating instance, a tangible sense of unity enveloped the group, a silent agreement passing between them like a current. The unfamiliar yet riveting connections they formed, born from shared experience and burgeoning trust, bolstered their resolve, transforming them from hesitant strangers into a cohesive force. Ellie felt a swell of understanding wash over her, a warmth that permeated deeper than mere camaraderie. They were no longer simply individuals drawn together by fate or circumstance but allies inextricably woven through the very fabric of enchantment, their destinies now intertwined in a way she couldn't quite understand but instinctively embraced.

"Now we must prove our worth!" Oliver declared, his voice ringing with conviction, determination etched upon his features like lines on an ancient map. "Whatever Valen demands, whatever trials he throws our way, we will meet them head-on, strengthened by our unlikely alliances! We will show him what we are capable of!"

As they stood together, bathed in the ethereal glow, the mural shimmered with renewed vibrancy, as if acknowledging their pledge and binding them to their shared mission. A murmur pulsed through their realised comradeship, a quiet energy that hummed with anticipation and a shared purpose. Quickly and efficiently, they formulated a plan, fuelled by adrenaline and a growing sense of belonging. They would delve deeper into the artefacts' tales, looking to understand their significance and unlock the secrets they held. They would nurture and enhance their connections, solidifying the bonds that had so unexpectedly formed. And, most importantly, they would unearth the next challenge woven into the tapestry of the night, ready to face whatever mysteries lay ahead.

With hearts intertwined, their individual stories now a shared narrative, they ventured forth, stepping into the next chapter of their whimsical tapestry. The fear that had lingered moments before was replaced by a burgeoning excitement, a thrill that pulsed with the promise of adventure. They were no longer simply a group of individuals; they were a team, a force, embarking on a journey to become true allies, forged in the fires of magic and bound by a shared destiny. The adventure had truly begun.

THE TRANSFORMATION

The hour hand of the antique clock in the curator's office crept towards midnight, each tick a hammer blow against Ellie's nerves. With each passing moment, the museum breathed a misty air of anticipation, a palpable energy that seemed to crackle in the static electricity clinging to her hair. Beneath the arching, cathedral-like ceilings of the Grand Hall, shadows danced atop the walls like flickering spectres, restless spirits preparing to unveil a long-kept secret, a truth buried beneath layers of dust and forgotten lore.

Ellie stood at the foot of the Grand Hall's imposing staircase, her breath catching in her throat. She strained her ears, trying to catch the echo of whispers that seemed to call out to her from the deepest corners of the ancient space, murmurs that promised answers and hinted at danger. They told tales of pharaohs and conquerors, of artists and revolutionaries, all trapped within the silent stone.

"Are we ready?" Ellie asked, her voice a mixture of excitement and trepidation, barely a whisper in the vast hall. She glanced at Professor Finch, a beacon of unwavering enthusiasm in the gloom. His curious eyes, magnified by thick lenses, sparkled under the dim glow of the overhead lanterns, exuding an infectious eagerness that made her heart race. He looked less like a respected academic and more like a child on Christmas Eve.

"Prepared as we can be," he replied, his voice a low rumble, barely heard above the rhythmic creaking of the old building. He adjusted his glasses, the gesture both familiar and comforting. "After years of research, countless late nights poring over ancient texts, it's time we engage with history in a way few have had the privilege to do. Tonight, Ellie, we don't just observe the past, we become a part of it." He winked, a conspiratorial glint in his eye. "Or at least, we try to. No guarantees, of course. History, as they say, is a fickle mistress." He patted the worn leather-bound book clutched tightly under his arm, its golden clasps gleaming faintly in the dim light. The book. The key. The reason they were here, alone, in the heart of the museum, as midnight approached, ready to unlock a secret that had been dormant for centuries.

Okay, here is a more polished version of the wording that was chosen earlier:

Each click of the hour hand on the ancient clock that was in the curator's office was like a hammer blow to Ellie's nerves. The clock kept moving closer and closer to midnight. There was a tangible energy that appeared to sizzle in the static electricity that was clinging to her hair, and the museum exhaled a foggy air of expectation with each passing instant. Under the cathedral-like ceilings that adorned the Grand Hall, shadows danced above the walls like flickering spectres. These shadows were restless spirits that were getting ready to reveal a long-kept secret, a truth that had been buried behind layers of dust and forgotten legend.

With her breath caught in her throat, Ellie stood at the base of the grand staircase that led up to the Grand Hall. It appeared as if she was trying to catch the echo of whispers that seemed to cry out to her from the darkest recesses of the old space. These murmurs offered answers and hinted at peril. She strained her ears to hear the word. They narrated stories about pharaohs and conquerors, artists and revolutionaries, all of whom were imprisoned inside the stone that was considered mute.

We are ready, are we? When Ellie enquired, her voice was barely heard above a whisper in the large hall. Her tone was a combination of enthusiasm and dread. A ray of unflinching excitement shone through the darkness as she cast a gaze in the direction of Professor Finch. He had thick lenses that emphasised his enquiring eyes, and they gleamed in the faint light of the lanterns that were hanging above them. His eyes exuded an infectious desire that caused her pulse to accelerate. His appearance was less that of a renowned scholar and more that of a little kid on the evening of Christmas Eve.

"We are as prepared as we possibly can be," he said, his voice barely detectable over the regular creaking of the ancient structure. "We are prepared as we can be." He adjusted his spectacles, an action that was both reassuring and familiar to him. The moment has come for us to connect with history in a manner that very few people have ever had the opportunity to do. This comes after years of study and many late hours spent looking over old writings. During this evening, Ellie, we are not only seeing the past; rather, we are becoming a part of it. The look in his eye suggested that he was plotting something. In any case, we try to. Of course, there are no promises. They say that history is a fickle mistress, and they are right. The golden clasps of the aged leather-bound book that he was holding closely under his arm glistened softly in the shadowy light as he caressed the book by its spine. For the book. This is the key. The reason they were here, all by themselves, in the centre of the museum, as midnight drew near, was because they were well prepared to discover a mystery that had been lying dormant for generations.

The moment Azrael the Lion, a creature frozen in time within a block of sandstone, unfurled from his stone form and roared softly into life, the air thickened. It wasn't just a change in atmosphere; it was a tangible shift, a palpable weight of magic that settled upon their shoulders. The hairs on Oliver's arms stood on end, and a shiver traced its way down his spine. "Indeed," Azrael said, his majestic voice reverberating like a rumble of thunder through the hall, each syllable echoing off the high, vaulted ceilings. "But it's not just a miracle, young one. It's a gateway, a key. It's a journey through the past, and a glimpse into futures yet unwritten. Follow me!"

With a majestic leap that defied his ancient stone form, Azrael bounded forward, his powerful muscles rippling beneath his golden mane. He moved with a grace that belied his size, guiding the adventurers – Ellie, the wide-eyed historian, and now, the bewildered but undeniably intrigued Oliver – toward the intricately carved oak doors at the far end of the hall. They were more than just doors; they were a portal, shimmering ever so slightly with an energy only visible in the corner of one's eye. Each step ignited Ellie's conviction, fuelling the fire of her lifetime passion. The museum was so much more than mere artefacts, dusty relics trapped behind glass. It was a living tapestry, interwoven with the vibrant threads of lives long since left, and now, with the promise of a new adventure, waiting to be relived. The air crackled with possibility, and for the first time in a long time, Oliver felt truly alive.

As Ellie hurried after Azrael, her heart pounding a frantic rhythm against her ribs, she felt a light touch upon her shoulder, a sensation both delicate and strangely powerful. She turned, anticipation and apprehension mingling in her gaze, to see Luci slithering gracefully into view. Her bronze scales, usually muted in the lower levels of the Citadel, glistened under the hall's soft, ethereal light, catching the ambient glow and reflecting it in a mesmerising dance of shimmering bronze and gold.

"You are about to witness the transformation of time itself," Luci intoned, her voice a melody that seemed to resonate not just in the air but within Ellie's very bones, echoing against the high, vaulted ceilings and the ancient stones from which they were built. "The very essence of history will swirl around you, waiting to be unveiled. Every forgotten secret, every pivotal moment, every ripple of cause and effect will become tangible." Her forked tongue flicked out, tasting the air, as if she could already sense the temporal currents gathering.

Ellie's breath hitched in her throat. "Are you ready for this?" she asked Luci, her voice a mere whisper, laced half with wonder at the sheer size of the event and half with a burgeoning fear of the unknown adventures that lay ahead. The implications were staggering. To glimpse the past, to potentially alter it...it was a power beyond comprehension.

The serpent's eyes, ancient and wise, twinkled like ancient stars, holding within them the secrets of millennia. They seemed to see right through Ellie, past her surface anxieties and into the core of her being, judging her readiness.

"I was created to guide you, to weave together the threads of the past and present, to illuminate the paths that lie hidden from mortal eyes, but you must be vigilant," Luci said, her voice becoming more serious, imbued with a weight that Ellie could feel settling on her own shoulders. "The artefacts you look for are not mere objects; they are keys. To uncover their true power and to understand the influence they hold, you must embrace their forms. Become one with their history."

Oliver, who had been impatiently pacing nearby, shot Ellie a sidelong glance, his expression a mixture of scepticism and grudging intrigue. His eyebrows were raised, a silent question hanging in the air. "How exactly do we do that?" he finally asked, his voice laced with a dry edge that masked his growing fascination. "Are we talking shapeshifting? Are we discussing some sort of ancient ritual? Because I'm really hoping it doesn't involve snakes."

"Transformation begins with understanding," Azrael replied, pausing at the threshold of the grand doorway that separated the present from the mysteries concealed beyond. "Each artefact whispers its story; your task is to listen."

Ellie took a deep breath, the cool air doing little to calm the frantic drum solo her heart was performing. Each beat echoed the momentousness of the moment. The aged wooden door, intricately carved with scenes of swirling galaxies and mythical creatures, creaked open, revealing a chamber unlike any she had ever imagined. It wasn't just lit; it was bathed in a luminous azure light, a vibrant, otherworldly glow that seemed to emanate from the very air itself.

Within this ethereal space stood a time-worn carousel, a relic of forgotten ages. Its painted horses, each a masterpiece of folk art, were frozen mid-gallop, their glossy coats and jewelled bridles glimmering under the azure light. They seemed to anticipate a joyous occasion, poised to celebrate the fleeting nature of time itself. Their painted eyes, wide and knowing, hinted at secrets held within their wooden frames.

As the grandfather clock in the corner, its face adorned with celestial constellations, struck midnight, the carousel sprang to life. But this wasn't the rusty, creaking motion of a machine worn down by age. Instead, a harmonious hum filled the hall, a low, resonant vibration that seemed to penetrate bone and awaken something ancient within her. The air thrummed with barely had energy.

"The transformation awaits!" Finn chirped, his voice a melodic blend of mischief and excitement. He bounded towards Ellie, his bushy tail twitching with impish glee, his emerald eyes sparkling in the azure light. "Step onto the carousel, my dear, and feel the magic coursing through you! It's a symphony of experience, a dance through the ages!"

With a mix of breathless excitement and a prickle of nervous hesitation, Ellie stepped forward. The smooth, polished wood of the carousel platform felt strangely warm beneath her feet. She joined the others – a motley crew of adventurers and dreamers – as they climbed onto the colourful horses. Each steed seemed to resonate with a unique energy, offering a silent invitation to embark on an extraordinary journey. Shimmering jewels adorned their saddles and manes, catching the light and scattering rainbows across the chamber walls.

"What will happen?" she asked, her voice barely a whisper. A mixture of fear and exhilaration fluttered in her chest, like trapped birds desperate for release. The unknown stretched before her, a vast and shimmering landscape of possibility. What wonders – or perils – lay beyond the turning of the carousel?

"The past will mould you," Azrael announced, his golden mane catching the ethereal glow. "You will see through the eyes of those who came before you."

As the carousel spun faster, a dizzying blur of painted horses and swirling colours, the light intensified, bathing Ellie in an ethereal glow. A palpable warmth enveloped her, more than just the summer air; it felt like a comforting embrace, a long-forgotten memory resurfacing. A shiver, not of cold, but of pure sensation, traced a delicate path down her spine as she squeezed her eyes shut. The cacophony of the amusement park – the shrieks of delight, the tinny music, the distant rumble of the roller coaster – coalesced into a harmonious symphony of childhood joy. She opened her eyes, hesitant, and gasped. The carousel was gone, vanished without a trace. In its place lay an enchanted village bathed in the honeyed light of late afternoon. Gentle wind rustled through seemingly endless golden fields that stretched to the horizon, the ripe grain swaying in rhythmic waves.

"Welcome to the land of the ancients," a childlike figure chirped, her voice like tinkling bells. She stood at the edge of a village square cobbled with stones worn smooth by time, waving a small, delicate hand. Her attire was a dazzling kaleidoscope of colours – a patchwork dress sewn with flowers and feathers and a headscarf embroidered with shimmering threads. Her laughter was infectious, a pure, unfiltered sound that resonated deep within Ellie's soul. It felt ancient and yet utterly new, as if she was hearing the echo of generations long past. The subject was no ordinary child; the conversation was the spirit of the past made manifest, a whimsical guide inviting her to explore its hidden corners, to unearth its buried secrets.

Ellie felt a tug of recognition, a faint humming in her chest that resonated with the very stones beneath her feet. "Is this...?"

she began, her voice a hushed whisper, afraid to break the delicate spell. But before she could complete her thought, the child, her eyes twinkling with mischief, grasped Ellie's hand and led her further into the village. The stalls, overflowing with handmade crafts and exotic wares, were bustling with life. Villagers chattered in a language she didn't understand, yet somehow comprehended. The air, thick with the promise of adventure, vibrated with energy. Fragrant spices wafted through the air from open-air kitchens, mingling with the joyous sounds of music and laughter, creating an intoxicating sensory overload that wrapped around Ellie like a warm, welcoming cloak.

Meanwhile, Oliver marvelled at the swirling panorama of figures bustling around him. Vendors hawked strange and wonderful wares, musicians played tunes that seemed to weave through the very air, and children chased each other with gleeful abandon. The market throbbed with a vibrant energy, a chaotic symphony of sights, sounds, and smells that overwhelmed his senses. He had expected a simple gathering, a mundane exchange of goods. But the crowd was something else entirely, a living, breathing organism fuelled by dreams and desires. Unbeknownst to him, however, a far greater adventure was unfolding just beneath the surface of the laughter and life, a subtle undercurrent of magic and mystery. "This is... incredible," he whispered, his earlier scepticism fading like morning mist under the warmth of the morning sun. The sheer spectacle of it all was enough to make him a believer, to ignite a spark of wonder he hadn't felt in years.

In a nearby stall overflowing with antique clocks, hourglasses, and curious instruments, Professor Finch was conversing animatedly with a bearded merchant. The merchant's eyes, deep-set and wise, seemed to hold the weight of centuries. Finch, usually reserved and scholarly, was positively electric with excitement. "Do you hold the secrets of time?" Finch boomed, his voice barely heard above the market din. A sparkle in his eye betrayed a childlike wonder, a blend of scholarly curiosity and genuine awe. He had dedicated his life to finding out about the universe, and this encounter felt like the culmination of a lifelong quest.

"Yes," the merchant said, his voice a low, resonant hum that seemed to vibrate in the air. He nodded seriously and stroked his beard as if he were thinking. "But the biggest secrets aren't in old books or hard maths problems. They are a part of you, woven into the very fabric of your being. To really understand time, you need to know the things that shape our lives, the moments that make us who we are, and the joys and sorrows that stay with us forever. He pointed to the busy market around him. "Time isn't straight; it's a tapestry made of memories, choices, and destinies."

In the middle of the controlled chaos, Lady Arabella, looking as regal as ever in her silk gown and jewelled headdress, hovered protectively over her friends. There was a quiet strength and understated elegance about her. She had seen a lot in her long life, including the rise and fall of empires and the dangers of politics. She knew how hard it was to find the right balance between progress and danger, between knowledge and duty. "Be careful," she said softly, her voice barely a whisper but full of experience. "Change can be as scary as it is enlightening." The road ahead may be full of problems, and the truths you find may be difficult to accept, but keep in mind that growth needs change, and change often requires giving something up. Her eyes were kind, but they also had a hint of foreboding, as if they were silently warning her of the tough times ahead.

Finn, a fluffy white ball of fur, ran around Ellie's feet, his tail wagging like crazy. He playfully pushed her towards the merchant's stall, putting a lot of pressure on her shins. "Woof!" he seemed to bark, a sound that said a lot without saying much. "You should really take a closer look!" He might be able to tell us more about the treasures we're looking for. His bright, smart eyes, which were usually full of mischief, were unusually serious and told her to keep going.

Ellie thought about Finn as she looked back at him. She had been unsure because she could feel a sense of magic coming from the messy stall. Finn, on the other hand, never gave up. She looked into his pleading eyes and saw more than just a dog's excitement. She saw a more profound understanding and a connection to the quest they were on. With new resolve, she stood up straight and walked up to the merchant, a thin man with eyes that were as old and wise as the dust motes that danced around him. There were many trinkets, scrolls, and shiny bits of old things all around him. "What do you know about the artefacts?" she asked, her voice steady even though she was shaking with excitement. She needed to know what they meant and why Finn seemed to feel so powerful about them.

The merchant's eyes, which were made bigger by thick, round glasses, sparkled with laughter. He didn't answer right away. Instead, he ran a rough hand over a tarnished silver amulet that had symbols on it that she didn't know what they meant. Finally, he spoke. His voice was rough but deep, like the echo of languages that had been lost. He said, "The artefacts you want have history pulsing through their forms." His hands moved through the air as if they were tracing stories on an invisible canvas. "They're not just things; they're vessels of identity that have been shaped by time and are waiting for brave souls to reconnect with them. They do remember, you know. They remember the ones who came before them, the good and troubled times, and the hopes and fears that are a part of who they are. And they pick... they pick who will hear their stories. He stopped and looked directly at Ellie, his gaze sharpening. "Are you sure you're ready to hear?"

Ellie felt a calming heat course through her body as she soaked up his words; this comforting heat obscured the unease she was experiencing. She had fleeting flashes of joy and sadness, memories of lives past that weren't her own, and her awareness wavered. She saw a light-hearted family reunion, with raucous laughter resonating around a sun-kissed table; a solemn ceremony, with the aroma of incense and the sound of whispered prayers filling the air; and a tragic farewell, with tears falling from an unfamiliar face. She created a jumbled mental tapestry with these stolen moments, fragments of life from somewhere she didn't know. Invisible yet powerful, time's muscles entwined with her soul, drawing her further into the depths where mysteries lay, tantalising with the promise of knowledge but also posing a threat to her very essence.

"Transformation has its cost," the merchant whispered, his voice barely heard amidst Ellie's whirlwind of sensations. His normally dazzling eyes were obscured by a veil of caution, reducing their vivacious radiance. If you let yourself become swept away by the waves of regret, you might never come up for air. The weight of innumerable lives can easily shatter the delicate self.

"In this world of stories," Azrael whispered, her voice a rock solid amidst the tempest she was experiencing inside. A reassuring power that sliced through the confusion was contained within its ancient knowledge. To find one's way through the maze, one must have knowledge. Keep in mind that what you find here is indiscernible. Find the answer you're looking for in every detail, every emotion, and even in fleeting impressions.

But as time went on, Ellie's sense of urgency intensified. Like a candle whose flame was about to go out, the light changed, blurring and dimming. She was almost overwhelmed by the borrowed memories, which were blurring the line between her true self and the ghosts of others.

With a voice that broke the rising echo of moments before, she cried out, "We must return!" as a desperate plea against the rising tide of the unknown. Sadly, by that point, it was too late. As the temporal currents drew her deeper into the abyss, the light of her own self started to fade. The maze of time was drawing her in, and the way out was getting harder and harder to see.

The whimsical tune of the carousel started to fade, like a worn-out clock. As a result, the once-vibrant hues of the painted horses and the sprightly dolphins took on a more subdued quality, their dismal figures creating lean, warped silhouettes on the uneven cobblestones. A subtle metallic tang had replaced the once-heavy aroma of spun sugar and laughter in the air. The vendor continued to stand behind his stall, which was brimming with strange objects and shiny ornaments. He stared at Ellie through deep-set eyes that appeared to contain the wisdom of many years and the mysteries of many adventures. The sense of urgency in her voice and the overwhelming sense of desperation that enveloped her were both picked up by him.

His voice sounded like dry leaves rustling on the pavement as he finally rasped, "To return, you must awaken the essence of transformation."

The word "essence" resounded in Ellie's mind like a frantic echo in the unexpected quiet, and she kept saying it. As the disparate parts started to fit together, she experienced a chilling realisation that was both cold and sharp. All signs, including the merchant's enigmatic remarks, the dwindling carousel, and her own growing anxiety, led to one terrifying conclusion. Maybe we're missing something important! An event that will spark this change.

Luci broke the silence with an abruptly powerful statement, "The artefacts hold memories." Her voice had been muted by the dwindling laughter. A sense of clarity appeared to have replaced the bewilderment that had previously obscured her features. "Reveal their tales, and you will discover a means of return. For going back means more than just going over the same old route; it's about embracing the journey you've been on and coming to terms with who you are now. Recognising the change within is more important than trying to escape. A guiding light in the darkening carousel world, her words lingered in the air, burdened with significance. The task at hand was clear: they needed to explore their history to understand what had led them to this point and, more importantly, to discover a means of escape.

A skeletal framework barely turning, the mechanical heart sputtering its last breaths, the carousel had been a vibrant blur of painted horses and echoing laughter once upon a time. The wind's whisper and Ellie's racing heart were the only sounds breaking the heavy silence. Her heart was a tapestry woven with joy, sorrow, and every emotion in between; she held onto the unseen threads of lives gone by. A potent vitality, a glimmer of promise, pulsed through her body, a vivid contrast to the deteriorating recollections all around her.

"What if we reweave their stories?" Her voice was filled with an impassioned plea as she inhaled. What if we reminded them of who they really are by telling them this? Understanding is more important than merely remembering. Their narratives unite us! They mirror our common path and serve as reminders of our shared humanity!

Everyone was on the edge of their seats as she spoke those words. The stillness was broken by the soft unfolding of a shimmering portal, rather than a rippling sound. It looked like a whirling light pool, a kaleidoscope of hues and feelings that throbbed with the reverberations of past lives. It conveyed sacrifice through the wrinkles of tired faces, love through the exchange of glances between soulmates, and joy through the unbridled laughter of kids. Every shade and pattern held a piece of an old story.

Ellie extended her hand, a slight tremor in her grip, with the intention of gathering the fragments of those stories that were beginning to fade away. The idea of her being a weaver, painstakingly putting together a tale that embodied vitality, strength, and the indestructible nature of the human spirit, was something she occasionally fantasised about. She closed her eyes and surrendered to the experience, allowing the tales to seep into her very being and allowing the elation of transformation to envelop her once more.

With a voice that resounded with a newly discovered conviction, she exclaimed, "We are the stories that we tell!" The resonance of her voice ignited the air around her. It was more than just a statement; it was a mantra, a declaration of power, and a demonstration of the indestructibility of the human spirit. In response to her belief, the portal began to pulse more brightly, ready to reveal its secrets and ready to be rewoven into a tapestry that would last forever. Her ability to retell the stories of those lives that had been forgotten, as well as her own, was the deciding factor in the outcome of their lives.

She was surrounded by a shimmering chamber that seemed to be a living entity reacting to the magic that was taking place. Each artefact vibrated in sympathetic resonance, reviving the powerful threads of history that had been dormant for a long time. The long-dormant power began to fill the air. The statues appeared to breathe once more, and the tapestries that depicted heroes who had been forgotten for a long time glowed with a renewed vibrancy. Oliver, whose face was etched with determination; Professor Finch, whose eyes twinkled with knowing anticipation; and the others, a diverse group bound by a shared purpose, formed a protective circle around Ellie, drawing strength from the unity that they shared. Their hands were tightly clasped together, serving as a conduit for the growing energy.

The carousel, which had been a silent sentinel of joy during childhood, was now being overpowered by a wave of energy that was undergoing transformation. The wooden eyes of its painted horses glowed with a newfound sense of animation as they reared and plunged towards the ground. The carousel began to spin once more, faster and faster, casting wisps of opalescent light that filled the room, transforming familiar shapes into ethereal forms. The carousel began to groan with the sound of ancient gears and wood protesting. The echoes of children's laughter, which were ghosts of past merriment, merged with whispers of courage, which were fuelled by the weight of their task and the danger that was currently approaching them. Unable to catch their breath and overcome with awe, Ellie and her companions submerged themselves in the enchantment of the moment, allowing it to wash over them and placing their faith in the unknown.

"The stories that they have to tell are in our hands!" The sound of Azrael's voice could be heard amplified and deepened, and it vibrated with an otherworldly resonance. The swirling light enveloped him, changing his features to those of both man and god. "Hold on tight! Refrain from letting go of the memory! It serves as the knot that holds us together!

Brilliant light erupted from within the chamber, a supernova of historical energy being released into the world. A wide opening appeared in the portal, which glistened like a tear and beckoned them to go ahead. During the process of engulfing every one of them, it served as a conduit, absorbing the spirit of the past and weaving a glorious tapestry that was woven with love, courage, and laughter. The very walls seemed to dissolve into a swirling vortex of time and memory, and the air itself crackled with possibilities that we could not even begin to imagine.

And just like that, the transformation started, not only of the artefacts, which were pulsating with renewed life and purpose, but also of every soul that was entwined in the fabric of that enchanted night. Not only did the museum hold memories, but it also had promises and secrets that were whispered on the wind, waiting to be revealed as the dawn began to break. The museum was no longer merely a repository of relics. The thick curtains that were blocking out the first rays of sunlight gave the impression of being an invitation rather than a barrier.

As their bodies twisted and shifted within the all-encompassing luminescence, their physical forms subtly changing to reflect the stories they were embracing, Ellie smiled, a calm and knowing expression gracing her lips. The change occurred as their bodies were constantly undergoing transformations. She had finally come to the realisation that they would always be a part of the stories that they embraced and that they would be inextricably linked to the heroes and heroines of earlier times. It was only the beginning of the night's adventure; the real journey was yet to come, and the real magic was still within their hearts. They were determined to change, but they would never stop looking for the limitless wonders that the enchanting universe had to offer. They were the guardians of history and memory, and their purpose was just becoming clear.

THE
FORGOTTEN GUARDIAN

The museum had a palpable stillness, like a heavy blanket that had been woven from centuries of dust that had not been disturbed and reverence that had been kept quiet. But as the clock got closer to the hour of midnight, there was a faint tremor of anticipation that rippled through the air. It was a barely perceptible hum that reverberated deep within the ancient stone walls. Ellie, the sharp-witted archaeologist; Professor Finch, the eccentric historian with an encyclopaedic knowledge of the arcane; and Oliver, the pragmatic security expert who still couldn't quite believe he was involved in this madness, huddled in the dim light cast by flickering torches. In a manner that was reminiscent of their wary glances, their long shadows danced around them.

"In your opinion, what does the Guardian appear to be like?" Ellie murmured, her voice barely heard above the quiet trickle of water that could be heard somewhere within the maze-like structure. Her heart was pounding against her ribs as she peered into the shadowy depths of the exhibit that was dedicated to forgotten civilisations. Her thoughts were racing with ideas, and she was imagining ancient guardians. She envisioned figures made of granite that were towering and animated by a magic that had been forgotten, serpentine creatures with scales made of shimmering obsidian, or perhaps something even more fantastical, a being that was woven from pure energy and the echoes of voices that had been heard for a very long time.

Professor Finch mused, "Legends tell of a guardian that awakens when forgotten stories are about to be uncovered," while adjusting his spectacles with a nervous tic that was characteristic of him. Despite his seventy years, he appeared to be much younger than he was;

flickering torchlight caught the glint of excitement in his eyes. It's possible that the creature we're looking for is not a living, breathing being, Ellie. It might be a sentient manifestation of the power that is contained within these walls; it could be an embodiment of the history of the artefacts. It is possible that the very spirit of the civilisations that have been forgotten is rising to defend its secrets. He took a momentary pause, thoughtfully stroking his beard. "Or perhaps", he continued with a sly grin, "it's just a really big dog with a particularly bad temper."

Oliver, who was known for his pragmatic approach, cleared his throat. His voice served as a counterpoint to the growing sense of unease that appeared to be settling over the group. It is important that we look for something that can be touched. There is a document, a clue, or an artefact. Let's not get caught up in imagining things that aren't real. These are not legends; we are here to find answers. To emphasise the importance of taking a methodical approach, he made gestures all around the dingy and expansive room.

However, just as those words were leaving his mouth, a low rumble reverberated throughout the room. It was a sound that seemed to vibrate not only in their ears but also in their very bones. Conversation came to a halt, and all attention was directed towards a tapestry that was hanging on the wall that was particularly magnificent. It depicted scenes from ancient battles.

Including fierce warriors battling against one another during chaos, as well as peaceful gatherings, such as families sharing meals under the beneficent sun. A strange vitality continued to pulse through the colours, even though they had faded with age. Almost as if she were being drawn in by a magnetic force, Ellie experienced a peculiar pull in the direction of it. She felt a prickling sense of premonition, a feeling that this tapestry held more than just woven threads and faded dyes, and her heart raced with a mixture of curiosity and a prickling sense of prognostication. I had the impression that it was a doorway, a silent invitation to something that was unknown.

As she pointed a trembling finger in the direction of the ancient tapestry, she exclaimed, "Look!" Her voice was a hushed whisper that was laced with awe and a tremor of fear. "The figures—they seem to be shifting!" Her eyes, which were wide and reflected the dim lighting of the museum, found themselves fixed on the intricate weave.

As the final, mournful chime of midnight resonated through the cavernous museum, a sound that seemed to vibrate in the very stones beneath their feet, the tapestry shimmered with an almost imperceptible energy. The woven threads, depicting scenes of forgotten lore and mythical creatures, seemed to writhe and pulse. Then, undeniably, the figures within it began to stir. No longer static portraits frozen in time, they stretched, shifted, and breathed imperceptibly. An ethereal light, emanating from the tapestry itself, illuminated the area, casting long, distorted shadows that danced upon the surrounding walls, transforming familiar exhibits into grotesque and unsettling phantoms.

Appearing from the heart of the shimmering tapestry, as if stepping from another dimension, was a majestic figure, radiating an aura of ancient power. He was draped in silver cloth, not woven but spun from moonlight itself, that glimmered like a constellation of captured stars in the night sky. The very air around him crackled with an unseen energy.

Azrael, a mythical being made real, stepped forward and filled the room with his powerful presence. His golden mane, which was no longer just thread but full of life and colour, shone with an inner fire as he finished changing from a woven statue to a living, breathing creature. With a knowing look, his old, wise eyes were fixed on them. "Welcome, brave souls," he said in a deep, rich voice that sounded like it had been around for a long time and had a lot of wisdom. "I am Azrael, the protector of the stories in this museum." Tonight, you will learn about a guardian who has been forgotten. His power grows as the shadows grow longer, and he holds the key to the darkness that lurks in the halls, a darkness that even I have trouble holding. His eyes darkened, and a low growl came from his chest, warning of the danger that lay ahead and the long journey that lay ahead.

Oliver's mouth dropped open a little. "You can't be serious. A guardian? "Here?" He looked around the giant room at the tall bookshelves and the softly glowing orbs that hung in the air. The thought of a powerful, mythical being hiding among the old artefacts was both extremely exciting and very scary.

"Yes," Azrael said, walking with an air of dignity. His long, flowing robes swirled around him as he walked, making him look even more otherworldly. "Magic is born from history and stories in this magical place, but if you don't remember them, old guardians fade away." They are connected to the stories they guard in a profound way. The magic gets stronger the more times a story is told. On the other hand, the guardian dies when the whispers stop.

Luci slid down from a pedestal covered in Egyptian relics, as if Azrael's words had called her. Everyone noticed her bronze scales shining in the light, which made them look even more beautiful. She moved in a way that was smooth and hypnotic. She said, "The Forgotten Guardian once curated the memories of eras long past," and her voice was a soft, sibilant whisper that seemed to echo through the room. She moved through the group of people, her cool scales brushing against their legs. "He was the keeper of lost empires and the writer of silent histories." But just like stories that were forgotten and lost to the sands of time, he too faded into obscurity. His strength faded, his shape shrank, and now he is just a shadow of what he used to be.

"Is it possible to find him?" Ellie asked, and her resolve grew. The idea of bringing back a strong protector and finding lost histories lit a fire in her. "What do we need to do?" "How can we help him get his strength back?"

"He lives in the Chamber of Echoes, where the voices of the past echo," Luci said, flicking her tail to show them a shadowy archway at the other end of the room. From inside, there was a faint, otherworldly glow. "But be careful—only those with good intentions can get through. The echoes will put your mind and heart to the test. They will dig into your deepest fears and desires, question your reasons for doing things, and test your willpower. Only people who are honest with themselves and their goals can expect to do well, and even then, there are no guarantees. A hint of a smile crossed Luci's snake-like face. "The past is a strong force, and it doesn't give up its secrets easily."

The four adventurers—Liam, the stoic warrior; Ellie, the curious historian; Oliver, the practical inventor; and Azrael himself, the mysterious guide—followed Azrael through dimly lit corridors. Finn, who was artfully mischievous and ran excitedly at their heels, his bushy tail a blur in the dark, was also with them. The corridors were more than just ways to get from one place to another; they were living records. The old stone was carved with strange symbols that seemed to move and change in the corners of their eyes. As they got closer to a heavy door, the air buzzed with an almost real energy, a hum that they could feel in their chests. The door wasn't just a barrier; it was a work of art that had been lost to time, with intricate carvings that showed battles, kings, and heavenly events that had happened long ago.

"What's out there?" Oliver asked, and his voice echoed a little in the small space. The beam of his torch shook nervously as he tightened his grip on it. He wasn't petrified, but he was on edge, which kept him sharp.

"A tapestry of voices," Azrael said, and his voice was so deep and powerful that it silenced even Finn's playful yaps. "A chance to bring the Guardian back to the world of memory." But be careful: not all voices are friendly.

Ellie moved forward, her historian instincts kicking in. Her eyes, which are usually soft and kind, now burnt with a powerful desire to learn. "Someone should tell a story or a memory. Someone should share a genuine and heartfelt story or memory. Maybe that will wake him up, touch his dormant essence, and bring him back. She took a worn leather-bound journal out of her bag and ran her fingers over the faded writing on the cover.

She spoke to the door with confidence, though she was a little nervous. Her voice was clear and strong, even though the air was heavy. "Listen to me, Guardian of Forgotten Tales! We would rather not steal or destroy; we want to learn. We want your wisdom, the knowledge that has been lost over time. We remember the history that happened in these walls, the good and terrible things that happened, and the hopes and fears of those who came before us. Come back to us! "Bring life back to this place!"

The old door shook as if it were responding to her voice fading away into the unseen depths beyond. As it slowly creaked open, a low groan, like the sigh of a giant who had been forgotten, came from its hinges. Inside was a giant room that seemed to go on forever. Shadows that flickered across the rough stone floor and the tall walls came from sources of light that couldn't be seen. The smell of dust and things that had been forgotten hung in the air, a real sign of time itself.

There were mirrors of all shapes and sizes all over the place, almost to the point of obsession. Some were small and fancy, with tarnished silver and bone frames, while others were huge, going from the floor to the ceiling, with surfaces that were cloudy with age. These weren't only normal reflections; they were ways to see into the past. Glimpses of long-lost moments—lovers laughing in a sun-drenched garden, a knight kneeling before a king, a child crying over a broken toy—twisted and turned in the glass, coming together to make hauntingly beautiful pictures that looked both real and like they were from a dream. The whole thing was mesmerising, disturbing, and undeniably strong.

The group, huddled together just outside the door, hesitated. Their faces showed a mix of awe and fear. The energy in the air was both attractive and repulsive. But Azrael, their leader and guide through this maze of time, stepped through without thinking. She moved with controlled grace, her head held high and her eyes shining with an inner light that seemed to cut through the darkness. She was both brave and had a keen sense of purpose. "Come with me," she said, her voice strong but almost pleading. "We must go beyond the limits of memory. The answers we need are inside us.

The heavy silence broke as they carefully stepped into the room. There was a lot of whispering in the air, with voices speaking both familiar and strange languages. The whispers surrounded them, pushing them closer and begging them to share their memories, secrets, and lives. It was too much, and I lost my way. Azrael raised a hand, stopping the growing panic in its tracks. "Oliver, tell us a story from your life," she said, her voice a clear and steady counterpoint to the whispers that were all over the place. Her gaze didn't waver, silently inviting him in and promising safety in the room's enchanting but unsettling embrace.

Oliver shifted uncomfortably because he felt exposed and vulnerable under the weight of so many unseen eyes. He cleared his throat and was surprised at how dry it was. He took a deep breath and steadied his voice, trying to sound calm even though he didn't feel that way. He started with a low rumble that filled the space between them. "I used to be a guide for school trips." "I told the kids stories about the artefacts, trying to make history come alive for them. I wanted them to hear the echoes of the past. A boy who was no older than seven asked me if the artefacts could talk one day. I told him that they could only whisper to people who wanted to hear them. "Only to those who really wanted to hear."

The shadows moved around a lot, like flames in a strong wind, and a deep, echoing voice filled the room, as if it were coming from the stones themselves. "I remember that day..." "The boy's dreams, so pure and full of hope, kept me alive when everything else faded," the voice said, sounding sad and joyful at the same time. The words hung in the air, and a ghostly figure began to take shape, pulling light from the darkness around it. A figure slowly took shape, showing a small man in a flowing robe that sparkled with a ghostly light, like moonlight caught in a net. Age had etched lines into his face, making it look like a roadmap of many years, but his eyes...his eyes sparkled with a strong life that went against the clear age of his body. "I am the Forgotten Guardian," he said, and each word was like a real thing, dancing in the air with an energy that could almost be felt. "Your sincere call, a beacon of true intent, has brought my spirit back to life."

Ellie felt a wave of feelings come over her, including awe, respect, and a deep sense of duty. As they gathered around the Guardian, she and the others looked at each other, and they all understood without saying a word. "We've come to honour the past, learn from it, and make sure the artefacts are kept safe, not just as relics, but as reminders of the lives and experiences they represent."

The Guardian's voice was calm but firm, and it held the weight of hundreds of years. "Curiosity and respect are the most important things," he said. "But know this: every artefact is more than just a thing. It is a container of stories, held together by the complex threads of time and space, each one whispering a secret to those who are willing to listen. He stopped and looked over them, judging how determined they were. "I will help you understand these themes and lead you through the maze of the past, but be careful: figuring out their truths is full of problems. Some memories are sharp and dangerous, and some stories are best left alone. "Be careful, because the past has a way of reaching out and grabbing those who dig too deep."

The room pulsed with a hidden energy, and the line between then and now was almost gone. There were a lot of echoes in the room, and each one was like a voice from the past, telling stories of victories and losses, love and loss, and empires that rose and fell. They often mixed up ideas with real life, which changed how people felt and made a dizzying array of choices. The echoes showed the adventurers how they were connected to the past in ways they couldn't yet understand. They hinted at destinies linked to people who had died long ago and events that had been forgotten. The spirits of the artefacts, which were shimmering and see-through, moved in and out of view like ghostly dancers. A Roman gladius shone for a moment, and its ghostly owner roared in a long-lost arena. A fragile porcelain doll showed up and sang lullabies from a nursery long ago. Each ghost gave hints about their stories, bits of their past lives that made you are keen to know more, but never the whole truth. There were whispers of battles, secrets shared in crowded markets, and the heavy weight of a crown. All these things hit the senses in a chaotic symphony of the past.

"Listen carefully," the Guardian said, his voice full of ancient wisdom. His eyes, which looked like pools of starlight, looked over the adventurers to see if they were ready. "You have to find the truth among all the lies." The past is a maze of lies, where shadows move and memories change. You can only understand the road ahead if you can tell the difference between fact and fiction.

"Truth threads?" Ellie said it again, her brow furrowed in thought. She was about to be overwhelmed by the volume of historical data. The weight of time pressed down on her shoulders.

"Yes," Azrael said, his voice a calm counterpoint to the whispers. "As historians, you must be able to tell the difference. It is your goal. Knowledge is more than dates and names; it's the stories that linger and echo through time. It's not just the dates and names carved in stone; it's also the stories that stay with us. It's the people, their reasons, and the results.

"To understand history, you have to listen to the whispers, untangle the threads, and weave them into a story that makes sense." He gestured around the room. "And be careful: some threads will give you unimaginable power, while others will lead you to total destruction."

The Guardian pointed to a large tapestry on the wall of the room with a flourish. It was a beautiful piece, made with gold threads and bright colours, showing the capital of an ancient civilisation at its height. Buildings with tall architecture reached for the sky, and their balconies and windows were full of people. These weren't just numbers; they were real, full of life. Merchants sold their goods in busy markets, kids played in sunny squares, and scholars argued about strange ideas under the shade of old trees. The air, even in the still threads, seemed to be full of energy and innovative ideas. "Tell me what you see," he said in a low, rumbling voice that echoed through the room. It was clear that he was challenging them.

Ellie stepped forward, her heart racing with a mix of fear and excitement. The Guardian's stare felt very heavy. She looked closely at the tapestry and let its details wash over her. "It's a city that is doing well in both culture and business. The buildings, the fabrics, and the way the people walk all show how rich the area is. But there's also a lot of stress there. Dark lines run through the happiness, almost invisible at first, like shadows in the corners of the squares. They are a warning of what is to come: a fight for power. "Greed or ambition may have planted the seeds of discord, which could tear their society apart."

"Yes," the Guardian said softly, nodding. His eyes, which looked like pools of ancient wisdom, seemed to see right through the tapestry. There is a warning in the tapestry, woven into its very fabric. It says that even the strongest civilisations are weak. When things get out of hand and family ties and respect break down, artefacts can lose their connection to the people who love them. They become just things, with no real purpose, open to abuse, and destined to be forgotten."

Oliver spoke up carefully, his forehead creased with worry. He knew what it meant. These artefacts, which are immensely powerful and important to history, would be in danger of being lost to time and possibly misused if they lost their connection to the present. "So how do we make sure these artefacts stay connected to us, our values, and our understanding, and don't fade away into obscurity, becoming just relics of a time long gone?" How do we keep them from falling into the wrong hands?"

"By learning their hard-earned history and witnessing their journeys, stories last through the generations," the Guardian's disembodied voice echoed through the giant hall. The otherworldly being, made of swirling light and memories that had been forgotten, went on to quote the old texts: "Share them boldly." Every item you keep tells a story that is waiting to be told again.

Ellie felt a sense of urgency. The air in the museum, which had been still and calm, now crackled with a faint energy. The air itself seemed to change, becoming thicker and more oppressive. In the corner of her eye, she saw shadowy figures that were difficult to see and made her uneasy. They grew more restless and clearer with each passing moment. Her heart raced in her chest. "What happens next, Guardian?" she asked in a voice so low it was almost a whisper. Her words were full of worry, like a poisonous vine.

"The night brings danger because it calls on the shadows that are still in the museum's walls, the ghosts of lost moments." The Keeper, a being of pure darkness, tests your resolve," he said. His glowing face flickered for a moment, showing a hint of what might have been worry. "But your unity, your strong faith in the power of these stories, and your pure intention will protect you. Hold on to the light they stand for.

In the middle of the room, where the weight of history felt almost real, a ghostly echo that was layered and distorted mixed with the Guardian's voice, making a chilling sound. It spoke with the weight of centuries; a statement made from the very fabric of time. "Remember", it whispered, the sound brushing against Ellie's mind like a freezing wind. "Only those who love the light and know the lasting power of truth and memory can drive away the shadows."

As Azrael finished his story, a heavy, oppressive weight fell on them, as if the weight of ages had settled on their shoulders. It was a real force, dark and hidden, putting their bond and their shared determination to the test. This presence seemed to look for weaknesses and threaten to pull apart the threads that held them together. "Hold on tight!" Azrael yelled, his voice cutting through the eerie quiet. He stood strong and firm against the darkness that was closing in on him.

Ellie instinctively grabbed Oliver's arm, holding it tightly and reassuringly. The rest of the group did the same thing, forming a protective circle without thinking about it. They found comfort and strength in that circle, drawing strength from being together. They looked for something stable amid the chaos, and their shared goal served as an anchor. Their shared determination began to lift their spirits, pushing back against the heavy weight of the unknown.

"Together!" Ellie cried, and even though she was scared, her voice was clear and steady. "We will remember and treasure. To the tales " Her words were a call to arms, a declaration of defiance against the darkness that was closing in, and proof of the strength of shared history and legacy.

The suffocating darkness around them started to fade away in a flash, and the heavy pressure lifted like a heavy shroud. The blurry shapes on the edges became solid, turning into ghostly figures that looked like guardians from the past. Their shapes glowed with ancient power. In the middle of these ghostly figures stood one, giving off a quiet sense of power. The Guardian smiled, a sign of approval in the darkening light, and acknowledged and confirmed their united stand.

"See how my ties to this world are fading," he said, his voice a deep whisper that seemed to shake the air itself. His robes moved like living shadows, twisting and turning as if they were made of the very fabric of twilight. "You have called my spirit by honouring the past and the stories that connect people." "Now, keep your stories safe and let them guide you through the dark times that are still to come."

Azrael, Ellie, Oliver, and their friends lit the way to the future, and their combined efforts pushed back the darkness that was closing in. They knew that the bonds they made in the Chamber of Echoes would last longer than just a memory. These shared experiences, full of ancient power and sacrifice, would tie them together forever, not just in the artefacts they now protected but also in their very souls.

As the ancient Guardian's glowing form flickered and began to fade into the air, a final, breathtaking vision appeared in the ethereal light. It was a landscape that had come back to life, full of colour and full of possibilities. A new view of hope and promise lay before them. The emptiness that had plagued their world seemed to fade away, leaving behind the promise of new life and growth.

"Hold on to the stories," the Guardian's voice echoed, a whisper carried on the very air. "The shadows will stay away, and together you will make new legends." The Guardian's essence twinkled like starlight scattering across the void with those last, powerful words. Its light faded until it was gone, leaving behind a breath of fresh energy that was invigorating and pure. The heavy burden of old duty was lifted, and a new sense of purpose and energy took its place.

Azrael turned around, and his face lit up with a warm smile that included Ellie, Oliver, and all their friends. His eyes, which still had the Guardian's light in them, showed that he had been through a lot and learnt a lot. He said, "We have a lot to do," and his voice sounded surer than ever. "The balance has changed, and the scales have tipped.

But our unity and the strength we have found in each other will echo through time, shaping the future just as the past has shaped us.

The group left the Chamber of Echoes with renewed determination, strengthened by their shared memories and the weight of what they had just learnt. Their steps were lighter, and they felt wonderful. They were bound together by a shared destiny to protect the fragile balance between light and shadow, past and future. Their hearts were woven ever tighter by the complex fabric of history. They had to carry not only the weight of their responsibilities but also the exciting possibility of making a better tomorrow, a tomorrow that would be lit up by the stories they would tell and the legends they would become. The road ahead would be long and challenging, but they were sure that they would win together.

Ellie felt a heavy weight settle on her as she stepped back into the museum's maze, the quiet whispers and echoing footsteps fading behind her. There was a lot of history in the air, and the building was full of the triumphs and tragedies of generations. She looked at her friend, and they both understood what the other was thinking. She reached out to touch an old stone wall and whispered to herself, almost with reverence, "Together, we will carry the stories of the past forever." The words were a promise to honour the lives lived and the lessons learnt, making sure that the echoes of history would continue to be heard in the present and shape the future they were now stepping into.

A GLIMPSE OF HOPE

In the museum's dimly lit halls, the staccato rhythm of hasty footfalls echoed, breaking the silence. The weighty silence that clung to the old stones made every step seem like a scream in an echo chamber. As the wind rustled through the room, Ellie could make out what sounded like the low murmurs of long-lost souls, sighs so otherworldly that they seemed to be coming from the walls themselves. As Ellie 's heart pounded frantically against her ribs, she used a moist palm to brush aside a stray lock of hair stuck to her forehead. Lady Arabella's glistening statue stood tall in the alcove, and she couldn't help but cast a sidelong glance in her direction.

The heavenly king or queen shimmered from head to toe in the stone sculpture that seemed to soak up and softly release the dim light. Lady Arabella's expression, frozen in stone, was just as reflective as before; her features were calm and unruffled, as if she were still deep in thought, unconcerned by the mayhem engulfing them. In the dim light, the statue's weathered features gave her an almost living appearance.

Asking, "Do you think they will find us in time?" Ellie's voice trembled nervously across the shadows, barely breaking the silence. An icy chill ran down her spine as she felt the terror rise to her core. She felt it deep within her that time was of the essence. Unseen powers were squeezing them, choking the air, and she could feel it. A constant reminder of the gravity of the situation was the sense of urgency that was plaguing her.

Lady Arabella's voice sounded like a low, resonant hum that seemed to tremble through the air, elevating her presence even though she was lifeless. "Fear not, dear Ellie," she replied. In her stone-blue eyes, there was a spark of insight, or maybe it was just the reflection of light on the smooth stone. She said, "Hope is often concealed within the folds of despair. Remember, sometimes light flourishes most brightly when shadows loom the heaviest." Her words were comforting, but they also felt like a riddle, a cryptic promise that offered a fragile lifeline in the overwhelming darkness. Ellie questioned whether it was sufficient. As far as she could tell, the shadows were getting longer.

In the resonant halls, Ellie flashed a timid smile towards the statue of Athena, its marble features behaving as a silent confidante. As a brief escape from the mayhem happening all around them, she took solace in its quiet wisdom. However, the solace was transient, like a ghostly embrace. They had seen the terrifying ascent of the shadows only moments before, black vines eating away at the priceless artefacts that lay in their path as they snaked across the golden ceilings. Under the weight of Valen, The Timekeeper, whose imposing authority and power seemed to threaten to shatter reality itself, the fabric of time itself buckled. Prior to the dawn bleeding into a world consumed by Valen's temporal tyranny, it was critical to restore balance, so they needed to gather their shattered resolve and piece together the fragments of their courage.

A towering display of ancient weaponry caused Azrael the Lion, whose golden fur shimmered with an almost otherworldly light, to pace nervously, a beacon in the encroaching darkness. "We need to be moving fast! Every second adds to Valen's control," he emphasised, his normally mischievous amber eyes now flashing a desperate sparkle. He searched the museum's winding halls, a labyrinth of history brought to life, for any trace of Finn, the active fox whose wisdom might save them. "Finn has information, gleaned from the whispers of the past, that may lead us to a way forward."

Once only a carefully carved wooden sculpture, Finn was now brought to life by powers they could not fathom, and he owned an endearingly naughty disposition. He dashed through an adjacent hall, his russet tail standing out against the subdued background. His eyes gleamed with a contagious enthusiasm, and a mischievous grin that verged on ecstasy shone through the darkness. "Look over here! Chop! Pay close attention, you won't want to miss this!" His voice had a playful rhythm that resounded throughout the halls, serving as both a summons and a challenge, and he left behind a wake of energetic, almost carefree, people.

Driven by a blend of optimism and urgency, the group swiftly pursued him, navigating complex displays of history along the way. Artworks from the Renaissance throbbed with an unnerving energy, while sarcophagi from Egypt whispered secrets and Roman emperors stood guard. The museum's grandeur, which was often both beautiful and reassuring, now seemed surreal, like a dreamscape warped by the creeping night. In an endless waltz, the shadows danced, their steps both playful and sinister. A chill ran through Ellie's veins, an unfamiliar feeling—a tingling awareness that reverberated in her very being—that she couldn't quite shake. There was a profound sense of urgency, as if they were on the brink of salvation or oblivion, the weight of fate hanging in the balance, and it wasn't just fear or simple anticipation; it was the Empyrean feeling of grasping at a fleeting destiny. They carried what felt like the entire universe—if not the entire universe itself—upon their shoulders.

As I approached the intersection, I could see Dr. Mariana Bell standing there, her worried expression amplified by the long shadows cast by the light. As if she were battling an especially defiant equation, her brow was furrowed in concentration. She spoke up about the ancient tapestry looming on the wall, saying, "I believe there is more than meets the eye here," her voice slightly echoing in the vast room. Some unseen energy seemed to be causing the air around it to quiver. "This artwork tells of a time of reckoning; a pivotal moment in the museum's history, shrouded in secrecy. It could be a key to our escape, a breadcrumb trail left by those who came before."

At her side, the formerly unflappable guard Oliver studied the tapestry in detail; he had become much more sensitive to the subtle magical currents that flowed through the museum. His scepticism had been eroded by the events of the past few days, and he now seemed eager to understand the impossible. He made the bold statement, "It looks like a map," as he pointed to the intricate pattern of interwoven symbols and landscapes within the tapestry. Running a calloused hand over the worn fabric, he spoke with an increasing sense of urgency, asking, "But why would they hide it here, in plain sight, yet so easily overlooked? What does it mean? Where does it lead?"

A serpent named Luci slithered closer, her movements as graceful as a dancer, and interjected, "Ah, but hope often flutters in unexpected places, doesn't it, darling?" Her bronze scales shimmered with an almost otherworldly light. "This tapestry is truly extraordinary, my dears. It holds the threads of fate, intricately interwoven with the history of this museum. Consider it a living record, a testament to the power that resides within these walls." She played with her tongue, tasting the stagnant air, as if trying to unearth hidden meanings from the dust motes that twirled in the gloomy illumination.

The tale unfurled like a tapestry within a tapestry as Luci painstakingly traced the twisting path of the narrative and untangled the complex details of the fabric. On the woven surface, pictures of heroes from the past appeared, their expressions reflecting their unwavering resolve. Moments of joy, celebration, and even solitude passed by as great conflicts fought for artefacts of tremendous personal importance flashed by. However, in the middle of everything, a black hole appeared, a missing piece of the puzzle, a missing piece of history. It foreshadowed the impending difficulty they would face, a dark cloud that might destabilise not just the museum's priceless artefacts but also the very fabric of time itself, causing the past, present, and future to become a jumbled mess. As a silent vow to heal the wound before it engulfed all they treasured, the burden of their mission descended upon them.

Perched on an elaborate pedestal of weathered stone was Huckleberry, a being with obsidian feathers and piercing amber eyes. There was an unseen, low-volume energy emanating from the pedestal. A sound imbued with an ancient power resounded through the vast chamber as he cared. According to him, "The shadows are more than a mere illusion." His voice, which had a gravelly rasp that had been around for ages, sounded warning and urgent. "They are remnants of forgotten secrets, echoes of realities fractured and lost, waiting for those who dare to confront them. To enter the darkness is to risk being consumed but also to gain knowledge beyond mortal comprehension."

Amidst the tangible fear emanating from the shadows that clung to the chamber walls, Ellie—a young woman with fiery red hair styled in a practical braid—stepped forward, her gaze staying fixed. A complex blend of eagerness and fear swelled within her as she expected. "What if the answer lies in the light?" she countered, her voice clear and strong. "If we can find out what's hidden in the pattern of the tapestry – if we can read the symbols that the darkness is making harder and harder to see – maybe we can break free from its grip." She pointed to a huge, complex tapestry that covered an entire wall, its vivid colours fading away as the shadows grew darker and darker.

"That's it!" Professor Finch interjected, his usually stooped posture straightening with newfound energy. A spark of enthusiasm, almost manic in its intensity, ignited in his eyes and momentarily eclipsed the weariness etched onto his face. He adjusted his spectacles, perched precariously on his nose. "The artefacts! The Amulet of Aethelred, the Scroll of Seraphina, the Chalice of Corvus – they all connect, each a piece of the puzzle! And with enough knowledge, with the combined power of these relics, we may weave our way back to the moment the shadows took form! To the genesis of this creeping blight!" He paced with enthusiasm, his tweed jacket waving behind him.

With purpose rekindled, Finn, a nimble and quick-witted rogue with a mischievous glint in his eyes, scampered between them, his energy infectious, a stark contrast to the oppressive atmosphere. "Then let's get weaving! No time to waste!" He clapped his hands together, a wide grin spreading across his face. With a small, intricately carved lockpick in his hand, its silver surface shimmering in the dim light, he readied himself to unveil the mysteries that lay ahead. "I have a few tricks up my sleeve, a knack for uncovering hidden truths. We'll force the secrets out of this ancient fabric, even if it takes all night! Get ready, darkness, because we're about to shine a light on your dirty little secrets!" The air thrummed with a renewed sense of hope, a fragile flame flickering against the encroaching darkness.

As the group set to work, combining Ellie's sharp historical memory with Finn's intuitive understanding of arcane symbols and Marcus's meticulous engineering skills, the museum thrummed with a renewed energy. The weighty silence that had clung to the place like a shroud was replaced by the low hum of focused concentration. The air shimmered, almost visibly responding to their efforts, crackling with a potential that had long lain dormant. With each new revelation, each decoded clue, the shadows seemed to retreat, inching away like the tide withdrawing from the shore, leaving behind the bare and gleaming sand of truth. Ellie marvelled at how their collective hopes intertwined, an invisible thread binding them together, strengthening with every shared insight. They pooled their knowledge, a confluence of ability designed to outsmart the challenges ahead, each member contributing a vital piece of the puzzle.

Hours slipped by unnoticed, lost in the intricate dance of deduction and discovery, completely absorbed in following the tapestry's complex narrative. They unlocked riddles hidden within its weavings, deciphering cryptic symbols and untangling historical inaccuracies planted deliberately as misdirection. Ellie found herself recalling obscure passages from long-forgotten textbooks, history she had diligently studied but believed relegated to the dusty corners of her mind. Now, that knowledge, woven into her very being, felt like a symbol of optimism, illuminating the path forward and guiding their investigation. The tapestry, once a silent observer, now seemed to actively take part, its threads subtly shifting and shimmering as they neared a breakthrough.

Suddenly, a gentle breeze swept through the hall, almost as if the museum itself were exhaling, rustling the edges of the tapestry and stirring the dust motes dancing in the shafts of moonlight. The shadows flickered and danced along the walls, no longer passive observers, but actively weaving form and substance as they seemed to echo the restless energy of the museum, testing its boundaries, probing for weaknesses. The temperature dropped perceptibly, a tangible sign of the encroaching darkness. "Away, shadows!" Finn exclaimed gleefully, his eyes sparkling with a defiant light. He held aloft a small, intricately carved wooden box, glowing with a faint inner luminescence. "Try to weave your darkness around this!"

"It's a moment of clarity," Azrael proclaimed, his voice strong and resonant, cutting through the oppressive atmosphere like a beacon. "Hope will always triumph where courage leads the way." His words, firm and unwavering, were a challenge thrown down at the foot of the encroaching darkness.

But the shadows, sensing their burgeoning strength slipping, coiled tighter, like constricting serpents determined to crush their prey. A lingering presence, malevolent and heavy, twisted among them, a palpable force challenging their resolve, whispering doubts and fears into their minds. It was a silent battle, fought not with steel, but with will. Yet, as if in direct response to their united front, their defiance against the encroaching gloom, the ancient tapestry in the centre of the chamber glowed warmly. Its golden threads, dormant for centuries, now sparked with life, illuminating the room with a soft, ethereal light, pushing back the oppressive shadows.

Ellie gasped, her heart hammering a frantic rhythm against her ribs. She had almost given up hope, almost succumbed to the despair that threatened to consume them all. But now, she glimpsed a flicker of possibility, a fragile ember refusing to be extinguished. "Look!" she cried, pointing a trembling finger. "The tapestry... it's opening!"

As the fabric shimmered and undulated, as if alive, an ethereal portal began to materialise within its woven surface. The edges of the opening were not clean-cut but rather woven with intricate depictions of time itself— swirling images of the past, the present, and the unwritten future colliding in a radiant blur of light and possibility. Hope, a fierce and burning thing, surged fiercely within Ellie as she stepped closer, emboldened by the sight. The portal hummed with power, beckoning them forward.

"Are we ready?" She glanced around at her companions; their faces etched with a mixture of apprehension and unwavering determination. The enormity of their task, the sheer weight of the responsibility they carried, weighed upon her like a physical burden. The fate of everything hung in the balance, resting on their shoulders. Yet, despite the fear, she felt a rising tide of determination swell within her, pushing back the doubt. This was her moment, their moment, to grasp what fate had in store, to step into the unknown and fight for a future worth living. It was a terrifying prospect, but a necessary one. The time for hesitation was over.

"Ready or not, let us take this leap together!" Finn chimed, grinning wide as he bounded forward, his youthful enthusiasm a beacon in the face of the unknown. He embodied the spirit of adventure they all bore in their hearts, the yearning for discovery, a tangible force that tied them together.

With a shared glance amongst the group – Ellie, Marcus, and Zara – they took a collective breath, drawing strength from the bonds that had formed through trials and triumphs. Each member held a unique strength, forged in the fires of their shared challenges. Ellie was the strategist, Marcus was the pragmatic, Zara was the heartfelt, and Finn was the unwavering optimist.

In that moment, the timeless echo of their newly forged friendship reverberated through the enchanted halls of the museum, melding into the fabric of their shared experience. They understood, at their core, that hope was not a solitary flicker; it was the unity between them, the interwoven tapestry of their individual skills and experiences, that would guide their way forward against the dark tides threatening to engulf them.

As they stepped into the opening, a portal shimmering with ethereal light, Ellie felt the warmth of hope envelop her, its tendrils intertwining with anticipation. Ellie felt a mixture of nervousness and excitement in her stomach. Now, unseen paths lay unfurling before them, beckoning them to step deeper into the uncharted realm of their destiny, a destiny intertwined with the secrets held within the museum.

"Together then, adventurers!" she declared, voice resounding with the promise of new beginnings, a newfound confidence bolstering her words. She met the gazes of her companions, seeing mirrored in their eyes the same blend of trepidation and excitement.

With hope lighting their way, casting dancing shadows that seemed to encourage them onward, they plunged into the radiant tapestry, leaving the shadows behind. They were ready to rewrite history, to uncover the mysteries that lay dormant within the enchanted museum, and to embrace the thrilling unknown that awaited them in its depths. Their journey had only just begun.

THE FINAL COUNTDOWN

While the ornate clock in the grand hall of the Enchanted Museum ticked with agonising slowness towards midnight, the air was thick with anticipation, heavy and still like a breath that had been held. Each chime reverberated throughout the vast area, serving as a jarring reminder of the rapidly diminishing amount of time. The earlier few hours had felt like a wild and disorienting ride through history, a whirlwind of long-lost empires and forgotten legends that had been brought back to life. Despite this, Ellie felt a potent mixture of excitement and trepidation course through her veins as she stood in front of a massive door that was etched with ancient runes that appeared to writhe in the flickering torchlight. It was a chilling cocktail of hope and fear. This warning had been given to them in cryptic whispers by Valen, the Timekeeper, whose voice reverberated throughout the very fabric of the museum. The very essence of their power was hanging precariously in the balance as they had only a few moments left to solve the final, intricate mystery that bound the enchanted artefacts to the realm of the mortals.

The regal and imposing Azrael the Lion paced beside her, his muscular form rippling beneath his golden fur. He was a lion. Between Ellie and the intimidating portal, his golden eyes, which were blazing with an inner fire of determination, flickered back and forth repeatedly. A low, resonant growl could be heard coming from his mouth as he rumbled, "Time waits for no one, Ellie." This door is the key to everything that we have experienced tonight, including the laughter, the terror, and the undeniable wonder that we have experienced. Further on lies the answer: how the connection can be severed. We must act, and we must take it quickly, before the first strike of midnight decides our entire future.

A nervous tremor could be heard in her voice as she responded, "Right," but it was barely heard. Her thoughts were racing as she desperately tried to make sense of the events that had happened throughout the night. They had been confronted with riddles that defied logic and forced them to question the very nature of reality. These puzzles had been crafted by time itself. They had seen the living history that adorned the halls of the museum, marvelling at ghosts and echoes of the past within the museum's walls. This, however, was not the case. At this point, the culmination, the final test, had arrived. It was now time to solve the final puzzle, and the solution was as elusive as smoke. They were being propelled forward with the weight of impending doom, and each tick of the clock was like a drumbeat, a relentless percussion section that heralded the urgency of their quest.

Beside them, Professor Finch adjusted his spectacles with a gesture that was both familiar and nervous, his face illuminated by the ethereal glow from the runes. Professor Finch, whose face was illuminated by the ethereal glow emanating from the runes, adjusted his spectacles with a gesture that was both familiar and nervous. He looked at the intricate carvings on the door with a thoughtful expression on his face, his brow furrowed in concentration. "The four elements are represented by these symbols," he murmured, his voice barely heard above the rhythmic ticking. "They are earth, air, fire, and water." Individually, each of the artefacts that we met embodies one of these elemental forces in its own distinct way. It is impossible to deny the obvious connection that the Sceptre of the Earth King has with the land. The Whispering Wind Chimes are a physical representation of the air that we breathe. Reborn from fire, the Phoenix Amulet is a symbol of the unending flame that never goes out. The Tears of Poseidon, a vessel possessing the unbridled power of the sea, is also present. It is necessary for us to make use of their abilities and combine their energies to open this doorway. However, the question stands: "How?"

When Ellie turned to face her companions, the flickering light from the torch was dancing in her eyes as she became more determined. Let's discuss what we've discovered so far. We are nearing the heart of this mystery, and we must combine everything. it is imperative that we combine everything. Luci, your stories have become entangled with our journey, directing us through challenges that appeared to be insurmountable before we met them. Your ability in these long-forgotten lands has proven to be extremely valuable. A grateful smile appeared on her lips as she paused for a moment.

Luci, the bronze serpent, unfurled gracefully from its coiled position, its scales glittering in the gentle, ambient light that pulsed from the cavern walls. Luci was a serpent. "The artefacts not only spoke truths about the past, but they also spoke truths about their very natures. Every one of them has a piece of the elements, and they are all waiting for the right catalyst to reveal their secrets. These are not merely artefacts; rather, they are living echoes of a time when magic was unrestricted, and the elements were in perfect harmony with one another. It is not enough to simply understand what they are; we must also understand what they are to realise their full potential.

Despite the seriousness of their predicament, Finn, who was known for his playful nature, scurried forward, his bright eyes shining with excitement and a hint of nervousness. The question is, "What if we each channel our strengths? We have all been working together to find a solution to this problem, but we should focus on everyone's contributions. It's possible that we should be concentrating on the contributions of everyone. You have a sharp mind, Ellie, and it is perfectly suited to the task of deciphering the complicated texts and symbols. There is a wealth of academic knowledge that Professor Finch has, including lore that has been forgotten but could be the key. In addition, Azrael, your bravery and strength could break down barriers, both literally and figuratively. In addition, we must have faith in the profundity of Lady Arabella and Huckleberry's puzzles, even though they appear to be cryptic and perplexing now. They have not yet led us in the wrong direction, have they, so far? It was a silent question that hung in the air, a plea for unity and renewed determination, and he displayed his tail in a wagging motion.

Oliver did not waver in his resolve. A newly discovered determination had blossomed within him, even though he had initially been reluctant to take part in the adventure. At first, he had a sense of dislocation because he was surrounded by people who appeared to possess innate knowledge and skills that he did not have. However, as the gravity of their mission became clearer to him, he experienced a sense of empowerment brought on by a responsibility that was both straightforward and essential. "I may not possess ancient wisdom, nor the scholarly prowess of Ellie, but I can hold the lantern," he declared, his voice ringing with an unexpected conviction. "I can hold the lantern." There is a tangible thing known as the light, which is a symbol of hope and clarity. It will shed light on the path that leads into the unknown, allowing us to see through the shadows that threaten to consume us.

The statue of Lady Arabella shone brightly in the moonlight that was streaming through the arched windows of the museum as the group paused for a moment to contemplate, to muster up their bravery, and to come together in understanding their mission. It appears the statue had been endowed with a life of its own, with its cool gaze watching and waiting for something to happen. A voice reverberated throughout the museum, "Every legend contains a lesson, a kernel of truth hidden within layers of myth and allegory," and it seemed as though the stones themselves were amplifying the statement. "The door will only unveil its treasures, reveal its secrets, to those brave enough to face their fears, to confront the darkness within themselves and around them."

Ellie nodded, taking in the words that Lady Arabella had spoken and concentrating her thoughts. Her worries were momentarily pushed aside by a surge of intellectual fervour which she was experiencing. "We need a plan," she said, her voice becoming more forceful as she spoke. Rushing in without any preparation will only result in disaster. Let's each give a voice to the essence of our artefact, its fundamental meaning, and try to understand how it is connected to this challenge. Together, as a unified force, let us confront the door by weaving together our individual strengths, combining our distinct points of view, and confronting it together.

Between them, a silent agreement was formed, which was a recognition of the fact that they were destined to be together. They took their positions in front of the enormous door, which was covered in intricate carvings that moved and writhed in response to the flickering lamplight. Ellie took the first step forward, grasping the ancient tablet tightly to her chest. Her voice was slightly trembling, but it was filled with an unmistakable determination; she was determined. "I call forth the knowledge of the past, the accumulated wisdom of generations, the secrets etched into languages that have been forgotten. I invoke the spirit that lives within this tablet! Uncover the mystery that lies hidden within these stones! Could you please guide us on how to proceed with this? proceed with this!"

In the same manner, Professor Finch, who was known for his meticulousness as a scholar, followed suit, his voice resonating with years of dusty books and sun-fried excavations. The palms of his hands were facing the ancient stone, and he raised them to channel the very essence of the terrain. By utilising the mysteries of archaeology, I can call upon the knowledge of the earth! Please allow the stones to remember and allow the past to direct us! The words he spoke lingered in the air, laden with the weight of civilisations that had been forgotten.

Azrael, who was standing tall and unyielding, committed his ferocious spirit to the achievement of the task. The inferno that he vowed to protect was reflected in his gaze to the extent that it burnt with an inner fire. Imitating the sound of a blacksmith's hammer, he pounded his fist against his chest, and the sound reverberated throughout the room. "I am the embodiment of bravery, and I guard the realm of fire! The flames should purify and protect, and the spirit should be allowed to burn brightly! It appears his presence was emitting heat, acting as a barrier against the unknown.

A silver thread was woven through the tapestry of their incantation, and the ethereal notes of Luci's voice intertwined with the other notes throughout the incantation. Her eyes, which were filled with ancient knowledge, shone with an almost supernatural comprehension of the difficulties that have occurred throughout history. It appears she was calling forth the spirits of long-forgotten winds as she raised her hands and traced patterns in the air with her fingers. It is from the currents of history that I call forth the winds of change! Allow the hushed voices to direct us and allow the future to take shape! The sound of her voice was a pledge; it was a sigh of optimism that was carried on the wings of time.

While he was holding the lantern high, Oliver exuded a sense of warmth and unyielding determination. Their faces were illuminated with an ethereal glow as the light cast shadows that danced around them. A guiding light of truth in the face of the growing darkness, he kept steadfast. "The depths of the waters are illuminated by the light of truth that streams from within me! Bring about the triumph of clarity, and let the depths reveal their secrets! His words were a promise to guide them through the murky depths of the unknown, and so, they were a lifeline for them.

As their voices blended, a potent spectre of energy encircled the door, a shimmering cocoon that was woven from the three of them working together to carry out something. Before this, the inscriptions were lifeless and dull, but now they were blazing with brilliant light. An entrancing rhythm was created by the intricate runes, which began to glow and pulse in time with their combined heartbeats.

This rhythm seemed to vibrate through the stone itself, creating a mesmerising effect. There was a palpable tension that was thick and heavy, and the seconds passed by like the last breaths of a life that had been lived, with each tick being a monumental weight that was placed upon their shoulders.

When the doorway, which had been silent for centuries, finally began to creak open with a groan that reverberated throughout the room, this was the moment that marked the turning point, the decisive moment. "It was a prelude to the unknown, and the sound was both ominous and liberating at the same time. The familiar chamber was transformed into a distorted landscape as tendrils of light, which resembled grasping fingers, streamed from the threshold. These tendrils cast elongated shadows on the polished marble floor. A wave of elation and profound relief washed over the adventurers, and it was a wave that drove away the fear and uncertainty that had been plaguing them. In front of them, a whirling universe of colours and light greeted them as they entered the unknown. It was a breathtaking panorama of possibilities and dangers, inviting them to cross the threshold and accept their fate. The journey had already started in earnest.

In the same manner as the other individuals, Professor Finch took a confident step forward. By utilising the mysteries of archaeology, I can call upon the knowledge of the earth! The sound of his voice resounded with a profound reverence, as if he were calling upon ancient forces that were concealed beneath the stone and soil. It appears the ground beneath their feet was responding to his invocation by emitting a delicate hum.

Azrael, who was standing tall and proud, channelled his fierce spirit with unyielding determination. In a declaration that was as bright as embers, he declared, "I am the embodiment of courage, and I protect the realm of fire!" A sliver of warmth emanated from him, as if the flames themselves acknowledged his commitment and bestowed upon him their power.

The next thing that happened was that the melodic notes of Luci's voice blended in perfectly with the others. Her voice was eerie and determined as she sang, "From the currents of history, I summon the winds of change!" Her tone was both haunting and determined. The atmosphere around them started to change in a subtle way, carrying with it the fresh and invigorating aroma of a breeze that was rising.

Oliver raised his lantern to his highest point, and the golden light that emanated from it cast a reassuring glow upon the old door. While exuding an air of tranquillity and reassurance, he made the following proclamation: "With the light of truth, I illuminate the depths of the waters!" The room was filled with a sense of clarity and hope as the gentle shimmer of reflected light danced across the surface of the water that was nearby.

While their voices blended in a harmonious resolve, an ethereal spectre of energy began to swirl around the enormous door, enveloping it in a radiant glow. The intricate inscriptions that had been carved into the stone suddenly came to life. The runes began to light up in vivid colours that pulsed rhythmically, and they were in perfect sync with the steady beating of their hearts. Every second seemed to stretch out in a taut manner, resonating loudly like the last, fragile breaths of a story that was waiting to be told. The atmosphere became thicker with anticipation.

Then, at the crucial juncture, the ancient doorway slowly opened with a creaking sound, much like it had awoken from a slumber that had lasted for centuries. From the threshold that had just been uncovered, brilliant tendrils of luminescent light streamed forth, casting long shadows that danced across the polished marble floor. A profound sense of elation and relief swept over the adventurers as they beheld the whirling cosmos that lay beyond; it was a magnificent vortex of stars and swirling galaxies that invited them to venture forth into the vast unknown.

The air was thick with anticipation, heavy and still like a breath that had been held, and it was happening while the ornate clock in the grand hall of the Enchanted Museum was ticking with agonising slowness towards midnight. Each chime reverberated throughout the vast area, serving as a jarring reminder of the rapidly diminishing amount of time that was passing. A whirlwind of long-lost empires and forgotten legends that had been brought back to life had been brought to life over the course of the earlier few hours, which had felt like a wild and disorienting ride through history. As she stood in front of a massive door that was etched with ancient runes that appeared to writhe in the flickering torchlight, Ellie felt a potent mixture of excitement and trepidation course through her veins. Despite this, she felt a mixture of both excitement and trepidation all at the same time. It was a chilling mixture of fear and hope all rolled into one. This cautionary message had been conveyed to them in a cryptic whisper by Valen, the Timekeeper, whose voice reverberated throughout the very fabric of the museum. They had only a few moments left to solve the final, intricate mystery that bound the enchanted artefacts to the realm of the mortals, and the very essence of their power was hanging precariously in the balance as they tried to solve it.

The regal and imposing Azrael the Lion went ahead to pace alongside her, his muscular body rippling beneath the golden fur that covered his body. What a lion he was! In the space that separated Ellie and the menacing portal, his golden eyes, which were blazing with an inner fire of determination, flickered back and forth repeatedly. A low, resonant growl could be heard coming from his mouth as he rumbled, "Time waits for no one, Ellie." This door is the key to everything that we have experienced tonight, including the laughter, the terror, and the undeniable wonder that we have experienced. Onwards lies the solution, how the connection can be severed, which can be found further on. Before the first strike of midnight, we must act, and we must take it quickly. This is because our entire future will be decided by this moment.

As she responded, "Right," her voice was barely heard even though it had a nervous tremor that could be heard in her voice. She was frantically trying to make sense of the events that had taken place throughout the night, and her thoughts were racing as she did so. They had been put in a position where they were forced to question the very nature of reality because they were confronted with riddles that denied logic. Time had been the one to create these puzzles in the first place. They had been able to experience the living history that was displayed throughout the museum's exhibition halls, marvelling at the ghosts and echoes of the past that were contained within the museum's walls. On the other hand, this was not the situation. Having reached this point, the culmination, the last test, had finally arrived. It was now time to solve the final puzzle, and the answer was as elusive as smoke until it was finally solved. The weight of impending doom was propelling them forward, and each tick of the clock was like a drumbeat, a relentless percussion section that heralded the urgency of their quest. They were being propelled forward with the weight of impending doom.

There, Professor Finch, whose face was illuminated by the ethereal glow emanating from the runes, adjusted his spectacles with a gesture that was both familiar and nervous. He was standing next to them. He looked at the intricate carvings on the door with a thoughtful expression on his face, his brow furrowed in concentration the entire time he was looking at them. "The four elements are represented by these symbols," he murmured, his voice barely heard above the rhythmic ticking of the clock. "They are earth, air, fire, and water." Each of the artefacts that we came across embodies one of these elemental forces in its own unique way. "They are earth, air, fire, and water." When it comes to the obvious connection that the Sceptre of the Earth King has with the land, it is impossible to deny the connection. The Whispering Wind Chimes are a tangible representation of the air that we breathe in that they are made of wind. The Phoenix Amulet, which was reborn from fire, is a symbol of the flame that never goes out regardless of the circumstances. Additionally, there is the Tears of Poseidon, which is a vessel that can harness the unrestrained power of the ocean waves. For us to be able to open this doorway, it is necessary for us to make use of their abilities and combine their energies. Nevertheless, the question that stays is, "How?"

The glimmering light from the torch was dancing in Ellie's eyes as she turned to face her companions. She was becoming more determined as she did so. Let's talk about what we've found out on this journey so far. We are getting closer and closer to answering the question at the heart of this mystery, and it is necessary that we combine everything. Luci, your tales have become intertwined with our journey, guiding us successfully through obstacles that, prior to our encounter with them, appeared to be insurmountable. You have proven to be an extremely valuable resource thanks to your ability in these long-forgotten lands. She paused for a moment, and within that moment, a grateful smile appeared on her lips.

Luci, the bronze serpent, unfurled gracefully from its coiled position, its scales glittering in the soft, ambient light that pulsed from the cavern walls. Luci was a serpent made of bronze. Luci himself was a serpent. "The artefacts not only spoke truths about the past, but they also spoke truths about their very natures. Every one of them has a piece of the elements, and they are all waiting for the proper catalyst to reveal their secrets. These are not merely artefacts; rather, they are living echoes of a time when magic was unrestricted, and the elements were in perfect harmony with one another. It is not enough to simply understand what they are; we must also understand what they are to realise their full potential.

Finn, who was known for his playful nature, scurried forward, his bright eyes shining with excitement and a hint of nervousness. The question that is being asked is, "What if we each channel our strengths?" even though their situation was extremely serious. Everyone here has been collaborating with one another to find a solution to this issue; however, it is possible that we ought to be putting more of an emphasis on the contributions made by everyone. You have a sharp mind, Ellie, and it is perfectly suited to the task of deciphering the complicated texts and symbols that have been presented to you right now. For example, Professor Finch is in possession of a vast amount of academic knowledge, which includes lore that has been forgotten but could be the key to solving the mystery. Azrael, your bravery and strength have the potential to break down barriers, both literally and figuratively. This is something that you could do. In addition, we must have faith in the profoundness of the puzzles that Lady Arabella and Huckleberry have created, even though they appear to be cryptic and confusing now. They have not yet taken us in the wrong direction, at least not yet. He made a motion with his tail that resembled a wagging motion, and it was a question that hung in the air, a plea for unity and renewed determination.

Oliver could not be persuaded to change his mind. Although he had initially been reluctant to take part in the adventure, he had recently discovered that he had developed a newly discovered determination within himself. His first reaction was one of dislocation because he was surrounded by people who seemed to have innate knowledge and skills that he did not have. This caused him to feel as though he was not a part of the group. On the other hand, as the significance of their mission became clearer to him, he felt a sense of empowerment that was brought on by a responsibility that was not only straightforward but also essential. "I may not possess ancient wisdom, nor the scholarly prowess of Ellie, but I can hold the lantern," he declared, his voice ringing with an unexpected conviction. "I can hold the lantern." The light is a tangible thing that is a beacon of hope and clarity. "I can hold the lantern." There is a tangible thing known as the light. In doing so, it will shed light on the path that leads into the unknown, thereby enabling us to see through the shadows that threaten to consume us.

The statue of Lady Arabella shone brightly in the moonlight that was streaming through the arched windows of the museum. At the same time, the group paused for a moment to reflect, to muster up their bravery, and to come together in developing an understanding of their mission. The statue seemed to have been endowed with a life of its own, as shown by its cool gaze, which was watching and waiting for something to take place. The words "Every legend contains a lesson, a kernel of truth hidden within layers of myth and allegory" were reverberated throughout the museum, and it appeared as though the stones themselves were contributing to the amplification of the statement. "The door will only unveil its treasures, reveal its secrets, to those brave enough to face their fears, to confront the darkness within themselves and around them."

Ellie gave a slight nod, concentrating her thoughts and taking in the words that Lady Arabella had just spoken during the conversation. She was experiencing a surge of intellectual fervour, which momentarily distracted her from her worries and allowed her to focus on other things. "We need a plan," she said, her voice becoming more forceful as she continued to speak a few words. You are setting yourself up for failure if you rush in without making any preparations. Together, let us each give a voice to the essence of our artefact, its fundamental meaning, and try to understand how it is connected to this challenge. We should confront the door as a unified force by weaving together our individual strengths, combining our different points of view, and confronting it together. Let us do this together.

They came to an understanding that they were destined to be together, and this understanding was expressed in the form of a silent agreement that was formed between them. They positioned themselves in front of the enormous door, which was covered in intricate carvings that moved and writhed in response to the flickering lamplight. They took their positions in front of the door. The first step forward was taken by Ellie, who clasped the ancient tablet tightly to her chest as she moved forward. Even though her voice was slightly shaking, it was filled with an unmistakable determination; she was determined. "I call forth the knowledge of the past, the accumulated wisdom of generations, the secrets etched into languages that have been forgotten. I invoke the spirit that lives within this tablet! Uncover the mystery that lies hidden within these stones! Tell us how to go ahead with this!"

Professor Finch, who was well-known for his meticulousness as a scholar, followed suit in the same manner. His voice resounded with the years of dusty books and sun-fried excavations that he had done. He raised his hands so that the palms of his hands were facing the ancient stone, and he did this to channel the very essence of the landscape. By making use of the mysteries that archaeology has to offer, I can access the knowledge that the earth has! Make it possible for the stones to remember and let the past guide us in the right direction! After he had finished speaking, the words lingered in the air, carrying with them the burden of civilisations that had been forgotten.

His ferocious spirit was dedicated to the accomplishment of the task, and Azrael, who was standing tall and unyielding, committed himself to it. The blaze that he swore to protect was reflected in his gaze to such an extent that it burned with an inner fire for the purpose of protecting it. He pounded his fist against his chest to imitate the sound of a blacksmith's hammer, and the sound reverberated throughout the entire room. "I am the embodiment of bravery, and I guard the realm of fire! The flames should purify and protect, and the spirit should be allowed to burn brightly! It appears his presence was emitting heat, acting as a barrier against the unknown.

A silver thread was woven through the tapestry of their incantation, and the ethereal notes of Luci's voice intertwined with the other notes throughout the incantation. Her eyes, which were filled with ancient knowledge, shone with an almost supernatural comprehension of the difficulties that have occurred throughout history. It appears she was calling forth the spirits of long-forgotten winds as she raised her hands and traced patterns in the air with her fingers. It is from the currents of history that I call forth the winds of change! Allow the hushed voices to direct us and allow the future to take shape! The sound of her voice was a pledge; it was a sigh of optimism that was carried on the wings of time.

While he was holding the lantern high, Oliver exuded a sense of warmth and unyielding determination. Their faces were illuminated with an ethereal glow as the light cast shadows that danced around them. A guiding light of truth in the face of the growing darkness, he kept his steadfastness. "The depths of the waters are illuminated by the light of truth that streams from within me! The triumph of clarity must be brought about, and the depths must be allowed to reveal their secrets! In other words, his words were a promise to lead them through the murky depths of the unknown, and as a result, they were a lifeline for them.

As their voices blended, a powerful spectre of energy encircled the door, a shimmering cocoon that was woven from the three of them working together to carry out something. This was what was happening as their voices blended. The inscriptions had been completely lifeless and uninteresting prior to this, but now they were blazing with brilliant light. The intricate runes began to glow and pulse in time with their combined heartbeats, which results in the creation of a rhythm that is both captivating and captivating. Since this rhythm seemed to vibrate through the stone itself, it produced an effect that was mesmerising. The seconds passed by like the final breaths of a life that had been lived, with each tick being a monumental weight that was placed upon their shoulders. There was a palpable tension that was thick and heavy, and the seconds also passed like the last breaths of a life that had been lived.

When the doorway, which had been silent for centuries, finally began to creak open with a groan that reverberated throughout the room, this was the moment that marked the turning point, the decisive moment." It was a prelude to the unknown, and the sound was both ominous and liberating at the same time. The familiar chamber was transformed into a distorted landscape as tendrils of light, which resembled grasping fingers, streamed from the threshold.

These tendrils cast elongated shadows on the polished marble floor. A wave of elation and profound relief washed over the adventurers, and it was a wave that drove away the fear and uncertainty that had been plaguing them. In front of them, a whirling universe of colours and light greeted them as they entered the unknown. It was breathtaking

In the same manner as the other individuals, Professor Finch took a confident step forward. By utilising the mysteries of archaeology, I can call upon the knowledge of the earth! The sound of his voice resounded with a profound reverence, as if he were calling upon ancient forces that were concealed beneath the stone and soil. It appears the ground beneath their feet was responding to his invocation by emitting a delicate hum.

Azrael, who was standing tall and proud, channelled his fierce spirit with unyielding determination. In a declaration that was as bright as embers, he declared, "I am the embodiment of courage, and I protect the realm of fire! " A sliver of warmth emanated from him, as if the flames themselves acknowledged his commitment and bestowed upon him their power.

The following thing that took place was that the melodic notes of Luci's voice blended in perfectly with the others. Her voice was eerie and determined as she sang, "From the currents of history, I summon the winds of change!" while she was singing. " Her tone was both haunting and determined. The atmosphere around them started to change in a subtle way, carrying with it the fresh and invigorating aroma of a breeze that was rising.

Oliver raised his lantern to his highest point, and the golden light that emanated from it cast a reassuring glow upon the old door. While exuding an air of tranquilly and reassurance, he made the following proclamation: "With the light of truth, I illuminate the depths of the waters! During the time that the gentle shimmer of reflected light danced across the surface of the water that was nearby, the room was filled with a sense of clarity and hope.

While their voices blended in a harmonious resolve, an ethereal spectre of energy began to swirl around the enormous door, enveloping it in a radiant glow. The intricate inscriptions that had been carved into the stone suddenly came to life. The runes began to light up in vivid colours that pulsed rhythmically, and they were in perfect sync with the steady beating of their hearts. Every second seemed to stretch out in a taut manner, resonating loudly like the last, fragile breaths of a story that was waiting to be told. The atmosphere became thicker with anticipation.

Then, at the crucial juncture, the ancient doorway slowly opened with a creaking sound, much like it had awoken from a slumber that had lasted for centuries. From the threshold that had just been uncovered, brilliant tendrils of luminescent light streamed forth, casting long shadows that danced across the polished marble floor. A profound sense of elation and relief swept over the adventurers as they beheld the whirling cosmos that lay beyond; it was a magnificent vortex of stars and swirling galaxies that invited them to venture forth into the vast unknown.

It was Valen who proclaimed, "Your hearts have guided you," and his voice was a resonant echo that seemed to emanate from the walls themselves. Following a period of inactivity and stagnation, the shadows that were present within the chamber started to churn and swirl around him, gaining momentum in a crescendo of radiant intensity. They pulsated with light, briefly eclipsing the room before restraining themselves and revealing Valen's form bathed in an ethereal glow. You will be remembered by time for your decision, which will be one that reflects the depth of your knowledge and the connections you have forged. Your actions in this very moment have had an impact that has been felt throughout the ages. To carry the weight and wonder of what you have learnt into the world, you are destined to shape the future. You are destined to shape the future.

A brilliant flash of blinding white light brought together the individual beams of earth, air, fire, and water, resulting in the merging of their energies into a single, unified force. Pathways of pure light began to unfurl from this nexus, spiralling outwards at an unfathomable speed, and eventually reaching across the vast expanse of space to touch the very stars. However, this was not the climax of their journey. They went ahead to delve even further, penetrating the cloak of the material world and penetrating the deepest parts of the human consciousness. A tangible distortion that warped the air and sent echoes of distant futures shimmering through the present, time itself rippled. This was a tangible result of the distortion. In the past, the world outside the museum was constrained by the rigid chains of linear history; however, this was no longer the case. Rather than being relegated to dusty textbooks and forgotten anecdotes, history did not disappear; rather, it danced vibrantly in the hearts of those who live it. It was a living, breathing entity that informed their choices, shaped their perspectives, and empowered them to build a better tomorrow. To propel them forward on the path that was predetermined for them, the burden of the past, which had become a source of strength, rested on their shoulders.

They found themselves standing once more amid the familiar grandeur of the museum as the enchanted realm's vibrancy began to fade, the kaleidoscopic colours began to fade away like a dream upon waking, and the light began to dim, retreating from the grand hall like a timid creature. Once upon a time, the ornate wooden door that stood behind them was a gateway to an infinite number of possibilities. With its intricate carvings returning to their static state, the door now stood sealed, protecting the secrets of the enchanted realm that was contained within. Despite this, the museum's core continued to send a low, resonant energy throughout the entire space. The artefacts, which had been admired in the past for their historical significance, now glowed softly with an inner light and pulsed with the echoes of the magic that they had seen. They were no longer merely objects or relics of bygone eras; rather, they were profound manifestations of stories, of triumphs and tragedies, of loves and losses, all of which yearned to be passed down from generation to generation, whispering their stories to those who had the courage to listen.

Ellie looked around at her companions, each of their faces visible because of the experiences they had shared together. Azrael, the stoic guardian, stood ever vigilant, his gaze scanning the hall as if he was still expecting the appearance of another danger. While Professor Finch was lost in contemplative silence, his glasses were perched on his nose. He was undoubtedly putting together the pieces of information that he had gleaned from their adventure. Luci, whose face radiated an ancient wisdom that belied her youth, smiled when she realised that she was aware of the situation. Oliver, whose posture was unmoving and unwavering, exuded a quiet strength that served as the foundation of their group. The silvery hair of Lady Arabella, which caught the gentle glow of the artefacts, gave off the impression that she exuded a grace that went beyond her aristocratic bearing. And Finn, despite the gravity of their recent trials, still had the inherent mischief that was visible in his twinkling eyes. He was holding a small, unassuming object, which was without a doubt a memento of their journey. They had appeared victorious, not simply triumphant over a challenge, but forged anew, their individual strengths intertwined, creating bonds of loyalty and affection that would seal their fate, weaving their lives together for years to come. They had appeared to have triumphed over a challenge.

The distant, melodic notes of a heralding bell could be heard as dawn began to break, painting the sky in shades of rose and gold. They heard the bell as it rang out. The sound of its resonant chimes reverberated through the peaceful streets, signalling the beginning of a new chapter that was about to be written. Not only did it signify a rebirth for the Enchanted Museum, which had been purified and revitalised because of their actions, but it also signified a rebirth for everyone who had visited the museum. Every one of them had within them a glimmer of the enchantment that they had become acquainted with, a fresh comprehension of both themselves and the world that surrounded them. As they moved forward into a world that was subtly but profoundly enriched by their unity, they were accompanied by the lingering whispers of the night, the faint scent of enchanted blossoms, and the thrilling echoes of adventure that were still resonating in their hearts. It was a world that would never be the same again, not because of grand pronouncements or sweeping gestures, but because of the quiet, enduring power of shared experience and the unwavering bonds of friendship. This was a testament to the magic that existed not only within the museum, but also within themselves.

Ellie murmured, "Together, we've created a legacy," to herself as a smile spread across her face. This smile reflected the journey that they had taken together as well as the significance of what they had carried out. Dust particles were seen moving in the air, illuminated by the late afternoon sun that was streaming through the grand museum windows. These dust particles were a silent testament to the stories that were contained within the museum's walls, stories that they were now entrusted to protect. As they took on their new responsibilities as guardians of the museum, they were overcome with a profound sense of responsibility. This feeling was intertwined with feelings of exhilaration and a growing anticipation for the future. Knowing that history, in its grand and intricate tapestry, would forever weave them together, binding them not just as colleagues but as kindred spirits, they felt a deeper understanding of their intertwined destinies. They knew history would forever weave them together. Because of their mutual interest in the past, they had developed a connection that was more powerful than any agreement or obligation.

As a result, they walked out into the light, hand in hand, leaving the quiet corridors of the museum behind them. There was a striking contrast between the silent stories that were behind them and the city that stretched out before them, vibrant and alive. Not only did they have an extensive knowledge of artefacts and historical events, but they also had a genuine and unwavering friendship. They were prepared to face whatever new adventures lay beyond the doors of the museum. The friendship was forged in the fires of shared experiences, a bond that would illuminate even the darkest nights, guiding them through challenges and celebrating their triumphs. It was a friendship that would illuminate even the darkest nights. The beginning of their journey had just begun, and they were intimately aware that they would face it together.

THE HEART OF
THE MUSEUM

The air was thick with anticipation, a palpable buzz that vibrated against Ellie's skin. She, Professor Finch, and Oliver stood in the Heart of the Museum, an expansive chamber that felt less like a room and more like a sacred space. Giant, ornately carved pillars reached towards the high, vaulted ceiling, disappearing into the shadows above. The soft glow of enchanted lanterns, each humming with arcane energy, filtered through the room, bathing the scene in an ethereal, almost dreamlike light. Here, within these hallowed walls, the museum's most extraordinary artefacts were housed, not merely displayed, but revered. Each object pulsed with a latent energy, whispering tales from eras long past, echoing with the triumphs and tragedies of forgotten civilisations.

"We're not merely studying the past," Professor Finch said, his voice hushed with reverence. He adjusted his glasses, the lenses catching the lantern light and reflecting a twinkle in his eye, a spark of pure, unadulterated academic joy. "We're standing in the very pulse of history itself! Every item here holds a story, a fragment of time, a captured emotion that, together, we can piece back together like a shattered mosaic. It's more than just dates and names; it's about understanding the hopes, the fears, the dreams that shaped the world we inhabit today." He gestured around the room, his hand sweeping across a tapestry depicting a forgotten battle, a shimmering orb that seemed to contain a miniature galaxy, and a set of ancient scrolls bound in dragon hide.

Ellie nodded, feeling the weight of history settle upon her shoulders, a powerful, almost overwhelming sensation. The exhilaration of discovery washed over her, a heady mix of excitement and responsibility. "But how do we decipher these stories?" she asked, her voice barely above a whisper, respectful of the ancient power that permeated the air. "How do we unlock the secrets they hold?"

Suddenly, a low rumble echoed through the chamber, a deep, resonant sound that seemed to emanate from the very core of the earth. The ground beneath them trembled slightly, a subtle vibration that sent shivers up their spines. Dust motes danced in the lantern light as the air grew thick with a palpable sense of magic. At the centre of the Heart, dominating the room with its imposing presence, stood the towering statue of Azrael the Lion. Carved from obsidian and inlaid with shimmering gemstones, he was the guardian, the silent sentinel of the museum. He stood magnificent, a symbol of power and wisdom, and now, impossibly, his eyes were flickering to life, like stars igniting at twilight, their golden light piercing the darkness.

"Fear not, dear friends!" Professor Finch exclaimed, his voice a mixture of awe and barely had excitement. "The Heart of the Museum is alive, and within it, within the very essence of Azrael, lies the key to our quest. The past is calling, and we must answer!"

"What's that glowing beneath your paw?" Oliver questioned, pointing a finger towards the ethereal luminescence emanating from the floor. His brow, previously etched with suspicion and doubt, now furrowed in genuine curiosity. The first reservations he'd harboured about the museum and its cryptic curator were beginning to dissipate, replaced by the undeniable thrill of the unfolding adventure.

"Indeed!" Azrael declared with a flourish, his voice brimming with an air of profound revelation. "This," he announced, gesturing dramatically with a paw towards the glowing stone, "is the Hearthstone, the very foundation of this museum's magic. It is the keystone upon which all its wonders rest. Only by understanding the tapestry of its history, by unravelling the threads of its creation and purpose, can we truly unlock the world of mysteries that surrounds us here."

As Azrael spoke, a subtle rustling echoed through the hall, and Luci slithered gracefully into view. Her scales didn't simply gleam; they shimmered with an internal fire, like molten bronze cooling in the twilight. Her serpentine eyes, intelligent and ancient, regarded them with knowing amusement. "Let me weave the first tale of the Hearthstone," she hissed, her voice as smooth and captivating as silk sliding over glass. "Once a powerful symbol of unity, it still echoes with the lingering sentiments of all those who have tread upon this hallowed ground, leaving an indelible mark within its crystalline structure."

With a subtle flick of her tail and an ethereal grace that defied gravity, Luci unfurled a shimmering scroll that appeared seemingly out of thin air. The papyrus was unlike any Oliver had ever seen, its surface shimmering with embedded starlight. Upon it, words danced and rearranged themselves, forming and reforming to reveal fragmented histories, anecdotes, and echoes of civilisations long past. He glimpsed fleeting images – bustling market squares, forgotten languages, and the faces of artisans whose hands had crafted the wonders that now lived within the museum's walls. "Once," Luci recounted, her voice resonating with the weight of centuries, "the Hearthstone was embedded in the very heart of a grand temple. A temple dedicated not to war or conquest, but to peaceful gatherings and the fostering of understanding. It served as a focal point, uniting warring tribes under a powerful bond of friendship, allowing for trade, the sharing of knowledge, and mutual respect that had been absent for generations. Its power was the power of connection and shared purpose."

As the whispers of the tales enveloped them, swirling around Ellie, Oliver, and even Finn, the air hummed with life, crackling with an unseen energy that prickled their skin. The museum, usually a silent tomb of history, felt vibrant and alive, reacting to the story Luci had woven. "But how do we harness its magic?" Ellie asked, her voice barely a whisper, captivated by Luci's narrative of the Hearthstone and its immense power. She imagined the possibilities, the potential for good, and felt a thrill course through her.

"The Hearthstone requires a specific alignment — a series of challenges to unveil the next piece of its history," Finn chimed in, appearing as if from thin air, his movements fluid and silent. One moment the hallway was empty, the next he was perched on a nearby display case, his eyes bright with mischief and an almost unsettling level of intelligence. "And I've heard there are riddles laid out for you!" He tapped a paw against his snout, a knowing glint in his amber eyes.

"Riddles?" Oliver's brows shot up, his usual calm demeanour momentarily disrupted. He nervously adjusted his glasses, looking around the seemingly endless exhibits. "Doesn't sound easy! We're not exactly known for our puzzle-solving skills." He exchanged a worried glance with Ellie, who, despite her first excitement, felt a knot of apprehension tighten in her stomach.

"Quite the opposite!" Finn teased, his tail twitching erratically, scattering dust motes in the air with each flick. "Each riddle will lead you deeper into the museum's layers, unlocking secrets you never knew existed. Think of it as an adventure, a grand game of hide-and-seek with the Hearthstone itself." He hopped down from the display case, padding silently towards them. "And I'll be right by your side, urging on your mischief and guiding you with playful hints. Just...try to keep me out of trouble, all right?" His mischievous grin widened, hinting at the chaotic energy he promised to unleash.

Professor Finch's usually measured tone was replaced by an uncharacteristic urgency. "Let's not tarry then," he articulated, a note of eagerness, even anxiety, threading through his voice. He adjusted his spectacles, his gaze sweeping over the small band of adventurers gathered before him. "Each moment wasted could seal the Hearthstone's fate. Time is of the essence, and the longer we delay, the greater the risk of irreversible damage."

As if summoned by his words, or perhaps simply waiting for the right moment, Lady Arabella appeared from her pedestal. The sculpted stone seemed to soften and flow around her, reforming as she stepped forward. Her figure radiated not just light, but a palpable warmth and grace, a benevolent presence that calmed the nervous energy in the room. "Dear adventurers," she began, her voice a melodious chime that resonated deep within their chests, "heed the call of the Hearthstone. It embodies the museum's spirit, forever binding the past with the present. It is the linchpin, the very lifeblood of this place." She paused, her eyes, ancient and wise, meeting each of theirs in turn. "Through its trials, you will not only decipher history, piecing together the fragments of forgotten eras, but also understand your own intertwined stories. The Hearthstone reflects, magnifies, and ultimately reveals the truth within."

Ellie, feeling a sense of unity ignite among the group, a shared purpose suddenly sparking to life, stepped forward tentatively. "Shall we begin?" she asked, the question hanging in the air, both a statement of readiness and a plea for reassurance.

"Indeed," Azrael proclaimed with fervour, his hand resting on the pommel of his sword. The glint in his eye betrayed a thrill of the challenge. "To unlock the Hearthstone, to even begin to understand its power, we must first uncover the riddles it guards. These are not mere puzzles, but trials of character, tests of knowledge, and ultimately, gateways to understanding."

Luci, ever the strategist, led them to a grand mosaic on the floor. The intricate designs, a swirling tapestry of colours and symbols, formed a circular pattern around a blank space in the centre. The air above the mosaic shimmered slightly, hinting at the magic woven into its creation. "Here lies the first riddle," she whispered, her voice hushed with reverence and a healthy dose of academic curiosity. "Only those proven worthy may step upon the heart." A subtle crease appeared on her brow as she scanned the design. "But what constitutes 'worthy' remains to be seen."

As they saw, captivated by the silent display, a series of words began to materialise within the blank space. At first, they were just faint glimmerings, like fireflies dancing in the darkness. Then, slowly, painstakingly, they resolved into letters, crisp and clear, forming into the riddle itself, etched in light upon the ancient mosaic, waiting to challenge their minds and test their spirits. The air crackled with anticipation.

The air in the ancient chamber thrummed with anticipation. "I am forever around you yet never touched; I shelter the secrets that you look for, watchful but unnoticed. What am I?" The riddle, spoken by the serpentine woman named Luci, hung heavy in the air, its weight pressing down on the small group huddled within the cavernous space.

"Ah, the answer must be... shadows!" Ellie exclaimed, her voice filled with the thrill of discovery. A wave of relief washed over her, quickly followed by the heady rush of solving the puzzle. The stakes were high, and each correct answer brought them closer to their goal, whatever that may be.

"Correct!" Luci hissed, the sound like wind whistling through dry reeds. Her smile widened, revealing a hint of sharp teeth. "Step forth, Guardian of Knowledge!"

At her words, the outline of Ellie's shadow on the rough-hewn wall flickered and brightened, ceasing to be a mere silhouette. It pulsed with an inner light, blossoming into luminescent forms of the artefacts that surrounded them. The shadows danced and swirled, casting intricate patterns that illuminated hidden pathways previously obscured by the gloom, and revealed concealed panels etched into the stone walls, their surfaces shimmering with an otherworldly glow.

"A remarkable display!" Professor Finch saw, his eyes wide with scholarly delight. He scrambled forward, a small, leather-bound notebook in his trembling hand, jotting down notes in a frenzied swirl of passion. Ink splattered as he scribbled, barely able to have his excitement. "The Hearthstone is indeed intertwined with our essence. The manipulation of shadow... extraordinary!"

"Watch closely!" Finn encouraged, his youthful energy a stark contrast to the Professor's academic frenzy. He darted his small frame through the intricate paths illuminated by the burgeoning shadows, his keen eyes scanning the newly revealed inscriptions. "Your next riddle awaits! Don't want to fall behind, do you?"

But Oliver hesitated, his hand instinctively reaching up to rub his neck. Unease crept into his chest like a chilling draft. The excitement that rippled through the others bypassed him, replaced by a growing sense of foreboding. "And what if we fail?" he asked, his voice barely a whisper. The consequences of failure hadn't been explicitly said, but the oppressive atmosphere of the chamber suggested they would be severe.

"Failure is but an invitation to learn," Lady Arabella replied softly, her voice like the chime of distant bells. Her ethereal presence, always slightly detached from the immediate events, radiated a calming aura. She moved with a graceful serenity, her long, silver hair flowing around her like liquid moonlight. "Remember, the past teaches as much as it challenges. Even in darkness, there is knowledge to be found." Her words, though comforting, did little to quell the apprehension gripping Oliver's heart. He couldn't shake the feeling that they were walking a treacherous path, and the price of failure might be more than just a simple lesson.

With newfound resolve, Ellie, her heart steeled by the trials they had already overcome, stepped into the inviting light emanating from what seemed to be the very heart of the shadow. It was an oxymoron, this shadow's warmth, but it pulsed with a power that drew them in, promised answers, and whispered of the ancient secrets they craved.

As they crossed the threshold, the echoes of history intensified, swirling around them like a vortex. The air shimmered with the residual magical energy of their past adventures, a tapestry woven with daring escapes, perilous battles, and moments of profound connection. It was a potent reminder of how far they had come and the strength they had found within themselves and each other.

"Focus on the moment! The next challenge awaits," Azrael said, his voice a calming counterpoint to the rising tide of historical clamour. He guided them further inward, deeper into the heart of the mystery. The grand hall narrowed, the walls closing in as if the very structure was conspiring to test their courage. The atmosphere thickened, becoming almost palpable, heavy with the weight of untold stories. Shadows danced madly around them, swirling and shifting like phantom figures, a chaotic ballet performed in the twilight. Undeterred, they embarked on the next leg of their journey, each step resonating with the anticipation of the unknown.

"Beyond this point lies inscription upon inscription, a cascade of histories, layered upon layered, like sedimentary rock," Luci explained, her voice a melodious whisper that cut through the oppressive silence. She gracefully glided ahead, her ethereal form illuminating the path. "Prepare for a symphony of forgotten voices! A chorus of kings and queens, scholars and warriors, lovers and betrayers... all vying for your attention."

As they traversed the narrow passage, the walls began to sparkle, tiny flecks of light igniting like forgotten stars. Slowly, almost imperceptibly, the portraits of those who once walked among the treasures they now looked for were unveiled. Faces appeared from the stone, figures from different epochs staring back with an unnerving intensity. Their eyes, made in shades of grey and sepia, seemed alive with emotion, their stories etched in the lines around their mouths and the furrow of their brows. They were silent witnesses to the ages, their voices locked within the stone, ready to be unleashed upon those brave enough to listen.

"Do not forget the riddle!" Finn reminded, his voice echoing with a newfound authority amongst the onboarding whispers of the past. "It is the key to understanding what lies ahead. We can only take on each stage with a clear heart and mind, free from the distractions of fear and doubt."

"Quite right, Finn!" Ellie agreed, feeling more grounded, more centred, with every heartbeat. The weight of the past was heavy, but the riddle was their anchor, their guiding star. "Their wisdom is our guide. Let us listen closely to the echoes and seek the answers within their silent gazes." She raised her head, her gaze meeting the unwavering eyes of a long-forgotten queen, and felt a sudden surge of connection, a silent promise to honour their sacrifice and uncover the truth they protected.

With newfound resolve, Ellie, her heart steeled by the trials they had already overcome, stepped into the inviting light emanating from what seemed to be the very heart of the shadow. It was an oxymoron, this shadow's warmth, but it pulsed with a power that drew them in, promised answers, and whispered of the ancient secrets they craved. As they crossed the threshold, the echoes of history intensified, swirling around them like a vortex. The air shimmered with the residual magical energy of their past adventures, a tapestry woven with daring escapes, perilous battles, and moments of profound connection. It was a strong reminder of how far they had come and the strength they had found in each other.

"Focus on the moment! The next challenge awaits," Azrael said, his voice a calming counterpoint to the rising tide of historical clamour. He guided them further inward, deeper into the heart of the mystery. The grand hall narrowed, the walls closing in as if the very structure was conspiring to test their courage. The atmosphere thickened, becoming almost palpable, heavy with the weight of untold stories. Shadows danced madly around them, swirling and shifting like phantom figures, a chaotic ballet performed in the twilight. Undeterred, they embarked on the next leg of their journey, each step resonating with the anticipation of the unknown.

"Beyond this point lies inscription upon inscription, a cascade of histories, layered upon layered, like sedimentary rock," Luci explained, her voice a melodious whisper that cut through the oppressive silence. She gracefully glided ahead, her ethereal form illuminating the path. "Prepare for a symphony of forgotten voices! A chorus of kings and queens, scholars and warriors, lovers and betrayers... all vying for your attention."

As they traversed the narrow passage, the walls began to sparkle, tiny flecks of light igniting like forgotten stars. Slowly, almost imperceptibly, the portraits of those who once walked among the treasures they now looked for were unveiled. Faces appeared from the stone, figures from different epochs staring back with an unnerving intensity. Their eyes, made in shades of grey and sepia, seemed alive with emotion, their stories etched in the lines around their mouths and the furrow of their brows. They were silent witnesses to the ages, their voices locked within the stone, ready to be unleashed upon those brave enough to listen.

"Do not forget the riddle!" Finn reminded, his voice echoing with a newfound authority amongst the onboarding whispers of the past. "It is the key to understanding what lies ahead. We can only take on each stage with a clear heart and mind, free from the distractions of fear and doubt."

"Quite right, Finn!" Ellie agreed, feeling more grounded, more centred, with every heartbeat. The weight of the past was heavy, but the riddle was their anchor, their guiding star. "Their wisdom is our guide. Let us listen closely to the echoes and seek the answers within their silent gazes." She raised her head, her gaze meeting the unwavering eyes of a long-forgotten queen, and felt a sudden surge of connection, a silent promise to honour their sacrifice and uncover the truth they protected.

The heavy oak door, groaning in protest at its hinges, swung open wider, unveiling a chamber of such breathtaking grandeur that it felt ripped from the pages of a myth. It was a kaleidoscope of history, a symphony of ages played out in stone, canvas, and forgotten metals. The chamber was resplendent, overflowing with artefacts pulled from the far reaches of time. Paintings depicting epic battles, their colours still vibrant despite the centuries, hung beside sculptures of long-dead heroes, their faces frozen in expressions of stoic defiance or serene contemplation. Scattered amidst these grand displays were smaller, more enigmatic relics – objects from cultures lost to time, their purposes unrecorded, their stories whispered only by the dust of ages.

Ellie gasped, her breath catching in her throat. A wave of awe washed over her as she beheld the sheer splendour surrounding them. Light filtered in from unseen sources, illuminating the room in a soft, ethereal glow, highlighting the intricate details of each object, each carving, each brushstroke. It was a visual feast, a tangible representation of the vast, complex quilt that is human history.

"This is the Heart of the Museum!" Professor Finch exclaimed, his voice echoing slightly in the cavernous space. His eyes shone with an almost feverish excitement. "This is where all histories converge! Every triumph, every tragedy, every whisper of the past is bound together in this very room!"

Yet, as they stepped fully inside, the atmosphere subtly shifted. The air grew colder, heavier, pregnant with an unseen energy. Shadows, previously still and predictable, began to lengthen and writhe, as if imbued with a life of their own. Dark forms, amorphous and indistinct, moved just at the periphery of their vision, dancing against the fluttering light like restless spirits.

Finn, usually the embodiment of playful exuberance, stood stock-still, his ears perked up, his brow furrowed in concern. His tail, normally wagging with boundless enthusiasm, hung low. "There's a...a sense of foreboding here," he murmured, his voice barely a whisper, his playful disposition momentarily and uncharacteristically shaken. "Something...uncomfortable."

Lady Arabella, her silver hair gleaming in the soft light, stepped forward, her gaze sweeping across the room with an air of quiet authority. "It is said that the Hearthstone, the very foundation upon which this chamber rests, vibrates with both light and shadow, metaphors for every history represented within," she said, her voice echoing with a timeless grace. "The echoes of joy and sorrow, of creation and destruction, resonate here. Yet, fear not! With courage and understanding, we shall navigate through the murk and unlock the secrets that lie hidden within."

As they ventured further into the Heart of the Museum, the ambiguous, looming shapes began to solidify, taking on more distinct forms. They coalesced into shadows of individuals, their features contorted by a range of emotions: some bore the look of deep sadness, their spectral faces etched with the pain of forgotten wrongs; others appeared wretched and menacing, their shadowy hands reaching out as if to reclaim what they had lost, their eyes burning with a malevolent hunger. The weight of untold stories pressed down on them, a palpable testament to the triumphs and failures, the hopes and fears, that had shaped the world they knew. The journey through history was about to become a much more personal and perilous one.

"Who dares enter this realm?" a voice snarled, echoing through the space like a thunderclap. The sound reverberated off unseen surfaces, a palpable wave of hostility that prickled the skin. It seemed to originate from everywhere and nowhere at once, amplified by the oppressive silence that had preceded it.

"It is us, guardians of time!" Azrael bellowed back with unwavering strength, his voice cutting through the echoing threat. Muscles tensed in his jaw, and his hand instinctively went to the hilt of the chronarium blade strapped to his side. "We come to restore the balance of narratives! A corruption festers within the timeline, and we will not stand idly by while it unravels!"

Suddenly, a figure appeared from the shadows that clung to the edges of the ethereal space, solidifying as if woven from the darkness itself. He was tall and slender; his frame draped in a midnight-blue cloak that seemed to swallow the meagre light. But it was his hair that truly caught the eye. Glimmering white, it flowed like cascading silk, almost shimmering with an inner luminescence. The atmosphere around him throbbed with ancient power, a tangible hum that resonated deep within their bones. The corners of his lips curved into an enigmatic smile, one that hinted at both amusement and a profound understanding. "I am Valen, The Timekeeper, the overseer of histories untold and secrets buried. I have been expecting you."

Ellie felt her heart race. The air grew heavy, thick with anticipation. This was it. This was the being who held the key, or perhaps the obstacle, to their mission. She stepped forward, her voice trembling slightly but firm, "Then you know who we are and why we seek the Hearthstone!"

"The Hearthstone binds the fates of those who hold it," Valen responded, his voice smooth and resonant, each word carefully measured. He studied them with eyes that seemed to hold the weight of centuries. "It is a nexus of temporal energy, a source of unimaginable power. But power comes with a price. It requires bravery and unity to harness its strength. Are you willing to confront the shadows of the past, to face the difficult truths etched into the very fabric of time, to illuminate the path forward? The past is not always kind, and its echoes can be dangerous. Could you please let me know if you feel fully prepared for what you might discover?

With a glance towards her friends, Ellie could see the resolve in their eyes reflecting her own. The flickering torchlight danced across their faces, painting them with fleeting patches of courage and determination. "Together, we will face whatever lies ahead. The museum is a tapestry of our lives—each of us a thread woven into its history. Every exhibit we've deciphered, every secret passage we've navigated, has brought us to this moment. We are inextricably linked to this place, and it to us."

Valen nodded, his usually jovial face etched with a serious intensity, acknowledging her bravery. "Then let us unveil the final riddle that will unlock the Hearthstone fully! We've come too far to falter now. Let's show it what we're made of!" His words were a rallying cry, a spark igniting the embers of their collective spirit.

And with that, the chamber began to glow, not with a gentle, comforting luminescence the light in a macabre ballet. Patches of the past flickered into existence, whispering tales of forgotten curators, daring explorers, and the countless artefacts that had found sanctuary within the museum's walls. The air crackled with energy, the very essence of history swirling around them.

Ellie could feel the warmth emanating from Azrael, a steady, grounding presence like the ancient stones of the building itself. She sensed the protective wisdom of Lady Arabella, a comforting wave of understanding and knowledge. Finn, with his ever-ready grin, radiated an aura of cunning tricks and unexpected solutions. And around them all, the rich history administered by Luci wrapped around her like a cherished embrace, a feeling of belonging that resonated deep within her soul. They were not merely adventurers, nor were they simply a team. They were the Heart of the Museum, the embodiment of its spirit, and together they would unravel its deepest enigmas, peeling back the layers of time to reveal the truth that lay hidden within.

As the hour neared dawn, painting the sky outside in hues of grey and rose, the journey was far from over. The puzzles they had solved were merely preludes to the grand finale. But united by a common purpose, a shared passion for discovery, and the unbreakable bond they had forged, Ellie felt an indomitable strength welling within her. They were entwined by threads of courage, determination, and the promise of discovery—the very essence of life pulsing in the heart of the museum, a vibrant counterpoint to the silent relics surrounding them.

"Let the next challenge begin!" they cried in unison, their voices echoing through the chamber, a defiant roar against the unknown. They stepped forward into a new era of adventure, where shadows would tell their stories and bond them closer than ever before, a testament to their bravery and the enduring power of friendship in the face of the impossible. The museum was no longer just a place; it was a living entity, breathing with them, challenging them, and ultimately, relying on them. Their future, and the future of the museum, was about to unfold.

THE CONFRONTATION

Normally, the museum was a quiet place to think, but now it was full of strange energy. Every creak of the old floorboards and every rustle of the air that couldn't be seen seemed to tell secrets of the magical night. The air was heavy with the mysteries that had grown under the moonlight, and Ellie could feel the tension in the air like a second skin. Every shadow seemed to have a hidden danger, and every exhibit seemed to hum with power. Ellie felt the heavy weight of expectation on her shoulders as the bright hands of the big clock in the central hall slowly moved closer and closer to the dreaded midnight hour. The mysterious riddle of Valen, a puzzle that has been around for hundreds of years in myth and legend, hung over the world like a dark, powerful thundercloud, threatening to unleash a storm of unpredictable and possibly deadly effects.

"Ellie!" " whispered Azrael, the beautiful lion statue. His voice was a low rumble that seemed to come from the stone itself. In the dim light, his golden eyes, which were usually fixed in a stoic stare, shone with an urgent intelligence that matched the frantic energy of the night. "We need to find Valen before the last bell rings. Every second slips through our fingers like grains of sand. Time, my dear, is not on our side at all! "

Ellie nodded, her heart beating wildly against her ribs. She looked at Professor Finch. His usually silly and strange mannerisms were gone, and his voice was serious and hard, something she had never seen before. He no longer had the playful twinkle in his eyes; instead, he had a laser-like focus. Ellie, the artefacts are much more than just dusty things stuck behind glass. He said, "They each thrum with a piece of our history, a piece of the puzzle, a whispered truth—a clue that could lead us right to Valen and let us face him." He adjusted his thick glasses with an unusual sense of urgency. His fingers shook a little as he reached for the worn leather-bound book he had been holding.

"Okay, Professor," Oliver, the museum's night guard who didn't want to be there, asked with a look of confusion and grim determination on his face. He still couldn't believe how strange things had gotten, how this magical reality had broken up his boring routine. But under the surface of his first fear, a new sense of bravery and responsibility was starting to grow. "Which artefact should we look at first? The cursed sarcophagus from Egypt? The self-playing harpsichord? Give me something to work with." He nervously adjusted his ill-fitting uniform, ready to face the unknown dangers that lurked within the museum's hallowed halls.

Finn, a ball of russet fur and energy, came out from behind a fluted marble column. His smart eyes shone with mischief, like polished amber, as he called Ellie and Oliver over. "Come with me! There's a tapestry nearby that tells the story of Valen, a legend I thought was just a story! I've seen it weave its secrets before, shining and changing with the sounds of memories that have been lost! He bounced on the balls of his paws, excited to continue their secret journey through the quiet halls of the museum.

As they rushed towards the tapestry, which was a bright mix of faded blues and golds hanging in the dark alcove, Luci slithered next to them. The museum lights were set up in such a way that her bronze scales, which had been polished smooth by time and magic, shone brightly, casting long shadows that danced on the walls. "Beware," she hissed, her voice a sibilant whisper that seemed to come from the very stones of the museum. "Facing Valen is not just about finding out his secrets and the truth he guards; you must also be ready to face the darkness that lives inside him and inside you."

"Shadows"? "" Ellie asked, her steps slowing down. A sudden wave of fear washed over her, taking the excitement of the adventure away and leaving her with a cold sense of dread. "What do you mean? " The museum's size, which used to amaze her, now felt overwhelming, as if secrets whispered from every corner were about to swallow her whole.

Luci said, "Each of you carries a darkness—secrets you've buried deep, regrets you've tried to forget, and fears that gnaw at your courage." She flicked her forked tongue out to taste the air and sensed their unease. She stopped to wrap her arms around the cold, granite foot of a Roman statue, whose blank eyes seemed to judge them. To face Valen and really understand the flow of time, you must first face yourselves. He reflects the past, future, and souls of those who seek him.

"What shadow do I have?" Oliver muttered, his bravado falling apart as Luci's words hit him hard. A familiar seed of doubt that he thought he had gotten rid of a long time ago started to grow in the rich soil of his insecurities. He had always thought of himself as brave, a leader, and a protector. But now, standing on the edge of the unknown, he felt more like a regular person stumbling through a world of gods, weighed down by flaws he was trying to hide. The tapestry loomed ahead. It was a door to untold power, but it was also a possible abyss of self-discovery that he wasn't sure he was ready for.

"Remember, Oliver," Azrael said, his voice a rich, commanding roar that echoed through the room and was strangely comforting. His eyes shone with old knowledge. "The heart of a lion knows fear well. It knows its fears and is remarkably familiar with them. "You can only hope to get stronger, braver, and wiser by facing those shadows head-on." He put a heavy, reassuring hand on Oliver's shoulder, and the warmth of his touch steadied him amid all the uncertainty.

As the group walked down the grand hallway of the old temple, their footsteps echoed softly on the polished marble. Every step seemed to wake up the stones below, which whispered secrets from long ago. They finally got to the grand chamber, which was dominated by a giant tapestry that hung from the floor to the ceiling like a waterfall in the sky. The tapestry opened in front of them, and the threads sparkled with a bright light like molten gold flowing endlessly, showing a beautiful scene. It showed a swirling dance of stars and planets weaving around complicated symbols like hourglasses, sundials, and spirals, all of which stood for the unstoppable passage of time. The whole thing was a beautiful symphony of colour and light.

"Look"! "Ellie gasped," her voice full of excitement as she pointed to a part of the tapestry that was especially bright and interesting near the centre. The mysterious Timekeeper stood there, hidden among the glowing stars and celestial patterns. His eyes seemed to see through time itself, hidden behind layers of shadow and starlight. The Timekeeper was a serious and commanding presence, a protector of both lost and future moments.

Professor Finch whispered, "Etched in the stars," and his normally friendly face was full of intense focus. His fingers were just above the tapestry, as if they were drawing invisible lines. "Valen is a myth to many, but here he shows himself only to those brave enough to go this far, to those who dare to look for the truth that is hidden behind the veil of time. We need to figure out what the secret is that is hidden in the fine threads of this work of art. "Every stitch has a meaning, and every symbol is a key."

Finn, who was always curious and impulsive, rushed forward with a sense of urgency. His little fingers reached out to grab a loose thread that had come off the edge of the tapestry. The thread glowed softly and otherworldly, which drew everyone's attention right away. He squeaked, his eyes wide and sparkling with excitement, "This thread is glowing— this has to mean something!" His excitement was so strong that even the experienced professor couldn't help but feel a flicker of hope.

As the group got closer, the room fell into a respectful silence. Each heart raced with the promise of discovery. The tapestry wasn't just an old thing; it was a living proof of the mysteries of time. Somewhere in its golden weave was the key to their quest.

Ellie knelt next to him, her fingers shaking a little as she gently held the glowing thread that was glowing softly in the museum's dim light. She pulled very carefully, and at first the thread resisted her touch, but then it gave in. A faint tremor ran through the hall around them almost right away.

The air itself seemed to vibrate, filled with an unseen current that crackled and hissed like static electricity before a storm. The thread gave off a strange light that made dust mites dance in the air.

The fabric of reality started to ripple right in front of them. In an instant, a swirling portal appeared, its swirling vortex made up of many colours—iridescent blues, fiery oranges, deep purples, and glimmering golds—that merged and twisted in patterns that were hard to look away from. The portal was both beautiful and scary. It was a door that opened to endless possibilities but also sent out scary signals. It silently called to them, luring them forward with the promise of answers they had been looking for for a long time, while also hinting at the dangers and mysteries that were just beyond its door.

The respectful silence was broken by Professor Finch's voice. His eyes were bright and full of a fierce mix of excitement and fear. "We must go in," he said firmly, his voice steady even though he knew what was coming. "Only together can we hope to take on Valen, the master of the moments we want to understand and the keeper of all temporal secrets."

Ellie, Oliver, Professor Finch, and their enchanted friends—creatures made from ancient magic—stepped forward with their hearts and minds set on the same goal. One by one, they stepped into the glowing space in front of them. The feeling came on quickly and strongly, like they were moving through ribbons of time and space, and their surroundings were twisting and turning in a confusing dance.

In a matter of seconds, they were taken to a place they had never been before, where time didn't flow in a straight line but bent, broke, and spiralled in ways they couldn't have predicted. Shadows moved in strange ways, whispering complaints, memories, and forgotten secrets into the air that was swirling around them. The air was heavy with the weight of many years.

As they landed softly, the ground beneath their feet sparkled like glass, showing not only their images but also brief flashes of memories and dreams that had not yet come true. The chaotic scene was both beautiful and scary.

They saw a single person through the thick, swirling fog. Valen stood proudly in the middle of a misty shroud, waiting for them. His presence filled the room—an enigma wrapped in eternal authority, shrouded in mystery and strength. The time had come.

"Welcome, seekers of truth," he said in a deep, resonant voice that seemed to match the strange realm's vibrations. The air was full of an unseen energy, like a tapestry made of echoes of things that had happened long ago. "You have come to face your fears and explore the maze you created. But remember this: to get the knowledge you so desperately want, to solve the puzzles that connect your fates, you must give up what you hold dear."

Ellie, always the realist, stepped forward, her boots softly crunching on the floor that wasn't there. "What do you mean?" she asked, her voice steady and calm amid all the confusion. She instinctively put her hand on the worn leather of her satchel, which made her feel better and reminded her of the world she knew.

"The very things you love," Valen said softly, looking around the room as if to bless it. He waved his long, graceful hand, which was covered in rings that glowed with a faint, otherworldly light. "Each one holds a memory, a piece of your soul, carved into its shape by the passage of time and the weight of experience. Let go of these objects and cut the ties that bind you to them, and the path to your destiny, which is now hidden in mist, will be revealed. If you hold on to them, you will stay trapped in your past."

Professor Finch stepped forward, his face red with anger and his usually neat appearance a little messy. His glasses were precariously perched on his nose. "No! You don't understand! These things aren't just trinkets. They are our history—they are our legacy! They are the physical links between us and those who came before us, the lessons learnt, the battles won, and the very ground we stand on!" He held a tarnished silver locket in his hand, its intricate carvings barely visible under a layer of grime, a desperate attempt to hold onto something solid in this ethereal place.

Valen's eyes were pools of liquid starlight that flashed with a wisdom older than time itself. This wisdom came from seeing civilisations rise and fall and countless lives come and go. "Yes, Professor. A legacy is a gift from the ancestors that is unbelievably valuable. But when you bury it in fear and longing, it becomes a burden, a ball and chain. When you let the past control your present and hold on to memories to avoid facing the future, you can't move forward and really embrace the possibilities that lie ahead. You have to face what you fear losing first."

Ellie's heart raced, pounding against her ribs like a frantic drum as she and Professor Finch looked at the artefacts around them again. They weren't just things; they were places where feelings were stored, echoes of happiness and sadness, success and failure. There was a chipped porcelain doll with painted eyes that stared blankly ahead. It was filled with the laughter of a child who had died long ago. There was a sword that had rusted and had scars from many battles. It told stories of bravery and loss. Lady Arabella, a life-sized marble statue, stood at the front, bathed in a soft, almost holy light. She was poised and graceful, and her calm expression gave off an otherworldly calm.

Lady Arabella's lips seemed to curve into the faintest of smiles, as if she could tell Ellie was scared. Her voice was deep and resonant, and it filled the room, making the air shake. "Don't be afraid of the past, dear Ellie," she said, and her voice calmed Ellie's racing heart and sent a wave of comfort through her. "It's just a guide, a map to help you get through the present. It's not a chain that ties you to the past. Let go of the fear, and you'll find the freedom you seek." Ellie realised that the challenge wasn't to forget the past but to understand it, learn from it, and finally break free from its hold. The question was, was she able to?

Ellie's heart raced, beating like a frantic drum against her ribs, as she looked at the swirling collection of artefacts around them. Each object seemed to have a strong energy that whispered stories of long-forgotten times and endless possibilities. The dusty books bound in leather, the shiny swords with hilts inlaid with precious stones, and the shimmering orbs that looked like they held tiny galaxies all added to the feeling of history coming to life. Lady Arabella, who was poised and graceful even when she was still, stood at the front. Her marble face, lit by lights that couldn't be seen, looked almost real, which was a little creepy.

"Don't be afraid of the past, dear Ellie," she said in a low, resonant voice that seemed to vibrate through the air. "It is just a guide, not a chain." The words, full of ancient wisdom, gave me a strange sense of peace during all the chaos.

"What if I can't let go?" Ellie asked, her voice shaking with fear. She felt like an anchor pulling her down because of the weight of her past, which was full of regrets and unfulfilled goals. Could she really get rid of it?

"Then you stay a prisoner of your design," Valen said, his voice getting softer after he had said something that sounded a little harsh at first. His eyes were the colour of old parchment and showed that he understood a lot. "But be careful; clinging to the past can ruin your future and drain your present." Only by confronting your demons—your regrets and painful memories—will you find your strength. You can only move forward after that.

A thick, suffocating silence surrounded them, broken only by a sudden rustle. A creature of myth and legend, Huckleberry , flew away from a high place that couldn't be seen. His wings were huge and strong, and as he flew around the room, they cast long, dancing shadows on the floor. He was a magnificent being, a protector of time itself. His presence was both awe-inspiring and a little scary.

"Time doesn't care, and neither do the stars," he said in a rough voice that echoed through the room. "Face your fears, the demons you keep hidden, and let your heart lead you." "True freedom lies in facing your deepest fears."

Visions filled the air suddenly, as if Huckleberry's words had called them. They spun around and came together to make short pictures—a kaleidoscope of happiness, sadness, confusion, and clarity. Each vision was very personal, giving a look into the heart of their problems. Ellie saw herself standing on the edge of her dreams, ready to jump into the unknown, but held back by her fear of falling and the deep-seated belief that she didn't deserve to succeed. Oliver saw that his protective instincts, which were usually his greatest strength, were being overshadowed by crippling self-doubt, making it impossible for him to protect the people he loved. Each vision made people sigh in understanding and gasp in recognition as they all followed a thread of their own intertwined shadows, looking for a way to untie the knots that held them together. The air was full of unspoken truths, the chance for freedom, and the scary thought of finally facing their deepest selves.

Ellie said, "It's not about making ourselves forget." Her voice broke the group's shared anxiety trance. Her eyes, which were usually full of curiosity, were now full of quiet determination. "It's about understanding. We need to come to terms with our pasts, accept our fears, and learn from them." "Putting them away and ignoring them just lets them grow and control us." She waved her hands to include everyone in her plea. "We must confront our dark sides, learn their origins, and choose to walk into the light with that knowledge."

Oliver's face, which had been brittle from years of discipline and fighting, softened a little. He had been fighting his demons, and the weight of his responsibilities was always threatening to crush him. He looked at his friends and said, "I've faced darker creatures than fear, just like I've faced you all." He looked at each face in turn, acknowledging their struggles. "If I can accept that I'm not just a guard but a protector because I care... if I can really believe that... Then I can do this! "I can handle whatever comes next." His voice was full of new strength, which was a turning point in his internal fight.

Finn, who was restless and full of energy, seemed to vibrate with nervous energy, but even he was affected by what Ellie said. He jumped up, and his quick body moved around them like a scout checking out the battlefield. "Yes!" "He shouted, his eyes shining with hope and excitement. "Together by our truths and our acceptance of each other, we can be more than what we've been!" We can make a future that isn't held back by the things that hold us back. We can be...better."

With a new sense of purpose, they moved closer to Valen, the swirling vortex of cosmic energy that held the universe's secrets. They threw their heart's fears into the cosmic void, not as a sacrifice but to show they understood. A strong, almost blinding light surrounded them, and waves of energy washed over them, probing their minds and souls with such intensity that no secret was left unexamined and no hidden corner was left untouched. They were forced to confront their pasts as memories, both good and bad, swirled around them. and joyfully, came back to them and swirled around them, making them face the things that had made them who they were.

Ellie felt lighter inside as the shadows faded away, revealing the uncomfortable truths behind her fears. It was as if a heavy weight she had been carrying for years had finally been lifted. The doubts and worries that had been bothering her for so long seemed to go away, and she felt more confident than ever. "We are stronger together," she said, her voice steady and brave, ringing with the clarity of someone who had finally understood something important. "We are not defined by our pasts, but by how we choose to face the future." And we choose to face it together.

Valen saw that the mist that had hung over this strange, timeless place was starting to fade away like frost in the morning sun. He looked at the determined faces in front of him: Ellie, whose eyes were shining with new strength; Oliver, whose youthful bravado was tempered by wisdom; and Professor Finch, whose scholarly face showed signs of weariness that hid the fierce spirit within. "You have proven yourselves," he said in a deep voice that seemed to shake the very fabric of this temporary place. He slowly bent his fingers, an old sign of power and understanding. "To overcome fear is to go beyond time itself." You have fought off the ghosts of your doubts and the ghosts of your past and come out on top. "Now you can go back to your time."

The portal, which was a swirling vortex of amethyst, emerald, and gold, made its light stronger, pulling them back towards their original realm. It pulsed with an energy that pulled at their senses, inviting them in a soft but firm way. Ellie felt the warmth of friendship wash over her as she held Oliver's hand in one hand and Professor Finch's arm in the other. The warmth made her fear go away. Eagerness grew in her chest, along with a sense of adventure, as she thought about the world that awaited them. She could see it more clearly and with more hope now.

They fell back into the museum, which they knew well, after coming out of the colourful waterfall. The air was full of new energy. The shimmering tapestry that had started their journey now unfurled gracefully behind them, its threads telling stories of bravery and strength. The things in the hall sparkled with new life, getting rid of their old sadness. Shadows that were once thick and scary faded away, pushed back into nothingness by the light they had brought back with them.

"Together, we faced the heart of our fears," Ellie said, and a wave of relief washed over her as she looked around at her friends. The fear that had threatened to take over them was gone, and in its place was a bond formed by going through something together. "And we came out together! "Better, stronger, wiser."

Finn, the lively sprite who had led them, danced around them in a flurry, a victorious streak of rustling, bright energy. His laughter rang out in the hall. "Now let's find out what's next!" He chirped, his eyes sparkling with mischief. The museum, which used to be full of old things, was now a door to endless possibilities. It called them forward, promising new adventures, new knowledge, and new friends. They were just starting their journey.

But just as the thrill of victory washed over their tired bodies and filled the grand hall with triumphant laughter, a shadow moved in the corner of the museum. It wasn't just a trick of the light or something they were imagining because they were tired. There was a ghostly presence, a whisper of unfinished business that hung around the ornate tapestries and echoed in the high, vaulted ceilings. With a shared look and an unspoken understanding that passed between them like an electric current, the group knew that even though they had won this time and stopped the evil forces that had been bothering the museum, their adventure was far from over. The event had changed them forever, bringing them together in ways they couldn't yet understand.

They knew their biggest battle was not with the ghosts of the past, the curses and tragedies that still haunted them, but with the bonds they had made and the hard things they had been through. They knew their biggest battle was not with the ghosts of the past, the curses and tragedies that still haunted them.

The real test for them was the promises of the future, the unknown areas of their potential, and the duties that came with using the new skills and knowledge they had gained in the museum's magical walls.

And as they got ready to start the next part of their journey, a spark of hope lit up inside them. At first, it was a flicker, but then it grew into a bright flame that echoed the whispers of the enchanted museum. The old building, which was now quiet but not empty, seemed to hum with unspoken support, a silent blessing on their future.

"Let's find out what lies ahead," Ellie said, stepping forward. This time, she didn't feel the fear and doubt she had felt before. Instead, she had the relentless resolve of a leader. She looked at her friends, giving them strength and comfort. The weight of her past battles had only made her stronger and clearer about what she wanted to do. They went into the unknown together, united by their shared experiences and a desire to learn more. The memories of their struggles changed from haunting ghosts into valuable lessons, and the shadows of the past slowly faded away in the bright, hopeful light of new beginnings. The world outside the museum was full of opportunities and problems, and they were ready to face it all together.

THE POWER OF UNITY

Ellie was standing at the entrance of the ancient Egyptian exhibit as midnight fell over the Enchanted Museum, which was enveloping its grand halls in an ethereal silence. Her heart was racing with anticipation as she stood there. The atmosphere was thick with the aroma of old papyrus, and dust particles were seen moving around in the moonlight that was coming in through the high arched windows. The hieroglyphs, which were embedded into the walls and sarcophagi of the exhibit, cast flickering, dancing shadows against the sandstone. Each hieroglyph whispered a story that had been forgotten for an exceptionally long time, a secret language that yearned to be understood. Even though his tweed jacket was slightly asymmetrical and his grey hair was falling out of the part of his head that had been meticulously combed, Professor Finch adjusted his glasses and peered into the growing darkness as if it were a complicated equation or a puzzle that was waiting for him to solve it with extreme care. He nervously tapped his fingers against the worn notebook he was holding by his side. His fingers were stained with ink, and there was a faint scent of parchment.

Ellie, pay attention! When he spoke, his voice, which was normally a soft hum, became eager and animated. The moment was accentuated by the hushed silence that prevailed in the otherwise empty room. His gesture was directed towards the enormous wall that was covered in intricate carvings depicting scenes of pharaohs, gods, and the journey to the afterlife. He said, "I believe there is a connection, a tangible bridge, between these ancient artefacts and the cryptic riddles we encountered earlier in the Hall of Lost Civilisations." It appears the images were writhing and shifting in the dim light, which was fuelled by the unwavering intensity of the professor.

"I've been thinking the same thing, Professor," Ellie responded, her mind a whirlwind of possibilities, ideas swirling and tangling together like the overgrown vines of a labyrinth. "I've been thinking the same thing." The ethereal glow of the hieroglyphs would be reflected in her emerald eyes as she ran her hand through her dark hair. With the name hanging in the air, it was a whispered plea, a desperate hope in the face of the unknown. "If only we could decipher this connection; if we could unlock the secrets held within these walls, perhaps it would finally lead us to Valen, the elusive Timekeeper," the person said.

A low growl that was guttural and resonant reverberated throughout the exhibit, sending shivers down their spines as they contemplated the complex patterns of history and magic that surrounded them. An unidentified energy could be heard crackling in the air. After that, right in front of their very eyes, Azrael, the magnificent golden lion that had been depicted on the sarcophagus of a queen who had been forgotten, came to life. The sculpted form of the animal disintegrated into flesh and bone, and his enormous paws padded silently against the stone floor. The golden eyes, which were both ancient and wise, glistened in the dim light, emanating a power that was both intimidating and reassuring, respectively. As Azrael boomed, his voice was a low rumble that seemed to vibrate through the very foundations of the museum. "Your thoughts are heading in the right direction, little seekers," he said. "However, to be successful, you will require more than just your intellect." Friends, tonight, unity is the most powerful tool you have at your disposal. "The sands of time are running out..." he paused, his gaze sweeping over them, assessing their readiness.

"The only way you can hope to unlock the Timekeeper's secrets is by combining your strengths and trusting in each other."

"Unity?" Oliver furrowed his brow, the midday sun glinting off the brass buckle of his guard's hat. He tugged at the brim, adjusting it further down his forehead, a nervous habit he'd developed over weeks of mounting tension. "Are you sure this approach is going to help? We're already strained as it is. Resources are dwindling, morale is low, and frankly, trust is thinner than this parchment." He gestured vaguely with a gloved hand, encompassing the makeshift camp and its inhabitants with a look of weary scepticism. "Pulling everyone together feels like adding more weight to a ship already threatening to capsize."

Before Azrael, his usual fountain of calm wisdom, could even formulate a response, Luci, her bronze scales shimmering like a thousand buried coins under the dappled light filtering through the canopy above, uncoiled from her perch on a nearby crate and gracefully coiled around Ellie's feet. Her voice, a low, resonant hum, cut through Oliver's anxieties. "In history, every moment of triumph, every bastion against the encroaching darkness, was built upon the strength of collaboration. Look to the empires, the legends, the very survival of humankind – all hinged on shared purpose. You must work together, not just with your words, flinging empty promises into the wind, but with your hearts, understanding and supporting each other's strengths and weaknesses."

Finn, a whirlwind of orange fur and boundless energy, appeared suddenly, darting between their legs, nearly tripping Ellie in the process. He yipped playfully, his bright eyes gleaming with unwavering optimism. "Don't worry, Olli! We've got this!

Sure, things are tough but look around; we've got more than just dusty old artefacts and cryptic maps — we have each other! Ellie's a genius with languages, Azrael knows more about ancient lore than any book, and even you, Oliver, are the best darn security guard I've ever seen! We just need to figure out how to use all our skills together!"

"Do we?" Oliver questioned, his voice laced with a deep-seated uncertainty that even Finn's cheerful pronouncements couldn't quite penetrate. He crossed his arms, his posture stiff and defensive. "We barely know each other. Ellie has just arrived, Azrael often communicates in riddles, and you, Finn, are more inclined to take my lunch than to provide me with support. time, and you, Finn, are more likely to steal my lunch than guard my back. How can we collaborate to tackle a challenge we scarcely comprehend, one that appears to come together to address a challenge we barely understand, one that seems to shift and change like the desert sands? We're a motley crew, thrown together by circumstance, not a unified force ready to face whatever horrors await." He sighed; the weight of his responsibility etched deeply into the lines around his eyes. The question hung in the air, a challenge and a plea, a desperate hope that somehow, impossibly, Finn might be right

Lady Arabella, regal and poised as a queen upon her throne, detached herself from a nearby pedestal. Her silk gown shimmered in the ambient light, each fold a testament to centuries of refined elegance. "Ah, dear guard," she addressed Ellie, her voice a melodic chime that resonated through the ancient chamber. "True power lies in the trust and cooperation of many, not in the knowledge of one." cooperation of many is that true power lies. Consider the artefacts that have been dispersed throughout the ages; they may appear to be unrelated to one another, but when they are brought together, they reveal a singular and compelling narrative. It is impossible to have a complete narrative without each individual fragment because each one holds a key or a perspective.

"We must embrace our differences," she declared, her determination igniting like a newly stoked fire in her chest. "Use our individual strengths to unravel the puzzles that are before us." Ellie felt the weight of the pressure to solve the ensuing mysteries grow stronger with each word. The responsibility pressed down on her shoulders, and it was possible that the fate of time depended on their ability to decipher the clues that were left behind. It is possible that Dr Mariana and the others are still out there, stuck in either the past or the future. We can increase our chances of finding Valen if we work together and combine our skills from different areas. We become more than the sum of our parts."

"So, are we forging a team then?" Finn, a rogue with a sharp wit and sharper fingers, looked up at Ellie with his eyes sparkling with mischief and a hint of genuine excitement. As her words hung in the air, a tangible energy crackled between them. The group, which consisted of a collection of individuals who were not related to each other but were brought together by fate, remained silent, absorbing the concept of teamwork and shared destiny. A band of adventurers, bound by a common goal and a thirst for the unknown?" He grinned, a flash of white teeth in the dim light. "Sounds like trouble. I'm in."

"Aye! A band of adventurers it is!" Azrael roared, his voice a thunderous clap echoing through the enormous hall, shaking the dust from the towering statues that stood as silent witnesses to countless ages. The sound reverberated through their bones, a call to action that stirred something primal within them. "Let your voices meld as one, your skills intertwine, and the flames of camaraderie shall light your path! Let us face the past and future together and retrieve all who are lost."

Professor Finch, ever the philosopher, pondered aloud, his voice echoing softly in the hushed museum, "Every historical journey is a testament to co-operation. Think of the builders of the pyramids! They thrived through collective effort; each block was placed through shared hands. Imagine the sheer logistical prowess, the intricate planning, and the dedication of countless individuals all striving towards a single, monumental goal. It wasn't just physical labour; it was a symphony of skills, a testament to shared vision." He paused, his eyes twinkling with intellectual fervour. "History isn't merely a collection of dates and names; it's a complex tapestry woven with the threads of human collaboration."

"What then?" Oliver challenged, his impatience a stark contrast to Finch's contemplative nature. "We understand the theory, Professor. But how do we apply it? How do we start this grand cooperative endeavour to find Valen?" He gestured around the dimly lit exhibit, filled with dusty relics and cryptic inscriptions, the very air thick with unanswered questions.

"By acknowledging each person's uniqueness," Ellie proclaimed, stepping forward with a confident glint in her eyes. "We each bring something different to the table. Oliver's sharp eye for detail, Professor Finch's encyclopaedic knowledge, my understanding of ancient languages... Together, we can decipher the artefacts and their stories. Each inscription translated, each symbol recognised a cohesive unit."

With newfound motivation, fuelled by Ellie's inspiring words and the professor's philosophical musings, the group fanned out across the exhibit. Oliver meticulously scanned the walls for anomalies, his fingers tracing the edges of aged reliefs. Ellie meticulously photographed inscriptions, already mentally translating them into modern languages. Finch, armed with his seemingly endless reservoir of historical context, moved slowly, his gaze constantly shifting, connecting disparate elements of the exhibit like dots on a map. Huckleberry , a creature of myth and legend, perched nearby on a towering display case, seeing keenly the renewed activity. His sharp, golden eyes seemed to sense the mounting tension but also something more: the nascent power of unity stirring within the group, a power that promised to unlock the secrets they looked for and bring them closer to Valen. The air crackled with anticipation, the weight of history pressing down on them, urging them forward.

"It starts with trust," Huckleberry croaked, his voice gravelly like ancient stone grinding against ancient stone. "Let your hearts whisper to each other. Shed the doubt and suspicion that cling to you like shadows. Only then will the whispers of the past guide your steps, for the path ahead is shrouded in deceit and echoes of forgotten betrayals." The air hung thick with the weight of his words, each syllable a stark warning.

The group exchanged glances, a silent conversation passing between them. Fear mingled with resolve in their eyes. An invisible thread tethered them, an unspoken agreement bound by magic and destiny, woven tighter by the palpable danger they faced. With Ellie leading the charge, her gaze sharp and determined, they efficiently divided the tasks. Each member was assigned according to their innate strengths, a testament to Ellie's intuitive understanding of their abilities and the precariousness of their situation. Liam, with his knack for traps and disarming wards, took point, while Maya, the group's resident healer, stayed close behind, ready to mend any wounds, physical or magical.

Ellie and Professor Finch, the esteemed and eternally curious historian, approached the majestic sarcophagus. It stood as a silent sentinel, dominating the chamber with its sheer size and imposing presence. Adorned with cryptic inscriptions that seemed to writhe in the flickering torchlight, it whispered tales of a forgotten civilisation. "We must translate these," Ellie said, her voice low and reverent. "Time and again, artefacts like this have embedded clues, secrets waiting patiently for the right mind, the right moment to unlock them." She ran a gloved hand across the cold, smooth surface, feeling the weight of history beneath her fingertips.

Professor Finch nodded, his brow furrowed in concentration. He crossed his arms, a habitual gesture when confronted with a particularly intriguing puzzle and scrutinised the carvings with the intensity of a hawk eyeing its prey. "Look here," he gestured with a trembling finger to a section of the inscription, "there's a distinct pattern. Each symbol corresponds to a word, perhaps even a sound. It's a phonetic puzzle, a complex linguistic riddle designed to protect the secrets within. If we can decipher this, we'll have taken the first step towards unlocking the secrets of the sarcophagus and perhaps the secrets of our destiny." He squinted, pulling a magnifying glass from his worn leather satchel. "The question is, what language, what era, holds the key?" His muttered musings filled the chamber, a counterpoint to the oppressive silence of the sarcophagus, a race between knowledge and the ticking clock of their quest.

Meanwhile, Azrael prowled steadily along the museum's perimeter, his powerful and commanding presence radiating a sense of both reassurance and strength that Oliver found deeply comforting and empowering. The giant cat's piercing eyes met Oliver's with a quiet intensity, as if silently urging him to embrace the moment fully. "You have a brave heart, guard," Azrael said in a low, gravelly voice that echoed slightly in the cavernous hall. "Are you willing to trust in this unity we are forging together?"

Oliver's eyes widened, and a spark of understanding ignited within him. The weight of responsibility balanced with a newfound hope. "Yes!" he exclaimed, his voice steady and fervent as the realisation slowly took root inside him. "We're stronger together." The conviction in his declaration seemed to ripple through the room.

Meanwhile, Finn, ever the restless and affectionate messenger, darted energetically around the room. With a quick scamper, he reached Lady Arabella, who stood gracefully by a glittering display of rare and ancient artefacts, her expression thoughtful and serene amid the precious relics. "Lady Arabella", Finn asked eagerly, his eyes bright with curiosity, "do you remember any stories that resonate with this unity we're discussing?"

Lady Arabella smiled gently, her gaze travelling over the intricate carvings and faded manuscripts encased behind glass. "The tales of heroism that I have studied through these artefacts often remind us that courage alone is not enough; it is made exponentially stronger through camaraderie," she mused, her voice soft yet rich with wisdom. "Unity transforms mere individuals into a force so formidable; it is capable of challenging the very passage of time itself." Her words hung in the air like a solemn vow.

As the myriad conversations and exchanges of ideas blended harmoniously, the museum seemed to pulse with a renewed energy, the ancient walls reverberating with the spirit of collaboration and hope. During this vibrant atmosphere, Ellie's hand brushed gently against a delicate piece of parchment lying beside a grand sarcophagus. The parchment bore detailed illustrations and writings describing past alliances forged in epochs long forgotten – forgotten alliances that had, through unity and sacrifice, changed the course of history forever.

"Look!" Elara exclaimed, her voice rising an octave with undisguised excitement. She held aloft a brittle, leather-bound tome, its pages yellowed and cracking with age. "I've discovered a reference to 'The Covenant of Kings' within these ancient texts! It speaks of a legendary alliance. Stories reflect how these leaders, once disparate and warring, united their empires not through conquest but through shared knowledge and mutual respect. Imagine, a union forged in understanding! "

A sudden flutter of wings drew her attention skyward. Huckleberry, her raven companion, wheeled in a wide arc, diving closer with an almost theatrical flair. He perched on a nearby branch, his obsidian eyes gleaming with both curiosity and a hint of foreboding. "The Covenant of Kings, how intriguing indeed! The halls of forgotten lore whispered a tale. But beware, seeker, not all unity is born out of harmony. Some speak of betrayal wrapped in silk, of agreements made in darkness, and bonds broken by ambition." He ruffled his feathers, a low croak escaping his beak. "Remember, the path to power is often paved with deception."

Ellie, the group's pragmatic strategist, turned to the others, her brow furrowed with concern. The first excitement had faded, replaced by a thoughtful unease. "Unity does not solely mean agreement or blind obedience. It transcends mere conformity. It's learning to embrace differences, to find common ground and work together despite disagreements. If the Covenant truly crumbled, we need to understand why."

Finn, ever the clever fox and master of analogies, chimed in, his eyes twinkling with inspiration. "I like to think of it like a puzzle box! Each piece is unique, with bizarre shapes and strange markings. The pieces scarcely align with each other; they may even appear to clash initially. last; maybe even seems to clash at first glance. But together, with careful consideration and a bit of patience, they create a vivid picture, a complete and compelling whole." He grinned, his silver earring catching the light. "The trick is to recognise the value of each individual piece, even the ones that seem to be missing."

"Exactly!" Professor Finch exclaimed, his spectacles perched precariously on his nose. He waved his hand with theatrical flair, as if to conjure forth the spirits of past artisans and diplomats. "This is precisely what we need, my young adventurers! This comprehension of unity and interconnectedness is crucial! unity, of interconnectedness! Perhaps these fragments of the Covenant, these lost pieces of history, can shed light on Valen's compass. Each artefact we uncover, each inscription we decipher, is not just a relic of the past but a story, a lesson on working as one! Let us learn from the triumphs and failures of those who came before us, lest we repeat their mistakes!" He adjusted his tie, a gleam of renewed purpose shining in his eyes. "The fate of the world, quite literally, may depend on it!"

With their plans becoming clearer, Ellie and the group directed their full attention to the ancient wall before them, meticulously analysing the intricate shapes and graceful curves etched into the weathered stone. Each carving seemed to whisper secrets of a long-forgotten tale, and together, they worked in perfect harmony, recalling legends and piecing together the story woven into each delicate letter. The atmosphere was thick with anticipation as they connected one fragment of the narrative to the next, bringing life to the silent inscriptions.

Suddenly, a low rumble shook the chamber, causing dust to fall gently from the ceiling. The massive sarcophagus positioned at the centre of the cavernous exhibit began to emit an eerie, pulsating glow. Its light spilled outward, casting long shadows and illuminating the room with a mysterious aura. A deep, resonant voice echoed from the sarcophagus, vibrating through the very air they breathed. "Only those who unite in passion and purpose shall unveil the path to their destiny. Seek the hidden keys among your strengths!" it intoned, a message both commanding and enigmatic.

Leaning closer to one another, Ellie and her companions felt a surge of buzzing energy coursing through their veins, stirring a profound sense of connection and purpose. They had just awakened something ancient and powerful. "We must think carefully about what makes each of us unique," Ellie urged, her eyes shining with determination. "What does each of you bring to the table? This is the key to moving forward."

"I possess wisdom and history," Lady Arabella announced confidently, her voice calm and steady. Her knowledge of the past promised insight into the mysteries ahead.

"I've got speed and stealth!" Finn chirped excitedly, darting in playful circles around the group. His quick reflexes and stealthy nature could prove invaluable.

"And I have courage," Oliver declared, his voice growing firmer with every word. "I stand ready to defend us all, no matter what challenges we face."

Together, they formed a circle of distinct talents, each strength a necessary key to unlocking the path destined for them. The carvings seemed to glow faintly in response, as if acknowledging the truth in the voice's words, beckoning them onwards into the unknown.

Suddenly, the walls began to shimmer, the ancient stone seeming to liquefy as hidden glyphs materialised, intricate patterns and symbols glowing with an inner light. These weren't static etchings; they detached themselves from the walls, cascading softly into the air like vibrant autumn leaves caught in an ethereal breeze. "Together, combine your strengths!" Azrael urged, his voice a resonant echo that vibrated through the chamber. He stood tall, his fierce spirit igniting a spark within each of them, a burning determination to overcome the challenges ahead.

With their newfound resolve, born from Azrael's encouragement and their shared peril, Ellie stepped forward, her voice ringing with confidence. "If you trust yourselves, then trust each other! Let us combine our thoughts, strengths, and aspirations! Let them merge into a single, powerful force!" Her outstretched hand beckoned them closer.

As they held hands in a circle, the faint glow surrounding them intensified, bathing the chamber in a warm, otherworldly radiance. The air became thick with anticipation, crackling with unseen energy. From seemingly nowhere, the booming, wise voices of Alfonso the Serpent resonated, ancient and profound. "Historically, bonds forged together held the fabric of unity in fit for the challenge of destiny. The tapestry of fate is woven with threads of cooperation and shared purpose." The Serpent's words seemed to solidify their commitment, reinforcing the importance of their alliance.

The ancient artefacts surrounding them responded to their combined energy, their silent stories now mingling in a symphony of light and power. Each artefact pulsed with its own unique energy signature, contributing to a beautiful tapestry woven from their voices, their histories, and their hopes. As the final surge of energy coalesced, focused and pure, a magnificent key slowly revealed itself within the outline of the glowing sarcophagus. It shimmered with an almost unbearable light, intricately crafted and radiating a palpable sense of power.

"Look!" Oliver pointed, his voice filled with awe and disbelief. "We've unlocked it!" The impossible had happened. Their combined efforts, their shared belief, had triggered something extraordinary.

The group's collective heartbeat echoed within the chamber, a rhythmic pulse that resonated with the weight of history. They stood on the precipice of discovery, united by a shared purpose and a powerful bond. The world outside remained oblivious to the momentous events unfolding within the ancient crypt, while within, they had created a bond that resonated through time, a testament to the power of unity and shared belief. The weight of centuries, the secrets held within the sarcophagus, now rested on their combined strength. The journey had just begun.

"Together", Ellie whispered, her voice thick with emotion, blinking back tears of joy that threatened to spill down her cheeks, "we truly can conquer anything." The weight of their journey, the perilous traps they'd navigated, and the riddles they'd solved together all culminated in this single, profound realisation. Realisation

As their fingers brushed against the cool, ethereal key, bathed in the soft glow emanating from within the hidden chamber, a rare and profound understanding washed over them. The ancient artefacts, scattered throughout the dusty halls of the museum, may have held forgotten secrets and cryptic clues, but it was their unity, their unwavering support for one another, that truly unlocked the museum's true potential, revealing more than just hidden rooms but the depths of their own capabilities.

In that moment, standing on the precipice of the unknown, nothing else seemed to matter. The whispers of doubt, the anxieties that had plagued them throughout their quest, faded into insignificance. They were no longer just individuals lost in a bewildering mystery, scrambling for clues in the dark. They were an unbreakable team, forged in the crucible of shared experience, bound by a silent understanding, and ready to face whatever challenges lay ahead, united not just by a common goal

ECHOES OF THE PAST

As Ellie, Professor Finch, and Oliver cautiously moved deeper into the museum's shadowy, maze-like hallways, the museum itself remained still and silent, surrounded by an aura of profound mystique. Under the dim, flickering lights, the vibrant, faded murals that had been carefully painted onto the ancient stone walls flickered eerily, casting ghostly and ethereal images of long-forgotten yesteryears across the polished floors. The museum had a variety of artefacts, each of which had its own distinct narrative, and each exhibit revealed hidden histories and secrets from bygone eras. The very air around them seemed to hum and vibrate with untold histories, as if the past itself were alive and breathing in the shadows. The visitor was given the impression that the cavernous chambers were filled with the soft echo of their footsteps.

An overwhelming surge of excitement coursed through Ellie's veins as they made their way steadily towards a magnificent grand chamber, which was a vast room that was adorned with Egyptian relics that had been meticulously arranged. Earlier that day, the mysterious figure known as Azrael the Lion had unearthed an ancient scroll that was fragile and fragile. She urged with determination, "We need to carefully align the details of what we already know about these artefacts," while her hands were tightly clutching an ancient scroll that was brittle. At the same time that her heart was beating faster at the thrilling thought of honouring the past and preserving its legacy through their upcoming rescue mission, her unending curiosity about history and its secrets served as the fuel that kept her unwavering motivation to piece together the intricate puzzle that was in front of them.

"What happened to the echoes that are still sounding? As he gently adjusted his round spectacles that were perched on the bridge of his nose, Professor Finch mused aloud, his voice deep and mindful as he did so. There are powerful impressions that were left behind by those who lived and breathed in their respective eras, and each statue and relic carries with them the memories of their respective eras. We must be mindful to respect and understand their stories if we are to genuinely appreciate their significance." His hands gestured animatedly, as though the very intricate and flowing tale of time itself were pouring forth through him, weaving an invisible thread of connection between the present moment and the distant past they looked to uncover.

Oliver scratched his head; his brow furrowed in concentration as he entertained his thoughts. Do you hear echoes of the past? To be more specific, what does that mean? To begin with, where do we even begin? He was more concerned with the immediate and tangible aspects of history than he was with the more abstract concepts of time because of his stubbornness, which often got in the way of the more significant themes of history. Battles and dates were things that he was able to understand, but the subtle currents of influence and the reverberations of events that had occurred in the past were often beyond his comprehension.

Nevertheless, he had a kind heart and an even better sense of loyalty than ever before. Even if he didn't fully understand the task at hand, he kept an unfaltering dedication to his friends and to the task at hand. He was a fiercely dedicated individual.

He wouldn't abandon them, even if he had to grapple with the tough concept of "echoes of the past". He would would not give up on them altogether.

A captivating sound filled the room before anyone could respond to it. It weaved its way through the silence like a tangible force, drawing everybody in with an allure that was impossible to resist. A low hum, a kind of melodic vibration that seemed to emanate not only from Luci, but from the very fabric of the ancient chamber, was the sound that was heard. As Luci herself gracefully glided through the air, her scales caught the dim light in mesmerising patterns, and the sound pulsed, shifting and subtly changing. There was a subtle change in the sound. It was a sound that reverberated deep within their bones, stirring something that had been forgotten as well as something that was fundamental.

Fear not, you courageous individuals. The past ever lingers," Luci began, her voice wrapping around them like a silken thread, smooth and hypnotic. It was a voice that held the weight of centuries, a voice that spoke not just of knowledge but of experience. "To decode the echoes that resonate here, we need to listen not only with our ears but also with our hearts." She coiled herself around a timeworn pedestal, its surface etched with symbols that seemed to shift and writhe in the flickering torchlight. The relentless march of time has reshaped the very landscape, and these artefacts have seen the rise and fall of eras, the disintegration of empires, and the reconstruction of the landscape itself.

They hold the keys, if you can but find the right lock." Her gaze, ancient and knowing, swept over each of them, assessing their willingness to embrace the intangible, their ability to feel the echoes that resonated around them. The challenge was laid bare: could they truly hear the whispers of history?

Without letting her enthusiasm dampen her enthusiasm, Ellie asked, "Are you able to assist us in deciphering those memories?"

"But first, you must unlock your minds to the history that surrounds you. Reach out, touch the artefacts, and let them talk," Luci replied, her eyes shimmering like emeralds. "In due time," she said. "But first..."

Ellie stepped forward, drawn ineluctably towards the statue of Anubis. It stood sentinel in the dim room, a silent guardian of ages past. The dark stone, polished smooth by countless years and reverent hands, shimmered under the limited light filtering from above. Anubis, the ancient Egyptian god of the afterlife, with his jackal head and knowing gaze, seemed to emanate an almost palpable aura of power. Intrigued and emboldened by a sudden surge of curiosity, Ellie placed her hand upon the cool, unyielding surface.

The moment her skin met the stone, a rush of energy surged through her, a jolt that resonated deep within her bones. Her vision blurred, the edges of the room dissolving into swirling colours, and then, in a dizzying plunge, she was transported. The sterile environment of the museum vanished, replaced by the claustrophobic, yet opulent, reality of an ancient Egyptian tomb. Gilding gleamed under the flickering light of unseen torches. Hieroglyphs, vibrant with colour despite the passage of millennia, danced across the walls, telling stories of pharaohs and gods. The air was thick with the scent of myrrh and dust, a potent blend that spoke of forgotten rituals and buried secrets. Outside, she could almost feel the oppressive weight of the desert, the endless expanse of sand pressing against

Flashes erupted within her mind – bustling markets overflowing with exotic goods, the pungent aroma of spices and dates hanging heavy in the air; winding alleys, their shadows concealing secrets and whispered deals. The sounds of a long-vanished civilisation filled her senses – the rhythmic clang of a blacksmith's hammer, the lilting music of a flute, the raucous cries of vendors hawking their wares. Then, amidst the sensory overload, came the whispers - soft, ethereal, and yet undeniably present. The consequences of every decision are felt throughout the ages, deciding the course of events for those who come after.

Abruptly, she gasped, the breath catching in her throat. The visions, the sounds, the sensations, all vanished as quickly as they had appeared. She stumbled back, her hand flying from the statue as if burned. The sterile reality of the museum slammed back into focus, the hum of the ventilation system a stark contrast to the vibrant chaos she had just experienced. Disoriented and shaken, she stared at the statue of Anubis, no longer merely an artefact behind glass, but a conduit to a world she never knew existed. "It spoke to me! A tremor of fear could be heard in her voice as she exclaimed, "The artefact... it shared a vision of the past!" Her voice was a mixture of awe and excitement. A vision...and a warning" The implications of what she had experienced, the weight of the choice that she was being asked to make in some way, settled upon her, making her feel heavy and uneasy. Her journey had just made its beginning.

The others, a tight-knit group of archaeology students and research assistants, clustered around Eleanor, their faces a mixture of awe and excited anticipation. The air practically crackled with unanswered questions; questions they hoped the enigmatic statue held the keys to. They had seen Eleanor's journey, the fleeting vision of a bustling Roman marketplace, the sensation of cobblestones beneath her feet, and it had ignited within them a fervent desire for their own taste of history.

Professor Finch, the acknowledged leader of their expedition and a man usually radiating calm academic composure, now seemed visibly shaken, his hands trembling not with fear, but with a profound and almost childlike anticipation. He approached the rough-hewn statue with a solemn reverence, a lifetime of research culminating in this single, improbable moment. As his fingers hesitantly brushed against the cool, weathered stone, the ambiance in the chamber shifted once more. The flickering torchlight seemed to dim, replaced by an inner illumination.

With patient reverence, almost a meditative stillness, Professor Finch allowed himself to be drawn into the artefact's embrace. He wasn't merely seeing, but feeling an ancestral echo, a whisper from a forgotten past. He saw sprawling sandstone temples bathed in the golden light of dawn, and then again silhouetted against the fiery hues of dusk. He heard, not with his ears, but with his very being, the sonorous chants of priests, their voices rising and falling in ancient rhythms. He could almost feel the weight of history pressing gently upon him, a comforting pressure that spoke of countless lives lived, loves lost, and empires built and crumbled. It was overwhelming, yet strangely grounding, revealing the intricate tapestry of time and the immeasurable value of the lives it cradled. The

Drawing a shaky breath, he stepped back from the statue, his eyes shining with newfound understanding. "Every artefact contains its legacy," he declared, his voice resonating with an enthusiasm that belied his age. "Each object, no matter how humble, holds within it echoes of the people who created it, used it, and cherished it. To understand the present, to navigate the complexities of our own world, we must embrace what has come before. We must learn from the successes and failures of those who walked this earth before us."

Oliver, the most pragmatic of the group, was still struggling to reconcile the rational world he knew with the extraordinary nature of the evening. The air thrummed with the implications of what they had all witnessed. Shaking his head slightly, as if to clear the lingering fog of the experience, he looked at Professor Finch, his brow furrowed in concentration. "Right then!" he exclaimed, his Yorkshire accent suddenly more pronounced. "This is all... well, rather remarkable. But if we're going to thoroughly investigate this thing, what's the plan, Professor? What do we do now?"

There was a rustle that reverberated from the shadows, a sound that resembled the sound of dried leaves skittering across cobblestones. From behind a forgotten exhibit that displayed dusty relics from a bygone era, Finn appeared. He was not a literal fox, of course, but rather a young man with a shock of fiery red hair and eyes that were as bright and alert as any woodland creature. His movements were quick and nimble, and he had a perpetual grin on his lips. "Did someone say they need help?" he asked. I am aware of the point at which the reverberations of the past merge! He chirped in a playful manner while darting between the adventurers with boundless energy. He twirled around Ellie's legs and gave Professor Finch's tweed jacket a playful tug, radiating an infectious enthusiasm at the same time.

It is unclear what you mean, Finn. She knew Finn; he was a local historian who was obsessed with the museum and its secrets, and he was known for his cryptic pronouncements. " Ellie asked, her voice a mixture of natural curiosity and a hint of exasperation.

As you are aware, the artefacts are all connected to one another. Finn gestured animatedly, his hands sketching invisible patterns in the air. "Each object holds a fragment of history, a whisper of the past," he said. "They are like pieces of a grand tapestry over the course of time." However, when they are brought together, they produce something that is...more. Hidden beneath the very foundations of this museum is a chamber that is tucked away, and it is this chamber that handles sealing the ultimate echo, which is the core of the mystery surrounding this museum. The point at which all those threads come together is here.

A chamber that is concealed? "That would be where the most profound echoes reside! " Professor Finch's eyes widened behind his spectacles as he adjusted them by placing them on his nose. He temporarily abandoned his usual air of scholarly detachment. A location where in addition to being remembered, the past is also experienced. Is there a way for us to get access to it? Furthermore, what kinds of safeguards might be in place? The possibility of unlocking the museum's deepest secrets and, by extension, a more profound understanding of history itself was a powerful lure. The hidden chamber, if it truly existed, promised untold revelations. His mind was already racing, picturing the historical significance of such a discovery. The possibility of unlocking the museum's biggest secrets was a powerful lure.

It was impossible to have the excitement that was glimmering in Finn's eyes. "Yes! I can also take you there if you want! "He exclaimed, his gaze bouncing between them, each face a mirror reflecting his own eagerness. The prospect of a new adventure was clearly irresistible to him." But "he cautioned, a hint of mystery entering his voice," it isn't accessible by normal means. This location is guarded and concealed from view. Before I can steer you in the right direction, you must first prove that you are deserving of discovery.

"The foothold of the forgotten can lead us there," she murmured, her eyes holding a knowing glint, "but we must earn our way with wit." Luci appeared to float closer with an ethereal grace, her voice a soft chime in the tense atmosphere. "But we must earn our way with knowledge." She took a moment to pause and allow her words to sink in before continuing, "The path is barred not by brute force, but by intellect." To unlock the door, we need to solve a riddle. We will be guided by history, with echoes of the past clinging to the air; however, this will only exist if we are willing to listen attentively and keep our minds open.

Oliver kept his watchful stance, as if daring the shadows that were gripping the corners of the room to make a move. He asked, "What kind of a riddle are we talking about?" Oliver's stance suggested that he was in a constant state of alertness. "Some dusty old rhyme? " He enquired, keeping his voice carefully measured and betraying a cautious curiosity. Or perhaps something... more complicated? "

Luci coiled back slightly, creating an impression of offering, of invitation to delve deeper into the unknown. "A riddle tied to the very essence of the museum itself," she replied, her voice resonating with an almost musical quality. "A question woven into the fabric of this place, its history, it's very soul. As she focused her gaze on them, she urged them to pay close attention to what was being said. "The echoes will lead you." "The answer is waiting to be heard within these walls, and it reverberates throughout them."

With a renewed sense of resolve, Ellie took another step forward, her first reluctance now replaced with determination. "Let's hear it, then," she said, her voice clear and unwavering, "Let the echoes speak." The challenge hung in the air, a tangible thing like a tangible thing.

As if responding to her unspoken encouragement, the ancient stones of the chamber began to resonate with a soft, rhythmic pattern. It was a subtle vibration at first, barely perceptible, but it quickly intensified, building into a deep, sonorous pulse. The sound was akin to a heartbeat, vast and ancient, echoing through time immemorial. The air itself seemed to shimmer and thicken, charged with an otherworldly energy. Then, an ethereal voice, disembodied and resonant, rose from the very depths o

"Time binds us like threads, tangible yet aloof. In the silence of light, a fading tune sings. Reveal what was lost, for wisdom it brings," the proverb goes. "In order to uncover what is hidden, you must first possess the truth."

The last syllable of the riddle dissolved into the echoing pulse, leaving a palpable tension in its wake. Professor Finch, his brow furrowed in concentration, murmured thoughtfully, tapping his chin with a bony finger. His eyes, usually bright with academic curiosity, were now clouded with a mixture of perplexity and excitement. "Threads, light, and silence," he repeated, almost to himself. "Threads, symbolising connection, perhaps? Light, not as illumination, but... a specific type of light? And the silence... the absence of something, or the presence of something unheard? What could that possibly mean? This isn't merely a puzzle; it's a key. But to what?"

Oliver scratched his head; his brow furrowed in confusion. "How does a fading tune fit into all this? We're talking about stolen artefacts, a shadowy organisation, and potentially a curse. What's a half-forgotten melody got to do with any of it?" He gestured around the hushed gallery, the weight of the museum's secrets pressing down on him.

Ellie closed her eyes, a faint crease appearing between her eyebrows. She focused, trying to sift through the impressions swirling within her, the echoes of the past clinging to the present. "Perhaps it's not about what we see, but what we don't see," she pondered, her voice soft, almost a whisper. "The answers are often hidden in plain sight, obscured by time. We're so focused on the obvious clues that we're missing something fundamental."

From her pedestal nearby, seemingly brought to life by the intensity of the moment, Lady Arabella's voice rose like an elegant melody. "Think of the females who shaped the museum, young ones. Their contributions, their struggles, their very existence, are interwoven with the grand narrative. They are a part of the tapestry too. Their stories offer light in the shadows, illuminating the whispers around us." A knowing smile played on her sculpted lips.

Ellie exclaimed, "Of course!" as her eyes suddenly opened, a breakthrough of clarity breaking through the cloud of confusion. "We must seek the stories of those who came before us—the women who contributed to the history preserved here, the women whose lives breathed life into these very halls! Their voices, which are often silenced, might hold the key to understanding the present!"

Luci nodded, her sinuous body moving effortlessly through the room, a silent observer until now. "You are well on your way, Ellie. Recall the statue of the nobleperson in the hall of antiquities. She embodies the tales of feminine strength in times lost, tales of resilience and influence that history often overlooks. Look closer, Ellie, listen harder. The answers are etched into the past, waiting to be discovered."

We must find her and ask her for guidance! She might know exactly how to solve the riddle! Oliver exclaimed, "Right!" as he suddenly found himself experiencing excitement. The adrenaline of the chase, combined with the tantalising prospect of finally cracking the riddle, had him buzzing with excitement.

He could almost feel their presence, their wisdom, resonating within the very walls of the museum as they sped through the winding paths of the museum, guided by Finn's spirited leaps and boundless energy. The whispers continued to echo around them, painting tales of ancient women who had left their indelible marks upon history. Their names, like echoes in the vast halls, seemed to urge them onwards. These women were pioneering scientists, fearless explorers, and visionary artists. Each whisper felt like a breadcrumb, bringing them closer to their primary aim.

They arrived at a grand chamber, the statues within it bathed in the ethereal, shimmering light of the full moon filtering through tall, arched windows. The moonlight danced across the polished marble floors, highlighting the intricate details of each sculpture. At the centre, bathed in the moon's silvery glow, Lady Arabella stood regal and poised as ever, her bronze figure illuminated with an almost otherworldly radiance. Her expression remained serene and wise, her eyes seemingly holding centuries of knowledge.

"Courageous visitors, what is it you seek?" She asked, her voice a melodic chime that resonated through the silent chamber. It wasn't a booming, authoritarian pronouncement, but a gentle invitation, filled with ancient understanding and a hint of curiosity. The sound sent a shiver down Oliver's spine, a mixture of awe and anticipation. He knew, with absolute certainty, that they had come to the right place.

Her eyes were wide and hopeful as she looked at the nobleperson in front of them. "We believe the answers we seek are hidden within these very walls, within the forgotten stories," Ellie replied with a voice that reverberated slightly within the ancient stone hall. "We are searching for the secrets of the echoes of the past," she said emphatically. Could you kindly direct us? "

"Indeed," the nobleperson said, her voice a low, resonant hum that seemed to emanate from the very stones beneath their feet. Her eyes, the colour of aged amber, glinted with an age-old understanding that transcended mere years. Deep wrinkles etched around them told of countless secrets saw and wisdom hard-earned. "Listen well—the threads that bind us, the very fabric of this world, are interwoven with the choices made by those who came before. Every deed and every choice have repercussions that are felt throughout time. Finding the voices that have been lost, the whispers that have been silenced by time and circumstance, is the first step in finding what it is that you are looking for. The silence will not reveal its secrets until that time has passed, and the echoes will become loud enough to understand.

They understood that the tapestry of history was not woven solely with the threads of kings and conquerors, but also, and perhaps more significantly, through the seemingly insignificant lives of ordinary people, particularly those women whose whispers lingered in silence, urging them to remember, to understand, and to learn. These were the ones who were cast aside, their contributions were minimised, and their voices were deliberately suppressed. The riddle took shape in the minds of the adventurers, and it looked like a complex puzzle that needed careful thought and a sensitive ear.

It became a shared experience, a collaborative effort woven with empathy and respect, as they honoured the legacy of those women. As they spoke, as they breathed life back into those forgotten stories, they began to feel a sense of purpose. They spoke of the nameless healers who knew the secrets of the earth, the artists whose creations were attributed to their male counterparts, and the mothers who shaped generations from behind the scenes. They pieced together fragments of lives that had been lost for a long time. They spoke of the artists whose creations were attributed to their male counterparts. They spoke of the artists whose creations were attributed to their male counterparts. They spoke of the mothers who shaped generations from behind the scenes. They pieced together fragments of lives that had been lost for a long time. Like archaeologists carefully reconstructing a shattered vase.

As they spoke, the ancient chamber seemed to pulse alive, a palpable energy thrumming in the very stones. Echoes, not just of their voices but of countless others before them, reverberated through the air, harmonising with their present conversation. It was as if the spirits of history, the forgotten architects and long-gone inhabitants of this place, were stirring, their flames of hidden voices flickering and guiding them towards the truth. With every whispered theory, every shared piece of knowledge, the complex riddle began to unravel, its intricate threads loosening until they stumbled upon the final, crucial piece, a key that resonated with the chamber's very core.

Ellie's heart raced, a frantic drum against her ribs, as she articulated the last fragment of the puzzle. Her voice, though trembling with excitement, rang clear and true: "In the silence of light lies the truth of those who faded into stories. A fading tune may refer to the vibrations of the past, the residual echoes of their lives, reaching out to us now!"

Suddenly, a soft, ethereal glow bloomed from the centre of the chamber. It wasn't harsh or blinding, but rather a gentle, inviting luminescence. The light coalesced, swirling and intensifying until it formed a luminous circle on the ground. This radiant halo cast long, dancing shadows across the aged walls, finally settling and bathing a previously unnoticed section of the stone floor in its ethereal light. There, etched almost imperceptibly into the rock, a hidden seam revealed itself, marking the entrance to the fabled hidden chamber – the culmination of their quest.

"Congratulations, brave explorers," Lady Arabella declared proudly, her voice ringing with genuine admiration. "You've unlocked the secrets guarded by time itself! For generations, this knowledge has been locked away, protected by ancient enchantments and the very fabric of history. But you, with your courage and intellect, have proven worthy. You stand on the precipice of a journey unlike any other."

In unison, the explorers reached out, hands hovering momentarily before stepping into the shimmering circle of light. It pulsed with an energy that resonated deep within their souls, a tangible connection to the age's past. Their spirits, drawn together by this shared quest, felt intertwined with the echoes of the past – the triumphs and tragedies, the whispers of forgotten languages, the weight of untold stories. They knew, with a certainty that settled in their bones, that this was not the end, but merely the beginning. Every moment from now on would be a significant thread, carefully binding the grand tapestry of history with the fragile threads of their own lives.

The museum itself seemed to breathe around them, the ancient stones humming with unseen power. It wasn't just a building filled with artefacts anymore; it was a living portal, a gateway to infinite possibility. With a mix of trepidation and excitement, they ventured forward, eager to embrace the mysteries that awaited them. Faint whispers seemed to snake through the halls, secrets carried on the drafts of time, calling them ever deeper into the heart of the enchanted museum.

THE REAWAKENING

The clock had struck midnight, its final chime swallowed by the oppressive silence that had reigned moments before. Now, the grand hall of the museum pulsed with a low, resonant hum, a vibration that tickled the soles of Ellie 's feet and sent shivers up her spine. Dust motes, disturbed from their slumber, swirled in the beams of moonlight filtering through the arched windows, transforming the air into a swirling galaxy. Ethereal shadows danced upon the polished marble floor, stretching and contracting as if alive, mimicking figures long gone.

Ellie stood at the centre of it all, a lone sentinel in the silent dawn of something unknown. Her heart raced, a frantic drum against her ribs, as she felt the energy in the air shift, thickening like a gathering storm. Static prickled on her skin. The air crackled with anticipation. The museum, usually a silent mausoleum of history, had awakened, shaken from its slumber by the witching hour. And with it, the echoes of its enchantments, the whispers of forgotten rituals, the memories etched into the very stones, were stirring, ready to be unleashed. Fear mingled with a thrill of excitement, a sense of being on the precipice of something extraordinary, something dangerous, something magical. The night had just begun.

"Can you believe it? After all our painstaking research, it's really happening," Ellie whispered excitedly to Professor Finch, whose eyes sparkled with a mix of curiosity and mischief.

"Yes, yes! Just think about all the secrets waiting to be uncovered!" he replied, adjusting his spectacles with a flourish. "But we must tread carefully—we don't yet know the full extent of this... reawakening."

From behind a nearby display, Oliver, the museum guard, peered nervously, gripping his flashlight like a lifeline. His hands trembled slightly as he scanned the dimly lit hall, eyes darting from shadow to shadow. "Do you really think those things... those artefacts can actually come to life?" he stammered, voice barely above a whisper, as if speaking any louder might awaken something unseen. He glanced anxiously around, his instincts screaming that something could leap out at any moment from behind a corner or under a nearby exhibit.

Before anyone could gather their thoughts or muster a reply, a deep, resonant growl reverberated through the vast hall, shaking the dust from the ancient displays. From the shadows, a figure appeared with majestic grace—the magnificent lion statue, Azrael, now alive. His sleek, stone-like mane glistened mysteriously in the ghostly moonlight filtering through the high museum windows. With a powerful stretch, Azrael shook off the remnants of a long slumber, muscles rippling beneath his polished surface, eyes glowing with an ancient wisdom. "Fear not, brave souls!" he declared in a voice both commanding and reassuring. "The night has many tales to tell, and I am here to guide you through its secrets."

Ellie, her heart inflamed with the passion of a true historian, stepped forward eagerly, her eyes wide with a mixture of astonishment and reverence. The spark of adventure shone brightly in her gaze as she addressed Azrael. "Lead us, then! We must uncover the mysteries of this night before the dawn breaks," she urged, feeling the weight of history pressing upon them and the thrilling promise that the night's revelations held. Together, they moved deeper into the museum's twilight realm, ready to embark on a journey through time and legend, led by the living spirit of the lion guardian.

Azrael nodded solemnly, his golden eyes, pools of liquid light, gleaming with ancient knowledge that spanned millennia. Every flicker in their depths hinted at forgotten empires and cosmic battles. "But first," he declared, his voice a low rumble that seemed to vibrate through the very stones of the chamber, "we need our allies. Luci!" he called, his voice echoing in the vast, unseen heights above. Almost as if summoned by magic, the magnificent bronze serpent, Luci, twisted down from her pedestal, a sinuous cascade of polished metal. Moonlight caught on her scales, turning them into a shimmering wave of liquid gold, each side sparkling with arcane energy.

"Now that you're all awake," Luci said, her voice smooth as silk, a sound that both soothed and tantalized, "I can finally share the tales woven into these walls. Legends whispered by the wind and etched in the very fabric of this place." She surveyed them with intelligent, serpentine eyes. "Many riddles and puzzles await, guardians of both time and truth. They guard the path forward, ensuring only the worthy can tread it."

"Riddles?" Oliver echoed, his brow furrowed in a mixture of perplexity and burgeoning intrigue. The word conjured images of dusty scrolls and esoteric symbols. "What do you mean? Riddles like... like what?"

Luci chuckled, a low, melodious sound that resonated with the power held within her metallic form. "The past is alive here," she explained, her scales shimmering with a hint of mischief, as if she relished the challenges to come. "To unlock its secrets, to unravel the threads of history that have become tangled and frayed, you must solve the puzzles that bind these artefacts. Each riddle, each challenge, is a key. Only then can we restore balance before daybreak before the forces of chaos consume all that we hold dear." Her gaze intensified, a silent plea for understanding and cooperation. The weight of the world, it seemed, rested on their shoulders.

As the group meticulously gathered their belongings and prepared to embark on the perilous quest that lay ahead, Lady Arabella, the esteemed and majestic statue who had been motionless and silent for centuries, suddenly stirred from her deep, centuries-old slumber. Her once unyielding marble eyes seemed to gleam with ancient wisdom as she slowly appeared from her timeless repose. "Time is a fickle friend, dear ones," she intoned solemnly, her voice resonating with a mystical quality, echoing through the grand hall like the gentle, haunting sound of distant chimes carried on the wind. "But remember, wisdom often lies beneath the surface of a well-formed enigma," she cautioned, her words weaving an air of mystery and depth.

With Lady Arabella's profound blessing invigorating their spirits, Ellie, the insightful and brave leader of the group, stood shoulder to shoulder with the ever-curious Professor Finch, the keen-eyed Oliver, the fierce and protective Azrael, and the enigmatic Luci. They were soon joined by a darting figure who had just burst from the shadows — Finn, a clever and nimble companion known for his quick wit and mischievous charm. Finn offered a spirited wave with his bushy tail, his bright eyes twinkling mischievously as his playful antics ignited the atmosphere with a much-needed spark of light-hearted joy and camaraderie.

"Let the adventure begin!" Azrael proclaimed with unyielding enthusiasm. His powerful roar reverberated through the vast entrance hall, a sound so commanding that it seemed to awaken the very walls around them. It was a call summoning the forgotten artefacts, those silent witnesses of history resting in shadowed corners, to join their noble quest. Each step they took echoed louder than the last on the polished marble floors, the sound growing in intensity as their anticipation and determination thickened the charged air. Finally, it was time to step boldly into the heart of the museum — a place where time itself seemed to twist and twirl like dancers locked forever in an endless, mesmerising waltz, weaving past and present together in a delicate, eternal dance.

They first approached a towering exhibit, its form entirely concealed beneath layers of shimmering silk cloth. The draping gave it an air of mystery, piquing their curiosity. Luci, ever dramatic, gestured with a flourish of her wrist. "Unveil history, and let the secrets breathe," she suggested, her voice filled with theatrical anticipation. Ellie, always eager to take the lead, didn't hesitate. She grasped the edge of the cloth and with a swift, decisive pull, revealed what lay beneath.

A gasp escaped Ellie's lips. Before them stood a massive tapestry, easily twenty feet wide and ten feet high. The fabric was aged and rich with colour, depicting an elaborate scene from ancient Egypt. Pharaohs, gods, and priests moved across its woven surface in a vibrant, stylized tableau. Hieroglyphs sprawled across the fabric like a cryptic alphabet, each symbol more intricate and mesmerising than the last. Some formed recognizable shapes – birds, eyes, snakes – while others were abstract and utterly enigmatic. The sheer scale and detail of the tapestry were breathtaking.

Professor Finch's eyes, usually hidden behind thick spectacles, danced with undisguised delight. He practically vibrated with excitement, his hands clasped together in front of his chest. "This tapestry! It's... it's magnificent! I've only read about it in fragmented texts. It tells of a ritual – the Reawakening of the Guardians! It speaks of the time when the powerful protectors of Egypt will rise again. This... this is an omen!" He gestured wildly, his enthusiasm infectious.

Finn, ever the quick thinker and the most agile of the group, instinctively scampered up to the tapestry, his fingers tracing the woven figures. "What do you see, Professor? Can you read it? What does it say about these Guardians? Are they... dangerous?" He peered intently at the hieroglyphs, a mixture of excitement and apprehension in his young voice. The air crackled with anticipation, the weight of history pressing down on them as they waited for the Professor to decipher the secrets woven into the ancient threads.

"Yes! The inscriptions speak of a moment—when the guardians return, the heart of the museum awakens," Finch explained, his voice filled with wonder. "But it requires a key—a riddle at the heart of this tapestry."

Together, they deciphered the ancient language, their fingertips tracing the weathered symbols etched into the ancient tapestry. Each glyph was a piece of a complex puzzle, a fragment of a forgotten story whispering from the depths of history. With focused intensity, they pondered over each clue presented, their voices hushed as they wrestled with the words intertwined in the threads. "To awaken the heart, you must state that which is unspoken yet serves as a bridge"—the riddle beckoned, its cryptic nature both frustrating and exhilarating. Slowly, painstakingly, the pieces began to fit together, forming a mosaic of understanding.

Ellie furrowed her brow, her historian's instinct igniting with a surge of excitement. Years spent studying forgotten civilisations had sharpened her mind, honing her ability to see patterns where others saw only chaos. "The bridge... it must mean the connection between the artefact and the history it stands for! The unspoken truth they embody." She tapped a finger against her lips, her eyes darting around the room, taking in the silent witnesses to the past. "We need to articulate the essence of what these artefacts meant to the people who created them, what their purpose was, and how they shaped the world around them."

Drawing strength from her growing conviction, Ellie turned towards the imposing lion statue. The creature, carved from a dark, volcanic stone, exuded a powerful aura of guardianship and forgotten royalty. Taking a deep breath, steeling herself for the unknown, she began to speak, her voice echoing in the cavernous hall. "What once was lost shall return when spoken! We remember our past and embrace its lessons. We acknowledge the power and artistry embodied in this statue, the pride of the kingdom it protected. We see in its eyes the wisdom of ages, the strength of a forgotten people, and the enduring legacy of their reign!" Her voice resonated with passion and respect, a heartfelt tribute to the past.

A wave of energy rippled through the air. The tapestry shimmered, the ancient symbols glowing with an ethereal light. A soft, rhythmic pulse emanated from its centre, like a beating heart awakening from a long slumber. Suddenly, arrows of pure, incandescent light splintered off from the tapestry and shot through the room, illuminating the forgotten artefacts lining the museum walls. Each beam focused on a specific object – a tarnished crown, a broken sword, a weathered scroll – bathing it in a radiant glow, as if breathing life back into their silent stories. The air crackled with untold possibilities, hinting that the activation of the tapestry was only the beginning of something truly extraordinary. The museum, once a repository of static objects, now pulsed with the vibrant energy of the past, ready to yield its secrets.

Huckleberry, a creature of the night, peeled himself from the deepest shadows. His feathers, the colour of a moonless midnight sky, seemed to absorb the light around him as he hovered impatiently. "Quick! Speak the truth of the artefact standing before you! Only then will it aid your progression to Valen. Time is fleeting, and Valen awaits those worthies of his presence."

He gestured with a sharp, ebony wing towards the object of their scrutiny: a crystal orb, pulsating with a faint, internal light. It rested upon an intricately carved pedestal of a stone that seemed both ancient and otherworldly. Runes, barely visible to the naked eye, spiralled around its base. Oliver, drawn by some unseen force, stepped forward, his gaze fixed on the mesmerising sphere. "This orb... it looks as if it once held the memories of the ages." He reached out a tentative hand, pausing just before touching its smooth, cool surface. He felt a faint thrumming, a resonance that whispered of countless stories and forgotten epochs.

"Speak, guard!" Huckleberry insisted, his voice a low rasp that echoed through the chamber. A hint of impatience, barely concealed, edged his tone. He hovered expectantly; his piercing yellow eyes fixed on Oliver. A moment of silence hung heavy in the air, charged with an unspoken tension. Oliver closed his eyes, drawing in a deep breath, and when he opened them again, a newfound confidence radiated from his stance. He declared, his voice resonating with conviction, "You encase the knowledge of our world, forever binding history to the present. You are not merely a repository of the past, but a living link connecting all that was, is, and ever will be." He felt certain, somehow, that this was the truth, not just what Huckleberry wanted to hear, but the very essence of the artefact's existence.

With his words, the orb pulsed with a life of its own, the smooth surface rippling as if having a miniature sun. Then, it surged with blinding light, illuminating the cavernous room with an ethereal glow that painted the walls in fleeting colours. With a final, resonating crack, the orb burst open, not with an explosion, but with a gentle release. Cascading from its shattered form were countless colourful wisps of memories and visions, swirling and dancing in the air like captured fireflies. Each fragment thrummed with a silent energy, having a glimpse of time – the carefree laughter of long-forgotten children playing under the shade of ancient trees, the chilling echo of fierce battles fought on grounds now silent, and the comforting warmth of love shared through ages, etched on faces now dust.

In awe, Ellie reached out a hesitant hand, her fingers brushing against a drifting memory. It was like catching a soap bubble filled with starlight. The moment she grasped it, it enveloped her momentarily, pulling her into its ephemeral embrace. Scenes flashed before her eyes, rapid and vivid: the calloused hands of ancient craftsmen meticulously shaping clay into intricate vessels, the heartbreaking story of a lost love preserved in a tarnished locket, the hushed whispers of secrets exchanged within these very walls. She saw the hopes, the fears, and the dreams that streamed life into the museum's very foundation, turning stone and mortar into a living, breathing entity.

"Now do you, see?" Luci crooned, her voice soft and melodic, laced with a touch of triumph. "The museum doesn't just hold artefacts; it holds the essence of every soul who walked these lands, the echoes of their existence imprinted on every object. History isn't just dates and names; it intertwines with each artefact, breathes within the walls, and pulses through the very ground beneath our feet. Only by honouring these echoes, by respecting the stories they hold, can we truly understand our past and, therefore, travel forward with wisdom and purpose."

The orb, its ethereal glow having pulsed with newfound energy, now dimmed to a gentle hum, leaving a lingering warmth in its wake. As the adventurers turned their backs on its mesmerising display, refocusing on their mission, an exhilarating thrill surged within them, a potent cocktail of anticipation and understanding. The museum, once a silent mausoleum of artefacts, now vibrated with an unseen energy, alive with untold stories, whispers of the past, and experiences waiting to be unveiled. Each exhibit beckoned, promising not just historical facts but a deeper connection to the human narrative.

"Let's keep moving," Azrael urged, his voice tinged with a newfound urgency. He took the lead, guiding the group through the labyrinthine corridors towards the next exhibit. "Time waits for no one, and dawn approaches! We must unravel as many secrets as we can before the sun steals our magic."

As they traversed the maze of memory-laden rooms, each filled with the ghosts of creators and observers, Ellie felt invigorated. The air itself seemed to crackle with possibilities, with the echoes of laughter, tears, struggles, and triumphs. "With every riddle we solve, with every lock we unlock, we awaken not only the history behind each piece, but also an understanding of our place within it," she mused, her voice soft with wonder. She turned to the others, her eyes alight as they paused to admire the surrounding wonders - a tapestry woven with threads of forgotten empires, a sculpture that seemed to breathe with ancient life, a painting that captured a fleeting moment in time, preserved for eternity. The museum was no longer just a repository of the past; it was a mirror, reflecting their hopes, fears, and potential.

Finn darted eagerly to the edge of a display, where a delicate porcelain dancer stood poised in mid-motion, frozen forever in her graceful stance. "Look! I've found another puzzle! This one looks fun!" he exclaimed, his voice bubbling with excitement and curiosity.

Oliver inched forward cautiously, his eyes fixed on the fragile figure. Despite the earlier tension that had gripped them, now replaced by a growing bond forged through their shared quest, he felt the need to remind, "Just don't break it." His warning came gently, underscored by trust and the hope that their teamwork would guide their actions.

Ellie stepped closer, her gaze analytical as she studied the porcelain dancer, who seemed almost alive, shimmering faintly as if illusionary dance steps trailed her delicate form. "What does she need to awaken?" she asked softly, sensing that this puzzle was more than a mere trinket; it held a secret waiting to be unlocked.

Finn's eyes sparkled with mischief and insight as he replied, "A heart that knows the pulse of joy. We must seek the dance of life in our words!" His declaration was filled with thrilling possibility, suggesting that the puzzle's solution lay not in physical keys but in emotion and expression.

Lady Arabella, standing nearby, added her gentle wisdom in a soothing voice. "Express what you feel within. Let her know the rhythm of your soul." Her words wrapped around them like a comforting melody, encouraging them to reach deep inside and share their truest feelings.

With their hands clasped tightly together in eager anticipation, Ellie closed her eyes and began to hum a soft, enchanting melody. The tune reflected the joy of discovery—the exhilaration of unearthing hidden histories, the friendships forged in the heart of chaos, and the laughter shared late into the night. The room seemed to glow with warmth, as if the porcelain dancer was beginning to respond to the rhythm of their combined spirits, waiting patiently to awaken at last.

The porcelain dancer flickered, her delicate features catching the light, her elegance enhanced by Ellie's heartfelt offering. The simple flower, plucked from the museum's forgotten garden, seemed to be the key. Slowly, almost imperceptibly, she began to move. Her porcelain limbs, previously frozen in eternal stillness, now flowed with an ethereal grace, dancing gracefully along a melody that lingered in the air, a tune only she could truly embody. It was a melody woven from the dust of centuries, a symphony of forgotten stories.

Suddenly, the museum trembled, not violently, but with a deep, resonant hum. Echoes of joyous whispers, like the rustling of silk in a forgotten ballroom, filled the grand hall. The artefacts, previously silent witnesses to the passage of time, began to resonate with the song of the dancer. A golden amulet pulsed with light, a tattered tapestry shimmered with forgotten hues, and a warrior's shield vibrated with the echoes of ancient battles. Energy surged around them, electrifying the space with a palpable life, a revitalisation that chased away the dust and shadows. It was as if the museum itself was awakening from a long slumber.

Ellie's heart soared, filled with a hope she hadn't dared to express until now. She felt a profound connection to the space, to the history it held, and to the people who had touched these objects long ago. She recognised the weight of their mission, the importance of their shared joy. "By expressing our bonds and happiness, we not only revive the artefacts but bring ourselves closer to the heart of the museum!" she exclaimed, her voice ringing with excitement. This mission wasn't just about bringing objects to life; it was about understanding the human connection woven into their very existence. They were unlocking the stories trapped within, powered by the purest emotions.

But just as they revelled in their progress, basking in the warmth of the revitalised space, a chill swept through the room, extinguishing the vibrant light like a blown-out candle. Darkness coiled around them like a thickening fog, wrapping its tendrils around their ankles and creeping up their spines. The joyous whispers faded into a terrified silence, replaced by the oppressive weight of the unknown. The air grew heavy with uncertainty, thick with a sense of foreboding. The dancer faltered, her movements growing stiff and unnatural. The awakened artefacts dimmed, their newfound light sputtering as if struggling against an unseen force. Something was wrong, terribly wrong. The awakening had attracted unwanted attention.

From the shadows, a chill deeper than the stone walls themselves emanated as Valen materialised. He wasn't merely walking; he seemed to coalesce from the darkness, his presence a heavy weight in the ancient chamber. The hood of his midnight-blue cloak obscured his face, leaving only the faintest glint of ageless eyes visible. "You tread dangerous paths, seekers of echoes. Too much reawakening may disrupt the delicate balance of time," he warned, his voice a low, resonating hum that seemed to vibrate through the very foundations of the place. The words weren't just spoken; they were *felt*, a pressure against Ellie's mind, a reminder of the power he wielded.

Ellie's heart hammered against her ribs, a frantic drumbeat against the silence that followed Valen's pronouncement. She understood the gravity of their journey, and the words of the Timekeeper only amplified their risk. "We came to revive the stories, to protect them from oblivion. To remind the world of what was so that what will be is shaped with wisdom. We wish to preserve, not disrupt!" She stepped forward, her voice trembling only slightly, fuelled by a desperate conviction. Her eyes met the shadowed gaze of Valen, pleading for understanding. "The stories are fading, disappearing. If they are lost, what will become of us?"

Valen regarded them closely, his unseen eyes seeming to pierce through their very souls, gauging their resolve. He was a being of epochs, accustomed to seeing intentions laid bare. A faint, almost imperceptible sigh escaped him. "Demonstrate your intent, then. Show that unity guides your path, that your quest is born of true purpose, not reckless ambition. For the night is still young, and the threads of time are easily tangled. Prove to me that your actions will mend the tapestry, not tear it asunder, and I will consider your plea." A spectral hourglass appeared in his hand, the sands within swirling with a strange, ethereal light. "The clock is ticking, little seekers. Show me what you're capable of. "

A wave of determination, sharp and invigorating as a winter sea, washed over Ellie as she glanced at her companions. Weariness clung to them like dust motes in the dim light, but their eyes still held a spark of hope. "Together, we're stronger," she declared, her voice resonating with newfound conviction. She investigated each of their eyes, offering a silent promise of support. "We must solve these riddles as one. Not as individuals chasing personal glory, but as a single, interwoven force."

With renewed urgency fuelled by Ellie's words, the group pressed on, the intricate puzzles of the museum yielding slowly but surely to their collaborative efforts. The hushed halls resonated with laughter, punctuated by the murmur of shared stories and whispered theories. An unyielding bond, forged not just in the fires of adventure but also in the crucible of shared vulnerability and mutual respect, held them together. The echoes of the past, whispers of forgotten grandeur and untold narratives, guided them – a delicate dance between the shadows of what had been, the ghosts clinging to ancient tapestries and dusty relics, and the bright, vibrant tapestry of what could be, a future painted with understanding and respect for history.

As dawn began to sneak through the cracks of the monumental museum, painting the marble floors with streaks of pale gold, Ellie felt a profound shift within her. It wasn't just about solving puzzles or uncovering secrets. She realised that they were not merely reawakening artefacts, dusting off relics of a bygone era. They were resurrecting history, breathing life back into the silenced voices of the past. They were binding together the old and new, forging a connection between the present and the generations that came before, in a harmonious symphony that transcended time itself, promising a future richer and more meaningful for their efforts. The weight of the museum's history, once a burden, now felt like a responsibility, a sacred trust they were privileged to uphold.

The heart of the museum was not just a mere collection of treasured artefacts encased in glass; it pulsed with the flames of human connection, a vibrant tapestry woven from shared experiences – each thread evolved through laughter echoing in its grand halls, the sorrow felt through stories of bygone eras, and the thrilling adventures unearthed within its ancient texts. Ellie smiled, a genuine curve gracing her lips as she embraced the ephemeral magic of the moment, her eyes sparkling with the understanding that this night, this shared journey, would be one forever etched within their souls like an inscription on a timeless monument.

With the spirit of the museum reinvigorated, its ancient energy humming with renewed life, and the profound connection to their intertwined histories reinforced, the group propelled forward, their steps lighter, their resolve strengthened. They were no longer simply visitors, but participants in a living narrative, ready to face whatever challenges the remaining hours held as they relentlessly looked for the final, elusive mysteries hidden within the museum's labyrinthine corridors before the break of dawn.

And as the first tentative fingers of light broke through the museum's grand architecture, painting the cavernous halls in hues of gold and rose, the adventure culminated in a dawning realisation. It wasn't just about finding a lost artefact or deciphering an ancient riddle; it was about the profound and unbreakable bond of history, friendship, and knowledge that had irrevocably intertwined, forming a powerful and eternal reawakening. The museum wasn't just a repository of the past but a catalyst for the future, telling stories that would never fade, stories they themselves were now a part of stories carried within their hearts, ready to be shared and reimagined for generations to come. The night had gifted them not just answers but a legacy.

A NEW DAWN

The sound of distant artefacts clinking stirred under the dim, pre-dawn light as the first rays of daylight, which were pale and hesitant, passed through the grand arched windows of the Enchanted Museum. The museum was a place where the Enchanted Museum was found. As soon as the first rays of sunlight entered the museum, you could see dust particles being painted in the air. The noise was not a loud clang or a jarring crash; rather, it was a soft and melodic sound, like the sound of tiny chimes ringing in a temple that had been forgotten for a long time. A whisper of the secrets held within the vast and eclectic collection echoed, a symphony of ages past rousing from their slumber. Ellie rubbed the sleep from her eyes, the lingering traces of dreams clinging to her like cobwebs. Her blonde hair formed a tangled halo around her face, and she rubbed it away. A halo of her hair surrounded her face like a halo.

She felt a profound, underlying weariness that hinted at more than just a lack of sleep, as the weight of the night's adventures settled heavily on her shoulders. She felt a physical burden of unearthed mysteries and whispered promises, as well as a profound, underlying weariness. The sensation that she was having was that she was having a tough time keeping up with everything that had taken place. What appeared to be a revitalised energy seemed to be buzzing through the museum, which was now illuminated by an ethereal glow. It was almost as if the museum were silently inviting visitors to explore its enchanting and possibly dangerous depths even further.

Is this the final say in the matter?" She whispered, half to herself and half to the room that was completely empty. The events of the night rushed through her mind like a river that was flowing; each conundrum, each puzzle, and each moment brought her one step closer to solving the mysteries that were being held within the museum.

As he bustled through the doorway, Professor Finch stood with a map that had been meticulously folded and clutched tightly in his hand as if it had the secrets of the universe. His glasses were slightly crooked and perched precariously on his nose. "Oh! It's Ellie!" His voice was a mixture of boyish excitement and professorial urgency, which always preceded a new discovery that had the potential to be dangerous. "It has been my powerful desire to find you!" he exclaimed, his voice characterised by a mixture of these two emotions. It is my feeling that there is something else that needs to be found out, and I am aware of it! The presence of a consistent thread that is drawing us in the direction of... the opposite of what you expected!"

When Ellie turned to face him, she gave him a worn nod, and her face was etched with the weariness that was caused by their most recent adventure. It was clear that the events that had happened prior to Valen's awakening had taken their toll. So, Harold, what exactly do you mean? The timekeeper, Valen, has been reawakened, his influence has been exerted, and we have carried out what we had set out to create. For now, the timeline is consistent.

The professor's eyes, which were magnified by his thick lenses, sparkled with a mischievous glint, betraying the restless mind that constantly churned beneath his calm exterior. "Yes, but..." the professor said. After a slight unfolding of the map, he revealed some mysterious symbols and annotations that had been hand-drawn. In the Hall of Echoes, we discovered an inscription. Do you remember what it said? Did you discover the "hidden one" deep within the chronometric resonators, the one that predicted a "new dawn"?

Ellie's brow furrowed in scepticism as she crossed her arms and responded with a "Yes." But it likely referred to the end of the night, Valen's defeat, and the restoration of time's balance. Ellie's expression did not change. On the surface, it appeared to be a metaphorical expression, a poetic way of expressing that we had achieved success.

A statue of Lady Arabella was visible in the distance, and Professor Finch rubbed his chin thoughtfully as his gaze wandered towards it. The statue was found somewhere in the unknown distance. The ethereal figure, which was carved from alabaster or possibly a material that is much more uncommon, gave off the impression of glowing softly in contrast to the light that was gradually coming in around her. This barely perceptible luminescence gave the impression that secrets that had been concealed for centuries were finally being brought to light. "Perhaps it is not just a resolution," he murmured, more to himself than to Ellie, "perhaps it is also an awakening—an invitation to explore what lies ahead," he said. "Perhaps it is not just a resolution." This event is a part of history that has not been completely explored.

Tonight, the grand library, which was typically a place of comfort and familiarity, appeared to have a different atmosphere than I had experienced in the past. An air that seemed to be charged with anticipation, buzzing with an energy that mirrored the professor's unusual pronouncements, seems to have been charged with anticipation. Ellie cast a single glance in the direction of the statue, pondering whether the late hour and Professor Finch's peculiarities in the academic world were finally starting to wear her down. "An invitation?" she asked again, her brow furrowing as she contemplated the words that he had just spoken.

Exactly at that moment, Lady Arabella made a graceful movement that defied the laws of physics and the very nature of stone. She shifted her position ever so slightly. There was no denying the fact that it was there, even though it was almost imperceptible, like a slight tilt of the head or a barely noticeable adjustment to her flowing gown. Her marble face reflected a knowing smile as it caught the first rays of the approaching dawn. as if emanating from the statue itself, although Ellie was certain that she had only heard Professor Finch speak just a few moments earlier. "When the sun rises, it signifies the conclusion of one adventure and the beginning of another. "Not only does the dawn bring light, but it also brings a promise – "A promise that has been whispered on the winds of time, a promise of answers that are waiting to be unearthed, and perhaps a few dangers that are best left undisturbed," the promise reads.

At that moment, Azrael Lion, his golden fur gleaming as though kissed by the sunlight itself, stepped forward. He was a majestic figure, a beacon of calm amidst the lingering tension of the night. His voice, a low rumble that resonated with ancient wisdom, filled the room. "There's wisdom in her words, Ellie. We have traversed the shadows, and the first light often reveals truths hidden in darkness. We've faced our fears and learnt from the whispers of the night. To ignore the lessons etched in our hearts now would be to squander the very essence of our trial." He paused, his amber eyes meeting Ellie's with unwavering certainty. "Let us not dismiss the insights gained in the darkness but instead use them to illuminate our path forward."

Ellie felt a thrill course through her, a spark of hope igniting in her chest. Azrael's words confirmed her own growing sense of urgency. "Valen mentioned gateways and paths—perhaps there's a way to bind the knowledge we've gained in the night with new adventures to come." She tapped her chin thoughtfully, picturing the cryptic images Valen had shared. "Maybe these 'gateways' aren't just physical portals but opportunities. Opportunities to apply what we've learnt, to test our limits, and to forge a new chapter in our journey." The possibilities seemed endless, a tapestry of potential woven with the threads of their shared experience.

As he made his way through the room, Finn, who was wearing a sly grin, bounded into the room and darted between the thoughts of the animates that had become awake. There was a striking contrast between the calm demeanour that Azrael owned and the vivacious energy that he exuded. "Oh, let's not dwell! We must explore quickly before the day's responsibilities ground us! The realm of adventure should never end!" He bounced on the balls of his paws, his bushy tail twitching with excitement. "Oh, let's not dwell!" "Oh, let's not dwell!" "While you philosophers are pondering the meaning of moonlight, I say let's chase the sunrise together! Who knows what wonders are waiting for us just beyond that hill!"

Let's not delay any further. The world isn't going to explore itself!" His enthusiasm, though seemingly impulsive, injected a much-needed dose of playful energy into the otherwise serious atmosphere. He stood for the constant urge to act, to not let introspection paralyse them.

Oliver, the ever-watchful guard, his brow furrowed with a mixture of scepticism and weary amusement, approached the small huddle of explorers with his arms crossed tightly over his chest. The moonlight glinted off the brass buttons of his uniform, making him appear even more imposing. "And what, pray tell," he drawled, his voice a low rumble, "do you propose we explore, exactly? We've already nearly tripped over every priceless vase and dodged enough rogue suits of armour for one night. The museum won't stay enchanted forever, you know. This whole place could snap back to normal any minute. I've got to get back to my patrol before the curator misses me! He's already suspicious enough as it is."

The group chuckled, a sound born partly of relief and partly of sheer exhaustion from the morning's bewildering events. Dr Bell, her usually meticulous hair slightly dishevelled and her eyes still sparkling with the thrill of discovery, entered the circle. Her heart, she suspected, wouldn't stop racing for days. "There's a fresh structure in the museum gardens— or rather, a re-emergence of one. A remarkable addition, if I might say so myself, that I believe may hold the key to understanding why we were gathered here, particularly considering the... ahem... mysteries we've just uncovered." She gestured vaguely in the direction of the hall they had just exited; her voice tinged with both excitement and a hint of trepidation.

Ellie felt a surge of hope that caused her chest to tighten. "Mariana, the gardens?" She asked, even though her own muscles were hurting and her mind was still reeling from the events that had occurred in the earlier hours of the day. How much do they have in their possession? Even though it is only a few rose bushes and a fountain, you give the impression that it is more than that.

"A series of installations, embodying the very essence of history's lessons, or so they were meant to," she responded, her voice warming with a hint of nostalgia that in the middle of the night seemed slightly out of place. "A series of installations, embodying the very essence of history's lessons." "A series of installations, embodying the very essence of history's lessons." "Up until tonight, it was nothing more than a work that had been forgotten, tucked away, and largely ignored. The enchantment of the museum is intricately intertwined with the revitalised installations, which are pulsating with equivalent energy.

While she looked at each of them in turn, her eyes were filled with a mixture of anticipation and a quiet plea for understanding. "I have a strong feeling that they are more than just decorations; they are a roadmap, perhaps holding the key to our next quest, or at the very least, illuminating the path that we are meant to take," she said. The gardens were likely their next stop, where the answer to their puzzling problem awaited.

Huckleberry , who was perched jauntily on Professor Finch's broad shoulder, produced a sound that was reminiscent of wind chimes in a temple that had been forgotten. He looked at Ellie with a sharp and knowing gaze and said, "And I hold the secrets to those very paths!" Huckleberry was perched on Professor Finch's broad shoulder. "Without the context of our trials through the night, the day may very well shatter into a routine – that monotonous hum of the mundane!

All these things, including whispers of forgotten lore and maps etched in starlight, are mine to share with you, should you decide to pursue them. Would you genuinely like to have that?

His question was punctuated with a dramatic preen, scattering a few shimmering feathers that floated like captured moonlight. "Do you really want that?"

Throughout the course of the conversation, Professor Finch, who had always been a proponent of exploration, adjusted his glasses and thoughtfully stroked his beard. Professor Finch expressed his belief that further investigation would be beneficial. He added, "It would not hurt to investigate further!" On the contrary, I have a strong suspicion. There is a new dawn, which means that there is added information, a new page in the grand book of existence. To find out what lies in store for us, shall we go to the gardens? He nodded in the direction of the expansive, meticulously cultivated gardens of the museum, which are a place of serene beauty even under ordinary circumstances. Perhaps the flora has reawakened with stories to share, or perhaps the dew reflects forgotten realities. Softly pulsating, almost as if it were breathing, it summoned

Despite not shattering the fabric of reality violently, a shimmering portal materialised in the centre of the museum's grand hall. Despite not shattering the fabric of reality with a violent rip, a shimmering portal materialised in the centre of the museum's grand hall. It did not tear open the fabric of reality with a violent rip; a shimmering portal appeared in the centre of the grand hall of the museum. Their collective thoughts seemed to summon it for an unknown reason. Instead, it blossomed into existence, much like a delicate flower pushing through concrete.

It pulsated softly, almost as if it were breathing, and it called out to them with a gentle, siren-like call, inviting them into the world beyond. Golds and oranges mixed with the portal's own hues of sapphire and emerald, creating a surreal interplay of colours. The dawn, which was bleeding through the tall arched windows, blended beautifully with the soft, ethereal glow of the portal, creating a surreal interplay of colours. When I was awake, the line between waking and dreaming seemed to blur

Ellie took a deep breath as the atmosphere suddenly became charged with an energy that she could almost taste. It was a combination of ozone, magic, and the idea that the future was unknown. She was filled with a tidal wave of excitement that was on the verge of bursting out of her body. "We are about to embark on an exciting journey! She exclaimed, her eyes glistening with excitement. The sheer allure of the opportunity was so powerful that it completely overpowered any fear that she might have felt just a few moments earlier." Her eyes glistened with excitement.

As they moved forward, the team moved on with an unspoken agreement and a silent understanding passing between individuals. As a result of the irresistible pull, Professor Finch, Huckleberry, who was still perched on his shoulder, Ellie, and even Mr Abernathy, who is typically reserved, were all drawn forward. As a group, they traversed the threshold, leaving the world they were accustomed to behind and entering the whirling, iridescent unknown. The captivating allure of the portal engulfed them, and by the time they reached the portal, the museum and the ordinary day that had just begun lost their significance.

The gardens spread out in front of them like an extravagant tapestry that had been woven from centuries of moments that had been forgotten. A living kaleidoscope of time was created by the fact that every leaf had a story to tell, and every bloom had a secret to reveal about different eras. The tranquil space was filled with statues of varying sizes and materials, including marble, bronze, and even obsidian. These statues served as silent guardians of antiquity to the atmosphere. Each sentinel's posture and expression evoked long-lost stories, drawing in the curious.

Finn exclaimed, "It's right there!" as he pointed towards a particularly intimidating figure. His bushy tail twitched with excitement as he continued to point in that direction. "That statue, it is a perfect representation of the Sphinx that we encountered during our earlier journey! However, what is it doing here, tucked away among these lilies and roses and other flowers?"

Oliver, who was known for his pragmatic nature, rubbed the back of his neck in a manner that conveyed his thoughtfulness. "I have walked through this particular section of the garden a significant number of times, but I must confess that I have never looked at it in great detail. It is impossible to deny that the sight of it bathed in the light of the morning has a certain whimsical quality. The contrast between the majesty of that creature and the delicate beauty of these flowers is striking.

As they drew nearer, an otherworldly light seemed to emanate from the Sphinx statue. Its eyes, previously dull and lifeless, now gleamed with a vibrant, golden hue, as if awakened by the dawning light. A voice, ancient and resonant, echoed through the garden, seemingly born from the very stone itself. "Seekers of truth, come closer! The dawn has birthed a new era of revelations. Your earlier trials have reached their conclusion, but new riddles, woven with threads of destiny, now await."

"Riddles?" Ellie exclaimed, her voice a mixture of apprehension and anticipation. Her heart, which had been expecting a peaceful morning stroll, now thrummed with a thrilling energy. She recognised, with a certainty that resonated deep within her soul, that this day would be anything but mundane. The gardens, once a place of quiet beauty, had transformed into the stage for a new and unforeseen adventure. The air crackled with unspoken possibilities, and the unfolding light promised a journey into the unknown.

The Sphinx, ancient and enigmatic, its gaze sweeping over the trio, continued, "To those entwined with history, to those who have tasted the whispers of ages past, there will always be more to discover, more to learn. The tapestry of time is endless, and its threads stretch far beyond what you can currently perceive. You stand at a crossroads; a pivotal moment etched in the annals of destiny. You must now choose which path to take. Linger here, within the sanctuary you've come to protect, and remain the unwavering protectors of the light, shielding this haven from encroaching darkness. Or you can pursue what lies beyond this garden's embrace, venturing into the unknown, facing trials yet unimagined."

If we pursue what lies beyond, what will happen? " " Oliver asked, his voice laced with a newfound hope. The enchantment, a tangible warmth, had woven its spell around him, loosening the knots of fear and doubt that had previously constrained his spirit. He was openly curious now, less guarded, eager to understand the implications of this monumental decision. "What happens if we pursue what lies beyond?"

"Every decision births a new story, a new challenge," the Sphinx replied, its voice a seductive whisper that seemed to slither into their minds, resonating with their deepest desires and fears. "Each path taken unravels a unique thread of fate, leading to unforeseen consequences and unparalleled opportunities. You may find that by stepping beyond these walls, you can not only restore balance to this museum, anchoring its magic and protecting its artefacts, but also those places you cherish beyond this realm, the homes and lives touched by the reverberations of this magical nexus. Remember, wisdom shadows each moment spent deciding. Contemplate the weight of your choice, for it will shape not only your destinies but the destinies of others."

"I vote for adventure!" Finn squeaked, his eyes wide with excitement. He practically leapt at the chance to truly make a difference!"

"The museum has already bound us together through our shared journey, forged a connection stronger than any magical chain," Ellie noted, her voice ringing with a newfound conviction and determination that radiated outwards like a beacon. "We arrived here separately, each with our burdens and insecurities, but we've become a team, a force capable of extraordinary things. It is time we honour these connections, these bonds we've formed, and seek out what lies ahead, together. Let us embrace this new dawn, this opportunity to transcend our limitations and become something more. Let us answer the call, whatever it may be, and face the future with courage and unwavering faith in one another."

The group of companions arranged themselves in a circle around the ancient Sphinx, its weathered face serving as a silent sentinel against the rising sun. The warmth of the morning, both literally and figuratively, filled their spirits, driving away the lingering shadows of the previous night. They took a collective breath, a silent agreement passing between them, and a bolstering of spirits before the unknown.

"Allow us to come to a conclusion that we should proceed into the forthcoming! It reflected the heart that lay beneath his flamboyant exterior that his pronouncements, which were often whimsical, had a surprising kernel of wisdom. His pronouncements held a surprising kernel of wisdom." Harold declared, his eccentricity shining through like the sunlight that pours through the branches above him in the morning, dappling the dusty ground around the Sphinx.

"Alright, then it must be the case!" Lady Arabella nodded, her presence regal yet comforting. Despite her noble bearing, there was a genuine warmth in her gaze, an understanding of the anxieties that often-accompanied new beginnings. She was the anchor, the unwavering presence that grounded their adventurous spirit.

With a shared glance, a silent conversation passing between them, each member stepped into the heart of their next adventure. Fingers brushed against one another, a fleeting connection that sparked courage in their chests, a reminder that they were not alone. They understood that the depth of unity forged through the trials of the previous night, the bonds strengthened in the face of adversity, would set the stage for whatever might come, good or ill. The horrors they had faced together had not broken them, but rather, bound them closer.

Huckleberry proclaimed, "I will be your eyes," while his wings were spread out in front of him, creating a majestic shadow that momentarily encircled the circle. His voice, which was typically a low rumble, held a note of fervent determination. "Together, we venture forth into the tales for which there are still stories to be told!"

Ellie felt a surge of hope course through her heart as she walked through a corridor lined with dew-kissed blossoms, the delicate petals of which shimmered in the sunlight, and verdant foliage that was bursting with life. Unseen energy hummed through the air, announcing the arrival of marvels that were yet to come. It was woven from the very essence of the garden's enchantment, a tapestry of magic that was waiting to be unravelled, and she felt it in her bones that their curiosity would be rewarded once more. The very garden seemed to be calling out to them, its mysteries sounding like a siren song that they were unable to ignore any longer.

A golden net was cast across the land as the sun rose to its fullest extent, painting the eastern sky with shades of apricot and rose. This net illuminated the path that lay ahead of us. Ellie's heart was filled with a newly discovered sense of purpose, and she whispered a silent promise to her friends, whose faces were etched with determination, as well as to the silent artefacts of the museum, which were watching over them. The narrative of their story, which was woven with strands of magic, mystery, and bravery, was not yet complete; rather, it was merely a new chapter that was waiting to be written.

They were ready to become the heroes whispered about around crackling fires, carving their destinies into legend. They were ready to carve their destinies into the fabric of legends now that they were free of the past. As they walked together into the golden and verdant landscape of a new era, where emerald forests met sun-drenched meadows, they embraced the limitless possibilities that the day had to offer.

Because deep within the core of the Enchanted Museum, where its ancient stones resounded with an unfathomable power, shimmered the echoes of countless adventures that had not yet been experienced. In the dazzling light of a new dawn, each adventure, which was a colourful tapestry of wonder and danger, promised to be even more astounding and even more captivating than it had been before. The Enchanted Museum silently beckoned us to delve into the unexplored realms that awaited us, a place where magic thrived and the air brimmed with dreams and excitement.

THE LEGACY PRESERVED

The museum was awash with the silvery luminescence of the moon, its ethereal glow seeping through the arched windows and bathing the polished marble floors in an otherworldly sheen. The light seemed to cling to the dust motes dancing in the air, transforming them into ephemeral jewels. This lunar wash cast elongated, distorted shadows across the floor, stretching and twisting the familiar shapes of exhibits into grotesque parodies. Where Ellie and her eclectic band of companions stood breathless, poised on the precipice of their final challenge, these shadows grasping claws, threatening to pull them back into the labyrinthine corridors they'd just navigated.

The air hummed, a low, resonant vibration that tickled the skin and hinted at untold power. It wasn't just the hum of electricity powering the security systems but something deeper, something ancient. It was the anticipation of the artefacts themselves, a chorus of whispers emanating from behind velvet ropes and glass displays. Each relic seemed to hold its breath, waiting for the first blush of dawn, waiting to see if this night, this chaotic and exhilarating game, would finally reach its conclusion. The air was rich with the enigmatic weight of history, the scent of old parchment and preserved wood, a tangible representation of the stories these objects held, stories that had delighted and terrorised them through the night, pushing them to their limits and revealing hidden strengths they never knew they had. Now, with the sunrise just hours away, they stood ready, knowing that the coming dawn would either bring an end to the chaos or plunge them into even deeper turmoil.

"Ellie", called Professor Finch, his voice a slight tremor of urgency barely contained by his characteristic eccentricity. "We must find Valen before it's too late! The dawn will force us back into the mundane world, and our adventure will end without resolution."

Nearby, Azrael, a figure of undeniable authority and allure, his stature both regal and imposing, trod the museum's marbled floor with a playful yet commanding presence. His every step resonated with an ancient power, suggesting a being both comfortable in his skin and capable of wielding immense influence. "Fear not, my friends!" he declared, the echo of his voice amplifying their hopes and concerns, a resonant wave that seemed to vibrate through the very stones of the building. "For every puzzle we've met thus far has led us closer to understanding. Each trial, each cryptic clue, has been a stepping stone, carefully placed to guide us onwards. possibilities that we must unravel with our combined intellect and courage."

Beside him, Luci, a creature of sinuous grace and captivating beauty, glimmered under the fluorescent lights. Her bronze scales, like ancient, burnished coins, reflected the dim rays like molten gold, each movement a ripple of shimmering light. "Yes, listen to Azrael," she hissed, her voice a silken whisper that held the weight of ages. "The path to Valen lies ahead, shrouded in mystery, yet illuminated by the flicker of wisdom. This journey is not merely a physical one carry within us the accumulated experiences and lessons that shape our understanding. Only then can we disentangle the shadows of the past, the echoes of forgotten truths that obscure the present and cloud the future." A subtle flick of her tongue punctuated her words, a silent promise of both danger and profound insight.

Oliver, the museum guard whose steadfast nature had been both a barrier and a beacon throughout their journey, leaned against a large tapestry depicting an ancient battle. The woven scene, a clash of warriors and a maelstrom of conflict, mirrored the turmoil brewing within him. His brow was furrowed with worry lines etched deeper than any crack in the museum's ancient facade. "What if we fail?" he uttered quietly, a whispered fear amidst the determination of his companions. The question hung in the air, heavy and unspoken, acknowledging the very real possibility that their quest might end in defeat, leaving them trapped within the labyrinthine corridors of time itself. The doubt in his voice was a sharp contrast to the unwavering confidence of Azrael and the enigmatic wisdom of Luci, a reminder of the human element in their extraordinary undertaking. He wasn't a god or a mythical serpent, just a man burdened by the weight of responsibility and the very real prospect of failure, a man who, despite his fear, stood ready to face whatever lay ahead.

With an empathetic glance, Ellie stepped closer to Oliver, her gaze softening the harsh lines etched on his face. She could sense the weight of their quest pressing down on him, the burden of responsibility threatening to overwhelm his usually bright spirit. "What we have gained so far is not merely a collection of artefacts or fragmented tales," she said, her voice gentle but firm. "It's friendship, Oliver. It's the bravery we've discovered within ourselves and each other. It's a shared purpose that binds us together, a reason to keep fighting even when the odds seem insurmountable. Trust in that, Oliver. Trust in the bond we have forged. Together, we're stronger than we realise, capable of facing anything that Valen throws our way." She squeezed his hand, silently assuring him that they were all there to help.

As they went ahead deeper into the museum, the air grew thick with anticipation, a palpable hum of energy that resonated in the very stones around them. Finn, a vibrant spark of mischief and unwavering loyalty, darted playfully between their feet, a flash of russet fur against the cold, grey stone. "Valen's chamber is close!" he yipped, his voice tinged with delight and a hint of nervous excitement. "I can feel his presence, lurking just beyond the next hall. He's waiting for us! Follow me!" He bounded forward, his bushy tail wagging furiously, a beacon leading them towards their ultimate confrontation.

Ellie felt a thrill of exhilaration surge within her, a potent mix of fear and anticipation that quickened her pulse. They pressed onwards, their footsteps echoing through the long corridors adorned with centuries of history, each stone whispering tales of triumphs and tragedies. "Look," she pointed excitedly to a grand mural stretching across the wall, a breathtaking tapestry depicting heroes of times long past. Each figure was frozen in a moment of pivotal decision; their faces etched with determination and the weight of their choices. "Each figure represents a moment in history where choices changed the course of events," Ellie explained, her voice hushed with awe. "Their actions, their decisions, rippled through time, shaping the world we know today. It's a reminder that even the smallest act can have a profound impact and that we, too, are empowered to shape our own destiny." The mural served as a silent testament to the power of courage and the importance of making the right choices, bolstering their resolve as they ventured further into the heart of the Timekeeper's domain.

Finn, practically vibrating with unrestrained energy, bounced around the poised statues that lined the ancient hall. He was a whirlwind of nervous anticipation, his hands gesturing wildly as he spun a playful narrative around them. "Look at them, frozen in time! They are just like us! Every decision we make now shapes what comes next, etching itself into the very fabric of our future. We can't linger! Let's hurry; I've never been so excited in my life!" A wide, almost manic grin stretched across his face, his eyes gleaming with a mixture of eagerness and trepidation.

Turning the corner, the group found themselves standing before a heavy wooden door, its surface a tapestry of intricate carvings depicting scenes of swirling galaxies and celestial beings. Here, the whispers intensified, a chorus of voices both familiar and alien, wrapping around them like a celestial embrace. It was as if the very walls were sharing secrets, urging them forward while simultaneously warning them to proceed with caution. Above the door, dominating the space, was an engraving of an hourglass, its sands suspended in mid-fall. The grains seemed to hover, defying gravity, as if time itself held its breath, waiting for their arrival, measuring their worthiness.

Dr Bell, her face etched with a weary concern, still reeling from the unforeseen and often disastrous consequences of her earlier conservation efforts, turned to face her companions. The weight of responsibility settled heavily on her shoulders. "We have to be vigilant," she said, her voice serious and laced with a hint of apprehension. "Valen The Timekeeper will not be easily appeased. His riddles demand not just surface-level knowledge, not just rote memorisation, but a profound understanding of what lies within us – our motivations, our fears, and our deepest desires. We must be prepared to look inwards, to confront the truths we might rather ignore, if we hope to pass his test." She paused, her gaze sweeping over each of them, a silent plea for them to understand the gravity of the situation. Their mission was more than just a historical quest; it was a journey into the heart of themselves.

"Then let us share," Professor Finch asserted, the spark of excitement igniting within his intellect. "Each of us has a shard of history—the wisdom of the ages—intertwined with our present journey. Let us unite our thoughts and explore these riddles together."

Huckleberry, a magnificent raven seemingly carved from obsidian, perched precariously on the edge of a nearby display case filled with ancient artefacts. His sharp, intelligent eyes, like chips of jet, darted between the assembled group. Without warning, he cawed loudly, the sound echoing through the chamber, before interjecting his pronouncements with the authority of a seasoned scholar. "Be mindful of your weaknesses and strengths," he croaked, his voice surprisingly deep and resonant, "for Valen the Timekeeper respects those who are aware of their essence. The first riddle is not merely a test of knowledge; it examines your collective spirit, probing the depths of your understanding and resilience."

"What is the riddle, Huckleberry?" Ellie enquired, her heart racing with a mixture of excitement and apprehension. The air crackled with anticipation, a palpable energy that filled the space between them. This was it, the first step in their quest.

"Listen closely," Huckleberry responded, spreading his massive wings in a display of anticipation, each feather a dark, shimmering marvel. "In days of yore, when shadows were cast, the echoes of power held every heart fast. Speak of the moments that altered the flow, or risk being trapped in the time you don't know." He fixed them with his piercing gaze, ensuring his words had fully sunk in.

The group shared contemplative glances, each brow furrowed in thought. The weight of the riddle, heavy with implications, seemed to leach the energy from the room, replacing it with a thoughtful silence. The words hung in the air, a challenge waiting to be untangled.

"The moments that changed history," Ellie breathed, her historian instincts kicking into gear. A spark ignited in her eyes as her mind began to race through the annals of time. "Those are the times that taught lessons, sacrifices made for the greater good. The turning points, the pivotal events... Perhaps it refers to events we've met? The battles we fought, the choices we made... could Valen be testing our comprehension of their consequences?"

Oliver furrowed his brow, still grappling with doubt. "But how do we express those moments? They're intangible. How can we possibly capture the essence of fleeting feelings, the weight of difficult choices, and the spark of connection we shared? It wants to try to grasp smoke."

"And yet, moments like these define us!" Luci interjected, her voice smooth but insistent, her scales rustling gently. "We must reflect on our journey—what have we learnt? What truths have been revealed through hardship and triumph? The tapestry of our adventures is woven not just with actions, but with the feelings and understanding they engendered."

"Each time we faced a challenge, we also faced ourselves," Ellie replied, her voice stronger now, tinged with newfound confidence. "Like when Azrael, with his maddeningly cryptic pronouncements, guided us through the riddle of the Sphinx, forcing us to confront our limitations in knowledge and belief. Or when Finn, in a daring act bordering on recklessness, stole the artefact from beneath the guardian's nose! The sheer audacity of it, the pressure, the consequences... Those are the kinds of moments that forge who we are."

"Indeed!" Professor Finch exclaimed, adjusting his spectacles with a gleam in his eye. "And remember Lady Arabella's wisdom about honour and sacrifice. The nobleperson, with her vast understanding of ancient lore, provided perspective on the artefacts, helping us piece together their histories and, we are to truly learn from them."

As they shared their personal reflections on the trials they faced, a mosaic of light began to form within the room, each shard being a moment of struggle and triumph. Vulnerable confessions unfolded, revealing hidden depths and resonating with shared humanity. Each recollection, whether a whispered fear or a bold act of defiance, came alive, illuminating the chamber not just with light, but with the vibrant hues of lived experience. These stories weren't just personal narratives; they were threads in a complex pattern, connecting them to the memories of their ancestors, their struggles echoing in the present, their triumphs offering guidance. The weight of generations settled upon them, a burden and a blessing, reminding them of the legacy they carried.

"Ah," Azrael sighed, his voice filled with gravitas and a hint of awe. "The power of unity has allowed us to transcend our limitations. We are no longer merely individuals but a collective consciousness, bound by shared experience. We are stronger together; our fears, once isolating burdens, now tempered by shared understanding, and our hopes, amplified by mutual support, combine to create a beacon for Valen." He paused, a hopeful glint in his eye, "A beacon that guides him through the chaotic currents of time itself."

As the final memories coalesced, the mosaic of light pulsed with renewed intensity, solidifying into a single, blinding sphere. The ancient wooden door, weathered by centuries and etched with forgotten runes, creaked open with agonising. In the swirling darkness, Valen materialised, his cloak a breathtaking swirl of stardust and shadows, constantly shifting and reforming like a miniature galaxy. His gaze was both penetrating, capable of seeing into the deepest recesses of their souls, and surprisingly kind, filled with an ancient understanding and a gentle empathy.

"Brave souls," he spoke, his voice resonating like a distant chime, simultaneously echoing through the chamber and whispering directly into their minds. "You have navigated the treacherous intricacies of the past, confronted your personal demons and embraced the weight of your stories, both the triumphant and the tragic. You have recognised the strength inherent in your togetherness, the power that arises when individual flames merge into a single, roaring fire. You have passed the test, proving yourselves worthy of what lies ahead. But the journey is far from over. Now comes the true challenge. What will you choose to do next? Will you use the wisdom you have gained to shape a brighter future, or will you allow the shadows of the past to consume you?" His question hung in the air; a profound and weighty choice offered with the quiet assurance that their answer would ripple through the very fabric of time.

As they shared their personal reflections on the trials they faced, a mosaic of light began to form within the room, each shard being a moment of struggle and triumph. Vulnerable confessions unfolded, revealing hidden depths and resonating with shared humanity. Each recollection, whether a whispered fear or a bold act of defiance, came alive, illuminating the chamber not just with light upon them, a burden and a blessing, reminding them of the legacy they carried.

"Ah," Azrael sighed, his voice filled with gravitas and a hint of awe. "The power of unity has allowed us to transcend our limitations. We are no longer merely individuals but a collective consciousness, bound by shared experience. We are stronger together; our fears, once isolating burdens, now tempered by shared understanding, and our hopes, amplified by mutual support, combine to create a beacon for Valen." He paused, a hopeful glint in his eye, "A beacon that guides him through the chaotic currents of time itself."

As the final memories coalesced, the mosaic of light pulsed with renewed intensity, solidifying into a single, blinding sphere. The ancient wooden door, weathered by centuries and etched with forgotten runes, creaked open with agonising slowness, revealing a dark chamber. Here, the usual laws of physics seemed suspended; time itself appeared to fold and ripple, like water disturbed by a submerged stone. Ethereal echoes of past events flickered at the edges of vision, hinting at the vastness of what lay beyond. From the swirling darkness, Valen materialised, his cloak a breathtaking swirl of stardust and shadows, constantly shifting and reforming like a miniature galaxy. His gaze was both penetrating, capable of seeing into the deepest recesses of their souls, and surprisingly kind, filled with an ancient understanding and a gentle empathy.

"Brave souls," he spoke, his voice resonating like a distant chime, simultaneously echoing through the chamber and whispering directly into their minds. "You have navigated the treacherous intricacies of the past, confronted your personal demons and embraced the weight of your stories, both the triumphant and the tragic. You have recognised the strength inherent in your togetherness, the power that arises when individual flames merge into a single, roaring fire. You have passed the test, proving yourselves worthy of what lies ahead. But the journey is far from over. Now comes the true challenge. What will you choose to do next? Will you use the wisdom you have gained to shape a brighter future, or will you allow the shadows of the past to consume you?" His question hung in the air; a profound and weighty choice offered with the quiet assurance that their answer would ripple through the very fabric of time.

Exultant joy filled the room, an effervescent, palpable energy that crackled in the air and warmed every heart present. They had done it. Against impossible odds, they had succeeded. Together they embraced the magic of the moment, a spontaneous outpouring of relief, gratitude, and profound connection. Their adventures had altered the course of time, not just for themselves

As dawn began to break, casting golden rays across the aged walls of the museum, painting the artefacts in a new, celebratory light, Ellie smiled, a genuine, radiating smile that reflected the joy swirling within her. She looked around at her companions, her chosen family. "Whatever happens next, whatever trials or wonders await us beyond these walls, we'll face it together." Her voice, though soft, resonated with conviction. "Our bond is forever inextricable, bound not just by the artefacts we uncovered and the secrets we unearthed but by the stories we will continue to write and the legends we will continue to forge."

The rest of the team nodded in agreement, a silent understanding passing between them. They knew their adventure did not truly end with the rising sun but transformed into the solid foundation upon which they would build new explorations and discoveries, new quests and triumphs. The museum, once a battleground, was now a touchstone, a testament to their courage and camaraderie.

Finn, his fur shimmering in the dawn light, gave a jubilant squeal, darting playfully between their legs, a furry embodiment of their unbridled joy. Oliver, the stalwart guardian, laughed, a hearty, genuine laugh that echoed through the halls. He realized, with a surge of warmth, that he had transcended his role as a mere guard, a protector of objects. He was now a part of something breathtakingly magical, a guardian of people, of stories, of a shared destiny.

As they stepped into the new day, carrying the spirit of the night within them like a precious ember, Ellie felt a whisper in her heart, a gentle nudge of intuition. *This was only the beginning.* Adventure awaited not just within the hallowed halls of the museum but throughout life's eternal corridors, in every unexplored corner of the world, in every unwritten chapter of their lives. And every moment experienced together, every hardship they overcame, and every victory they celebrated, would forever echo through time, shaping who they were and who they would become.

And while the museum's doors may close at dawn, silencing the whispers of the past for the day, the whispers of the night, the secrets they had uncovered, and the bonds they had forged would continue to guide their souls on new paths, igniting their imaginations and inspiring them to create stories yet to unfold, legends yet to be written. The world was waiting, and they were ready to answer its call.

RESOLUTION IN
THE NIGHT

T he museum was awash in the silvery luminescence of the moon,
     its ethereal glow penetrating the arched windows and bathing
the polished marble floors in a sheen that seemed to come from
another world. It appears the light was clinging to the dust particles
that were moving through the air, thereby transforming them into
ephemeral jewels. By stretching and twisting the familiar shapes of
exhibits into grotesque parodies, this lunar wash cast shadows that
were elongated and distorted across the floor. When Ellie and her
diverse group of companions stood there, gasping for air and poised
on the brink of their final challenge, these shadows grabbed their
claws and threatened to pull them back into the labyrinthine corridors
that they had just navigated.

   There was a low, resonant vibration in the air that tickled the skin
and conveyed a sense of power that was beyond comprehension. The
sound was more than the security system's electric buzz; it was deeper
and older. It was the anticipation of the artefacts themselves, which
were sounding like a chorus of whispers coming from behind velvet
ropes and glass displays. This night, this chaotic and exhilarating
game, appeared to be waiting for the first blush of dawn, waiting
to see if it would finally end. Each relic appeared to be holding its
breath, waiting for the dawn to touch the ground. It was a tangible
representation of the stories that these objects held, stories that had
delighted and terrified them throughout the night, pushing them to
their limits and revealing hidden strengths that they had never known
they had. The air was thick with the mysterious weight of history,
the scent of old parchment, and the scent of wood that had been
preserved. Now, with the sunrise only a few hours away, they stood

ready, aware that the dawn would either put an end to the chaos or plunge them into even more turmoil. They were aware of this fact.

"Ellie," Professor Finch called out, his voice carrying a slight tremor of urgency that was barely contained by the extraordinary eccentricity that was characteristic of him. It is imperative that we locate Valen now, before it is too late! Because of the dawn, we will be compelled to return to the everyday world, and our journey will end without any resolution.

Nearby, Azrael, a figure of undeniable authority and allure, walked across the marbled floor of the museum with a presence that was both playful and commanding. His stature was both regal and imposing. Each step he took reverberated with an ancient power, showing that he was a being who was not only at ease in his concerns. "Because each and every conundrum that we have encountered up to this point has brought us one step closer to comprehension. Every difficulty, every decipherable clue, has been a stepping stone that has been strategically positioned to lead us forward. In the future, Valen, the Timekeeper, will be waiting for us, and his puzzles will weave the very fabric of time itself, creating a tapestry of paradoxes and possibilities that we will have to unravel with our combined intelligence and bravery.

Beside him, Luci, a creature of sinuous grace and captivating beauty, glimmered under the fluorescent lights. Her bronze scales, like ancient, burnished coins, reflected the dim rays like molten gold, each movement a ripple of shimmering light. "Yes, listen to Azrael," she hissed, her voice a silken whisper that held the weight of ages. "The path to Valen lies ahead, shrouded in mystery, yet illuminated by the flicker of wisdom. This journey is not merely a physical one but a voyage into the depths of knowledge and self-discovery. We must embrace the history we carry within us, the accumulated experiences and lessons that shape our understanding. Only then can we disentangle the shadows of the past, the echoes of forgotten truths that obscure the present.

Oliver, the museum guard whose steadfast nature had conflict, conflict mirrored the turmoil brewing within him. His brow was furrowed with worry lines etched deeper than any crack in the museum's ancient facade. "What if we fail?" he uttered quietly, a whispered fear amidst the determination of his companions. The question hung in the air, heavy and unspoken, acknowledging the very real possibility that their quest might end in defeat, leaving them trapped within the labyrinthine corridors of time itself. The doubt in his voice was a sharp contrast to the unwavering confidence of Azrael and the enigmatic wisdom of Luci, a reminder of the human element in their extraordinary undertaking. He wasn't a god nor a mythical serpent, just a man burdened by the weight of responsibility and the very real prospect of failure, a man who, despite his fear, stood ready to face whatever lay ahead.

With an empathetic glance, Ellie stepped closer to Oliver, her gaze softening the harsh lines etched on his face. She could sense the weight of their quest pressing down on him, the burden of responsibility threatening to overwhelm his usually bright spirit. "What we have gained so far is not merely a collection of artefacts or fragmented tales," she said, her voice gentle but firm. "It's friendship, Oliver. It's the bravery we've discovered within ourselves and each other. It's a shared purpose that binds us together, a reason to keep fighting even when the odds seem insurmountable. Trust in that, Oliver. Trust in the bond we have forged. Together, we're stronger than we realise, capable of facing anything that Valen throws our way." She reached out and squeezed his hand, a silent reassurance

There was a palpable hum of energy that resonated in the very stones that surrounded them as they went ahead further into the museum. The air became thick with anticipation as they went ahead further into the museum. There was a flash of russet fur against the cold, grey stone as Finn darted between their feet in a playful manner. Finn was a vibrant spark of mischief and unwavering loyalty. A tinge of delight and a hint of nervous excitement could be heard in his voice as he exclaimed, "Valen, the chamber of the timekeeper is right around the corner!" He charged forward with his bushy tail wagging furiously, acting as a beacon that led them towards their ultimate confrontation. "I can feel his presence, lurking just beyond the next hall. He's waiting for us! Follow me!" he exclaimed.

A potent mixture of fear and anticipation caused Ellie's heart rate to quicken, and she felt a surge of exhilaration and excitement surge through her body. As they continued forward, the sound of their footsteps reverberated through the lengthy corridors that were adorned with centuries of history, with each stone reciting stories of triumphs and tragedies. "Look," she exclaimed with a gleeful gesture, pointing to a magnificent mural that stretched across the wall. It was a breathtaking tapestry that depicted heroes from a long time ago. The figures' faces were etched with resolve and the weight of their choices, frozen in a moment of pivotal decision. They were frozen in time, etched with resolve and the weight of their choices. "Each figure represents a moment in history where choices changed the course and are empowered to shape our destiny." The mural served as a silent testament to the power of courage and the importance of making the right choices, bolstering their resolve as they ventured further into the heart of the Timekeeper's domain.

As he bounced around the poised statues that lined the ancient hall, Finn gave off the impression that he was practically vibrating with unrestrained energy. As he spun a playful narrative around them, he was a whirlwind of nervous anticipation, his hands gesturing wildly over the course of the conversation. A wide, almost manic grin stretched across his face, and his eyes gleamed with a mixture of eagerness and trepidation. "Look at them, frozen in time! They just claimed enthusiastically.

As the group turned the corner, they found themselves standing in front of a massive wooden door. The surface of the door was covered in intricate carvings that depicted scenes of galaxies that were swirling and celestial beings. In this location, the whispers became more intense, sounding like a chorus of voices that were both familiar and foreign, enveloping them like a divine embrace. It was as if the walls themselves were divulging concealed information, encouraging them to move forward while at the same time cautioning them to proceed with caution. An engraving depicting an hourglass with its sands suspended in mid-fall was a prominent feature of the room, which was found above the door. It appears the grains were suspended in midair, defying the force of gravity. It was as if time itself was holding its breath, expecting their arrival and evaluating their value.

Dr Bell was still reeling from the unexpected and often disastrous outcomes of her previous conservation efforts. There was a significant amount of responsibility that was placed on her shoulders. As she spoke, her tone was solemn and tinged with a trace of apprehension. "We have to be vigilant," she said. "Valen will not be easily appeased." A profound understanding of what lies within us, including our fears, our deepest desires, and our motivations, is needed to solve his riddles. His riddles require not only surface-level knowledge but in addition to rote memorisation. We must be prepared to look inwards, to confront the truths we might rather ignore, if we hope to pass his test." She paused, her gaze sweeping over each of them, a silent plea for them to understand the gravity of the situation. This expedition was more than just a historical quest; it was a journey into the heart of themselves.

"Then let us share," Professor Finch asserted, the spark of excitement igniting within his intellect. "Each of us has a shard of history—the wisdom of the ages—intertwined with our present journey. Let us unite our thoughts and explore these riddles together."

Huckleberry, a magnificent raven seemingly carved from obsidian, perched precariously on the edge of a nearby display case filled with ancient artefacts. His sharp, intelligent eyes, like chips of jet, darted between the assembled group. Without warning, he cawed loudly, the sound echoing through the chamber, before interjecting his pronouncements with the authority of a seasoned scholar. "Be mindful of your weaknesses and strengths," he croaked, his voice surprisingly deep and resonant, "for Valen respects those who are aware of their essence. The first riddle is not merely a test of knowledge; it examines your collective spirit, probing the depths of your understanding and resilience."

"What is the riddle, Huckleberry?" Ellie asked, her heart racing with a mixture of excitement and apprehension. The air crackled with anticipation, a palpable energy that filled the space between them. This moment was the culmination of their journey, the first step in their quest.

Huckleberry responded by spreading his enormous wings in a display of anticipation, each feather a marvel of darkness and shimmering. "In days of yore, when shadows were cast, the echoes of power held every heart fast. Speak of the moments that altered the flow, or risk being trapped in the time you don't know," he said, fixing them with his penetrating gaze, making sure that his words had fully imprinted themselves on their minds.

The group exchanged thoughtful glances, each brow furrowed in thought. The weight of the riddle, which was heavy with implications, seemed to leach the energy from the room, replacing it with a thoughtful silence. The words hung in the air, offering a challenge that was waiting to be untangled.

"The moments that changed history," Ellie breathed, her instincts as a historian beginning to kick in. A spark ignited in her eyes as her mind began to race through the annals of time. "Those are the times that taught lessons, sacrifices made for the greater good. These times marked significant turning points and points, the pivotal events... Perhaps it refers to events that we have met? The battles that we fought, the choices that we made... Could Valen be testing our comprehension of the consequences of those choices?"

As Oliver continued to struggle with uncertainty, he furrowed his brow and asked, "But how do we express those moments? They are intangible. How can we possibly capture the essence of fleeting feelings, the weight of difficult choices, and the spark of connection we shared? It wants to try to grasp smoke."

"And yet, moments like these define us!" Luci interjected, her voice smooth but insistent, her scales rustling gently. "We must reflect on our journey—what have we learnt? What truths have been revealed through hardship and triumph? The tapestry of our adventures is woven not just with actions, but with the feelings and understanding they engendered."

"Each time we faced a challenge, we also faced ourselves," Ellie replied, her voice stronger own limitations in knowledge and belief. Or when Finn, in a daring act bordering on recklessness, stole the artefact from beneath the guardian's nose! The sheer audacity of it, the pressure, the consequences... Those are the kinds of moments that forge who we are."

"Indeed!" Professor Finch exclaimed, adjusting his spectacles with a gleam in his eye. "And remember Lady Arabella's wisdom about honour and sacrifice. The nobleperson, with her vast understanding of ancient lore, provided perspective on the artefacts, helping us piece together their histories and, more importantly, the moral implications behind their creation and use. She taught us that knowledge without ethics is a dangerous weapon." He paused, stroking his beard thoughtfully. "These experiences, these lessons... It is necessary for us to be able to articulate them, understand them, and ultimately feel them to truly learn from them.

As they shared their personal reflections on the trials they faced, a mosaic of light began to form within the room, each shard being a moment of struggle and triumph. Vulnerable confessions unfolded, revealing hidden depths and resonating with shared humanity. Each recollection, whether a whispered fear or a bold act of defiance, came alive, illuminating the chamber not just with light upon them, a burden and a blessing, reminding them of the legacy they carried.

"Ah," Azrael sighed, his voice filled with gravitas and a hint of awe. "The power of unity has allowed us to transcend our limitations. We are no longer merely individuals but a collective consciousness, bound by shared experience. We are stronger together; our fears, which were once burdens that made us feel isolated, are now tempered by shared understanding, and our hopes, which are amplified by mutual support, combine to create a beacon for Valen." He paused, a hopeful glint in his eye, and then continued, "A beacon that guides him through the chaotic currents of time itself."

As the final memories coalesced, the mosaic of light pulsed with renewed intensity, solidifying into a single, blinding sphere. The ancient wooden door, weathered by centuries and etched with forgotten runes, creaked open with agonising slowness, revealing a dark chamber. Here, the usual laws of physics seemed suspended; time itself appeared to fold and ripple, like water disturbed by a submerged stone. Ethereal echoes of past events flickered at the edges of vision, hinting at the vastness of what lay beyond. From the swirling darkness, Valen materialised, his cloak a breathtaking swirl of stardust and shadows, constantly shifting and reforming like a miniature galaxy. His gaze was both penetrating, capable of seeing into the deepest recesses of their souls, and surprisingly

"Brave souls," he spoke, his voice resonating like a distant chime, simultaneously echoing through the chamber and whispering directly into their minds. "You have navigated the treacherous intricacies of the past, confronted your personal demons and embraced the weight of your stories, both the triumphant and the tragic. You have arrived at the realisation that the power that arises from the merging of individual flames into a single, raging fire is the strength that is inherent in your togetherness. The test has been successfully completed, proving that you are deserving of what is to come. Despite this, the journey is not yet over.

Now comes the real test of your abilities. I am curious as to what you intend to do next. Will you use your knowledge to create a better future or let the past consume you? His question lingered in the air; it was a profound and weighty choice that was offered with the quiet assurance that their response would ripple through the very fabric of time.

As they shared their personal reflections on the trials they faced, a mosaic of light began to form within the room, each shard being a moment of struggle and triumph. Vulnerable confessions unfolded, revealing hidden depths and resonating with shared humanity. Each recollection, whether a whispered fear or a bold act of defiance, came alive, illuminating the chamber not just with light but with the vibrant hues of lived experience. These stories weren't just personal narratives; they were threads in a complex tapestry, connecting them to the memories of their ancestors, their struggles echoing in the present, their triumphs offering guidance. The weight of generations settled upon them, a burden and a blessing, reminding them of the legacy they carried.

"Ah," Azrael sighed, his voice filled with gravitas and a hint of awe. "The power of unity has allowed us to transcend our limitations. We are no longer merely individuals but a collective consciousness, bound by shared experience. We are stronger together; our fears, which were once burdens that made us feel isolated, are now tempered by shared understanding, and our hopes, which are amplified by mutual support, combine to create a beacon for Valen." He paused, a hopeful glint in his eye, and then continued, "A beacon that guides him through the chaotic currents of time itself."

As the final memories coalesced, the mosaic of light pulsed with renewed intensity, solidifying into a single, blinding sphere. The ancient wooden door, weathered by centuries and etched with forgotten runes, creaked open with agonising slowness, revealing a dark chamber. Here, the usual laws of physics seemed suspended; time itself appeared to fold and ripple, like water disturbed by a submerged stone. Ethereal echoes of past events flickered at the edges of vision, hinting at the vastness of what lay beyond. From the swirling darkness, Valen materialised, his cloak a breathtaking swirl of stardust and shadows, constantly shifting and reforming like a miniature galaxy. His gaze was both penetrating, capable of seeing into the deepest recesses of their souls, and surprisingly

"Brave souls," he spoke, his voice resonating like a distant chime, simultaneously echoing through the chamber and whispering directly into their minds. "You have navigated the treacherous intricacies of the past, confronted your personal demons and embraced the weight of your stories, both the triumphant and the tragic. You have arrived at the realisation that the power that arises from the merging of individual flames into a single, raging fire is the strength that is inherent in your togetherness. The test has been successfully completed, proving that you are deserving of what is to come. Despite this, the journey is not yet over. Now comes the real test of your abilities. I am curious as to what you intend to do next. Will you use your knowledge to create a better future or let the past consume you? His question lingered in the air; it was a profound and weighty choice that was offered with the quiet assurance that their response would ripple through the very fabric of time.

Exultant joy filled the room, an effervescent, palpable energy that crackled in the air and warmed every heart present. They had done it. Against impossible odds, they had succeeded.

Together they embraced the magic of the moment, a spontaneous outpouring of relief, gratitude, and profound connection. Their adventures had altered the course of time, not just for themselves, but perhaps for the world at large, weaving their destinies together with a tapestry of shared experiences, each thread a memory, a challenge overcome, a moment of unwavering loyalty.

As dawn began to break, casting golden rays across the aged walls of the museum, painting the artefacts in a new, celebratory light, Ellie smiled, a genuine, radiating smile that reflected the joy swirling within her. She looked around at her companions, her chosen family. "Whatever happens next, whatever trials or wonders await us beyond these walls, we'll face it together." Her voice, though soft, resonated with conviction. "Our bond is forever inextricable; bound not just by the artefacts we uncovered and due to forge."

A silent understanding passed between the members of the team as they nodded in agreement. They were aware that their journey did not truly end with the rising sun but rather transformed into the solid foundation upon which they would build new explorations and discoveries, new quests and victories. The museum, which had been a battleground in the past, was now a touchstone, a testament to their bravery and brotherhood.

Finn, his fur shimmering in the dawn light, gave a jubilant squeal, darting playfully between their legs, a furry embodiment of their unbridled joy. Oliver, the stalwart guardian, laughed, a hearty, genuine laugh that echoed through the halls. He realised, with a surge of warmth, that he had transcended his role as a mere guard, a protector of objects. He was now a part of something breathtakingly magical, a guardian of people, of stories, of a shared destiny.

As they stepped into the new day, carrying the spirit of the night within them like a precious ember, Ellie felt a whisper in her heart, a gentle nudge of intuition. This was only the beginning. Adventure awaited not just within the hallowed halls of the museum but throughout life's eternal corridors, in every unexplored corner of the world, in every unwritten chapter of their lives. And every moment experienced together, every hardship they overcame, and every victory they celebrated would forever echo through time, shaping who they were and who they would become.

And even though the doors of the museum might close at dawn, putting an end to the echoes of the past for the day, the echoes of the night, the secrets they had discovered, and the connections they had made would continue to lead their souls down new paths, sparking their imaginations and motivating them to create stories that had not yet been told and legends that had not yet been written. The world was waiting for them, and they were prepared to answer its call.

REFLECTIONS
ON ADVENTURE

The starlit sky twinkled through the high, arched windows of the Enchanted Museum, bathing the priceless artefacts in a gentle, ethereal glow. The grand hall, usually hushed and reverent, was still faintly humming with residual magic. The madcap escapades of the night – the chase through time, the talking tapestries, and the near-disaster with the sentient sarcophagus – had finally come to a standstill, but the echoes of laughter, gasps of surprise, and the thrum of adventure still danced in the air, clinging to the velvet ropes and the polished floors. Ellie leaned against the age-worn, cool marble of a towering column, her breath catching in her throat, her heart still racing a frantic rhythm as she took in the surreal aftermath of their extraordinary journey. Dust motes swirled in the silvery light, illuminating the faint sheen of sweat on her forehead.

"Do you think... do you think everything will return to normal?" she mused aloud, her voice barely a whisper, a hint of trepidation clinging to each syllable. She ran a hand through her dishevelled hair, a testament to the chaotic events that had unfolded.

Professor Finch adjusted his spectacles, the lenses catching the starlight and reflecting it in miniature rainbows. He still managed an air of scholarly contemplation, even amidst the fantastical remnants of their night – a misplaced Roman helmet here, a half-unravelled Egyptian scroll there. "Normalcy, dear Ellie, is such a fluid concept," he replied, his tone lively, his eyes twinkling with an almost childlike glee. "Consider all that we've experienced! The temporal anomalies, the enchanted objects, and the very fabric of reality have all been over a precariously balanced display of ancient pottery.

From the shadows cast by a colossal dinosaur skeleton, a soft rustling brought Oliver into view. The museum guard, usually a picture of stoic composure and unflappable professionalism, wore a somewhat bemused expression, his normally impassive face creased with a mixture of exhaustion and incredulity. He clutched his flashlight like a lifeline, its beam dancing nervously across the floor. "You mean to say... all of *this* is normal?" he asked incredulously, gesturing towards the magnificent, roaring lion statue that had, just moments ago, returned to its dormant, stone form beside him, its breath slowly fading into the cool museum air. "I'd dare say my nights patrolling the east wing will never be the same again. I used to worry about teenagers sneaking in, not... not living statues going for a midnight stroll." He looked from Ellie to the Professor, his gaze pleading for a reasonable explanation, a sense of order restored to his universe. The silence in the air, broken only by the distant chime of a grandfather clock, is a stark reminder of the ordinary world waiting just beyond the museum walls.

Azrael the Lion, a magnificent creature crafted from gleaming gold, lazily reclined against the velvet ropes meant to have mere mortals. He flicked his tail, its golden tassel shimmering like captured starlight, with regal nonchalance. "Normal is but a mere statue awaiting midnight's arrival," he chuckled, his voice rich and twinkling with mirth, a sound like the chime of hidden bells. "You have unlocked treasures tonight that will change you forever." His amber eyes, usually fixed and unseeing, now held a knowing glint, as if peering directly into Ellie's very being.

Ellie's mind echoed with a kaleidoscope of memories, a vibrant and chaotic replay of events from the moment she had crossed the museum's threshold and tumbled headfirst into madness. She recalled their first bewildering encounter with Luci, a sinuous bronze figure that had unwound from its pedestal, weaving intricate tales of ancient history. His voice, a hypnotic whisper of polished metal, breathed life into forgotten narratives and painted vivid tapestries of the past. The enchantment of those moments still enveloped her, clinging to her like a finely spun web, as if a spell had been cast upon her very soul. She could almost feel the ghost of Luci's cool bronze scales against her skin.

Finn, a whirlwind of mahogany and mischief, still zipped around the plinths like a playful autumn breeze. He danced between exhibits with an irrepressible energy, a blur of polished wood and boundless curiosity. He paused beside her, his wooden form glimmering in the low light, the candlelight reflecting off his smooth surface, creating a playful contrast with the more sombre surroundings. "Sometimes", he said, his tone mischievous yet profoundly insightful, "the adventure is not just about the destination, the lost artefact, or the solved riddle. It's about the friends you find along the way." His ears perked up, twitching with anticipation, a sure sign that he was eager for more explorations, more mysteries to unravel, and and more laughter to share.

Meanwhile, Lady Arabella, a porcelain doll of exquisite detail and forgotten elegance, appeared from her contemplative silence. She had been perched upon a display case filled with antique jewellery; her painted gaze lost in the swirling patterns of the Persian rugs. "Listen closely, dear ones," she said, her voice like fine silk, full of wisdom gotten through centuries of silent observation. "You each carry a piece of the stories you've uncovered within you. It's not just about history, dusty dates, and forgotten kings; it's about the very essence of bravery, the unwavering loyalty of friendship, and the profound beauty of shared experience. Reflect upon the ties that bind you beyond mere adventure, for those connections will shape who you become." Her porcelain hand, delicate and frail, trembled slightly as she gestured towards them, a subtle reminder of the fragility of time and the enduring power of connection.

"Indeed!" exclaimed Oliver, his voice laced with genuine surprise and burgeoning affection. "I never thought I'd be friends with a lion, a creature of such majestic roar and fierce independence, let alone a serpent, a being steeped in ancient mystery and whispered secrets! Or a wooden fox, for that matter, so meticulously crafted, so full of sly cunning and silent observation!" The relief and sheer absurdity of their unlikely camaraderie finally burst forth. Laughter, bright and unburdened, broke through the lingering tension that had clung to them like cobwebs, instantly bringing the group closer, weaving invisible threads of shared experience and developing trust.

But memories of the treacherous challenges they had faced were difficult Huckleberry . With his piercing gaze and cryptic pronouncements, he had guided them through a labyrinth of riddles and perilous pathways, reminding them at every turn of the immense stakes involved. "You must always remember," Huckleberry had croaked, his voice raspy with the dust of ages, as they carefully extracted him from his centuries-old display case, "knowledge is the pathway to wisdom, that elusive serpent that coils within our minds. And wisdom, dear friends, is power. The power to choose, to act, to ultimately shape your destiny." The weight of his words still hung in the air, a constant reminder of the lessons learned.

"Huckleberry had it right," Ellie chimed in, her eyes sparkling with newfound understanding, a genuine smile finally creeping up her face. "We encountered trials that tested our limits and strengths, pushing us to the very edge of what we thought possible. But it wasn't just about surviving the challenges; it was the knowledge we gained about ourselves, the hidden reserves of courage we discovered, and especially the knowledge we gained about each other, understanding our individual quirks and vulnerabilities, that truly mattered. Understanding, after all, is the first step to acceptance, and acceptance... well, acceptance is the first step to true friendship."

Valen had been an enigma, a spectre haunting their every move. Clad in shadows, he moved through their lives like a phantom, always present but never truly seen. He'd orchestrated their journey towards the ultimate challenge, a complex and dangerous quest that stretched their abilities to the breaking point. Only at the very end, when the dust had settled and the actual cost was tallied, did he reveal his true purpose: a test, a catalyst, a bizarre and convoluted way to forge them anew. "Time shifts and sways," Ellie murmured, her brow furrowed in thought, still reflecting on their bizarre and unsettling encounter with this cloaked figure. She traced a finger along the cool glass of a display case. "And yet, amidst that chaos, we remained steadfast."

"Ah, the bonding!" chimed Finn, his voice full of delight, a bright counterpoint to Ellie's subdued introspection. He clapped his hands together, his eyes sparkling with remembered excitement. "Am I right in saying that we all sharpened our wits, honed our teamwork, and discovered strengths we didn't know we had? I, for one, discovered I'm surprisingly adept at cracking ancient codes under pressure... who knew?" He chuckled, clearly relishing the memory.

"Absolutely," Professor Finch responded, his voice a warm and comforting rumble. He adjusted his spectacles, his gaze sweeping over the group with a hint of pride. "This was about connecting the sinews of history with our hearts—mending ages that had once stood still, fractured by conflict and misunderstanding. Our varied experiences, our individual perspectives, served as the mortar, didn't they? They enriched our understanding of the past and, more importantly, of each other." He paused, a thoughtful expression on his face. "We learnt that collaboration, empathy, and a willingness to challenge our own assumptions are the keys to unlocking the secrets of the ages."

As they meandered between exhibits, each one more awe-inspiring than the last, Ellie felt the combined weight of their shared experience settling upon her shoulders. The museum was a treasure trove, overflowing with artefacts that whispered stories of bygone eras. She felt crushed, not by burden, but by the sheer size of history and by the powerful bonds they had forged through the trials of the night. A new perspective began to take hold of her. The artefacts weren't merely relics; they were vibrant vessels of stories that transported them through time—each with its heartbeat, each whispering a secret that needed to be unearthed. And now, she felt uniquely equipped to listen. The night with Valen hadn't just tested them; it had opened their ears to the whispers of the past.

Dr Bell, her usual scholarly pallor replaced with a rosy hue, looked a touch more vibrant than before, as if the thrill of the adventure had sparked a new fire within her. The desert sun seemed to have kissed her cheeks, bringing out the flecks of gold in her usually serious brown eyes. She leaned against a crate filled with carefully wrapped pottery shards, her gaze sweeping over the makeshift camp. "The purpose of preservation is more than just safeguarding fragile objects from decay, isn't it?" she mused, a thoughtful furrow creasing her brow. "We are the storytellers who breathe life into these artefacts. Each piece whispers of a life lived, a decision made, a moment experienced. It's our duty to tell the world of the daring and the courageous—the lost echoes of those who lived, loved, and ultimately, shaped the world we inhabit today."

The appreciation for their quest surged within Ellie, a warm feeling spreading through her chest like the desert sun. She reflected on what they had achieved – the meticulous excavation, the painstaking restoration, and working with genuine passion. She looked at each member of her newfound family – Mariana, Arabella, and the others – seeing in their eyes the same shared dedication. "And emphasising that the past isn't simply a backdrop; it's an ever-expanding canvas where our adventures paint the future. We learn from their triumphs and their failures and use that knowledge to forge a better path forward."

"Poetic!" Lady Arabella declared, her elegant posture accentuating the grace of her wisdom. Even seated on a dusty folding chair, surrounded by the rugged landscape, she managed to exude an air of refined sophistication. She adjusted the silk scarf around her neck, a hint of a smile playing on her lips. "Indeed! Our memories, both individual and collective, serve as brushstrokes in the grand portrait of life, adding colour, texture, and depth to the overall composition. They are the threads that weave us together, reminding us of the bonds that survive the currents of time and the enduring power of the human spirit." Her words hung in the air, resonating with the weight of history and the promise of the future.

As the first hues of dawn, soft pinks and gentle golds, began to seep through the museum's grand windows, painting long streaks across the polished floors, Ellie felt a gentle tug at her heart. It was a bittersweet sensation, a delicate ache laced with gratitude. Though the night was ending, its secrets unveiled, and its challenges overcome, the essence of their adventure lingered like the warmth of sunlight chasing away shadows, promising a new beginning imbued with the memories they had made.

They had appeared from a night cloaked in mystery, a night where ancient artefacts whispered forgotten tales and mischievous spirits danced in the dimly lit halls, right into the embrace of a new day—together. They were no longer just acquaintances, but allies, strengthened by their triumphs and trials, their fears faced, and their bonds tested. Their lives were now intertwined by the magic of the Enchanted Museum, a shared experience etched into their souls. The air hummed with unspoken understanding; a silent promise of loyalty forged in the crucible of their shared adventure.

Across from her, Oliver watched the dawn break, his gaze steady and resolute. The weariness of the night still clung to him, etched faintly on his face, but his eyes shone with newfound purpose. "I don't wish to return to yesterday," he said, his voice carrying a quiet strength, staring firmly at the shifting shadows of the conquered night. "The horrors we faced, the puzzles we solved... they've changed us. Whatever comes next, outside these walls, I want us to face it as a team. The museum's enchantment may abide only until dusk, its magic fading with the setting sun, but the camaraderie forged here, the trust we've placed in each other, will endure far beyond. It will become a part of who we are." He paused, a hint of a hopeful smile playing on his lips. "We've learnt we can rely on each other, and that's a power no magic can erase."

"And so promise, a pact forged in the heart of the enchanted museum. "For what is adventure", he continued, his voice softening with a hint of wistful longing, "but the echoes of the past, no longer silent, but whispering tales of bravery, loss, and triumph, beckoning us forward into the unknown? They are the ghosts of dreams urging us to chase our own."

As Ellie, her cheeks flushed with excitement and a touch of trepidation, tucked a stray strand of hair behind her ear, her gaze swept across her companions. She saw in their eyes the same spark of determination that burnt within her own heart. Each face was etched with the memory of the stories they had unearthed, the secrets they had shared in the museum's hallowed halls. She nodded with renewed resolve, a strength she hadn't known she had radiating outwards. "We've only just begun," she affirmed, her voice ringing with conviction. "Let's venture into the day, carrying the weight and the wonder of these stories, keeping them alive not just in our memories, but in our actions, our choices. Let's ensure they are forever infused with the spirit of the enchanted museum – a spirit of courage, curiosity, and unwavering hope."

Together, as one, they turned towards the rising sun, its warmth promising a new beginning. They embarked on a journey not just through history, piecing together fragments of forgotten lives, but forward into the future they would create, a future shaped by the lessons learnt they faced it together, armed with the wisdom of the past and the unwavering hope for a brighter tomorrow.

THE PROMISE
OF TOMORROW

There was a palpable, magical energy that permeated the enchanted museum, and it was like a silent symphony that only those who were in tune with its ancient heart could truly hear. As if they were figures from a dream that was only partially recalled, Ellie and her companions, Professor Finch and Mr Davies, the stoic security guard who was undeniably affected, appeared from the swirling shadows of the past. There was a faint pre-dawn light that was filtering through the tall stained-glass windows of the museum, and it illuminated the dust motes that were dancing in the air. These dust motes were disturbed by their journey through time. The adventures that they had experienced in a single, whirlwind night felt nothing short of extraordinary, a tapestry woven with threads of danger, intrigue, and unimaginable wonder. They had avoided mischievous sprites in the Renaissance exhibit, deciphered cryptic runes etched into a Viking longboat, and narrowly escaped the clutches of a reanimated Egyptian mummy, to name a few of the adventures that they had experienced.

Ellie stood in the middle of the grand space as the first light of dawn began to penetrate the opulent foyer, painting it in hues of soft lavender and rose gold. rose-gold. Her heart was full of promise, but it was also weighed down by a profound sense of responsibility. Her shoulders were pressed down by the weight of history, which she had both experienced and seen.

"Am I able to sense it? Her voice was barely heard above the creaks and groans of the ancient building as it adjusted to the new day.' she whispered, her language barely heard. She turned her attention to Professor Finch, who was frantically writing in his notebook, creating a whirlwind of ink and a flurry of frantic energy. His wild, silver hair, which was always in a state of disarray, was doing a poor job of keeping up with his thoughts. Each strand of his hair appeared to vibrate with the residue of his intellectual excitement. We have solved riddles that have been around for centuries, seen things that are beyond comprehension, and uncovered a great deal tonight. On the other hand, it seems as though there is still a great deal more to understand. Perhaps we have only just begun to scratch the surface."

Professor Finch looked up, his spectacles perched precariously on his nose, his eyes sparkling with an almost manic enthusiasm. He clutched his notebook to his chest like a precious relic. "Indeed, Ellie! Indeed! Each artefact holds countless stories – layers of time waiting to be unravelled, like geological strata revealing the secrets of the earth. The possibilities are... staggering! But we must tread carefully, my dear. Remember the cautionary tale; it is a powerful force, Ellie, and it does not always appreciate being disturbed." He glanced nervously at Mr Davies, who was standing silently by the entrance, his normally jovial face etched with a profound, unsettling unease. It was obvious that the events of the night had shaken him more than he let on.

As if stirred by their conversation, Azrael the Lion stretched, his majestic form shimmering in the soft hue of dawn's light filtering through the arched windows. The grand hall, usually bustling with visitors, was still and expectant. Muscles rippled beneath his golden fur as he extended his massive paws, claws retracting and extending with a soft, rhythmic click against the ancient stone floor. "The promise of tomorrow lies not in what we've discovered, but in what we choose to do with that knowledge," he proclaimed, his voice a deep rumble that reverberated through the vast space, shaking the very dust motes dancing in the sunbeams. It was a pronouncement that hung in the air, a challenge and an invitation all at once.

Ellie's gaze drifted to the shimmering mosaic tiles beneath her feet, each piece a fragment of history, painstakingly placed centuries ago. Cobalt blue interspersed with fiery gold, depicting scenes of forgotten empires and mythical creatures. She traced a worn pattern with her finger, a faint hum resonating beneath her touch. She felt a stirring in her heart, as though they were the key to unlocking further mysteries, a tangible connection to the individuals who had walked these same halls before

Suddenly, Luci slithered forth, her bronze scales glinting with an otherworldly sheen, catching the dawn light and refracting it into a thousand tiny rainbows across the floor. She moved with a fluid grace, a hypnotic dance of curves and shadows, her eyes, like chips of obsidian, fixed on Ellie. "The future is woven from the past," she intoned, her voice a low, melodic hiss that sent a shiver down Ellie's spine. "But it is you, dear friends, who will choose the threads. This museum is merely a tapestry, reflecting the decisions of those who walk within its walls. Guard its stories, learn from its lessons, and weave a future worthy of its legacy." She raised her head, a knowing glint in her eyes. "For the past, present, and future are inextricably linked, each informing the other

Oliver scratched his head in bewildered frustration as he stumbled out of the labyrinthine network of museum exhibitions. Although the revelations that had occurred the night before were still swirling around in his mind, Oliver was still unable to process them. The burden of what he had discovered, the inconceivable realities that he had seen, clung to him like the mist of the morning. In a resolute manner, he asserted, "All I know is that we need to fix what was broken," while his brow furrowed into a determined frown. "In light of everything that we have been through, the changes in time, and the glimpses into what might be... It would be irresponsible of us to simply allow everything to be forgotten. There is no way that we can allow it to become merely another exhibit.

The voice of Lady Arabella, who chimed in, was like the melodious ringing of tiny silver bells. "Do not be afraid, my dear Oliver," she encouraged. As she approached him, she exuded an air of refined composure, even during chaotic circumstances. "The actions you take today will have repercussions for all of eternity. Each choice and action causes ripples to be felt throughout the timelines. The decisions that we make have the potential to change the very course of history. Considering the monumental task that lay ahead of them, her words served as a sharp reminder of the importance of proceeding with caution and intent.

Suddenly, a flash of crimson fur dashed across the polished floor. Finn, a whirlwind of mischievous energy, scampered around their feet, his bright eyes twinkling with playful delight. "I think all of you are overthinking it!" he exclaimed, his bushy tail wagging enthusiastically. "Just enjoy the museum's wonders! Feel the magic crackling in the air. It feels alive, doesn't it? Tomorrow will take care of itself! Besides, worrying won't brew us any extra cups of tea!" His joyful spirit was contagious, an effervescent antidote to the heavy atmosphere, and soon even their solemn discussions took on a lighter, more hopeful note.

As the group shared amused glances and knowing smiles over Finn's cheeky antics, a shadow fell across them. Huckleberry , a majestic creature of ebony plumage and piercing golden eyes, perched himself regally on a nearby pedestal, his formidable presence silencing the immediate mirth. His ebony feathers ruffled slightly in the fresh morning air that drifted in from the open museum doors. "There is wisdom in your words, Finn," he conceded, his voice a deep rumble that resonated through the hall, "but do not disregard what lies ahead. The power that has been bestowed upon Valen has not yet been shown in its entirety. Although we have only scratched the surface of our understanding, he is in possession of the skills necessary to manipulate the very fabric of time itself. There is still work that needs to be done, and the significance of this discovery cannot be overstated. In the balance is not only the future of this museum but also the future of the entire world and possibly the entire universe.

Just then, Dr Bell burst into the room from a side corridor, a whirlwind of energy despite her dishevelled appearance. Her dark hair, usually meticulously pinned, was tousled about her face, and lines of exhaustion etched themselves around her eyes. Yet, her expression was anything but defeated; it shone with a fierce, determined light. "I've been thinking," she said breathlessly, her voice raspy with lack of sleep but brimming with renewed fervour. Her sudden arrival and impassioned words had an immediate effect, reigniting the group's flagging spirits and dragging them back from the brink of despair. "What if we can harness the magic we've awakened? Not only do you have it, but you also study it, and you use it? What if we were able to preserve not only the artefacts themselves but also the stories that they tell and then share those stories with the world beyond these institutions and beyond these walls?" She paused, her eyes moving over each of them, and her sense of urgency was palpable. "We can have the ability to create an experience, a living tapestry of history that connects people through time, sparking their imaginations and fostering understanding."

"An exhibition!" Ellie exclaimed, her heart pounding with the excitement of a flurry of possibilities, ideas bubbling to the surface like champagne. "We can share our journey, teach others about the history we've uncovered, and showcase how the threads of our experiences, both past and present, interweave to create the world we live in..." she exclaimed, the word barely escaping her lips before her brain had fully formed the thought. "We can do all of these things." Rather than being merely a dry and static display behind glass, it has the potential to be an exciting adventure! People can establish a genuine connection with the past through this dynamic experience.

Indeed, this is a wonderful concept! As Professor Finch exclaimed, his normally pale cheeks became flushed with excitement. He straightened his tie, which was already straight, and his eyes shone brightly. "Imagine the lessons we can impart, the understanding we can foster!" Furthermore, consider the community we have the potential to build! An environment in which individuals from all occupations can congregate to investigate, get knowledge, and feel appreciation for the intricate web of human history.

Lady Arabella, whose first apprehension had been palpable, now sat forward, her eyes shining with genuine approval. "Your vision, combined with this noble intention, will do far more than simply restore what was lost," she said, her voice resonating with a newfound conviction. "It will illuminate paths yet walked, revealing hidden opportunities and inspiring future generations to connect with their heritage."

Oliver leaned forward, his usual cynicism momentarily forgotten, and said, "Okay, I'm in." Oliver is known for his pragmatic approach. However, what are the steps that we need to take? Even so, could you please advise on where we should begin? The puzzle that was in front of them was obviously more alluring than any earlier uncertainties that he had. His curiosity was piqued.

Ellie took a deep breath as she felt the weight of the task that lay ahead of her, but she was also buoyed by the collective enthusiasm. "First", she said, meeting each of their gazes in turn, "we must seek guidance." To obtain Valen's blessing, we must pay him a visit. In the absence of a comprehensive understanding of the repercussions of our plans, there is no possibility of successfully completing this task or of sharing this power with the world in a responsible manner. We need his perspective because he is the one who holds the key to understanding the delicate balance of time.

Thus, let us get moving!" Azrael roared, the sound bouncing off the silent exhibits, a primal urgency striding ahead of them, pulling the team into its wake. "We cannot allow the night to fall without leaving our mark," Azrael said. We have gone too far and taken too much of a risk. Tonight, we are here to make history, not just see it!"

Together, they wove through the labyrinthine hallways of the museum, a newfound determination propelling them forward like an invisible wind. The hushed silence, once oppressive, now felt expectant, a stage set for their daring performance. Every step echoed with the familiarity of adventure, a rhythm they knew well, while the soft, strategically placed emergency lights lightened not only their path but also the emotional burden of the night's trials. The claustrophobia of the cramped storage rooms and dimly lit galleries had receded, replaced by a focused anticipation.

As they reached the central chamber, the grand, cathedral-like space that housed the museum's most prized possessions, the shadows in the room began to deepen, swirling and coalescing until they solidified into a discernible figure cloaked in mystery—Valen. He stood tall, an imposing presence that seemed to emanate from the very stones of the building. His features were obscured by the deep cowl of his cloak, but his eyes, glinting with centuries of knowledge, pierced the gloom.

"Ah, brave souls," his voice resonated through the chamber, deep and melodic, carrying a weight of authority mixed with an unexpected gentleness. It was a voice that had likely witnessed empires rise and fall, the laughter of children and the lamentations of mourners. "You have navigated well through the challenges of the night. Your dedication and resourcefulness have been proved by your actions." "But tell me, "He asked, his gaze sweeping over them, analysing and evaluating, "what are you willing to give up in exchange for the power to shape your tomorrow?" The question lingered in the air, replete with implications that were not explicitly said.

She met Valen's intense gaze, her voice steady and clear despite the tremor of excitement that ran through her. "We would like your blessing to create a living exhibition, a space where the history of each artefact can breathe once more, where stories aren't confined to dusty labels and glass cases," Ellie said as she stepped forward, her earlier trepidation having been replaced by a newly discovered confidence that blossomed within her like a defiant flower from within.

This is a place where the past can ignite the imagination of the present, thereby establishing a connection between people of all ages and the human stories we have unearthed. The past is something that we want to honour, but not as a static relic; rather, we want to honour it as a dynamic foundation upon which we can build a better future. We are here to offer you our enthusiasm, our commitment, and our unyielding dedication to the preservation and dissemination of the stories that mean something to you.

Thus, let us get moving! " Azrael roared, the sound bouncing off the silent exhibits, a primal urgency striding ahead of them, pulling the team into its wake. "We

Together, they wove through the labyrinthine hallways of the museum, a newfound determination propelling them forward like an invisible wind. The hushed silence, once oppressive, now felt expectant, a stage set for their daring performance. Every step echoed with the familiarity of adventure, a rhythm they knew well, while the soft, strategically placed emergency lights lightened not only their path but also the emotional burden of the night's trials. The claustrophobia of the cramped storage rooms and dimly lit galleries had receded, replaced by a focused anticipation.

As they reached the central chamber, the grand, cathedral-like space that housed the museum's most prized possessions, the shadows in the room began to deepen, swirling and coalescing until they solidified into a discernible figure cloaked in mystery—Valen. He stood tall, an imposing presence that seemed to emanate from the very stones of the building. His features were obscured by the deep cowl of his cloak, but his eyes, glinting with centuries of knowledge, pierced the gloom.

"Ah, brave souls," his voice resonated through the chamber, deep and melodic, carrying a weight of authority mixed with an unexpected gentleness. It was a voice that had likely witnessed empires rise and fall, the laughter of children and the lamentations of mourners. "You have navigated well through the challenges of the night. Your dedication and resourcefulness have been proved by your actions. However, I would like to know, "His gaze swept over them, scrutinising and assessing. " "What can you offer?" "What are you willing to sacrifice in exchange for the power to shape your tomorrow?" The question lingered in the air, replete with implications that were not explicitly said.

Ellie stepped forward, her earlier trepidation replaced by a newfound confidence that bloomed within her like a defiant flower. She met Valen's intense gaze, her voice steady and clear despite the tremor of excitement that ran through her. "We would like your blessing to create a living exhibition, a space where the history of each artefact can breathe once more and where stories aren't confined to dusty labels and glass cases." This is a place where the past ignites the imagination of the present, connecting people—both young and old—to the human stories we've uncovered. We wish to honour the past, not as a static relic but as a vibrant foundation upon which to build a brighter future. We offer you our passion, our dedication, and our constant commitment to preserving.

As they made their way back, the air in the museum was thick with the lingering scent of dust and adventure, and the group could be heard cheering and laughing as they made their way back. An ecstatic testimony to the adventures that took place during the night, the echoes reflected off the ancient artefacts. Although they understood their adventures were not yet over, they were overcome with a profound sense of excitement. The experience had tied them together in a way that could not be broken, regardless of whether their first venture had been characterised by foolishness or driven by genuine triumph. As a group, they had become a formidable force that had the potential to alter the destinies that were woven into the very walls of the museum and possibly even the world beyond.

The experience was only the first step, a tentative toe that briefly touched the surface of a vast and uncharted ocean. A more extensive journey was waiting to unfold in front of them, forming a complex mosaic of opportunities and challenges that were woven together with strands of mystery and intrigue. It was a promise of tomorrow that would never end, illuminated by the vibrant colours of their newly formed partnerships, which were forged in the crucible of their shared experiences.

They were united as friends and allies, and their hearts were filled with a camaraderie that went beyond simple acquaintance. They faced the future with unwavering hope. The memory of this night, the whispered secrets of the museum, and the discoveries that were fuelled by adrenaline would be permanently etched into their minds, evoking the enchanted atmosphere of the night that would reverberate throughout their lives and beyond, resonating in their actions and shaping the legends that they would eventually become. The museum, which had been a static monument to the past, had transformed into a living, breathing testament to their potential. It was a place that would forever be imbued with the spirit of their shared adventure for all time.

WHISPERS OF DESTINY

A round the time that the clock tower struck midnight, the echoes of laughter and chatter that had been heard during the day's grand reopening gradually faded into silence. A solemn countdown to the night's true unveiling was being performed by each chime, which reverberated throughout the vast halls. There was a palpable energy that shimmered in the air deep within the heart of the Enchanted Museum. It was a living, breathing force that hummed against the skin. Ornate chandeliers, which were dormant during the day, began to flicker to life, their warm glow illuminating the labyrinthine corridors that housed treasures that had been buried for an exceptionally long time. These treasures were relics that spoke of secrets and artefacts that yearned to be freed from their confinement. There was a slight ripple in the tapestries that were woven with previously forgotten magic, and the air itself seemed to be thick with anticipation.

Ellie took a moment to compose herself as she leaned back against the cool, moss-kissed stone of an ancient pillar in a secluded corner of the museum, close to the Hall of Antiquities. Dancing around her like teeny-tiny, inquisitive spirits were the dust particles that swirled in the light of the chandelier. She was filled with a potent mixture of fear and exhilaration as she experienced the thrill of adventure coursing through her veins. It had only been a few hours since she had been standing in the same room, brimming with excitement at the prospect of what the night might bring, eager to finally explore the museum after hours. She had seen artefacts blossoming with life, such as a Roman bust reciting poetry and a Viking longship model sailing across the reflecting pool. Now disorder prevailed, and she had seen these things. What a typical example of the museum's unpredictable nature! She ought to have known better than to expect a peaceful evening spent conducting research.

As he clung to his torch like it was a lifeline, Oliver, the night guard who was unaware of what was going on, fumbled around closely beside her. His brow furrowed in an expression of concern. A haphazard dance was performed by the beam, which reflected off the polished shields and the shining weaponry. "What should we do now? At first, the suits of armour in the Mediaeval exhibit began to engage in a battle, and then... then the Egyptian sarcophagus began to speak! A nervous glance was cast in the direction of the shadows that danced along the walls, elongated and distorted by the flickering light. "Everything that was once so familiar has turned into something that is completely strange," he murmured. His face, which was normally bright and cheerful, was pale and showed a mixture of fear and disbelief.

In response, Ellie said, "Believe me, Oliver, if there's one thing I've learnt tonight, it's that every shadow has its story." Her enthusiasm for history was bubbling to the surface, and it overpowered her own apprehension. Her heart raced with excitement, and she felt a profound sense of discovery. She adjusted her glasses, her eyes shining with curiosity even though she was aware of the imminent danger. She straightened up and pushed herself off the pillar.

"What we need to do is figure out what those stories are and, more importantly, why they are waking up now," she said. "Come on. Let's see what else the night has in store for us."

Exactly at that moment, a resounding roar reverberated throughout the corridors of the museum, causing the very foundations of the establishment to shake. Ornate tapestries appeared to be rippling, ancient artefacts appeared to be shaking on their pedestals, and the air seemed to crackle with an almost palpable energy. The ethereal light that seemed to emanate from Azrael the Lion, the ancient Egyptian guardian of the museum, materialised from the shadows that lined the grand hall. His golden fur shimmered in the light that seemed to emanate from him. His eyes burnt with the knowledge that had been accumulated over the course of millennia, and he was enormous, a magnificent specimen frozen in a perpetual state of powerful grace. Don't be afraid, my dear ones! His tone was loud and authoritative, resonating with a commanding presence that demanded attention. "The Night of Whispers presents opportunities that none of you have ever experienced before. Intertwined destinies, rewritten fates, and revealed secrets were all part of the story. Arrive! The future is waiting for us!"

The weight of destiny settled on the group with the force of a physical presence as Azrael's voice rumbled through the air, washing over them like a wave of ancient power. A physical presence was the manifestation of this weight. They found themselves drawn closer to one another as well as to the mesmerising spectacle that was taking place in front of them as the cloak of adventure, which had been spun from the threads of mystery and intrigue, wrapped that around them. Luci, who was standing next to them, slithered down from her pedestal, the ancient stone groaning softly under her weight. Her bronze scales, which were intricately etched with hieroglyphs, glowed with an inner light that reflected the flickering candlelight. As she whispered, her voice was a melodic tinkle, like the delicate chime of distant bells. "To see your paths is to understand where you have been," she said. "But first, before you can shape your futures, we must solve the riddle of the heart."

Her instincts, which had been honed over the course of years of solving puzzles and having an unquenchable thirst for knowledge, kicked in. While she was dissecting the cryptic words, classifying potential solutions, and already formulating a plan of attack, her inquisitive mind turned repeatedly with possibilities. It was with barely held excitement that she exclaimed, "What riddle? What heart are we talking about? I'm ready!" Her voice was bubbling with excitement.

The movements of Finn were as fluid and unpredictable as a flickering flame, and he darted through the corridors with a mischievous glint in his wooden eyes. He came to a stop close to Ellie, his carved features giving off an air of playful caution in some way. A word of caution, however! Much like an onion, the heart is shielded by layers of protection! Every successive layer presents a unique obstacle and a different test. In addition, each one needs to be removed with caution. It only takes one incorrect response or one careless assumption to ensure that the secrets are kept hidden for all time, encased in a wall that cannot be broken through.

Ellie, Oliver, and Professor Finch, who had materialised silently out of the deeper shadows near a massive statue of Anubis, nodded with a shared glance that spoke volumes. It was a silent agreement to face the unknown together, a commitment to uncovering the truth. These three individuals had nodded. There was a low, eager rumble in Professor Finch's voice as he urged Luci to provide additional information. His eyes sparkled with the unadulterated eagerness of discovery, reflecting the same childlike wonder he had had when he first discovered his passion for ancient history. His demeanour, which was normally scholarly, was elevated to a higher level. Even though it was obvious that the Night of Whispers was stirring something deep within him, he was prepared to give it his full attention.

"Three artefacts hold the key," Luci explained, her voice reverberating throughout the vast hall as she was speaking. She moved with the grace of a serpent, winding herself around in a slow circle in front of them, her eyes shining with the disturbing knowledge that she had. "Every moment is a moment in time, a lesson learnt that is essential to re-establishing the equilibrium," the instructor said. Beginnings, also known as the fragile hope, that appears from the darkness, are represented by the new moon. The first snowfall symbolises the transformation, the letting go of the old and the acceptance of the new things that are on the horizon.

And finally, the ascent of the sun... unity, the coming together of disparate elements into a unified whole.

The implications of Luci's words caused Ellie's mind to race as she furrowed her brow to understand them. "We need to uncover these artefacts. But where might we find them? This museum is enormous."

"Child, learn to trust your gut instincts. They will not lead you astray." Lady Arabella spoke, her voice like a graceful breeze of elegance, a whisper of silk against skin. As she stepped forward, the essence of the 18th-century nobleperson came to life before their eyes, the flickering candlelight reflecting in her powdered wig. "The museum is a tapestry of history, woven intricately with threads of memory and magic. When you are looking for the new moon, you should look in the Sculpture Room. There, silent forms hold the weight of ages. During the snowfall, you should look for the Chamber of Stories, which is the place where stories are told on the wind and legends are created. You will be able to see the sun rising from the grand balcony that looks out over the sleeping city. On the other hand, you should be wary of the shadows because they have the potential to mislead you by luring you with promises of false hope and whispers of power.

Oliver straightened his back, and his gaze hardened with determination as he declared, "Let's move, then!" The burden of the task began to settle on his shoulders, but a spark of determined energy began to rekindle within him. He went on to say, "We might even find a way to return this chaos to silence before dawn paints the sky. We owe it to the city and to everyone."

As they ventured deeper into the museum, the air grew thick with anticipation, crackling with unseen energies. Ellie felt the weight of destiny in the air, an invisible hand guiding her steps, pulling her towards the unknown. The Sculpture Room revealed itself first, a hushed sanctuary filled with marble figures frozen in eternal tableau. Almost instinctually, she stepped towards an exquisite piece standing for a new moon, its silver glimmer catching her eye in the dim light. The coolness of the stone resonated against her fingertips. "Could this be it?" she whispered, running her fingers gently over the smooth, crescent surface.

"Artefacts such as these must be treated with respect. They hold stories that you cannot yet fathom, energies that are volatile and potentially dangerous." Professor Finch cautioned, his voice laced with concern. He adjusted his spectacles and approached with a cautious reverence. "Artefacts such as these hold them."

At that moment, a low hum reverberated through the room, vibrating through the floor and up into their bones. The very air seemed to shimmer and distort. "To unlock the past, one must pay heed to the present," Huckleberry croaked from his perch above, his voice a raspy echo that seemed to emanate from the very stones of the museum. He ruffled his feathers, scattering dust motes in the air like tiny stars. "What shines bright may also hold darkness. Answer truthfully, and this moon shall reveal its wisdom or consume you in its shadow."

Ellie's voice was tinged with anxiety as she asked, "What do we need to answer?" She was enjoying the cryptic clues that were unfolding in front of her, but the stakes felt like they were impossible to deal with. The fate of the museum, and possibly the fate of the city, rested on their shoulders.

"In moments of twilight, when the world is shrouded in doubt and uncertainty, what guides you true when shadows spill across the blue and the path ahead is obscured from view?" Huckleberry asked as he spread his wings wide and cast a long, menacing shadow over the artefact. The room appeared to become colder, and the air seemed to become heavier.

Ellie pondered the riddle in enormous depth, ultimately closing her eyes and leaning into the pulsating energy emanating from the surface of the moon. Images flashed through her mind, including Oliver's unyielding determination, Finn's boundless optimism, and Professor Finch's unwavering knowledge. "Friendship", she finally spoke, her voice clear and resolute, breaking through the oppressive silence. "In times of uncertainty, it is our bonds with each other that guide us." It is the hope that we have in common with one another and the trust that we have in one another that keeps us on the right path.

Suddenly, light exploded from the artefact, bathing the room in an ethereal glow. The new moon shimmered, its surface rippling and transforming. It detached itself from the pedestal, reshaping itself into a glowing orb that hovered in front of Ellie, pulsating with a gentle, warm light. "You have answered wisely," Huckleberry proclaimed, his voice a swirl of enchantment and approval. "The first piece has been unveiled. The power of the new moon is now yours to wield."

As they held the orb, its glow expanded, pushing back the shadows and revealing a hidden passage behind the statue, a secret doorway shimmering with ethereal light. The scent of ancient parchment and forgotten magic wafted from within, beckoning them forward. "On to the next!" cried Finn, his youthful exuberance bubbling to the surface as he leaped playfully into the light, eager to face the next challenge. "Snowfall, here we come!"

Navigating the maze-like corridors, their footsteps echoing in the oppressive silence, they finally landed at the Chamber of Stories. The air within felt different, charged, expectant. Its walls were adorned with tapestries, not mere decorations, but living chronicles, each thread woven with ancient verses that hummed with barely perceptible energy. A deep sense of nostalgia, a feeling of being both profoundly lost and inexplicably home, washed over Ellie as she stepped inside. The chamber seemed to remember her, or perhaps a part of her she had forgotten. "We must find the artefact of the first snowfall," she said to the group, her voice echoing slightly, carrying a weight of urgency that belied her youthful appearance.

The air was heavy with anticipation, shimmering with possibilities that danced just beyond the reach of their senses. Dust motes swirled in the shafts of light that pierced the gloom, each a tiny universe reflecting the weight of untold tales. "Look for anything that speaks of winter," the wise Lady Arabella suggested, her gaze sweeping the room, missing nothing. Her eyes, usually bright with mirth, now held a serious focus, betraying the importance of their quest. She ran a gloved hand along a tapestry depicting frost-covered trees, her brow furrowed in concentration.

Oliver's eyes, ever quick to spot the unusual, twinkled at the sight of a snow-laden wooden carving nestled in a dusty corner, almost hidden in shadow. He rushed over, his boots scraping softly against the stone floor, driven by an almost childlike excitement. He knelt, his fingers itching to touch it. "This could be it!" he announced, his voice a hushed exclamation.

As he brushed the dust away, revealing intricate details of hand-carved snowflakes and frosted branches, a flurry of shimmering snowflakes materialised around them. No ordinary snow, these flakes radiated an ethereal light, swirling in a magical dance that defied gravity. The temperature dropped perceptibly, and the air crackled with unseen energy. A voice appeared from the artefact, soft yet insistent, resonating not just in their ears but in the very bones of the chamber. "In the stillness of winter's breath, what reflects the beauty of life and death?"

Ellie grits her teeth, her mind racing, piecing together the fragments of lore she had studied for so long. The riddle hung in the air, a challenge thrown down by an ancient power. "It speaks of renewal... the cycle of life!" she exclaimed, her eyes widening with understanding. "It's about understanding the fragility and beauty of existence. Winter is a time of dormancy, of what appears to be death; however, one can find the promise of rebirth within the sleep that winter brings. The artefact probes us to decide what exemplifies the delicate equilibrium that exists between deterioration and fresh starts!"

The quest, however, refused to falter.

The artefact, a mysterious source of power humming within the museum, responded to what it perceived as genuine understanding. In that moment, a radiant snowflake, intricate and ethereal, unfurled before Ellie. The air around her shimmered with an almost tangible light, illuminating the delicate patterns of ice crystals. As she reached out hesitantly, drawn by an irresistible force, the snowflake underwent a magical metamorphosis. It dissolved, transforming into a delicate silver pendant, cool against her skin, and settling perfectly around her neck. The pendant pulsed with a soft, inner light, a symbol not just of the beauty of winter but of the potent, transformative power of deeper understanding.

Oliver shouted, "Two down, one to go!" with a voice that rang with contagious enthusiasm. He pumped his fists in the air, his youthful excitement bubbling over. The success fuelled their determination to continue.

Racing towards the grand balcony, a palpable sense of anticipation electrified the air. Their footsteps echoed through the vast hall; each beat a counterpoint to the pounding in their chests. Outside, the sun's soft rays began to paint the sky with hues of pink and gold, signalling the dawn. An awakening light seeped through the grand windows, gently caressing the museum's static exhibits, breathing a semblance of life into them. And yet, this beautiful sunrise stirred a sense of urgency within Ellie. Time felt like it was slipping through her fingers, and the final challenge loomed large.

Reaching the balcony, they found themselves facing a magnificent golden sun sculpture. It stood in the very centre, its radiant face dominating the space. Thick, verdant vines, rich with leaves and blossoms, were intricately intertwined around its form, softening the otherwise imposing image. As they approached, the sun glimmered, an almost imperceptible shift in its golden sheen, suggesting a keen awareness of their presence. A booming voice, resonating with the power of a thousand suns, filled the balcony as the air crackled with energy. "Answer me this," it declared, the words echoing around them, "What joins as one, despite differences, brings forth unity within diversity?"

Ellie's heart raced, a frantic drum solo against the backdrop of the silent, expectant faces surrounding her. The weight of the moment, the culmination of their quest, pressed down on her. "It's the connections we forge, isn't it?" she responded instinctively, the words tumbling out, born of a deep-seated belief rather than conscious thought. "Diverse stories woven together create history."

As if in agreement, a triumphant beam of sunlight erupted from the intricate sculpture that dominated the balcony, defying the late hour. It illuminated the space with a golden radiance, wrapping around the group like a warm embrace, a tangible representation of hope. They could feel the bonds encircling them, the invisible threads of friendship and shared purpose tightening, echoing the undeniable truth in Ellie's answer. The power of their unity was palpable, a force as real as the ancient stones beneath their feet.

Then, the artefact she had sought so desperately, the one that had started this perilous journey, burst forth with renewed energy. It transformed into a glimmering orb, a miniature sun that glowed fiercely in Ellie's hands, radiating warmth and an almost sentient hum. One by one, each of the artefacts they had painstakingly recovered throughout the night levitated from their resting places and drifted towards her, drawn by an unseen force. Now, all the artefacts lay nestled in her grip, pulsating with light and energy, as if alive and anxious to fulfil their purpose.

A voice, soft yet undeniably powerful, intoned from the shadows. "Destiny unfolds through your choices and bonds." Valen, a figure shrouded in mystery and legend, stepped forward, his presence commanding yet enigmatic. He seemed to emanate an aura of timeless wisdom, his gaze holding the weight of centuries. "You have navigated the trials and unveiled the whispered truths of timing and unity. You have proven yourselves worthy. Now comes the task of restoration."

With a voice that was barely above a whisper, Ellie enquired, "Restoration?" She was breathless with anticipation and a hint of apprehension. The culmination of their efforts was approaching, but please clarify what it specifically involves.

"The chaos unleashed this night must be balanced," Valen replied, his words resonating with solemnity. "The delicate threads of time have been frayed, the harmony disrupted. With these artefacts, conduits of ancient power, you will mend the rifts created this night. Their powers, combined with the strength of your unity, will restore tranquillity before the dawn breaks and the damage becomes irreparable." The fate of the world, it seemed, rested squarely on their shoulders.

The weight of the evening and the challenges they had met coalesced into a single, urgent question that hung in the air. "It's the connections we forge, isn't it?" Ellie's heart raced, and a frantic drum pressed against her ribs. She responded instinctively, the words tumbling out as a confirmation of the feeling that had grown within her ever since this whole thing started. "Different stories woven together create history," she said.

A triumphant beam of sunlight, impossibly radiant despite the late hour, erupted from the heart of the intricate sculpture that dominated the balcony. It sliced through the darkness, illuminating the faces of her companions and wrapping around the group like a warm, palpable embrace. They could feel the invisible bonds encircling them, tightening, strengthening – echoing the profound truth in Ellie's answer. A shared understanding, forged in danger and sacrifice, connected them in a way that transcended words.

The artefact she had painstakingly found – a seemingly insignificant piece of carved obsidian – burst forth with sudden energy, transforming into a shimmering, opalescent orb. It glowed fiercely in Ellie's hands, bathing her face in its ethereal light. Now, the other artefacts, each a testament to a different, interconnected moment in time, lay cradled in her grip, pulsating with a life force that was both exhilarating and terrifying. They thrummed in unison, a symphony of ancient power resonating within her very being.

"Destiny unfolds through your choices and bonds," a voice intoned softly from the shadows. The sound was ancient and resonant, seeming to vibrate through the very stones of the balcony. Valen stepped forward, his presence commanding yet enigmatic. His face, etched with the weight of centuries, held a mixture of anticipation and knowing. "You have navigated the trials and unveiled the whispered truths of timing and unity. You have proven yourselves worthy. Now comes the task of restoration."

When Ellie asked, "Restoration?" she was breathless with anticipation and a touch of trepidation. The burden of responsibility had settled upon her shoulders, and it was heavy yet strangely invigorating.

"The chaos must be balanced," Valen replied, his gaze unwavering. "The threads of time have been frayed, the delicate balance disrupted. With these artefacts and the power they hold, you will mend the rifts created this night. Their powers, combined with your unity, your understanding of the interwoven nature of existence, will restore tranquillity before dawn. The fate of more than just this city rests in your hands."

Ellie's breath hitched in her throat. The weight of the past few hours, the frantic energy, and the sheer impossibility of their success seemed to coalesce into a single, overwhelming emotion: gratitude. It wasn't just a polite thank you but a profound and soul-deep realisation of the incredible people surrounding her and the extraordinary experiences they had shared. Her gaze swept across the room, taking in the silent witnesses to their endeavours – the ancient artefacts, the crumbling scrolls, and the weathered statues that had somehow guided them through the perilous night. Each object seemed to hum with a forgotten energy, a testament to the enduring power of history, and Ellie understood with startling clarity that their journey was destined to become part of that narrative, a legend.

The oppressive darkness that had clung to them just moments before began to recede, replaced by the tentative glow of dawn. Sunlight, hesitant at first, streamed through the grand, arched windows, painting the dust motes dancing in the air with a golden hue. It illuminated the faces of her friends, etched with exhaustion but alight with a profound sense of accomplishment. Seeing their weary smiles, the shared understanding in their eyes, Ellie felt a surge of hope bloom within her. This moment wasn't just the culmination of their quest, the end of a chapter. It was a turning point, a springboard launching them into a future brimming with possibilities. This ending was, in fact, a beginning. Their destinies, irrevocably intertwined beneath the watchful gaze of the moon, had led them here, to this pivotal moment. And if they had each other, they would continue to chase the thrill of the unknown, to explore the forgotten corners of the world, and to listen to the whispers of the night, for within those shadows lay the promise of untold adventures waiting to be discovered.

SPECULATIONS OF THE FUTURE

When the first rays of dawn began to shine through the magnificent arched windows of the museum, painting the dusty floors with golden strokes, Ellie stood at the centre of the enchanted hall, surrounded by the people she had recently made new friends with. A subtle thrum that tickled the skin and whispered of forgotten realms could be heard in the air, and it was a hum that was caused by the remnants of magic. Once shrouded in mystery and pulsing with unrest, the artefacts now sparkled with a sense of peace, their surfaces gleaming with a gentle, internal light. The hum was a clear sign that the artefacts had been abandoned. A nod of respect was extended to them by Valen, whose cloaked figure shimmered with the last tendrils of night like fading starlight. The gesture was a silent acknowledgement of their bravery and unity in the face of formidable challenges. The air around him crackled with the energy of time, serving as a constant reminder of the immense power he had and the sacrifices he made to safeguard the timeline.

"Each of you has demonstrated tremendous bravery," he intoned, his voice resonating softly against the ancient stone walls, imbued with a resonating quality that spoke of centuries past. "I am completely impressed by your bravery." It is because of your combined efforts that the museum's soul has been brought back into harmony, putting an end to the discord that had the potential to unravel the historical pieces. Your determination has ensured that the tales contained within these artefacts will be woven into the fabric of time for all of eternity. Their teachings should serve as a guide for future generations to understand the delicate equilibrium that exists between the past, the present, and the future.

Harold Finch, the professor, adjusted his glasses with a proud smile spreading across his face and crinkling the corners of his eyes. He was still slightly rumpled from the adventure that had occurred earlier in the evening. His normally dishevelled hair was even more awry than it typically was, a bumbling guard who tripped over more clues than he discovered, and a motley crew of enchanted beings plucked from the annals of folklore could change the fate of history! To put it simply, it is extraordinary! His heart was filled with a mixture of pride and gratitude for their unlikely but undeniably effective partnership, and he beamed at the group as he looked at them. A friendship that had been forged in the flames of magical chaos had been formed between them because of the adventure, which had saved the museum and created an unbreakable bond between them.

The sound of Oliver's laughter was a familiar rumble, which is typically reserved for correcting apprentices who have gotten things wrong. On this evening, however, his typical abrasiveness was tempered by the sense of camaraderie that was shared among the improbable group. The swaying candlelight danced across the ancient artefacts that were all around them, serving as a silent testament to the adventure that they had both experienced together. As he scratched his beard, he admitted, "I'll admit that I was sceptical on the subject." Is it possible that a group of...enthusiasts...believed they could save this old place? Then again, tonight? It's going to be for the record books. the best kind, which is packed with danger, wit, and just the right number of near-death experiences to keep things captivating. Even though it was a rare sight, he winked, which caused the corners of his eyes to wrinkle.

It appears the statue of Lady Arabella, which was momentarily infused with a shimmer that was reminiscent of life in the early morning light, was emitting warmth. Her tone, even though it was the sound of stone, was regal, but it was also tinged with an almost maternal affection. "And it will be our legacy, something that will be woven through the whispers of those who have the courage to believe in enchantment. Even though generations will walk these halls without being aware of the events that took place that night, the echoes of our bravery and unity will continue to reverberate, serving as a reminder that magic, in its purest form, is still present. A silent blessing was bestowed upon each of them as her gaze lingered on them.

Azrael the Lion, who was extremely majestic even when he was at rest, slowly turned his enormous head in the direction of Ellie, his golden eyes brimming with extraordinary insight. He appeared to have an inherent power that was amplified by the moonlight that was still clinging to his mane. Thank you, Ellie, for bringing us together. Maybe it was a shared purpose and a little bit of fate that brought them together. On the other hand, it was your unyielding heart and your refusal to give up that served as the compass that led us through the darkness. Even when we had doubts about ourselves, you were able to recognise the potential that each of us had, and for that, we will be eternally grateful.

The bushy tail of Finn, who was a whirlwind of energy, twitched with undisguised delight as he darted around their feet in a playful manner. His eyes, which were sharp and intelligent, sparkled with a joyful twinkle. "Let's not overlook having some fun! It was a night filled with exciting activities, such as sneaking through the corridors, solving riddles in the dead of night, and engaging in wild races with shadows that almost resulted in a tumble or both. Never in the history of the world have I felt so alive! Please, is it possible for us to make those experiences a regular occurrence?

Valen's iridescent cloak was given a final, dramatic flourish, and with that, the enchantments that had come to life during the night began to gradually fade away. Even though they were still glowing softly, the ancient artefacts went back to their eternal slumber, their power having been secured and accomplished. It was as he began to fade back into the shadows that he whispered, "Remember, dear friends," his voice resonating with the weight of ages, "the true magic lies not just in the artefacts, in their inherent power, but in the bonds that are forged through adventure." Keeping the spirit of collaboration, the courage to face the impossible, and the unwavering belief in the extraordinary are all skills that should be kept. Keeping this spirit with you always will ensure that the magic will never entirely disappear.

Ellie experienced a quiet swelling of determination within her as the last remnants of night faded away, painting the eastern sky in hues of rose and gold. More than just a collection of artefacts that were meticulously displayed in glass cases, the museum was much more than that. It was not only the lives of those who had created the artefacts but also the lives of those who were now connected to them by a common experience. It was a living, breathing tapestry of lives. Stories were woven into the fabric of the tapestry, waiting to be told, to be treasured, and to serve as a source of motivation for future generations.

It was not only that they had preserved its legacy, but they had also created new chapters that were full of laughter, bravery, friendship, and the undeniable truth that even in the darkest of nights, hope can always, always be found. The aroma of dry parchment and spells that had been forgotten, mingling with the crisp morning air, was a sign that there would be more exciting experiences to come.

They gathered for one final moment in the grand hall, which was bathed in the pre-dawn light that was filtering through stained-glass windows depicting forgotten eras. The warmth of camaraderie enveloped them like a comforting cloak as they gathered there. The profound connection that they had developed through the crucible of their extraordinary adventures was reflected in their faces, which were etched with the marks of their shared struggles and victories. Each of Ellie's companions received a smile from her, and her eyes lingered for a moment on each of their recognisable faces.

There was Professor Finch, his glasses perched precariously on his nose, and he had a perpetual twinkle in his eye that hinted at knowledge that had not yet been revealed. Oliver, the pragmatic inventor, was standing next to him. He was already sketching new contraptions in his worn leather notebook, and his mind was buzzing with the possibilities that they had gained from their journey. Azrael, the mysterious shadowmancer, kept his stoic demeanour as he always had, but a subtle softening of his features revealed the affection he had for the group.

Even Luci, the mischievous imp, appeared to be momentarily subdued. Instead of her typical impish grin, she displayed a more sincere expression than she normally does. A silent promise of future expeditions was etched onto Lady Arabella's determined face as she adjusted her pith helmet. Intrepid explorer Lady Arabella was adjusting her helmet. Finn, the nimble rogue, was seen leaning against a nearby pillar while casually polishing a dagger. His commitment to the group was unwavering. And even the gentle spirit of Huckleberry , who floated nearby, seemed to emanate a sense of profound peace. He appeared to be an ethereal guardian who was watching over them with eyes of kindness.

As Ellie surveyed her friends, she spoke with a voice that resounded with conviction and her eyes that sparkled with excitement. "Let's promise to return," she said. "Let's commit to uncovering more adventures and uncovering more mysteries." A heartbeat and a rhythm that is uniquely its own can be found in this museum, which is a repository of history and magic. In addition, we have only just started to pay attention to its hushed utterances, and we have only scratched the surface of its limitless mysteries. Who knows what marvels wait for us within the walls of this building?

As the sun rose, it painted the enchanted museum in a glorious golden hue, illuminating forgotten relics and casting long, dancing shadows, while the group of friends dissipated into the dawn, each beginning their own individual journeys. However, their hearts were inextricably linked, inextricably linked by the experiences that they had in common, the secrets that they had discovered, and the bonds that were formed within those spellbinding walls.

They carried with them the echoes of languages that had been forgotten, the weight of ancient artefacts, and the unwavering knowledge that destiny had chosen them. They would be ready, without hesitation, to answer the call of their next adventure, and they would be forever drawn back to the museum and its promises that had been whispered. They were the champions of the world's hidden history, and they were prepared to embrace the world that was waiting for them, which was ripe with possibilities.